OKISHIMA   OKAYAMA   KOBE   OSAKA

T0009369

MA

08 09 10

CLIFF

LIGHTHOUSE

TOURIST
ASSOCIATION

TANGERINE
TREES

CLINIC

HARBOR

RESIDENTIAL
AREA

N

FORBIDDEN ZONES
22ND
0308AM-;G=07
0700AM-;J=02
0900AM-;F=01
1100AM-;H=08
0100PM-;J=05
0300PM-;H=03
0500PM-;D=08
0700PM-;G=01
0900PM-;I=03
1100PM-;G=09
23RD
0100AM-;F=07
0300AM-;G=03
0500AM-;E=04
0700AM-;C=08
0900AM-;D=02
1100AM-;C=03
0100PM-;D=07
0300PM-;H=04
0500PM-;F=09
0700PM-;B=09
0900PM-;E=10
1100PM-;F=04

BATTLE
REMASTERED
ROYALE

WRITTEN BY KOUSHUN TAKAMI

A NEW TRANSLATION BY NATHAN COLLINS

HAIKA
SORU

SAN FRANCISCO

BATTLE ROYALE
Copyright © 1999 by Koushun Takami
All rights reserved.
First published in Japan by Ota Shuppan in 1999.
English translation © 2014 by VIZ Media, LLC

Cover art by Tomer Hanuka
Cover and interior design by Fawn Lau

HAIKASORU
Published by VIZ Media, LLC
P.O. Box 77010
San Francisco, CA 94107

www.haikasoru.com

Library of Congress Cataloging-in-Publication Data
Takami, Koushun.
  [Batoru rowaiaru. English]
  Battle Royale : remastered / Koushun Takami ; a new translation by Nathan Collins.
      pages cm
    ISBN 978-1-4215-6598-9 (paperback)
  1. Reality television programs—Japan—Fiction. 2. Junior high school students—
Japan—Fiction. 3. Allegories. 4. Science fiction. 5. Suspense fiction. .I. Collins,
Nathan, translator. II. Title.
  PL876.A396B3913 2014
  895.63'6—dc23
                                    2014002592

Printed in the U.S.A.

First English-language edition, February 2003
First Haikasoru edition, November 2009
Remastered edition, April 2014
Seventh printing, June 2021

I DEDICATE THIS TO EVERYONE I LOVE.
EVEN THOUGH IT MIGHT NOT BE APPRECIATED.

"A STUDENT IS NOT A TANGERINE!"

—KINPACHI SAKAMOTO
(FROM MIEKO OSANAI'S *KINPACHI SENSEI OF CLASS 3-B*)

"BUT TILL THEN TRAMPS LIKE US
BABY WE WERE BORN TO RUN"

—BRUCE SPRINGSTEEN,
"BORN TO RUN"

"IT'S SO HARD TO LOVE"

—MOTOHARU SANO,
"IT'S SO HARD TO LOVE"

"DURING ALL THOSE LAST WEEKS I SPENT THERE,
THERE WAS A PECULIAR EVIL FEELING IN THE AIR—AN
ATMOSPHERE OF SUSPICION, FEAR, UNCERTAINTY, AND
VEILED HATRED....YOU SEEMED TO SPEND ALL YOUR TIME
HOLDING WHISPERED CONVERSATIONS IN CORNERS OF
CAFÉS AND WONDERING WHETHER THAT PERSON AT THE
NEXT TABLE WAS A POLICE SPY....

"I DO NOT KNOW IF I CAN BRING HOME TO YOU HOW
DEEPLY THAT ACTION TOUCHED ME. IT SOUNDS A SMALL
THING, BUT IT WAS NOT. YOU HAVE GOT TO REALIZE
WHAT WAS THE FEELING OF THE TIME—THE HORRIBLE
ATMOSPHERE OF SUSPICION AND HATRED."

—GEORGE ORWELL,
HOMAGE TO CATALONIA

NINTH GRADE CLASS B, SHIROIWA JUNIOR HIGH SCHOOL

CLASS ROSTER

BOYS:

1	YOSHIO AKAMATSU
2	KEITA IIJIMA
3	TATSUMICHI OKI
4	TOSHINORI ODA
5	SHOGO KAWADA
6	KAZUO KIRIYAMA
7	YOSHITOKI KUNINOBU
8	YOJI KURAMOTO
9	HIROSHI KURONAGA
10	RYUHEI SASAGAWA
11	HIROKI SUGIMURA
12	YUTAKA SETO
13	YUICHIRO TAKIGUCHI
14	SHO TSUKIOKA
15	SHUYA NANAHARA
16	KAZUSHI NIIDA
17	MITSURU NUMAI
18	TADAKATSU HATAGAMI
19	SHINJI MIMURA
20	KYOICHI MOTOBUCHI
21	KAZUHIKO YAMAMOTO

GIRLS:

1	MIZUHO INADA
2	YUKIE UTSUMI
3	MEGUMI ETO
4	SAKURA OGAWA
5	IZUMI KANAI
6	YUKIKO KITANO
7	YUMIKO KUSAKA
8	KAYOKO KOTOHIKI
9	YUKO SAKAKI
10	HIRONO SHIMIZU
11	MITSUKO SOUMA
12	HARUKA TANIZAWA
13	TAKAKO CHIGUSA
14	MAYUMI TENDO
15	NORIKO NAKAGAWA
16	YUKA NAKAGAWA
17	SATOMI NODA
18	FUMIYO FUJIYOSHI
19	CHISATO MATSUI
20	KAORI MINAMI
21	YOSHIMI YAHAGI

OPENING REMARKS

(As Given by a Pro Wrestling Fan in an Alternate World)

What? Battle royale? You're asking what a battle royale is? Don't you know? Then what are you doing coming to a wrestling show? What? No, it's not the name of an offensive move. No, it's not the name of a championship title, either. A battle royale is a type of match. What, you mean today? Here? No, there's not gonna be one here today. They're held at bigger arenas than this—you know, a special occasion kind of thing. Hey! Hey, look! See, that's Takako Inoue. She's pretty hot, am I right? Oh, sorry, where was I? Right, battles royale. All Japan Pro Wrestling still puts them on. A battle royale is, well . . . Okay, so wrestling is usually one on one, or with two teams of two, something like that. But a battle royale has ten, maybe twenty fighters, just a big, big number of 'em, all in the ring at once. And anyone can go after anyone, one on one, or one on ten—anything goes. But no matter how many people get pinned—wait, you don't even know what a *pin* is? That's when your shoulders are on the mat and then comes the count, *one, two, three*, and on that third count, that's it, you're done. Same in a battle royale as with a normal match. Wrestlers can also forfeit, and sometimes there's even a knockout. Oh, and countouts too, when someone stays outside the ring too long. And there're disqualifications. In any case, pins are usually what does it in a battle royale.

Go! Takako, go! Take her out! Oh, ah . . . Sorry, sorry. Anyway, the ones that get pinned lose and have to leave the squared circle. And the match keeps going like that, with fewer and fewer competitors as it goes on. Of course, in the end, it's down to two. One on one, and there's the real match. One of those two is gonna go down. When it's over, only one man's standing. The winner. Victory. They give out a giant trophy and hand over the prize money. Get it? Huh? You mean the ones who are friends? Well, you see, at first, they work together. But when the end comes, they'll have to fight each other. Those are the rules. That means that sometimes, if you're lucky enough, you can see some really rare match-ups. You know, like way back with the tag team Dynamite Kid and Davey Boy Smith. And it happened once with Road Warriors Animal and Hawk. Well, with that one, one or the other of them stepped out of the ring to let the other guy win. A real display of love, like they were brothers, you know? A letdown, if you ask me. Now see, two people who didn't always get along can still team up. But you're workin' with one guy to take out another, and your "partner" can stab you in the back just like that! Who would *I* like to see in a battle royale? Well, with all the rival federations that've popped up now, I'd like to see the best of each face off. Keiji Mutoh, Shinya Hashimoto, Mitsuharu Misawa, Toshiaki Kawada, Nobuhiko Takada, Masakatsu Funaki, Akira Maeda, The Great Sasuke, Hayabusa, Kenji Takano, also Genichiro Tenryu and Riki Choshu, and Tatsumi Fujinami and Kengo Kimura could probably still pull it off. It'd be fun if Yoji Anjo and Super Delfin could be in it too. You never know, they might make it to the end. For the women, you have to go with Takako there. Then there's Aja Kong, Manami Toy, Kyoko Inoue, Yumiko Hotta, Akira Hokuto, Bull Nakano, Dynamite Kansai of course, Cutie Suzuki and Hikari Fukuoka, Mayumi Ozaki, Shinobu Kandori and Chigusa Nagayo, and . . . what's that? You don't know any of them? And you *really* came here to watch pro wrestling? Hey! No no no, Takako, fight back! Takako! *Niiice.*

GOVERNMENT MEMO
TOP SECRET

INTERNAL MEMORANDUM
1997.00387461

FROM: DIRECTOR OF DEFENSE, SPECIAL PLANNING DEPART-
MENT OF THE SECRETARIAT TO THE LEADER; CHIEF OF COMBAT
EXPERIMENTS, NONAGGRESSIVE FORCES STAFF OFFICE

TO: SUPERVISOR, REPUBLIC COMBAT EXPERIMENT 68TH
PROGRAM, TRIAL #12, 1997

ON MAY 20, AT 18:15, A ROUTINE INSPECTION BY CENTRAL
PROCESSING IDENTIFIED EVIDENCE OF AN INTRUSION INTO THE
OPERATION SYSTEMS. THE INCIDENT OCCURRED IN THE EARLY
HOURS OF MARCH 12, AND OUR UTMOST EFFORTS ARE FOCUSED ON
THE INVESTIGATION FOR TRACES OF ANY POSSIBLE SUBSEQUENT
UNAUTHORIZED ACCESS.

THE IDENTITY AND OBJECTIVE OF THE PERPETRATOR, AS
WELL AS THE EXTENT OF THE COMPROMISED DATA, REMAINS
UNDER INVESTIGATION. THE METHOD OF INTRUSION EMPLOYED A

HIGH DEGREE OF SKILL, AND UNCOVERING THE FULL PICTURE OF THE DAMAGES WILL LIKELY REQUIRE SIGNIFICANT TIME.

UPON RECEIVING A REPORT THAT WE COULD NOT RULE OUT THE POSSIBILITY THAT DAMAGES EXTENDED TO DATA FROM THE 68TH PROGRAM, THE OFFICE OF DEFENSE IN THE SPECIAL PLANNING DEPARTMENT OF THE SECRETARIAT TO THE LEADER AND THE COMBAT EXPERIMENTS DIVISION IN THE NONAGGRESSIVE FORCES STAFF OFFICE JOINTLY HELD AN EMERGENCY EXPLORATION INTO A POSSIBLE DELAY OF THE 1997 TRIAL #12 OF THE SAME.

HOWEVER, IN VIEW OF THE FACT THAT PREPARATIONS FOR TRIAL #12 ARE ALREADY COMPLETE, AND WITH NO EVIDENCE YET FOUND OF A LEAK OF RELATED INFORMATION TO THE GENERAL PUBLIC, THE DELIBERATIONS RESULTED IN THE DECISION TO CONDUCT THE TRIAL AS PLANNED. DESPITE THIS CONCLUSION, WE WILL PURSUE A SWIFT INVESTIGATION INTO NECESSARY CHANGES FOR TRIALS #13 AND BEYOND, AND WILL BE DEVOTING SPECIAL ATTENTION TO REVISIONS OF THE CURRENT GUADAL-CANAL SYSTEM.

NEVERTHELESS, GIVEN YOUR ROLE AS SUPERVISOR OF TRIAL #12, AND AS THE DIRECTOR OF ITS EXECUTION, YOU ARE TO PROCEED WITH THE UTMOST CAUTION.

FURTHERMORE, THIS INCIDENT IS CLASSIFIED TOP SECRET AND IS TO BE TREATED AS SUCH.

PART ONE
THE GAME BEGINS

STUDENTS BEGIN.

As the bus entered the prefectural capital city of Takamatsu, the scenery slowly shifted from pastoral to urban. With the city came lights in multicolored neon, headlamps from oncoming traffic, and in offices left to shine through the night. A group of men and women in sharp business suits stood talking in front of a roadside restaurant, perhaps waiting for a taxi. Weary, cigarette-smoking youths squatted in the sterile parking lot of a convenience store. A blue-collar worker, perched on his bicycle, waited for the crosswalk signal to change. The evening was still a bit chilly for May, and the man's disheveled, threadbare windbreaker made him stand out—just one of many fleeting impressions flowing beyond the bus windows, swept away by the low rumble of its engine. The digital clock above the driver's seat changed to 8:57.

Shuya Nanahara (Boys #15, Ninth Grade Class B, Shiroiwa Junior High, Shiroiwa Town, Kagawa Prefecture) was seated on the left-hand side of the bus, gazing off into the nighttime scenery. He had to lean forward a bit to see around Yoshitoki Kuninobu (Boys #7), who occupied the window seat, rustling through his travel bag. With his right leg stretched out into the aisle, Shuya flexed his toes against the inside of his Keds sneaker, the canvas torn inside the heel, frayed threads sticking out like cat whiskers. Those shoes were hard to come by these days, although supposedly that hadn't always been the case. The brand was American, and the sneakers were made in Colombia. Though this was 1997, and the Republic of Greater East Asia certainly wasn't lacking for goods—if anything, it overflowed with them—imported commodities were extremely difficult to acquire. Well, such was only to be expected with the national policy of quasi-seclusion—especially so with a hostile country like America (government officials called it the "American Empire," as did school textbooks).

From his seat near the back of the bus, Shuya surveyed the cabin. Under the dim fluorescents filtering through dingy ceiling panels, he had a view of the other forty-one students who had been his classmates since the eighth grade. After leaving their school in Shiroiwa less than an hour before, the kids were all still excited and chatting away. They weren't overjoyed that their school trip was beginning with an overnight ride imposed on them either out of cheapness or possibly due to an overly packed schedule. But once the bus passed over the Great Seto Bridge, got onto the Sanyo Expressway, and was on its way to their destination in Kyushu, they would calm down a little.

Toward the front, a rowdy cluster of girls bubbled around the teacher in charge of their class, Mr. Hayashida. Among them was Yukie Utsumi (Girls #2), class leader and representative for the girls' side, with braided hair that looked good on her. Also in the group were Haruka Tanizawa (Girls #12), her teammate on the volleyball team and quite tall for a girl; Izumi Kanai (Girls #5), daughter of a town councilman with a prim attitude to match; Satomi Noda (Girls #17), a gifted student whose round-framed glasses suited her calm and collected countenance; Chisato Matsui (Girls #19), ever meek and demure; and a few others. They formed the popular group, or anyway the middle-of-the-road group—though to call them a group at all might not be quite right. Girls tend to form cliques, but not so in the Shiroiwa Junior High Ninth Grade Class B, where there weren't really any to speak of. The closest to a clique would be the group led by Mitsuko Souma (Girls #11), who was a little rough around the edges and, to be frank, a juvenile delinquent. Hirono Shimizu (Girls #10) and Yoshimi

Yahagi (Girls #21) made three. From his position, Shuya couldn't tell where the girls were sitting.

The first row behind the driver's seat was slightly elevated, and its shorter backrest revealed two heads side by side, belonging to Kazuhiko Yamamoto (Boys #21) and Sakura Ogawa (Girls #4), the closest couple in class. Every so often their heads shook, likely in shared laughter at some joke. Well, with a pair as reserved as Kazuhiko and Sakura, the most trivial talk might seem hilarious.

Shuya glanced up the aisle to see an immense school uniform protruding into the space just ahead. Inside that uniform was Yoshio Akamatsu (Boys #1). Yoshio was the largest kid in the class, but he was sensitive, the type that ends up teased and picked on. He was scrunching his bulky frame forward, buried in the latest popular portable video game.

The jocks, Tatsumichi Oki (Boys #3, Handball Team), Kazushi Niida (Boys #16, Soccer Team), and Tadakatsu Hatagami (Boys #18, Baseball Team), sat together, flanking the aisle. Shuya himself had been in Little League (and was even called the ace shortstop) and used to be good friends with Tadakatsu until the two had drifted apart—possibly because Shuya had quit playing baseball. Replacing the sport with more "unpatriotic" hobbies, like the electric guitar, was likely part of it too. Shuya had seen Tadakatsu's mom get uptight about those kind of things.

After all, rock music was banned in the Republic. There were, of course, ways around the ban. Shuya's guitar wore an official permit sticker that read USE OF THIS MUSICAL INSTRUMENT IN THE PRODUCTION OF DECADENT MUSIC IS STRICTLY PROHIBITED. "Decadent music" being rock.

Now that he thought about it, Shuya realized he had made a completely new set of friends.

A quiet laugh came from the seat behind big Yoshio Akamatsu. It belonged to one of those new friends, Shinji Mimura (Boys #19). Around the edge of the seat, Shuya caught sight of Shinji's short hair and the finely crafted earring in his left earlobe.

When they became classmates the year before, Shuya had already heard of "The Third Man," the ace guard on the basketball team. Shinji was proud of his exceptional athleticism, on par with the ace shortstop Shuya—though Shinji would certainly jest, "I'm better, baby." During a school field day held soon after class placement, the two discovered they made a great duo and hit it off right away. But there was more to Shinji than just sports. Though his grades were merely average (aside from mathematics and English), Shinji possessed a staggering breadth of knowledge and a perspective far beyond his years. Ask him most any question, and he'd have the answer right away, even down to typically unobtainable information about foreign countries. And he'd always have advice in a time of need. Despite all that, Shinji didn't have an arrogant bone in his body. Well, he did have his own way of joking, like the time he said, "Everyone knows I'm a genius. Haven't you heard?" But there was nothing offensive about it. Basically, Shinji Mimura was a good guy.

Seated beside Shinji was Yutaka Seto (Boys #12), who had been the athlete's friend since elementary school. Yutaka was the class clown, and one of his quips was probably what had sparked Shinji's laughter.

One row behind the pair was Hiroki Sugimura (Boys #11). Hiroki, reading a paperback, had somehow managed to fold his lanky frame into the narrow seat. Taciturn and a student of martial arts, Hiroki had an intimidating presence and kept mostly to himself. But once Shuya had tried talking to him, he found the boy to be nice, if shy, and the two got along surprisingly well. The paperback was probably one of Hiroki's prized anthologies of Chinese poetry. (Chinese literature books were fairly easy to find despite being translations of foreign works. But then they would be, as the Republic proclaimed China "our sovereign territory.")

There was a line Shuya read once in an American book he'd salvaged from some corner of a used bookstore, relying on a dictionary to make it through: "Friends come in and out of your life." Maybe that was true. Perhaps he would drift apart from Shinji and Hiroki and his other friends like he had with Tadakatsu.

Or not.

Shuya glanced at Yoshitoki Kuninobu in the adjacent seat, still rustling through his bag. They, at least, had been together this far, and he
didn't see anything changing that. Shuya and Yoshitoki had been friends
ever since they were still wetting their beds in the pompously named
"House of Mercy and Love," a Catholic institution for children who had
lost—or who were no longer *allowed* to live with—their parents. They
seemed destined to be friends, whether Shuya wanted it or not.

While we're on the subject, an explanation on religion in the
Republic might be in order. The government was a unique brand of
national socialism, with the Leader, wielder of supreme power, as its
leading symbol. (Once, Shinji Mimura had scowled and said, "This is
what successful fascism looks like. Is there anything as evil anywhere
in the world?") But the Leader didn't enforce a state religion—aside
from belief in his political system, which itself didn't clash with any
established faith. Citizens were free to worship, as long as their activities remained within certain bounds—though the complete lack of any
legal protection meant that only the most devout persisted, and only in
meager efforts. Shuya himself had never been particularly religious, but
he did feel gratitude toward religion. He recognized that the Church had
given him a comfortable childhood and had raised him into a decent
young man, if he could be called one. Secular, state-run orphanages did
exist, but by reputation were lousy facilities poorly run, notorious as
training grounds for future soldiers in the Nonaggressive Forces.

Shuya looked over his shoulder toward the rear of the bus. Sitting
in the long bench seat of the last row were bad boys Ryuhei Sasagawa
(Boys #10) and Mitsuru Numai (Boys #17). A third was at the right-
hand window (Ryuhei Sasagawa had left a couple seats empty between).
Though the seat backs blocked his view of this third boy's face, Shuya
recognized the distinctive haircut, slicked-back and hanging long, atop
a head that remained perfectly still, unperturbed by the dirty jokes
and coarse laughter of other two at his left. The youth may have been
sleeping, or perhaps, like Shuya, had been captivated by the city lights.

Why that boy—Kazuo Kiriyama (Boys #6)—had shown up to

something as childish as this school trip was the greatest mystery to Shuya.

Kiriyama was the leader, of sorts, of the area delinquents, Ryuhei and Mitsuru among them. Though by no means big—he couldn't have been taller than Shuya—Kiriyama could easily subdue a high schooler and even took on local yakuza. He had become a prefecture-wide legend. His father's being the president of a leading local enterprise probably helped, but there was more to his stature than that. (Shuya had heard rumors that Kiriyama was a bastard child. Uninterested, he'd never bothered to look into it.) Kiriyama had a handsome, intelligent face, and his voice, though not deep, was intimidating. His grades were the best in the class—the class leader for the boy's side, Kyoichi Motobuchi (Boys #20), spent late nights studying just to compete. Even in sports, when forced to participate, Kiriyama was better and more graceful than just about any of his peers. The only boys in Shiroiwa Junior High who could rival him in a serious match-up would be the former ace shortstop Shuya and the basketball team's ace guard Shinji Mimura. In every aspect, Kazuo Kiriyama was the perfect man.

But why then did this perfect man end up a leader of hooligans? Shuya couldn't begin to know the answer, though he could perceive in Kiriyama—a sense, almost tactile—something out of place. Shuya couldn't put his finger on it. Kiriyama never acted out in school, nor would he bully someone as Ryuhei Sasagawa and others sometimes did to Yoshio Akamatsu. But Shuya felt *something* was . . . lacking, perhaps?

Kiriyama frequently skipped school. The thought that he would ever actually study was preposterous. When he did show up for class, he just sat there, silent, his mind seemingly somewhere completely different. Without a powerful and meddlesome government insisting upon a compulsory education, Kiriyama might never have attended school at all. Or he might have come all the time, just because he felt like it. Shuya couldn't guess which. He had thought the boy would certainly pass on the school trip without a second thought, yet here he was. Kiriyama acting upon another whim, then?

Shuya was staring off at the lights in the ceiling, thinking about Kiriyama, when a sunny voice called his name and pulled him back to reality.

From the seat across the aisle, Noriko Nakagawa (Girls #15) offered something wrapped in cellophane. Small enough to fit in the palm of her hand, the pouch was packed full with little, light brown, round objects—cookies, probably. Light from the ceiling glinted along the surface of the clear, stiff wrapping like the sun over water. A neatly tied bow of gold ribbon held it closed.

Noriko Nakagawa was in Yukie Utsumi's group of mainstreamers. Shoulder-length hair framed a round and very girlish face, with striking eyes that were gentle and dark, almost black. She was petite, with a playful streak, the picture of an average girl. If anything about her merited special mention, it was her talent with Japanese; Noriko was the best writer in class. (As a result, Shuya and Noriko talked relatively often. During breaks, Shuya would compose song lyrics in the margins of his notebook, and sometimes Noriko would ask to read them.) Noriko usually kept with Yukie and the other girls, but showing up a little late for the trip, she had been forced to take the open seat.

Shuya reached toward the bag, but stopped, raising his eyebrows in question.

Somewhat flustered, Noriko said, "Um, my little brother begged me to bake these today. I had these extra, and they're no good stale, so you and Mr. Nobu can have them, if you like."

Mr. Nobu was Yoshitoki Kuninobu's nickname. Despite his good-humored, goggling eyes, Yoshitoki could be surprisingly wise and mature. Referring to him as you would an adult seemed appropriate. The girls didn't often use the boys' nicknames—"Mr. Nobu" included—but Noriko did, and freely. She made it feel natural and never offended anyone by it. That was Noriko; she had this buoyant quality. Shuya never had a nickname—actually, he did have something of a strange one from elementary school, after a brand of cigarettes, but like Shinji's "The Third Man" moniker, no one ever actually used it when talking with him—but some time ago he had noticed that Noriko was the only girl who ever called him by his first name.

Listening in, Yoshitoki interjected, "Really? You mean it? Nice! If you made them, they must be good."

Yoshitoki snatched the bag from Shuya's reach, quickly undid the ribbon, and withdrew and sampled a cookie.

"Wow! These are *amazing*!"

Caught in the middle, Shuya grinned. Could that boy be any more obvious? As soon as Noriko had taken the seat across from Shuya, Yoshitoki began acting all weird, sneaking glances at her and straightening his posture.

A month and a half earlier, during spring vacation, Shuya and Yoshitoki were fishing for black bass at the city reservoir when Yoshitoki blurted, "Hey, Shuya, I . . . kinda . . . got a crush."

"Oh," Shuya said, "who is it?"

"Nakagawa."

"From our class?"

"Yeah."

"Which one? There are two Nakagawas. You mean Yuka?"

"Whatever. You're the one who's into the fat ones, not me."

"You jerk. You trying to say Kazumi's fat? She's just a little chubby, that's all."

"Sorry, sorry," Yoshitoki said. "Anyway, well, it's Noriko."

"That so? Well, she's a nice girl."

"Don't you think so? Right?"

"Yeah, yeah."

Yoshitoki was utterly transparent. Yet Noriko seemingly remained unaware. Shuya couldn't tell if she was that oblivious or what. Maybe that was just part of what made her Noriko.

Shuya took a cookie from the bag in Yoshitoki's hand and held it up to his eyes. Then he looked at Noriko and asked, "You said they're no good stale?"

"Yeah." Noriko gave two sharp nods. For some reason, her eyes seemed tense. "That's right."

"Guess you must be confident they were any good in the first place, then."

Shuya had been making a lot of snide remarks lately, perhaps picking it up from Shinji Mimura. The habit annoyed some, but Noriko giggled and said, "That's right."

"Hey," Yoshitoki said, cutting in again, "I said they were amazing, didn't I? You heard me, right, Noriko?"

Noriko smiled. "Thanks. You're so sweet, Mr. Nobu."

Yoshitoki suddenly stiffened as if he had poked his finger into an outlet. Then, without further comment, he stared down at his feet and crunched on a cookie.

With another grin, Shuya popped a cookie in his mouth. It was sweet and light.

"This *is* good," he said.

Noriko, who hadn't taken her eyes off him the entire time, said, "Thanks!"

Shuya thought she sounded different when she was thanking him. Maybe he had just imagined it . . . But no, her eyes were so serious, watching him eat that cookie. Were they really left over from ones made for her brother? Or had she made them because she wanted *someone* in particular to eat them? No, that was just his imagination. Wasn't it?

Shuya's mind jumped to Kazumi. She was a grade ahead of him, and until last year, they had been in the music club together.

Rock music would never make it into the repertoire of a school in the Republic, but when the music club's advisor, Mrs. Miyata, wasn't around, the band often played rock to kill time. That's really why the students joined up. The only female saxophone player in the ensemble, Kazumi Shintani was better than any of the boys at rock sax. She was tall (nearly as tall as Shuya's one-hundred-seventy centimeters), and a little chubby, but when she had that alto sax in her hands, and her hair gathered at the sides of her neck, and she got that mature, world-wise expression, she was really cool. The sight made Shuya's heart race. Then she taught him difficult guitar chords. ("I played a little before I started sax," she'd said.) After that, he practiced day and night, and by the middle of eighth grade, he had become the best in the club—all because he'd wanted Kazumi to hear.

One day after school, Shuya and Kazumi found themselves alone in the music room. He sang and played "Summertime Blues" for her, and she said, "That was incredible, Shuya. Really cool."

That night, he bought himself his first can of beer to celebrate. It was delicious. But three days later, when he told her straight out, "Um, I . . . like you," she was as straight with him.

"Sorry, I have a boyfriend."

She graduated and went on to a high school with a music program—the same school as her boyfriend.

There's more to the story of Shuya and Yoshitoki fishing at the reservoir that spring day. After telling Shuya about Noriko, Yoshitoki asked, "Do you still like that older girl?"

Shuya answered, "Yeah, I like her. Probably will for the rest of my life."

Yoshitoki looked perplexed. "But hey, she's already got someone."

Shuya had said, "So what?" and with an overhand cast, sent his silver lure as far as it could go.

Shuya grabbed the cookies from Yoshitoki, who was still looking downward, and said, "If you eat them all, Noriko won't get any."

"Oh, yeah, sorry."

Shuya returned the package to Noriko and said, "Sorry about that."

"Oh no," she said. "It's all right. You two eat them."

"Really? The two of us shouldn't get to have all—"

Just then, Shuya noticed who was sitting next to Noriko. Shogo Kawada (Boys #5), his large frame clad in the school's uniform, leaned against the window glass, arms folded, eyes closed, and still. Asleep, maybe. Kawada's hair was cropped so short as to be almost nonexistent, and his face, vaguely reminiscent of some carnival food vendor, wore a faint layer of stubble. *Stubble, everyone!* Didn't he look a little old to be in junior high?

Well, actually, that could be explained. Though the same group of students in Class B had been carried over from the eighth grade,

Shogo Kawada had transferred in from Kobe only the month before. And whether due to illness or injury (likely the latter—he didn't seem the type prone to illness), he had missed over half a year of school and had been held back. This made him a year older than most of the class. Though Kawada had never spoken of any of this himself, Shuya had heard it all the same.

And what he had heard was, frankly, not good. According to rumor, Kawada had been nothing but a thug, and he'd received the injuries that had taken him out of school in a fight. Scars all over his body seemed to confirm the speculation. One long slash across his left eyebrow came from what appeared to be a blade. And in the locker room, Shuya had shivered when he saw the scars on the youth's arms and back. (As an aside, Kawada's muscular body, reminiscent of a middleweight boxer's, impressed even Shuya.) On his left shoulder were two peculiar round marks, one right next to the other—just like gunshot wounds, as impossible as that would be.

These rumors came paired with another, shared by whispers: *Someday, Kawada and Kiriyama are going to fight.* Just after Kawada transferred in, Ryuhei Sasagawa, reckless and posturing, got in the new student's face. What went down and how it ended were only hearsay, but Ryuhei came back looking pale and ran crying to Kiriyama, who gave no response, save for a disinterested glance. At least so far, the two would-be rivals had not yet given any impression that anything serious was going to happen. Kiriyama didn't appear to have any interest in Kawada, and the feeling seemed mutual. Thanks to that, Class B remained at peace, happily ever after.

In any event, between the age difference and the rumors, the other students would avoid Kawada. But Shuya didn't like to judge people from rumor. Someone once said, "*If you can see it with your own eyes, you don't need to listen to the word of others.*"

Shuya looked at Noriko and gestured to Kawada with his chin. "Is he asleep?" he asked.

"Hmm," she said, and glanced over her shoulder. "Yeah, I didn't want to wake him."

"He doesn't seem like the kind of guy who eats cookies, anyway."

Noriko giggled, and just as Shuya began to crack a smile, the voice came.

"I'm fine."

Shuya again looked at Kawada.

The firm, deep voice lingered in Shuya's ears, unfamiliar, but evidently belonging to Kawada. He must have been awake, though his eyes remained closed. Shuya realized he'd almost never heard him speak, despite the new student having transferred in over a month before.

Noriko glanced again at Kawada, then back to Shuya, who shrugged and stuffed another cookie into his mouth.

After that, he and Noriko and Yoshitoki went on talking, or so he thought.

It was just before ten when Shuya noticed something was off.

Something felt wrong inside the bus. In the seat to his left, Yoshitoki breathed softly, asleep. Shinji Mimura's body had slumped over, dangling into the aisle. Noriko Nakagawa's eyes were closed. No one was talking. Everyone seemed to have fallen asleep. Of course, it was past bedtime for kids who really cared about being healthy, but with the excitement of having just left on their school trip, wasn't it a bit early for everyone to be sleeping? They all should be singing. Wasn't this bus equipped with one of those hateful, vulgar karaoke machines?

Worst of all, Shuya himself felt incredibly tired. In his stupor, he tried to look around, but his head, too heavy, flopped against the backrest. His vision swam, and at the shadowy front of the confined cabin, in the windshield mirror, Shuya saw the bus driver reflected in miniature.

A mask covered the driver's mouth, with some hoselike object trailing down and a thin strap hooked around his ears. What was it? Aside from the hose hanging downward, it looked just like one of those emergency oxygen masks from an airplane.

Was the air inside the bus unbreathable? *Ladies and gentlemen, the bus will be making an emergency landing due to engine trouble. Please fasten your seat belt, put on your oxygen mask, and listen for the flight attendants' instructions.* Yeah, right.

A scratching noise came from the right, and Shuya, with considerable effort, inclined his neck in that direction. His body felt heavy, like he was moving through jelly.

Shogo Kawada had lifted himself from his seat and was trying to open the window. But whether it was rusted shut or had a broken lock, the window wouldn't budge. Kawada began to pound on the glass with his left hand, trying to break it. Why?

But the window didn't break. Kawada attempted to strike it one more time, but his arm lost its strength and fell slack. He slumped back into his seat. Shuya thought he could faintly hear that low voice say, "Damn."

And then Shuya slept.

Around that same time, the children's families back in Shiroiwa were visited by men in black sedans. The parents must all have been equally speechless, called to their doors in the middle of the night and presented with the government document stamped with the peach emblem.

Nearly all would silently nod and think of the children they would likely never see again. But some would lash out, only to be beaten unconscious with a single blow of a tactical baton—or, if they were unlucky, showered in a stream of hot lead spat out by submachine guns and taken from this world just a little ahead of their beloved young.

The bus for Shiroiwa Junior High's Ninth Grade Class B had long since peeled off from the school trip caravan and turned back toward

Takamatsu City. It entered the city, wound through the local streets, then stopped, its engine fading to silence.

The driver was in his forties, a good-natured-looking fellow with salt and pepper hair. The oxygen mask still strapped to his slightly haggard face, he looked back at the students of Class B with a hint of sadness in his eyes. But when a man arrived outside the window, the driver's expression cleared. He gave the Republic's distinctive salute and pushed the switch to open the door. As the men in military uniforms and gas masks swarmed inside, the driver gazed off into the distance.

Beneath the moonlight and beyond the bone-white concrete pier, the ship that would carry the "players" swayed atop the vast jet-black sea.

42 STUDENTS REMAIN.

1

For a brief moment, Shuya found himself in the familiar surroundings of his classroom.

Of course, this classroom wasn't that of Ninth Grade Class B, though it did have the teacher's podium and lectern, washed-out blackboard, large-screen TV elevated on a stand to the left, and rows of desks and chairs of plywood and steel. On the corner of the desk where Shuya sat, someone had used a metal tool to carve antigovernment graffiti: *The Leader is hot for women in uniform.* Together on the bus until only moments ago (at least as far as he could tell), all forty-two students were seated at the desks, the boys in their standing collar button-up jackets and the girls in their sailor *fuku*, but asleep, slumped haphazardly onto their desks or back in their chairs.

Seated beside the frosted glass windows on the hallway side of the room (assuming this place had the same layout as his own school), Shuya surveyed his surroundings. None of the other students appeared to be awake. To the left and a little forward, near the center of the room, was Yoshitoki Kuninobu, with Noriko Nakagawa behind and Shinji Mimura on his left, each of them deep asleep on their desks. Lanky Hiroki Sugimura had been deposited at a desk next to the exterior windows at the room's left. Shuya came to the belated realization that everyone had been placed in the same assigned seats as their class in Shiroiwa Junior High. Then he noticed what had been feeling off about the room—the windows on Hiroki's side were covered with black panels. Steel plates, perhaps? Dingy light from rows of ceiling fluorescents reflected coldly off the panels' surface. The frosted glass windows near Shuya were also submerged in darkness, possibly covered from the hallway side. Shuya couldn't tell what time of day it was.

He looked at his watch. Exactly one o'clock. Morning? Or afternoon? The date read *THU/22*. If his watch hadn't been tampered with, either three hours had passed since that peculiar exhaustion overcame him in the bus or this was the afternoon of the next day. Okay. No point in dwelling on it.

Shuya looked around at his classmates.

Something was strange. Well, everything about this was strange. Yet something was *wrong*.

Shuya quickly recognized what it was. Noriko was slumped on her desk, and just above the sailor collar of her uniform, a metallic silver band snugly encircled her neck. Barely visible at the edge of Yoshitoki Kuninobu's buttoned collar was a matching object. And Shinji Mimura, Hiroki Sugimura, and every one of his classmates all had one around their necks.

Struck with a sudden realization, Shuya touched his right hand to the back of his neck.

He felt something hard and cold. There was no doubting it—he had one too.

He gave the object a little tug, but, firmly in place, it refused to come off. Now that he had become conscious of the band, he felt like he was suffocating. *A collar! A goddamn collar. I'm no dog!*

Shuya fidgeted with the thing for a time before giving up.

And what had happened to the school trip?

Shuya noticed his gym bag lying at his feet. The night before, he'd stuffed it with clothes and a towel, a travel notebook handed out by his school, as well as a flask of bourbon and whatever else he thought he would need. Everyone else's bags were beside them as well.

Suddenly, the sliding door at the front of the class clattered open. Shuya looked toward the entrance.

A man entered the room. He was alone.

He was well built, though a little on the short side, with under-sized legs that seemed only an afterthought to his torso. He wore plain, light beige slacks, a gray suit coat, a crimson tie, and black loafers, all of them shabby. A peach-colored pin on his collar identified him as a government official. He had rosy cheeks. But what stood out the most was his hair, straight and down to his shoulders in a style popular with younger women. Shuya was reminded of the grainy photocopied cover of a Joan Baez cassette he'd copped off the black market.

The man stepped onto the teacher's podium and surveyed the class. His eyes landed upon Shuya, the only student awake (unless it was all a dream).

The two stared at each other for at least one full minute. But as the other students began to stir, and the sounds of uneasy breathing grew, the man looked away. Some of the students called out to wake up others who were more deeply asleep.

Shuya looked across the classroom. The other kids had started to awaken, their eyes yet unfocused, and with no idea of what was happening. Yoshitoki Kuninobu turned in his chair and met Shuya's gaze. Shuya pointed to his own collar and tilted his head to the side. Yoshitoki's hands scrambled for his neck, and shock sprang to his expression. Then, for some reason, Yoshitoki shook his head several times, finally looking to the front of the class. Noriko Nakagawa also gazed at Shuya, her eyes distant, but Shuya could only offer a shrug in response.

Finally, when everyone was awake, the man spoke, his voice cheery, "All right, is everyone awake? Did you sleep well?"

No one said a thing in reply. Not even the two class clowns, Yutaka Seto and Yuka Nakagawa (Girls #16).

42 STUDENTS REMAIN.

2

The long-haired man at the teacher's lectern continued with a broad smile, "All right, all right, all right, okay, I'll explain. First off, My name is Kinpatsu Sakamochi, and I'm your new instructor."

The man who called himself Sakamochi turned to the blackboard and wrote his name in large, vertical characters with the chalk—a riff on the name of a teacher on a long-running TV series. What kind of stupid name was that? An alias, maybe, given the situation.

The class leader for the girls, Yukie Utsumi, stood suddenly and said, "I don't understand."

All eyes turned to her. Yukie's long hair parted into two neat braids. Her expression was a little tense, but her voice was firm. Maybe she'd imagined up some scenario, impossible as it seemed, that had brought the students there, like they had all been knocked unconscious in a bus accident.

"What's going on?" Yukie asked. "We'd just left on our school trip. Isn't that right, everyone?"

Yukie looked over her shoulders to her classmates all around. Her question had triggered an outburst, as nearly everyone was shouting over each other:

"Where are we?"

"Did you fall asleep too?"

"Hey, what time is it?"

"Was everyone sleeping?"

"Shit, I don't have a watch!"

"Do you remember getting off the bus and coming here?"

"Who the hell is that guy?"

"No, I don't remember anything."

"I don't like this. What's going on? I'm scared."

Shuya noted that Sakamochi had stopped his speech to listen. Silent himself, Shuya watched his classmates. A few were keeping quiet.

The first to catch his notice was Kazuo Kiriyama, a little behind him and to the side, at the middle of the back row. Beneath his slicked-back hair, Kiriyama's calm eyes were fixed on the man at the podium—watching, not glaring; his eyes were far too placid to call it that. Despite their attempts to get him to say something, Kiriyama paid no attention to his lackeys seated around him: Ryuhei Sasagawa, Mitsuru Numai, Hiroshi Kuronaga (Boys #9), and Sho Tsukioka (Boys #14).

Then there was Mitsuko Souma, second seat from the front on the window row. You remember, that vaguely rough-around-the-edges girl. Her desk was separated from the other two in her clique (Hirono Shimizu and Yoshimi Yahagi), and none of the other girls—or boys, for that matter—tried to talk to her. (Hirono and Yoshimi were in adjacent seats to Shuya's left and were saying something to each other.) Mitsuko had the captivating face of a pop idol, though it wore its usual vaguely listless expression. Arms folded, she stared at Sakamochi. (Hiroki Sugimura sat directly behind her and was talking with Tadakatsu Hatagami to his right.)

Next was Shogo Kawada, in the same window row, two seats from the back. He too silently stared at Sakamochi. As Shuya watched, Kawada took a piece of gum from his pocket and started to chew, his eyes fixed dead ahead as his jaw worked up and down.

Shuya faced the front of the class and noticed Noriko was still staring back at him. Her dark eyes trembled in fear. Shuya glanced at Yoshitoki in the seat ahead of her, but he was talking about something with Shinji Mimura in the next row. Quickly returning his eyes to Noriko, Shuya attempted a tiny nod. A little relief edged into her eyes.

Sakamochi clapped his hands a few times and admonished, "All right, all right, all right, quiet down, everyone!" The uproar quickly subsided, and he continued. "Okay, I'll explain. We've had you come here for one and only one reason."

Then: "Today, you're all going kill each other."

This time, no outburst came. The students froze like subjects of a still life photograph—except Kawada, Shuya noticed, who kept on chewing his gum. Kawada's expression remained impassive, though Shuya thought he might have seen the flash of a faint smile.

Sakamochi maintained his broad grin and continued, "Your class has been chosen for this year's Program."

Someone whimpered.

42 STUDENTS REMAIN.

Every junior high school student in the Republic of Greater
East Asia knew about the Program, which was covered in textbooks
starting in the fourth grade. A somewhat detailed description appears
in the government-compiled *Republic of Greater East Asia Compact
Encyclopedia*:

Program (prō'grăm, -grəm) *n.* 1. A written list providing details of
items or performers (names, order of appearance, etc.) [. . .]

4. A battle simulation necessary to our defense and conducted by our nation's Ground Nonaggressive Force. Officially
titled "Combat Experiment 68th Program." First held in 1947,
the annual simulations are conducted by fifty ninth-grade classes
selected voluntarily nationwide (prior to 1950, the number of
classes was forty-seven), with various statistics collected from
the trials. The experiment itself is simple: the students in each
class fight each other until only one remains, and the findings,
including the elapsed time of the simulation, are determined. The
last survivor (winner) in each class is awarded a lifetime pension
and a personally signed autograph from His Majesty The Leader.
The 317th Leader's famous "April Speech" was given in response

to protestors and agitators from an extremist sect during the first year of the Program.

The "April Speech" appears in the seventh grade textbook as follows:

My beloved comrades, who strive toward revolution and development. *[Two-minute interruption for applause and cheers for the great 317th Leader]* Comrades. *[One-minute interruption]* Throughout the world, shameless imperialists who seek to menace our Republic still continue to assemble. Observe what they do to their own countrymen. They exploit them, they cheat them, they brainwash them, the people who would otherwise have been our comrades, into becoming the advance guard of their imperialism, and then they use them at their whim. *[Unanimous cry of righteous indignation]* Given the slightest chance, the imperialists would invade the soil of our Republic, the most advanced revolutionary state in the world. By weaving their plots to bring ruin to our people, they lay bare the depths of their devious ways. *[Scattered shouts of anger]* With our nation surrounded by this state of affairs, the 68th Program is absolutely vital. In truth, I myself will be unable to hold back my bitter tears of remorse over the loss of the lives of thousands, even tens of thousands, each at the age of only fifteen. But if their lives serve to protect the independence of our people living in this nation of abundance, then will not their flesh and blood live on for eternity, becoming one with this land of beauty passed down to us by our gods? *[One-minute interruption for a wave of applause and cheers.]* As you all know, we do not have a military draft in the Republic. The Ground, Maritime, and Air Nonaggressive Forces consist of young volunteer soldiers who aspire to patriotism and burn with a resilient purpose of revolution and development. They risk their lives day and night on the front lines. Think of the Program as a kind of draft, one unique to our nation. To defend our nation [. . .]

Enough of that windbag. (Middle-aged Nonaggressive Forces re-cruiters could be often found right outside train stations, saying, "How about we get some pork and rice?" as their standard bait.)

Shuya had heard about the Program before he was even in fourth grade. It was after his parents died in a traffic accident and when he'd just begun to adjust to life in the House of Mercy and Love, where an acquaintance of his father had put him. (None of his relatives would take him in. Some said it was because his parents had been involved in antigovernment activities, but he'd never confirmed the story.)

Shuya must have been five at the time, watching TV in the rec room with Yoshitoki Kuninobu, who had already been well established at the House of Mercy and Love when he showed up. The latest episode of Shuya's favorite giant mecha anime had just ended, and the director of the facility, Ms. Ryoko Anno, changed the channel. (The daughter of the previous director, at the time she was probably still in high school. Regardless, the kids used the honorifics with all the workers there, and Ms. Anno was no exception.) Shuya kept on watching the screen, where an adult man in a stiff suit was talking into the camera. The child recognized that this must be that "news" thing, that boring show that was on all the channels from time to time.

The man was reading from a script. Shuya couldn't remember what the newscaster said, but it was pretty much always the same and was probably something like:

"We have received confirmation from officials with the government and the Nonaggressive Forces that the Program, run in Kagawa Prefecture for the first time in three years, completed yesterday at 3:12 p.m. The participating class was from Zentsuji Fourth Junior High, Ninth Grade Class E, of the city of Zentsuji. The Program took place at the previously undisclosed location of Shidaka Island, four kilometers off the coast from the town of Tadotsu. Three days, seven hours, and forty-three minutes elapsed before the winner was determined. Earlier today, the bodies were retrieved, and autopsies were held to determine the preliminary cause of death for the thirty-eight deceased students as follows: seventeen by gunshot, nine by edged weapon, five by blunt object, three by suffocation . . ."

The newscast displayed the apparent "winner," a young girl in a tattered sailor-suit uniform, flanked by two soldiers, her face twitching as she looked into the camera. At the edge of her long, disheveled hair, her right temple was smeared dark red. But something peculiar about this image would remain fresh in Shuya's memory: the corners of the girl's mouth working in contorted flashes that looked like a smile.

Shuya recognized now that this was the first time he had witnessed the face of insanity. But at the time, he hadn't distinguished it as such; he simply felt afraid, as if he were looking at a monster.

Shuya believed he had asked, "Ms. Anno, what is that?"

Ms. Anno shook her head and said, "It's nothing." Then she looked away from Shuya and whispered, "That poor girl."

Yoshitoki Kuninobu, preoccupied with a tangerine, hadn't been paying attention to the TV for some time.

As Shuya grew older, these local news reports, coming roughly twice a year with no schedule and no warning, felt increasingly ominous. With fifty ninth-grade classes around the country, and assuming forty students in each, it was a death sentence visited annually upon two thousand children—no, one thousand nine hundred fifty, to be precise. And this was no mere killing, but familiar classmates murdering each other in competition for a single survivor's throne, like the most heinous game of musical chairs.

But there would be no resisting it. The actions of the government of the Republic of Greater East Asia were not to be defied.

So Shuya viewed the Program with dismissive contempt. That was how most of the kids in the ninth-grade "reserves" dealt with it. Okay, sure, a kind of draft unique to our nation? Our nation of abundance and land of beauty? How many junior high students were there in the Republic? Even with the declining birth rate, the odds weren't even one in eight hundred or so. In all of Kagawa Prefecture, at most only one class "wins" that lottery in two years. Frankly, getting killed in a car accident was just as likely, and seeing how he never got the luck of the draw, Shuya never thought he'd get chosen. Hell, when the local shopping arcade held a raffle, he'd never won more than a box of tissues. So who gives a shit? Fuck it.

But every once in a while, someone in his class—usually one of the girls—would cry and say, "My cousin's in the Program," or something like that, and inside Shuya that black terror would return. And with it, anger. *Who had the right to make that cute girl sad?*

But then, after days of depression, that girl would begin to smile again, and Shuya's feelings of terror and anger would gradually fade away. Only the faint, indistinct sense of helplessness and distrust toward the government remained behind.

That's how it went.

And when Shuya entered ninth grade this year, he—and likely his classmates—believed Class B alone was safe. They had to believe.

Until this very moment.

A chair noisily scraped against the floor as one of the boys stood and shouted, his voice shrill, "That can't be!"

Shuya turned to see the source of the outburst, somewhere behind Hiroki Sugimura. It was the class leader for the boys, Kyoichi Motobuchi. Kyoichi's face had crossed from pale into ashen in a surreal contrast with his silver-rimmed glasses. He could have been one of Andy Warhol's silkscreen creations from their art textbook, *Decadent Art of the American Empire*.

Some in the class may have hoped Kyoichi would offer some rational argument. *Kill the kids who were our friends just the day before? That's impossible. This has to be a mistake. Explain it to this jerk, class leader.*

But what Kyoichi said was utterly worthless.

"M-my father is the director of the Kagawa Department of Natural Resources." Kyoichi was trembling, and his voice sounded even more nervous than it usually did. "There's no way my class would be selected for the P-Program."

The man who had called himself Sakamochi shook his head with a dry smile. His long hair billowed.

"You're Motobuchi, yeah?" Sakamochi said, his voice syrupy. "Surely you know of the concept of equality, right? Listen, all people are born equal. Just because your father is a government official doesn't mean it's all right for him to receive special treatment. Clearly the same goes for his son. Listen, everyone, you all have your own circumstances. Some of you come from rich families, and some poor. But your value isn't determined by such things—by things beyond your control. Each one of you must discover your own worth through your own efforts. So, Motobuchi, don't make the mistake of thinking that you alone are special." Then he shouted, "Because you're not!"

Stunned to silence, Kyoichi slumped to his chair. Sakamochi glared at the boy for a time until his broad grin suddenly returned.

"They'll be talking about you on the morning news," Sakamochi said. "Of course, with the Program being a secret experiment, they won't announce any of the details until it's over. But, well, your fathers and your mothers have all been informed."

Everyone appeared stunned. *We have to kill our classmates? Can it really be?*

"What," Sakamochi said, scratching his head in apparent consternation, "you still don't believe me?"

He faced the doorway and called out, taking time with the words, "You men—come on in!"

On command, three soldiers noisily rushed into the room. Their dress—a camouflage combat uniform, combat boots, and a metal helmet with the peach emblem emblazoned on the front—identified the men as members of the Nonaggressive Forces. They carried assault rifles slung from their shoulders and wore belt holsters with pistol grips visible. One was tall, with tousled hair—odd for a soldier, that—and his default expression seemed to be an insincere smile. Another was of average height and baby-faced, a leading man type. The last seemed a touch effeminate and fairly unimpressive compared to the other two. The three men were stooped over, hauling a large sack made of heavy plastic. It resembled a black sleeping bag, only it bulged here and there, as if stuffed with pineapples.

Sakamochi stepped aside to the window, and the three soldiers placed the bag atop the teacher's podium. The ends of the bag hung off the edges of the platform. Whatever was inside must not have been very rigid, because the ends—especially the side facing the windows—drooped.

Sakamochi said, "These men will be assisting with your Program. Allow me to introduce them. This is Mr. Tahara, Mr. Kondo, and Mr. Nomura. All right, show them what's in the bag."

The insincere soldier called Tahara grabbed the zipper on the hallway side and tugged it open. A red liquid covered the interior.

With the zipper only partway open, one of the girls in the front row screamed. Others quickly joined in, the soprano chorus swelling over a backdrop of confused exclamations and clattering desks and chairs.

Shuya gulped.

Then he saw it, inside the half-open bag—the teacher in charge of Class B, Mr. Hayashida. No, the former teacher. No, the former Mr. Hayashida.

His cheap, blue-gray suit was soaked in blood. Only the left half of his black-rimmed glasses (the source of his nickname, "Dragonfly") remained. Unsurprising, given that only the left half of his head was still there. Behind the single lens, the red marble of an eye stared languidly at the ceiling. What was left of his hair was mottled with a gray jelly that must have been brain matter. His left arm, watch still on, spilled out from the bag, as if relieved to be free of the confines, and dangled off the front of the podium. Anyone in the front row would have been close enough to see if the watch's second hand still moved.

"All right, all right, all right, quiet, quiet." Sakamochi clapped his hands, but the girls' shrieks persisted. "Quiet, please! Really, you all—"

Suddenly, Kondo, the baby-faced soldier, drew his sidearm.

Shuya thought the soldier was going to fire a warning shot at the ceiling, but instead, Kondo seized the body bag with his free hand and dragged it off the platform. He then lifted Mr. Hayashida's body so that the teacher's head was level with his own. He looked like a hero in some sci-fi monster movie battling a giant cocoon-spinning worm.

The soldier put his gun to Mr. Hayashida's head and squeezed the trigger twice. The teacher's head blew apart, insides spraying out, the energy of the high velocity round scattering bits of brains and bone in a bloody mist that fell upon the faces and chests of the students in the front row.

When echoes of gunfire subsided, Mr. Hayashida didn't have much of a head left at all.

The soldier tossed Mr. Hayashida's body beside the podium. The screams had stopped.

42 STUDENTS REMAIN.

4

The standing students fearfully lowered themselves back into their seats. The unimpressive soldier on the end dragged Mr. Hayashida's body bag to the corner of the room, then rejoined his two comrades beside the teacher's podium. Sakamochi returned to the lectern.

The room was again silent, save for the sounds of one student somewhere near the back: miserable moaning punctuated by splashes of vomit spilling wetly on the floor. The smell came soon after.

"All right," Sakamochi said, calmly smoothing back his hair, "Mr. Hayashida was, you see, very opposed to your selection for the Program. Well, this all happened so suddenly, I feel bad about it myself."

The students had gone still. They had accepted reality. This was not a joke. They were going to be forced to kill each other.

But now, finally, Shuya desperately made himself think. His mind, dazed when confronted with the impossibility of the scenario, had been awakened by the ghastly sight of Mr. Hayashida's corpse and the cruel performance in which it had featured.

I have to escape, whatever it takes. But how? Right, first, I need to talk to Yoshitoki . . . and Mimura and Sugimura. But how exactly does the Program go, anyway? The details haven't ever been made public. I know we're given weapons to kill each other with, but are we allowed to talk? And how does the government monitor what happens?

"I-I," said a voice, interrupting Shuya's thoughts. He raised his head and opened his eyes.

Yoshitoki Kuninobu half stood, blankly staring at Sakamochi, unsure if he should finish what he had been about to say, as if the words had spilled out of their own accord. Shuya's body tensed. *Yoshitoki, keep quiet!*

Sakamochi offered a warm smile and said, "Yes, what is it? Ask me anything."

On automatic pilot, without even thinking, Yoshitoki continued. "I . . . don't have any parents. Who did you contact?"

"Ah, yes." Sakamochi nodded. "There was a student living in a welfare institution. You're Nanahara, then? The school records said you had . . . ideological problems. And—"

"I'm Nanahara," Shuya interrupted, half shouting.

Sakamochi glanced at Shuya, then looked back at Yoshitoki. Yoshitoki looked at Shuya too, still something vacant in his expression.

"Oh, sorry, sorry," Sakamochi said. "There was another. You must be Kuninobu. Right, I made sure to contact the administrator of the facility where both of you live. She was . . . rather pretty."

Sakamochi grinned at the implication he had seen her personally. As utterly cheerful as the smile was, there was something nasty to it.

Shuya grimaced. "Is she . . . Did something happen to Ms. Anno?"

"She was like Mr. Hayashida, Nanahara. She resisted on your behalf. To make her obedient, well . . ." Sakamochi paused before calmly continuing, "I had to force myself upon her. Now, don't you worry, she's not dead or anything."

A crimson rage sprung up inside Shuya, but before he could say anything, he heard Yoshitoki yell, "I'll kill you!"

Yoshitoki stood. His face had changed, with a heartfelt anger rarely displayed by the typically genial boy. His classmates had likely never seen him like this before—nor would they have even imagined him generally capable of the emotion—though Shuya, having lived together with his friend for so many years, had encountered that expression maybe a couple of times. Once was in the fourth grade, when a hit-and-run driver struck the orphanage's dog, Eddie, outside the front gates, and Yoshitoki chased after him. The second time was just a year ago. A man had been using the House of Mercy and Love's debts as an excuse to make dogged advances on Ms. Anno. When she finally scraped together the money and rejected him once and for all, he deliberately cursed her out where the children would hear. If Shuya hadn't stopped him, Yoshitoki would have knocked the man's front teeth out, whatever the cost. Yoshitoki was incredibly, incredibly kind, and could laugh off most any offense, whether it was being made fun of or being pushed around. But hurt someone he loved, and his response would be ferocious. Shuya admired that.

"I'll kill you, you bastard!" Yoshitoki went on shouting. "I'm going to fucking kill you and bury you in shit!"

"Oh?" Sakamochi said, flashing an amused smile. "Do you really mean what you're saying, Kuninobu? Listen, people have to take responsibility for the things they say."

"Fuck you! I'm really going to kill you, and don't you fucking forget it!"

Shuya yelled, "Yoshitoki! Let it go!" But Yoshitoki didn't seem to hear.

Sakamochi spoke again, this time in a soothing yet oddly gleeful tone. "You know, Kuninobu, what you're saying right now, that's in defiance of the government."

"I'll kill you!" Yoshitoki didn't relent an inch. "I'll kill you kill you *kill you*!"

Just as Shuya lost his patience and was about to shout again, Sakamochi shook his head, then turned to the three soldiers standing beside the podium and made a sharp gesture.

The three camouflaged men, Tahara, Kondo, and Nomura, extended their right arms in unison, like the Four Freshmen or some other vocal group striking an impassioned pose for a song's climax—though *this* ensemble happened to be holding pistols. If this were the chorus, it might go, *Baby please, Baby please / Spend this night with me.*

From his seat diagonally behind, Shuya could see Yoshitoki's goggling eyes bulged open even wider.

The three guns flashed simultaneously. Halfway into the aisle, Yoshitoki's body danced the boogaloo.

It was over before anyone, including Noriko Nakagawa directly behind, could duck.

And as the gunfire's echoes faded, Yoshitoki slowly leaned to the right, then flopped to the floor between his own desk and that of Izumi Kanai to his right. Izumi gasped.

The trio held their pose, arms outstretched and level. Three identical wisps of smoke wafted from the muzzles of their pistols. The room was oddly silent. Between the desk legs, Shuya saw his friend's familiar face pointed straight at him, those goggling eyes open, staring at a point on the floor. A pool of bright blood began to spread. Yoshitoki's arm, splayed at his side, began to spasm, shaking from the shoulder down to the fingertips.

Yoshitoki!

Shuya stood and began to run to Yoshitoki's side, but Noriko got there first. She cried, "Mr. Nobu!" and stooped over him.

The soldier with the fake smile was the only one to shoot her. She fell forward as if she had tripped and slammed atop Yoshitoki's convulsing body.

The man immediately pointed his weapon at Shuya. Becoming more and more confused, Shuya froze in place. Moving only his eyes, he looked at Noriko. She was on her hands and knees atop Yoshitoki. Blood gushed from a wound in her right calf.

To Noriko, Sakamochi said, "Leaving your desk without permission is not allowed." Then to Shuya, "The same applies to you, Nanahara. Take your seat."

Shuya tore his eyes from the sight of Noriko's rapidly bloodying leg and from Yoshitoki beneath her, and looked Sakamochi straight on. He could feel his neck muscles twitch from the shock.

"What the hell is going on?" Shuya shouted, on the verge of crying, unable to make himself move. The insincere soldier kept his pistol trained right between Shuya's eyes. "What the hell are you doing? You have to—Yoshitoki needs first aid! And Noriko . . ."

Sakamochi frowned and shook his head. Then he repeated, "Take your seat now. And you too, uh, Nakagawa."

Noriko, her face pale from the sight of Yoshitoki, slowly lifted her head to look at Sakamochi. Anger overshadowed what must have been incredible pain. She glared at Sakamochi and said, clipping each word, "Please help Kuninobu."

Yoshitoki's right arm continued to spasm. But as Shuya watched, the movements were quickly abating. Without immediate attention, his wounds would clearly be fatal.

With a sigh, Sakamochi turned to the insincere soldier and said, "Tahara, make sure of it."

Before Shuya had time to think *Of what?* the soldier aimed his pistol down and fired once. Yoshitoki Kuninobu's head jolted, and something sprayed out and splashed onto Noriko's face.

Noriko was dazed, her mouth agape. Dark red flecked her face.

Shuya realized his own mouth was hanging open.

Though part of his head was now gone, Yoshitoki kept on staring at the same spot on the floor. But he had stopped spasming. He had stopped doing anything at all.

"Look," Sakamochi said. "He was dead already. Now, if you've seen enough, take your seats."

Noriko looked down at Yoshitoki's gnarled head. "Oh," she let out. "This . . ."

Shuya was still in shock. His eyes were locked on Yoshitoki's face, glimpsed between the desk legs. His thoughts were paralyzed, as if it were his brains that had been blown out. His mind whirled in a tornado of memories of times spent with Yoshitoki. Little adventures camping and rowing downriver, rainy days engrossed in old, well-worn board games, watching a copy of an American movie that had made its way to the black market, *The Blues Brothers*. (Amazingly, the film

had even been dubbed in Japanese, though the voice actors were terrible.) The two lead characters had been in an orphanage, and for a
time, Shuya and Yoshitoki played pretend Jake and Elwood. Then he
remembered the expression on Yoshitoki's face, not so long ago, when
he said, "Hey, Shuya, I . . . kinda . . . got a crush." And after that . . .

"Can't you two hear me?" Sakamochi said, or perhaps repeated, as
Shuya might in fact not have heard. He just stared at his friend's face.

As did Noriko. If they had continued like that, the two may have
soon followed after Yoshitoki Kuninobu. Beside Sakamochi, the insincere soldier was pointing his gun at Noriko, and the other two soldiers
pointed theirs at Shuya.

But a calm voice—carefree, even—saying, "Teacher Teacher
Teacher," brought Shuya back to reality, or at least made him turn
dimly to face the voice's source.

On the other side of Yoshitoki's now empty chair, Shinji Mimura
had raised his hand. Noriko finally looked his way.

"Um, Mimura, right?" Sakamochi said. "What is it?"

Shinji lowered his hand, and The Third Man's voice sounded no
different than any other day when he asked, "Since Nakagawa is hurt,
could I help her to her chair?"

Sakamochi's eyebrows rose a little, but he nodded his consent.
"Sure, go ahead. I want to keep things moving."

Shinji nodded, stood, and walked to Noriko's side, kneeling between Yoshitoki's body and her. As he moved, he had taken a neatly
folded handkerchief from his pocket, which he then used to wipe
Yoshitoki's blood from her face. Noriko didn't react.

"Come, Nakagawa, stand," he said, taking her by her right arm
and helping her up.

Then, with his back turned to Sakamochi, Shinji looked at Shuya,
who was still half standing at his desk. Beneath crisp, upturned eyebrows, Shinji's typically good-humored eyes had turned solemn. With
an arching of an eyebrow and a minute shake of his head, he jerked
his left hand down, palm open. When Shuya didn't understand, Shinji
repeated the gesture.

The second time, Shuya realized through his daze that Shinji was telling him, *Settle down*. He returned Shinji's gaze and eased back into his chair.

Shinji gave him a slight nod and helped Noriko to her seat, then turned his back again and returned to his own.

Noriko's right leg dangled from her chair, blood gushing from the wound, staining her white sock and sneaker in bright red, like she had put on one of Santa's boots.

Finally regaining her senses, Noriko started to thank Shinji. But, as if he could see behind himself, the boy dismissed her with a shrug. She withdrew, and her eyes fell back down to Yoshitoki, lying just to her right. Her gaze froze there, and though she didn't make a sound, Shuya could see her eyes filling with tears.

He too looked at Yoshitoki's corpse, the legs of the desks fragmenting the view. A corpse, that's all it was now. There was no denying it. Though unable to fully process what had just occurred, Shuya knew this was a corpse—the corpse of the boy with whom he had shared the last ten years of his life.

As he looked into Yoshitoki's gaping eyes, anger came to him, pulsing, building steadily, resolute, taking control of his body. He thought he might be shaking. Emotions quelled by shock returned to him. His lip curled as he turned to face Sakamochi.

The man watched him with amusement. *I'll never forgive you,* Shuya thought. *I'm going to kill the bastard!*

Shuya was only moments away from exploding as his friend had done, but then he remembered Shinji's gestured message—*Settle down*. An outburst now would only bring him the same fate as Yoshitoki. And now Yoshitoki's crush, Noriko Nakagawa, was badly hurt. If Shuya died, what would happen to her?

With effort, he broke away from Sakamochi's gaze and buried his eyes in the top of his desk. He felt miserable. Denied an outlet, the rage and sorrow threatened to crush his spirit.

Sakamochi chuckled, apparently turning his attention elsewhere.

To keep his body from trembling, Shuya clenched his fists under his desk. Strongly, strongly, he clenched. But with Yoshitoki's body so near, forcing down his emotions was not easy.

He really couldn't process it. *Can it really be? Can you lose someone just like that? Someone that close, gone?*

The two boys had always been together. What they had done together may not have amounted to much, but when they had been playing in the river and Yoshitoki nearly drowned, Shuya was the one who saved him. When they were collecting grasshoppers and carelessly stuffed too many into a single box, killing nearly all of them, they both felt bad about it. They had fought over who Eddy the dog loved more. When they snuck into the attic over the school's faculty room for a laugh, and it looked like they were about to be caught, they pulled off the escape and laughed about it together. The two really had been inseparable. They had been.

And now, he's gone?

Shinji raised his hand. "Teacher, I have another question."

"Again, Mimura? What is it?"

"Nakagawa is hurt. Wouldn't her being in the Program make it unfair?"

Sakamochi laughed in amusement. "Yeah. Well, that may be true, Mimura, but what of it?"

"Couldn't you see that her wounds get treated and have the Program postponed until she's healed?"

Shuya, having barely been able to control his tumultuous emotions, marveled at Shinji Mimura's composure—though he was surprised he could be any more impressed with the boy than he already had been before. It was true; Shinji was far calmer than Shuya had managed. If Shuya could match it himself, maybe he could buy himself and his classmates more time to find an escape.

Sakamochi burst into laughter. "What an amusing suggestion, Mimura," he said. Then he offered a different solution. "All right, then, how about I kill Nakagawa. That would make everything fair, right?"

Not only Noriko, but all the students tensed. Shuya could see Shinji's back muscles stiffen beneath his school uniform.

Right away, Shinji said, "I take it back, I take it back. I give."

His joking tone sent Sakamochi into another burst of laughter. The insincere-looking soldier, who had already begun reaching for his holster, returned his hand to rest on his rifle's shoulder strap.

Sakamochi clapped his hands twice and said, "All right, listen, you all have different aptitudes. Whether intellect or physical ability, you all start unequal. So Nakagawa won't be receiving any medical atten— You there! No talking!"

With a shout, he threw a white object at Fumiyo Fujiyoshi (Girls #18), who was about to whisper something to the female class leader, Yukie Utsumi. For a second, Shuya thought it was a piece of chalk—a guess that would have been apt, back in another world.

Thuk! Making the sound of a nail driven into a coffin, a thin knife sprouted from the center of Fumiyo's high and fair-skinned forehead.

Yukie's eyes widened as she saw it, while Fumiyo made for a bizarre show, looking up, trying to identify the knife in her own brow, her head tilting back.

Then, in an instant, Fumiyo collapsed sideways. Her temple slammed against Yukie's desk, jolting it.

This time, no confirmation was needed. Who could have a knife sticking out of her forehead and survive?

No one moved. No one spoke. With held breath, Yukie stared down at Fumiyo. Noriko watched with a stunned expression. Shinji Mimura pursed his lips and looked at Fumiyo, who had fallen into the same aisle as Yoshitoki.

Shuya forced his dry throat to swallow and thought, *He did that just because he felt like it. On a fucking whim! Our lives are at the mercy of this bastard, Sakamochi or whatever his name is.*

"Whoops, I really did it now," Sakamochi said. "Sorry, everyone. It's against the rules for the teacher to kill his students."

He closed his eyes and scratched his head. Then, his expression suddenly plain again, he said, "But no more doing *anything* without permission. That includes whispering. I don't want to have to do it, but if you talk in class . . . I have plenty of knives."

Shuya gritted his teeth and told himself, *Wait.* Two of his class-mates were dead already, their corpses sprawled on the floor. Again and again, he repeated it to himself. *Wait.*

But Yoshitoki's face kept drawing his eyes in. He couldn't help it. He felt ready to cry.

40 STUDENTS REMAIN.

"I'll explain the rules," Sakamochi said, his voice again cheerful.

Unlike the already dried blood of their teacher, "Dragonfly" Hayashida, Yoshitoki Kuninobu's blood was fresh, the smell of it thick in the air. Shuya couldn't see Fumiyo Fujiyoshi's face from where he sat, but she didn't seem to be bleeding much.

"As you all may already know," Sakamochi said, "the rules are simple. Kill one another. That's it. No holds barred." Sakamochi beamed a smile. "And only the sole survivor will be able to go home. And you'll even get a signed card from the Great Leader. Pretty cool, right?"

In his mind, Shuya spat.

"You all might think those are some harsh rules. But the unexpected will happen—that's what life is. Listen, if you're going to manage life's accidents, you need to keep a good grip on yourself. Think of this as practice for that. An exercise, okay? Also, in the name of gender equality, there will be no handicaps for the boys or girls. But I do have good news for the girls. According to actual Program results, 49 percent of the past winners have been girls. If they can do it, so can you. You have nothing to fear."

Sakamochi signaled, and the camouflaged trio began carrying in large black nylon daypacks from the hall. The backpacks soon formed a large pile beside Mr. Hayashida's body bag. Some of them bulged out at angles, as if they might contain a pole-shaped object.

"One at a time, you will each leave here," Sakamochi explained. "But before you depart, you'll be given one of these bags, inside which you will find some food and water, and a weapon. Every bag has a unique weapon. You see, as I said before, you all come into this with differing capabilities, and this way, we can add a little . . . factor of uncertainty. If that sounds confusing, let me put it another way. We're adding things into the experiment without knowing their effects. Now, we have not predetermined which of you will receive which weapon. As each of you leaves, we'll take one bag from the top and hand it to you. Also inside your pack will be a map of this island, a compass, and a watch. Raise your hand if you don't already have a watch. Nobody? Oh, and I almost forgot to tell you—we *are* on an island. It's just about six kilometers around. This is the island's first time as the venue for the Program, but everyone has cleared out for us. There is no one else here."

Sakamochi turned to the blackboard and took a stick of chalk. Next to where he had written his own name, he sketched a large, rounded diamond shape. Above it and to the right, he drew an upward-facing arrow and the letter N. Just to the right of the diamond's center, he made an X. With his chalk still pressed to the blackboard, he looked over his shoulder to speak.

"All right, this is the island's school. Got it? That's where we are." Sakamochi tapped his chalk against the X. "I'll be staying here the whole time, watching over you."

Next he drew four spindle shapes, one in each cardinal direction.

"These are ships," Sakamochi said. "They have the very important job of shooting anyone who tries to escape by sea."

Now he drew several parallel vertical and horizontal lines across the island, making it look like a misshapen wire mesh grill. Sakamochi labeled each square, starting at the top left, "A1," then "A2," and so on, continuing in the next row with "B1," then "B2," and so forth.

"This is just a quick sketch," Sakamochi explained, "but the map inside your pack is along the same lines."

He set down the chalk and clapped the dust from his hands. "All right, so, when you leave here, you'll be free to go where you please. But I will make announcements, broadcast throughout the island, at twelve and six, day and night. That's four times a day. I'll be letting you know which zones, according to your maps, will be dangerous, from what time. Take a good look at your maps, refer to your compasses and the topography, and hurry away from those areas!

"And why is that, you ask?" Sakamochi placed his hands on the lectern and looked around at the students' faces. "That's right—the collars on each of your necks."

Several of the students must have not yet noticed the collars, because they touched their hands to their necks and looked startled.

"Those collars," Sakamochi said, "are the result of our Republic's advanced technologies. Completely waterproof, shockproof—No, hey, stop, stop, you can't take it off. It won't come off. And if you try to *force* it loose . . ." Sakamochi winced. "It'll explode."

The students who had been fidgeting with their collars quickly dropped their hands.

Grinning broadly, Sakamochi continued. "Those collars monitor the electrical signals emitted by your heartbeat and inform the computers inside this school whether you're alive or dead. They also can identify your location on the island, which brings us back to the map."

He gestured toward the blackboard with his right hand. "Those same computers will be randomly determining the dangerous areas before I announce them to you. And if any of you stay in those zones past the determined time—oh, just those of you still living; the dead ones won't matter—if you remain in one of the forbidden zones, the computers will automatically recognize it and will send a signal of their own back to your collar."

"And," Sakamochi said, giving a dramatic pause, though Shuya felt he knew what was coming. "The collar will explode."

Shuya had been right.

Sakamochi stopped to gauge the students' expressions. Then, after a short time, he said, "But maybe you're wondering why we have that rule. Well, if everyone just found their own spot to hide, the game wouldn't progress. So we're going to make you move about. And the areas you can move in will shrink, smaller and smaller. That's why."

Sakamochi had called this a *game*. As despicable as it was, the word fit. And though nobody said a word, they all seemed to get the rules.

"I want to make sure you fully understand," Sakamochi said. "Going inside a building won't help you. Neither will digging a hole. The signal will still reach you. Oh, and that reminds me, you're free to hide inside any of the buildings, but phones have all been disabled. You can't call your mom and dad. You're in this battle alone, just as in life. Also, though we start without any forbidden zones that would trigger your explosive collars, this school is an exception. Twenty minutes after the last of you leaves, this will become a forbidden zone, so be sure to distance yourself from here first. Get two hundred meters away. All right? And in each announcement, I'll read the names of the students who died over the previous six hours. Though the announcements will occur at regular six-hour intervals, when there is only one student left, I will inform them by broadcast. Oh, and one more thing. There is a time limit. Did you hear me? A time limit. In the Program, students die, but if there's ever a twenty-four-hour period with no deaths, time's up. No matter how many are still alive . . ."

Shuya saw this one coming too.

"The computers will do their thing, and all of the survivors' collars will explode. There will be no winner."

Right again.

Sakamochi stopped speaking, and silence returned to the classroom. The smell of Yoshitoki Kuninobu's blood remained heavy in the air, and the students still seemed in a daze. They were afraid, though unable to fully comprehend their situation—that they were about to be thrown into a killing game.

Sakamochi, sensing their collective mood, clapped his hands. "Well, that's it for the tedious details. What I'm about to tell you next is more important. A bit of advice. Some of you might consider it preposterous to kill your own classmates. But don't you forget: the others—they're ready to kill."

Shuya wanted to scream *Bullshit!* But Fumiyo Fujiyoshi's execution for talking in class left him with no choice but to restrain himself.

Everyone remained quiet, but something had changed, and Shuya saw it.

The students were looking around, their eyes sweeping across each other's pale faces. But whenever two gazes met, each hastily looked away to Sakamochi. This episode only went on for a few seconds, but even after it passed, the looks on their faces remained—expressions taut with paranoia and fear. Expressions that wondered if the boy or girl beside them was ready to kill. Only Shinji Mimura and a few others appeared calm.

Shuya gritted his teeth. *Damn it,* he thought. *That's just what these bastards want you to do! Come on, think, all of you—we're friends. There's no way we could kill each other!*

"All right then," Sakamochi said, "let's make sure you got the message. Inside your desk is paper and a pencil. Take them out."

The students shifted uneasily in their seats and withdrew their paper and pencils. Shuya decided to go along with it for now.

"Okay," Sakamochi said, "I want you to write this down. If you want to remember something, you have to right it down. 'We will kill each other.' Write it three times."

Shuya heard the scratching of pencils taken to paper, and he could see Noriko gripping hers. Her expression remained grim. He started to scrawl down the insane mantra, when halfway through, his eyes flicked to Yoshitoki's corpse, and he recalled his friend's bright smile.

Sakamochi continued, "Okay, now write, 'If I don't kill, I'll be killed.' Three times."

Once more, Shuya looked toward Fumiyo Fujiyoshi. Her pale fingers, poking out from the sleeve of her sailor fuku, had curled, forming a shallow cup. One of the school nurse's aides, Fumiyo had been cool-headed and was always there to lend a hand.

Shuya looked up at Sakamochi.

You bastard, I'm going to drive this pencil into your heart!

40 STUDENTS REMAIN.

"All right," Sakamochi said. "So you're going to leave the class-room, one at a time, at uh, two-minute intervals. If you go through the door and turn right, the exit will be down the hall. Loiter inside, and you'll be shot and killed. Now, according to the rules of the Program, we'll select one student to go first, then the rest of you go in the order of your seat numbers. Boy, girl, boy, girl. When we hit the end of the list, we'll loop back to the top."

Shuya recalled that Noriko Nakagawa was number fifteen on the girls' side. *She's the same number as me. We'll leave at almost the same time. Unless she's first, and then I'm last, that is. But . . . can she even walk?*

Sakamochi withdrew an envelope from his breast pocket. "The first student was randomly selected. The result is in this envelope. Just a moment, now."

Sakamochi took out a pair of scissors tied with a pink ribbon. He had started ceremoniously cutting open the end of the envelope when Kazuo Kiriyama spoke, his voice calm like Shinji Mimura's, though cold and commanding. "When does the game begin?"

All of the students turned to look at the back row where Kiriyama sat. (All, except for Kawada, who just kept on chewing his gum.)

Sakamochi kept working the scissors as he replied, "As soon as you leave. So you all might want to find someplace to hide and come up with your battle plans. It's nighttime, anyway."

Kiriyama didn't respond, but now Shuya finally knew it was one in the morning—no, make it nearly half past one now.

Sakamochi finished cutting the envelope, pulled out a white paper from within, and unfolded it. His mouth rounded in surprise.

"What a coincidence! Boys, number one. Akamatsu."

Sitting in the front seat of the window aisle (or should I say, the steel plate aisle), Yoshio Akamatsu looked stunned. At one hundred eighty centimeters and ninety kilograms, he was big bodied, but in gym class, Yoshio did nothing but screw up—he couldn't catch a fly ball if it was coming right to him, nor could he even run a single lap around the track. His thick lips had drained of color.

"Quickly now, Akamatsu," Sakamochi said.

Yoshio grabbed the bag he'd packed for the school trip and unsteadily rose to his feet. The three camouflaged soldiers, rifles held at their hips, prompted him to take his daypack, and he did. The doorway opened into darkness, and he stood there, looking back at his classmates for a quick second, fear in his face. Then he was gone. The echo of a few footsteps became a clomping run, fading into the distance. It sounded like he tripped and fell once before darting off again.

As the room fell silent, several of the students let out pent-up sighs.

"Okay, we'll wait two minutes. Next will be girls number one, Mizuho Inada."

This pattern of attendance call and departure went relentlessly on and on.

But near the beginning, when number four for the girls, Sakura Ogawa left, Shuya noticed something. Hers was the second desk behind him, in the last row, and when she walked to the front of the class, she walked right by Shuya. He saw her touch her hand to the desk of her boyfriend, Kazuhiko Yamamoto, slipping him a scrap of paper. She must have left him some message on the sheet of paper she had used to write "We will kill each other."

Shuya might have been the only one who noticed. Sakamochi, at least, gave no sign he'd seen anything. Kazuhiko palmed the note and squeezed it tightly in his fist beneath his desk. Shuya felt a tiny bit of relief, knowing that madness had not yet completely consumed them all. The bonds of love persevered.

She left the room, and Shuya wondered, *What did she write to him?* He looked at the map on the blackboard. *The name of one of those squares on the grid? A meeting place? That drawing is much too crude, and besides, there's no telling if it'll match the real map at all. Maybe a direction and a distance? But wait, if the two of them are going off to meet somewhere in secret, that must mean they're convinced some of us are out to kill them. That's just how Sakamochi wants us to think.*

Shuya thought. *I don't know what's right outside, but surely I can wait there and talk to everyone who comes out after me. None of Sakamochi's rules would do anything to stop that. Sure, everyone's gone paranoid and confused, but if I can talk to them rationally, I know we can all come up with a plan. And Noriko's the first one after me. Can she walk? Shinji's also after me. Too bad Sugimura will have already gone.*

Shuya tried to conceive of some way to get a note to Hiroki Sugimura, but the boy's seat was too far away. Besides, if he screwed it up, he'd just become another Fumiyo Fujiyoshi.

Soon came Hiroki's turn. As he was about to step through the open door, he glanced at Shuya, and their eyes met. But that was all. Inside himself, Shuya sighed. He wondered if Hiroki was thinking the same thing and would be waiting for him outside. He hoped Hiroki could pull aside some of the others.

Ahead of Hiroki, and after, went the three who had remained quiet through all of the uproar: Shogo Kawada, Kazuo Kiriyama, and Mitsuko Souma.

Kawada had kept on chewing his gum as he departed. His expression remained calm, and he didn't give Sakamochi or the camouflaged trio a single look.

Kiriyama had also left quietly, as did Mitsuko.

When Sakamochi had said, "*The others are ready to kill*," those three were likely the very first to be suspected by the others. They were the bad kids. Killing would be nothing to them if it ensured their survival.

But Shuya thought Kiriyama, at the least, was different. Kiriyama had his boys—Hiroshi Kuronaga, Ryuhei Sasagawa, Sho Tsukioka, and Mitsuru Numai. More than just some group who kind of got along, they had a real bond. The rules of this game might turn everyone else into enemies, but those five would never betray each other. When Kiriyama left, Shuya paid close attention to the cluster of followers seated around his desk. Curiously, their expressions lacked concern. Maybe Kiriyama had been able to pass a note to the others. Surely the five of them were planning to escape together. With Kiriyama, they'd be able to give the government the slip—though he wouldn't be trusting anyone outside his gang.

Mitsuko Souma also had her group. But her seat left her separated from Hirono Shimizu and Yoshimi Yahagi, and she wouldn't have been able to pass them a message. Anyway, Mitsuko was a girl. No way she'd be playing this game. Impossible.

Shogo Kawada alone gave Shuya pause.

No one in the class associated themselves with Kawada. After he transferred in, he'd hardly even talked to any of his classmates. And so much of him remained an enigma. Never mind the rumors, but those scars covering his body . . .

For a moment, Shuya began to doubt. *Is Kawada going to be the one among us who'll actually dive right in? No way. Or would he? There's at least a possibility, isn't there?*

Shuya quickly banished the thought. Falling into mistrust and jumping at shadows—that would be letting the government win. But in his heart, the whisper of a worry remained.

Time passed.

Many of the girls cried as they left.

Though to Shuya it felt like not much time had passed at all, he reckoned it had been nearly one hour (minus Yoshitoki Kuninobu's two minutes) when Girls #14, Mayumi Tendo, vanished out the door, and Sakamochi said, "Boys number fifteen, Shuya Nanahara."

Shuya picked up his duffel bag and stood. He tried to think of anything he could do before leaving the room.

Instead of walking straight for the door, he headed left. Noriko turned her head and watched him approaching her.

"Nanahara," Sakamochi said, flourishing his knife. "You're going the wrong way."

Shuya stopped. The three soldiers had put their hands to their weapons. He went to speak, but he felt his throat stiffen. He had to force out the words. "Yoshitoki Kuninobu was my friend. At least let me close his eyes. 'Accord the dead every courtesy.' Isn't that what the Leader wrote in his Analects?"

For an instant, Sakamochi looked unsure, but in the end, he chuckled, lowered his knife, and said, "All right. That's very kind, Nanahara."

Shuya let out a small breath and resumed walking. When he reached Yoshitoki's body, on the floor directly in front of Noriko's desk, he stopped.

Though he had said he was going to close Yoshitoki's eyes, he couldn't help but freeze. The boy's skull had burst open just above the ear, caused by the insincere soldier's violent confirmation of the kill. His short hair was matted with blood, and up close now, Shuya could see a thin layer of tissue and something white. Skull. When the bullet ate its way into the boy's head, it had made his eyes bulge out even more than usual. Yoshitoki's eyes were vacant and pointed upward in their sockets, like those of a starving refugee receiving his food ration. A pink mixture of blood and spittle oozed from the crack of his open mouth, and dark blood trickled from his nose, the liquids lazily flowing into and being absorbed by the vast sea of blood that had escaped his chest. An awful sight.

Shuya lowered his bag and crouched down. Yoshitoki had slumped forward, and Shuya sat him back up. The boy's uniform was torn in three places on the chest and stained dark red, and when Shuya lifted him up, blood gushed out and splashed to the floor. The body felt enervated and incredibly light—probably because of all the blood that had drained out.

With Yoshitoki's corpse in his arms, Shuya's mind became icily clear, his sadness and fear overcome by rage.

Yoshitoki, I will avenge you. I'll do it. I promise.

He hadn't much time. Using his palm, Shuya wiped the blood from his friend's face and gently closed his eyelids. He laid Yoshitoki back down and folded the boy's arms atop his chest.

Then, taking some time to gather up his bag, Shuya turned his mouth to Noriko and whispered quickly, "Can you walk?"

That was enough to send the three soldiers' hands back to their sidearms, but Shuya caught Noriko's nod. He faced Sakamochi and the three soldiers, but with his hand low where only she could see, he made a fist and jabbed his thumb toward the door. *I'll be waiting for you. I'll wait for you outside.*

Shuya couldn't see Noriko, but out of the corner of his eye, he thought he caught Shinji Mimura, seated across from Yoshitoki's empty chair, still looking straight ahead with his arms folded, forming a smile at the corners of his mouth. Maybe he had noticed Shuya's gesture. The thought helped Shuya pull himself together. *He's Mimura. If we have Mimura, we just might be able to escape.*

But Shinji Mimura might have been more fully aware of their situation. His smile might have been a goodbye. But for now, the possibility didn't occur to Shuya.

Shuya continued walking up the aisle. Before he collected his black daypack, he thought for a moment, then went to Fumiyo Fujiyoshi's body and closed her eyes as well. He wanted to pull the knife out of her forehead but decided not to.

The instant he stepped through the doorway, part of him wished he had.

7

The hallway was unlit, save for the light from the doorway shining onto the wooden floor. The classroom windows, like those on the outside wall, had been covered by black metal panels—possibly to provide protection from any students who, like Shuya, were determined to escape and attempted to assault Sakamochi's location. Whatever the case, none of them would be able to get near once they left and the school became a forbidden zone.

To the right, Shuya saw a door to an identical, adjacent classroom, and farther down, another. Beyond that, double doors—the exit, perhaps—stood open into darkness. To the left, the hallway dead-ended with another room.

Was it the faculty room for this small, remote school? The door was open, and the lights were on. Alert soldiers sat at cheap folding tables, fidgeting in metal folding chairs. Were there twenty of them, or thirty? No, there were more—one man for each student in Ninth Grade Class B.

Shuya had been considering that if his daypack contained a gun (which was a possibility—the Program news reports always included the number of "deaths by firearms" alongside the "deaths by blades" and "deaths by strangulation"), or if any of the students waiting outside had one, they could storm Sakamochi and his guards before everyone had left—before the school became one of the forbidden zones. But now, all such hopes were dashed. The three with Sakamochi weren't the only soldiers around. It seemed obvious now that he knew it.

One of the men turned his head to glance across his teacup at Shuya. Like the trio in the classroom, this soldier wore an expression that was oddly blank.

Shuya quickly turned on his heels and hurried to the exit. An impatient frustration occupied his thoughts. *Well, all that's left to think about now is to meet up with everyone else. But what if soldiers are waiting outside to prevent anyone from sticking around until the next of us comes?*

Shuya left the dark hallway through the double doors of the exit and descended a small staircase of three or four steps.

The schoolyard was a desolate moonlit space the size of three tennis courts. Woods lay beyond it, and a small mountain loomed to the left, while the right opened into inky darkness—the sea. Tiny points of light dotted the distance. Land, probably. The Program was always held in the same prefecture as its chosen junior high. The locations varied; Shuya had heard of a few, including a mountain surrounded by high-voltage fences and a prison slated for demolition. But in Kagawa Prefecture, islands were the norm, as local news invariably revealed (though only after each Program had ended). Sakamochi hadn't given the island's name, but Shuya thought that he might be able to recognize its shape once he got a look at his map. A sign on one of the buildings might even reveal the name.

A light breeze bore the smell of the sea. The night was cold for May, though not unbearable, at least as long as he was careful not to let the chill sap his body of too much strength in his sleep.

But first things first.

No one was around. No soldiers, nor any of his classmates, as he had hoped to find. Everyone had taken Sakamochi's advice and hidden themselves. Even Hiroki Sugimura had gone. Only the salty breeze crossed the playground dirt.

Shit. Shuya scowled. Once they scattered, they would be playing right into the government's hands. If any of them managed to meet up with their close friends and form a group, like Sakura Ogawa and Kazuhiko Yamamoto, or Kiriyama's gang, then some hope remained. But if they all hid alone and stumbled upon each other one by one, anything could happen in the resulting confusion. And wasn't that confusion an essential element of the game?

Okay then. I, at least, will wait for the rest. Starting with Noriko Nakagawa.

Shuya turned around for a quick look into the darkness back inside the school. Sakamochi had said, "*If you loiter in the hallway, you'll be shot and killed,*" but none of the soldiers at the end of the hall seemed to be paying particular attention in Shuya's direction. Not even chatting, the men were simply sitting around, with weapons not at the ready.

Shuya licked his lips and decided it would be a good idea to step away from the doors. He turned back around.

That was when he noticed it.

Before, he had been too preoccupied with the scenery to notice the object at his feet. It looked like a garbage bag.

At first, he thought someone might have dropped their daypack, but soon his eyes widened.

It wasn't a garbage bag, and it wasn't anyone's daypack. One end had hair. Human hair.

A person. Wearing a girl's sailor-suit school uniform. She was face down and curled into a fetal position, but Shuya recognized the single braid and the wide ribbon that tied it. How could he not—he had just watched her from behind when she left the classroom three minutes before. She was still, with not even a twitch. Girls #14, Mayumi Tendo.

From the back of her sailor fuku, beside the lobster tail of her braid, a dull metallic pole stuck out at an angle like a radio antenna twenty centimeters long. Four tiny objects resembling the tail of a fighter plane were affixed at its end.

What . . . what is that?

Instead of immediately seeking cover as he should have done, Shuya froze in astonishment.

Sakamochi's answer to Kiriyama's question echoed in his mind. *When does this game begin? As soon as you leave here.*

Had someone really done this? Did someone return and do this to Mayumi Tendo the moment she left?

Shuya hurriedly cowered and glanced around.

Whatever the reason, the attacker was nowhere to be seen. No arrow had flown at him during his momentary distraction. Had the killer fled, satisfied once he took out the lone girl? Or was this some kind of false flag tactic, done by those soldiers at the end of the hall to convince the others that some of their classmates had already started playing the game? That didn't quite sound right.

Shuya realized that Mayumi Tendo might not be dead yet. She might be seriously wounded and unconscious. He should check her, at least.

Shuya was about to step forward. He would have found a swift exit from the game had he not sensed something and stopped—

A whizzing sound split the air, and a silver object flashed past his eyes, downward, from above. A new antenna sprouted from the ground.

Shuya was shaking. If he hadn't waited for Noriko at the doorway, he would already be dead. The attacker was on the roof.

Shuya pinched his lips and plucked the arrow from the dirt, then sprinted to his right. He moved without thought, only hoping that it was in a direction the shooter hadn't anticipated. He spun and looked up. On the gabled roof of the one-story school, a black silhouette loomed across the pale moonlit sky.

Is that . . . Sho—

He had no time to think. The shadow turned its aim on him.

Shuya launched the arrow at the figure. He had only hoped to startle his attacker and buy some time. But the arrow moved incredibly fast and traced a graceful arc straight at the shadow. Had anyone other than the ace shortstop, Shuya, attempted it, events might have gone differently.

The figure grunted, brought its hands to its face, and bent over. Then it began to sway, and fell.

Shuya recoiled back a step and watched the figure slowly tumble down the more than three-meter drop before thudding to the earth, the weapon clattering alongside.

Light spilling from the school's entrance revealed the large, uniformed figure keeled over on the ground. He was Yoshio Akamatsu, the first to leave, who had left so terrified. He was completely still—unconscious, or worse. Lying at his fingertips was some combination of a rifle and a bow. A kind of crossbow, maybe. Yoshio's daypack had fallen by his feet, half open, the bundle of silverish bolts visible inside.

Shuya felt the blood drain from his face. *He started it, he really did! Yoshio Akamatsu started the game! He got his weapon, came back, and killed Mayumi Tendo!*

He sensed someone approaching from behind.

He spun to see Noriko Nakagawa, who gasped at the scene before her. Shuya's eyes fell back to Mayumi Tendo, and he dashed to her side and touched his hand to her neck. She was dead. She really was dead.

His mind was a spooled fuse, and he felt it burn. *What if there are others who're thinking like Yoshio? When they come back, what if they have guns?*

His perspective on the game had been forcibly altered. *This is how it is. This is what Sakamochi meant. As soon as you leave here.*

Shuya sprang to his feet, ran to Noriko, took her by the hand, and said, "Run! Run as fast as you can!"

He ran, tugging along the injured girl. But which way to go?

He didn't have time to think it through. For now, he ran for the woods. Shuya thought, *We could wait behind that tree, and*—but he had to dismiss the idea. In her current state, Noriko wouldn't stand a chance if anyone should attack. Nothing would be more dangerous than to remain anywhere near that school.

Any thoughts of waiting outside the building for his classmates had vanished. He rushed Noriko into the woods, with trees mixed with bushes and a carpet of ferns.

Shuya turned, thinking to shout some warning in the direction of the school, where eleven of his classmates remained. (With twenty-one pairs of boys and girls, twelve more should have come after Shuya and Noriko, but Fumiyo Fujiyoshi had made it eleven.) He discarded the idea. *The others aren't stupid. They're not stupid like me. They'll run for their lives the instant they step out of those doors. Besides, Mayumi Tendo's corpse is waiting for them too.* Shuya convinced himself he was right. For a moment, he thought of Shinji Mimura's face, but he dashed the image from his mind. He forced himself to believe that they would be able to meet. He would find a way, later. But for now, he didn't want to spend one second longer near that school.

Holding Noriko Nakagawa tight, he continued haphazardly through the brush. A nearby bird cried and flapped its wings into flight. He didn't see it, but he hadn't the time to watch anyway.

39 STUDENTS REMAIN.

Yoshio Akamatsu regained consciousness almost immediately, but after blacking out from a terrible blow to the head, he felt like he was coming out of a deep slumber.

The first thing he noticed was the incredible pain. He was in a daze. *What happened? Did I stay up too late playing video games last night? So was yesterday Saturday, or even Sunday? Is it Monday now? I have to get to school. What time is it? It's still dark out. Maybe I can sleep a little more.*

The sky and the ground were sideways, and before him he saw an empty dirt field, and beyond it the curved, bowlike shape of a mountain, darker than the night sky.

Suddenly, everything came back—meeting Sakamochi; seeing Mr. Hayashida's corpse; leaving the room; taking cover in a shack and finding the crossbow inside his daypack; returning to the school; watching Takako Chigusa (Girls #13), her face harsh yet beautiful and then tense, and she was sprinting away, carried by those ace track runner legs; desperately climbing the narrow steel ladder on the side of the school to get to the roof; loading the first arrow as quickly as possible, but too slow, and Sho Tsukioka (Boys #14) was getting away. And then—

He turned his head and saw a girl lying there in her sailor fuku.

To no great surprise to himself, the flood of memories had been accompanied not by guilt over killing his classmate, but by terror. For inside him terror was a giant billboard rising in a wasteland, and on it his classmates, armed with axes and pistols and all kinds of weapons, jumped out at him like in a 3D movie, with the tagline, *I'll kill you!* written in blood.

He was under no illusion that killing his classmates wasn't wrong. And maybe it was foolish to even try to survive when every one of them would die once the game's time expired. But that was only logic. Yoshio didn't want to die. He feared his classmates because he thought they would turn on him. *You have to understand, these killers are prowling all around.*

The decision to pick off his would-be enemies in the most efficient way possible had not arisen from a conscious decision, but from somewhere deeper, from the primal fear of death. This wasn't a matter of determining friend from foe. All were foes. When someone like Ryuhei Sasagawa bullied him, hadn't the others only looked away?

Yoshio scrambled to his feet. First things first, he needed to deal with Shuya Nanahara. *Where is he, anyway? My crossbow, my crossbow, I need to pick up my crossbow. Where is my crossbow?*

Suddenly, something like a club struck the back of his neck.

Yoshio lurched forward and fell. His body twisted into a V, and his face raked against the moist earth. That the skin scraped off his forehead and cheek didn't bother him at all. By the time he had fallen, he was already dead.

Sticking out the back of his neck was a silverish bolt, just like the one he had put in Mayumi Tendo.

38 STUDENTS REMAIN.

Kazushi Niida (Boys #16) had emerged from the school two minutes after Noriko Nakagawa. He stood now, frozen in place, trembling. The crossbow next to Yoshio Akamatsu's body had been loaded, and Kazushi picked it up without intending to use it. But when Yoshio had stood, Kazushi's finger squeezed the trigger reflexively.

Kazushi tried to move his clouded mind into action. *That's right,* he thought, *I have to get away from here. That's the first thing. That's what I should have done in the first place, instead of paying any attention to Yoshio Akamatsu or Mayumi Tendo. I need to get out of here. See, Yoshio is clearly the one who killed Mayumi. So I didn't do anything wrong.*

Kazushi was very good at making excuses, and doing so stirred sense back into one part of his numbed brain.

He lowered the crossbow and scooped up Yoshio's daypack with its bundle of bolts nearly without a thought. He started to move on, but stopped and picked up Mayumi's bag as well. Then he ran.

38 STUDENTS REMAIN.

10

They had been running for what seemed like ten minutes. With the arm he had around her, Shuya motioned Noriko to stop. Faint moonlight filtered through the treetops. She looked up at him. Their ragged, heavy breathing seemed an overwhelming wall of sound, but Shuya tried to listen past that wall for any noises concealed in the surrounding darkness.

He heard no pursuing footsteps. Though too busy gasping for air to be able to let out a sigh of relief, he did feel a little reassured. He had been carrying both of their bags over his right shoulder, and when he set them down, his muscles protested sharply. Shuya was out of shape. Sure, his electric guitar was heavier than a bat, but he didn't spend the whole time swinging it. He put his hands on his thighs and took a rest.

Shuya prompted Noriko to sit, and helped her down into the shadowy brush. He listened again for any sound around them, then sat beside her. The thick mass of leaves crunched faintly beneath him.

He felt like they had run a long way, but having zigzagged through the undergrowth, they had likely gone off course on their way up the mountain. They might have been no more than a few hundred meters from the school. At least he couldn't see its artificial glow, whether it was because of the rolling mountainside or the folds of trees between.

Shuya felt safe in this darker place. Coming this way had been a snap decision, but one assuredly safer than heading for the open seaside.

He looked at Noriko and whispered, "You all right?"

Softly she said, "Yeah," and nodded.

Shuya wanted to remain sitting there for a while, but he knew that wasn't an option. Instead, he opened his daypack. Behind what felt like a water bottle, his hands brushed against a long, thin, and firm object.

Shuya pulled it out. He felt a leather sheath and a leather-wrapped grip sticking out of it. A combat knife. Sakamochi had said a weapon would be inside. Was this it? He groped around the inside of the bag but felt only a flashlight and what must have been a bundle of bread rolls. Nothing else that seemed to be a weapon.

Shuya popped open the snap and withdrew the knife. He noted the length of the blade—fifteen centimeters—and that it was in usable condition, before returning it to the sheath, which he then fastened, clasp open, around the belt of his school slacks. He undid the lower-most button of his jacket so he could reach the handle at a moment's notice.

Without asking permission, Shuya pulled over Noriko's daypack and opened the zipper. Peeking into a girl's things was taboo, but it wasn't like she'd packed it herself.

Inside, he found something unusual. It was a stick, about forty centimeters long and curved into a V, wooden, and firm and smooth to the touch. Was this what a boomerang looked like? A throwing weapon of primitive hunters and warriors, an Aboriginal village's champion huntsman could send it flying through the air and bag a kangaroo, but what were kids supposed to do with one? Shuya sighed and returned it to Noriko's bag.

He had finally caught his breath, no longer sounding like an invalid wheezing on his deathbed.

"You want some water?" Shuya asked.

Noriko nodded and said, "Just a little."

He took the plastic bottle from his daypack, twisted open the lid, and sniffed at its contents. He poured a little of the liquid onto his hand

and tested it with his tongue. He then took a sip, and when nothing unusual happened, he passed the container to Noriko. She took it and drank only a small mouthful. She must have understood how precious water might become over the coming days. The bottles only held about one liter, with only two provided to each student. Sakamochi had said the phone lines wouldn't work, but what about the water pipes?

Shuya said, "Let me take a look at your leg."

Noriko nodded and stretched out her right leg, unfolding it from under her skirt. Shuya took the flashlight from his daypack and, wrapping his palm around it to prevent light from spilling out too far, used it to get a look at the wound on her leg.

It was on the outside of her calf, a vertical gash about four centimeters long and one centimeter deep. Blood was still trickling from the edges of the exposed pink flesh. She would need stitches.

Shuya switched off his flashlight and pulled over not the daypack but his own gym bag. He took out the flask of bourbon and two clean bandanas he'd packed for the school trip. Uncapping the flask, he said, "This is going to hurt."

"I'm ready."

When he tipped the flask and poured the bourbon to disinfect her wound, she let out a small gasp. He placed one of the folded bandanas directly over the gash, then spread open the other before refolding it into a long strip and wrapping it firmly around her calf. Not a proper bandage, but it would stop the bleeding for now.

As he pulled the two loose ends tight and tied the bandana in place, Shuya muttered a curse.

Softly, Noriko asked, "Thinking about Mr. Nobu?"

Shuya gritted his teeth. "Him, and Akamatsu, and everyone. This sucks. This really sucks."

While his hands worked the knot, Shuya studied her face until he had to look down again to finish the tie. She thanked him and pulled her leg back.

"Mayumi," Noriko said. "She . . . Did Akamatsu . . ." Her voice trembled. "He killed her, didn't he?"

"Yeah. He was above the doorway. He fell when I threw the crossbow bolt at him."

Thinking back to what had happened, Shuya realized that he'd left without dealing with Yoshio Akamatsu. At the time, he assumed the boy had been knocked out cold, but Akamatsu might have quickly regained his senses. He could have climbed back up to the roof, crossbow in hand, and continued his slaughter.

Was I too naïve again? Should I have killed him then and there?

Shuya held his watch up to the moonlight. The finely crafted old model K. Hattori diver's watch (a gift, like most of his possessions, with him living in an orphanage) read just past 2:40. Whatever had happened to Yoshio Akamatsu, nearly all of the students would have left the school by now, save for two or three. Shinji Mimura would already be gone by now. *At least,* Shuya was almost certain, *Shinji would never let himself be killed by Akamatsu.*

Shuya shook his head, thinking himself a fool for still believing he could get his classmates to band together.

"I never thought he was that kind of guy," Shuya said. "Willing to kill everyone just so he could survive. I mean, I understand the rules of the game. I just didn't think anyone would actually go along with it."

"I don't think," Noriko said, "that's quite how it was."

"What?" Shuya looked into her face. Her expression was hard to read in the moonlight.

"It's like . . . You know how Akamatsu was such a timid boy. I think maybe he was scared. I *know* he was. You have no idea who's going to turn on you out here. I think Akamatsu was convinced that everyone was going to come after him. That had to be terrifying. He thought that if he didn't act, he'd be . . . killed."

As Noriko had done, Shuya leaned back against a tree trunk and stretched out his legs.

He himself had seen the logic—fear could turn a student into a killer—but he also thought that by nature, the scared ones would just hide. Yet maybe it was true that extreme terror could drive them into taking the initiative.

Shuya asked, "You think so?"

"Yeah." Noriko nodded. "Still, to not even give her a chance, that's awful."

They remained silent for a time. Then a thought came to Shuya, and he said, "Do you think if he saw the two of us together, he wouldn't have attacked? With us together, that would prove we weren't participating."

"Yeah. Maybe."

Shuya considered what she'd said. If indeed Akamatsu had merely been taken by paranoia, then . . .

In that moment, Shuya thought, *I thought some of the others were going along with this. That's why I ran. But maybe I was wrong. Killing your own classmates—who could do a ridiculous thing like that? Then . . . shouldn't I have waited for the others, even if that meant I had to deal with Akamatsu?*

Either way, what's done is done. Even if we went back now, everyone will have already left. But was Noriko really right about Akamatsu? Had he simply been afraid?

Shuya didn't know what to think anymore.

"Noriko."

She looked up.

"What's your take on this?" he asked. "I was worried we'd be in danger of someone else like Akamatsu, so I thought that whatever else we did, we had to get away from that school first. But . . . if he was just afraid . . . I mean, do you really think anyone is going to play this game? I mean, I was hoping that if I could get everyone together, we could escape this damn game. What do *you* think?"

"You mean everyone?"

"Yeah."

Noriko fell quiet. Gathering her pleated skirt, she pulled her knees in to her chest. Then she said, "I must be a terrible girl!."

"What?"

"I could never do that. Maybe Yukie," she said, meaning Yukie Utsumi, the class leader, who they'd both known since elementary school, "and some of the other girls I'm always with, them I could trust, I think. But not the others, no way. I couldn't be with them, not at all. Don't you think that? I can't know exactly what Akamatsu was feeling, but *I'm* afraid of everyone else. I didn't realize it until now, but I don't really know anything about them, or what kind of people they are, really. You can't see inside a person's heart."

"I don't really know anything about them," she had said.

She's right, Shuya thought. *What the hell do I know about the other kids? They're just people I happen to be with during the school day.* Shuya suddenly found himself again wondering if some of his classmates were enemies.

"And so I'd suspect them," Noriko said. "Even if they were with us, if I didn't really trust them, I'd suspect them. I'd suspect that they were . . . they were trying to kill me."

Shuya sighed. As horrific as this game was, it was extremely well designed. In the end, he couldn't let any and all join up with them, not unless he was absolutely confident they could be trusted. What if, *what if*, someone were to catch him off guard? It wouldn't be just him he'd be endangering but Noriko as well. That the kids who'd left the school ahead of him had immediately vanished was natural. They were just being pragmatic.

Shuya's thoughts were interrupted as his mind made a new connection.

"Wait a second," he said. Noriko's eyes flashed up to him. "That means that just because we're together, that doesn't prove we don't mean harm. They still might suspect that I was planning to eventually . . . kill you."

Noriko nodded. "That's right. And I'd be suspected too, the same way. With the two of us together, one of the others might not attack us. But if we asked any to join with us, I think they probably wouldn't. It would depend on who we asked."

Shuya gulped. "Scary, isn't it."

"Terrifying."

Maybe running from the schoolyard had been the right choice

after all. What mattered most to Shuya was getting Noriko Nakagawa, the girl Yoshitoki had loved, safely out of here. And right now, she was safely at his side. Shouldn't he have been satisfied with that? He had taken the safest approach. But . . .

"But," he said, "I at least wanted Mimura with us. He'd come up with some brilliant plan. You'd be fine with him, right, Noriko?"

"Of course," she said with a nod. Given how much time she spent with Shuya at school, she'd had plenty of opportunities to talk to Shinji Mimura.

Shuya recalled how Shinji had stood Noriko up and signaled him to calm down. He realized that if Shinji hadn't done that, both he and Noriko may very well have remained frozen in place and been shot just like Yoshitoki.

Noriko lowered her head, possibly having the same thoughts, remembering the events that had led them here, and whispered, "Mr. Nobu . . . he's gone, isn't he?"

Quietly, as if he didn't quite believe it himself, Shuya answered, "Yeah, I guess so."

The two were again silent for a time. They might have talked about memories of their friend, but this wasn't the time or place. Besides, what had happened to Yoshitoki weighed far too heavily on Shuya for superficial reminiscences.

"What should we do?" he asked. "From here."

Noriko tightened her lips and tilted her head in silent question.

"I was just thinking," he offered. "Maybe we could find Mimura or some of the others. The ones we feel we can trust."

Noriko said, "That's . . ." but the word trailed into contemplation, and she never finished the sentence.

Right, Shuya thought, *neither of us knows how to find them. At least not for now.*

All Shuya could do was sigh.

Between the branches overhead, the moonlit sky was dim and gray. Shuya felt he now understood what they meant by "Damned if you do, damned if you don't." If it didn't matter who they joined up with, the two could have simply walked around and shouted. But that would have been an open invitation to any would-be opponent to come kill them. Shuya hoped that no such enemies were out there, but still, he was afraid.

The thought led to an idea, and Shuya turned to Noriko and asked, "Weren't you afraid of me?"

"What?"

"You never worried I might try to kill you?"

He couldn't see it very clearly in the moonlight, but he thought Noriko's eyes went wide. "You would never do anything like that!"

Shuya thought about it a little, then said, "But you said it before, 'You can't see inside a person's heart.'"

She shook her head. "I just know that you of all people would never do anything like that."

Shuya looked her straight on. He must have looked dazed. "You know?"

"Yeah . . . I know," Noriko said. She hesitated, but then continued. "I've been . . . watching you for so long."

The sentiment probably deserved to be delivered with more formality. And would it be asking too much for a situation that was at least a tiny bit more romantic?

Shuya recalled the anonymous love letter, written on pale blue stationery, that he'd found inside his desk one day in April. As the former ace shortstop in Little League and the current self-proclaimed (and occasionally acknowledged) rock star of Shiroiwa Junior High, Shuya had received love letters before. But this one had made something of an impression on him, and he'd held on to it. He thought it was because he liked the poetic writing:

Be it only a lie, be it only a dream, please turn back and look
    at me
Not a lie, not a dream, your smile that day
But maybe my lie, but maybe my dream, that it was sent
    my way

It won't be a lie, it won't be a dream, on the day you call my
    name
Never a lie, never a dream, that.

Shuya had wondered if she had written the note. The handwriting
was similar, and the poetic style would have fit. Had it really been her?

Shuya briefly considered asking her about the letter, but decided
not to. This wasn't the right time, and he had no right to bring it
up, since he was utterly smitten by Kazumi Shintani, a girl who, to
borrow from that pale blue love letter, would never "turn to look at
him." Not that girls, or the matter of that love letter, were of much
concern anymore. What was important to him now was protecting the
girl who Yoshitoki Kuninobu had had a crush on, not worrying about
who might have a crush on him.

Shuya thought back to Yoshitoki's bashful expression when he
said, "Hey, Shuya, I . . . kinda . . . got a crush."

"Shuya," Noriko was asking him now, "aren't you afraid of me?
No, I should really ask . . . why did you rescue me?"

"Well . . ."

Shuya considered telling her about Yoshitoki. *My best friend was
in love with you. So I have to help you. That's the way it is.*

He discarded that thought also. That was a discussion best saved
for another time, when they could really talk. If such a time ever came,
that is.

Instead, he told her, "You were hurt. How could I leave you like
that? And at the very least, I trust you. Hey, not trusting a cute girl like
you would bring some serious bad karma."

The glimmer of a smile flashed across Noriko's face, and Shuya
did his best to return it. Even in these dire circumstances, working his
muscles into a grin made him feel a little more at ease.

Then he said, "Well, I'm glad that we're together, even if it's only
us two."

Noriko nodded and said, "Yeah."

But what were they supposed to do now?

Shuya began repacking his bags. Even if their next move was to stop again to rest and think things out, they needed somewhere with good visibility. He reminded himself that he had no idea what the others were planning, but he knew he had to be careful. He needed to be realistic, even if he hated what that meant.

He kept out the map, compass, and flashlight. *The world's worst orienteering meet,* he thought.

Shuya asked, "Can you walk some more?"

"Yeah, I'm fine."

"Then let's keep moving a little longer. We'll find a place we can rest."

38 STUDENTS REMAIN.

11

Mitsuru Numai (Boys #17) carefully advanced from tree to tree, where the woods met the beach, moonlit and narrow, with only a few dozen meters of sand until the water. Over his shoulders, he carried his personal gym bag along with the daypack he'd been given, and in his right hand he clutched a small semi-automatic pistol. (A Walther PPK 9mm, the gun was one of the better weapons issued to participants. Most of the other weapons used in the Program were imported on the cheap, and in high volume, from neutral countries not aligned with either the Republic or the American Empire.) Mitsuru had seen a hobbyist replica version of the Walther and understood how to use it without having to read the included manual. He even knew he didn't need to cock the hammer before firing and had been able to load the firearm from the supplied box of ammunition.

The weapon felt reassuring in his right hand, but something far more important was in his left: a compass. It was the same cheap, tin model as Shuya had received, but so far, it had done the job. Forty minutes before Mitsuru left the classroom, his personal Great Leader, Kazuo Kiriyama (Boys #6), had handed him a note that read, *If this really is an island, I'll be waiting on the southern point.*

Of course, in this game, no one is your ally. That's the rules. But the Family—the Kiriyama Family—had a real bond. When others labeled them as thugs, they didn't mind it. It only strengthened their ties.

And Mitsuru Numai and Kiriyama shared an even more special connection. In a way, Mitsuru had made Kazuo Kiriyama who he was today. He was fairly sure about something that Shuya Nanahara and the rest of those typical kids would have no way of knowing: before junior high, Kazuo Kiriyama had been no delinquent.

Mitsuru could remember clearly the day he had met Kazuo Kiriyama. It was a memory so vivid he could never forget it if he tried.

Ever since elementary school, Mitsuru had been a real bruiser, though as the school bully, his rule was not that of a tyrant. To him, born to a family of no real worth and a poor student with no talents to speak of, fighting was the only way he could prove himself. He measured worth in toughness—a standard to which he held himself and never failed.

Naturally, on his first day of junior high, Mitsuru did his best to subdue any would-be competitors ("bitches," to him) coming in from other elementary schools. From what he saw in the kids he met in what amounted to the entertainment district for his town, he didn't have much to worry about. But there might have been some, coming from the other schools, who hadn't heard about him. One king was enough; that was how order was preserved. Of course, he never thought of it in exactly those terms, but he understood how it worked.

Sure enough, among his new class were a few such "bitches." After the entrance ceremony and the subsequent orientation back in the classroom, school was let out, and Mitsuru was finishing up the last of them when it happened.

In the secluded hallway outside the art room, Mitsuru grabbed the kid by the lapels and shoved him against the wall. The boy was already bruised above an eye that brimmed with tears. He'd been no problem at all. Just two punches, and it had been over.

"You got that?" Mitsuru was saying. "Don't you go acting like you're tougher than me!"

The kid was nodding his head, *okay, okay, okay.* He was begging to be let free, but Mitsuru needed a promise first.

"I asked you if you got it!" He lifted the boy up with one arm. "Answer me. I'm the toughest in this school. You got it?"

Annoyed at the kid's lack of a response, Mitsuru raised him higher still. That was when he felt *his* eyes upon his back.

Mitsuru spun. Suddenly released, the boy fell to the floor and took off running, though Mitsuru wasn't about to chase after him.

There were four of them, all far taller than him. They surrounded him. Lapel pins on the stand-up collars of their sloppy uniforms announced they were in ninth grade. With one glance, he knew exactly what they were. They were like him.

"Hey, kid," a pimply-faced one said with a creepy grin. "You shouldn't pick on the weak."

Another, with shoulder-length, auburn-dyed hair, pursed his unusually thick lips and said, "Naughty, naughty."

The mocking, effeminate way he said it sent all four into roaring, deranged laughter, *Hee-hee-hee!*

"We'll have to teach you a lesson," the first one said.

"Oh, we must," lisped the second, and they all laughed again, *Hee-hee-hee!*

Mitsuru tried to take the pimpled teen by surprise with a front kick, but before he could, the one on his left swept his leg out from under him.

Mitsuru fell flat on his ass, and the pimply one was right on him, kicking him in the face, knocking out one of his front teeth. The back of his head slammed against the same wall he'd been holding the other kid against. He felt dizzy. The back of his head felt warm and wet. He got on his hands and knees to try to stand, but the one on the right kicked him in his stomach. Mitsuru groaned, then puked everything he had. He heard someone say, "Gross."

Fuck, he thought. *Cowards, bastards! I could take on any of you, one on one.*

He was helpless now. He had chosen this location to rough up the other kid because no one would be around. No teachers were going to come.

Then his wrist was being held to the floor. One of them carefully curled Mitsuru's index finger and pressed it beneath his leather shoe. For the first time in his life, Mitsuru felt total terror.

They wouldn't. They wouldn't.

They did. The foot pressed down, and Mitsuru's finger audibly, sickly, *snapped*. He shrieked. The pain was incredible, like he'd never experienced before. He heard more laughter, *Hee-hee-hee!*

They're insane, Mitsuru thought. *They're nothing like me. There's something wrong with their fucking minds—*

They prepared his middle finger.

Pride and everything be damned, he was ready to beg. "S-stop," he pleaded, but they ignored him. Another snap, and his middle finger was ruined. He screamed again.

He heard one of them say, "Now, how about another?"

That was when it happened.

That was when the door to the art room slid wide open, and a quiet voice said, "Would you guys keep it down?"

At first, Mitsuru wondered if a teacher had been in the classroom. But a teacher would have intervened more quickly, and besides, the request would have been bizarre coming from one of the faculty.

Still pressed against the floor, Mitsuru turned his head to look.

There stood a boy, not too tall but incredibly handsome. He was holding a paintbrush.

Mitsuru had seen him at orientation. The boy was one of his classmates. He was from out of town, and no one knew who he was. But he was quiet and meek, and Mitsuru hadn't taken much notice of him. The boy had the refined looks of someone from a well-off family. He would certainly be no good in a fight and wasn't worth Mitsuru's time.

But what the hell is he doing in the art room after the first day of school? Well, painting, of course, but that's kind of weird.

Whatever the case, the pimpled bully approached the boy, saying, "What was that, asshole?" He stood in front of the kid and repeated,

"What was that, asshole? You some first-year? What the fuck are you doing here? Huh? You want to say that again?"

He slapped the paintbrush from the younger boy's hand. Dark blue paint splattered across the floor.

The boy slowly looked up to the older boy's pimply face.

What happened next might seem obvious. Suffice it to say, that little kid beat up the four ninth graders—knocked them all out cold.

The boy approached Mitsuru and gazed at him for a time before saying, "You should go to the hospital." Then he was gone, having glided back to the art room.

Mitsuru remained sitting on the floor for a time, staring off at the four bodies in stunned awe. That boy was something altogether different. Mitsuru felt like a novice boxer, who, even granted a decade-long career, would likely never progress past six-round bouts, meeting the world champion for the first time.

Mitsuru had seen genius.

Ever since, Mitsuru served that boy—Kazuo Kiriyama. Mitsuru didn't need to test him. Kiriyama simultaneously took out four guys who Mitsuru thought he could handle one at a time. And, since one king was enough, anyone who wasn't the king had better serve. He'd believed that for a long time. That's how it worked in the boys' manga he so avidly read.

Kazuo Kiriyama was a mystery.

When Mitsuru asked him how he had learned to fight like that, he simply said, "I just learned," and wouldn't answer any further questions on the subject. Mitsuru tried to coax more out of him by suggesting he must have had a reputation in elementary school, but he only denied it. Any karate competition wins, then? That didn't work either. Later, Mitsuru learned that Kiriyama had been sneaking into the art class to work on a painting, as had happened on the day they met. When Mitsuru asked him why, he said, "I just felt like it." Mitsuru was drawn to Kiriyama, due in part to those mysteries. (As an aside, the painting, a view of the empty courtyard from the art room, was a far better work than a sixth-grade student would otherwise be expected to produce. Mitsuru never saw the painting, however, as Kiriyama tossed it into the wastebasket as soon as he had completed it.)

Mitsuru showed Kiriyama around the small town, with the coffee shop where he and his friends hung out, the secret stash where he kept his stolen objects, the shady dealer of illicit goods, and so on. He was only a small fry, but he left out nothing he knew. Kiriyama never gave a reaction, though he must have been interested enough to come along. Sometimes Kiriyama ran up against some of the older kids in school (aside from the ones he'd already beaten up), and some from one of the other junior highs, and sometimes even high schoolers.

Each time he laid them flat on the ground in a flash. Mitsuru was crazy about Kiriyama, elated like a trainer feels when a boxer he coaches becomes a champion.

And there was more to Kiriyama than that. He was smart, and he excelled at anything he did. When they did a break-in, like at the liquor store warehouse, he came up with, and executed, the brilliant plans. Kiriyama had gotten Mitsuru out of many a scrape. (Since he and Kiriyama teamed up, he had never been caught by the police.) Also, his father was supposedly the president of a major company within the prefecture—and even the entire region of Chugoku and Shikoku combined. He was afraid of nothing. Mitsuru believed that some men were born to be kings. He thought, *This man is destined for greatness. Something more than I could even imagine.*

Kiriyama was appointed the leader of their group. As they went around causing trouble, Mitsuru had asked himself once, just once, if it was right to involve him. The single restriction Kiriyama imposed on the gang was his own house (strictly speaking, a mansion); he never allowed Mitsuru or the others inside. (He had never said this straight out, but his demeanor made it understood.) Mitsuru didn't know if Kiriyama's father was aware of what his son was up to, but either way, this delinquent wondered if he should be teaching the sheltered boy all this bad behavior. After mulling it over, he voiced his concern to Kiriyama.

But the boy only replied, "Whatever. It's interesting."

Mitsuru decided to accept that.

And so, he and Kiriyama had been through a lot together—the king and his trusty advisor.

As for his classmates, he wasn't sure, but he could never believe that Kiriyama and his Family would kill each other, even in this desperate situation. That's precisely why Kiriyama had handed them notes. Mitsuru was certain Kiriyama had already figured out what they needed to do—how to outwit that Sakamochi and escape. Once Kazuo Kiriyama got started, the government wouldn't stand a chance.

Such were Mitsuru's thoughts as he left the school and headed south. Just once, in the twenty-five minutes he walked, he saw another person. The figure vanished into a cluster of houses to the southeast of the school. Mitsuru thought it might have been Yoji Kuramoto (Boys #8). Mitsuru was of course nervous. After all, he had seen Yoshio Akamatsu dead out in front of the school. The game had begun.

Nothing had changed Mitsuru's plan. He hurried toward the meeting location. The others didn't matter a bit. He and his friends were escaping.

As he moved farther south, cover became more sparse, and he grew more tense, both in body and mind. Underneath his school uniform, he was drenched in cold sweat, and beads of it ran from his short, permed hair and down his forehead. A little ahead, the shoreline curved right, to the west. In the middle of the curve, a craggy outcropping jutted eastward from the mountain and submerged into the sea. The rock formation looked like the exposed spine of a buried dinosaur, or a *kaiju* maybe. The rocks stood far taller than Mitsuru and blocked his view of the other side. He glanced seaward where, across the dark, flat expanse, tiny lights indicated small islands and other landmasses. Mitsuru was certain he was on an island in the Seto Inland Sea. At least of that much he could be sure.

He carefully surveyed the area before leaving the trees and stepping onto the sand. Exposed in the moonlight, he walked toward the outcropping. Clinging to the steep rock face, he began to climb. The ascent was difficult; the rocks were cold and smooth, and his bags and the pistol he held got in the way.

After some struggle, he reached the top of the rocks to find that the formation was only three meters wide, with sandy beach spreading out below on the other side. He stepped forward to begin the descent.

"Mitsuru."

The voice came suddenly from behind, and Mitsuru nearly jumped. Reflexively, he turned and raised his gun.

Then, with a sigh of relief, he lowered it.

Kazuo Kiriyama was sitting on a ledge in the shadow of a bulge of rock.

With relief in his voice, Mitsuru began to say, "Hey, Boss—"

Then he noticed the three lumps on the ground at Kiriyama's feet.

Mitsuru squinted at the darkness, then his eyes shot wide open.

Those lumps were *people*.

Ryuhei Sasagawa (Boys #10) was on his back, staring up at the sky. Hiroshi Kuronaga (Boys #9) was twisted on his side. He recognized them without a doubt—like him, they were part of Kiriyama's Family. The third was a girl in a sailor fuku. She was face down, and he couldn't be sure, but he thought she was Izumi Kanai (Girls #5). Beneath the three bodies was a pool of liquid. In the dark, the puddle was black, but Mitsuru knew that in daylight, it would be the same crimson color as on the flag of the Republic of Greater East Asia.

Clueless of what had happened, Mitsuru began to tremble. *What . . . what was . . .*

"This is the southern point," Kiriyama said, looking up at Mitsuru beneath slicked-back hair, his eyes as calm as ever. He wore his school jacket on his shoulders, with his arms free of the sleeves, like a boxer draped in his robe at the end of a bout.

"W-wha-what . . ." Mitsuru said, the tremble of his chin transmitting into his voice. "What . . . they . . ."

"You mean them?" Kiriyama thumped Ryuhei Sasagawa's body with the end of his plain (though high quality), leather cap-toe boot. Ryuhei's right arm swung from its resting place on his chest and traced a half-arm's-length arc before splashing into the puddle. His pinky and ring finger disappeared into the liquid.

"They tried to kill me," Kiriyama explained. "Kuronaga, and Sasagawa too. So I . . . killed them."

It can't be!

Mitsuru couldn't believe his ears. Hiroshi Kuronaga was a nobody who just tagged along with their group. And he'd sworn an oath of loyalty to Kiriyama. Ryuhei had a lot of bravado and a violent streak (sometimes Mitsuru had to go to a lot of trouble to keep him from kicking Yoshio Akamatsu's ass). But when his little brother got caught shoplifting, Kiriyama pulled some strings to deal with the police, and ever since, Ryuhei had been extremely grateful. Those two would never have betrayed Kiriyama.

Mitsuru sensed something sticky in the air. Blood. The stench of blood. Far from the smell of Yoshitoki Kuninobu's blood in the classroom, this was on an entirely different level. The difference was in the quantity. A full bucket's worth of blood had been splashed around.

Overcome by the smell, Mitsuru's head shook up and down. *That's right,* he thought, *you can't ever know what someone else is thinking, and maybe Kuronaga and Sasagawa thought they were going to be killed and went crazy, and that's just how weak they were. They came here to the meeting place but tried to surprise Kiriyama to take him out.*

Mitsuru's eyes were pinned to the other corpse. Now flat on her stomach, Izumi Kanai had been a pretty and petite girl. She was the daughter of a town councilman (though, in a country with such an ultra-centralized bureaucracy, the title was only honorary), and though she wasn't nearly in Kiriyama's league, if you counted off the wealthiest families in town on your fingers, you'd reach her family on one hand. But she never acted stuck up, and Mitsuru himself had, on occasion, thought she was cute. Of course, he knew better than to get hung up on a girl of her class.

And now she's . . .

Mitsuru somehow managed to speak. "B-but, Boss, Kanai . . . she—"

Kiriyama's cold, dull eyes stared at him, overwhelming Mitsuru, who tried to come up with an answer to his own question. "Sh-she . . . She tried to kill you too, right?"

Kiriyama nodded. "Kanai just happened to be here."

Mitsuru's faith wavered, but he ultimately forced himself to believe that it wasn't impossible. It's what the boss said.

Mitsuru blurted, "Y-you don't have to worry about me. I'd never think of killing you, Boss. Th-this stupid game can eat shit. We're going to take out Sakamochi and those soldiers, right? Let's do it! I—"

He knew that with the forbidden zones, they couldn't approach the school. That's what Sakamochi had said. But Kiriyama would already have thought of a way around it.

But Mitsuru stopped talking. He'd noticed Kiriyama shaking his head. Mitsuru's tongue had turned sticky, but he continued, "Okay, all right, so we're escaping then? Great! Let's find a boat and—"

Kiriyama said, "Will you let me talk?" and when Mitsuru stopped again, he continued, "Either way would have been fine with me."

That's what Mitsuru thought he heard, and he could only blink in response. He didn't understand what Kiriyama had said. He tried to read Kiriyama's eyes, but they were just a calm twinkle in the shadow of his face.

"W-what do you mean, either way?"

Kiriyama's neck stretched as he lifted his chin to the night sky. The moon shone brightly, creating delicate shadows on his handsome face.

In that pose, he continued, "Sometimes, I lose track of what's right."

Mitsuru was even more confused now, but as he listened, an entirely different thought skimmed across his mind—a sense that something was missing.

He realized what it was—who it was.

With him there, and Sasagawa and Kuronaga on the ground, one of the Family was missing: Sho Tsukioka (Boys #14). He had left the school ahead of Mitsuru. *Where is he?*

Of course he might have been frightened and was taking longer to get here. Or might he have been killed on the way? Whatever had happened, his absence felt like a bad omen.

Kiriyama was saying, "Like now. I just don't know."

The sight of Kiriyama, talking on like this, seemed strangely sad.

"Anyway," he said, and turned to Mitsuru. He seemed to be talking faster now, as if he'd reached an allegro mark in the score. "When I came here, Kanai was already here, she tried to run away, and I kept her from escaping."

Mitsuru swallowed.

"Then I flipped a coin," Kiriyama said. "Heads, and I'd fight Sakamochi. And . . ."

Before Kiriyama had finished speaking, Mitsuru finally understood.

No. He couldn't . . .

He didn't want to believe it. It shouldn't have been. Kiriyama was the king, and he was his trusty advisor. It was supposed to be his eternal loyalty, and Kiriyama's grace. Take Kiriyama's slicked-back hair. Right about when Mitsuru's broken fingers had healed, he'd recommended the new hairstyle to Kiriyama and had him try it out. "That's better, Boss," he'd said. "You look badass." And Kiriyama had never changed it. Maybe a hairstyle didn't amount to much, but to Mitsuru, it was a symbol of their bond.

But, Mitsuru now realized, *what if he just thought it would be too much of a bother to change it? What if he had too much on his mind to care about something like that? And it doesn't stop there. All we did together, I believed was out of a kind of sacred team spirit. What was it to him? A diversion? Just—just—an experience? Not more than an experience, no feelings attached? Hadn't he said it himself? "It's interesting."*

From the depths of his mind, an old doubt came back to life. He had thought it unimportant and left it gathering dust in some corner of himself.

He had never seen Kazuo Kiriyama smile.

Mitsuru's next thoughts drew closer to the core of the truth.

He's always seemed like he has a lot on his mind. I think that's true, but down in his heart, is there a darkness deeper than I can imagine? No, not a darkness, but nothing, just an empty space.

Maybe Sho Tsukioka sensed it.

Mitsuru had no more time to think. He focused all his thoughts on his trigger finger (the one that had been broken) on the lowered Walther PPK.

The sea breeze blew in, stirring up the smell of the pool of blood, mixing with it. The sound of crashing waves carried on.

Extending from his hand, the nose of the PPK shook. But Kiriyama was already throwing back his jacket.

There was a faintly pleasant sound. *Brattattattat.* The sound of 950 rounds firing per minute, though of an altogether different nature, resembled the clacking of an old mechanical typewriter in an antique store. Izumi Kanai, Sasagawa, and Kuronaga, had all been stabbed. For the first time since the game's opening, gunfire echoed across the island.

Mitsuru was still standing. Though he couldn't see them through his clothes, he had four finger-sized holes running from his stomach to his chest. Whatever the reason, only two holes came out his back, each wide enough to fit a tin can through. The Walther PPK wavered at his side. His eyes stared off toward the North Star, though on such a brightly moonlit night, he probably couldn't see it.

Kiriyama was holding a crude hunk of metal that looked like a small gift box with a grip slapped on—an Ingram MAC-10. He said, "Tails, I'd play the game."

As if he had been waiting for those words, Mitsuru tipped over forward. When he fell, his head bashed against a rock and bounced back five centimeters.

Kazuo Kiriyama remained seated for a time. Then, he abruptly stood, walked over to Mitsuru Numai's corpse, and touched the fingertips of his left hand to the bullet-riddled body, as if he were checking for something.

This was no emotional response. He wasn't feeling anything—no pangs of conscience, no remorse, no sympathy.

He just wanted to know what happened to the human body when penetrated by bullets. Actually, it wasn't that he *wanted to know*, just that *knowing it wouldn't be bad*.

Before long, he withdrew his hand and touched it to his left temple—to be precise, a little behind it. To anyone who didn't know, he might have appeared to be straightening his slicked-back hair.

But that wasn't what he was doing. He had a strange sensation— not pain, not an itch, but a peculiar feeling that came to him only rarely, not more than a few times a year, drawing his hand reflexively to the spot. That sensation, along with the feeling of his fingertips touching there, had become deeply familiar to Kiriyama.

Though he knew a great many things about the world, due to the thorough and exceptional education provided to him by his "parents," what Kiriyama didn't know was the cause of that sensation. But how could he? By the time he was old enough to look in the mirror, the wound's scar had almost completely healed. The rest of the story remained in the distant past: the freak accident that had caused the wound and nearly killed him in the womb; his mother's immediate death; with less than a month to his due date, the consultation between his father and the famous doctor over the shard that had pierced his skull; the fact, unbeknownst to both his father and that doctor who bragged about his flawless operation, that the shard had gouged out the most minute cluster of nerve cells. The surgeon died of liver failure soon after, and his father—his biological father, that is—passed away under complex circumstances. By now, none were left who could tell Kiriyama the whole story.

But one thing was clear—though to Kiriyama, it was just the natural way of things—and even if he never consciously acknowledged it, and may have even lacked the ability to acknowledge it, this is what it came to:

He, Kazuo Kiriyama, standing in front of the four corpses, including that of Mitsuru Numai, had no reason to feel any pangs of conscience, any remorse, any sympathy, or any emotion at all. From the day he came into the world, he had never experienced anything that resembled an emotion.

34 STUDENTS REMAIN.

On the northern edge of the island, opposite Kiriyama and his Family, a steep, towering cliffside plunged into the sea roughly twenty meters below. The small clearing atop the cliff wore a crown of wild grass. The sound of crashing waves came carried up by the rocky face; their mist drifted in the breeze.

Bathed in moonlight, Sakura Ogawa (Girls #4) and Kazuhiko Yamamoto (Boys #21) sat side by side at the edge of the grassy cliff, their legs dangling below, Sakura's right hand resting gently on Kazuhiko's left hand.

Their daypacks and belongings, including their two compasses, were scattered around them. Just as Kiriyama had told the others to meet him at the southern tip, Kazuhiko had given Sakura a scrap of paper that read, "At the northern point," (next to the words: "We will kill each other"). That he had not chosen the same location as Kiriyama was a bit of good luck, and no matter what else would happen next, they at least had been able to talk alone. A .357 Magnum revolver was tucked into Kazuhiko's belt, but he didn't think he'd be using it now.

"It's peaceful here," Sakura murmured. Her hair was cropped quite short for a girl, and her profile traced a beautiful outline from her high forehead down to the sideways glimpse of a gentle smile. She was tall and slender, and she always sat up straight. When Kazuhiko had finally arrived, the couple had shared all too brief of an embrace. In his arms, she had trembled like a wounded little bird.

"Yeah, it is," Kazuhiko said. Aside from the bridge of his nose, which was slightly too wide, he had a handsome face. He turned away from her and faced ahead. The open sea remained pitch black in the moonlight, dotted with silhouettes of islands even darker and a large landmass beyond, which Kazuhiko thought must be the Honshu mainland. It was not quite half past three in the morning. Lights floated in the darkness, where all the different people were in peaceful slumber—though some may have been students his age, up late studying for their high school entrance exams. Not so far away, yet a world beyond their reach now.

Kazuhiko shifted his attention a little closer and saw the small black dot roughly two hundred meters away. It must have been one of those ships Sakamochi said would shoot anyone who tried to escape. Even at night, the Seto Inland Sea bustled with nautical traffic, but on this night, the lights of sailing ships were nowhere to be found. The government had likely prohibited all passage.

The sight gave Kazuhiko the chills, but he tore his eyes away from the black dot. When he'd left the school, he saw Mayumi Tendo's and Yoshio Akamatsu's bodies, and on his way here, he'd even heard far-off gunfire. Now that the game had begun, all that would continue to the end. He'd talked to Sakura about it a little before, but none of it seemed to matter anymore.

"Thank you so much for these," Sakura said. She was looking at the tiny bouquet of tiny flowers in her other hand. Kazuhiko had found them along the way and picked a few he liked, white clovers or something like that, the bundle of white petals like cheerleader pom-poms atop the airy stems. The flowers didn't make for a particularly impressive bouquet, but they were all he could find.

Kazuhiko flashed her a grin. "Thank you very much."

She remained looking at the flowers for a time, then said, "We won't be able to go back together. No more walking through town together, no more eating ice cream together."

"That's not—" Kazuhiko started to say, but she cut him off.

"There's no fighting it. I know that too well. I heard that my father tried to oppose the government's methods. Then one day . . ." Through her hand, Kazuhiko could feel her trembling. ". . . the police came. They killed him. They didn't have a warrant or anything. They didn't even say anything, but just came in and shot him dead. I can remember it. I was in our tiny kitchen. I was still small. I was sitting at the table. My mother held me tight. And I grew up, still eating at that same table."

She turned to Kazuhiko and said, "There's just no way to fight it."

They had been dating more than two years, and he'd never known. She never told him about it, not even after they'd first slept together in her house the month before.

Kazuhiko knew there had to be something else he could say, as all he could muster up felt incredibly trite: "That must have been hard."

Sakura surprised him with a smile. "You're so kind, Kazuhiko. You really are. That's why I love you."

"I love you too. I love you so much."

Kazuhiko wished he weren't so young and inarticulate, so that he could explain how he felt: the effect that she had on him, her expressions, her words, her movements, so tender, her soul, beautiful and perfectly pure; how important her very existence was to him. But he felt unable to express it. He was only a ninth grader and, worse yet, one with low marks in Japanese.

"Anyway," she said, closing her eyes. She took in a breath, more composed now, and let it out. "I wanted to make sure I got to see you first."

Kazuhiko remained quiet, listening to what she had to say.

"Terrible things are going to happen. With what you told me, they're already happening. Yesterday, everyone was friends . . . but they're killing each other, aren't they?"

Through her hand, Kazuhiko could feel her shudder again.

She gave him a smile mixed with emotion—fear, and maybe a little irony at the senseless fate that had visited them. "I can't take it," she said. "Not that."

Of course she couldn't. Not someone as compassionate as Sakura. Kazuhiko didn't know any sweeter girl.

"Besides," Sakura continued, "we won't be able to go home together. Even if by some miracle one of us could go back, it wouldn't be together. Even if . . . even if I somehow survived, I couldn't take you being gone. So . . ."

She didn't finish the sentence. Kazuhiko knew what she had been about to say: *So I'll die. Here. With you here, before anyone else can interfere.*

Instead, she said, "But you will live."

Kazuhiko smiled sadly, squeezed her hand tight, and shook his head. "That's cruel. I feel the same as you. Even if I survived, I couldn't take *you* being gone. Don't you go and leave me alone."

Sakura's wide eyes stared into his. She began to cry.

She looked away from him and wiped her tears with the hand holding the clover bouquet. Then she said something that took him a little by surprise. "Did you watch it last week? You know, the one on Wednesdays at nine. The last episode of *Tonight, At Our Rendezvous*?"

Kazuhiko nodded. *Rendezvous* was a drama broadcast by the DBS commercial network. As would be expected from a show produced in the Republic of Greater East Asia, it was a shallow love story—though fairly well made for its flaws, and it had been a ratings hit for years.

"Yeah, I saw it," Kazuhiko said. "You kept telling me I should."

"Uh-huh. Well, you know . . ."

She went on, and as Kazuhiko listened, he thought, *This is just how we always talk.* He found such bliss in their ordinary, pointless chatter. *She wants us to be us through the very end.*

Before he knew it, he was on the verge of tears.

"I'm totally fine," Sakura was saying, "with how the two main characters ended up together. That's how it always goes, you know? But I don't like what happened with Miki's friend, Mizue—the one played by Anna Kitagawa—and how she gave up on the guy she loved. I would have gone after him."

Kazuhiko grinned. "I thought you'd say that."

Sakura laughed bashfully. "I can't hide anything from you." She sounded so happy. "I can still remember when I first saw you, on my first day in junior high and in your class. You were tall, and cool, but more than that, I saw you and I thought, 'Here's someone who could really understand me. Deep down, he'd understand me.'"

"I . . . don't know how to say this very well, but . . ." Kazuhiko twisted his tongue around inside his mouth and thought for a moment, then said, "I don't know how to say this very well, but I felt the same way, I think."

He had said it well.

For a while, he leaned in against Sakura. With his left hand still holding hers, he reached his right hand to her shoulder.

Sitting together like this, they kissed. The moment lasted a few seconds. Or was that half a minute? Or an eternity?

Then, their lips separated. They had heard rustling in the bushes behind them. Someone had come. That was their signal. *The train's about to depart, so all aboard, you'd better get moving.*

There was nothing left to say. Sure, they could have fought back. He could have taken his revolver in hand and faced whoever was there. But that wasn't what she wanted. She wanted to pass quietly, before she got sucked into this damned senseless massacre. Nothing was more important to him than her. He couldn't trade her for anything now. This was what her trembling heart wanted, and he would obey. If he were a little more eloquent, perhaps he would have thought: *For her principles, I offer my life.*

Their bodies fell through the air beyond the cliffside, the pitch-black sea at their backs, their hands still clasped together.

Yukie Utsumi (Girls #2) was peeking out from the brush. Her breath caught in her throat. She hadn't the slightest intention of harming anyone, at least not unless someone attacked her first, and had never imagined her sound would have signaled their departure. She could only stare in stunned silence as the best couple in class, their two bodies side by side, vanished from the grassy cliff top. She could hear the faint sound of waves crashing against the sheer cliff below. A gentle breeze blew. The tiny white clovers had spilled from Sakura's fingers and came to rest upon the grass.

Behind Yukie, Haruka Tanizawa (Girls #12) asked, "What's wrong, Yukie?"

Yukie heard her, but just stood there, trembling.

32 STUDENTS REMAIN.

Megumi Eto (Girls #3) sat in the dark, arms wrapped around her shins. Her small body trembled. She was inside a house on the outskirts of the island's only village, a cluster of residences along the eastern shore. Though the lights might still have been working, Megumi didn't dare find out. The moonlight coming in through the kitchen window didn't reach under the table where she hid, leaving her in near total darkness. She couldn't see her watch, but figured she'd been sitting there for two hours, which made it nearly four in the morning. Almost an hour had passed since she'd heard the small and distant burst of what sounded like fireworks. Megumi didn't want to think about what that noise really was.

She lifted her face and saw the moonlit shapes of a teakettle and cupboards above the kitchen counter. Megumi knew that whoever had lived here must have been sent away to some temporary housing, but she could still sense their presence in the home. It felt unnatural and creepy, and reminded her of an old ghost story she'd heard as a child—the one about the crew of *Mary Celeste,* who had suddenly vanished, leaving behind on their abandoned ship everything in mid-use, meals and all.

When she left the school, Megumi ran, unaware of where she was going. The next thing she knew, she had ducked into a village. Her first thought was that not many of the others had left before her—five, only five. With fifty, maybe sixty, buildings in the village, she could fly into one of them with hardly any risk of running into anyone. Once inside, she could lock the door and hold the fort, as it was, and remain safe—at least until she was forced to move by one of those forbidden zones. The exploding collar made for an oppressive presence, but there was nothing she could do about it. *If you try to force it loose, it'll explode,* Sakamochi had said. What mattered now was not to miss the scheduled announcements of where and when the forbidden zones would activate.

Megumi had tried to enter the nearest house first, but it was locked. So was the second. At the third house, she used a rock to smash the sliding glass door around the back of the home. The loud noise sent her instinctively scrambling beneath the veranda to hide. No one seemed to be approaching. She went inside. With no way to lock the back door now, she struggled with the heavy storm doors on the outer rails but managed to slide the panels closed. Plunged into total darkness, the house felt sinister, more haunted mansion than home. Megumi turned on her flashlight to search the house and found two sturdy fishing rods to jam the storm doors shut.

Now she was under the kitchen table. *I can't kill anyone,* she thought. *There's no way. But maybe, just maybe, if this won't be in a forbidden zone until the end* (she had checked her map and seen that nearly the entire village lay within zone H-8), *I might be able to survive.*

But, Megumi thought, her body still quivering, *it's so terrifying. The way the game is, everyone's my enemy. I can't trust anyone, I know that . . . but I just can't make myself think that way. That's why I'm stuck here, shaking like this. But even if . . . even if . . . that time comes, and the final whistle is blown, and I'm still alive, that would have to mean everyone else is dead . . . my friends, like Mizuho and Kaori . . . and that boy—even thinking of him now makes my heart race—Shuya Nanahara.*

In the darkness, Megumi pulled her knees into her chest and sat thinking of Shuya. What she really loved about him was his voice. It was a little gravelly, not too high-pitched, but not too low. He seemed really into that banned music—rock or something—and when he had to sing songs praising the government or the Leader in music class, he always had this displeased look on his face. But even then, his voice was remarkable. And with his guitar, he could improvise rhythms like nothing she'd ever heard, and they made her body dance of its own accord. Yet there was a grace to the sound, the beauty of a church bell's resounding ring. He had long, wavy hair ("the Bruce Springsteen look," he'd said, though Megumi hadn't a clue who he meant), kind, double-lidded eyes (sometimes Megumi thought they looked cute, like a cat's), and the agility of a former Little League MVP.

Thinking of Shuya's face and his voice, her trembling subsided. *Ah, how nice would it be if Shuya were with me now . . .*

But . . . but why did I never tell him how I felt? I never sent him a love letter. I never had him meet me somewhere so I could tell him face to face. I didn't even tell him over the phone. And now I never will.

A thought caught her attention.

The phone.

Sure, Sakamochi said we couldn't use the phones, but what if . . .

Megumi scrambled for her nylon handbag, which she'd left next to the daypack, and pulled the bag closer. She opened the zipper and shoved aside her clothing and toiletries.

Her fingertips felt the hard, squarish object, and she pulled it out.

It was her cell phone. Megumi's mother had bought it for her in case something should happen on the school trip (though this was hardly just *something*). Sure, she'd envied the couple kids who had one, and there was a thrill to it, like having her own secret passageway. On the other hand, she wondered if her parents were being overprotective and thought her mother worried too much, and besides, what did a junior high kid need with one of those things anyway? So she had stuffed the shiny new phone into the bottom of her purse, completely forgetting about it until this very moment.

With shaking hands, she flipped open the phone.

The device switched automatically from standby to dial mode, and the dial pad and tiny LCD screen sprang to life with a dim green light. In the glow, Megumi could see her own legs and skirt, and her bags too. But more importantly, there, on that screen, was that unmistakable icon, the antenna and bars. *A signal!*

"Please, God," Megumi whispered.

Impatiently, she pressed the numbers for her home in Shiroiwa. Zero, 8, 7, 9, 2 . . .

She pressed the phone to her ear. Silence. Then, ringing. Hope swelled up in her chest.

One ring. Two. Three. *Hurry, answer. Mom, Dad, I don't care which. I know it's the middle of the night, but you know your daughter's in trouble. Hurry.*

The receiver clicked to life, then the voice came. "Hello."

"Oh, Dad!"

Still cramped in the confines of the kitchen table, Megumi closed her eyes. She felt like she might go mad from relief. *I'm saved, I'm saved!*

"Dad!" Delirious, she shouted into the phone. "It's me. Megumi. Oh, Dad! Save me. Dad, come save me!"

But when there was no response, she regained her senses. *Something is . . . wrong. What . . . Why isn't Dad . . . Wait, what's going on?*

Finally, the man on the phone spoke. "I'm not your dad, Eto. This is Sakamochi. Didn't I tell you that phones wouldn't work?"

With a yelp, she dropped the phone, then clawed for it on the ground, mashing the button to end the call.

Her heart pounded, and despair crushed her chest once more. *It didn't work. Of course it didn't. I'm going to . . . die here. I'm going to die.*

But the hammering of her heart was about to be sent leaping to a whole new level.

She heard the sound of breaking glass.

Her head jerked to face the noise's direction. The living room.

She'd checked it earlier to make sure everything was locked. *Someone's here! Why? Of all these houses, why this one?*

Hurriedly, she snapped shut the faintly glowing phone and stuffed it into her pocket. From atop her daypack, she drew her weapon—a double-edged diving knife—from its plastic sheath and gripped it tightly.

I have to run, quick as I can.

But her body remained frozen. All she could do was quiet her breathing. *Please, please God, make sure they can't hear my heartbeat.*

Megumi heard a window open, then close, and then the sound of cautious, quiet footsteps.

The footsteps seemed to wind their way through the house, until finally approaching right outside the kitchen where Megumi hid. Her heart pounded louder and louder.

A flashlight's thin beam pierced into the room. The light glided above the kitchen counter and the teakettle and pots.

The intruder sighed and said, "Good, no one's here."

The footsteps entered the kitchen, but Megumi had already been stricken with panic at the sound of the girl's voice. Gone now, smashed to pieces, was any hope that the intruder was one of her good friends and that she could talk her way out. The voice belonged to none other than Mitsuko Souma (Girls #11). The worst girl in the entire school, Mitsuko wore a lovely, angelic face but could make teachers wither under a single glance.

Even with all the rumors that surrounded Kazuo Kiriyama and Shogo Kawada, Megumi was most afraid of Mitsuko Souma. Maybe it was because Mitsuko was also a girl, or maybe it was because one of the girls in Mitsuko's clique, Hirono Shimizu, had picked on her when they became classmates at the start of eighth grade, tripping her as she walked past in the hall and ripping her skirt with a box cutter. Hirono had since lost interest in her—though Megumi had still been sad to learn that the same class would carry over to ninth grade— and Mitsuko herself had never bullied her. Nevertheless, Mitsuko was someone not even Hirono could defy.

Someone like Mitsuko Souma, Megumi thought, *would enjoy killing me off.*

Megumi's body began trembling again. *No, of all things. Stop. Don't shake. If she hears . . .* She squeezed her arms tightly around herself, striving to subdue her shaking.

From underneath the table, Megumi could see Mitsuko's hand holding the flashlight and an illuminated band of skirt near the girl's waist. Then Megumi heard the sound of Mitsuko rummaging through the drawers below the sink.

Hurry up. Please, just hurry up and leave. At least get out of this room. Wait, that's it. I could run for the bathroom. I can lock the door from the inside and escape through the window. Just please, leave the kitchen so I can—

Ririririri-ring! The sudden electronic chirp sent Megumi's heart leaping nearly to her throat.

She thought she saw Mitsuko Souma jump too. Immediately, Mitsuko's flashlight went dark and with it her skirt. Megumi sensed the girl retreating to the corner of the room.

When she realized the ringing was coming from her pocket, Megumi frantically took out her phone. Her mind went blank and she reflexively flipped open the phone and jabbed randomly at the buttons.

"Ah, this is Sakamochi," said the voice on the phone. "Listen, Eto, I wanted to add that you'd better turn it off. The phone, I mean. If I were to call you, it would give your position away to everyone, wouldn't it? Right? So you should—"

Megumi's fingers found the end call button, cutting off Sakamochi.

Silence, suffocating, continued for a while. Then came Mitsuko's voice.

"Megumi? Is that you, Megumi? Are you there?"

Mitsuko seemed to be in the corner of the dark kitchen. Megumi quietly placed her cell phone on the floor and clutched her knife. Her hand shook even more, and the weapon seemed a fish trying to wiggle free from her grasp. But tightly, tightly, she gripped it.

Mitsuko was taller than Megumi, but she couldn't have been that much stronger. Whatever her weapon was . . .

What if it's a gun? No, if she had a gun, she'd be firing in my direction. And if it's not a gun, then . . . I have a chance. I have to kill her. If I don't kill her, she'll kill me.

If I don't kill her . . .

With a click, the flashlight's beam reappeared. The light shot in beneath the table, blinding Megumi for a moment. *Now! Stand up! Stick my knife at that light!*

But something unexpected interrupted her thoughts.

The beam of light fell low, and into it Mitsuko sank, dropping to the floor, gazing at her, crying.

From trembling lips, Mitsuko breathed out the words, "Thank goodness." She was sobbing. "I—I . . . was so scared."

She extended her arms toward Megumi, as if reaching out for salvation. She wasn't holding a weapon; her hands were empty.

She said the rest in one breath. "It's you, it's you, I don't need to worry, right, you wouldn't kill me, you'd never do a thing like that, and you'll stay with me, won't you?"

Megumi was stunned. *Mitsuko Souma—that Mitsuko Souma—is crying. She wants my help. Oh . . .*

Her tremors melting away, Megumi felt welling up inside of her a lump of emotion that was hard to describe.

So that's it. Ah, that's how it is. No matter what names people called her, no matter what the rumors, Mitsuko is just another ninth-grade girl like me. How could she ever do something so terrible as kill her own classmates? The girl was all alone, frightened out of her mind.

But—how could I? I thought it, didn't I? I thought to kill her.

I'm . . . I'm an awful person.

Emotions filled her, both self-disgust and, at the same time, relief at having someone with her, at not having to be alone anymore. Teardrops began to fall from her eyes.

The knife tumbled from Megumi's fingers. She crawled out from beneath the table and took Mitsuko's outstretched hands. As if a dam had burst inside her, the words spilled out, passionate. "Mitsuko! Mitsuko!"

She felt herself trembling again, but because of a different emotion now. *But what does that matter when I . . . when I . . .*

"There, there," Megumi said. "It's all right. I'm here now. I'm with you. We're together now."

"Yes. Yes," Mitsuko said, scrunching up her tear-streaked face. She squeezed Megumi's hands in return. "Yes. Yes." She nodded.

There, on the kitchen floor, Megumi embraced her. She could feel Mitsuko's warmth, and as the girl's helplessly trembling body pressed against her chest, her feelings of guilt redoubled.

I thought terrible things. So terrible . . . I was going to kill her.

"Hey." The words came unbidden from Megumi's lips. "I . . . I . . ."

"What?" Mitsuko looked up at her with tear-filled eyes.

Megumi pressed her lips tight to stifle her own sobs and shook her head. "I'm so ashamed of myself. For a moment there, I was going to kill you. I thought I'd kill you. I was so scared."

Mitsuko's eyes flickered wide, but she didn't become angry. With her tears still running down her cheeks, she simply bobbed her head.

Then, with a grin, she said, "It's okay. It's okay, really. Don't be upset. It's not a big deal. It's natural, in a screwed-up situation like this. Don't be upset. Okay? Just stay with me. Please."

Mitsuko lifted her hand and gently held the back of Megumi's head, then leaned in until they were touching, cheek-to-cheek. Mitsuko's tears ran down Megumi's face.

Oh, Megumi thought, *I was wrong about everything. To think, Mitsuko Souma has been so kindhearted all along. Here I was going to kill her, and she forgave me with two little words: "It's okay." Isn't that what Mr. Hayashida, though he's dead now, always said? Never judge people by rumors. Only people with ugly hearts do that.*

Again she felt emotions welling up inside her chest. She held Mitsuko tight. That was all she could do for now. *I'm sorry. I'm sorry. I was an ugly person. I really—*

She heard a sound—*slkkk*—like a lemon being sliced.

It was a very pleasing sound, right out of a TV cooking show; a sound only the best, newest knife and the freshest fruit could provide. Today, viewers, we'll be making salmon with a lemon marinade.

It took a good two or three seconds before Megumi realized what had happened.

Just beneath her chin and to the left, she saw Mitsuko's right hand and the blade that extended out from it in a gentle curve, like the shape of a banana, casting the dull reflection of the flashlight's beam.

A sickle. Like for reaping rice. And the end of it . . . in my throat.

Her left hand still cupping the back of Megumi's head, Mitsuko drove the sickle deeper with another *slkkk.*

Megumi's throat felt fiercely hot, but it didn't last long. Unable to speak, she could only feel the incredible warmth on her chest as the blood streamed down, and then she didn't feel anything. She was gone before she could place any meaning to the blade inside her throat. Without a final thought of her family, or even Shuya Nanahara, Megumi died in Mitsuko's arms.

When Mitsuko let go, Megumi's body crumpled sideways to the floor.

Mitsuko didn't hesitate before switching off her flashlight and standing up. Annoyed by her tears, she wiped them away. (Mitsuko could cry at a moment's notice—that was one of her many special talents.) She held the sickle up to the moonlight that trickled in from the window and wiped the blood from the blade. The falling blood drops splattered softly as they hit the ground.

Not bad, for a start, Mitsuko thought. She'd intended to look for something easier to wield, a kitchen knife, perhaps, but this sickle wasn't as bad as she'd expected. She'd just been a little too careless inside that house, not knowing if someone else was there or not. The next time, she'd be more cautious.

She looked down at Megumi's corpse and murmured, "Sorry about that. I was going to kill you too."

31 STUDENTS REMAIN.

PART TWO
THE MIDDLE GAME

STUDENTS REMAIN.

The first night broke into dawn.

Shuya Nanahara looked up through the trees and watched the blue sky gradually take on white. Leaves and branches—of evergreen oaks, camellias, and some cherry trees and others Shuya couldn't identify—wove an intricate net concealing where he and Noriko hid.

Shuya had checked his map, which confirmed the island's rounded diamond shape and indicated two mountains, one to the north and one to the south. Shuya and Noriko were near the foot of the northern mountain's western slopes, and just a little south relative to its peak—zone C-4, according to the coordinate grid. The exceptionally detailed map included not only the topographic contour lines, but also each house in the village and around the island (these were marked with light blue dots), various buildings (only a few earned the commonly recognizable icons—a medical clinic, a volunteer fire station, a lighthouse—while the rest were places like the community center, the fisherman's co-op, and the like), and streets big and small. Between the lay of the land, the roads, and the occasional scattered house, Shuya had been able to find his bearings.

Moreover, while he was fairly high up on the mountain during the night, he had double-checked that the map was indeed a faithful representation of the island. The silhouettes of islands of many sizes dotted the dark black sea—and, as Sakamochi had said, the outline of a guard ship (due west) stationed with its lights off.

Directly to Shuya and Noriko's west, the thicket terminated at a steep slope. A small field opened below, beyond which the downslope continued toward the sea. Passing through the field during the night, they had found a building, almost a shack, which had been built off the ground. Shuya had noticed the weathered wooden *torii* gate ten meters away and figured it to be a small, very small, Shinto shrine. (The map confirmed this.) The front door stood open, and no one was inside.

But, as he had done with the other houses they'd come across on the way, he decided not to hide inside the little shrine. One of the others might have the same thought, and with only one entrance, if someone were to notice them, they'd be trapped.

When it was time to rest, Shuya found a place, relatively near the ocean, where the undergrowth parted with just enough space for both of them to lie down. Higher up the mountain, the greenery would have been thicker, but he had the feeling that many of the others would end up converging there. And if the two encountered someone who turned out to be an enemy, and they had to run, he figured it would be better to do so on more level ground—especially with Noriko's wounded leg.

Shuya was sitting against a tree about ten centimeters wide. Noriko was just to his left, also leaning against a tree, with her injured right leg stretched out in front of her. They had pushed themselves through exhaustion, and Noriko had closed her eyes.

Even after lengthy discussions over what they should do next, they hadn't come up with much.

His first thought was to find a boat to escape the island. But he quickly realized that would have been pointless. The guard ships were at sea, but more than that . . .

Shuya touched his hand to the collar around his neck and felt its cold surface. He'd gotten used to the feel of it against his skin, but the weight of it remained, an embodiment of the senseless fate that bound them.

That was right, the collars.

A specific signal transmitted by the computers inside the school would trigger the bomb inside the collar to explode. When Sakamochi had explained the rules, he said it would happen if any of them entered a forbidden zone, but nothing prevented the same from happening to students who attempted a seaward escape. Those guard ships weren't even necessary. Even if Shuya managed to find a boat, escape would be utterly impossible unless he could do something about their collars.

Then it followed that their only move was to attack Sakamochi at the school and disable their collar locks. But the school, in zone G-7, had been designated a forbidden zone directly after the game's beginning. Even if they could approach it, they were being tracked anyway.

Shuya was turning this over in his mind when he noticed the world around him had become bright. Moving about in the daylight would be dangerous. *We just have to wait it out until the next nightfall.*

But that thought led to another problem: the time limit. Twenty-four hours without a single death, Sakamochi had said. The death Shuya witnessed as he left the school had been more than three hours earlier. If the day passed with no more killings, they all would die in a little more than twenty hours. Waiting until night to prepare an escape could be too late. Ironically, each classmate's death bought the others more time to live—but Shuya didn't want to think about that.

For now, damned if he did, damned if he didn't. They were all damned.

Shuya kept hoping he could somehow meet up with Shinji Mimura. A guy with Shinji's extensive knowledge, and the boundless wisdom to use it, would surely be able to find a way through this situation.

He also kept on regretting, despite the risk, that he hadn't waited for Shinji after Yoshio Akamatsu's attack. *Did I really do the right thing? Had there really been any chance that some "enemy" would strike? Hadn't Akamatsu only been an exception?*

No . . . I can't be sure of that. There might still be trouble yet. I can't even tell who the bad guys are. Who's thinking straight, and who isn't anymore? But . . . in this game, maybe we're the ones who've lost our senses. Are we the crazy ones?

Shuya felt like he was losing his mind.

All that's left—for now—is to wait here a little while longer and see what happens. Maybe I'll think of something. If I don't, then we wait until night and find Shinji. But can we find him? Sure, this is a small island, only six kilometers around, but finding someone here won't be easy. And once night comes, how long will we have until it's game over?

Even in the—I hate to think it—one-in-a-million chance I find Shinji, or if Noriko and I escape on our own, we'll only be criminals. Unless we defect to some other country, we spend our whole lives on the run. And then, one day, some agent of the government guns us down in a deserted alley. A bloated rat comes out to nibble at my fingers.

Maybe I'd be better off insane.

Then Shuya thought about Yoshitoki Kuninobu. He was saddened by Yoshitoki's death, but maybe the boy had actually been incredibly lucky to have been spared this mad reality—mad, and without hope.

Should we just kill ourselves? Would Noriko agree to a double suicide?

Shuya turned his head and, for the first time, studied Noriko's profile in the soft, burgeoning light.

He noticed her well-shaped eyebrows, the gentle curve of her eyelashes on her closed eyes, and her lovely nose with the rounded tip, her full lips. She was a very cute girl. He thought he understood how Yoshitoki had liked her looks.

But now that face had been smeared with sand, and her hair, hanging just below her shoulders, was in tangles. Then there was that collar. The ugly silver band coiled around her neck like she was a slave in some long ago time.

This bullshit game is spoiling her beauty, Shuya thought, and with that he felt a sudden surge of rage that brought him back to his senses.

I won't let this beat me. I'm going to survive, and I'm going to make these fuckers pay for dumping us into this game. And not just pay. You come at me with a right cross, and I'll smash you with a fucking baseball bat.

Noriko's eyes blinked open, and she met his gaze.

For a while, they stared at each other. Then quietly, Noriko asked, "What's wrong?"

"Nothing . . . Well, I was thinking . . ." Being caught staring into her face had taken him off balance. He blurted the first thing that came to him. "Okay, this might sound weird, but you're not actually thinking of killing yourself, are you?"

Noriko looked down. Her ambiguous expression might have held the hint of a smile. He could see her clearly now; the sun was rising. Then she said, "Of course not. Although . . ."

"Although?"

She appeared to think for a moment. Then she continued, "Well, if we were the last two alive, I might want to kill myself. That way, at least you would—"

Taken aback, Shuya shook his head. He shook it hard. He'd just brought up the subject on impulse, never expecting that kind of answer.

"Don't talk that garbage," Shuya said. "Don't even think it. We are in this together until the very end. No matter what. That's final."

Noriko smiled and reached out her hand, touching his. "Thank you."

"Look, we're going to survive this. Don't you even think about dying."

Again, she gave him a little smile. Then she said, "You haven't given up."

He shook his head, putting a little force into it. "Of course not."

With a little tilt of the head, Noriko said, "You know, I've always thought of you as having a positive force about you."

"A positive force?"

She grinned. "I can't explain it very well, but it's like you have this drive toward living. Right now, it's your determination to survive. And," she said, turning her soft smile to him, "that's what I really like about you."

Embarrassed, Shuya replied, "I think that's just me being an idiot."

Then he said, "If we find a way off this island, well, it's not like I have anyone. I mean, I don't have any parents. But you—you have your mother and your father, and your brother. You won't be able to see them. Can you handle that?"

Another smile. "I'd already accepted that—as soon as this started." After a moment, she added, "But what about you? Will you be all right?"

"All right with what?"

"That you won't be able to see *her*?"

Shuya gulped. She knew all about him. She'd said it herself: *I've been watching you for so long.*

He'd have been lying if he said it didn't hurt. For so long he'd thought of no one but Kazumi Shintani. And now he'd never see her face again.

But he shook his head. "That's—"

He had been about to say that it was just a one-sided crush, just his own delusion, but he was interrupted. The sudden blare of Sakamochi's voice resounded all around.

31 STUDENTS REMAIN.

"Good morning, everyone!"

It was Sakamochi's voice. Shuya couldn't tell where the loudspeakers were, but the words came loud and clear, if distorted and metallic. The speakers must have been distributed throughout the island.

"This is your instructor, Sakamochi speaking. It's now six a.m. How are you all doing?"

Shuya grimaced, though only after he'd recovered from being dumbstruck by Sakamochi's cheerful tone.

"All right," Sakamochi said, "I'm now going to announce the names of your dead friends. I'll start with the boys. First, number one, Yoshio Akamatsu."

Shuya thought that Yoshio Akamatsu hadn't been dead when he left. *So after that,* he wondered, *did he try to kill someone else, and then get killed himself? Or—could it be—had he remained lying there, unconscious, until that first forbidden zone activated, and his lovely little collar blew him to bits?*

Since Shuya had been the one to knock him out, the idea didn't sit well with him..

But the names of the dead piled into a heap that buried these thoughts.

"Continuing on, number nine, Hiroshi Kuronaga; number ten, Ryuhei Sasagawa; number seventeen, Mitsuru Numai; number twenty-one, Kazuhiko Yamamoto. And, let's see here, the girls. Number three, Megumi Eto; number four, Sakura Ogawa; number five, Izumi Kanai; number fourteen, Mayumi Tendo."

The list of names of course meant that the time limit would be postponed for the near future, but such thoughts were far from Shuya's mind. He felt dizzy. The faces of the classmates whose names had been read formed and vanished in his mind. They were all dead, and for each one, there'd be a killer. Unless, that is, they had committed suicide.

This game is happening. There's no stopping it. Shuya saw in his mind a long funeral procession, a crowd all dressed in black. A man in a black suit with a somber, know-it-all expression said, *"Oh, it's Shuya Nanahara and Noriko Nakagawa. That's right, you two haven't gone yet, have you? But look over there, those are your own graves that you just walked past. We already carved in your seat numbers, both fifteen. Don't worry, the carving's free. It's on special."*

"That's a good pace," Sakamochi said. "Your teacher is very proud. Right, next up are the forbidden zones. I'll be giving the sectors and times. Take out your maps and follow along."

Still in shock at the number of the dead and still disgusted at Sakamochi's tone, Shuya nonetheless took out his map.

"First, an hour from now. That's seven a.m. From seven, zone J-2. Get out of sector J-2 by seven a.m. Got that?"

J-2 was located just to the west of the island's southern tip.

"Next, in three hours. From nine, sector F-1."

F-1 was on the same western shore as Shuya and Noriko, but much farther to the south.

"Next, in five hours. From eleven, sector H-8."

H-8 included nearly the entire village on the eastern shore.

"That's all for now. Now, I want you all to do your best today!"

Sakamochi's broadcast clicked off.

None of the forbidden zones were near the pair's current location. Whether or not the areas were, as Sakamochi had said, selected at random, it seemed Shuya had made the correct choice by not escaping into the village. But this place might be included in the next set.

"He mentioned . . ." Noriko said, and Shuya turned to her. "He mentioned Sakura and Yamamoto."

"Yeah." Shuya's voice caught in his throat. "Do you think they killed themselves?"

"I don't know. But I'm sure they were together to the end. Somehow, somewhere, they were able to meet."

Shuya had himself seen Sakura leave Yamamoto a note. But anything after that amounted to nothing more than wishful thinking. They could have been killed in separate places by separate crazed classmates.

Banishing the lingering image of the two lovers' hands touching as the note was passed, Shuya took out the class roster from his pocket. The sheet had been in the daypack along with the map. Though it seemed vulgar, he had to keep track. He took out a pen, intending to strike through the names. But he couldn't do it. *It's just too . . . it's just too . . . Well, it's cruel.*

Next to the names, he drew a small checkmark. He did the same next to Yoshitoki Kuninobu's and Fumiyo Fujiyoshi's names. Shuya felt as if he had become that black-suited man in his vision. *"Okay, you, and you. And you there. What size coffins are you? If you can make do with a model eight, it's a big seller, so I can give you a steal."*

Be that as it may, Shuya noticed that of Kiriyama's four lackeys, three were dead. Hiroshi Kuronaga, Ryuhei Sasagawa, and Mitsuru Numai. The only one left was Sho Tsukioka—kind of a weird kid who went by the nickname "Zuki"—and Kiriyama himself.

Shuya thought back to Numai's smug expression after Kiriyama left the classroom. Shuya had assumed that Kiriyama would surely assemble his gang to escape. But what did their deaths signify? Had they gotten together, only to be possessed by paranoia, turning their meeting place into a battleground? And had Kiriyama and Tsukioka managed to flee? And were Tsukioka and Kiriyama still together? Shuya had no idea; something completely different might have gone down.

And there was that faint noise, sounding like gunfire, that had reached his eardrums. If it had been a gun, had it taken the life of one of those ten kids?

Just then, his thoughts were interrupted by a rustling sound. Noriko's expression had gone visibly tense. Shuya stuffed the pen and paper back into his pocket.

Shuya listened closely. The sound continued—and it was approaching.

Under his breath, he told Noriko, "Quiet."

Shuya gripped his daypack. Thinking they needed to be able to move at any moment, he had gathered up all of his things into the backpack. He'd left some clothes in his gym bag, but those could be left behind. Noriko had done the same with her possessions.

Shuya hoisted the two daypacks over his left shoulder. He lent Noriko his hands to help her stand up, and they crouched side by side.

Shuya withdrew his knife. He held it in a reverse right-hand grip. But then he thought, *Sure, I know how to use a guitar pick, but will I be any good with this?*

The rustling grew louder. *How close is it now—within meters?*

The anxious impatience he'd felt in front of the school again gripped his mind. He grabbed Noriko by the arm and pulled her back. They stood and backed into the underbrush. *Faster! We need to move as fast as we can!*

They came out of the bushes that had shielded them and emerged onto a trail. The footpath wound up the mountain's slope. Overhead, treetops sandwiched a ribbon of blue sky.

Shuya shielded Noriko behind him as he retreated several meters up the path. In the bushes, the rustling continued, growing louder, until . . .

Shuya's eyes widened.

A lone white cat popped out from the undergrowth. Filthy, scraggly, and with matted fur, but nevertheless, a cat.

Shuya and Noriko looked at each other. Breaking into a grin, she said, "A cat." Shuya returned her a chagrined smile. As if only just now noticing the two, the cat looked their way.

It stared at them for a while, then pattered up to them.

While Shuya was putting his knife back into its sheath, Noriko crouched down slowly, on account of her injured leg, and offered her hands to the cat. It jumped into her hands and nuzzled her feet. She cupped its front legs and lifted the little animal.

She puckered her lips into a kiss and held them out toward the cat. "You poor thing. You're so skinny."

The cat opened its mouth into a happy *meow.*

"I wonder if it belonged to someone," Noriko said. "It's so friendly."

"I wonder."

The government had evicted the island's residents to stage this game. (Since each Program operated in secrecy until its conclusion, the locals probably hadn't been given a reason.) Noriko might have been right, and this creature might have been left behind without its owner. No houses were nearby, but could it have wandered all the way up the mountain?

As Shuya thought about this, his eyes drifted from Noriko and the cat. He turned his head.

Then he recoiled.

A mere ten meters down the path, a figure in a school uniform stood as if glued to the spot. He was roughly Shuya's height, with a muscular build that had been forged on the handball court, dark suntanned skin, and short, spiked-up hair. He was Tatsumichi Oki (Boys #3).

31 STUDENTS REMAIN.

Following Shuya's eyes, Noriko turned. In an instant, her expression went tense. *Which was he,* Shuya wondered, *an enemy, or not?*

Tatsumichi Oki stood there, staring at them. Shuya sensed his field of vision narrowing in response to the threat—as it did when he rode in a speeding car—but at the periphery of his awareness, he perceived the large hatchet in Tatsumichi's right hand.

Almost without a thought, Shuya reached for the knife in his belt.

That set it off. Tatsumichi's arm jerked—then the next instant, he was charging straight at them.

Shuya shoved Noriko, cat still in arms, into the bushes.

Tatsumichi was already within reach.

Shuya quickly raised the daypacks to catch the hatchet's blow. But the bags split open, spilling their contents to the ground. The blade struck Shuya's bottle, sending water spurting out, and continued through to Shuya's arm. His skin felt ablaze, sizzling.

He discarded the sliced-up bag and jumped back to create some distance. Tatsumichi's expression had turned hard, and his eyes were wide open, the whites forming a full circle around his black pupils.

Shuya was in disbelief. *I know how things are here—for a second,*

I suspected him too, but why? Tatsumichi was always so cheerful and carefree. Why would he do this?

Tatsumichi glanced to the side, where Noriko had fallen into the bushes. Following his eyes, Shuya looked over at Noriko. Her face and lips had frozen under the attacker's gaze. The cat had already bolted into hiding.

Tatsumichi suddenly turned to face Shuya, and the hatchet was swinging sideways.

Shuya jerked the knife free from his belt, taking it in a reverse grip, and met the blow. Unluckily, the weapon hadn't left its leather sheath. Even so, he halted the hatchet's strike with a resounding *clang*. Its edge stopped five centimeters from his cheek. Shuya could make out the blue ripples on the blade's surface, formed when the steel had been tempered.

Before Tatsumichi could swing again, Shuya dropped his knife and took hold of his opponent's hatchet arm. But Tatsumichi powered through another slash. Though slowed, the hatchet made contact with the side of Shuya's head. Several strands of his long, wavy hair tore loose and fluttered in the air. He felt his earlobe tear open. It didn't hurt much. A blithe and incongruous thought ran through his mind: *Well, all kinds of guys get their ears pierced. Shinji did.*

Tatsumichi switched the hatchet to his off hand. Before he could ready another swing, Shuya kicked the inside of his leg. Tatusmichi's leg dropped. *Yes! Down!*

But Tatsumichi didn't drop. He staggered into a half turn, then fell against Shuya, backing him into the undergrowth on the seaward side of the path. Branches snapped all around them.

Shuya kept moving back. Pressed by Tatsumichi's brute force, Shuya practically ran backward. Noriko's face was disappearing into the distance. In this unreal situation, another inappropriate thought entered Shuya's mind, a memory from a Little League practice. *Let's hear it for Shuya Nanahara, the backward-running champion!*

Suddenly, the ground felt different.

Then Shuya remembered that steep slope down to the field with the tiny shrine.

I'm falling!

The two tangled boys rolled down the bush-covered slope. The clear morning sky and the green foliage spun around and around. But he had both hands around Tatsumichi's wrist, and he didn't let go.

Shuya felt like he had fallen an incredible distance, though it might only have been about ten meters. With a thump, he came to a crashing halt. He was in bright daylight. They had tumbled all the way into the open field.

He was flat underneath Tatsumichi. *I have to get up,* Shuya thought, *before he does!*

But instead, he hesitated. Something didn't feel right. Tatsumichi's full-powered machine press of an arm now lay limp and motionless.

When Shuya looked up from his position under Tatsumichi's chest, he saw what had happened.

Directly above his head, the hatchet was lodged exactly halfway deep into Tatsumichi's face. The half of it outside his face looked like a wafer of chocolate garnishing a Christmas cake. The blade entered through his forehead, split his eyeball cleanly in two (blood and some viscous fluid were pouring out), and its steel glimmered pale blue in the cavity of his gaping mouth.

And while Tatsumichi's hand held the hatchet, Shuya was gripping that wrist. From Tatsumichi's face to Shuya's wrist, a terrible and creepy sensation raced at the speed of light.

As if tracing along the course of that sensation, Tatsumichi's blood oozed all the way down the hatchet to Shuya's hands. With a low yelp, Shuya released the boy's wrist and scrambled out from underneath him. Tatsumichi's body flopped over, face up, his face gruesome in death, soaking in the morning sun.

Shuya gasped for air, his shoulders heaving up and down. Dull waves of nausea came swelling up from the pit of his stomach.

Though the unrivaled horror of Tatsumichi's death visage had certainly had its effect, Shuya was far more distressed by himself. He had *killed* someone—and not just anyone, but someone who had, until yesterday, been a fellow classmate.

Shuya tried to tell himself it was an accident, but he didn't believe it. After all, during their fall he had done everything he could to deflect the blade from himself—by twisting Tatsumichi's wrist back as hard as he could.

He felt like he was going to puke.

But Shuya swallowed, holding it down. He lifted his head and looked up the slope he'd tumbled down.

Shrubbery covered the slope, blocking his view. He'd left Noriko behind, alone. More than anything else now, he needed to protect her. This was no time to throw up. *I have to hurry,* he thought, trying to calm himself down. *I have to hurry back to her.*

Shuya stood. For a moment, he looked down at Tatsumichi's face and the hatchet that had split it in two.

After a brief hesitation, he pried Tatsumichi's fingers from the weapon's handle. No matter what had happened, he couldn't leave Tatsumichi like this. A burial was out of the question, but leaving that hatchet buried in his face would have been too cruel. Shuya couldn't physically bear it.

Shuya gripped the handle and pulled.

Tatsumichi's head lifted with the hatchet. The blade had dug so deeply that it wouldn't come free.

Shuya exhaled deeply. *Oh, God.*

Then he thought again. *No, where the hell is God in all this? Ms. Anno was such a devout Christian, and what did her faith get her aside from being raped by Sakamochi? Well, halle-fucking-lujah.*

Rage erupted within him.

Gritting his teeth, Shuya knelt beside Tatsumichi's head and placed a trembling hand on his dead classmate's forehead. With his other hand, he yanked out the hatchet. With an ugly spurting sound, blood sprayed from the boy's face, and the blade came free.

For a second, Shuya was overcome by the feeling that this was all a bad dream. The left and right halves of Tatsumichi's head had tilted askew. It was too unreal, like a plastic facsimile. For the first time, Shuya realized how fragile and malleable the human body was.

Closing Tatsumichi's eyes didn't seem a good idea. Tatsumichi's eyelid, which had been split in two along with the eyeball, had contracted and twisted upward and would never close again. The other eye was manageable, but who would want a winking corpse—especially here?

Shuya felt sick again.

Instead, he stood and turned. To get back to Noriko, he'd have to take the long way around up the trail.

But his eyes shot open wide again.

Fifteen meters in front of him, in the middle of the field, stood a boy with glasses and a school jacket—Kyoichi Motobuchi (Boys #20), the boys' class leader.

And the class leader was holding a revolver.

30 STUDENTS REMAIN.

17

Behind silver-rimmed glasses, the class leader's eyes met Shuya's. His hair, usually neatly parted to the side, was now a tangled mess, and his glasses were smudged and filthy, but those eyes—those wide, bloodshot eyes? They looked just like Tatsumichi's had. His face was as pale as it had been in the classroom, inhuman as an Andy Warhol painting.

Shuya perceived the gun's barrel begin to move. He twisted over backward and dropped to the ground. The next instant, he heard the explosive bang and saw a small flame envelop the muzzle. He thought he felt something hot skim just over his head, but he might have imagined it.

His back still on the ground, and with no time to think, Shuya tried to retreat. The tall grass rustled against his back.

He wasn't moving nearly quickly enough. He couldn't escape. Kyoichi had advanced within a handful of meters and was settling his aim on Shuya's chest.

Shuya's face went as stiff as a plaster sculpture. More than the need to protect Noriko, more than anything now, true terror swelled up inside him. *The next tiny, tiny lead bullet that gun spits out will kill me. It'll kill me!*

"Stop!" came a voice.

Kyoichi gave a start and looked back over his shoulder. Dumb-founded, Shuya followed the class leader's glance.

A large figure stood at ease in the shade of the small shrine. It was Shogo Kawada (Boys #5), with his butch-cut hair—practically shaved off—a prominent scar over his eyebrow, and that intimidating carnival-food-vendor's face. He was holding a pump-action shotgun, a sawed-off Remington M31.

Kyoichi spun to face this intruder and fired. Kawada quickly dropped to his knees. His shotgun barked, and sparks showered from the muzzle as if it were a flamethrower. An instant later, Kyoichi's arm was gone. Blood sprayed into the air, and for a moment, the class leader stared in wonder at the new short-sleeved look of his school uniform. The rest of the sleeve—along with the arm, and the hand holding the revolver—had fallen to the grass. Kawada swiftly pulled back the handgrip and chambered the next shell. The spent red casing flew out to the side.

As if only now realizing what had happened, Kyoichi let out an animal shriek. Shuya thought the class leader would just fall over now.

But he didn't. Instead, Kyoichi ran to his severed arm. With the hand he still had, he wrenched the revolver from his own fingers. *Like a relay baton pass,* Shuya thought. *One guy filling two positions, way to go!* Once again, Shuya felt like he was watching a bad horror flick. Or maybe reading a bad horror novel.

Damn, this really is bad.

"Stop, I said!" Kawada yelled.

But Kyoichi didn't stop. He pointed the revolver at Kawada.

Kawada fired again. Kyoichi folded over in the middle like a midair long jumper—only this jumper was blown backward. He landed on the tips of his dangling feet, and then the next instant, as if the film had skipped a few frames, he had crumpled face up on the ground. He sank into the tall grass and moved no more.

Shuya scrambled to his feet.

He saw the class leader's body amid the waving leaves. Near his stomach, a gaping hole had been shredded open through his school jacket. His insides looked like a slop bucket at a sausage factory.

Kawada didn't spare the corpse a glance and walked straight toward Shuya, shotgun still at the ready. He pumped the forearm grip, ejecting another empty casing.

Shuya was overwhelmed by the series of events that he had just witnessed and the horrific deaths of Tatsumichi and Kyoichi. But between heavy breaths, he managed to say, "Please, wait, I—"

"Don't move," Kawada said, stopping on the other side of Kyoichi's body. "Drop your weapon."

Shuya became aware of the hatchet in his hand. He did as he was told. The bloody hatchet thudded to the ground.

Just then, Noriko appeared where the trail hit the steep slope. She had pushed through the thicket, dragging her hurt leg behind her. She must have followed after Shuya and Tatsumichi. (Shuya then realized not even a full minute had passed since his fight with Tatsumichi Oki.) Noriko's face had already gone pale, probably from the sound of the gunfire, but when she saw the sprawled corpses of Tatsumichi and Kyoichi, and Shuya and Kawada facing off, her breath caught.

Noticing Noriko above, Kawada wheeled his shotgun, pointing it right at her. Noriko froze.

"Stop!" Shuya yelled. "Noriko is with me. We don't want to fight!"

Kawada slowly turned his head to Shuya. His expression seemed strangely vacant.

Then Shuya shouted, "Noriko! Kawada saved my life. He's not our enemy!"

Kawada looked in Noriko's direction and back to Shuya, then, slowly, he lowered his gun.

Noriko remained still for a time, then raised her hands to display that she was unarmed, and climbed—nearly slid—down the steep trail. Dragging her injured leg behind her, she limped to Shuya's side. They both stared at Kawada.

Kawada regarded them as if they were twin armadillos. Shuya

noticed that the stubble on the young man's cheeks and chin had grown a little longer.

Finally, Kawada spoke. "First, let me explain—I had no choice but to shoot Kyoichi. Understood?"

Shuya glanced down at Kyoichi's corpse and considered what Kawada had said. *What if,* he thought, taking time with it, *what if Kyoichi had just been confused?* The class leader might have seen Shuya take out Tatsumichi and gotten the wrong idea. Noriko wasn't with him. That misunderstanding would only have been natural.

Yet Kawada spoke the truth. Shuya couldn't blame him for his actions. If Kawada hadn't shot Kyoichi, Kyoichi would surely have killed him. *After all, I killed Tatsumichi, didn't I?*

Facing Kawada, Shuya said, "Yeah, I understand. And thank you. You did save me."

Kawada gave him a small shrug. "I was just stopping Kyoichi—though I guess it ended up that way, huh."

Adrenaline was still rushing through Shuya's body, but he managed to cobble a few words together. "I'm just glad to see someone who's still normal here."

In truth, Shuya was astonished. Back in that classroom, he'd pegged Kawada as the only classmate who would take part in this game. But rather than becoming an opponent in the game, Kawada had saved his life.

Kawada stared at them thoughtfully for a while, then asked, "You two are together, then?"

Shuya raised his eyebrows. "Yeah, I said we were, didn't I?"

"Why are you two together?"

Shuya and Noriko looked at each other, then back to him. Shuya said, "What do you mean—" at the same time Noriko began, "What do you—" and they both stopped mid-sentence. The two looked at each other again. Thinking she was letting him talk, he turned back to Kawada and said, "What do—" But again she had said it too. They exchanged another glance, then faced Kawada in silence.

Something of a grin flashed across Kawada's face. If it had indeed been a smile, this would be the first time Shuya had ever seen one from him.

Kawada said, "Okay, fine, I get it. Anyway, let's find a place to hide. No reason to stand around here out in the open."

29 STUDENTS REMAIN.

Yuko Sakaki (Girls #9) hurtled through the undergrowth. Running wildly like this was dangerous, but she needed to escape, and it didn't matter how.

The scene Yuko had just witnessed flashed through her mind—what she had seen from the bushes. *Tatsumichi Oki's head split wide open. Shuya Nanahara extracting the blood-soaked ax.*

Yuko had felt the hair on the back of her neck stand up. *Shuya Nanahara killed off Tatsumichi Oki. Truly and utterly.*

Until Shuya pulled out the hatchet from Tatsumichi's head, Yuko, as if possessed, had been unable to tear her eyes away. But when she saw the red on that blade, terror finally overcame her. She grabbed her daypack, clamped her mouth shut to contain her unbidden scream, and ran. Her eyes brimmed with tears.

In her state, she scarcely heard the exchange of gunfire she'd left behind.

29 STUDENTS REMAIN.

Shuya and Noriko led Kawada back to the thicket where they had hidden. They picked up their bags, and Kawada remarked that the view from there wasn't very good. Shuya had put a lot of thought into choosing that location, but Kawada seemed surprisingly acclimated to the situation, so the two did as he instructed and followed him a little ways up the mountain. That dirty cat had disappeared somewhere.

Not far away, in the undergrowth, Kawada said, "Wait here. I'm going to find Motobuchi's and Oki's bags."

When Kawada had left, Shuya helped Noriko sit and then sat beside her. He gripped the revolver (a .38 Spl Smith & Wesson Chief's Special) Kawada had given him after recovering the handgun from Kyoichi's body. Carrying the weapon made him uncomfortable—after all, he'd witnessed that ghastly one-man baton pass—but he endured holding it.

"Here, Shuya," Noriko said.

She held out a pink adhesive bandage. She must have retrieved it from her daypack, which Tatsumichi had slashed with his hatchet. Shuya touched a hand to his ear. The bleeding had mostly stopped, but his fingertips were met with a jolt of searing pain.

"Stay still," Noriko said. Leaning in, she unwrapped the bandage and began carefully wrapping it around his earlobe. "I wonder why everyone came to this part of the island. Including us and Kawada, that makes five."

Shuya stared back at her. Having been graced with one action scene after another, the thought hadn't occurred to him. But she was right.

He shook his head. "I don't know. But we came here to get as far away from the school as possible. We avoided climbing the mountains and we stayed off of the coast, where we would have been too exposed. Maybe we all thought the same things, and we all decided this same location would be safe—us and the class leader and Oki."

The moment he mentioned Tatsumichi, he felt a sudden wave of nausea. *That face, each half askew like a split-open peanut shell. And his body is right nearby. Come one, come all, and see the amazing Peanut Man!*

With the queasiness came a sudden return to clarity of mind and senses, each having been numbed in the rush of combat.

"Shuya, you're looking pale. Are you okay?"

Shuya couldn't answer. A shiver ran through his body, then became a tremble. Harder and harder he shook, until his teeth chattered erratically, as if doing a maniac tap dance.

Noriko placed her hand on his back and asked, "What's wrong?"

His teeth still clattering, Shuya answered, "I'm scared."

Shuya turned his head left to look into her face. She gazed back at him with concern.

"I'm scared," he said. "I'm freaking scared. I *killed* someone."

Noriko looked into Shuya's eyes for a long moment. Then, moving her injured leg with care, she slid forward to sit, cross-legged, diagonally in front of Shuya. Gently she opened her arms and wrapped them around his shoulders. Her cheek touched Shuya's trembling cheek. He could feel her warmth. The stench of blood clung to the inside of his nostrils, but now the faint smell of perfume—*or is it shampoo?*—came through.

This gesture had surprised him, but he was grateful for the comforting warmth and smell. He sat still, hugging his knees.

Shuya was reminded of the hugs his mother had given him before her accidental death. He stared off into the edge of Noriko's sailor collar and thought of his mother. She had spoken clearly and moved with such vibrancy. Though he had only been a child at the time, he thought she had been a cool mom. Her face, well, she looked a lot like Kazumi Shintani. She was always exchanging smiles with his father, who, with his mustache, didn't look much like a typical salaryman. (Holding Shuya wrapped in her arms, she had told him, "Your dad works with laws. He helps people in trouble. In this country, that's a very important job.") Seeing them together like this made him think, *One day, I'll marry someone like her, and we'll always smile at each other like they do.*

Gradually, his trembling subsided and then stopped.

"Are you all right now?" Noriko asked.

"Yeah. Thanks."

Noriko slowly let him go.

After a while, Shuya said, "You smell nice."

Noriko smiled bashfully. "Don't say that. I couldn't take a bath yesterday."

"No, you really do smell nice."

Another smile was flashing across her face when the bushes rustled. Shuya covered Noriko with his left arm and readied the Smith & Wesson in the other.

"It's me," said a voice. "Don't shoot."

Parting the thick undergrowth, Kawada appeared. Shuya lowered the revolver.

Kawada wore his shotgun in a shoulder sling and carried two daypacks in his arms. He pulled out a small cardboard box from one of the bags and tossed it to Shuya.

Shuya plucked the box out of the air and opened it. Inside, bullets formed neat rows and displayed their gold-colored posteriors. Five were missing, like pulled teeth.

"They're for your gun," Kawada said. "Load up."

Kawada set down his shotgun and took up a piece of string. He lifted it up and pulled, and Shuya could see that the string ran into the bushes. Kawada then took out a pocket knife and unfolded the blade from its handle. Since his provided weapon had been the shotgun, he must have brought the knife on his own.

Kawada moved to a nearby tree, its trunk about as thick as a soda can, and carved in a notch. He then fit the taut string snugly into the groove and cut off the extra, which he also tied around the tree in the same manner.

Shuya looked up to Kawada and asked, "What's that?"

"This?" Kawada said, putting the knife away. "It's kind of a primitive alarm system. The string makes a circle around us twenty meters out, in double layers. This end is connected to the outer rings—if someone catches on the string, this end will pull loose from the tree. Don't worry, the intruder won't even notice. But we'll know to be on the alert."

Shuya thought for a second, then asked, "Where did you find that string?"

With a small tilt of his head, Kawada said, "There's a general store down by the harbor. I wanted a few things, so I went there first off. I found the string there."

Shuya's jaw had dropped. No matter how small, any island would have at least one place to buy goods as a matter of course. A store would have all kinds of useful things. The thought of it, though obvious, hadn't crossed his mind—though even if it had, with Noriko to look after, he wouldn't have been able to wander around the island.

Kawada sat facing the two of them and began to search through either Oki's or Motobuchi's daypack. He withdrew a water bottle and a roll of bread and asked, "Wanna eat? It's time for breakfast."

Still hugging his knees, Shuya shook his head. He wasn't at all hungry.

"What's wrong? Are you feeling sick because you killed Oki?" Kawada inspected Shuya's face and spoke casually. "Don't let it get to you. Say everyone is killing one person at a time, then this is like a tournament. With forty-two students—no, make that forty—kill five or six, and you'll win. Only four or five to go."

Shuya glared at Kawada, even though he knew this was supposed to be a joke—no, *because* he knew it was a joke.

Shrinking beneath Shuya's withering look, Kawada pulled back and said, "Hey, sorry. I was kidding."

His voice acidic, Shuya asked, "What, you *don't* feel sick? Or was killing our class leader not the first time for you?"

Kawada shrugged. "Well, first one this time, at least."

Shuya thought that was a weird thing to say, but he couldn't place what exactly was odd about it. He felt confused. Whatever the case, if Kawada was as much of a delinquent as the rumors suggested, it might take a lot more to upset him than it would Shuya.

Shuya shook his head, then switched topics. "Um . . . there's something I don't get."

Kawada lifted his eyebrows, and the scar over his left brow raised with them. "What's that?"

"The class leader . . . Motobuchi, he—"

"Hey," Kawada interrupted, lifting up his chin. "I thought we'd been over this. I didn't have any choice. Are you trying to say I should have let him kill me? I've got no interest in trying to be Jesus Christ. For one, I can't resurrect myself. Not that I've tried."

"No, that's not what I was going to say."

As he tried to figure out what to say, Shuya wondered if that was supposed to be another joke. *Was Shogo Kawada the joking type?*

Then Shuya said, "When Motobuchi fired at me, that was because he saw me kill . . . well, he saw Oki dead right in front of him. No, I did kill Oki. But that was because he attacked me first."

Kawada nodded, and Shuya continued, "That's why Motobuchi thought he had to take me out. He wasn't being crazy."

"That's right. That might be. But still, I had to—"

"No." This time Shuya interrupted him. "I'm not talking about that anymore. But Oki attacked me even though I hadn't done anything. And Noriko was with me. We were together. He shouldn't have had any reason to suddenly attack, right?"

Kawada shrugged and placed the water bottle and bread near his feet. "Oki was up for it. That's all. What's not to understand?"

"Well no, I just . . . logically, I understand it. But I just can't accept it. I guess it's not that I don't understand. But *Oki*? I don't . . ."

Shuya hesitated, and Kawada jumped in. "You don't have to understand why."

"What?"

Kawada's lips tightened into a morbid smirk. "I haven't been in your class very long, so I don't know what everyone's like—both of you included. But what the hell do *you* know about Oki, really? Maybe someone in his family is badly ill, and he felt he absolutely couldn't let himself die here. Or maybe he was the kind of person who only thinks of himself. Or maybe he went crazy from the fear and lost all reason. Or there's this possibility—you were with her, and you had teamed up. But how could he be sure you'd let him into your group? If you decided he was a threat, you could have killed him. Or, if he thought you were taking part in this, he could see you using the same logic and killing him. What about you? Did you do anything that could have provoked him?"

Shuya started to say, "No, I . . ." Then he remembered. When he saw Oki, he had reflexively put his hand to his knife. Shuya had been afraid of Oki too.

"Is it coming back to you?"

"I—I touched my knife." Shuya looked at Kawada. "But that's all. I didn't—"

Kawada lightly shook his head. "That's plenty of reason right there, Shuya. Seeing you taking your weapon in hand, Oki might have thought he had to kill you. In this game, everyone's on a very short fuse."

Then, as if making a closing statement, he said, "But in the end, the easiest explanation is that he was simply ready to do it. You don't need to understand why. All that matters is that if someone comes at you with a weapon, you can't show any mercy or you'll be dead. Rather than trying to figure out everything about the people you run across, you'd better first be wary of them. Don't be too trustful of others. Not in this game."

Shuya sighed. Had Tatsumichi Oki really been out to kill him? Maybe Kawada was right, and thinking about it was foolish.

Shuya again looked at Kawada. "That's right."

"What?"

"I forgot to ask you."

"So what is it? Spit it out."

Shuya did. "Why are you with us?"

Kawada raised his eyebrows, then touched his tongue to his lips. "That's right. Maybe I'm not on your side too."

"No, that's not it." Shuya shook his head. "Anyway, you saved us, didn't you? And didn't you risk your life trying to stop Motobuchi? I'm not suspecting you or anything like that."

"You're wrong, Nanahara. You really don't know this game."

"What do you mean?"

"Partners are an advantage to surviving the game."

Shuya considered this, then nodded. Kawada had a point. They could take turns watching while the others rested, and were anyone to attack, they'd have strength in numbers.

"Is that all?" Shuya asked.

"Think about it." Kawada nudged the shotgun on his lap. "Do you really think I was in that much danger by stopping Motobuchi? Do you think Motobuchi was ever going to stand down just because I ordered him to? Can you be sure I didn't mean to kill that crazy kid no matter what he did? Did I really have no choice but to kill him? And sure, I was never going to be able to convince Motobuchi to team up with me, but when I shouted for him to stop, couldn't that have been just an act to see if I could get you on my side? Isn't it possible that I only want the numbers for now and plan to kill you both in the end?"

Shuya stared at Kawada's face, taken somewhat aback by the logical and explicit manner in which the other boy spoke. Kawada may have been a year older than him, but the way he talked was like an adult—and a gifted one at that. He reminded Shuya a little of Shinji Mimura in that regard.

Shuya shook his head. "Once you start getting suspicious like that, there'll be no end to it. I don't believe you're my enemy." He glanced at Noriko. "That's what I think."

"Me too," Noriko said and nodded. "The minute we can't trust anyone, we'll have lost. That's what I think."

"A noble philosophy." Kawada nodded. "And if that's good enough for you, that's fine. But just remember, in this game, you'd better always be on your guard." With that he asked, "So what is it, then?"

Shuya realized he'd forgotten what he meant to ask.

"Oh, right," Shuya said. "The issue isn't us, it's you. Why do you trust us? It's like you said, just because we're together, that doesn't mean one of us—or both, even—aren't really set against you. You don't have any reason to trust us."

"I see," Kawada said, amused. "The practical question, is it, Nanahara? You're getting the hang of it."

"Don't avoid the question. Please answer." Shuya gestured, spreading his arms open. Kawada drew back as if to say, *Hey, watch it with that revolver.*

When Shuya persisted, Kawada again raised his eyebrows, and that faint smile returned. He gazed up at the treetops overhead for a time. When he looked back to Shuya and Noriko, his expression was serious.

"Okay, first—"

Shuya saw something dart through Kawada's calm eyes. He didn't know what it was, but it was incredibly intense.

"I have my own reasons to object to this game's rules—no, the game itself." Kawada stopped, then kept going. "It's like you said, and though I'm embarrassed to admit it, I follow my conscience. And by that I mean . . ."

Kawada stood the shotgun between his legs and, like it was a cane, wrapped both hands around its barrel. He watched Shuya and Noriko.

Somewhere off in the woods, a bird chirped. Kawada looked solemn. Nervously, Shuya listened.

"You two looked like a nice couple," Kawada said. "Back there. And now as well."

Shuya stared blankly at him.

A couple?

Noriko spoke first, her face flushing bright red. "It's not like that. Shuya would never . . ."

Kawada grinned. Then he broke into laughter, an unexpectedly affable laugh. "So that's why I'm trusting you. Anyway, you just said it—start to have doubts and there'll be no stopping it. Does that answer your question?"

Shuya finally grinned. Then, feeling he owed it to Kawada, he said, "Thanks. I'm glad that you trust us."

Still smiling, Kawada said, "Hey man, you're welcome."

"You know, I pegged you as an individualist from the day you transferred to our school."

"Easy with the fancy words there. I can't help it if I don't look friendly. I was born with these looks, man."

Noriko beamed at him. "I feel so much better to have another person with us."

Kawada scratched the stubble below his nose, then did something unexpected. He offered Shuya his right hand. "Same here. It's lonely by myself."

Shuya shook his hand. Kawada's palm was thick, and like this gesture, every bit that of a fully mature man.

Kawada leaned forward around Shuya and held out his hand to Noriko. "And one for you."

Noriko shook it.

Then Kawada's eyes fell to her leg, wrapped in the bandana. "I forgot about that," he said. "First, let's have a look at that wound. Then we'll talk about what's next."

29 STUDENTS REMAIN.

The sunlight coming through the finely patterned frosted glass gradually brightened and took on white. A ray of direct sunlight suddenly streamed in through the upper edge of the window, landed on the wall where Yumiko Kusaka (Girls #7) sat, and caused the girl to squint. Yumiko thought of that platitude always trotted out by their local bishop. (Her parents belonged to the Halo Church, as had she from before her name was even registered with the town hall.) "One day the light will find you, as it brings blessings to all Creation."

Yeah, I'm so blessed getting to play such a fun game as this, ha ha.

With a sarcastic smirk, Yumiko shook her boyishly short hair and glanced at Yukiko Kitano (Girls #6), who was wrapped in a blanket beside her, also sitting against the wall. Yukiko was vacantly staring at the floorboards beginning to take in the light. Despite the self-aggrandizing name on the front door that read OKI ISLAND TOURIST ASSOCIATION, this unwelcoming building seemed more like a community center. Over where the floor sank down a step for the entranceway, there was an office desk, a chair, and a rust-speckled filing cabinet. A phone sat on the desk, which she had tried, of course, but as Sakamochi had warned, the receiver was dead. A few fairly unappealing tourist flyers peeped out from the cracks.

Yumiko and Yukiko had been friends since nursery school, despite being in different classes and living in different neighborhoods. It was the Halo Church that had brought them together—or rather their parents who brought them to the church. When they met, it was Yumiko's third time coming to church but Yukiko's first, and the girl had seemed nervous, whether from the gongs ringing with the chants, or possibly the general atmosphere of the sanctuary's gaudy ornamentation. After the service, Yukiko's parents, attending to some other matter, left her by herself. Yumiko approached the timid girl and said, "Don't you think this is all dumb?"

Yukiko seemed startled, but then smiled. They had stuck together ever since.

Other than their names, the two girls didn't share many similarities. Yumiko had always been feisty and was often called a tomboy. Even now she batted fourth on the softball team (not that she saw much of a chance that she'd make it through this—not much of a chance at all). Yukiko liked more domestic things and often treated Yumiko to her homemade cakes and such. They were even very different heights; Yumiko was fifteen centimeters taller. Yukiko often said she wished she had Yumiko's tall figure and chiseled looks, but Yumiko far more envied Yukiko her petite body and round cheeks. Yes, they were completely different types, but they were the best of friends. That never changed.

Fortunately *(Well, that's a disrespectful way to put it)*, Yoshitoki Kuninobu (Boys #7) had died before he left, meaning that only two minutes passed between the girls' departures. After exiting the classroom, Yumiko waited for Yukiko in the shadows next to the front door. Not knowing what else to do, the two ran. (That Yoshio Akamatsu would return to begin his massacre a scant twenty minutes later was something the two girls had no way of knowing.) Far north of the village and toward the mountain off the eastern coastal road, they found a solitary building plopped atop a small hill and locked themselves inside.

Four hours had passed since. Though they hadn't done anything but sit there together and wait, the girls were exhausted from anxiety.

Yumiko looked away from Yukiko, and they both stared at the floor.

As dazed as she felt, Yumiko had been thinking, *What should I do now?* Even inside the building, they had heard Sakamochi's six o'clock announcement. Not counting Yoshitoki Kuninobu and Fumiyo Fujiyoshi, nine of her classmates were already dead. And aside from Sakura Ogawa and Kazuhiko Yamamoto, she didn't believe the others could all have been suicides. *People are killing other people. Right now, this second, someone might be dying.* Soon after the morning announcement, she thought she heard far-off gunfire.

Can someone really kill their own classmate? Yumiko knew the rules, of course—she just couldn't believe a human being was capable of following them.

But.

But if someone was trying to kill me, or if I at least thought they were, then I could do it. I think.

So that means . . .

Yumiko glanced at a megaphone lying in the corner of the room. *Does it still work? If it does . . .*

Then isn't there something *I can do?*

But she was scared. She was scared to do it. Though she couldn't believe anyone was possibly playing this game, she felt a touch of fear she couldn't shake. That's why she fled here with Yukiko right at the start. *What if? What if one them did?*

But . . .

She recalled a scene from her childhood. She saw the face of her second best friend, after Yukiko, in elementary school. The girl was crying. For some reason, all Yumiko could remember about her friend's outfit were the pink sneakers.

"Yumi," Yukiko said, interrupting Yumiko's thoughts. Yumiko turned to her.

"Let's have some bread," Yukiko continued. "If we don't eat, we won't think of anything."

Yukiko smiled tenderly. It was her familiar kind smile, if a bit forced.

"Right?" Yukiko asked.

Yumiko returned the smile and nodded. "Yeah, let's."

They each took out a bread roll and water from their daypacks. Yumiko's eyes briefly landed on the two can-like objects inside her bag. The cylinders were greenish-silver in color, with a thumb-sized bar jutting out the top, attached to which was a lever and a ring about three centimeters wide. She assumed they were grenades. (Yukiko's weapon must have been some kind of joke—a dart set. At least the round wooden target was included.)

After she'd eaten half of her roll and drunk a mouthful of water, Yumiko asked, "You feeling a little better now, Yukiko?"

Yukiko was chewing a bite of bread, but her eyes widened in response.

"You were trembling all night," Yumiko explained.

"Oh." Yukiko broke into a smile. "Yeah, I'm fine now. I've got you with me."

Yumiko smiled and nodded. As she ate, she almost brought up what she felt they must do, but she didn't. She didn't feel confident enough in her reasoning. What she was thinking could be extremely dangerous. Going through with it wouldn't only endanger herself but Yukiko too. On the other hand, this very fear could drive them all straight to the deadline. Which was the right thing to do? Yumiko was unsure.

The two girls remained quiet for a while. Then Yukiko suddenly said, "Hey, Yumi."

"Yeah? What's up?"

"You're probably going to tell me this is a stupid thing to ask at a time like this, but . . ." Yukiko nibbled her small but full lips.

"What is it?"

Yukiko hesitated but finally spoke. "Did you have a crush on anyone in our class?"

Yumiko's eyes widened a little.

Wow. This is exactly the kind of thing you'd talk about on a school trip. After the card games, the pillow fights, the explorations of the inn and such had concluded, this was *the* late-night topic. Anything else, even badmouthing their teachers or talking about the future, ranked a distant second. It was the holy topic, a little sacred ritual observed in the dark of night. Until she'd fallen asleep on the bus, Yumiko had assumed it would likely come up over the course of the trip.

"You mean, like a boy?" Yumiko asked.

"Uh-huh." Yukiko, seemingly embarrassed, looked over to Yumiko with downcast eyes.

"Well . . ." At first, Yumiko didn't know what to say, but she decided to tell the truth. "There is one."

"Oh." Yukiko's eyes fell to the knees of her pleated skirt, and she went on, "Hey, I'm sorry I never told you, Yumi, but I—I like Nanahara."

Yumiko wordlessly nodded. She'd already had a hunch.

She pulled out her mental file on Shuya Nanahara. *Height: 170 cm, weight: 58 kg, vision: right eye 20/17, left eye 20/13, build: thin, but well muscled. In elementary school, played shortstop in Little League, batting first. Quit baseball, and now prefers playing music, excelling in singing and the guitar. No nickname but is often called "Wild Seven," like the brand of cigarettes. The handle came from his status as his Little League team's ace player along with the first kanji in his family name—the number seven. Blood type B, born on October 13th—autumn, as the first kanji in his given name suggests. Lost both parents to an accident at an early age, and now lives in the House of Mercy and Love, a Catholic orphanage near the edge of town. Close friends with Yoshitoki Kuninobu, also in the orphanage—well, he's dead now. As for his studies . . . in a word, so-so. Strongest subjects: the humanities, including English and Japanese. His mouth has a kind of quirky curve to it, but his sharply defined double eyelids make him look kind. Not bad looking at all. Hair wavy, down to his shoulders in the back, almost a girlish length.*

Yumiko's portfolio on Shuya was practically bursting. (She was confident hers was more comprehensive than Yukiko's.) (Mostly confident.) The bit about Shuya's height held special importance—because unless Shuya kept growing, Yumiko wouldn't be able to wear high heels when she walked beside him, since they would make her taller.

But she didn't think she could share these thoughts with Yukiko—not in such specific terms.

"Huh," Yumiko said as calmly as she could. "Really?"

"Yeah." Yukiko looked down, then said what she'd been wanting to say all along. "I want to see him. I really want to see him. I wonder what he's doing right now."

Yukiko kept her hands pressed against the sides of her skirt as her eyes flooded with tears.

Yumiko gently put her hand on her friend's shoulder. "He's Nanahara. I'm sure he's fine. No matter what." Then, thinking that sounded a little suspicious, she hastily added, "I mean, he's the best athlete in class, and he seems really brave, not that I really know, but . . ."

Yukiko wiped her tears, nodded, and said, "Yeah." Then, bouncing back, she asked, "What about you, Yumi? Who do you like?"

Buying some time, Yumiko looked up to the ceiling and affected a "Hmm," as she racked her brains. *This is bad. I'd better come up with a name quick just to get out of this.*

Oki was the handball champ, and his face, though a little rough-hewn, wasn't bad. Mimura was the ace guard on the basketball team and knew just about everything. He even had a following among a certain group of girls (though none in Class B, where he had a reputation as a playboy). Numai acted tough, but Yumiko had the impression he wasn't so bad. He was nice to the girls—*oh, wait, he's dead now.* She liked Sugimura's brooding vibe. A lot of the girls thought he was scary because he practiced at some martial arts school, but Yumiko found it attractive. But he was always with that Takako Chigusa girl. She would never let Yumiko hear the end of it if she found out. Takako was a tough one. But she was a good kid. Now that she thought about it, they all were, the boys and the girls.

She returned to that same question. *Do I trust them?*

"C'mon, who is it?" Yukiko prodded.

Yumiko faced her.

She hesitated again but decided she'd tell her friend. At least, she'd bring it up. Whenever she needed advice, no one was a better listener than Yukiko.

"Hey," Yumiko said. "Can I ask you something?"

Yukiko tilted her head in confusion. "Yeah, what?"

Yumiko folded her arms, gathering her thoughts, then said, "So, do you think any of them really want to kill anyone? Any of our classmates, I mean."

Yukiko frowned. "Well . . . they're really . . . they're dying . . ." At that word—dying—her voice trembled. "They're all dying. You heard the announcement this morning. Nine already, just since we left. I can't believe they all killed *themselves*. And you heard that noise. It sounded like gunfire."

Yumiko tilted her head and spread open her hands. She noticed a small tear in the cuff of her left sleeve. "But look," Yumiko said, "we're scared here, aren't we? With both of us together. Right?"

"Yeah."

"I think everyone else is too. They all must be so afraid. Don't you think so?"

Yukiko seemed to mull it over, then said, "Yeah. Maybe you're right. I've been so caught up in my own fear that I never really thought about it."

Yumiko nodded once, then continued, "We've been able to stick together, so we don't have it so bad, but I think anyone who's alone has got to be absolutely terrified."

"Yeah."

"So let's say you were that afraid. What would you do when you stumbled upon someone else?"

"I'd run, of course."

"What if you couldn't?"

Yukiko seemed to consider it extremely carefully. Then, slowly she said, "I might . . . yes, I might fi-fight. If I was holding something, I'd throw it, and if I . . . if I had a gun, yes, I might shoot. Of course I'd try to talk. But if it was all of a sudden, and I had no other choice."

Yumiko nodded. "Right? So I think—what I think is—none of them actually wants to kill anyone else. They're just scared, and they're convinced the others are trying to kill them. And someone who believes that, even if no one attacks him, might go after the others."

Yumiko paused, uncrossing her arms, setting her hands on the floor. "I believe they're all just scared."

Yukiko pursed those small, full lips. After a moment, she looked down at the floor and said in a faltering voice, "I don't know. I don't trust them. Like Souma's group, or Kiriyama, or . . ."

Yumiko gave her a smile, shifted her legs beneath her pleated skirt, and settled back in a different position. "I'll tell you what I think, Yukiko."

"Sure."

"If we keep on going like this, we'll die. Remember the time limit? When twenty-four hours pass without anyone dying? Even if we survive until then, we'll be killed."

Yukiko nodded, her face frightened again. "That's true."

"And our only possible chance is for everyone to work together and come up with a way to escape. Right?"

"That's right. But—"

"I have to tell you something," Yumiko interrupted. She tilted her head ever so slightly. "Something bad happened to me because I didn't trust someone. Back in elementary school."

Yukiko looked into Yumiko's eyes. "What happened?"

Yumiko raised her eyes to the ceiling. She saw the face of her crying friend—and those pink sneakers.

She looked back at Yukiko. "I had this—it was really important to me . . . Well, you remember those Egg Cats that were so popular, right?"

"Yeah. They put those characters on everything. I had an Egg Cat pencil board."

"I had a tricolor pen—limited edition. It seems so unimportant now, but back then, I treasured it."

"Uh-huh."

"But one day, I couldn't find it." Yumiko looked down. "I thought one of my friends stole it. She'd wanted it so badly. And I realized it was missing right after first period gym class, and she'd excused herself early from gym because she wasn't feeling well, and she was the first one back in the classroom. And on top of that . . . well . . . this is terrible . . . but she didn't have a dad, and her mom worked at a bar, so she didn't have a good reputation."

Yukiko slowly nodded.

"I grilled her, but she said she didn't know about it. I even went to the teacher. He probably had his own pre-formed opinions of her, because he commanded her to tell the truth. But she was crying, saying she didn't know anything about it."

Yumiko faced Yukiko. "When I went home, I found the pen on my desk. I'd just forgotten it there."

Yukiko was quietly listening, so Yumiko kept going, "I apologized to her. She said it was fine. But I'd made things awkward, and in the end—I think her mother remarried or something—she soon transferred away, and I never heard from her since. But we had been really good friends. As much as you and me. But I didn't believe her."

With a frown, Yumiko continued, "After that, I decided I'd do my best to trust others. I want to believe in other people. If I can't do that, I know that nothing will work out. And I'm not talking like the old people at that stupid Halo Church. This is what I truly believe. I hope you understand."

"Yeah, I do."

"So, about now. Souma and the others—they look like they're bad. People say they are. But they can't be so bad that they actually would enjoy killing. There's nobody like that in our class. Isn't that right?"

After a moment, Yukiko answered, "Yeah."

"So," Yumiko went on, "if we could only reach out to them and explain, everyone would stop fighting. Then we could all figure out if there's anything we can do. And even if we can't find a way out, at least we could avoid all this killing. How about it?"

"Yeah . . ." Yukiko nodded, but she still seemed hesitant.

A little worn out from all the talking, Yumiko sighed and shifted her legs again. "Anyway, that's my opinion. But tell me what you think. If you're against the idea, I won't do it."

For a while, Yukiko stared thoughtfully at the floor. After two full minutes, she cracked open her mouth.

"Yumi," she said, "you told me once that I worry too much about what other people think."

"Hm? Yeah, I guess I did."

Yumiko stared into Yukiko's face. Yukiko lifted her head, and their eyes met.

Yukiko grinned. "I think you're totally right. That's my opinion."

Yumiko smiled back at her. "Thank you." She was grateful Yukiko had thought for herself before saying that. She saw it as proof that her own reasoning had been correct.

That's right. I have to do this. I'm not going to die without at least trying, not me. If there's a chance, I'm going to take it. It's like I told Yukiko, I want to believe. Let's try and see.

Then Yukiko asked, "But how are we going to do it—how can we reach everyone?"

Yumiko pointed to the megaphone lying in the corner of the room. "It's all up to whether or not that works."

Yukiko bobbed her head, then looked up at the ceiling. After a time, she said only this:

"If it works, I'll be able to see Nanahara."

Yumiko nodded. With a little feeling, she said, "That's right. We will."

29 STUDENTS REMAIN.

21

"All right, that's good," Kawada said to Shuya, tossing the needle and thread onto the daypack at his side. "Hand me that whiskey again, Nanahara."

Noriko's leg was stretched out on its side in front of Kawada. The wound on her right calf was sewn closed by coarse cotton thread; Kawada had managed to put in the stitches. They hadn't had any anesthetic, of course, but over the course of the ten-minute operation, Noriko didn't cry out once.

Shuya offered Kawada the flask. Next to him was a small fire pit fashioned from piled up rocks, and above the charcoal sat an open can filled with water at a rolling boil. (Kawada said he'd found the charcoal, along with the needle and thread, at the general store.) The boiling water had disinfected the needle and thread, but since pouring it directly onto Noriko's wound wasn't exactly an option, Kawada had cleaned the gash with Shuya's whiskey before he stitched it up. Noriko took a deep breath and scrunched her face, preparing for the next splash.

Shuya looked at his watch. The water had taken a fairly long time to boil, and the time was already past eight.

"Okay," Kawada said. He pressed one of Shuya's bandanas,

sterilized, against her wound in place of a proper gauze, then swiftly wrapped the other around her leg. "We're all done."

Then, with a note of concern, he added, "As long as no strange bug infected it already."

Noriko took back her leg, thanked him, then said, "You're good at that."

"I was always good at playing doctor," Kawada said.

Kawada pulled a pack of Wild Sevens from his pocket, put a cigarette in his mouth, and lit it with a cheap one-hundred-yen lighter. Shuya wondered if he'd pilfered those from the store as well, or if they were his own. They were a popular brand, up there with Busters and Hi-Nites.

Shuya stared blankly at the package, which for some reason was emblazoned with the silhouette of a motorcycle rider. None of his friends ever gave him a nickname, but that was probably because everyone already called him by the name of those cigarettes. The origin of this moniker was absolutely simple. Back in Little League, he was his team's ace in the hole. When they were in reach of evening up the score, he'd nail it. When he was on base, even if his teammates couldn't get in a hit, he'd steal bases to score another run. (He held the notable record of stealing home three times in one season.) With runners on base, he'd be counted on for a double play. When their pitcher tired out, he'd switch from shortstop and step up on the mound. He was the wild card. Mix that together with the first kanji in his family name—the number seven—and you get Wild Seven.

In eighth grade, Shuya became classmates with Shinji Mimura, the basketball team's expert guard. Shinji had his own *nom de guerre*: The Third Man. The story went that Shinji got that name back in seventh grade, when he occupied the bench as the team's third-string shooting guard. With five minutes left on the clock and twenty points down against opponents who were favored to win, he—the literal third man—was sent to the court, and the Shiroiwa Junior High team breezed to victory. After that, he became a starter, and Shiroiwa now held a regular position among the top teams in the prefecture-wide tournaments. Still, because of the lasting impact of that dramatic win, and an association with the first kanji in *his* family name—the number three—everyone kept on calling him "The Third Man."

For this year's April intramurals, as a joke the class girls made the two boys a pair of jerseys—#3 and #7. Shuya and Shinji both wore them for the games. It all seemed so far away now. Again Shuya wondered, *Where is Shinji now? I know we could count on him.*

As if suddenly remembering something, Kawada dug through his pockets and produced a small leather pouch, almost like a coin purse. He took out a small foil and plastic blister pack of white pills, handed it to Noriko, and said, "Pain relievers. Take some, they'll help."

Noriko blinked in surprise. But she accepted the pills.

"Hey," Shuya asserted.

"What?" Kawada said. He exhaled, seeming to relish the smoke, and leveled his gaze at Shuya. "Don't look at me like that. It's just a cigarette. Junior high kids smoke them all the time. Besides, I'm old enough to be in high school. And didn't you bring booze out here anyway?"

Setting aside the assumption that it was fine for a high schooler to smoke, Shuya shook his head and said, "That's not it. Did you get those drugs at the general store?"

Kawada shrugged. "Well, yeah. They weren't for sale, but I took them out of a first aid kit behind the register. It's no big deal—just some headache medicine. It's called Anvil. Doesn't sound very good for your head, does it? Anyway, I'm sure it'll make her feel better for now."

Shuya pursed his lips. *He might be telling the truth, but . . .*

"Aren't you a little *too* prepared?" Shuya asked. "And where the hell did you learn how to stitch up a wound?"

The corners of his mouth turning up into a wide grin, Kawada offered another shrug. "My dad was a doctor."

"What?"

"Well, it was a small dump of a clinic in the slums of Kobe. I've seen him sew people up since I was a little brat. I have to admit, I was an outstanding doctor's aide myself—or at least I acted like I was from time to time. You see, my dad couldn't afford to hire a nurse."

Shuya didn't know what to say to that. *Was that story true?*

Holding the cigarette between his fingers, Kawada lifted his hand to cut off Shuya's response. "I'm not lying. If you think about it, you can see that medicine can become essential in this situation."

Shuya kept quiet for a moment, but then he recalled something else that had bothered him. "That's it."

"What's it?"

"Pardon me, um, but if I might ask you—"

"Skip the formalities, Nanahara. We're in this together."

Shuya shrugged once and went to his question. "You were trying to open the bus window. Did you notice the knockout gas?"

Noriko gave Kawada a questioning look.

Now Kawada shrugged. "You saw that? You could have helped."

"Sorry," Shuya said, "but I couldn't. How did you know what was going on, though? I couldn't smell anything."

"Oh, there was a smell, Nanahara." Kawada rubbed his half-spent cigarette into the ground. "It was faint, but anyone who knows it would have recognized it."

This time Noriko asked, "How do you know it?"

"Actually, my uncle works at a government lab, and—"

"Come on," Shuya interjected.

With a wry smile, Kawada said, "If I have to, I'll explain later. Anyway, I really screwed up. I should have caught on sooner. I never thought this would happen, you know? But enough about that. We need to focus on the present. Do you have a plan?"

The way he said, *If I have to, I'll explain later,* tugged at Shuya's mind, but Kawada was right: coming up with a plan for their escape was the priority. Everything else, Shuya set aside. "We're going to escape."

Kawada nodded as he lit another cigarette. Then, suddenly remembering it, he tossed dirt onto the charcoal in the fire pit. Shuya heard Noriko take a drink of water, swallowing the pill.

Shuya added, "Do you think it'll be hard?"

Kawada shook his head. "The question you should ask, Nanahara, is: 'Do you think it's possible?' If you did, I'd answer: 'The chance is extremely remote.' But what then?"

"These collars—" Shuya said, gesturing to his neck—and the object he had in common with Noriko and Kawada, "—mean they'll find us wherever we run."

"That's right."

"And we can't go near that school."

Sakamochi had said it: *"Twenty minutes after the last of you has left, this will be a forbidden zone."* And he hadn't needed to sound so cheerful about it, the bastard.

"That's right," Kawada said.

"But what if we could draw them out? We could take Sakamochi hostage. We'll make them disable these collars."

Kawada raised his eyebrows. "And?"

Shuya licked his lips and continued, "And . . . that's it. We'll find a boat ahead of time, and we'll take Sakamochi with us when we escape."

Even as he said it, he knew the plan was a long shot. Without any idea how to draw Sakamochi out of the school, the thought didn't even amount to a plan.

"You finished?" Kawada said, and Shuya could only nod.

Kawada took another drag on his cigarette, then said, "First, and most importantly, there won't be any boats."

Shuya bit his lip. "You can't know that."

Kawada grinned and exhaled smoke. "Didn't I tell you I went to the store by the harbor? No boats. Not a one. Even the old, busted-up ones, like you'd expect to see up along the shore—they've all been taken away. No, these guys were amazingly thorough."

"Then we'll use one of the guard ships. If we can take Sakamochi hostage—"

"Impossible, Nanahara," Kawada interrupted. "You saw how many soldiers there are. Besides . . ."

Kawada pointed to the silver collar at his neck. "Those bastards can trigger these however they please, forbidden zone or not. That's anytime, and anyplace. The cards are stacked against us. Anyway, even in the off chance you succeeded, I bet the government wouldn't think twice before writing off someone like Sakamochi as an acceptable loss."

Again Shuya was speechless.

"Do you have any other ideas?" Kawada prompted.

Shuya shook his head and said, "No."

"What about you, Noriko?"

Noriko also shook her head but said something else. "Well, we were talking . . . and we were thinking about gathering the people we trust and thinking up a plan together. If we think as a group, we might come up with something good."

That's right, Shuya thought. *I forgot to say that.*

Kawada lifted a single scarred eyebrow. "But isn't it hard to know who to trust out here?"

Shuya answered enthusiastically, "There's Mimura. And Hiroki Sugimura. As far as the girls go, there's our class leader, Utsumi. But Mimura—he's really amazing. He knows everything. He's good with machines too. I'm sure he'd think of something."

Rubbing his hand though his stubble, Kawada watched Shuya's face. Then he said, "Mimura, huh?"

Shuya's eyes widened. "Did something happen?"

"No," Kawada said. He seemed to find this hard to say, but he continued, "But I saw him."

Immediately Shuya shouted, "What! Where?" He and Noriko looked at each other. "Where? Where did you see him?"

Kawada pointed eastward with his chin. "It was last night. He was just west of the school. He had gone into a house and seemed to be searching for something. He had a gun, and I think he noticed me."

"Why didn't you call out to him?"

Kawada regarded Shuya's critical tone with a quizzical expression. "Why should I have?"

"You saw him back at the school—he helped Noriko back to her seat. Didn't you see? And—"

Kawada anticipated the rest. "He suggested postponing the game because of her injury. Probably to buy everyone enough time to escape?"

Yes, he's got it. Shuya nodded.

But Kawada shook his head. "You're saying that should be enough for me to trust him? That won't do. He could have just been putting on a show to convince everyone he could be trusted. That would put him in the perfect position to kill us all later."

"Ridiculous!" Shuya yelled. "That's some twisted mind you've got. He's not that kind of guy. He—"

Without saying anything, Kawada pushed out his palms in a calming gesture, and Shuya quieted. *Right, shouting was dangerous— incredibly dangerous.*

Then Kawada said, "Cut me some slack. I don't know Mimura that well. And like I said, rule one of this game is to suspect everyone, rather than trust them. You have to be especially cautious of the ones who seem clever. Anyway, even if I asked him to join up with me, I doubt he would have agreed."

Shuya started to respond but decided against it, letting out his breath. What Kawada was saying wasn't entirely unreasonable. The real mystery to Shuya was why Kawada trusted Noriko and him— though the older boy had said it was because they "looked like a good couple."

"Well then," Shuya said, "we should go to where you saw Mimura. He can absolutely be trusted. I guarantee it. I know he'll think of something. I know—"

But Kawada shook his head, cutting him off again. "If this Mimura is as sharp as you say, do you think he'd stick around where I saw him?"

Kawada was right.

Shuya sighed a deep, deep sigh.

Noriko said, "Kawada, is there any way for us now to contact the others, like Mimura, or anyone?"

Kawada jiggled another cigarette out of the pack and shook his head. "I don't think so. If you were just trying to get people to gather and didn't care who came or how many, that's one thing. But restricting your message to one specific person would be difficult."

They fell silent for a while, and Shuya watched Kawada holding the cigarette in his lips. The lit tip of the Wild Seven made a faint crackling sound as it grew a little shorter.

When Shuya spoke, his mouth felt heavy. "So there's nothing we can do."

But Kawada lightly remarked, "That's not true."

"What?"

"I have a plan."

Shuya stared intently at Kawada's smoke-shrouded face. Then, unable to hold back his excitement, he blurted, "What do you mean? You have a way out?"

Kawada surveyed Shuya's and Noriko's faces. With the cigarette still perched in his lips, he looked up to the sky in contemplation. He traced his fingers along the smooth surface of his collar. Wisps of smoke drifted in the air.

"There might be a way," Kawada said, then added, "with one condition."

"What kind of condition?" Shuya asked.

Kawada gave a slight shake of his head. He held the cigarette near his lips as he said, "We have to survive to the end first."

Shuya furrowed his brows in confusion. "What do you mean?"

"It should be obvious." Kawada returned his gaze to them. "It could only work when we're the last three alive—and everyone else is dead."

Noriko immediately spoke up. "That's too cruel. So we're going to just look out for ourselves?"

Kawada lowered his cigarette, holding it between his crossed legs. He raised his eyebrows and said, "That's no different than Shuya saying he wants to escape."

"No," Shuya interjected. "That's not what Noriko's saying. She's just asking if you mean to trade everyone else's lives for our own. Isn't that right, Noriko? That's cruel, to start."

"Hey, hold on." Kawada waved his hands, then rubbed out his cigarette on the ground. "I don't mind if people join us—as long as they can be trusted. Either way, the plan only starts when everyone who's not in our group is dead. That's all I meant."

"If that's the case," Shuya said excitedly, "we could just tell everyone the plan. If it's a sure thing, no one will oppose it. That way we could save all of them, right? Isn't that so?"

Kawada's lips tightened. Then, sounding a little weary, he said, "And what are you going to do if someone attacks you before you can say any of that?"

Shuya held his breath.

Kawada said, "As long as you don't actively want to kill someone, the smartest way to survive in this game is to stay put and hide. That's why the government put bombs in these things—" he pointed to his collar "—to force us to move. It's one of the game's cardinal principles. Never forget it. Carelessly stroll about, and someone might strike from the shadows. Even worse, Noriko's injury makes us prime targets."

Shuya knew he was right.

"And what's more," Kawada continued, "when you talk about saving everyone, you're really only talking about saving them from dying *here*. We'll be fugitives, and the government will come after us. Ultimately, our chances of being killed are high. Do you think everyone is going to accept that? Did you forget? In this game, you don't know who your enemies are. If you thoughtlessly allow everyone to join up with you, you'll do more than suffer for it."

"But nobody's—"

"Can you really say nobody's like that, Nanahara?" Kawada's eyes were hard. "All right then, if your whole class was made up of good little boys and girls, it would be just peachy. But if we want to be realistic, don't you think we should be on our guard? After all, weren't you attacked by Akamatsu and Oki?"

While Kawada was preparing to attend to Noriko's wound, Shuya had told him about getting ambushed outside the school by Akamatsu. And it was as Kawada said—Shuya didn't really know why Yoshio Akamatsu had done what he had done. Maybe Akamatsu really meant to play the game.

Shuya sighed. His shoulders dropped, and he feebly pushed out the words. "So we're just going to watch and let the good ones—who are probably most of our classmates—die? That's how it's going to be?"

Kawada nodded slightly several times. "I know it's hard, but yes—though whether that's actually most of them or not, I don't know."

They were quiet for a while. Kawada lit another cigarette. *You smoke too much,* Shuya thought. *You're in junior high, man.*

After a time, Noriko said, "Hold on."

Shuya turned his head toward her.

"You said the plan was for after everyone else was dead," she said, "but couldn't we also run out of time? Sakamochi said if no one dies for twenty-four hours . . ."

"Yeah." Kawada nodded. "That's definitely possible."

"And if that happens, your plan won't be any good?"

"Correct. But that won't happen. Supposing everyone is getting along and playing nicely, they can all be a part of my plan. But that won't happen either. So there's no need to worry about that. I heard that of all of the past Programs nationwide, only half of one percent ended by the time running out."

Shuya's mouth opened a crack. Then he said, "You heard? Where did you hear a thing like that?"

"Hey, hold up." Kawada pushed the air with both hands to stop Shuya again. "We have more important matters at hand. Neither of you has asked me what my plan is yet."

Shuya went quiet but then asked, "So what's your plan?"

Kawada shrugged. With the cigarette between his lips, he spoke from the side of his mouth. "Can't say."

Shuya frowned. "What?"

"I can't say yet."

"Why not?"

"I just can't."

"You can't say *yet*? When exactly, then, can you tell it to us?"

"Good question. When it's down to the three of us, I suppose. But I'll tell you this for now. What I have in mind, if anyone interferes, it's not going to work. That's why we can't do it until we're the only three left alive."

Shuya again fell silent. As Kawada continued to smoke, Shuya stared at this new companion's face. Somewhere inside his thoughts, a voice whispered, barely at the edge of his perception.

Kawada grinned as if he too had heard the voice's whisper. "I know what you're thinking, Nanahara. You're thinking this: there's another possibility. I could be baiting you with the hope of escape, tricking you into helping me so that I can survive. But there's no such hope, and when it's down to the three of us, I will kill you, and I will win. It's all so convenient for me." Kawada paused. "So, am I wrong?"

Shuya felt a dash of panic. "That's not—"

"Am I wrong?"

Shuya held his tongue and glanced over at Noriko. She remained quiet and stared at Kawada's face.

"That's not it. It's just—"

But Shuya cut off mid-sentence.

He had heard a voice. Far in the distance, and electrically distorted, the voice said, "Hey, everyone!"

29 STUDENTS REMAIN.

The voice continued, "Hey, everyone, listen up!" It was a girl's voice.

Noriko said, "That's Yumiko."

The tall, perky Yumiko Kusaka (Girls #7), who batted fourth for the girl's softball team.

Kawada's face stiffened. "I'm going to check it out. I'll be back."

He took his shotgun in hand, stood, and started walking into the thicket to the east, in the direction of the voice.

"We'll come too," Shuya said.

They hadn't finished their conversation, but for now, Shuya tucked the Smith & Wesson in his front waistband and gave Noriko his shoulder, helping her to her feet. Kawada glanced back at them but continued forward without a word.

When they reached the edge of the thicket, Kawada halted. Shuya and Noriko stopped behind him.

With his back to them, Kawada said, "They're . . ."

Shuya moved right behind Kawada, and he and Noriko joined the boy in poking their heads out from the brush.

The mountaintop was ahead. Among the sparse trees near the summit of the northern mountain stood a structure—some kind of observation deck. Despite their position in the foothills some five or six hundred meters away, the three students could see it clearly. Crudely constructed, the platform resembled a shack stripped of one of its walls. Two figures stood within. Shuya's eyes went wide.

Yumiko's voice traveled to them. "Everyone! Stop fighting! Come up here!"

Shuya could see that the taller of the two figures—Yumiko Kusaka, probably—was holding something in front of her face. *Is that a kind of megaphone? As in the ones cops use to address besieged bank robbers and the like?* Something about it seemed ludicrous—*Hey everyone, stop fighting and come out with your hands up*—but Shuya realized they had found a way to reach not only where he and Noriko and Kawada were, but far across the island.

"Who's that other one?" Shuya whispered.

"Yukiko," Noriko said. "Yukiko Kitano. They're together then. They're really close friends."

Kawada wore a pained expression. "What the hell are they doing? They're going to get themselves killed like that. They're completely exposed."

Shuya bit his lip. So Yumiko Kusaka and Yukiko Kitano were trying to persuade everyone to stop fighting. They were attempting what he himself had considered doing but had ultimately abandoned after Yoshio Akamatsu ambushed him. Those two girls assumed no one would really want to play the game. They must have chosen that location to be able to be seen by the most possible people. That, or they had been near there all along.

"I know none of us want to fight," the voice said. "Come up here!"

Shuya hesitated. He still needed to figure out the situation. The conversation with Kawada had left a lot hanging. *What if—it's unlikely, but what if—Kawada is our enemy?*

But ultimately Shuya told Kawada, "Can you look after Noriko?"

Kawada turned. "What are you going to do?"

"I'm going to go up there."

Kawada furrowed his brows. "Are you stupid?"

Shuya didn't appreciate that remark, but he let it pass. "What do you mean? They're putting themselves in danger. They're not in this game. They're clearly not. So they can join us. Didn't you just say it? They're in danger now."

"That's not what I'm talking about," Kawada said, baring his teeth. Somewhat inappropriately, Shuya noted that his teeth were large and quite nice. "*Didn't* I just explain it all? In this game, the most important thing is to stay where you are. How far away do you think they are? Anyone could be between here and there."

"I know that!"

"No, you don't get it. Everyone has already noticed them by now. If we can assume someone's going to attack those two, then that killer will be waiting for someone like you to bumble through. They'll get more targets that way."

Shuya shuddered, though less because of what Kawada said as how calmly he stated it.

"Please," the voice said. "Come up here. There's two of us. We don't want to fight!"

Shuya separated himself from Noriko and said, "I'm going."

He gripped the Smith & Wesson tightly and moved to step from the thicket, but Kawada grabbed him by the arm.

"Stop."

"Why should I!" Shuya shouted. "You want me to just sit back and watch them get slaughtered?" Shuya had lost control over not only his voice, but the words that came tumbling out. "Or do you not want me to leave because you're not finished using me to get farther ahead? Is that how it's gonna be? Are you our enemy?"

Noriko spoke, her voice sorrowful. "Shuya, stop it," she said. Shuya started to say something else when he noticed it—Kawada's expression remained placid, even as he clutched his arm.

Kawada's face suddenly reminded him—though they looked not a bit alike—of the former director of the House and Mercy and Love, Ms. Anno's elderly and now deceased father. After Shuya had lost his own parents, the manager of the orphanage had been his only authority figure and guardian. When he lectured the young Shuya, the manager had worn the same expression.

Kawada said, "You can die if you want to. But if you go now and never return, Noriko's odds are going to get a hell of a lot worse. Did you forget about her?"

Shuya gulped. Kawada was absolutely right. "But . . ."

Kawada calmly continued, "I'm sure you're all too aware, Nanahara, that loving someone means not loving someone else. If you care about Noriko, don't go."

"But . . ." Shuya wanted to cry. "So then what are you suggesting? We just let them get killed?"

"I never said that."

Kawada released Shuya's arm, turned to face Yumiko's mountain, and raised his shotgun. "This is going to hurt our chances of survival just a little. Just a little."

He aimed his shotgun at the sky and pulled the trigger. This close up, the gunpowder blast was incredible. For a second, Shuya thought his eardrums had been blasted clear out of his head. The gunfire echoed off the mountainside. Kawada pumped the shotgun and ejected the empty casing. He fired again. The sound shook the air.

I get it, Shuya thought. *He's using the gunfire to scare Yumiko Kusaka and Yukiko Kitano, so they'll stop calling out and hide.*

Yumiko's megaphone-amplified voice halted. Shuya thought she and Yukiko were looking their way. But the three were hidden in the thicket, so the girls would not likely be able to recognize who they were.

"Come on!" Shuya said. "Shoot some more!"

"I can't. Those two shots alone might have been enough for someone to figure out our location. Anything more will be too dangerous."

Shuya thought about it, then raised his Smith & Wesson above his head.

But Kawada took his arm again.

"Stop! How many times do I have to tell you, Nanahara?"

"But—"

"All we can do for them now is hope that they'll hide quickly."

Shuya looked toward the summit. Then the voice—Yumiko's voice—returned.

"Stop! We know you don't want to fight!"

Shuya shook his arm free. He couldn't stand it any longer. No matter what it took, he wanted them to hide somewhere safe. He put his finger on the trigger of the Smith & Wesson and—

Brattattattattattattattattat.

The far-off sound resembled a typewriter, and as it went on and on, Shuya heard Yumiko groan. The megaphone persistently amplified her cry. Then she was quiet, and the scream came. It sounded like Yukiko Kitano. That sound too carried crisply all the way to Shuya's ears thanks to the megaphone's tiny, hardworking amplifier.

Beneath the platform's roof, the taller of the figures slowly slumped to the floor, and the screaming continued, saying, "Yumi!" The megaphone issued a burst of static as it crashed to the floor. Another *brattattat* came, only this time, much quieter. Shuya realized that the first clattering noise had also been picked up by the megaphone. Now that the device had broken, the sound was much fainter.

Yukiko collapsed behind the shapes of the low trees surrounding the deck, and like Yumiko, she vanished from Shuya's sight.

Both Shuya and Noriko had turned sickly white.

29 STUDENTS REMAIN.

On the concrete floor of the observation deck, Yukiko Kitano crawled toward Yumiko Kusaka. Her stomach felt like it was on fire, and all the strength had fled her body, but somehow she managed to crawl, her trail on the white concrete a wild brushstroke painted in red.

"Yumi!" The scream tore through her stomach, but Yumiko didn't care. Her best friend had fallen and wasn't moving. Nothing else mattered.

Yumiko was lying on her stomach with her face turned toward Yukiko. But her eyes were closed. A pool, thick and red, began spreading underneath her.

When Yukiko reached her friend, it took all of her strength to sit up. She grabbed Yumiko by the shoulders and shook.

"Yumi! Yumi!"

As she screamed, flecks of red fell on Yumiko's face. Yukiko didn't realize they had come from her own mouth.

Slowly, Yumiko opened her eyes and whispered, "Yukiko . . ."

"Yumi! Wake up!"

Yumiko winced. But she held on through the pain and said, "I'm sorry, Yukiko. I was a fool. Hurry . . . run."

"No!" Crying, Yukiko shook her head. "We have to go together. Come on!"

Yukiko frantically looked around. She saw no sign of their attacker. Whoever it was must have targeted them from a distance.

"Hurry, Yumiko!"

She tried to help up Yumiko, but it was hopeless. She became suddenly aware that she could barely support her own body. The pain in her stomach redoubled, and she groaned and collapsed forward. She could only manage to turn her head to face her friend.

Yumiko's face was right there, staring at her with glazed eyes. "Yukiko," she said, her voice feeble. "Can you move?"

"No." Yukiko forced her cheeks into a smile. "I guess not."

"I'm sorry," Yumiko repeated softly.

"It's all right. We did what . . . we had to do . . . didn't we, Yumi?"

She could tell from Yumiko's face that her friend was about to cry. She thought her own wounds weren't as severe, but she felt her consciousness rapidly slipping away. Her eyelids were heavy.

"Yukiko?"

Yumiko's voice pulled her back, and she managed to say, "W-what?"

"There's . . . something I couldn't . . . tell you . . . before."

"Hm?"

Yumiko formed a slight grin. "I also . . . had a crush . . . on Nanahara."

For a moment, Yukiko didn't understand what her friend was saying. Whether that was because she hadn't expected it, or that her hearing had already started to go, she didn't know.

But eventually the words knocked at the door of Yukiko's heart and stepped inside. *Oh, I see now.*

As her awareness sank into the mist, a scene replayed in her mind. The two of them had just gone out shopping. They found a pair of earrings, some cheap things on sale for three thousand yen, but absolutely gorgeous. Though the two rarely shared the same tastes, they both wanted them. In the end, they decided they would each pay half and they would both get one of the earrings. It was the first time either of them had bought jewelry. Even now, that earring was tucked away at the back of her desk drawer in her house near the edge of town.

Somehow, Yukiko felt at peace. She found that an odd thing to feel as she was about to die.

"Oh . . ." Yukiko said. "You . . . did . . ."

Yumiko faintly smiled again.

Yukiko opened her mouth one last time. *Come on,* she told herself. *You can at least say one more thing, can't you?* She wasn't very religious, but if the Halo Church had ever offered her one thing of beauty, it was Yumiko. They had been together since the day they met in that church.

"Yumi . . . I . . . I'm . . . so glad we were . . ."

She had been about to say "friends" when the *bang* sound came and shook Yumiko's head. A red hole opened in Yumiko's temple, and those now hollow eyes simply pointed at her, seeing nothing. That far-off stare might have been unintentionally appropriate, considering she was on an observation deck.

Yukiko opened her mouth in terror and shock. She heard another *bang* and felt the impact of a blow to her head. Those were the last things she ever sensed.

Kazuo Kiriyama (Boys #6) was crouched so as not to be seen from outside the platform. He lowered Mitsuru Numai's Walther PPK and picked up the girls' daypacks.

27 STUDENTS REMAIN.

24

After the two single shots had fired, Shuya and Noriko remained frozen. A hawk cried overhead.

Kawada took a look around, then turned back to them and said, "It's over. Let's go back."

Shuya took Noriko's arm and looked up to the taller boy. His lips trembled. "It's over? There's gotta be a better way to say that."

Kawada shrugged just up to the base of his neck. "You'll have to excuse the way I talk. I don't know that many words. Anyway, I guess you understand now. Some of them are playing. And I'll go ahead and tell you that this isn't something Sakamochi and his boys did just to get us to fight. They don't want to die either, so they won't be leaving that school."

Shuya wanted to respond, but he held himself in check and began walking, supporting Noriko by the arm.

As they walked, Noriko said in a scratchy voice, "It's . . . it's so terrible."

When they reached their original spot, Kawada began packing up his things.

Shuya asked him what he was doing, and he answered, "Get ready. We're going to move three hundred meters. Just in case."

"But you said it's safest not to."

Kawada pursed his lips and shook his head. "You saw what happened. Whoever it was, that bastard is merciless. Even worse, he's got a machine gun. He probably knows where we are. If he does, we're better off moving."

Then he added, "Just a little. We'll move just a little."

27 STUDENTS REMAIN.

Yutaka Seto (Boys #12) was running frantically down the slope, or rather, crawling, since he was on his hands and knees, concealing himself among the bushes. The dry dirt had turned his size-small black school uniform almost completely white. His round, boyish eyes and class-clown face contorted with fear.

After Yutaka had left the school, he hid himself near the top of the northern mountain—in the bushes not fifty meters below where Yumiko Kusaka and Yukiko Kitano had called out to everyone with their megaphone.

Although he had been at an angle from them, Yutaka had a clear view of the girls. He went back and forth and back and forth, hesitating, deliberating what he would do. He had just decided to come out and answer their call when he heard the two distant gunshots, and the girls turned to look that way—opposite from Yutaka. He reconsidered his move, thinking it would be a good idea to wait things out a little longer. Then not more than ten or twenty seconds later, that typewriter gunfire came, and as the megaphone amplified her cry, Yutaka watched Yumiko Kusaka fall. Right after that, Yukiko Kitano was also shot.

He knew that at that moment, the two girls yet lived. But Yutaka couldn't make himself come out to help them. After all, he was a born joker, never good in a fight. Even worse, his weapon, the one that had been supplied to him, was a single fork—a plain, ordinary fork like you'd use to eat spaghetti. Then, somewhere out of his sight, he heard two more shots, and he knew that the attacker had finished off Yumiko and Yukiko.

That instant, Yutaka scooped up his bag and took off, skidding down the mountainside. *Whoever that is, he's coming for me next. I'm sure of it! I'm the next nearest one!*

Suddenly he noticed the great clouds of dust he'd stirred up. *Oh, no! No, no! This is bad! Worse than a slipper in your soup! Damn it, man. Forget the comedy and focus!*

Doing the best he could not to lose his footing, he changed tack and scrambled down the slope on the palms of his hands (well, his right hand, gripping the fork, was more of a fist) and the soles of his shoes. He could feel the skin scraping off his hands, but he didn't care. *Shit, I must look hilarious right now. I'm a human water beetle.*

After proceeding like this for two or three minutes, Yutaka stopped. Furtively, he looked over his shoulder. The summit, where Yumiko Kusaka and Yukiko Kitano had died, appeared distant beyond the trees. Nothing moved. Yutaka listened. Nothing made a sound.

Did I make it? Am I safe?

As if answering his unasked question, something dug into his arm.

Fear flooded his mind, and a shriek escaped his lips.

"You fool!" someone hissed. The pressure against his arm lifted, and a warm hand covered his mouth. Too disoriented to understand, he believed the killer had caught him, and in his panic, he swung the fork.

With a clang, the fork hit something and stopped. *What happened?*

But when nothing else happened, he fearfully opened his eyes.

The figure standing before him wore a school uniform. The boy's body was turned to the side, and he covered his face with a semi-automatic pistol (a Beretta 92F), blocking the fork. He held the gun in his left hand. Judging by their proximity, and that the boy's right hand was over Yutaka's mouth, the fork would have stabbed the boy more than a little deep had he not been left-handed. And he was left-handed. And only one boy in Class B had never had his left-hand-edness corrected.

"Watch it there, Yutaka."

The boy's hair glistened with whatever styling product he used to keep his bangs up off his face. Beneath it, he had straight, upturned eyebrows. And beneath those, his piercing, but humorous, eyes held Yutaka's gaze. Then there was that earring in his left ear. He was The Third Man, Shinji Mimura (Boys #19)—Yutaka's best friend in class. Shinji grinned and gently removed his hand from Yutaka's mouth. Stupefied, Yutaka slowly lowered the fork.

Then finally, overcome with relief, he shouted, "Shinji! Shinji, it's you!"

"You idiot!" Shinji Mimura whispered, pressing his hand back across Yutaka's mouth. When he let go again, he said, "Over here. Keep quiet and follow me."

Yutaka followed in a daze. Between the bushes and trees, he noticed how the island, which he'd gotten used to viewing from above, had leveled off. In those few short minutes, he'd descended a long way.

Yutaka looked straight ahead, glancing at Shinji's back, when suddenly, a grim hypothesis overwhelmed him, and for a second, his legs froze.

What if Yumiko Kusaka and Yukiko Kitano's killer was . . . Shinji? What if he followed me here? No, then why hasn't he killed me yet? Well, that's because I think he's my best friend, and he knows it, and if he partners with me, he can, say, use me to keep watch while he sleeps. That way, he'll be more likely to survive. Then, when it's down to the two of us, he'll kill me. Say, that's a great idea! If this were a video game or something, that's totally what I'd do.

Stop it, idiot! What are you thinking?

Yutaka stamped out the thought. Shinji didn't have a machine gun—that's what that noise had been, no doubt about it—and besides, Shinji was Shinji. He was Yutaka's best friend. He would never kill a girl as if she were no more than an insect.

Shinji looked back at him and whispered, "What's wrong? Hurry up."

Yutaka followed after him, still in a daze.

Shinji slowly and cautiously walked ahead. When they had covered about fifty meters, he stopped, pointed down near his feet with his pistol, and said, "Step over this."

Yutaka squinted and saw the thin, inconspicuous thread that had been strung up taut and level.

"What's . . ."

"It's not a trap or anything," Shinji said from the other side of the string. "If you catch on it, the empty can all the way at the end of it will fall and make noise."

Yutaka's eyes widened as he nodded. Shinji must have been hiding out here, and this was a kind of tripwire alarm. *Impressive. The Third Man is more than some big-shot basketball player.*

Yutaka stepped over the thread.

About twenty meters further, they reached a thicket, and Shinji stopped and told Yutaka to sit.

Yutaka sat facing Shinji. Realizing he still clutched the fork, he placed the utensil on the ground. Sharp pain suddenly returned to his left palm and the outside of his right hand. His skin had scraped off, particularly on his knuckles, where red flesh lay exposed.

Noticing this, Shinji set down his gun and pulled his daypack out from under a nearby bush. He took out a towel and the bottle of water, moistened an edge of the cloth, and said, "Give me your hands, Yutaka."

Yutaka held out his hands, and Shinji wiped the wounds, taking care not to apply too much force. Then he tore off a couple thin strips from the dry side of the towel and wrapped them around Yutaka's hands.

"Thanks," Yutaka said. Then: "So you've been hiding out here."

With a smile and a nod, Shinji said, "Yeah. I saw you from here—caught a glimpse of you moving through the bushes. You were pretty far off, but I know you when I see you. I took a minor risk and followed your trail."

Yutaka felt a little choked up. *Shinji put himself in danger for* me.

"Going around carelessly like that," Shinji said, "that's dangerous too, you know."

"Yeah." Yutaka thought he might cry. "Thank you, Shinji."

"I'm glad." Shinji let out a deep breath. "If I'm going to die out here, I at least wanted to see you first."

Now Yutaka really did tear up. But he managed to hold back his tears, and he changed the subject. "Just now . . . I was right near Kusaka and Kitano. I—I . . . I couldn't help them."

"Yeah." Shinji nodded. "I saw it too. That's how I found you. Don't be too hard on yourself. Hell, I heard them, and I didn't do a thing about it."

Yutaka nodded. The scene of Yumiko Kusaka and Yukiko Kitano's deaths replayed, still vivid in his memory, and he trembled.

27 STUDENTS REMAIN.

26

By the time Shuya's group had moved about a hundred meters to the southwest, and Kawada had finished running the wire through the undergrowth, it was already past nine in the morning. The sun was high in the sky, and the verdant smells of May were in the air. The sea, when they caught glimpses of it through the tress as they moved, shimmered a brilliant blue, dotted with the scattered islands of the Seto Inland Sea. It would have been the perfect setting, if they were only hiking.

But they weren't. All passing boats steered far clear of the island, appearing as mere points in the distance. The only one close by was the gray guard ship in charge of the western shore. It too was quite far off—though close enough to make out the machine gun mounted atop its prow.

Now that he'd finished setting the wire, Kawada let out a deep breath and sat in front of Shuya and Noriko. He returned the shotgun to rest atop his legs.

After neither of the two said anything, Kawada asked, "What's wrong, you two?"

Shuya looked up at Kawada. He thought for a moment, then said, "Why do you think they did that?"

Kawada lifted his eyebrows. "Kusaka and Kitano, you mean?"

Shuya nodded. He hesitated, then said, "Didn't they know what would happen? At the very least, they must have expected the possibility. According to the rules of the game . . ." He let out a sigh. "We're supposed to kill each other."

Kawada withdrew a cigarette, put it between his lips, and lit it with his hundred-yen lighter. "They seemed very close. Weren't they part of some religious group together?"

Shuya nodded. They had been two entirely average girls but had always kept a certain distance from Noriko and Yukie Utsumi's group of mainstreamers. He thought their religion might have been why.

"Yeah," Shuya said, "the Halo Church or something—some Shinto sect, I think. Their church is south of the highway, along the Yodo River."

"Maybe that had something to do with it." Kawada exhaled smoke. "'Love thy neighbor.'"

"No, that's not it," Noriko said. "Neither of them seemed passionate about their faith. Especially Yumiko—she made that very clear. She told me it was just a social thing."

Kawada mumbled, "I see," then his eyes dropped. He continued, "The good people aren't always the ones who get saved. The same goes for everywhere, not just here. It's the capable ones who make it. But I respect those who preserve their conscience even through rejection and failure."

He stared at Shuya and Noriko. "Those two decided to believe in their classmates. They must have thought that if they could gather everyone together, they'd have a chance to save everyone. They should be commended. They did what we were unable to do."

Shuya let out a breath and said, "I agree."

After a while, Shuya again looked up at Kawada and said, "I don't think you're our enemy after all. So I'm going to believe in you."

"Me too," Noriko said. "I can't imagine you as a bad person."

Kawada shook his head and grinned. "At the very least, I'm no good at lying to girls."

Shuya flashed him a grin. "So won't you tell us? I mean, if you don't want to share your escape plan, that's all right. Just tell us why. Do you think we'll let it slip in front of one of our classmates, and then something will go wrong? Is it because we can't trust the others? Or at least, you think we can't trust them?"

"Hey, don't ask me so many questions at once. I'm not smart enough to handle more than one at a time."

"Liar."

The cigarette in his mouth, Kawada rested his elbows on his legs, cupped his chin, and looked to the side. When he turned back, he said, "Nanahara, the reason I can't tell you is just what you said. I don't want the others to know my plan. And even if you two never tell, I don't want the others even sensing that you know it. So I can't tell you."

Shuya thought about that a little while, then exchanged glances with Noriko. He gave Kawada a nod. "Okay then, I understand. We're going to trust you. But . . ."

"Something still bothering you?"

"It's just that, any way you think about it, there's no possible way. So I'm really . . ."

"Curious, is that it?"

Shuya nodded.

Kawada let out a deep breath and rubbed his cigarette on the ground. He ran his hand through his short hair.

"Everything has a hole," he said. "Well, most everything."

"A hole?"

"Yeah, a weak spot. I'm going after that weak spot."

Shuya narrowed his eyes in confusion.

Kawada continued, "I know this game a lot better than any of you."

Noriko asked, "How so?"

"Don't stare those pretty round eyes at me. I'm likely to get shy."

She gaped at him, then formed a slight smile. "How?" she repeated.

Kawada brushed his hair again while the two waited.

Finally, he spoke.

"Do you know what happens to the survivor of this game?"

Shuya and Noriko looked at each other. They both shook their heads. Each Program had only one survivor. Whoever made it through this absurd game was shoved in front of news cameras, with the rifles of Nonaggressive Forces soldiers pointed at their backs. ("Smile. Smile nice for the cameras.") But whatever happened to the survivor after that remained a mystery.

Kawada watched Shuya's and Noriko's faces as he continued, "They're forced to transfer to a school in a different prefecture. They're told never to speak of the game and to lead a normal life. That's it."

Shuya felt suddenly heavy, and his face stiffened. He stared intently at Kawada's face, and realized that Noriko was holding her breath.

Kawada said, "I used to be in Ninth Grade Class C of Kobe Second Junior High in Hyogo Prefecture. I'm the survivor of last year's Hyogo Program."

27 STUDENTS REMAIN

27

Softening his expression, Kawada continued, "I got the Leader's autograph too. Isn't that swell? His handwriting looks straight out of a nursery school—though I don't remember it all that well, since I tossed the thing on burnable trash day."

In sharp contrast to Kawada's lighthearted tone, Shuya didn't even breathe. Sure, the Program could come to any ninth grader. But to the same person, two years in a row? Not only would that require being held back a year, getting chosen for the Program was as likely as winning the lottery. But everything fit: Kawada's familiarity with the game, his noticing the knockout gas on the bus, and all those scars on his body. If what Kawada was saying were true, it was outrageous!

Shuya said as much.

Kawada shrugged and said, "Yeah. The game was last July. I was badly hurt and hospitalized for a long time. I was able to do a lot of studying—including about this country—from my bed, you know. The nurses and everyone were really nice and brought me books from the library. The hospital was my school. Anyway, because of all that, I had to repeat ninth grade. But still . . ." Kawada looked at Shuya and Noriko again. "Even I didn't expect to be playing this happy little game again."

That's right, Shuya thought, recalling the conversation they'd just had—well, three hours past, now. When Shuya had asked Kawada, *"Was killing our class leader not the first time for you?"* Kawada said, *"Well, first one this time, at least."*

After a moment, Noriko asked, "So the ones who've already been drawn—" But she must have thought that sounded too much like she was talking about someone who'd won a sweepstakes, because she rephrased it. "Those who've already been in this once aren't exempt?"

Kawada grinned. "Since I'm here, I'd suppose not. Don't they say that the classes are randomly selected by computer? I'd say a previous winner like myself would have quite an advantage—but it seems they don't make a special case for it. I guess some people are just more equal than others."

Kawada cupped his hands around his lighter and lit another cigarette. "Now you know why I recognized the gas's smell. And why I have this." He pointed to the scar over his left eyebrow.

Tearfully, Noriko said, "It's terrible. It's too awful."

"Don't say that, Noriko." Kawada broke into a smile. "This way, I can help you."

Shuya held out his hand.

"What's that for?" Kawada said. "I'm no palm reader."

Shuya laughed and shook his head. "I'm sorry for every accusing thing I've said. It's a handshake. We're together to the end."

With an understanding nod, Kawada said, "All right," took the boy's hand, and gave it a little shake. Noriko smiled in relief.

27 STUDENTS REMAIN.

Kinpatsu Sakamochi (instructor) was sitting at his desk in the faculty room, rummaging through scattered piles of documents. Along the north and south walls of the room, Nonaggressive Forces soldiers stood, weapons at the ready, manning the loophole openings in the steel-plated windows. Little sunlight reached the room, and the fluorescent lights remained in use. A handful of soldiers sat at a desk across from Sakamochi, staring into a row of desktop computer monitors. Another three wore headphones connected to some other kind of machine. A large generator sat along the western wall, powering all the lights, computers, and other equipment. Unconfined by its soundproofing, a low hum filled the air. The rest of the soldiers were resting in the classroom the students had left.

"Let's see," Sakamochi said, "Yumiko Kusaka died at 8:42 a.m. and Yukiko Kitano, she was also at forty-two after." He brushed his long hair back behind his ears. "Ahhh, there's so much to be done!"

The old black phone at his desk rang. With his pen still in hand, he distractedly snatched up the receiver.

"Yes, this is Oki Island School," he said offhandedly. "Shiroiwa Junior High, Ninth Grade Class B Program Headquarters."

The next instant, he jolted upright in his chair and put both hands around the receiver. "Yes, sir. This is Sakamochi speaking. I appreciate everything you've been doing for us, Superintendent. Oh, yes, sir, our second one just turned two, and our third is on the way. Oh, no, we're just doing our part for the country. The declining birth rate's a big problem. Yes, sir. And how can I help you, sir?"

Sakamochi listened for a while and then chuckled. "Oh, wow. You put your money on Shogo Kawada? I'm betting on Kazuo Kiriyama. Yeah, I put it on the chalk. Well, Kawada, you see, he's a contender, being experienced, after all. That's almost unheard of, isn't it? Of course he's still alive. How much did you put on him? Wow, that's incredible. Impressive. What's that? The current status? Can't you access it there? It's on the government's secret website—oh, I see, you're not very good with computers.Well, umm, that's . . . yes. Hang on."

Sakamochi held the receiver away from his face and called to a craggy-faced soldier at one of the monitors. "Hey, Kato. Do you know if Kawada is still with those two?"

The soldier typed on his keyboard, then curtly replied, "He is."

His monitor would be displaying a map of the island, overlaid with the students' locations as provided by the signals from their collars. Sakamochi was about to scowl at Kato's gruff attitude, but he stopped himself. Kato had been this way ever since Sakamochi, back in his days as a mere junior high school teacher, took on a class of problem students. Kato had been at the top of the list. This was nothing new. Sakamochi put the receiver back to his ear.

"Sorry to keep you waiting, sir. Let's see, Kawada is operating with two other students. That's . . . Shuya Nanahara and Noriko Nakagawa. Yeah, they've been talking about escaping together. Would you like to listen to the recording? Oh, well, yes. Do I think he means it? Well, I can't say for sure, but common sense says he's lying, probably. Because escape is utterly impossible. Oh, yes, about that. Hold on, let me check. The papers, the papers. Here it is, Shogo Kawada, right? There wasn't anything particularly suspicious about his behavior at his previous school. No subversive statements or actions, right. I see his father died sometime around the last game. It looks like he got drunk and said some seditious things. But Kawada's comment was 'Good riddance. Nobody cared about that bastard.' Well, maybe they just didn't get along. Maybe his dad tried to demand some of the compensation money. Yes, well, when you put it that way, having two more with him does give him an advantage. Nanahara is an excellent athlete, so he'll be useful—though Nakagawa is injured. Yeah, our Tahara shot her. Yes. Oh, yes. They completely trust him. He rescued an injured girl—now, really, that's brilliant. He's feeding them all kinds of great stuff too. Yes."

Sakamochi had been laying on the obsequious laughter, but suddenly, his eyebrows shot up high. With his free hand, he brushed back his hair over his ear.

"What?" he said. "That can't be. Look, well, you're talking about that thing in March, right? Yes, I received the memo. If that's true, then right now . . . Yes. Well, those guys over in Central are always overreacting. Besides, they're junior high schoolers. There's no way they could be aware we're listening to them. From what I can see now, I'm telling you, there isn't a single student that knows. Yes. That's why—Yes. Yes. Yes, sir. All right. Oh, no, please, I couldn't possibly accept . . . well, if you insist. Thank you very much. Yes. Yes. All right. Yes. Goodbye."

Sakamochi let out an audible sigh, returned the receiver to its cradle, and picked up his pen. "So much to do!" he said, sweeping back his hair. He scribbled on the documents as if his pen were glued to them.

27 STUDENTS REMAIN.

When Shinji first met up with him, Yutaka Seto had seemed on edge from the shock of witnessing the deaths of Yumiko Kusaka and Yukiko Kitano up close, but now that some time had passed he had calmed down. As the warm sunlight filtered through the treetops, Shinji listened for any movement. He sensed no one near, hearing only the peeping of small birds. Whoever had killed Yumiko Kusaka and Yukiko Kitano had apparently not noticed the two boys. Still, Shinji needed to remain alert.

Shinji loved and respected his uncle, who had taught him everything, starting with basketball, and whose influence was largely responsible for The Third Man being who he was today. One of the things his uncle said was, "Relax when you need to, but be tense when you need to. The point is to never mix up the two." This mentor often stressed to him—for example, when driving basic computer skills into him, demonstrating how to access illegal foreign networks— that there was no such thing as being too careful. And Shinji knew, he was certain, that this was one of those times when he needed to be tense.

He heard Yutaka call his name and returned his attention to the boy, who sat against a tree, hugging his knees, with his eyes looking down between them.

"Now that I think about it," Yutaka said, "I should have waited for you in front of the school. Then we would have been together from the start." He looked up at Shinji. "But I was scared."

Shinji crossed his arms, Beretta still in hand. "I'm not so sure. It might have been dangerous."

That's right, Shinji thought. *I'd better explain it to him. He might not know that Mayumi Tendo and Yoshio Akamatsu died in front of the school. And—*

Then Shinji noticed Yutaka was crying. Tears filled his eyes and spilled down his cheeks, making thin white trails down his muddied face.

Shinji gently asked, "What's wrong?"

"I . . ." Yutaka lifted an injured hand and dried his eyes with the torn edge of the cloth bandage. "I'm pathetic. I'm clumsy and a coward, and . . ." He paused. Then, as if forcing out words that had caught in his chest, he said, "I couldn't save her."

Shinji's eyebrows inched up, and he glanced down at his downcast friend. He had known not to bring this up himself. Slowly, he said, "You mean Kanai?"

With his head still down, Yutaka nodded.

Shinji thought back to the time he was in Yutaka's room when his friend told him, with a little bit of pride and a little bit of embarrassment mixed into his voice, "I . . . like Izumi Kanai." And that Izumi Kanai had died so quickly. Her death had been announced in the six a.m. report. They didn't know where she had died. They only knew it had to have been somewhere on the island.

"There wasn't anything you could do," Shinji said. "Kanai left ahead of you."

"But I—" Yutaka spoke without raising his head. "I couldn't even look for her—I was too scared—I never thought something crazy like that would happen to her. I thought she'd be fine. I made myself think that. Then by six, she was already . . ."

Shinji quietly listened. Somewhere beyond the treetops, the bird was chirping again. Another bird joined in, and their calls overlapped as if in a mutual song.

Suddenly Yutaka lifted his face. Looking up at Shinji, he said, "I've made up my mind."

"About what?"

Tears still clouded Yutaka's eyes, but they looked straight into Shinji. "I'm going to avenge her. Sakamochi and the rest of those bastards in the government—I'm going to fucking kill them."

Somewhat startled, Shinji stared into his friend's face.

Shinji himself was, of course, completely pissed off at this bullshit game and the government behind it. He had never really hung out with Shuya Nanahara's best friend Yoshitoki Kuninobu (the boy's too-laid-back attitude left Shinji with a bad taste in his mouth), but still, Yoshitoki was a nice guy—a really, really nice guy. And the government had murdered him with a casual brutality. Then the rest of their classmates, one after the other, Fumiyo Fujiyoshi, and as Yutaka had just mentioned, Izumi Kanai, and then the others, like Yumiko Kusaka and Yukiko Kitano, whose lives had been taken as he watched. *But . . .*

"But . . . that would be suicide," Shinji said.

"I don't care if I die. There's nothing else I can do for her now." Yutaka paused and examined Shinji's expression. "Is it funny for a wimp like me to say something like that?"

"No . . ." Shinji said, drawing the word out. Then he shook his head. "Not at all."

Shinji stared back at his friend for a time, then tilted his head back and gazed at the branches and leaves above. He wasn't surprised by the clownish boy's display of intense emotion—that was just who Yutaka was. That's why they'd been friends for so long. *But—*

"I don't care if I die. There's nothing else I can do for her now."

What's it like to feel that way about a girl? Shinji wondered, looking up at the layers of leaves turned a yellowish green by the sun's glow on their other side. He had had many girlfriends and even slept with three of them (not bad for a ninth grader, huh?), but he'd never felt that kind of love for any girl.

That his parents had never gotten along might have had something to do with it. His father, being who he was, had women on the side. (He did very well in his managerial position, but—and this was probably strange coming from a boy who didn't yet support himself—in nearly every aspect, his father was an unremarkable man. Shinji couldn't believe the man could share the same blood as his uncle, who radiated vibrancy.) And his mother, unable to bring herself to confront her husband, closed herself inside her own world, flitting from one new hobby to the next, from ikebana flower arrangement to various women's clubs. His mother and father had normal conversations. They each did what was necessary. But they didn't trust each other, and they didn't help each other. They just quietly built up their resentment as they grew ever older. Maybe, in this world, that's how most parents were.

When the ace guard Shinji Mimura picked up basketball in elementary school, he captivated the girls—getting a girlfriend was easy. Kissing them was easy too. After a little while, sleeping with them became just as easy. Still, he'd never fallen in love.

He regretted never talking about it with his uncle, who always had an answer for everything. But he hadn't started thinking about it until recently, and his uncle had passed away two years ago.

The earring Shinji wore in his left ear had been something his uncle treasured. He once explained to the boy, "This belonged to a woman I loved. She died a long time ago."

After his uncle's passing, Shinji decided he'd take the earring. If he were still alive, his uncle would probably say, *That earring might be a bad influence on you, Shinji. To truly love, and to be loved, isn't a bad thing, you know. Hurry and find yourself a pretty girl.*

But earring or not, he still hadn't been able to fall in love.

Shinji remembered when his little sister, Ikumi, three years younger than him but mature for her age, asked, "Do you want to marry for love? Or would you be okay with an arranged marriage?" He had answered, "I might not get married at all."

Ikumi. Shinji thought of his sister. *If it's possible, I hope you'll fall in love and have a happy marriage. Your brother's going to say goodbye to this world without ever knowing true love.*

Shinji looked at Yutaka. "Can I ask you something, Yutaka? Sorry if it might come out sounding rude."

Yutaka looked blankly at him. "What is it?"

"What was so great about Izumi?"

Yutaka stared at him for a while, then his teary face formed a slight smile. Maybe he was thinking this could be his way of properly honoring her in death, now that flowers weren't going to be possible.

"I don't know how to put it," Yutaka said, "but she was so pretty."

"Pretty?" Shinji asked, then hurriedly added, "I mean, I'm not saying she wasn't."

Izumi Kanai wasn't all that ugly, Shinji thought, *but as far as our class goes, the pretty ones are Takako Chigusa (or maybe she's just my type), Sakura Ogawa (well, she had Kazuhiko Yamamoto—and they're both gone now), and Mitsuko Souma (and no matter how good-looking she is, she's out of the question).*

With that little grin, Yutaka said, "When she looked sleepy at her desk, and she rested her cheeks on her hands, she was pretty." Then he added, "And when she was watering the plants on the little balcony outside our classroom, and she would look so happy touching the leaves, she was pretty." And then, "And at the field day, when she dropped the baton in the relay race, and she was crying after, she was pretty." And then, "And during breaks, when she was listening to Yuka Nakagawa or one of the other girls, and she'd hold her stomach as she burst out laughing, she was beautiful."

Oh.

As he listened to Yutaka rattle on, Shinji felt like a part of him understood completely. Though Yutaka's explanations weren't really explaining anything, Shinji thought, *I get it. Hey Uncle, I think I'm actually starting to get it.*

When Yutaka had finished, he turned to face Shinji.

Shinji stared back at him with soft eyes and tilted his head slightly.

Then he grinned. "I always said you'd be a comedian someday, but you know, you could be a poet."

Yutaka grinned back.

Then Shinji said, "Hey."

"What?"

"I don't know how to say this, but I think Kanai must be happy right now—to know someone loves her that much. She's probably crying up there in heaven."

After the incredible poetry of Yutaka's words, his own sounded banal, but he'd had to say something. Even so, Yutaka's eyes began to well up with tears again. Then, an instant later, the tears spilled out, trickling down, tracing several white lines down his cheeks.

Choked up, Yutaka said, "You really think so?"

Shinji placed a hand on his friend's shoulder and gave him a gentle shake. "I do." He let out a breath and continued, "One more thing. If you say you're getting revenge, I'll help."

Yutaka's tear-filled eyes opened wide. "You mean it?"

Shinji nodded. "Yeah."

It had been on his mind for a while now. No, not that girl issue, but something else—what his future would be in this fucking grand Republic of Greater East Asia.

He'd talked about the future before—now that he thought about it, with Yutaka too. Yutaka had said something like, "I can't even imagine." Then, "At the very least, I'll be a comedian, right?" Shinji had given the glib reply the chuckle it sought, but inside, he felt this was a more serious matter. Maybe Yutaka thought it was serious too but couldn't bring himself to talk about it. What it all came down to was this: this country was insane. (As Shinji had once said to Shuya Nanahara, "This is what successful fascism looks like. Is there anything as evil anywhere in the world?")

And the insanity wasn't limited to this damn game. Anyone who showed the slightest disobedience toward the government ended up being disappeared. Even if the charges were false, the government showed no mercy. Every citizen lived under its fearful shadow, in total compliance, finding sustenance only in the small happinesses of the day-to-day. And should those small happinesses be unjustly stolen, the only option was to acquiesce in subservience.

But Shinji had started to believe the way things were was wrong. Probably everyone thought it too—only no one ever dared to come out and say it. Even Shuya Nanahara listened to illegally imported rock music to let off steam. But it never went beyond that. As Shinji began to understand the ways of the world he became more and more convinced that he needed to speak out despite the danger, even if no one else would.

Then, two years ago, it happened—his uncle's death. On the surface, it appeared to be an accident. When the police came to ask his family to claim his body, they explained that he had been electrocuted while working alone at his factory at night. But Shinji's uncle had been acting strange for a little while. The man had seemed unusually preoccupied. While Shinji was doing his customary poking around on his uncle's computer, he asked him what was wrong.

His uncle replied, "Well, one of my old friends . . ." But then he stopped himself, suddenly evasive, and said, "Ah, never mind. It's nothing."

My old friends.

Shinji's uncle hardly ever discussed his past. He always managed to change the subject. When Shinji realized his uncle didn't want to talk about it, he stopped asking. (And when he asked his father, he was told, "That's nothing you need to know.") But his uncle's breadth of knowledge spanned the legal and the illegal, and behind his explanations on the world and society Shinji perceived a buried dislike, even a hatred, toward their nation. And also . . . something of a shadow. Once, Shinji had said, "You're incredible, Uncle. You're so cool." But his uncle gave a pained smile and said, "That's not true, Shinji. I'm not cool or any of that. You can't survive in this country and live with integrity. No, if I were a good person, I'd be long dead by now." The conclusion Shinji drew from all this was that at some point, his uncle had been involved in some form of resistance against the government. But something had caused him to stand down. At least that's what Shinji suspected.

Because of this, Shinji was a little worried when he heard his uncle mention his old friends. But, thinking his uncle could handle anything, he decided not to pester him with questions.

But his fears had been well placed. At the time, Shinji had suspected one of his uncle's old friends, with whom he'd lost contact, had reached out to him, and after some hesitation, he'd decided to take on the assignment.

And then . . . something happened. Since the police in this nation had the right to execute civilians without trial, they didn't hesitate to do so wherever they were, whether it was at someone's workplace or out on the street. But when the person involved was related to a prominent figure, it wasn't unlikely for them to cover up the execution as an "accidental death." What really disgusted Shinji was that his father had a fairly important role in a fairly important firm. (According to the Republic's worker classification system, he was a Class-1 worker—the highest rank outside of the upper-level bureaucrats.) What disgusted Shinji even more was that, if his theory was true, his uncle had been "taken care of," while his good-for-nothing father had, in whatever roundabout way, consented to the government's actions.

No matter what else, his uncle's death couldn't have been an accident. That man would never die some stupid, careless death via accidental electrocution.

Thinking about it now, Shinji sensed that his earring's former owner may have been linked to his uncle's past. Trembling with rage at his uncle's murder, he swore to never bow down to this country.

Shinji was convinced that his uncle's words—*"You can't survive in this country and live with integrity"*—had been a warning. And just as he had warned, he died. But after all that he had taught Shinji, the boy thought this: *I'm going to find a way to do what you gave up long ago. I want to be virtuous. After all, isn't that what you taught me?*

But of course that was only a general emotion, and he hadn't taken any direct action to bring it into reality. He had heard of resistance groups but had no idea where to find them. Besides, his uncle had warned him, "You're better off not trusting any groups or movements. They're not all that reliable." He also thought he was a little too young. But more than anything else, he was scared.

But then even if he got lucky enough to escape this damn game, he'd be a fugitive. *If that's the case, then I can do whatever I want, ironically enough. Whether through some group or on my own, it won't matter. I'll do whatever I want to with this country as my enemy.* This determination had begun to harden inside him.

And now, Yutaka's words had given those feelings a final push.

But Shinji decided to set aside such complex emotions for now and instead admit something else he'd been feeling.

"I'm jealous of you, you know—that you had a girl to love. So if you're doing this, we're doing it together."

Yutaka's lips trembled. "Shit, you mean it? You really mean it?"

"Yeah. I do." Putting his arm on Yutaka's shoulder again, Shinji added, "But for now, we need to think of our escape. Killing that one little bastard, Sakamochi, won't hurt the government. They wouldn't even feel an itch. If we're doing this, we've gotta have a much bigger goal. Right?"

Yutaka nodded. After a while, he wiped his eyes, and Shinji said, "Hey, you haven't seen anyone, have you? Aside from Kusaka and Kitano?"

His eyes red from rubbing the tears away, Yutaka looked at Shinji and shook his head. "No. I . . . ran away as soon as I left the school. And I kept on running. What about you, Shinji? Did you see anyone?"

Shinji nodded once. "Just as I left. It must have happened after you were gone—Tendo and Akamatsu's corpses were right outside the entrance."

Yutaka's eyes widened. "They were?"

"Yeah. I think Tendo was killed as soon as she stepped out."

"And Akamatsu?"

Shinji folded his arms. "I think he killed her."

Yutaka's face stiffened again. "Really?"

"Yeah, he was the first one out, so what other reason would he have for being there? He came back and shot her, probably hiding in some shadow. They had arrows sticking out of them, Tendo and Akamatsu both. The same kind of arrows. So he did in Tendo, then tried to attack the next one out, but instead he got his weapon taken from him—probably a crossbow, looking at the arrows—and got killed himself. That's the simplest scenario."

"But the next one out . . . that was . . ."

"Nanahara."

Again Yutaka's eyes went wide. "Shuya? Shuya killed him? He killed Akamatsu?"

Shinji shook his head. "I don't know. The most we can know for sure is that Akamatsu wasn't able to kill Nanahara. And he wasn't able to kill the one after him either. So it was probably Nanahara who did it. Nanahara could have just knocked him out. He can be a little soft sometimes. Then someone who came out later finished off Akamatsu."

Shinji thought for a moment, then added, "Nanahara would have escaped with Noriko. He might not have had time to deliver the killing blow."

"Noriko? Oh, that's right, she was shot, wasn't she? That's when you—"

"Yeah." Shinji formed a sardonic smile. "If only the game had been delayed. I never expected that to work, but I thought I'd try it. Anyway, Noriko came next after Nanahara. He signaled to her before he left. My desk was close enough to see it."

Yutaka nodded. "I get it. Noriko was shot, so Shuya . . ."

"Yeah. And there's the thing with Kuninobu."

Now really understanding it, Yutaka bobbed his head several times. "That's right. Nobu, he had a crush on Noriko, didn't he? So Shuya couldn't abandon her."

"Yeah. Well, even without that, a kid like Shuya, I bet he had some plan to join together with everyone who came after him, or something like that. But Akamatsu made it obvious that that was never an option. Especially with Noriko injured. So I think he took off with Noriko, just the two of them."

Yutaka nodded again. Then his eyes dropped. "I wonder where Shuya is. If you two teamed up, we'd be unstoppable."

Shinji raised an eyebrow. Yutaka was probably thinking about the masterly combo Shinji and Shuya Nanahara made in the intramural games.

He's right, Shinji thought. *I'd feel a lot better if Nanahara were with us.*

And it wasn't just because of the boy's athleticism—he had this unfailing brand of courage and the ability, which Shinji shared, to make snap judgments under pressure. But more than anything else, few could be trusted in this game. Such a gentle person (a little *too* easygoing, from Shinji's perspective) would never kill his own class-mates just so he could survive.

But Shinji reached out again and placed his hand on Yutaka's shoulder. His friend looked up at him, and he said, "I'm just thankful you're with me. I'm glad we found each other."

Yutaka looked like he might begin crying anew. Shinji put on a reassuring smile. Yutaka held back the tears and grinned back.

Then Shinji continued, "Enough about the dead bodies. I noticed someone else. You know the woods on the other side of the schoolyard?"

"Yeah, I remember."

"Someone was there. Several people, actually."

"Really?"

"Yeah. I think . . . they were waiting for someone. And only five people left after me—Motobuchi and Yamamoto, and Matsui, Minami, and Yahagi. Anyway, they didn't try to get my attention. They were in a group, so they probably weren't going to suddenly come after me, but I didn't see any reason to want to go over to them and join them, either. You said you wished you'd waited for me—but the way things were, that would have been impossible. The fact is that Akamatsu probably came back and killed Tendo. When I saw that group in the woods, I thought, *The same could just as easily happen to them.* Sure, they could have been well armed. Either way, I got away from there as quickly as I could."

Shinji paused to wet his lips, then went on. "I saw two others."

Yutaka's eyes widened again. "Really?"

Shinji nodded. "During the night, I moved around a bit. And I saw a girl. She'd done her hair up all weird—standing straight up, you know? So I think it was probably Shimizu. When I was walking along the base of the mountain, I saw her moving through the bushes."

"Didn't you . . . call out to her?"

Shinji shrugged. "Well, maybe I'm not being fair, but Souma's friends scare me."

Yutaka nodded.

"I saw one more person," Shinji said. "It was that Shogo Kawada."

Yutaka opened his mouth as if to say, *Wow*. Then he said, "Kawada, huh." He spoke the older boy's name with a certain amount of awe, as did many of the other students. "He's a little intimidating. So you—"

"Yeah, so I didn't try joining up with him. But . . ." Shinji glanced up to the sky, then looked back to Yutaka. "He seemed to notice me. I'd gone into a house to look for something. Just as I was about to step outside, I saw him straight ahead. He quickly ducked behind a ridge in the crop fields. He was carrying a shotgun, I think. I hid behind the door, but I could tell that he was watching me for a moment. But then he was gone. He didn't attack me or anything."

"Hmm," Yutaka said. "So, at the very least, Kawada's not hostile."

Shinji shook his head. "We can't be so sure. He could have seen I was armed and decided not to risk an attack. Either way, I wasn't about to follow him."

"I see." Yutaka nodded. Then, as if suddenly remembering something, he looked up. "Hey, I didn't see anything, but just before Kusaka and Kitano were killed, did you hear two other shots?"

Shinji nodded. "Yeah."

"They didn't sound like that machine gun. Do you think someone else was shooting at Kusaka?"

"No," Shinji said, shaking his head. "It wasn't that. I think someone was trying to stop them. What they were doing was so obviously dangerous. I think whoever fired those shots was trying to scare them into hiding."

Yutaka leaned forward, nearly frantic. "Then at least whoever fired those shots isn't hostile."

"That's right. But we don't have any way to meet up with them. We could probably find where they fired from, but surely they've already moved. They exposed their location to that machine-gun bastard too."

Yutaka sat back, dejected. The two remained silent for a while, and Shinji crossed his arms to think. He had been hoping that Yutaka had seen any of their classmates they could trust. If they had stayed in the same place, the two boys could have met up with them. The people he would have trusted were probably the same people that Yutaka would have trusted, and if his friend had come across any of them, he would have joined up with them. But Yutaka had been alone, so none of that really mattered.

But who can we trust anyway? Nanahara . . . and Hiroki Sugimura? Is that all? What about the girls? Maybe the class leader, Yukie Utsumi, and her friends . . . but the girls in class aren't crazy about me, maybe because I get around too much. Well, Uncle, I guess you were right—I should have found one girl and stuck with her.

Oh well, I must have been lucky just to run into Yutaka. Him I know I can trust.

Then Yutaka said, "Hey, Shinji. You said you were searching for something, right?"

Shinji nodded. "Yeah, I said that."

"What was it? What were you looking for? Some kind of weapon or something? I should have done that, but I was too scared."

Shinji looked down at his watch. *Well, it should be about finished. The password cracker's been running for an hour now.*

Shinji stood up, tucked his gun in the front of his waistband, and said, "Yutaka, could you move over?"

Yutaka scooted away from the tree he'd been leaning against. Beyond it, bushes extended their roots along the earth, forming a small thicket.

Shinji walked to the cluster of bushes and reached his hand inside. Carefully, he slid it out, accessories, cables, and all.

Yutaka watched in astonishment.

Shinji had pulled out a car battery (that provided the power), a half-disassembled cell phone, and a laptop computer, all interconnected with red and white cords.

The LCD screen was on, though its display was blank.

Blank. That means . . .

Shinji pursed his lips to let out a barely perceptible whistle and pressed the space bar. The computer awoke from its energy-saving sleep mode, its hard disks whirred back to life, and the grayscale desktop came back on the display.

Shinji's eyes twinkled mischievously as he searched for the last line in the tiny window in the center of the screen. "Shit, that's all? A vowel substitution, *really*? That's so easy, I never would have guessed it."

Finally, Yutaka said in amazement, "Shinji, is this . . ."

Shinji opened and closed his fists, his customary warm-up to prepare his fingers for their flurry on the keys. He gave Yutaka a grin. "It's a PowerBook 150. I never would have thought I'd find a sweet machine like this on some island in the middle of nowhere."

27 STUDENTS REMAIN.

Waiting for her watch to point to ten o'clock, Yoshimi Yahagi (Girls #21) cautiously poked her head out the back door of the house where she hid. The structure was located at the southern edge of the village, far from where Megumi Eto had been killed—though Yoshimi had no idea Megumi had been killed there anyway. She'd only heard the girl's name in the morning announcement.

Far more pressing from that announcement were the forbidden zones. At eleven a.m., the collars of any players remaining in sector H-8, which included the village, would explode. No pleas could convince the computer to wait.

The rear entrance faced a narrow alleyway that ran between the houses. The house on the other side might not have been even a meter away. She renewed her grip on her firearm (a Colt M1911, .45 caliber), putting both hands on it. It felt sturdy and solid. With her right thumb, she pulled back the heavy hammer. She'd only taken a quick glance, but she didn't sense anyone down the alley in either direction.

Cold sweat bubbled up on a round, girlish face that didn't quite suit the bad-girl reputation Yoshimi had earned as part of Mitsuko Souma's group. Only an hour or two ago, from the second-floor window, she'd seen Yumiko Kusaka and Yukiko Kitano calling out from the top of the northern mountain. Then she heard the *brattattat* of the gun. No doubt about it—the killing was on, and not everyone was simply hiding as she was. Some of the others had no trouble killing their classmates. And she couldn't know where they might suddenly appear.

She stepped out and sidled along the wall to her right. When she reached the corner, she peeked out to the south and saw crop fields extending up the gentle slope of the island, dotted with patches of green. She noticed several houses, though far more scattered than the village where she was. Yoshimi decided she needed to reach the mountain. There she would be safe for the time being.

Yoshimi resituated the daypack on her shoulders and glanced all around. Then she sprinted for a small thicket alongside the fields.

She made it there in seconds and pushed her way into the bushes. Holding her pistol in both hands, she looked to the left and then to the right. No one was there.

She hadn't gone that far, but her shoulders heaved as she gasped for breath. *Keep going, keep going.* She was still in H-8. Actually, she might have left the sector already, but it wasn't like a white line had been drawn across the ground, and she wouldn't be able to feel right until she made it good and far away. A blue dot marked each house on the map, but with so many of them clustered in the area around the village, she couldn't be sure which dot denoted which house. And the sector's border cut straight through that cluster.

Yoshimi wanted to cry. She believed that if she hadn't been part of Mitsuko Souma's clique, she would have been able to find the trustworthy girls—those average girls—and moved as a group. But nobody would trust her now. Not after all the bad things she'd done with Mitsuko Souma and Hirono Shimizu—like shoplifting and what was basically extortion. Even if she told the others she didn't want to hurt them, they probably wouldn't believe her. In fact, they might attack her on sight.

During the night, Yoshimi had seen another girl before she'd hid inside that house. As she was running into the village, the other girl ran out from it. She wasn't sure, but she thought it might have been Kayoko Kotohiki (Girls #8). The girl might have initially hidden in the village, then changed her mind and relocated. (That turned out to be the correct decision, since the village became the first forbidden zone.) If she'd wanted to call out to the girl, the timing and distance would have been right. But Yoshimi couldn't bring herself to do it.

So, then, what about Mitsuko Souma and Hirono Shimizu? Sure, her friends were bad, but they were her friends. If she could find the girls, would they trust her? Could she trust them? Maybe not.

Almost utterly overwhelmed by despair, Yoshimi pictured the face of a certain boy. That face had remained in her mind since the game's start. He had told her that he didn't care that she hung out with Mitsuko Souma, he loved her anyway. He kissed her gently on the bed and softly reproved, "Don't do anything *too* bad." He made her believe that she might be able to change.

She had thought he might wait for her outside the school, but when she left, no one was there. The reason was obvious. Mayumi Tendo's and Yoshio Akamatsu's bodies lay at her feet, and anyone who lingered risked meeting the same fate. (Yoshimi wondered where their killer had gone.)

The boy in her thoughts was somewhere on the island. *But where? Or . . . is he already . . .*

Yoshimi felt a sharp pang in her chest. Tears blurred her vision.

She wiped her eyes with the sleeve of her sailor top and proceeded to the outer edge of the thicket. But she had a little farther yet to go.

She tightened her grip on the pistol and looked about for the next patch of cover. To her right stood a group of tall trees with dense undergrowth beneath.

Again she sprinted across the field. Tiny branches scratched her face as she dove into the underbrush. Cautiously, she stood into a crouch and looked around. The thick layers of foliage partially blocked her view, but she didn't see anyone near.

Still ducking, she continued deeper into the copse. *It's all right, it's all right. There's no one here.*

Yoshimi reached the edge of the thicket. Straight ahead, she could now see the greenery of the southern mountain, with trees large and small set behind a dense grove of what looked to be bamboo. She would find plenty of places to hide there. *Okay, I got this. Just one more time. Just once more, and I'll—*

Suddenly, a rustling noise came from behind. Her heart leaped straight up.

Quickly she crouched down. Gripping her Colt M1911, she cautiously turned around. The hair on the back of her neck stood.

Between the trees a mere ten meters away, she caught a flash of black—a school uniform. Her eyes widened in fear. *There! Someone's there!*

Clenching her teeth to quell her fear, Yoshimi ducked her head. Her heart pounded, its pace quickening.

Again she heard the rustling sound.

She was sure that no one had been in the copse. Whoever this was had entered the bushes after her. *Why? Was I seen? Was I followed?*

Her face turned pale.

No, that's not the only possibility. Whoever it is might simply be on the move, like me. If I was seen, then he—or she—would be coming straight for me. I haven't been seen. So . . . so I'll just wait. Wait, and let the other pass by. I can't move. For now, just don't move.

With another rustle, the intruder moved again. With her head low, Yoshimi saw through the crowded leaves the figure flitting from tree to tree. From her position, the person moved from right to left, revealing his profile.

Yes! Good, he's not coming this way—

She was about to let out a sigh of relief when she jolted her head up.

The figure had passed into the trees and out of sight. The rustling sound gradually receded into the distance.

She couldn't have seen wrong. Had this just been a panic-induced hallucination? No, this was no trick of the mind.

Yoshimi bolted up into a standing crouch and moved toward the noise. After a few meters, she stopped again in the shade of the overgrowth and listened. The leaves blocked most of her view, but she caught sight of the school coat.

Her hands moved without thought, pulling in to her chest. If she hadn't been holding the pistol, she would have looked like she was praying.

Which, at that moment, she was. If this incredible coincidence had been an act of some god out there, that's the god to whom she was praying. She had no particular religion, but whichever god it was, she didn't care. She offered her prayer of thanks. *Oh, God, it's really true! I love you, God!*

She stood, and the name tumbled from her lips. "Yoji!"

Yoji Kuramoto (Boys #8) trembled for a moment, then slowly turned around. His face had a vaguely Latin air, and his thick eyelashes moved as his eyes widened and then returned to their normal size. For the briefest instant, his expression seemed to go blank, but Yoshimi was positive that must have been her mind playing tricks on her. A smile blossomed on his face—that familiar smile of the boy who loved her more than anyone else.

"Yoshimi—"

"Yoji!"

With the daypack still over her shoulder, and the M1911 still in her right hand, she ran to him. She felt her face scrunch up, and tears came to her eyes.

In a tiny clearing amid the thicket, he caught her in his arms, his embrace tender yet reassuring.

Without another word, Yoji softly placed his lips on hers. Then he kissed her eyelids and then the tip of her nose. His kisses hadn't changed at all. This may not have been the right time or place, but her body filled with joy.

When their lips parted, he gazed into her eyes and said, "You're all right. I was worried about you."

Still snug in his arms, Yoshimi replied, "Me too. Me too." Tears spilled out the corners of her eyes and traced down her cheeks.

When Yoji left the classroom, he had glanced back at her. On the verge of crying, she watched him go. Then, from the moment she'd left, through the night and this morning, she'd felt so scared. But now, she'd met the person who she thought she'd never live long enough to see again.

As if the surprise had only now caught up with him, Yoji said, "This . . . what were the chances?"

"Yeah, it's incredible, right? I thought—I thought I'd never see you again. Not in this . . . this horrible game."

As Yoshimi cried, Yoji gently ran his fingers through her hair. "It's all right now," he said. "Whatever happens, we'll be together."

His words were comforting, but Yoshimi felt her eyes tear up even more. *The rules say only one will survive, but for now, I can be with the one I love most. We'll stay together until that time limit comes. If anyone attacks, Yoji will protect me. Oh God, please tell me this isn't a dream. Right, God?*

Yoshimi thought back to all that had happened since she met Yoji, when they became classmates in eighth grade. It all really began on a day in the fall of that year, when they chanced upon each other on the street and went to a movie together. On Christmas, they split a strawberry shortcake in a café, and then kissed that night. For New Year's, she dressed up in a long-sleeved kimono for the first temple visit of the year. (The fortune she drew was a "Small Blessing," while Yoji got a "Great Blessing"—which he exchanged with hers.) Then, a night she'd never forget, on Saturday, the eighteenth of January, she spent her first night at Yoji's house.

Yoshimi asked him, "Where have you been?"

Yoji pointed toward the village. "I was in one of those houses. But you know, this collar—at eleven, it was going to explode. So . . ."

His expression was serious, but Yoshimi thought it was all funny. *We were so near. This whole game I've been wondering where he was, and he's been so near all along!*

"What's wrong?" he asked.

"I was there too. I was hiding in one of those houses. We must have been right by each other."

They both grinned. She watched his smiling face, savoring the happiness of being able to share a smile with someone she loved. It may have seemed such a trivial thing, but it wasn't at all. Nothing was more important. And now, she had reclaimed that happiness for herself.

Yoji gently loosened his embrace. He looked down to her right hand, finally noticing it, and Yoshimi realized she was still holding the gun. She gave him an embarrassed smile and laughed. "I totally forgot."

He returned the smile. "That's a fine weapon. Look at what I ended up with."

He showed her what he'd been holding. She hadn't noticed the weapon at all. It was a sheathed *tantō* short sword straight out of an antique store. The cord wrapped around the grip was frayed, and the oval-shaped guard had taken on a patina. Yoji revealed a bit of the blade, spotted with rust. He slid the blade back into its sheath and tucked it under his belt.

"Let me see yours," he said.

Pointing the barrel to the side, Yoshimi offered him the pistol. "Here, just take it. I don't think I'd be very good with it, anyway."

Yoji nodded and took the Colt M1911. He held the grip and checked the safety. He pulled back the slide and exposed the chambered round. The hammer was still cocked.

"Got any ammo for this thing?"

With the magazine already fully loaded, Yoshimi nodded, searched through her daypack, then gave Yoji the cardboard box of ammunition. He took it with one hand, flipped open the lid with his thumb, and looked inside. Then he stuffed the box into the pocket of his uniform.

Then, the next moment, Yoshimi couldn't believe what she was seeing. Completely unable to comprehend the reason for what was happening, she stared at his hands as if watching him perform some baffling magic trick.

Yoji was pointing the Colt M1911 at her.

"Yoji?"

She stood there in shock as he took a few steps back.

"Yoji?" she repeated.

Finally, she perceived that his face was no longer his own. It had contorted. The parts were all the same—those long eyelashes, the large, hooked nose, the wide mouth—but that face, with the twisted mouth and bared teeth, was one Yoshimi had never seen before.

From that contorted mouth, he spat out, "Go. Get the fuck out of here."

For a moment, Yoshimi couldn't understand his words.

Irritated, he continued, "I don't care where. I said go!"

Still stunned, Yoshimi heard her mouth form the word "Why?"

The irritation in his voice grew stronger. "You think I can stand to be with some bitch like you? Get the fuck away from me!"

Something inside her began to crumble, first slowly, then faster. "Why?" Her voice trembled. "Did I . . . did I . . . do something wrong?"

Keeping the gun pointed at her, Yoji spat to the side. "Don't make me laugh. I know you're a worthless bitch. You've been arrested by the cops. Better yet, you've been sleeping with guys old enough to be your dad. Did you think I didn't know? Do you expect me to trust a bitch like you?"

Yoshimi's jaw dropped. She gaped at him.

What he said was . . . true. She had been arrested several times for shoplifting and for blackmailing a high schooler with her friends. And then there was the prostitution. It had happened a long time ago, but she had slept with some middle-aged men Mitsuko Souma had introduced her to. She'd only done it a few times. The money was good, and everyone else was doing it. Besides, at the time, she was fed up with her life, so she didn't hate putting on the unfamiliar makeup, acting like an adult, and being with those men who were generous in their own way. She had assumed Yoji knew all this about her.

And she had put an end to all of that on that autumn day when they started dating. She still hung out with Mitsuko Souma and Hirono Shimizu, and she couldn't suddenly pretend she was a good student, but at the very least, she stopped selling herself, and she did what she could to keep herself out of trouble. And so she believed that Yoji had forgiven her and loved her despite her past.

She believed that the whole time.

A single tear rolled down her cheek. "I—I don't do that kind of thing anymore." Now she cried tears very different from the ones before. "I wanted . . . I wanted to be the woman you deserved."

For a moment, Yoji stared at her, looking as if he'd been struck.

But then that twisted expression returned. "You lie! Stop pretending to cry!"

Yoshimi stared at him with her teary eyes. Again her words came tumbling out. "If that's how . . . if that's how you think, why did you go out with me?"

His answer came immediately. "I thought a slut like you would be an easy lay. Why else? Now go! Get out of here. Fuck!"

Something overcame Yoshimi, and she rushed toward him. Maybe it was because she didn't want to hear him say another word, or maybe it was because she couldn't deal with the reality that he was pointing the gun at her.

"Stop it!" she yelled through her tears. "Please stop it!"

She tried to grab the gun from his hands.

He dodged to the side and shoved her away. Her daypack slid down to her arm, and she fell on her back in the grass.

Then he was on top of her.

"What the hell are you doing!" he yelled. "Shit. You're trying to kill me, aren't you? Fuck! I'll kill you right here."

He pointed the gun at her, and she frantically grasped his wrist with both hands. Then he added his other hand to the weapon, and the pistol inched downward until it was almost to her head. The rushing of her blood pounded in her ears.

Pushing as hard as she could, she yelled, "Yoji! Please! Stop, Yoji!"

Yoji said nothing. His bloodshot eyes glared down at her. His arms came down on her with a steady, mechanical force. Five centimeters left. Four centimeters. Three centimeters. If he fired now, the bullet would graze her hair. Two centimeters, and . . .

The sadness and fear tore her apart. But suddenly, a thought pushed through the fractures.

She understood everything now. She didn't want to believe it, but she knew that the person she had so loved had only been an illusion.

And yet, it was a wonderful illusion. She had believed that with him, she could have started a new life. No matter what he was, Yoji had given her that dream. Without him, she never would have thought it possible.

She thought back to the time they were eating ice cream at the only burger stand in Shiroiwa. She got ice cream on the tip of her nose, and he said, "You're so cute." She thought that, at least, hadn't been a lie.

She had loved him.

Yoshimi relaxed her arms. The gun snapped down to aim at her forehead. His finger was on the trigger.

She gazed up at him, and quietly she said, "Thank you, Yoji. I was happy when I was with you."

His eyes went wide as if he'd finally realized something important, and he froze.

"It's all right," she said. "Shoot me."

She smiled and closed her eyes.

He was still pointing the gun at her, but his arms began to tremble.

She waited for the hot bullet to bore its way into her head. But as long as she waited, the sound of the gunshot never came.

Instead, she heard a scratchy whisper. "Yoshimi . . ."

Slowly, she opened her eyes.

Their eyes met. Through the blur of the thin layer of tears, she saw Yoji's eyes return to the familiar ones of the boy she loved—only now, they were tinged with shame and regret.

Oh!

He understands! Yoji, is this real?

A sudden *thunk* noise sounded satisfying, though slightly disturbing and wet, like someone had stomped their heel against a damp wooden floor.

Almost simultaneously, Yoji's finger pulled the trigger—not that he had meant to. It was only a reflex. The gunshot, like an exploding firecracker, made Yoshimi shriek. But Yoji had already pointed the gun away from her, and the bullet lodged into the grass above her head, sending up a little cloud of dirt.

Yoji's lifeless body toppled over onto her, then was completely still.

As she scrambled out from under him, Yoshimi looked over the shoulder of his black uniform and saw a smiling face. It was her long-time partner in crime, Mitsuko Souma.

Yoshimi didn't understand what was happening. Though she didn't know why, the smile on that sweet, beautiful, angelic face brought on a deep-seated terror.

Mitsuko asked, "Are you all right?" took her hand, and pulled her free from Yoji's body.

There in the tall grass, Yoshimi rose unsteadily to her feet. Then she saw it. Planted deeply in the back of Yoji's head was an extremely sharp sickle. (*A sickle!* As a city girl, atypical for Shiroiwa, Yoshimi had never seen one before.)

Leaving the sickle where it was for now, Mitsuko went for the Colt M1911 in his hand. His muscles had stiffened, so she pried up one stiff finger at a time. Once she had it securely in her grasp, she grinned.

Yoshimi just stood there, looking down at Yoji's body—just an empty shell now—and trembled. She shook, and she shook. She had lost someone so important so easily. She felt like she had when she was a small child (back when she was more innocent), and her favorite glass figurine fell and shattered on the ground—though the scale of her emotion couldn't be compared.

Yoshimi's senses returned, back on earth from somewhere high above the sky. She saw Mitsuko (she had been seeing this whole time, of course, but the visual information hadn't reached her consciousness) put both hands on the sickle in the back of Yoji's head and start to wriggle the weapon free. His head shook along with it.

"No!" Yoshimi screamed and shoved Mitsuko aside. The girl fell back onto the grass, and the hem of her pleated skirt shifted up to her thighs, revealing her well-formed, beautiful legs.

Heedless of Mitsuko, Yoshimi shielded Yoji's body. The sickle remained planted in his skull. Teardrops fell from her eyes. The sickle was telling her, *Shaking me won't bring me back to life. Don't shake me. This thing's stuck in me—can't you see it hurts?*

Giant waves of emotion swept through her. She was drowning in the feeling that the world was coming apart. Her mind came to the reason for all her pain, and with tear-filled eyes, she glared fiercely at Mitsuko. She tried to kill her with her stare. Any awareness of the game, and concerns over who were her friends and who were her enemies, had vanished from her thoughts. If anyone was her enemy, it was Mitsuko Souma, who had stolen from her the one she loved.

"Why did you kill him?"

Yoshimi's words sounded hollow to her own ears. She had nothing left inside—she felt like an empty pit in the shape of a human. Yet still she managed to speak. Humans were capable of such strange things.

"Why? Why did you kill him? You're cruel! You're too cruel! You devil! Why did you have to kill him? Why?"

Mitsuko scrunched her lips in dissatisfaction. "He was about to kill you. I saved your life."

"No! Yoji understood. He understood me! You're the devil. I'll kill you! I'm going to kill you! Yoji understood me."

With a shrug and a shake of her hand, Mitsuko pointed the Colt at her. Yoshimi's eyes widened.

And so Yoshimi heard that dry firecracker pop one more time. She felt as if an entire car had crashed into a single point high on her forehead. That was all there was.

Yoshimi Yahagi fell onto her beloved Yoji Kuramoto and moved no more. The .45 caliber bullet had demolished half of the back side of her head. But her mouth remained intact, open, as if to scream, blood oozing from the corner, soaking a dark patch into Yoji's school coat.

Mitsuko Souma lowered the smoking Colt and shrugged again. She'd thought she could have used the girl for a little while at least, to soak up a bullet or two.

Then she said, "Yeah, I guess he did understand you."

She bent over and brought her mouth next to Yoshimi's ear. The girl's head had been half obliterated, and a gray, gelatinous mixture of blood and brain matter formed a sinister layer of topping on her earlobe.

"It seemed like he'd decided not to kill you. That's why I killed him."

Then she got back to pulling the sickle out of Yoji's skull.

25 STUDENTS REMAIN.

31

The wind carried a faint sound to Shuya and the others. He looked up. Then the sound came again. He listened for a while, but that had been it. The only noise in that deep thicket belonged to the treetops rustling in the breeze above.

Shuya looked over to Kawada, who was sitting by his side. "Was that . . . gunfire?"

"That was gunfire," Kawada said.

Noriko began, "That means another—"

Kawada shook his head. "We don't know that."

The three had been silent for several minutes, but prompted by the gunfire, Kawada opened his mouth to speak. "Okay, listen up, you two. It's good that you trust me, but it's like I said—we need to survive until the end. So there are a few things I want to set straight."

He looked at Shuya. "Are you prepared to be merciless, Nanahara?"

Shuya gulped. "Who to? The government?"

"Them too, of course." Kawada nodded. "But I'm asking if you're ready to kill your classmates—not if but when they attack us."

Shuya lowered his head a little, and when he spoke, his voice sounded feeble. "If it comes to that, I won't have any other choice."

"What if it's a girl?"

Shuya's lips tightened. His eyes went to Kawada and then back down. "I won't have any other choice."

"All right then. Just as long as we're clear."

Kawada nodded and gripped the shotgun resting on his crossed legs. Then he added, "If you're too busy getting all upset every time you kill someone, someone else will come along and kill you."

Shuya debated whether or not to ask Kawada something. He decided it wasn't right to ask, but the question came tumbling out against his will.

"What about you? Were you merciless—one year ago?"

Kawada shrugged. "Yeah. Do you want to hear the details? How many guys I killed? How many girls I killed? All the way until I won?"

Noriko crossed her arms in front of her chest and clutched her elbows.

"No . . . never mind." Shuya shook his head. "Hearing that won't help anything."

They fell silent for a time. Then, uncharacteristically apologetic, Kawada said, "I couldn't help it. Some of them had gone half insane— and some had no problem with killing as many of the others as they could. The ones who were more like my friends died right away, and I wasn't able to team up with anyone. But I couldn't accept letting myself get killed as an option."

He paused, then added, "I also had something I needed to do. And so I couldn't die."

Shuya lifted his head. "What was that?"

"Isn't it obvious?" Kawada smiled a little, but a fierce sparkle flickered across his eyes. "I'm going to tear down this fucked-up country—this country that dropped us into this fucked-up game."

Seeing Kawada's lips twist in anger, Shuya thought, *Oh, him too.* Shuya had also been wanting to strike back against the bastards running the game—the bastards who had no qualms about running this sadistic game of musical chairs, this bullshit game that turned the students against each other. He wanted to smash them straight to the bottom of hell.

And what about those friends Kawada had mentioned, who had died right away. He'd said it in passing, but maybe they were as important to him as Yoshitoki was to Shuya.

Shuya thought about asking Kawada about it but decided against it. Instead, he said, "You told us you did a lot of studying . . . Is this what you studied for?"

Kawada nodded. "It wouldn't have been long before I did something against this country."

"Like what?"

"Beats me." Kawada grimaced and shook his head. "Bringing down a system that's already been built up is easier said than done. But I would have done something. I think I would have. And I still mean to. That's why I'm going to survive this time too."

Shuya looked down, between his upraised knees, at the revolver hanging limply in his hands. Another question flitted into his mind, and he looked back up and asked, "If you know this one, can you clue me in?"

"What is it?"

"What's the point of this game? Is there a point to all this?"

Kawada's eyes widened a little, but then he looked down and let out a chuckle. He must have found the question pretty funny. Then finally, he said, "Of course there isn't."

"But," Noriko interjected, "don't they say it's necessary for national security?"

Keeping the amused smile, Kawada shook his head. "That's crazy talk. Although with how crazy this whole country is, maybe that's what passes for rational."

"Okay, fine." Shuya felt his anger rising. "Then why is it still happening?"

"That's simple. It keeps happening because nobody speaks up."

Seeing that Shuya and Noriko were at a loss for words, Kawada added, "Look, the government is run by nothing but idiots. Not only that, but you can't get into the government unless you're an idiot in the first place. I think whenever this lovely little game was concocted—

probably by some lunatic military theorist—nobody said a word against it. Butting in on the business of the experts only brings trouble. And in this country, it's terribly difficult to discontinue something once it's been established. Stick your nose into something that doesn't concern you, and you'll be out on your ass. Or maybe you'll be sent to a labor camp on charges of deviant ideological tendencies. Even if nearly everyone is against it, nobody says anything. And so nothing changes. There are a lot of screwed-up things in our country, but they're all structurally the same. It's textbook fascism. And . . ."

Kawada looked at both of them. "You two—and the same goes for me—even if we feel that something doesn't make sense, we can't speak out. Your own life is too important, right?"

Shuya couldn't respond to that. The anger that filled him had lost its fire.

Noriko said, "It's shameful."

Shuya glanced at Noriko. Her sad eyes were looking down. *Right,* he thought. *Absolutely right.*

Kawada said, "You know how there used to be a Republic of South Korea?"

Kawada was staring straight ahead, where a single pink azalea flower bloomed between the leaves on a nearby tree.

The sudden change of subject puzzled Shuya, but he answered anyway. "Yeah, I've heard of it. It was the southern half of what's now the DRKP."

Their textbooks had explained the long-running war between the two nations of one people—officially, the People's Republic of South Korea and the Democratic Republic of the Korean Peninsula—on the other side of the sea to the west of their Republic of Greater East Asia. The textbooks read, "Though we regarded the Republic of South Korea as a friendly nation, the sovereign state was forcibly annexed by the DRKP in 1968, following a scheme hatched by the American Empire and a segment of the DRKP's imperialist class." (Naturally, this passage was followed by this: "For the sake of the freedom and democracy of the entire Korean people, our nation must quickly drive out the

DRKP imperialists and annex their territory, and advance one step further toward the ideal of coexistence between all peoples of Greater East Asia.")

"Right." Kawada nodded. "The Republic of South Korea was a lot like our country. Tyranny, utter submission to the Leader, indoctrination, isolationism, information control, and encouraging domestic informants. But after only forty years, the state failed. And yet our Republic of Greater East Asia cruises along with nothing to stop it. Why do you think that is?"

Shuya considered it, though he'd never really put much thought into that kind of subject before. Regarding the defeat of the People's Republic of South Korea, his textbook had said it was "entirely due to the devious schemes of the American Empire and other imperialists." (And in vocabulary clearly beyond the level of a junior high student.)

Okay, so, how then does our Republic of Greater East Asia continue to thrive? Of course the Republic of South Korea shared a land border with the DRKP, but there had to be more to it than that . . .

Shuya shook his head. "I can't figure it."

Kawada looked him in the eye and gave him a small nod, then said, "First of all, it's a matter of keeping balance."

"Balance?"

"Right. The Republic of South Korea was totalitarian, while we— well, for sure in our country, oppressive social control is the rule. But where they were clever was—and who knows if this was intentional or not, but by now the result is clear. The really clever thing was, they left us a few scraps of freedom. Meanwhile, they tell us, 'Of course freedom is a natural human right, but for the common good, we occasionally need to observe limitations.' Sounds legit, right? At least as far as the statement goes."

Shuya and Noriko quietly listened to what Kawada had to say.

Kawada added, "And so our country took off. That was seventy-six years ago now."

Noriko cut in. "Seventy-six years ago?" As she hugged her knees through her pleated skirt, her head tilted quizzically.

"What," Kawada said, "didn't you know?"

Noriko looked at Shuya, who gave her a little nod and then said to Kawada, "I heard a little something about that. The history in our textbooks is one huge lie, and the current Leader isn't the three hundred and twenty-fifth Leader, but rather only the twelfth."

Shinji Mimura had educated him on that. Noriko's not being aware was only natural. They didn't teach that at school, and the adults typically kept their mouths shut. (Besides, some of them might not even know.) When he heard it from Shinji, Shuya was astonished. Not even eighty years ago, before the emergence of the first Leader—and there must have been some grand-scale revolution—their country had been entirely different, in name and structure and all. (Shinji had explained, "Before the revolution, this was a feudal state, and everyone had this tripped-out hairstyle called *chonmage*. There was also a discriminatory caste system, but frankly, it was a lot better than what we have now.")

Shuya glanced at Noriko's surprised face, but his own eyebrows shot up when Kawada added, "Well, that might not be true either."

"What do you mean?" Shuya asked.

Kawada smiled, then offered, "There is no Leader. He's just a fictional character—at least that's what some say."

"What?"

"That can't be," Noriko gasped. "I've seen him on the news. And on New Year's he appears at his palace, in front of a crowd of normal people—"

"It seems that way." Kawada grinned. "But who are those 'normal people'? Have you ever met any of them? What if they were merely actors, just like the Leader himself?"

Shuya considered the possibility. He immediately felt sick, with the nauseous, uneasy feeling that everything was a lie, and truth was nowhere to be found.

Dejectedly, Shuya asked, "Is that really true?"

"I don't know. It's just something I heard. But it's certainly a plausible theory."

"Where the hell did you hear something like that, anyway?" Shuya asked. Then, remembering Shinji, he added, "Did you get it from the Net?"

Kawada smiled again, but only with his mouth. "Unfortunately, I'm no good with computers, but there are ways to find out if you care to look. Anyway, I think it's certainly plausible, because that way, they can avoid making a supreme figure of authority. Then, everyone in the government's inner circle would be equal—with equal freedom. And equal responsibilities. No unfairness. No one to complain. There's just that one ingenious ruse. Because as long as they had that central unifying figure, they wouldn't be forced to inform the common people what was really going on."

Kawada let out a deep breath, then continued, "Anyhow, that's not important. To get back to what I was saying, this country took its first successful step. And its successes built, and built, and built. But when I say it succeeded, I mean as a modern industrial nation. Even with the policy of partial seclusion, we slowly drew into our economy the neutral countries, not aligned with ourselves or the Americans, importing raw materials and exporting manufactured goods. And our products sold well. But that's only to be expected, since the products we make are all high quality. On that point, we rival America. The only sectors where we lag a hair behind are space technology and computers. But that high quality is the result of the individual's obedience to the group, and the coercive directions of the government. But still . . ." He stopped himself, then shook his head. "And once the system begins to succeed, the people are going to begin fearing any change. When it becomes successful enough, and the people enjoy a high quality of life, the idea of completely upending everything might seem preposterous. So what if there are little problems here and there—a few small sacrifices are inevitable."

Kawada looked at Shuya and gave him a sardonic smirk. "Of course one of those 'little problems,' and 'small sacrifices,' is this happy little game. Sure, it's bound to be hard on the participants and their families, but sadly, they're too few. Given time, even most of the families move on. You know that old phrase, 'Those who've gone become more distant with each day.'"

Kawada's winding explanation had come full circle, back to this bullshit game of which the Republic of Greater East Asia was so proud. But now, noticing Shuya's contorted frown, he asked, "What's wrong?"

"I think I'm going to puke," Shuya said. He'd finally begun to understand what Shinji Mimura had meant when he said, "*This is what successful fascism looks like. Is there anything as evil anywhere in the world?*" Shinji must have been long aware of everything Shuya had just now learned.

"Well. How about I give you another one that'll make you sick?" Kawada seemed to be enjoying this. He continued, "I've been thinking that another difference between us and the Republic of South Korea might be ethnic."

"Ethnic?"

Kawada nodded. "Yeah. In other words, I think the system used by our government has been tailor-made to fit its people. Obedience to our superiors. Following blindly. Dependence on others and following the herd. A conservative nature and avoidance of conflict. That hopeless stupidity that enables a person, who, say, snitched on someone else, to convince himself that he did the right thing, provided someone else offered the noble-sounding rationale that it was for the good of the group. And so on, and so on. Have they no pride? Have they no reason? They can't think with their own heads. They just follow, like little *baa-baa*-ing sheep. Just makes me want to puke."

Shuya agreed, and so did his stomach.

But then Noriko cut in. "I think you're wrong."

Shuya and Kawada looked at her. From the way she sat, hunched over, hugging her knees, Shuya thought the fatigue was starting to catch up with her. But she returned their gazes and spoke clearly. "I didn't know any of this. I've heard a lot of things for the first time just now. If everything you're saying is true, and if everyone knew the whole story, they wouldn't stay silent. Things must be the way they are because everyone is kept in the dark. I don't want to believe that we're all fundamentally bad people as you say. I'm not saying we're an especially noble people, but I know we're just as capable of rational thought as anyone else on the planet."

As he listened to Noriko, Kawada smiled. It was a deeply tender smile. Then he said, "I like the way you talk, Noriko."

Meanwhile, Shuya regarded her anew. She hadn't stood out that much in class, and he'd always figured her as the kind of girl who rarely expressed her opinions as openly as she had done just now. As strange as it was, he felt like he was seeing more and more of a different side of her since the game began. Maybe he had just been too foolish to see it before. And maybe Yoshitoki had seen that side of her all along.

Either way, hers was a far more admirable view than the one that made him "want to puke." But more than that, he thought she was right. No matter what, this was their country, where they were born, and where they grew up. (Though given the circumstances, he couldn't be sure how much more growing up was left for them.) Maybe someday the American Empire, or America, or whatever it was called, would liberate them, but the future was up to themselves. They couldn't rely on others—and ultimately, perhaps they had no one on whom they could rely.

Shuya returned his gaze to Kawada and asked, "Hey, Kawada, do you think we can really change this country?"

But to his disappointment, Kawada simply shook his head. Shuya had expected a more encouraging response from the guy who swore he'd "tear down this fucked-up country."

Sounding a little foolish, Shuya said, "But didn't you just say you'd tear down this country?"

Kawada took out a cigarette, his first in a while, then lit it and crossed his arms. "Shall I tell you what I think?"

Shuya nodded.

Kawada folded his arms, took the cigarette from his lips, and exhaled a puff of smoke. "I think that history moves in waves."

Not quite understanding, Shuya was about to ask what he meant. But before he could, Kawada continued, "Come a certain time, and come a certain set of circumstances, this country will change, whether we do anything or not. I don't know if it'll be a war or a revolution. And I don't know when that time will come. Maybe it never will."

Kawada took another drag and exhaled it. "But in any case, right now, it's impossible, as far as I can tell. Like I just said, this country has gone insane, but it's also well designed. It's extremely well designed."

Kawada pointed at the other two with his cigarette. "Okay, here we have a nation that's rotting. If you can't stand the smell, you should take the wisest action—to throw it away and go someplace else. There has to be some way to flee the country. Do that, and you'll be able to live free from the stench. You might get homesick every now and then, but you'll go every day, free from hardship. But that's not for me."

Shuya rubbed his hands on his thighs. This was what he'd been waiting for—for Kawada to echo his thoughts, that this is his country, so he wanted to do what he could. Hadn't Bob Marley sung about this?

"Why not?" Shuya asked.

But Kawada's answer came from a somewhat different place.

"I want satisfaction. I want revenge. Even if the only result is getting to feel self-satisfied, I want to strike a blow against this country. That's all. As for whether that'll bring about any reform, well, I have major doubts."

Shuya took in a little breath, then said, "The way you talk, it sounds hopeless."

"It is hopeless," Kawada said.

25 STUDENTS REMAIN.

When he heard the two distant gunshots, Yutaka cowered. Shinji
interrupted his keystrokes.

"That's—" Yutaka said.

Shinji nodded. "More gunfire."

Then Shinji quickly resumed his work. He might have been a little
brusque, but he couldn't afford to be concerned with others.

Yutaka looked down at Shinji's fingers, while his own towel-
bandaged hands held the Beretta his friend gave to him to look after.

"Hey, Shinji," Yutaka said impatiently, "what are you doing with
that computer, anyway? Can't you tell me yet?"

After rebooting the communications software and dialing up
through his cell phone, Shinji had started banging away at the keyboard, occasionally exclaiming, "Yes! Yes! Yes!" or "Oh, shit, oh,
right," or "Okay!" But he hadn't given Yutaka any explanation at all.

"Hold on. Almost . . . done."

Shinji was typing again. Inside a window near the center of the
monochrome display, English words streamed by, interspersed with
special characters like "%" and "#" and so on. Shinji typed in response.

"All right," Shinji said.

Having initiated the download, Shinji's hands rested. He had performed the basic operations in Unix (natch), but since this *was* a Mac after all, he'd set up a graphical download progress meter that popped up in a separate window. Shinji stretched his arms over his head. All that remained was to wait for the download to finish—though once it did, he still had to overwrite the log entry to erase his tracks. Then he'd use the data to come up with a plan. He could simply over-write the data, or possibly put together his own program to outwit his opponents. The latter would take some doing, but he figured half a day would suffice.

Yutaka repeated, "Shinji, tell me what's going on."

With a grin, Shinji backed away from the laptop and leaned against his old tree. He still felt a little keyed up, so he took a deep breath to calm himself. His excitement was only natural; after all, when he'd revealed the PowerBook 150 to Yutaka, he hadn't yet known for sure, but now he did. Victory was as good as his.

Slowly, he opened his mouth to speak. "The thing is, I've been thinking about how to escape from here."

Yutaka nodded.

"But this, you see," Shinji said, pointing to his neck. He couldn't see the collar there, but it was probably identical to the silver band around Yutaka's neck. "I wanted to get these off, no matter what. Thanks to them, that bastard, Sakamochi, knows where we are. Right now, he knows we're here together. And if we try to escape, these will make it easy for them to capture us—or, they could send a signal to the explosives inside and kill us in an instant. I wanted to get them off."

He opened his hands, then shrugged. "But I gave up. As long as I don't know how they're built on the inside, I can't mess with them. Sakamochi said they would explode if we took them apart, and I doubt he was bluffing. The detonating cord is probably lining the inside of the outer casing. If the wire gets cut, the explosives will go off. Why cross a collapsing bridge? I thought about sliding a metal plate between the collar and the neck, but to fit, the metal would probably be too thin to stop the explosion."

Yutaka nodded again.

"So then I had an idea. What about getting that computer inside the school, the one that supervises our capture and operates the detonation signal, to work *for* us? Do you get what I'm saying?"

Shinji had learned the basics of how to use a computer from his uncle. But when his mentor died, leaving him his computer, Shinji worked at mastering it with the same level of passion he applied to the basketball court. From time to time, he infiltrated the restricted international line to access the real Internet (what this country called the "Internet" was in reality nothing more than a closed network—the laughably named "Greater East Asia Net"), where he acquired even more advanced techniques along with the latest news from around the world. This was of course illegal, and though the punishment didn't go as far as execution, a child Shinji's age would get two years in a juvenile detention center for ideological criminals.

For that reason, Shinji honed his skills at avoiding detection, and he never told anyone what he was doing—though he did show Yutaka some pictures he'd downloaded (dirty pictures, mostly, but what else would you expect?). By any measure, Shinji had acquired considerable hacking skills.

"So I went looking for a computer," Shinji said. "I already had my cell phone, you know. I guess we were allowed to keep all of our stuff in this stupid game, so it's too bad I didn't bring along my own laptop. Anyway, I found this baby, so it worked out. I still needed power, so I took that battery from a car. I had to mess with the voltage, but that was no big deal."

As Shinji explained, Yutaka began nodding. He seemed to be finally coming to grasp, if vaguely, what those objects on the ground in front of him were up to. But then, as if a thought suddenly came to him, he interrupted. "But, but . . . didn't Sakamochi say that we couldn't use the phones? So then do *cell* phones work?"

Shinji shook his head. "No. That's a no go. I tried a number—the weather information—and Sakamochi picked up. 'Fair weather at the Shiroiwa Junior High Program Headquarters,' he said. I hung up right away, 'cause I was so pissed that I felt sick. Anyway, that means that they're controlling the nearest cell tower. I don't think a phone with *any* provider would work."

"So—"

Shinji held up a finger, cutting him off. "Think about it. They must have some way to reach the outside. And their computers must be connected to other government computers—for their own security, among other reasons. So how do they communicate with the outside world? It's simple. The mobile networks selectively allow only the calls originating from military numbers."

"So we can't—"

Shinji cut him off again, then grinned. "But—there's always a 'but.' I thought that even with those measures, wouldn't they have set it up so that someone from the phone company, at the very least, could operate the system in case something went wrong?"

Shinji reached for the cell phone on the ground and said, "I never told you this, but my phone's a little special. Its ROM has two sets of phone numbers and network IDs. You can't tell by looking at it, but I can switch between them by turning this screw ninety degrees. As for that second number, I programmed it when I was playing around with making phone calls for free." He let go of the phone. "It's the number used by phone company technicians to test phone lines."

"So . . . that means . . ."

Shinji winked. "Exactly. The rest is simple. Well, connecting the landline modem to the cell phone was a little tricky. I don't exactly have the proper tools out here. But I managed it. And I reached the network. Then I accessed my home computer. Hacking isn't just like regular network access—you need special tools, like password-cracking software, so I needed to download that stuff before I could do anything else. Then my first target was the prefectural government's site. The national systems like Central Processing must be well guarded, but I figured down at the prefectural level security would be softer. I was right. Then I figured that no matter how directly the Program is managed by the central government, they would have to be in some level of contact with the local prefecture. I was right there too. I saw unfamiliar addresses in the communications log files. Reading through the mailbox, I found an e-mail to the superintendent notifying him that the game had begun. So I broke into the sender's site next—the provisional server in that school. The next part was a bit of a pain in the ass, but I looked around as best I could and found a backup of a work file someone had screwed up and left behind. I nabbed it. I'll spare you the details, but I found a piece of encrypted text that looked like it might be important. The Mac's been working at breaking it for me since before I met up with you. And here's what it found . . ."

Shinji reached for the PowerBook. Leaving the connection status window open, he summoned a text file written in a gigantic 24-point font and showed Yutaka the display. Yutaka leaned in to see.

KINPATI-SAKAMOCHO

"Sakamocho . . . ?" Yutaka asked.

"Yeah. I think it's Spanish or something. Just a stupid little vowel change to make it harder to guess. But that's the root password. Now I can do whatever I want. That's what I've been up to now. I've just scraped every bit of data from inside the school computers. After I poke through the files, I'll be able to log back into those computers and disable these collars locked around our necks. They think they're all safe inside the forbidden zone, where we can't come near. We can attack them by surprise. We'll have a chance against them. Then, once we've taken over the school, we should be able to help the others. And if not, we'll fake our deaths, and the two of us can wave this island goodbye."

Shinji paused to catch his breath, then grinned again. "What do you think?"

Yutaka wore an expression of astonishment. "Incredible."

Pleased by his friend's reaction, Shinji smiled. *Thanks, Yutaka. Whatever else is happening, it's always nice to have my skills appreciated.*

"Shinji," Yutaka said, still looking astonished.

Shinji raised his eyebrows. "What's up? Do you have a question?"

"No." Yutaka shook his head. "I was just—I was wondering . . ."

"What?"

Yutaka dropped his eyes to glance at the Beretta in his hand, then looked back up. "Well . . . why are you friends with a guy like me?"

Shinji didn't understand what Yutaka was getting at. His mouth hung open, then he said, "What are you talking about?"

Yutaka looked down again. "It's—it's just . . . you're really incredible. I get how you could be friends with someone like Shuya. He's just about as good at sports as you are, and he's awesome at the guitar. But . . . but I'm nothing. So I was wondering why you'd be friends with someone like me."

Shinji watched Yutaka's downturned face. Then slowly and softly, he said, "Don't talk nonsense like that, Yutaka."

Yutaka looked up.

Shinji continued, "I am who I am, yeah? And you're who you are. Even if I'm pretty good at basketball, or pretty good at computers, or pretty popular with girls, those kinds of things don't determine a person's worth. You have the ability to make people laugh, and you'd never hurt anyone. And when you get serious, you can be far more serious than me—like with girls, for one thing. And I'm not jerking you around with some garbage about how everyone has some good side to offer. I'm telling you there's a lot about you I like."

Shinji shrugged, then offered a grin. "I like you. We've always been together. You're an important friend. Just so we're clear—my best friend."

He could see the tears coming back to Yutaka's eyes. Then Yutaka said, "Shit," like he had when he was tearing up just before. "Thanks, Shinji. Thanks."

The boy wiped his tears and laughed, then said, "But if you stick around a crybaby like me, you'll end up drowning before you can escape."

Shinji was forming a grin when—

Beep.

Shinji frowned with his eyebrows and hurriedly sat up. That was the Macintosh's default alert sound.

Shinji knelt in front of the PowerBook and peered at the screen.

His eyes went wide. The message on the screen said that the line had been disconnected, and the download interrupted.

"Why?" Shinji groaned. Frantically, he typed on the keyboard. But he couldn't repair the connection. He closed the Unix communication software and tried a different program to dial the modem.

This time, the message read NO CONNECTION. No matter how many times he tried, the result remained the same. The connection between the modem and the cell phone seemed fine. To test it, he disabled the link and dialed directly with the phone's touch pad. He tried the weather report. He put the phone to his ear.

The phone was silent. *What, so is the phone—no, the battery still has plenty of charge . . .*

Impossible. With the phone still in his hand, he stared blankly at the PowerBook's screen, which was now black on standby. *They couldn't have noticed my hack. They* can't—*that's why it's called hacking.* Shinji was more than skilled enough.

"Shinji, what happened? Shinji?"

Yutaka's voice came over his shoulder, but Shinji couldn't respond.

25 STUDENTS REMAIN.

33

When Hiroki Sugimura (Boys #11) saw the star-shaped blip appear at the edge of the handheld device's LCD screen, his eyes widened. This mark matched another that had been at the center of the display since he'd first held the gadget.

He was inside the village on the island's eastern shore. The area would soon become one of the forbidden zones, so he moved quickly, though extremely cautiously, between the houses. Meanwhile, he kept a close eye on the device, which looked like one of those PDAs often used by salarymen. And now, finally, the display had changed. This was the first such response since booting it up sometime past six in the morning, when he'd finished flipping through the instruction manual included with it inside his daypack. He'd prioritized searching the impending forbidden zones, as announced by Sakamochi, but the device had remained silent as he dashed from sector J-2 on the southern shore to sector F-1 on the western shore, to here, sector H-8.

The device couldn't really be called a weapon, as such. But right now, depending on how he used it, it could be far more effective than even a gun—though he wasn't sure if he was currently using it effectively or not.

Hiroki made sure he had a good grip on the long stick in his other hand and stepped away from the clapboard wall at his back. (The weapon was the handle from a broom he'd found in a shack off the north side of the residential area. If he'd wanted some kind of blade, he could have had his pick, but having studied kempo since he was in elementary school, he knew how to wield a staff, so he thought this would be both easier to use and more useful.) He spurred his large, one-hundred-eighty-centimeter-tall body to speed, and soon he had pinned himself against the wall of the house diagonally adjacent. The star icon at the side of the screen moved closer to its pair in the center.

He thought back to what the manual had said about how the display worked, then he looked over his shoulder. *It's inside a house. This house.*

The house had a small yard with a vegetable garden where tomato stalks grew waist high, and vines of sweet potatoes or some such covered the ground alongside onions and the multicolored blooms of pansies and chrysanthemums. A children's tricycle sat in front of the garden, its chrome handlebars gleaming in the near-noon sunlight.

The storm doors on the veranda were closed. Worried that opening them might make a loud noise, Hiroki went around the right side of the house.

There was a window—a broken one. No doubt remained. Someone had gone inside. And if the instruction manual was worth the paper it was printed on, that person was still there.

With the forbidden zone deadline approaching, he could reasonably assume that anyone alive would have left the sector by now. The odds were strong that only a corpse awaited him. But he had to know for sure.

Hiroki stuck his head through the broken window and looked inside. The room appeared to be a living room with tatami-mat floors.

He cautiously slid the window open. To his relief, it made no sound. Keeping the stick in one hand, he grabbed the window frame with his other and, in one catlike motion, climbed inside.

The room had a decorative alcove, and in the center of the room sat a low table. A large-screen TV was situated in the corner next to the window where Hiroki had entered. Taking care to silence his footsteps, he slipped out of the room.

As he entered the hallway, he smelled something mixed in with the air, as if he'd put his nose up to a rusted scrap of iron.

Hurrying now, he moved down the hall. The smell grew stronger.

It was coming from the kitchen. Hiroki stood at the side of the doorway and peeked inside.

On the floor behind the kitchen table, he saw a pair of white sneakers and socks and, above them, legs, nearly up to the calves.

Hiroki's eyes widened and he ran to the other side of the table.

A girl in a sailor fuku was lying facedown. Her face was turned away from him. She had a petite body, with shoulder-length hair, and blood had formed a pool across the wooden boards of the floor with her face at its center. It was an incredible amount, and its surface had already started to coagulate and turn black.

She was dead all right. But . . .

That petite body. That shoulder-length hair.

She could have been one of the two girls he was searching for. He couldn't say which of the two was more important to him, but this could have been one of the two. *Think. Did she wear sneakers like these?*

Hiroki set aside his stick and daypack and slowly knelt beside the body. He reached a trembling hand for her shoulder. After a moment of hesitation, he clenched his teeth and flipped over the corpse, and revealed fresh, red, and still liquid blood underneath. The smell was intense now.

The body was gruesome. Above her collar (which was what had led him here), her slender throat had been slit open. The blood had long since drained out, and for a second, the open, hollow gash seemed an infant's toothless mouth. The blood had left a downward trail, staining the collar's silver surface before continuing down toward her chest. Blood stuck to her mouth, and the tip of her nose, and her left cheek, where they had been submerged in the pool of blood after she fell. Around the edges of her gray, vacant eyes, drops of now-hardened blood had formed in the tips of her eyelashes.

She was Megumi Eto (Girls #3).

She wasn't who he'd feared she might be.

Though deeply shaken by the horrific sight, he felt relieved. He closed his eyes and let out a breath. Then, feeling guilty over his relief, he gently picked up Megumi's body and moved her out of the pool of blood and rested her on her back some distance away. Rigor mortis had begun to set in, and he felt a little like he was posing a doll, but when he was done, he softly closed her eyelids. He thought for a moment, then tried to fold her arms over her chest, but her body was too stiff now, and he had to give up.

Reclaiming his stick and his daypack, Hiroki stood back up. He gazed down at Megumi for a time, then turned and hurried back to the living room. It was almost eleven a.m.

25 STUDENTS REMAIN.

34

Time quietly passed. Beside Shuya, Kawada continued to smoke without a word, and Noriko too remained silent. Now and then birds exchanged their calls through the thicket. Overhead, leaves swayed in the breeze and cast their mesh of sweeping, pendular patterns of light over the three students. If Shuya listened hard enough, he could hear the sound of waves from the sea. He had grown comfortable in this space in the grove and its convincing illusion of tranquility.

The hope of escape, from his conversation with Kawada, doubt-lessly provided this feeling. And the plan called for them to do nothing but wait. Despite Noriko's injuries, they were safe as long as they kept up their guard. After all, they were three with two guns.

But Shuya couldn't stop thinking about the distant gunshots that had come an hour before.

Has someone else died? If so, it could have been Shinji Mimura or Hiroki Sugimura, though Shuya hated to admit it. Even if it hadn't been one of his friends, it could have been another of his innocent classmates. He and Noriko might be saved thanks to Kawada, but everyone else could be terrified in this moment, and dead in the next.

As Shuya thought this, he couldn't help but feel distressed. Of course, he hadn't forgotten what Kawada had said—remaining still was the best strategy. Shuya knew Kawada was correct. And with Noriko's injury, if they went on the move, they'd make for prime targets. Again he knew Kawada was correct.

But was remaining there, just the three of them in peace and safety, really the right thing to do? Yumiko Kusaka and Yukiko Kitano decided to have faith in the others, even when they had no expectation of escape. His group, on the other hand, had a means of escape—at least if Kawada was to be believed. So shouldn't they at least take a chance?

Certainly one person had already killed—*willfully* killed. Shuya had witnessed Yumiko's and Yukiko's execution. And other such murderers might be among his classmates. Possibly like the ones he'd encountered—Yoshio Akamatsu, Tatsumichi Oki, and Kyoichi Motobuchi. He could never expect someone like that to join his group. Or a person like that might act friendly, only to kill them when the right moment came.

At the very least, shouldn't they do *something* to find the ones they could trust?

But even if they did, knowing exactly who they could trust was impossible. If they tried to save everyone they could, one of their would-be enemies might slip into their group. That would mean certain death—and not just for himself, but for Noriko and Kawada as well.

In the end, all Shuya could do was sigh. His mind was chasing itself. No matter how many times he thought it through, the conclusion was the same. He couldn't do anything. The best he could hope for was to stumble across Shinji Mimura or Hiroki Sugimura by chance. And what were the odds of that?

"Hey," Kawada said as he lit up another cigarette. Shuya looked over to him.

"Don't think about it so much," Kawada said. "Thinking's no use. Just concentrate on yourself and Noriko."

Shuya raised his eyebrows. "What are you, a mind reader?"

"Sometimes. Especially when the weather's nice like today." Kawada took a drag from the cigarette. Then, as a thought suddenly came to him, he looked at Shuya and said, "Was that true?"

"What?"

"What Sakamochi said—that you have 'ideological problems.'"

"Oh." Shuya dropped his eyes, then nodded. "That."

"What did you do?"

Kawada's eyes took on a hint of mischief, and Shuya returned the look.

He could think of two possibilities as to what Sakamochi had meant. The first was that when he graduated to junior high, he joined the music club and the baseball team, but was turned off by the baseball team's underlying militaristic discipline and obsession with winning. (This was no surprise, as baseball was the Republic's national pastime, with performances in international tournaments putting the country's dignity on the line. Unfortunately, the sport was also popular in the hated American Empire, and when the Republic's Olympic team lost to the imperialists in the finals, the league's managers would have to prepare themselves to commit *harakiri*.)

Their coach, Mr. Minato, had repeatedly harassed the kids who joined because they loved baseball but weren't any good at it. And when Shuya announced he was quitting two weeks later, he lost his temper, and slipped and cursed out Mr. Minato and the Republic National Baseball League.

And so this former golden rookie of Shiroiwa Junior High embarked on his path to becoming (according to himself) a rising rock star. This left a giant black mark on his school record. But Kawada might have been referring to a certain something else . . .

"Nothing," Shuya said, shaking his head. "He was probably just talking about how I like rock. He must have had a problem with me being in the music club."

Kawada chuckled and gave him a knowing nod. "That's right, you play guitar. That's what got you into rock?"

"No, I listened to rock, which got me into the guitar. When I was in the orphanage . . ."

Shuya recalled the handyman, in his forties, who had been employed at the House of Mercy and Love until three years back. He was upbeat, with thinning hair that turned up at the back of his neck (he'd called it a ducktail). Now, he was in a forced labor camp up in South Karafuto. None of the children, not even Shuya and Yoshitoki, knew why. When he said goodbye to them, he didn't explain. He only said, "I'll come back, Shuya, Yoshitoki. I'll just be swinging my pickaxe, singing 'Jailhouse Rock' for a little while first." He gave his old, self-winding watch to Yoshitoki, and his Gibson electric guitar to Shuya—Shuya's first guitar. Shuya wondered if the man was still doing all right. He'd heard that people sent to the forced labor camps often died from overwork and undernourishment.

Shuya explained, "Someone gave me a tape. He also gave me his electric guitar."

"Hmm." Kawada nodded. "Do you have a favorite? Dylan? Lennon? Or maybe Lou Reed?"

Shuya stared at him, somewhat surprised. "You know a lot."

Getting hold of actual rock music in the Republic of Greater East Asia wasn't easy. An organization called the Popular Music Judgment Society strictly monitored foreign music. Most anything even resembling rock and roll never made it through customs and was treated like an illegal drug. (He'd even seen a poster in the town hall with a staged photo of a long-haired, sleazy-looking rock-and-roller plastered over with that diagonal slash from a no parking sign and the text STOP THE ROCK. Nice one, guys.) Supposedly, the Peach Government didn't much care for the rousing beat, but Shuya thought it was the lyrics more than anything. The aforementioned Bob Marley was one example, but a classic example would be the chorus of Lennon's "Imagine," about dreamers. How could this nation not consider lyrics like that a threat?

In the record stores, nearly all the albums for sale were of the vapid, domestically produced pop idol sort. The most extreme imported music Shuya had ever seen was Frank Sinatra—that was the extent of it. (Well, maybe this country could stand to give "My Way" a listen.)

For a while, Shuya had thought the ducktailed handyman had been sent to the labor camp because of this, and he regarded the tapes and guitar the man had left behind as objects to be feared. But it seemed that he had been wrong. When he moved up to junior high and entered the music club, a fair number of the others also liked rock music and had electric guitars. (Kazumi Shintani was a huge rock fan, of course.) Through his new connections, Shuya was able to obtain dubs of *The Times They Are-a-Changin'* and *Stand!*

But this all remained within only a trusted circle of friends. If all the students in Shiroiwa Junior High were asked if they had ever listened to rock music, more than nine in ten would likely say they hadn't. (Actually, every one of them would say they hadn't, since even those who *had* heard rock music would obviously never admit it.) With Kawada's previous displays of his extensive knowledge, Shuya wouldn't have been surprised if he'd had some mere passing familiarity with rock music. But Dylan and Lennon were extremely serious stuff.

"Don't look so shocked," Kawada said. "I'm a city boy from Kobe. I'm no Kagawa hick. I'm going to know something about rock."

Shuya showed him a sneer and said, "You just had to go there." His gloominess had lifted just a little. "I like Springsteen. Van Morrison's not bad either."

Without skipping a beat, Kawada said, " 'Born to Run' is a good one. As for Morrison, I like 'Whenever God Shines His Light.' "

Shuya's eyes widened again, and he felt himself grinning. "You know a lot!"

Kawada smiled back. "I told you. I'm a city boy."

Shuya noticed that Noriko had been keeping quiet. Worried that she might be feeling excluded, he asked her, "Didn't you say you've never heard rock music?"

Noriko gave him a small smile and shook her head. "I'm not that familiar with it. What's it sound like?"

Shuya grinned. "The lyrics are wonderful. I'm not very good at describing it, but it's a kind of music where people really express their troubles. Sometimes it's about love, of course, but other times they sing about politics, or society, or the way we live our lives, or even life itself. They have the words, and use the melody and beat to express them. Take Springsteen's 'Born to Run' . . ."

Shuya knew the song's ending by heart.

Then he added, "It goes like this," and sang the last line softly.

He looked at Noriko and said, "We'll listen to it together some time."

Her eyes went a little wide and she nodded. Another time, and she might have been beaming at him, but all she could offer was a frail smile. Shuya was too exhausted himself to notice something was wrong.

He told Kawada, "If everyone listened to more rock and roll, we'd be better off. This country would never last."

He thought back to what Noriko had said earlier, that the people didn't stand up to the government because nobody knew anything. He figured that all those important things that were kept from the people were inside rock music, and that was precisely why the government banned it.

Kawada's Wild Seven cigarette had burned down to the stub, and he leisurely rubbed it into the dirt. Then he lit a fresh one and said, "Hey, Shuya."

"What?"

He let out a slow puff of smoke and said, "Do you really think rock has that kind of power—power enough to be feared by the government?"

Shuya nodded deeply. "It does."

Kawada gazed into the boy's face, then looked away and shook his head. "I'm not so sure. I get the feeling it's just a way for us to vent our frustrations. Sure, it's illegal or whatever, but anyone who wants to listen to rock can find a way. It's an outlet. This country's crafty like that. Who knows, they might start to encourage it one of these days—as a tool, you see."

Shuya felt stunned, like he'd been slapped in the face. Rock was Shuya's religion. Music was his Bible, and Springsteen and Van Morrison were the apostles. Granted, he had gotten used to being shocked thanks to the indiscriminate killings of his classmates, so this was a comparatively minor blow.

Deflated, Shuya slowly said, "You think?"

Kawada nodded several times. "Yeah. But what bothers me is that rock isn't something to be banned or encouraged. It's not that kind of thing. People who want to listen to rock will listen to rock when they feel like listening to rock. Right?"

Shuya pondered this for a while, then said, "I hadn't thought of it that way. But I can see where you're coming from." Then he added, "You're something, Kawada. You're really perceptive."

Kawada shrugged.

They fell silent for a while.

Then Shuya said, "But . . ."

Kawada, who was unwrapping a new pack of cigarettes, looked at him.

Shuya continued, "I do think rock has power, after all—a positive force."

That was what Noriko had said about him.

Kawada grinned. He put a cigarette in the corner of his mouth and lit it, then said, "To tell you the truth, Nanahara, I think so too."

Shuya returned his grin.

"It's ironic," Kawada said. "We're in that exact situation."

"What's that?" Shuya asked.

"All we can do now is run. *We were born to.*"

25 STUDENTS REMAIN.

Kaori Minami (Girls #20) lifted herself to a crouch when she heard the faint rustling noise. She was slightly to the east of the island's center (sector F-8 on the map), within the mixed woodland near the base of the northern mountain.

She adjusted her grip on her pistol, a SIG-Sauer P230 .380 ACP. Despite its diminutive size, it felt large in Kaori's hands.

Without knowing it, Kaori gnawed at her lip. Many times she had heard similar sounds since hiding here at the start of the game. Every time, after realizing the noise had been only a trick of the wind or from some small animal (maybe even a stray cat?), she had been able to calm herself down. But she hadn't gotten used to it. The many scabbed-over wounds on her lip, from where she bit it, were joined by a fresh cut. This time . . . it might be an enemy. *An enemy.* Her classmates were coming to get her. The image of Mayumi Tendo's and Yoshio Akamatsu's bodies, seen at the moment she left the school, remained vivid in her mind.

And when she stepped out those doors, she heard a voice call to her from the woods ahead. She thought it sounded like Yukie Utsumi, the class leader. Kaori spied other shadowy figures beside Yukie in the darkness of the undergrowth. She thought she heard Yukie say, in a hushed yet sharp whisper, "Kaori! Come join us. We're all girls. You'll be safe with us!"

But joining them was out of the question. In these circumstances, no one could possibly trust anyone else. Once she was with them, she'd never know when they might catch her off guard. Ignoring Yukie's appeals to stop her, she turned and ran in another direction. And that brought her here. But now, this time, was it an enemy? Was that the sound?

She gripped her pistol tightly in both hands and waited. But the sound stopped.

She waited a little longer. Nothing.

Kaori let out a sigh of relief and lowered herself back into the undergrowth. A crooked leaf brushed against her cheek, and annoyed, she shifted her position. With the palm of her hand, she rubbed at the spot where the leaf had touched her. Pimples were bad enough; the last thing she needed was some rash making her face all puffy. Even if she was going to die anyway, she didn't need that.

Her thoughts sent a chill down her spine. *Am I going to die? Me? Die?*

The realization set her heart beating faster. It was almost enough to give her a heart attack.

Am I going to die? Am I going to die? She heard the words in the back of her head like a ringing in her ears or some second-rate CD player unable to read past the scratches on the disc, skipping over and over. *Am I going to die?*

Almost frantically, Kaori reached into the top of her sailor uniform and clutched at the brass locket she wore around her neck. She pulled it out and opened it, and the cheerful face with the long hair smiled out at her.

As she stared at the picture in the locket, her heart rate finally began to settle down, gradually returning to its previous pace.

The photo was of Junya Kenzaki, the most popular member of the boy band Flipside. The locket was only given to members of their fan club, and Kaori was proud to know she was the only girl in

Shiroiwa to have one. (Of course, most girls these days would only shake their heads at it. If nothing else, lockets were passé. But Kaori didn't think so.)

Oh, Junya. I'll be fine, won't I? You'll protect me.

His picture seemed to be telling her, "*You'll be fine.*" ("*Of course you'll be fine. Now, how about I sing your favorite song, 'Galactic Magnum'?*")

Kaori's breathing had steadied, and she asked the photo, *Hey, Junya. Do you think I should have joined Yukie? Would there have been a way out for me? No, of course not.*

Suddenly, she was crying.

Why was this happening? She wanted to see her mom. She wanted to see her dad and her sister and her kind grandma and grandpa. She wanted to take a bath and to rub acne cream on her face, and to sit on that comfy sofa in the living room and drink hot cocoa while she watched her VHS of Flipside's TV special. (Even though she'd already seen it many, many times.)

"Junya," she said, "protect me. Please. I—I feel like I'm going crazy."

Hearing herself say that aloud, Kaori thought she really *was* going insane. Freaked out, she felt nausea rising in her stomach. She cried even harder.

A rustling sound came from behind, and she jumped. This noise was far louder than before.

Her eyes still clouded with tears, she quickly turned.

A boy in a school uniform was peering at her through the bushes. It was Hiroki Sugimura (Boys #11). *He snuck up behind me—without me noticing!*

Overcome by terror, she raised her gun without thought and squeezed the trigger. Letting out a pop, the weapon kicked against her wrists. The brass shell spun through the air, glittering in the sunlight that filtered through the leaves.

Hiroki had already disappeared deep into the foliage. The rustling continued, then abruptly disappeared.

Kaori trembled as she held her pistol at the ready. Then she snatched up her belongings and ran into the brush in the opposite direction. As she ran, her mind formed disoriented thoughts. *Hiroki Sugimura was trying to kill me. I know he was. If not, why would he have snuck up behind me without a saying a word? He must not have had a gun. And when he saw that I did, he panicked and fled. If I hadn't noticed him—and if I hadn't fired so quickly—he would have stuck a knife or something right into my chest—a knife! I have to stay on my toes. I have to shoot the moment I see someone. If I show any mercy, I'll be killed. Killed! Dead!*

I've had enough of this. I want to go home. Bath. Acne cream. Cocoa! Videotape. Flipside. Junya. No mercy. Shoot. Shoot! Cocoa. Junya. Acne! Cream! No mercy. Junya.

Tears streamed from her eyes. The locket remained open, flopping against the chest of her sailor fuku, Junya Kenzaki's bright face swinging wildly up and down and left and right.

No mercy. Junya. I'll be killed! Shoot. Mother. Sister! Father. Shoot! Shoot! The new album debut!

Kaori was losing her mind.

25 STUDENTS REMAIN.

"... And that's all the students who have died," Sakamochi's cheerful voice was saying for the noon announcement.

The new additions on the waiting list for their funerals were Tatsumichi Oki, Kyoichi Motobuchi, and of course, Yukiko Kitano and Yumiko Kusaka. Yoji Kuramoto and Yoshimi Yahagi had also died.

"I'll now report the forbidden zones beginning this afternoon. Now please take notes. Take notes, now."

Shuya took out his map and a pen. Kawada also had his map out.

"First off, from one o'clock is J-5. Then from three, H-3. From five is D-8. Did you get that?"

J-5 was on the southeastern shore, H-3 was near the southern mountain's summit, and D-8 was the southeastern ascent of the northern mountain. Their location, C-3, hadn't been announced. They could get by without moving for a little longer.

"Everyone, I know it might be rough having your friends die, but you have to keep your spirits up. If you're too scared to spread your baby wings, you'll never soar. Bye now!"

Having spewed out another round of blithe platitudes, Sakamochi ended his report.

With a sigh, Shuya put away his map and stared at his check-marked class roster. "We're already down to twenty-five. Damn it."

Kawada put a fresh cigarette between his lips and cupped his hand around its end as he put a light to it. Then he said, "It's like I told you. They're gonna keep on dying like they're supposed to."

Shuya looked up at Kawada, who exhaled smoke, returning the stare. Shuya understood what he meant. The more their classmates died, the closer the three came to their opportunity for escape—and the farther they became from the time limit.

Shuya said, "You shouldn't talk like that."

Kawada merely shrugged. Then he averted his eyes. "Sorry."

Shuya felt like saying more, but he made himself tear his eyes away from Kawada. He pulled up his knees and looked between them. A few tiny yellow flowers peeked out through the leaves. An ant crawled up one of their stalks.

What bothered Shuya was this: when they had been talking about rock, Shuya felt almost as if they had actually become good friends. But something within Kawada kept the boy from getting close. Was he simply aloof by nature?

Shuya let out a quiet sigh. Then he moved his thoughts to another subject. Of the six names Sakamochi had announced, the only ones whose deaths he hadn't personally witnessed were Yoji Kuramoto and Yoshimi Yahagi. He was pretty sure they had been going out. Did that mean they were together on the island? And then there were those two gunshots he'd heard just past eleven. Had those shots done the couple in? Then who was the shooter?

He thought back to the sound of the machine gun that had killed Yukiko Kitano and Yumiko Kusaka. Was it the same person, or . . .

"Nanahara," Kawada said, getting his attention. "You haven't eaten breakfast yet, have you? The government bread is shit, but I grabbed some strawberry jam and coffee from the general store. Let's eat."

From his daypack, Kawada withdrew a squat glass jar, its contents shiny and deep red and its label illustrated with strawberries, along with a slim can (two hundred grams worth) of instant coffee. Shuya figured the coffee was destined for the empty can that Kawada had filled with water and left to boil over a fresh pile of lit charcoal. Kawada then took out a pack of plastic cups.

"You definitely loaded up."

"Yeah." Kawada nodded, then dug back into his bag and presented a rectangular box. "Look, a whole carton of Wild Sevens."

Shuya decided to cheer up. He made a slight grin and nodded, then took the bread from his daypack.

He offered one of the rolls to Noriko, saying, "You should eat too."

"Oh." Still hugging her knees, Noriko looked up. "I'm . . .fine. I'm not that hungry."

"You're not hungry? What's wrong?"

As she looked down again, Shuya noticed her pale face. Now that he thought about it, he realized she'd been keeping awfully quiet.

"Noriko?"

Shuya moved over to her. Kawada watched them as he continued working at the top of the coffee can.

"Noriko."

Shuya put his hand on her shoulder. Her hands were clenched around her knees. Only now did Shuya notice her pallid face and her pinched lips, with only a tiny gap from which her pained breaths hissed out. Noriko closed her eyes and put her hands on Shuya's arm, leaning on him a bit.

Her hand, and her shoulder, through the black fabric of her sailor fuku, felt hot. Shuya reached out with his right hand and gently lifted her bangs to feel her forehead.

She was burning up. Her cold sweat dampened his palm.

Flustered, he looked over his shoulder to Kawada. "She has a fever, Kawada!"

Feebly, Noriko said, "I'm . . . fine."

Kawada rested the coffee can at his feet and stood. He traded places with Shuya and put his hand to her forehead. He rubbed his stubbled chin, then took her wrist and looked at his watch. He must have been reading her pulse.

"Sorry about this," Kawada said, and gently placed his fingers to her lips and opened her mouth. Then he pulled down the skin under her eyes and examined behind her lower eyelid.

Then he asked her, "Do you feel cold?"

Her eyes were half lidded, but she managed to nod. "Yeah . . . a little."

"Nanahara," Kawada said.

Shuya had been watching, holding his breath. Distressed, he asked, "How is she?"

"Just give me your coat," Kawada said, removing his own. Shuya hurriedly stripped off his own and handed it to Kawada, who carefully wrapped the two coats around Noriko's body.

"The bread, Nanahara. And the jam and some water."

Shuya hurriedly grabbed the roll he'd offered her, his bottle of water, and the jar of jam from atop Kawada's daypack. He gave Kawada the bread and water, then opened the jar of jam and handed it over. Kawada wedged the roll into the jar and covered it with the red jam. He held it out to Noriko and said, "You need to eat this, Noriko."

"Yeah, but . . ."

"No buts. Just a little bite."

Noriko's unsteady hand took the roll, and she took a couple nibbles. She seemed to have to force it down her throat. She gave the rest back to Kawada.

"Can't have any more, huh?"

She gave a slight shake of her head. Even such a small gesture appeared to be an effort.

Kawada looked like he wanted her to eat more, but he gave up for now, setting the bread aside. He then took his pouch of pills.

"This is cold medicine," he said. "Take it."

He handed her a capsule different from the pain reliever he'd given her that morning. She nodded, and with Kawada's help, she swallowed it with some water from the bottle. Some of the liquid spilled from her mouth, and Kawada gently wiped it away with his handkerchief.

"Okay, Noriko," he said. "Now lie down."

She bobbed her head and lay down on the grass, with the two coats still wrapped around her.

Anxious, Shuya asked, "What is it, Kawada? Is she okay?"

Kawada shook his head. "I can't tell for sure. It might just be a cold. But her wound might have gotten infected. Just maybe."

"What?" Shuya looked down at the bandana bandage around Noriko's right calf. "But didn't we do everything right?"

Kawada shook his head. "Right after she was shot, she did a lot of walking through the woods, yeah? Some germs could have gotten inside the wound during that time."

Shuya stared at Kawada for a while, then knelt back down next to Noriko. He reached out for her forehead. "Noriko . . ."

She opened her eyes and gave him a feeble smile. "I'm all right. Just . . . a little tired. Don't worry."

But from her shallow breaths, Shuya didn't think she was anywhere near all right.

Shuya looked over his shoulder at Kawada again. Somehow managing to restrain the anxiety in his voice, he said, "Kawada. We can't stay here. We need to go someplace else—like a house, or something, to warm her and—"

Kawada interrupted him with a shake of his head. "Hold on. For now, let's wait and see how she does."

Kawada adjusted her makeshift blanket of coats so that no gaps remained.

"But—"

"I told you before. Moving isn't safe."

Noriko cracked her eyelids open. She looked at Shuya and said, "I'm sorry, Shuya . . ." Then to Kawada, she said, "I'm so sorry." She closed her eyes again.

Shuya pressed his lips together and watched her pale face.

25 STUDENTS REMAIN.

37

Takako Chigusa (Girls #13) peeked out from behind the tree trunk. She was on the slope of the southern mountain, to the east of the summit, somewhere near the border of H-4 and H-5 on her map. A diverse mixture of trees both tall and short comprised the forest around her, though the trees gradually grew shorter up the ascent, in the direction Takako now looked.

She took a good grip on the weapon she'd been supplied, an ice pick. Crouching, she looked once more over her shoulder.

Obscured by the woods now, the house where she'd been hiding was no longer in sight. Dilapidated and overgrown with tall weeds, the house seemed to have been abandoned even before the island had been chosen for the Program. Attached to its side was a smaller structure—a chicken shack, maybe—and even its rusty metal roof lay beyond her sight. How far had she come? Two hundred meters? Or only one hundred? As the star short-distance runner on the Shiroiwa Junior High track team (she held the second fastest time in the prefecture for the Girls' Junior High Two-Hundred-Meter Dash), she had gained an almost innate sense for that particular distance, but with the rolling mountainside and the vegetation—not to mention the stress—she could no longer tell.

After finishing her lunch of water and that awful government bread, Takako made up her mind to leave the house once her watch read one o'clock. Hiding herself in the corner of the abandoned structure, she had heard what she thought to be gunshots several times since the game began. But she decided that hiding would do nothing to improve her situation. She needed to find someone—a friend she could trust—and work together.

She knew that not everyone she trusted would necessarily trust her, but . . .

Takako was good-looking. Her long, tapered eyes may have seemed a little severe, but they suited her sharp chin, firm lips, and the well-defined profile of her nose. All together they gave her an aristocratic look. At first glance, her long, brown, highlighted hair might not have matched her appearance, but that along with her accessories—two piercings in her left ear and one in her right, rings on her middle and ring fingers of her left hand, five bracelets between her two wrists, and a pendant fashioned from a foreign coin—asserted her own look that accentuated her beauty. Her teachers didn't seem to care much for her hair or her gaudy, B-grade accessories, but they had never once directly scolded the girl, who was sheltered by her good grades and, more importantly, her status as the track team's star runner. Consequently, Takako was conceited and had a reputation for flouting those silly little school rules to which the other girls had to adhere.

Whether due to her beauty or her pride, or because she was simply shy, Takako had few close friends in her class. Her best friend, Kahoru Kitazawa, she'd known since elementary school, but she was in a different class.

She had one classmate, only one, whom she could absolutely trust. Not a girl, but a boy. Only one boy. They'd been friends since they were little.

That related to a subject that now weighed heavily on her mind.

When she was about to leave the school, Takako thought that one of her classmates who'd left earlier could have returned, weapon in hand. To be safe, she couldn't carelessly stroll out through the sole exit. She had to act in a way that her supposed ambusher wouldn't expect, and she had to get away from the school as quickly as possible.

So after Takako left the classroom and stepped into the hallway, she stood at the side of the entrance and surveyed the outside. Woods lay ahead, a mountain on her left, and a relatively open space on her right. The ambusher, if there was one, would be hiding in the woods ahead or the slope on the left.

She ducked through the doorway and sidled along the outer wall of the school, then sprinted off to the right, making a mad dash, unleashing the power of those prized track-runner legs. Moving purely on instinct, she ran along the road that passed through the village, threw herself into an alleyway, and dashed for the foot of the southern mountain. Her only thought was to hurry away from that school and to find a place to hide.

But.

What if in those woods in front of the school, or up toward the mountain, had been someone who *wasn't* going to attack her? In other words . . . what if . . . *he* had been hiding in those woods or that mountainside, waiting just for her? When she ran away full tilt, had she lost her chance to find him?

. . . *No.*

Takako didn't think so. That would have been impossible. Everyone would have known that lingering around that school was dangerous. They'd known each other their whole lives, but that was the extent of their connection. They were just friends, never too close or too distant. He—that is, Hiroki Sugimura (Boys #11)—would never endanger himself to wait for her. That she had even considered he might have was only a figment of her arrogance, and nothing more.

For now, she needed to find someone. Ideally, that person would be Hiroki Sugimura, but she knew that was too optimistic. If not him, then the class leader, Yukie Utsumi, would do, or any of those other plain girls. If she was careful not to get shot right off the bat, she could talk to them. Takako hoped she would run into someone who was still calm. (Though she had the feeling that anyone *too* calm in a situation like this was the most dangerous.) But all she could do for now was search.

Even still, Takako knew not to shout. She'd seen the proof of that. From that abandoned house, she had watched Yumiko Kusaka and Yukiko Kitano die atop the northern mountain.

Her idea was to leave her hiding place in the abandoned house and head for the top of the southern mountain. If she made it that far, she could spiral her way back down, all the while checking the bushes to see if someone was hiding inside. She figured that tossing handfuls of little rocks into the undergrowth would do the trick and had been doing so since she left the house. Once she saw who was there, she could decide whether or not to announce herself. According to Sakamochi's noon announcement, the area around the summit would be a forbidden zone starting at three o'clock. But if everything went well, she'd be able to perform a complete survey of the sector by then. And anyone who was up there would have to leave before three. Someone on the move would be much easier for her to spot.

Takako checked her provisioned wristwatch, which read 1:20. With all the bracelets she typically wore, she hardly ever used a watch, but she didn't have a choice now. She touched her hand to the shackle around her neck.

"And if you try to force it loose, it'll explode."

Not only did the collar dig into her skin and stifle her breath, its very presence pulled her down. The chain of her pendant clinked against the metal collar.

Takako pushed it from her mind and gripped her ice pick (not that she saw much use to a weapon like that). She took some pebbles from her pocket and scattered them into the undergrowth in front of her and to the sides.

The stones rustled through the leaves.

She waited. Nothing. She moved forward and let out her breath. She prepared herself to set foot into the next clearing on the way up the mountain.

Suddenly, she heard a rustling. Ten meters to her left, a head poked out from the bushes. She could see the back of his uniform coat and his tousled yet smooth hair. His head turned to the left, then to the right.

Surprised, Takako froze in place. *This is trouble. A boy. Boys are always trouble.* This thought was without any particular basis, but Takako felt that way about every boy aside from Hiroki Sugimura. And she knew this wasn't Hiroki.

Takako held her breath and slowly stepped back into the thicket. Expecting this possibility did nothing to quell her trembling now that it had happened.

The boy swiftly turned. Their eyes met. The astonished face belonged to Kazushi Niida (Boys #16).

Oh, shit. Of all people, it had to be him.

Her first concern was that she had left herself completely exposed to him. Regardless of anything else, that was a danger. She turned on her heels and ran back the way she'd come.

Kazushi's voice came from behind. "Wait."

She could hear him wading through the thicket after her.

"Hey, wait!" He was shouting now. "Wait!"

Ugh, that idiot.

For a few seconds, Takako weighed her options, then finally decided to stop. She turned to face him. She figured that if he'd had a gun or something like that and meant to shoot her, he would have already. That made his loud voice the biggest threat. Kazushi wouldn't only get himself discovered, but her along with him. She glanced around but saw, as she had confirmed when she'd passed through moments before, no signs that anyone else was around.

Slowing, Kazushi descended the gentle slope.

As he approached, Takako noticed he was carrying what looked like a rifle with a bow attached to its end. *He's not pointing it at me, but if he does, can I dodge his shot and get away again? Was stopping a mistake?*

No, she told herself. Kazushi Niida was a forward on the soccer team. Top ballgame athletes like him were often faster than top track runners. Even if she was the fastest among the girls, he would have eventually caught up with her.

Either way, it was too late now.

Kazushi stopped with around four or five meters between them. He was relatively tall and solidly built, with broad shoulders. His hair was long, as was popular with soccer players these days, and silky, though it was now disheveled, as if he'd just stepped off the pitch after an intense overtime matchup. Aside from bad teeth, his was a handsome face. And right now, it wore an ambiguous smile.

Takako watched him, wondering, *What does this jerk want?*

He might not mean her harm. He might be thinking he'd finally found someone he could trust.

But Takako didn't have an especially high opinion of the boy. She hated his particular brand of chumminess. His cockiness didn't help things either. The two had been classmates since seventh grade (Hiroki became her classmate in eighth), and he did fairly well in his studies and his sports without putting in much effort. Whether it was because of this, or completely unrelated, he possessed a striking lack of maturity. He was always trying to act cool, and whenever he screwed up, he'd always have some plausible excuse at the ready. And though it was hardly worth mentioning, back in seventh grade, for some reason, a rumor had spread that Takako and—the admittedly handsome, as far as it goes—Kazushi were dating. (Junior high kids liked to gossip. Well, let them say what they want.)

When that was going on, he had come right up to her desk, placed a hand on her shoulder (the nerve!), and said, "People are talking about us."

Putting on a demure act, she had pivoted free of his hand and gently parried him, saying, "Oh, I'm flattered," but on the inside, she was scoffing. *Nice try, creep. How about you take another hundred years to work on your lines?* But she had the feeling that that level of approach wasn't going to cut it right now.

Now, Takako chose her words carefully. She needed to get away from this guy as quickly as possible. That was what it came down to.

"Don't shout, stupid," she said.

"Sorry. But I only had to because you ran off."

"I'm sorry too," Takako replied straight away. *Keep it short and get to the point. That's what I do best.* "But I don't want to be with you." She fixed her eyes on his face and managed to shrug her tense shoulders. "Wouldn't it be best for both of us if we just split?"

Not satisfied with that, Kazushi frowned and asked, "Why?"

Inside her mind, she clicked her tongue at him. *Because you put on this naïve, little-boy act.*

Aloud, she said, "I think we both know why. Got it? See you."

Takako went to turn around, but her trembling knees told her how unsure she was.

She stopped.

Out the corner of her eye, she saw the weapon in Kazushi's hand, pointing at her.

Slowly now, she turned back to face him. Her eyes were fixed to his finger on the crossbow's trigger.

Takako asked, "What do you think you're doing?"

As she spoke, she casually slipped her daypack off her left shoulder, taking the strap in her hand. *Would the bag be able to stop one of those arrows?*

"I don't want to do this," Kazushi said. The way he spoke to her was exactly what she despised about him. His words were apologetic, but in fact he was putting himself in a position of power over her. "So how about you stick with me."

Now that pissed her off. But even in her anger, she noticed something. Back when she was hiding in the abandoned house, her skirt had snagged on a broken door and tore a long split up one side, like the slit on a Chinese dress. Kazushi had glanced down at her exposed thigh. She caught an unidentifiable *gumminess* in his gaze. It gave her the creeps.

She shifted her footing to hide her leg from him as best she could. Then she said, "You've got to be kidding. No way I'm going to stick with you when you're pointing that thing at me."

Typically arrogant, Kazushi said, "So you're not going to run?" He hadn't lowered the crossbow.

Takako summoned her patience. "Please just put that down."

"And you're not running away."

"Are you deaf?" she said sharply, and Kazushi reluctantly lowered his weapon.

Then, taking an oddly smug tone, he said, "You know, I've always found you attractive."

Takako raised her well-defined, elegantly arched eyebrows.

She'd had enough. *What, you think I'll just forget how you threatened me?*

Kazushi's eyes fell to her leg again. This time, his gaze lingered, a little brazen, looking her up and down.

Takako lifted her chin slightly and asked, "What of it?"

"It means I'm not going to kill you or anything. Just stick with me."

She shrugged again, this time too angry for the gesture to feel stiff. Flatly, she said, "I told you already. I'm not interested."

Then she said, "See you."

She almost turned around again but thought better of it, instead keeping her eyes on him as she backed away. Kazushi immediately raised the crossbow. His expression was that of a child in a department store begging for a toy. *Mom, I want it, I want it.*

Quietly, Takako said, "Don't do this."

"Okay, then stay with me," he repeated. The tilt of his head betrayed an attempt to rein in his escalating anxiety.

"I told you I don't want to."

Kazushi didn't lower his crossbow. For a time, they glared at each other.

Losing her patience, Takako said, "What are you after? Come on, say it. You're not going to kill me right away, and you're insisting I stay with you even when I say I don't want to. Why?"

"I . . ." Kazushi held her eyes with that lecherous gaze. "I want to protect you. So stay here. The two of us will be safer together, right?"

"You have to be joking," Takako said, the outrage edging into her voice. "You can't point that thing at me and say you're going to protect me. I can't trust you. Get it? Can I go now? I'm going."

"Move and I'll shoot." He held the crossbow aimed straight at her chest.

By vocalizing the threat, Kazushi stepped free from the last shackle that held him within the bounds of reason (as far as the bounds had been pushed already). Keeping the weapon pointed at her, he said, "Know your place, girl. Women should listen to what men tell them."

Takako was absolutely furious. But Kazushi hadn't finished speaking yet.

Casually, as if asking her sign, he said, "You're a virgin, aren't you?"

Takako was speechless.

What? What did this dumbass just say?

"Am I wrong?" he asked. "Sugimura doesn't have the balls to sleep with a girl."

Kazushi must have mistakenly believed, along with most of their classmates, that she and Hiroki were dating. But what he said pissed her off on two levels: one, that he made that baseless assumption about her and Hiroki's relationship; and two, the contempt that oozed from his voice when he said Hiroki's name.

Takako felt her lips twist into a smile. She had the habit of grinning when she was furious.

Turning that smile on Kazushi, she said, "And you think that's any of your business?"

Possibly misreading her smile, he gave her a twisted grin back. "Sure."

Still smiling, she glared back at him. *Yes, sir, you're absolutely right, sir. Despite, as you can see, the way I dress, I am indeed a virgin, sir. A blushing fifteen-year-old virgin, sir. But what the fuck kind of business is that of yours, asshole!*

Kazushi went on, "You see, both of us, we're going to die anyway. Don't you want to do it once before you die? I wouldn't make for a bad partner."

Though driven to the utmost extreme of rage, for a moment she just stared at him, dumbstruck. Her mouth might have hung open. If her disgust existed in an area around her, its field would have previously been within arms' reach, but now extended beyond the horizon. *Land ahoy, Captain Columbus. It looks like San Salvador Island. Okay now, there're savages. Beware the savages.*

Takako dropped her eyes. Then, without thinking, a quiet laugh slipped from her lips. This was ridiculous. No, really, it was the smash hit comedy of the year.

She raised her head. Despite the furious glare she leveled at him, Takako deigned to permit him one final chance.

"This is the last time I'll say it," she said. "I don't want to be with you. Be a good boy and put that thing down, and leave me alone. If you don't, I'll have to assume you mean to kill me. All right?"

Kazushi didn't lower his crossbow. To the contrary, he raised it as high as his shoulders and threatened, "And this is the last time *I'll* say it. Do as I tell you, Chigusa."

Maybe it was something in her innate personality that she felt something of a rush as their exchange reached this crucial junction. She couldn't be held responsible for whatever happened next.

Whatever it took, it was time for her conversation with this shithead to end. She took one step forward.

"I see. So you want to rape me, do you? That's it, right? You think you can do whatever you want just because you're going to die anyway, yeah?"

He glared at her. "I never . . . said that."

Didn't you? On the inside, she sneered at him. *Let me guess what's next—first you'll say you don't want to rape me, and then you'll tell me to take off my clothes.*

Still smiling at him, Takako calmly tilted her head. "You know, at a time like this, you might want to worry more about your life than your little dick."

From his neck to his face, Kazushi turned crimson. His mouth twisted, and he exploded, "You think I'm joking? You really want to get raped?"

Takako grinned. "The truth comes out."

"You think I'm fucking joking? I could kill you too, right now!"

He sickened her. Only moments ago, he'd tried cajoling her, saying, *"I'm not going to kill you or anything."*

Kazushi paused before adding, sounding proud of himself, "I already killed Akamatsu."

This startled her a little, but she raised her eyebrows and said, "Huh." Even if what he said was true, the way he'd been cowering in the bushes, he'd probably bumped into the terrified boy and killed him. Then, worried that someone more capable than himself might come along, he hid. And if by running and hiding he survived to the end, and his only remaining opponent was weaker than him, he'd say something like, "I don't have any other choice, do I?" and kill without a second thought.

What Kazushi said next confirmed her suspicions. "I thought it through and decided to consider this a game." Then he added, "So I won't hold back."

Still wearing that smirk, Takako kept on staring at him.

Aha. Now she understood everything. *So, with or without my consent, you were going to fuck me and then, when the time came, kill me—when everyone else had been killed, and all I had to do was die for you to survive? I see. And did you work out how many times you could fuck me before then?*

Her spine tingled with disgust and fury.

"A game?" Her lips curled into a wide smile. "But aren't you ashamed to go up against a girl?"

For a brief moment, he looked as if he'd been struck, but his harsh expression quickly returned. His cold eyes flashed. "Do you want to die?"

"Go ahead, try and shoot me."

Kazushi hesitated. Takako didn't miss her chance. She threw the handful of pebbles she'd snuck from her pocket at his face. As he raised his hands to shield himself, she spun around, dropped her daypack, and sprinted back the way she had come, ice pick in hand.

She thought she heard him cursing behind her. Just as she thought she'd cleared fifteen meters with her star track-runner's start, her right leg was blown forward, and she fell onto her face. Sliding on the dirt, she felt an exposed tree root scrape her cheek. This facial injury enraged her even more than the sharp pain from her leg that followed. *This asshole ruined my* face*!*

Takako twisted onto her back and sat up on the ground. A silver-colored bolt had pierced through the back of her skirt to impale itself on her right thigh. She could feel the blood coursing down her well-toned muscles.

Kazushi caught up with her. Seeing her sitting there, he dropped the crossbow, letting it clatter to the dirt. From his belt he pulled out two wooden sticks connected by a short chain—nunchucks. As he wielded them in his right hand, their chain hung down, rattling in the air. (He had found the nunchucks inside Mayumi Tendo's day-pack after he'd killed Yoshio Akamatsu. His own weapon, for some bizarre reason, was an ordinary three-stringed *shamisen* of absolutely no use. It wasn't even big enough to smash over somebody's head, like a guitar. Takako knew none of this, however.)

Takako glanced at the discarded crossbow and thought, *You're going to regret dropping that.*

A little out of breath, Kazushi said, "This is your fault. You provoked me."

Still sitting on the ground, Takako glared up at him. Even now, he continued to search for excuses. She didn't know how she'd put up with being classmates with him for more than two years.

"Please wait," she said.

As Kazushi frowned at her, she rose to her knees, reached her hand behind her back, gritted her teeth, and yanked the bolt free. She felt her flesh rip and the blood begin to gush. Her skirt tore again. *Great, now my skirt's in two pieces.*

She tossed the arrow aside and stood up, glaring at Kazushi. She was all right. The pain was fierce, but she could still stand. She shifted the ice pick to her right hand.

"Give it up," Kazushi said. "It's no use."

Takako held the ice pick level and pointed it at his chest. "You said this is a game. Fine. I'll be your opponent. I'll never lose to some punk like you. I'll give everything I have to stop you. You got that? You understand me? Or are you too stupid?"

But Kazushi's expression remained confident. He probably thought he couldn't lose against her, an injured girl.

"I'll say it one more time," Takako said. "Don't even think about beating me half to death as a way to rape me. Look, little boy, you should worry more about your life than your prick."

Kazushi's face contorted, and he raised the nunchucks as high as his head.

Takako gripped her ice pick. Tension hung in the air between them.

He stood nearly fifteen centimeters taller than her and weighed probably twenty pounds more. Even as likely the best athlete among the Class B girls, she thought she had little chance of winning. Even worse, that gash in her leg was severe. But losing was not an option.

Suddenly, Kazushi made a move. He came forward, swinging his nunchucks down.

Takako took the strike with her left arm. One of her two bracelets sailed into the air (handmade by a South American Indian, the bracelet was a favorite, damn), and a wave of numbness shot from her upper arm to the middle of her brain. Undeterred, she raised her ice pick. Kazushi grimaced and dodged backward. Once again they stood two meters apart.

Her arm throbbed, but she was all right. Kazushi hadn't broken anything.

His second attack came. This time he brought the nunchucks up in a backhand tennis swing.

Takako ducked her head and twisted to the side, dodging the blow. The nunchucks grazed her long, highlighted hair, tearing out several strands and sending them flying. Swiftly Takako swung her ice pick at his extended wrist. She felt it hit home, and Kazushi grunted and stepped back.

They were apart again. Takako saw a streak of red on the wrist holding the nunchucks. But he didn't seem badly hurt.

The gash on her leg pounded. She felt the blood covering nearly her entire leg from the thigh down. She didn't think she could last much longer. She heard the sound of panting breath, then realized it came from her own lips.

Once more Kazushi came swinging. Takako could see he was aiming for somewhere between the upper left side of her head and her shoulder.

She stepped forward. She had remembered something that Hiroki Sugimura, who attended a martial arts school, had once taught her: *An attack aimed at the wrong distance will lose most of its effect. Sometimes you need to bravely step forward.*

The nunchucks struck her shoulder, but only by the chain, which hardly hurt. Takako threw herself into Kazushi's chest. His stunned, wide-open eyes were directly in front of hers. She swung the ice pick up.

Kazushi shoved her away with his off hand. Her injured leg buckled, and she toppled onto her back.

Rubbing his nearly injured chest, he looked down at her and said, "What kind of girl are you?"

When Takako slowly pulled herself up, he came rushing at her, swinging the nunchucks down. He aimed for her face.

Takako raised the ice pick to block the attack. With a metallic clang, the ice pick was gone, rolling to a stop on the dirt beside her. Only the intense pain remained in her hand.

Takako bit her lip. Her eyes glaring at him, she backed away.

Kazushi twisted his mouth into a grin and took one step forward, then another. *Shit, this guy's a total psychopath.* He showed no compunction about beating a girl—with a weapon, even. Rather, he was enjoying it.

Again Kazushi swung the nunchucks. Swiftly, Takako bent back to dodge them, but they came after her. In a fluid movement, he had extended his reach. Maybe he was getting used to the weapon.

CRACK! The nunchucks struck the left side of her head. Her body lurched. A warm liquid began to gush from her left nostril.

Takako was about to drop. Kazushi's expression might have been one of victory.

Still swaying, Takako narrowed her lovely, long, tapered eyes.

As she fell, she thrust out her long leg and kicked the outside of his knee as hard as she could. He let out a guttural moan and dropped onto that knee, losing balance, and pivoting halfway around on it—leaving his back half exposed to her.

Had her thoughts only been on retrieving her ice pick, she might have lost. But that wasn't what she did.

She leaped onto Kazushi's back.

As if riding piggyback, she clasped her arms around his head. Her weight sent him toppling forward.

In that instant, she had a decision to make—about her fingers. *My pointer and middle finger? No, no, the thumb and middle finger are the strongest ones.* Takako had always taken good care of her nails. No matter how many times her track coach, Mr. Tada, scolded her, she'd never trimmed off her sharp, pointed nails.

Mounted atop his back, Takako grabbed him by the hair and yanked his head up. She couldn't see exactly where to put her hands, but she could make a guess.

She felt him instinctively close his eyes. He must have realized what she was about to do.

It was futile. Takako's right thumb and middle finger split through his clenched eyelids and plunged into his sockets.

"Aiiieeeeeeee!"

Kazushi screamed. He got up on his hands and knees, released his nunchucks, and tore at her arms. He thrashed around, trying to shake her off his back.

Wrapped tightly around him, Takako didn't let go. She pushed her fingers deeper. Her fingers sunk down to their second joints. Suddenly, she felt something jolt her fingers and realized his eyeballs had popped. If anything about all of this came as a bit of a surprise to her, it was that the human eye socket was smaller than she'd expected. Unfazed, she curled her fingers inward. His blood, along with some viscous semitransparent liquid, made for a peculiar form of tears as they oozed from his eye holes.

Kazushi howled, rising to his feet, flailing his arms. He scratched at Takako's hand and pulled her hair.

Takako sprang free, tearing off several strands of her hair—or even a bundle—in Kazushi's grasp. No use worrying about that now.

She hunted for her ice pick and found it quickly. She picked it up.

Kazushi roared and thrashed his arms as if fighting an invisible foe (which, in fact, he was). Then he fell back on his ass with a thud. His eyes were wide open, but pure red, from his eyelids in, like those of an albino monkey.

Dragging her right leg behind her, Takako approached him. Then she lifted that injured leg and stomped it down onto his unguarded groin. Her white sneaker with purple stripes (she also used them for warming up at track practice) had already been soaked red with her own blood. She felt something squish beneath her shoe, like a flattened little animal. Kazushi moaned, moved his hands down to cover his crotch, and curled into a fetal position. Now she stepped on his throat with her good leg. She put her weight on it. Kazushi reached out with both hands, thrashing at her leg, trying to push it away, feebly punching and clawing at it.

"Hel . . ." Kazushi wheezed. With his throat crushed, the utterance came out like a draft of air through a door crack. "Help me . . ."

Fat chance, Takako thought. She realized her lips had twisted into a smile. *I'm not even angry this time. I'm enjoying this. I really am. Well so what? I never claimed to be Pope John Paul the Second or the Fourteenth Dalai Lama, so what's the problem?*

She gripped the ice pick with both hands, knelt, and thrust it inside his mouth (she noticed he had a few fillings). Kazushi's arms, struggling to pry off her leg, suddenly jerked, and then went still. Takako pushed the ice pick deeper. It plunged wetly into his throat with little resistance. From his chest to his toes, Kazushi convulsed like a backstroke swimmer doing an underwater dolphin kick. Then it stopped. His albino eyes remained open, surrounded by a spiderweb pattern drawn in the sticky poured-out paint of his blood.

With a sudden surge of pain in her right leg, Takako collapsed on her back beside his head. Her breath wheezed between her teeth, like it did after she ran time trials for the two-hundred-meter dash.

She had won.

But she also felt let down—the fight might not have lasted but thirty seconds. She reminded herself that she wouldn't have been able to beat him had the battle been prolonged. In any case she'd won. That's what mattered.

Holding on to her blood-soaked leg, she looked down at Kazushi's corpse, with the ice pick coming up out of his throat like it was in some sideshow magic act. *Witness, ladies and gentlemen, as I bring up what I just swallowed.*

"Takako," said a voice from behind.

Still seated, Takako looked over her shoulder as she reached for the ice pick, plucked it from his mouth, and readied her grip. (When she did this, Kazushi's head lifted from the ground before flopping back down.)

Mitsuko Souma (Girls #11) was looking down at her.

Takako's eyes jumped to Mitsuko's hand, where delicate fingers held a large pistol.

Takako didn't know Mitsuko's intentions. But if she, like Kazushi Niida, was playing the game (and the odds of that were high—this was, after all, *the* Mitsuko Souma), Takako didn't stand a chance—not against someone with a gun.

I have to run. I should run. Takako pulled in her injured leg and began to stand up.

Her voice oh-so-kind, Mitsuko asked, "Are you okay?" She held the gun pointed away from Takako. But Takako needed to remain cautious.

Takako scooted back, then put her hand on the trunk of a nearby tree and managed to get to her feet. Her right leg was rapidly growing heavier.

She answered, "I guess."

Mitsuko studied Kazushi's corpse, then glanced at the ice pick in Takako's hand. "You killed him with just that? Wow. As another girl, I'm impressed."

She spoke with heartfelt admiration. She seemed ebullient, even. Her eyes twinkled from that lovely, angelic face.

Again Takako replied, "I guess." Having lost a substantial amount of blood from her leg, she felt woozy.

"Say," Mitsuko said, "I noticed something a while ago. You're the only girl who never sucks up to me."

Still unable to get a read on the girl's intentions, Takako stared at her. (The two girls vying for first and second place as the most beautiful in Shiroiwa Junior High stared each other down. It was just them, their jewelry, and a boy's corpse with crushed eyeballs. My, how lovely.)

Mitsuko was right. Takako would've rather died than be a toady. When she talked to Mitsuko, she was never timid like the other girls. She was too proud for that, and besides, she wasn't afraid of Mitsuko.

Then she recalled something an older teammate she'd had a crush on once (actually, until only a few months ago) liked to say. This wasn't like her faint and indistinct feelings for Hiroki Sugimura; she was in love with this boy. He even said it that time he showed up before one of their meets in rough shape, his friend having gotten him into some fight: "Don't fear a thing. There's nothing to be afraid of."

He was charming, and he didn't suck up to anyone. Takako had had her eye on him ever since she entered junior high. Much of her current style could be traced back to his influence. But he had had a girlfriend—a beautiful girl, a little like Sakura Ogawa, with this serenity like a lake nestled deep within a forest. But that was all in the past now.

Then she thought, *If something made me remember this now, and not when I was fighting Kazushi, does that mean . . . I'm afraid of Mitsuko?*

"It's been a little frustrating," Mitsuko was saying. "You were so pretty. You were a better girl than me."

Takako didn't say anything. Something felt off, and she quickly realized what it was. *Is she speaking in the past tense?*

"But . . ." Mitsuko's eyes twinkled playfully. She switched back to present tense for the rest. "I really like girls like you. Maybe I'm a little bi." She laughed. "That's why this is such . . ."

Takako's eyes widened. She spun around and took off running. Her right leg dragged a little, but it was a respectable sprint for the track team's ace runner.

"That's why this is such . . ."

Mitsuko raised her Colt M1911. Three times she squeezed the trigger. Deep within the grove, already twenty meters down the gentle slope and rapidly distancing, the back of Takako's sailor fuku opened in three places, and Takako dove forward like a baseball player sliding headfirst into base. Facedown, she slid along the ground. Her skirt flapped against her well-formed legs, the left one white and the right one red in vivid contrast, as they shot up into the air then fell right back to the earth.

Mitsuko lowered her gun and said, "Such a shame."

24 STUDENTS REMAIN.

38

Noriko's breathing was becoming ever more ragged. Kawada's cold medicine hadn't produced any apparent effect. Though hardly any time had passed—Shuya's watch read nearly two in the afternoon— her cheeks seemed sunken in. Shuya used up one of his water bottles to moisten Noriko's handkerchief, then wiped her sweaty face with it and placed the cloth back on her forehead. She kept her eyes closed, but nodded as if to thank him.

Shuya looked at Kawada, who was still sitting cross-legged at the base of a tree, smoking. The boy's right hand rested near the grip of the Remington shotgun on his lap.

"Kawada."

"What?"

"Let's go."

Kawada raised his eyebrows and exhaled smoke. "Where?"

Shuya's lips tightened. "Come on, I can't take this anymore." He gestured to Noriko with his chin. "She's getting bad."

Kawada glanced at Noriko, who was still lying down with her eyes closed. "If it's sepsis . . ." He paused. "Keeping her warm and letting her rest won't make her better."

"That's my point." Somehow managing to fight down his impatience, he continued, "There's a symbol for some kind of clinic on the map. If we can get there, we should be able to find some better medicine, right? It's a good ways north of the little town, and it's not in any of the forbidden zones yet."

"Oh, yeah. I guess I did see that." Kawada let out a languid trail of smoke from the side of his mouth. "You might be right."

Shuya repeated, "Let's go."

Kawada tilted his head, then took another drag and rubbed the cigarette into the ground. "That clinic is a kilometer and a half away. It'll be dangerous to move now. We wait until dark."

Shuya gritted his teeth. "If we wait until dark, and it ends up in one of the forbidden zones, what then?"

Kawada didn't reply.

"Hey," Shuya said. Whether out of frustration or the fear of alienating Kawada, his voice became a little shaky. But he had to go on. "I'm not saying that I think you're going to kill us. But are you that set against taking any risks? Does anything matter to you besides yourself?"

Shuya stared him down. Kawada's expression remained calm.

Noriko's voice came from behind. "Shuya . . ."

He looked over his shoulder.

Noriko turned her head to the side to face Shuya. The handkerchief slid off her forehead and fell on the ground.

Her words broken between pained breaths, she said, "Don't. Without Kawada . . . we won't survive anyway."

"Noriko." Shuya shook his head. "Don't you see? You're losing your strength. What happens if it gets too late for you by the time he can get us off this island?"

Then to Kawada, he said, "If you won't come, I'll take Noriko myself. Our deal is off. You're on your own."

Without bothering to hear a response, he began packing up his and Noriko's bags.

"Wait," Kawada said. Slowly he stood, then walked over to Noriko and took the pulse from her left wrist. While Shuya had remained at her side, Kawada had repeated this once every twenty minutes or so.

Kawada rubbed his stubbled chin and said, "You wouldn't begin to know which medicine to use."

Then he turned his head to Shuya and said, "Fine, then. I'm coming with you."

24 STUDENTS REMAIN.

Despite the more than thirty minutes that had passed since three bullets had been shot into her back, and despite the large amount of blood she'd lost from those wounds and the one from Kazushi Niida's crossbow, Takako Chigusa still lived. Mitsuko Souma had long since gone, though Takako was in no position to be aware of that.

Half unconscious, Takako dreamed. Her family—her father and mother and her sister, two years younger, waved at her from the front gate of their house.

She saw that her sister, Ayako, was crying, saying, "Goodbye, Sis, Goodbye." Her handsome father, whose looks she'd largely inherited, and her mother, whose round face more resembled that of her sister, were both silent, wearing sad expressions. Beside the three, her dog, Hanako, hung her head and wagged her tail. Ever since she had been a young girl, Takako had taken care of that clever dog.

Damn, Takako thought in her dream, *what a waste. I've only lived fifteen years. Hey Ayako, take care of Mom and Dad, okay? I know you're used to everyone looking after you, but you have to be strong like your sister now.*

What a waste, for real. I never even had an actual boyfriend.

The scene changed, and she saw the slender figure of Kahoru

Kitazawa, her best friend for seven years now and the only girl to whom she'd been able to vent.

And you, Kahoru. I guess this is goodbye. Wasn't it you who told me once that as long as you give it your all, not even hell would scare you? You were right, it doesn't scare me. And yet . . . it's still kind of hard, dying alone like this.

Kahoru seemed to be shouting something. Takako couldn't hear what she was saying, but it sounded something like, "What about him?"

Him?

The scene changed, and she was in her track team's locker room. She knew this was the summer of eighth grade. The room had been torn down that fall, replaced by a new clubhouse.

This isn't a dream. This really happened. This . . .

An older teammate was there. He had short hair, spiked up in the front, and wore a white T-shirt with the words FUCK OFF! across the chest and green track shorts with a black stripe. He had mischievous, yet kind, eyes. He was *that* older teammate. He was good at hurdling. Now he concentrated on taping up a knee he'd injured a while before. They were alone in the room.

"Hey, hey," Takako said, "your girlfriend is beautiful. I think you two make a great couple."

When I'm talking to him, even I turn into such a typical girl. How lame.

"Yeah?" He looked up at her and grinned. "You're way prettier."

Takako smiled back at him, but her feelings were mixed. She was happy hearing him compliment her looks for the first time, but to her mind, the way he had so casually said that she was prettier spoke to the strength and commitment he shared with his girlfriend.

Still smiling, he asked, "Are you seeing anyone, Chigusa?"

The scene changed again.

She was in a park. Her perspective seemed quite low.

Oh, this must be when I was a child. Second or third grade, maybe?

Hiroki Sugimura was crying in front of her. He wasn't tall like he was now—rather, Takako was taller. Some bully had taken his brand-new comic book.

"Hey, boys shouldn't cry. It's pathetic. You need to be stronger. Look, come with me. Our dog just had puppies. Wanna see?"

"Okay." Hiroki wiped his tears and came along.

Now that she thought about it, Hiroki had started martial arts school the next year. Around that time, he started getting tall, eventually surpassing her.

Until the end of elementary school, they often went over to each other's houses. One time, when Takako was feeling low, he said, "What's wrong, Takako? What happened?"

Takako thought about it, then said, "Hey, what would you do if someone told you they liked you?"

"Hmm. No one ever has, so I don't know."

"Hey, is there anyone you like?"

"Hmm. No. Not right now."

Takako thought a little longer. *What about me? Nothing?*

Well, whatever. "Huh. You should find someone to like and tell them."

"I'm too chicken. I don't think I could."

The scene changed again. It was the first day of eighth grade, and she and Hiroki had just been put in the same class. They were talking, when at some point, he said, "I heard one of the older guys in your club is pretty cool."

He implied the question: *And you like him, right?*

"Where'd you hear that?" she asked.

"Just somewhere. Do you think you have a chance?"

"Not at all. He has a girlfriend. What about you? Are you still single?"

"Whatever. Leave me alone."

We always remained at arm's length. I think we both liked each other, a little . . . or am I just full of myself? I know I liked you a little. Liking my teammate was something different. I hope you can understand.

Hiroki's face appeared as she knew it now. He was crying.

"Takako, don't die."

Hey, come on now, that's not very manly. Don't cry. You might be a lot bigger now, but you haven't progressed at all.

Is God just messing with me now? She stirred herself awake and opened her clouded eyes.

In the soft afternoon light, Hiroki Sugimura was looking down at her. Beyond him, and in between the treetop leaves, the fragmented blue sky made intricate Rorschach patterns.

Her first thought was that Hiroki wasn't crying. The disbelief came next.

"How—" Pushing the words through her lips was like trying to force open a rusted door. She realized she didn't have long to live. "— did you get here?"

All he said was, "It wasn't any trouble." He seemed to be kneeling next to her, cradling her head. She remembered falling facedown, but she was on her back now. Her right hand could feel leaves—*Did he carry me deeper into the undergrowth?* (Her left hand, no, her entire left side was numb and felt nothing—an aftereffect of Kazushi Niida's strike to her head, perhaps.)

Softly, Hiroki asked, "Who did this to you?"

Right. That's important information.

She answered, "Mitsuko." Kazushi Niida didn't matter for shit anymore. "Watch out for her."

Hiroki nodded. Then he said, "Sorry."

She stared up at him, not understanding.

He said, "I waited for you. I hid outside the school."

He pressed his lips together, as if he were trying to suppress something. "But . . . then Akamatsu came back—back to the school. I . . . was distracted, just for an instant. Then you took off running and I lost you. I ran after you, shouting . . . but you were probably pretty far off by then."

Oh no, Takako thought. She'd thought she heard a distant voice as she ran through the darkness. But she had been so flustered, she thought she had just imagined it—and if she wasn't imagining it, that meant someone was there, so she ran as fast as she could.

Oh no.

He waited for me. Just like I wondered, he risked his life to wait for me there. Sure, he said getting here wasn't any trouble, but I bet he's spent this whole time searching for me.

Takako felt like crying.

But instead, she did her best to work her face into a smile. "You did?" she said. "Thank you."

She knew she wasn't going to be able to talk much longer, and she tried to think of the right thing to say. She was weighing a few options when a strange question popped into her head, and she found herself asking it.

"Hey, is there anyone you like?"

Hiroki's eyebrows moved a little, and quietly, he said, "There is."

"It couldn't be me, could it?"

A smile crossed his sad expression. "It's not."

"Oh. Well, then . . ."

Takako took one deep breath. Her body felt strangely cold and yet hot at the same time. She felt poison welling up within her.

"Hold me tight, just for a little while. It'll be over soon."

Hiroki's lips tightened. He sat her up, took her in his arms, and squeezed her close. Her head felt limp, tipping backward, but he held it up.

She felt she could say one more thing.

"Survive, Hiroki."

God, can I get away with one more?

She gazed deeply into his eyes and smiled. "You know, you've become a fine man."

"And you're the greatest girl in the world."

She smiled faintly. She wanted to thank him, but she could no longer push enough air through her vocal chords. She just stared into his eyes. She was grateful. *At least I won't die alone. And I'm glad the person to be with me in the end is Hiroki. I'm really glad.*

Thank you, Kahoru. I heard you.

Takako Chigusa remained there like that, in his arms, and died around two minutes later. She kept her eyes open through the end. For some time, Hiroki held her limp, lifeless body, her full weight entrusted to his arms, and wept.

23 STUDENTS REMAIN.

"Duck," Kawada said.

He raised his shotgun and carefully surveyed the area.

Carrying Noriko on his back, Shuya obeyed. They were in the shade of a large elm tree, its trunk just wide enough to fit their arms around. Shuya figured they must have made it two thirds of the way to the clinic. On the map, they'd be somewhere around F-6 or F-7. Unless they had gotten turned around (and with Kawada as their guide, they wouldn't have), they would soon see the building down to their right.

The three had followed the shore, passing through C-4, where they had first met Kawada, then followed the base of the northern mountain eastward. Traveling in broad daylight did turn out to be no easy task. They would move a little, then quiet their breaths, and when they had no choice but to pass through thick vegetation, Kawada threw several small rocks ahead to find out if anyone was there. It had already taken them half an hour just to get this far.

Noriko's pained breathing persisted on the other side of Shuya's head.

Like a mother with her child on her back, he turned his head partway around and said, "Noriko, we're almost there."

She mumbled in reply.

Kawada said, "Okay, let's move. We're heading for that tree next, got it?"

"Okay."

Shuya half rose and proceeded along the soft, grassy soil of what seemed to have once been a crop field. Kawada, carrying all of their bags in his left hand and holding the shotgun in his right, attended his flank. As Kawada turned his head in every direction, the shotgun swiveled in perfect tandem.

They reached the next tree, this one a little narrower, and halted again. Shuya caught his breath.

Kawada asked, "Are you getting tired, Nanahara?"

Shuya displayed a grin. "Nah, she's light as a feather."

"If you're tired, we can take a break."

"No." Shuya shook his head. "I just want to get there."

"If you're sure," Kawada replied.

But a doubt began to well up inside Shuya. He felt like such an idiot. He was always making snap judgments, forgetting to check the important details.

"Kawada."

"What?"

"That symbol on the map—do you think it's really a clinic?"

Keeping his back to Shuya, Kawada chuckled. "I recall that's what *you* said it was."

Flustered, Shuya said, "No, I just—"

"It's a clinic. I've seen it myself."

Shuya's eyes widened. "You have?"

"Yeah. I was going around the island last night until I met up with you two. I wish I'd had the foresight to grab some more powerful drugs. I didn't think I'd need to."

Shuya sighed in relief. But inside his head, he gave himself a solid thwack. *Get it together. You're going to get not only yourself killed, but Noriko too.*

During this exchange, Kawada had continued searching for their next destination.

"All right—" Kawada was saying when the gunshot rang out.

Shuya stiffened. Then he quickly crouched and looked around. Had he been too optimistic in thinking they'd be able to reach the clinic without incident?

No one was in sight.

He looked at Kawada, who had stretched out his arm to shield them and was looking ahead and to the left, where a row of tall trees ten meters away—Japanese cedars, maybe—blocked their view up the gentle slope. Did that gunshot come from the other side?

Shuya let out the breath he'd been holding.

"We're fine," Kawada whispered. "Looks like we're not the targets."

Keeping his pistol tucked away and still carrying Noriko on his back, Shuya said, "They're close."

Kawada nodded. Then the gunfire continued. Two shots, then another three. The last three sounded a little bigger. Another shot echoed. That one was smaller.

"A gunfight," Kawada whispered. "They're really going at it."

Shuya felt relieved that they weren't in danger for the time being, though unknowingly, he chewed at his lip.

Two of his classmates were trying to kill each other—and just over there. And here he was, just trying to keep quiet, waiting for it to end. This was just like . . .

Again Shuya pictured that man in his black funeral suit. *"All right, it's your turn. And then you next. Oh, Shuya, it's not your time yet. Good for you."*

Still facing away from Shuya, Kawada said, as if reading his thoughts (after all, he had said something silly about being good at that when the weather was nice), "You're not thinking about going over there to stop them, right, Nanahara?"

Shuya gulped, then muttered, "No."

Kawada was right. Their top priority was to get Noriko safely to the clinic. If he stuck his nose into other people's battles, he'd be inviting danger.

From his back, Noriko said, "Shuya . . ." Her fever was hot enough he could feel it, her voice only a whisper.

Shuya looked over his shoulder and saw her narrowed eyes.

"Let me down . . . have to see if someone . . ."

Her words cut off into ragged breaths, but Shuya knew what she wanted to say. *What if someone who wasn't playing the game— someone innocent—was about to be killed?* That could have been either of the two—or both—who were exchanging bullets right now.

They were almost due south of the northern summit where Yukiko Kitano and Yumiko Kusaka had been killed. But none of the gunshots they'd heard belonged to that machine gun. Neither of these two was likely the one who killed Yukiko and Yumiko. But whoever that was might hear the shooting and appear at any moment.

Again the bullets crossed, and again silence returned.

Shuya gritted his teeth. He let Noriko off his back and set her to rest against the trunk of the tree where they hid.

Kawada looked back at Shuya. "Hey, you're not . . ."

Ignoring him, Shuya told Noriko, "I'll go check it out." Pulling the Smith & Wesson from his belt, he told Kawada, "Look after her."

Shuya heard Kawada say, "Wait—" but he was already running.

Looking in all directions, he went up the slope, then passed through the tall coniferous trees.

Thick bushes carpeted the other side. Shuya waded into them. He dropped to the ground and weaved through the long, razor-sharp needles.

He heard the gunshots again. Finally reaching the edge of the thicket, he gingerly popped out his head.

Ahead stood an old wooden house, single-story with a tall, gabled roof—your typical farmhouse. An unpaved driveway went off to the right. Fencing in the far side of the grounds was an escarpment, atop which deep forest extended up the mountainside. Far above, Shuya could make out the observation deck where Yumiko Kusaka and Yukiko Kitano had died.

The farmhouse was to Shuya's left. Hirono Shimizu (Girls #10) was crouched against the fence on his side. She was looking across the yard at a storage shed beside the driveway. A figure—another girl—peeked out from the side of the shed door. When she looked up, Shuya saw that she was Kaori Minami (Girls #20). Both girls were armed. Not even fifteen meters separated the two.

Shuya didn't know what had caused them to start shooting at each other. Either could have attacked the other. But Shuya didn't think that was what had happened. They had probably stumbled into each other, and in the panic and confusion, neither had trusted the other, and the gunfight kicked off.

His belief may have been founded simply on his partiality for girls, but either way, he couldn't stand there and watch in silence. No matter what, he had to stop this.

Even as he gauged the situation, Kaori popped her head out from the shade of the doorway and fired once at Hirono. She handled the weapon like a child might a squirt gun, but this was no squirt gun. The proof came when the gunshot resounded and the brass shell spun into the air.

Hirono fired twice back at her. Her stance was much more regular, and her shells didn't go flying. One shot landed in one of the shed's vertical beams and kicked out a burst of splinters. Kaori quickly ducked her head back inside.

Hirono was almost completely visible from Shuya's position. She opened her revolver's cylinder and ejected the empty cases. Shuya noticed her right arm was drenched in red. Maybe Kaori had shot her somewhere in her arm. Still, her hand worked quickly as she inserted fresh rounds. She returned her aim to Kaori.

This had all transpired in a few seconds. Before Shuya could act, he was struck by that now-familiar feeling—this was a nightmare. Kaori Minami was into pop idols, always chatting with her friends about their favorites, and would get all bubbly when she'd found a new photograph. Hirono, on the other hand, was one of Mitsuko Souma's girls and had a bit of a wicked streak . . . but despite everything, they were both cute ninth graders in junior high. And they were shooting at each other. They were really shooting at each other, with real bullets. But of course they were.

This is no time to think about that.

Shuya purposefully rose. He pointed his Smith & Wesson into the air and fired. A stray thought crossed his mind: *Who are you, the sheriff?* But without hesitation, he shouted, "Stop!"

Hirono and Kaori froze stiff, then, in unison, turned their heads in Shuya's direction.

Looking from one to the other, Shuya said, "Stop it! Stop it right now. I'm with Noriko Nakagawa." He thought it would be best to leave Kawada's name out of it for now. "You need to trust me."

Even before he finished saying them, he realized how damn trite his words must have sounded. But he couldn't think of any other way to say it.

Hirono immediately looked away from Shuya, her eyes on her opponent, Kaori. And Kaori was standing there, stupefied, watching Shuya.

In that instant, Shuya noticed Kaori had left herself halfway exposed outside the shadows of the doorway. Defenseless.

What happened next reminded Shuya of a car accident he'd once witnessed. It happened one autumn evening shortly before his eleventh birthday. He was walking home from elementary school, a short distance behind a younger girl also on her way home. Maybe the semi driver had fallen asleep, because he lost control, crashed through the guard rail, rode up onto the sidewalk, and hit the little child. Unbelievably, her backpack came off her shoulders and went sailing on a completely different trajectory than the girl. She landed first, coming down on her shoulders, sliding along the concrete wall on the inside of the sidewalk, until she stopped, and blood poured out. She'd left a trail of it a meter long along the base of the wall.

He'd seen the whole thing as if it were in slow motion—particularly from when the truck left the road until it struck the girl. He knew exactly what was going to happen, what he was about to witness, but he could do nothing to stop it. That was how it felt.

Kaori had completely let her guard down. Hirono aimed her gun at her and fired. She fired again. The first shot hit Kaori in her right shoulder, twisting her halfway around to her right. The second shot caught her in the head. As Shuya watched, part of Kaori's head—from her left temple up—exploded.

Kaori collapsed into the open doorway of the shed.

Then Hirono glanced at Shuya and turned on her heels and ran off to his left, westward, from where Shuya's group had started. She plunged into the undergrowth and vanished from sight.

"Shit!"

Shuya let out a low groan, then, after some hesitation, he emerged from the thicket and ran toward the shed where Kaori had fallen.

Kaori's legs jutted out from the door of the shed, a structure barely large enough to house the old and rusted tractor within. She was on her side. Her body had twisted. Blood flowed from her mouth and joined with that from the wounds in her head and shoulder and began to form a pool beneath her face on the concrete floor. Motes of dust from the floor floated atop the pool of blood. Kaori's open eyes vacantly stared up. A delicate gold chain hung from the chest of her sailor suit onto the floor, and the locket at its end seemed a tiny island amid a lake of blood. Inside it, a male pop idol was sending out a cheerful smile.

Shuya was shaking as he knelt beside her.

Oh, man, what the hell? Now she can't gossip over her idols or go to their concerts, and . . . if I had handled this just a little better, would she not have had to die?

He heard a noise and turned around. Kawada and Noriko, supported on the boy's arm, looked out from the thicket.

Leaving Noriko there, Kawada jogged over to Shuya.

Kawada's expression looked as if he wanted to say, *See, I told you so,* but he didn't. He calmly scooped up Kaori's gun and daypack, then as if by afterthought, squatted down and closed her eyelids with the side of his hand.

All he said was, "We're going. Hurry up."

The danger was obvious. Someone—that machine gunner, in particular—could have heard the gunfire and might show up at any moment.

But Shuya remained frozen, staring down at Kaori's corpse, until Kawada tugged him away by the arm.

22 STUDENTS REMAIN.

41

The clinic was an old, single-story residence. Its wooden walls had blackened, and the black tiles of its roof showed their age, having weathered white around the corners. Much like the farmhouse where Kaori Minami had died, the building was nestled against the northern mountain and located at the end of an unpaved driveway. Shuya's group had come across the mountainside, but that driveway likely led down to the paved road that followed the island's eastern shoreline. A white compact van—the doctor's, maybe—was parked in front of the clinic. Beyond the van, Shuya could see the sea.

The water sparkled in the afternoon sun. Its beautiful color here, a brilliant blue tinged with green, shared no similarities with the murky waters that broke against the concrete seawalls of Shiroiwa's harbor. With scarcely a wave, the sea's surface placidly reflected the sun's light in twinkling specks that grew ever more dense into the distance. The silhouettes of the other islands floating in the Seto Sea seemed unexpectedly near. Shuya had once heard that on the open water, the lack of objects to provide points of reference caused perceived distances to shrink. Shuya figured the closest island was probably still four or five kilometers away.

In any case, they had arrived. Only by luck had they made it there unharmed. They had immediately left the area where Kaori had died, and no machine-gun fire had followed them. According to the map, they had traveled a mere two kilometers, but Shuya had carried Noriko on his back, while under the pressure of a possible attack at any moment, and the hike had exhausted him. He hoped they could quickly make sure the clinic was clear of any other students not only so that Noriko could rest, but so that he could as well.

But something had caught his eye.

On the sea's peaceful surface, a ship floated. It was, no doubt, one of the guard ships of which Sakamochi had warned them. But beside it were two more. Sakamochi had said one patrol would be in each cardinal direction, and off the western shore, Shuya had seen only one vessel. Had something happened?

With Noriko still on his shoulders, Shuya peeked his head out from the shade of the leaves and said to Kawada, "There are three ships."

"Yeah," Kawada said. "The smallest is the guard ship. And the big one there, that'll transport the soldiers in the school back home. The middle one will carry the winner off this island. It hasn't changed. They're the exact same ships from last year."

"So the Hyogo Program last year was on an island like this?"

"Yeah." Kawada nodded. "Hyogo borders the inland sea too. Apparently all the prefectures along the sea have their Programs take place on an island, pretty much without exception. After all, there are more than a thousand islands in this narrow sea."

After that, Kawada instructed them to wait. With his shotgun at the ready, he descended the slope that led toward the clinic. Crouching down, he inspected the van first, even checking underneath the vehicle. Then he darted over to the building and circled it. When he got back to where he started, he looked around the front entrance. The sliding frosted glass door was apparently locked, so he flipped the shotgun and smashed a hole in the glass with its sawed-off stock. He ducked and waited. Then he reached his hand through the triangular opening he'd made, opened the door, and went inside.

Having watched over this whole process, Shuya turned his head to check on Noriko. Her head limply rested on his back.

"Noriko, we're here."

Noriko responded with only a short moan. Her breaths still sounded painful.

After five full minutes, Kawada appeared from the front door and waved Shuya over. Careful not to lose his balance, Shuya climbed down the two-meter drop onto the clinic's property.

A thick wooden sign hanging beside the entrance bore weather-faded, hand-painted lettering that read OKI ISLAND MEDICAL CLINIC. Kawada stood in the doorway, holding his shotgun level, looking out in every direction. Shuya slipped past him and through the entrance. Kawada followed him in and slid the door all the way shut.

The space immediately inside was a waiting room roughly eight square meters large. Along the left side of the room, a green padded bench with a white cover sat on the worn, cream-colored carpet. Above the bench, a wall clock was tick-tocking away as its hands approached three. A doorway to the right seemed to lead to the examination room.

Kawada jammed the door shut with a broom he must have found nearby and waved Shuya to the examination room, saying, "Over here."

Though he was probably supposed to remove his shoes, he kept his sneakers on and stepped up from the entranceway, then went into the room on the right. A wooden desk was at the window, and a doctor's black leather stool sat near another stool with green vinyl. Despite its small size, the clinic still carried the odor of disinfectant.

Two beds were on the other side of a thin green curtain hanging from a rail of metal pipe. Shuya carried Noriko to the closer of the two beds and carefully laid her down. He thought about taking back his school coat that he'd put around her but decided to leave it be.

Kawada quickly pulled the window curtains shut, said, "Here're some blankets," and offered Shuya two thin brown blankets that had been folded into small squares. Shuya took them, and after a moment of thought, laid one of the blankets across the empty bed. Then he lifted Noriko, transferred her there, and put the other blanket over her and tucked her in. Kawada was rifling through the drawers of a gray cabinet—probably a medicine cabinet, though nothing on the outside appeared any different from an ordinary piece of office furniture.

Shuya leaned in toward Noriko and brushed the sweat-matted hair from her cheeks back over her ears. She seemed to be only semi-conscious. Her eyes were closed, and her breathing remained pained.

Shuya cursed. "Noriko, are you all right?"

Noriko's eyelids cracked open, and she vacantly gazed up at him and said, "Mm-hm . . ." Her high fever was keeping her in a daze, but her thoughts remained clear enough for her to respond.

"How about some water?"

Noriko gave him a tiny nod. Kawada had left the daypacks on the floor, and Shuya went to his, retrieved a new bottle of water, and broke open the cap. He propped Noriko up and gave her a drink. Water spilled from the side of her lips, which he wiped with the back of his finger.

"Is that enough?"

Noriko nodded. Shuya laid her back down and looked up at Kawada. "Any medicine?"

"Hold on," Kawada said. He moved to another cabinet, this one low to the ground, and rummaged through it. He pulled out a cardboard box, opened the lid, and read the directions. He seemed to find it acceptable, because he took out a small jar and some kind of ampoule. The jar was filled with a white powdery substance.

Shuya asked, "Does that dissolve in water or something?"

"No. It's for an injection."

Shuya was startled. "You know what to do with that?"

Kawada opened the faucet at the corner of the room. No water came out, so he clicked his tongue and used a bottle of water from his daypack to thoroughly wash his hands. He set a needle into a small syringe and drew the liquid from inside the ampoule.

"Don't worry," he said. "I've done this before."

"Really?" Shuya felt like that was all he ever said to Kawada.

Kawada broke the seal on the small jar of powder, pressed the syringe through the cap, and expelled the ampoule's liquid inside. He withdrew the needle, took the jar in one hand, and gave it several small, quick shakes. He stuck the syringe back into the jar and extracted the liquid mixture.

After he'd prepared a second syringe, Kawada finally approached the bed.

Shuya asked, "Is that really going to be all right? What about side effects, or shock, or—"

"That's what I'm about to find out. Quit worrying and help me. Hold out Noriko's arm."

Shuya didn't understand, but he lifted up the side of the blanket and rolled up the sleeves of one of Noriko's arms, both his coat's and her own sailor-suit blouse's. The skin of her slender arm had lost its tanned, healthy color and turned sickly pale.

"Noriko," Kawada said. "Have you ever been allergic to any medicine?"

Noriko opened her vacant eyes.

Kawada repeated the question. "Are you allergic to any medicine?"

Noriko shook her head.

"Okay. I'm going to do a little test first."

Holding Noriko's arm steady with her palm up, Kawada took a cotton ball soaked with some disinfectant and rubbed it over a wide patch of her wrist, where he then carefully inserted one of the syringes. He injected a minute amount of the medicine and her skin swelled in a tiny bump. He picked up the other syringe and made an identical bump right beside the first.

Shuya asked, "What's that for?"

Kawada replied as he promptly disposed of the two needles. "Only one of those contains the medicine. If both spots are identical after fifteen minutes, we won't have to worry about, well, any of the more extreme side effects. It means we can at least try the drug. But . . ."

"But?"

This time Kawada took a slightly larger bottle from the cardboard box. He set it down on a nearby side table and began preparing a new syringe in the same manner as before.

As he worked, he said, "Sepsis is difficult to diagnose. To tell you the truth, I'm not even sure if this is sepsis, or if it's just a regular cold. And antibiotics are strong stuff. That's why I had to test it first. Either way, I don't exactly have the right level of knowledge or experience you'd want for something like this. But . . ."

Shuya held Noriko's hand and waited for him to continue.

Kawada exhaled, then said, "If this is sepsis, we need to treat it as fast as we possibly can. We have a limited window."

The fifteen minutes passed quickly. In the meantime, Kawada checked her pulse again and took her temperature—thirty-nine degrees. No wonder she was faint.

As far as Shuya could determine, the two injection marks on her wrist were identical. Kawada must have concurred, because he picked up a slightly larger syringe than before.

Kawada leaned in to her and said, "Noriko. Are you awake?"

With her eyes still closed, she said, "Mm-hmm . . ."

"I'm going to give it to you straight. I can't be sure if what's got you is sepsis or not. But I think it's highly likely."

Noriko made a slight nod. "It's all right. Go ahead . . ." she said. She must have been able to follow the two boys' earlier conversation.

Kawada nodded, then inserted the needle more deeply. He injected the liquid and withdrew the syringe. He pressed a cotton ball on the spot, then instructed Shuya, "Hold it in place."

Kawada walked the empty syringe over to the sink and tossed it inside. Then he returned to the bedside.

"Now she needs to rest. Look after her for a while. If she seems thirsty, you can use the rest of our water bottles."

Shuya started to say, "But—"

Kawada shook his head. "It's fine. I found a well out back. If we boil it first, we should be able to drink it."

Then Kawada left the room. Shuya turned back to the bed. With his right hand pressing the cotton ball to her wrist, and his left hand gently holding hers, he watched her face.

22 STUDENTS REMAIN.

Noriko fell asleep almost immediately. For a while, Shuya watched over her. Then, making sure the bleeding had stopped, he discarded the cotton ball, tucked her arm back under the blanket, and exited the room.

A door at the back of the reception area appeared to lead into the doctor's living quarters. Shuya went inside.

Past the door, a hallway ended with a kitchen on the right. Kawada was there. Unsurprisingly, the gas cooktop next to the sink seemed to be inoperative—the familiar red glow of Kawada's charcoal peeked out from beneath a stockpot filled with water on one of the two burners.

Kawada had climbed atop the kitchen table to search through the built-in ceiling cabinet opposite the sink. Shuya noticed that Kawada was wearing New Balance sneakers. He hadn't paid much attention to them, assuming they were some domestic brand like Mizumo or Kageboshi. But these were *New Balance*! He'd never seen a pair of those before.

Putting that aside for now, Shuya asked, "What are you doing?"

"I'm looking for food. I found some rice and miso, but not much else. The vegetables in the fridge are rotten."

Shuya shook his head. "I feel like we're stealing."

"We *are* stealing. Did you think we weren't?" Still digging through the cabinet, he added, "Never mind that. Just prepare yourself. Someone could come here any moment. Just see what'll happen when that machine-gunner attacks. We don't have anywhere to run. So be ready."

"Okay."

Kawada rummaged through the cabinet a little while longer, then hopped down from the table. His New Balance sneakers squeaked on the floor. He asked, "Did Noriko fall asleep?"

Shuya nodded.

Kawada pulled out another pot from beneath the sink, walked it over to a plastic rice container at the corner of the room, and poured rice into it.

"Cooking some rice, huh?" Shuya asked.

"Yeah. Noriko won't get her energy back on that bread alone."

Kawada used a rice bowl to scoop out water from a bucket on the floor and into the pan. He must have filled the bucket from the well. He stirred the rice, then replaced the water. Then he took several pieces of charcoal from his daypack and placed them beneath the open burner. He pulled out a pack of cigarettes, stashed its contents back into the same pocket, then crumpled up the empty package, lit it with his lighter, and tossed it into the charcoal. After the flames spread through the coals, he put the lid on the pot of rice and placed the pot on the burner. He clearly knew what he was doing.

"Damn," Shuya said.

Taking a break, Kawada lit a cigarette and sent Shuya a questioning glance.

"You're so good at everything."

"That so?" Kawada said dismissively, but a different thought crossed Shuya's mind, and he was back where Kaori Minami had been killed. *I know what's going to happen, but I can't stop it. Everything's in slow motion. Kaori whirls, and the side of her head blows apart. Did you see that? It blew apart.*

If it had been Kawada who tried to stop them, and not you, he told himself, *maybe that tragic outcome could have been avoided.*

Kawada asked, "Is what happened with Minami bothering you?" His mind-reading abilities were in full effect today. The lack of sunlight inside didn't seem to affect him.

Shuya looked up at Kawada, who shook his head and said, "Don't let it get to you. It was an awful situation, and you did your best."

Shuya dropped his eyes. *Kaori Minami's corpse sideways on the floor of some filthy farm shed. The pool of blood oozing forth. By now it had probably started to coagulate. But she'd still be there like that, with no funeral. Just like some discarded mannequin, her body left to sprawl on the floor. In that way, she was the same as Tatsumichi Oki, Kyoichi Motobuchi, Yukiko Kitano, and Yumiko Kusaka, and all the others.*

He felt sick. They were all sprawled about, already nearly twenty of them.

"Kawada."

The name had spilled out of Shuya's lips. Kawada answered with a tilt of his head and a gesture with the cigarette in his hand.

Shuya asked, "The ones who died—what happens to their bodies? Are they just left there until this bullshit game is over? Just rotting or whatever as the game stretches on?"

Matter-of-factly, Kawada replied, "About a day or so after the game ends, an appointed cleanup crew comes in."

"A cleanup crew?" Shuya bared his teeth.

"Yep. I heard it from one of the workers, so it must be true. The soldiers have too much pride to do some menial job like that. Of course, government officials accompany the crews to reclaim the collars and perform a cursory autopsy. You know, like you hear on the news? This number died from asphyxiation, and so on."

Shuya was disgusted. He thought back to how those news reports always ended, with some meaningless enumeration of the causes of death and the numbers of students.

But a realization caused him to knit his brows.

Noticing his expression, Kawada said, "What's up?"

"Well, it's just that doesn't make any sense, does it? This—" Shuya raised his hand to his neck, and his fingers brushed the cold surface, the feeling of which no longer seemed out of place. "This collar is classified, right? Wouldn't they have to retrieve them before any contractors showed up?"

Kawada made a slight shrug. "The cleanup crews wouldn't have any idea what they are. They probably just assume they're used as some kind of tag. As a matter of fact, the contractor I talked to didn't even remember the collars until I asked about them. So there's no rush. The government can deal with the collars after the cleanup crew's collected all the bodies, right?"

Maybe he was right. But if he was, then something else bothered Shuya.

"Hold up," Shuya said. "What if a collar breaks or something? Say one malfunctions and thinks one of the living students is dead. Couldn't that student escape? Shouldn't they at least check the dead bodies as soon as the game is over?"

Kawada raised his eyebrows. "You sound like one of them."

"No—I," Shuya stuttered. "It's just . . ."

"I doubt these things ever break. If they could malfunction, it could throw the whole game out of whack. And remember, we're all armed. If one of us is still alive, it wouldn't be about checking the bodies. There'd be at least some kind of battle."

Kawada took a thoughtful drag of his cigarette, then exhaled the smoke. "This is just my guess, now, but I think each collar has been loaded with redundant systems. If something breaks, the electronics can just switch to the backup. Say one component breaks—and I think the chances of that would be far less than one percent—but say it does break. If you add redundancy, the probability of the collar malfunctioning becomes negligible."

He looked at Shuya. "The odds of us escaping that way are as close to zero as possible."

Shuya nodded in understanding. Kawada was probably correct. (And Shuya was continuously impressed by Kawada's ability to reason.)

But then . . .

Shuya's thoughts returned to the question he'd promised he wouldn't ask:

What countermeasures has Kawada prepared that can go up against such a flawless escape-proof system?

Before he had time to contemplate the matter, Kawada said, "Anyway, look, I have to apologize."

"For what?"

"Noriko. I was wrong. We should have treated her sooner."

"No . . ." Shuya shook his head. "It's okay. And thanks. I couldn't have done anything on my own."

Kawada lit a fresh cigarette. He blew out a puff of smoke and stared at a point on the wall. "Now all we can do is wait and see. If it's just a cold, her fever will go down with rest. But even if it's sepsis, that medicine should do the trick."

Shuya nodded, grateful to have Kawada there. Without him, he could only have sat on his hands, watching Noriko grow weaker and weaker. He felt childish and a little ashamed for having berated Kawada, saying, "Our deal is off," back when he started heading for the clinic. He knew Kawada had only made the difficult decision after carefully weighing Noriko's condition against the risk of moving during the day.

Shuya decided he needed to apologize.

"Um, sorry. Saying you're on your own and all that. I just got so worked up . . ."

His face still in profile, Kawada shook his head and grinned. "You made the right decision. End of discussion."

Shuya let out a breath and decided to drop the subject.

Then another thought came to him, and he asked, "Your father—is he still a doctor?"

Kawada took another drag, then shook his head and said, "No."

"What's he doing now? Is he still in Kobe?"

Casually, Kawada said, "No. He's dead."

Shuya's eyes widened. "When?"

"When I went into this game last year. By the time I got home, he was already dead. I figure he got in a scrap with the government."

Shuya's expression hardened. He felt he was beginning to understand that spark that had crossed through Kawada's eyes when
he vowed to destroy this fucked-up country. His father must have
attempted some kind of protest when Kawada was taken away for the
Program and had received his government's certain response in the
form of a bullet.

Shuya wondered if some of his classmates' parents died the
same way.

"Sorry," Shuya said. "I shouldn't have asked."

"It's okay. I don't mind."

Shuya paused and then asked another question. "So did your
mother move with you to Kagawa?"

Again Kawada shook his head no. "My ma died young. I was
seven. She was sick. My dad was really beat up over it—how of all the
people, the one he couldn't save was his own wife. Most of his work
was in surgery and abortions, you see. Disorders in the cranial nervous
system were beyond his expertise."

Shuya apologized once more. "Sorry."

Kawada chuckled. "I said it's okay. You don't have any parents
either. And that lifetime government pension deal is no lie. I've got
enough money. It's not as much as they like to say it is, but still."

Tiny bubbles began to form on the surface of the stockpot of water
above the charcoal. The briquettes beneath the rice pot were still black
in quite a few places, but the ones beneath the stockpot were glowing
bright red, and their heat reached the table where Shuya and Kawada
stood. Shuya sat on the flower-patterned vinyl tablecloth.

Out of the blue, Kawada said, "You were good friends with
Kuninobu."

Shuya turned his head to Kawada, regarded the boy's profile, then
looked ahead. He hadn't thought of Yoshitoki for a while now. The
realization came with some guilt.

"Yeah," Shuya said. "We were always together, you know."

After some hesitation, he added, "Yoshitoki had a crush on
Noriko."

Kawada listened as he continued to smoke.

Shuya wasn't sure if he should speak what next came into his mind. It had nothing to do with Kawada. But in the end, he decided to tell him. Kawada was his friend now. He could hear this. Besides, they had time to kill.

"Yoshitoki and I lived at this place called the House of Mercy and Love—"

"I know."

Shuya bobbed his head, then went on. "There are all kinds of kids in a facility like that. I was put there when both my parents died in an accident when I was five. But actually, I was unusual. Most of the kids—"

"—are there because of family issues," Kawada finished for him. "Illegitimate children, mostly."

Shuya nodded. "You know a lot about this."

"I know a little."

"Well . . ." Shuya took a deep breath. "Yoshitoki was illegitimate. Of course, nobody with the orphanage ever talked about it. But something like that—you can just tell. Seems like there's a lot of cheating going on these days. Anyway, neither of his parents ever came to take him back. And . . ."

The sound of water boiling came from the stockpot.

"Yoshitoki told me something once. It was way back now—back when we were in elementary school, I think."

Shuya recalled that moment. In the corner of the playground, the two friends had climbed astride a swing fashioned from wire rope and a rough log and were rocking back and forth.

"Hey, Shuya. I . . ."

Shuya prodded him casually, "You what?" He kicked at the ground to rock the log. Yoshitoki wasn't doing much of the work, instead letting his legs dangle off each side.

"Well . . . uh . . ."

"What? Out with it already."

"It's just . . . is there anyone you like?"

"Aw, geez," Shuya said with a grin. He knew his friend meant girls. "That stuff? What, you got a crush on a girl now?"

"Well," Yoshitoki evaded the question. "Anyway, I asked you first. Do you?"

Shuya thought about it, and then said "Hmm."

Shuya had already earned his "Wild Seven" Little League nickname and had received a number of love letters. But as he remembered it, back then he didn't truly understand how it felt to like someone. That, he'd saved until he met Kazumi Shintani soon after.

Just to give some answer, he said, "There're some girls I think are all right."

He took Yoshitoki's silence as a sign his friend wanted him to go on, so he casually added, "Komoto's not bad. She wrote me a love letter. I haven't, uh, I haven't really responded to her though. And Utsumi, on the volleyball team, you know, from the other class? She's not bad either. Now that's my type. Real outgoing, you know?"

Yoshitoki seemed deep in thought.

"Hey now," Shuya said. "You got me to talk. Your turn. Who do you like?"

Instead, Yoshitoki said, "That's not what I was talking about."

Shuya frowned his eyebrows. "What then? What is it?"

Yoshitoki seemed hesitant. Then he said, "Um, I don't get it."

"Huh?"

"I mean," Yoshitoki said, still letting his legs limply dangle, "I think if you love someone, you'd marry her, right?"

"Well, yeah," Shuya replied with a dull expression. "Yeah. If I really loved someone, I'd want to marry her. Though I don't feel that way about anyone yet."

"Right?" Yoshitoki said, as if it were obvious. Then he asked, "But look, if for some reason you couldn't marry her, and you had a kid, you'd raise the child, wouldn't you?"

Shuya felt a twinge of embarrassment. He was at the age when the idea of how babies were made was beginning to dawn on him. "Had a kid? Come on, that's grown-up stuff. That kind of talk, it—"

Shuya finally remembered how Yoshitoki had been born to parents that weren't married to each other, and that neither had wanted him. Shuya stiffened and swallowed the rest of his words.

Yoshitoki simply stared at the log between his legs.

Then he said, "My parents didn't do that."

Shuya suddenly felt sad for his friend. "Hey, Yoshitoki—"

Yoshitoki looked up at Shuya and his voice became firm. "That's why I—I don't understand how to like a girl, and all that stuff. I don't feel like I can trust it."

As Shuya kept on pushing the swing with his legs, he couldn't help but stare at Yoshitoki. He felt like he'd been addressed in some alien language. At the same time, the words had sounded like a chilling prophecy.

To Kawada, Shuya said, "I think . . ."

Shuya's hands rested beside him on the vinyl tablecloth. He wrapped his fingers around the edge of the table. Kawada, still holding the cigarette in his mouth, exhaled smoke and squinted in the cloud.

"I think, back then, Yoshitoki was a lot more mature than I was. I was just this dumb little kid. But Yoshitoki, after that, he never—even when we went on to junior high, and I told him I really fell for someone," he said, meaning Kazumi Shintani, "he never talked about that kind of thing again. That worried me."

The boiling water bubbled. Shuya looked over to Kawada. "But then one day he told me he had a crush on Noriko Nakagawa. I acted like it wasn't a big deal, but when he said it, I was so happy. It was just—it was just . . ."

Shuya looked away. He knew he was about to cry.

Once he managed to fight back his tears, he said the rest without looking at Kawada's eyes.

"It was just two months ago that he told me."

Kawada remained silent.

Shuya faced him again. "That's why I have to protect Noriko to the very end."

Kawada returned his gaze for a time, then said, "I see," and rubbed his cigarette out on the tablecloth.

Shuya said, "Please don't tell her. After we escape this game, I'll tell her myself."

Kawada nodded and said, "Okay."

22 STUDENTS REMAIN.

43

Nearly five hours had passed since the Macintosh PowerBook 150's network connection had been neatly severed with a beep. Shinji Mimura scrolled through a document in a window on the display of the 150, which was no longer a remote terminal but a mere calculator. Shinji sighed.

Over and over he'd tinkered with the phone, checked the connections, and rebooted, but no matter what he tried, the black-and-white laptop screen displayed the same message. Finally, after disconnecting his cell phone from the modem, he concluded that the phone itself was completely dead. If he couldn't connect to the wireless network, he couldn't even access his home PC. Also out of the question was calling all of his girlfriends and tearfully saying, "I'm going to die soon, but I loved you more than anyone." Shinji considered stripping his cell phone just to make sure he hadn't made a mistake—but then he dropped everything.

Shinji's skin crawled.

The reason he could no longer dial in to the network had been clear to him for a while. The government had discovered the line service number used by the DTT technicians, the one accessed by the counterfeit alternate ROM he'd painstakingly built into his custom phone. They'd blocked that number just like any other standard line. The question was, how had the government been able to detect and respond to his method? He felt sure he hadn't done anything careless that would have exposed his hack. Of that much he could be confident.

That left only one possible explanation. They had discovered his hacking attempt through some method other than their computers' internal security systems, alert systems, or someone manually monitoring the network. And now that they knew—

The moment the realization hit him, Shinji reached for the collar around his neck.

Now that the government knew, it would come as no surprise if they remotely triggered the explosives to kill him—and probably Yutaka too.

Thanks to this, the government-supplied bread and water he ate after noon tasted even worse.

When he'd seen Shinji turn off the laptop, Yutaka looked to his friend for an explanation. But Shinji only said, "It's no good. I don't know why, but it's not working anymore. I think my phone might have broken."

Yutaka seemed pretty bummed after that, and he sat back down in the same place he'd been all morning. Outside of a few words exchanged after the occasional echo of gunfire, the two boys remained silent. Shinji Mimura's glorious escape plan, that Yutaka had called "incredible," had gone up in smoke.

I'm going to make you bastards regret not killing me right away. No matter what.

Shinji thought for a while, then stuck his hands into his pockets and pulled out a small, old pocketknife he'd carried around with him ever since he was in elementary school. On the same key ring as the knife was a small metal cylinder covered with scratches. He held the tube up to his eye.

The knife had been another gift from his uncle. The cylinder, however, like the earring in his left ear, he'd kept as a memento after his mentor had died. His uncle had kept it attached, in the same manner, to a knife that never left his side either.

Inside the cap of the thumb-sized container, a rubber ring kept any water from getting inside. It was a case typically used by soldiers to keep a piece of paper with their name, blood type, medical conditions, and the like, in the event of injury. Some used it to store matches. Until his uncle died, Shinji thought something like that would be inside. But what he found was something altogether different. The case itself had been carved from a single piece of a special alloy, inside of which were two smaller, similar cases. Shinji took out the two cylinders. At first glance, he couldn't figure out what they were for, but he quickly realized that they were meant to be attached together. The screw on one fit perfectly into the other. His uncle had stored them separated within a case and under close guard, because if he left the two halves attached, something bad might happen. After some research, Shinji came upon what they were (and recognized immediately that they of course had to be kept separate—otherwise they would be too dangerous to walk around with), but he never figured out why his uncle carried them with him. On their own, they couldn't be used for much. Maybe the man had kept it on his person simply as a reminder of someone, much like Shinji did now, both with the cylinder and with the earring the boy now wore. Either way, the object provided a clue into his uncle's past.

The cap squeaked as Shinji opened it. He hadn't done so since his uncle's death. He dropped the two nested cylinders into his hand and broke the seal on the smaller of the two.

The inside of the cylinder had been packed with cotton to absorb any shock, behind which peeked out the dull yellow of brass.

Shinji appraised the object for a moment, then closed it again. He returned the two smaller cylinders to their original places inside the larger case. He'd thought that if he ever had to use the thing, it would be after they'd escaped the island—though he had considered the possibility that he would need it after he disrupted the computers inside the school, once he got together everything else he needed to launch an assault on Sakamochi and his thugs. But now, this was all he had.

He screwed the cap on tight, then flipped out the blade of his pocket-knife. The sun had begun its descent in the west, and in the light of the thicket, the silver steel took on a yellow hue. Next Shinji took out the pencil from his pocket, the one he'd used when they all wrote, *We will kill each other*, before the game began. Because he'd also used it to write down the list of forbidden zones on his map and to check off the names of the dead from his class roster, its tip had gone blunt. Shinji sharpened it with his knife. Then, from a different pocket, he took out his map and turned the paper over. It was blank.

"Yutaka," he said, and his friend, seated there, hugging his knees and staring at the ground, looked up at him.

His eyes twinkling with hope, Yutaka said, "Did you think of something?"

Shinji didn't know what it was about Yutaka right then that ticked him off. Maybe it was the boy's tone or the words themselves. Whatever it was, for just a moment, a voice deep inside Shinji said, *What's this shit? I'm banging my head against the wall trying to think of a way out of here, and you think it's okay for you to just sit there and space out? Sure, you got all fired up swearing you'd avenge Izumi Kanai, but you haven't thought for jack. You think you're ordering fast food and I'm working the register? Well fuck then, you want fries with that?*

But Shinji suppressed that voice.

Yutaka's round cheeks had deeply sunken in, making distinct the lines of his cheek bones. But that was only natural. The stress of this killing, and not knowing when it would end, could exhaust anyone.

Ever since he was little, Shinji never felt second to anyone in gym class. (Two exceptions came in eighth grade—Shuya "Wild Seven" Nanahara, and of course, Kazuo Kiriyama. Basketball aside, he never knew if he would beat them or not.) His uncle often took him hiking in the mountains, and he felt confident in any matchup that came down to physical stamina. But not everyone was as physically fit as The Third Man. As for Yutaka, he was hardly an athlete, and when the cold seasons came, he would miss a lot of school. The fatigue he was facing would be on an entirely different level than Shinji's, and it could be affecting his ability to think.

Then Shinji came to a realization that froze him in place. Wasn't the fact that he was even a little upset at Yutaka just now an indication of his own fatigue? With their chances of survival practically nonexistent, it would have been more strange if he hadn't been on edge.

That's not good enough.

I need to be careful. Or else . . . This isn't some basketball game where losing means I have to feel bad. No, in this game the consequence of losing is death.

Shinji shook his head.

Yutaka asked, "What's wrong?"

Shinji looked up and made himself grin. "Nothing. Anyway, you want to help me take a look at something on the map?"

Yutaka scooted over toward Shinji.

"Hey," Shinji said, raising his voice, "there's a bug—on your neck!"

Yutaka jumped and raised his hand to his neck, but Shinji stopped him, saying, "I'll get it." He leaned in, and his eyes went to something—not a bug—at the base of Yutaka's neck.

"Damn, it ran to the other side," Shinji said. He circled behind Yutaka and looked in close.

Yutaka squeaked, "Shinji, did you get it? Shinji?" Shinji took an even closer, more careful look.

Then he brushed the back of Yutaka's neck with his hand and squashed the imaginary insect beneath his shoe. He then (pretending) picked up the bug and (pretending) flung it into the brush.

"Got it," he said. Returning around front, he added, "It looked like a small centipede."

"Gross." Rubbing the back of his neck, Yutaka glanced to where Shinji (pretending) had tossed the bug and made a face.

Shinji grinned and said, "Okay, the map."

Yutaka peered down at the map . . . and seeing it facedown, he furrowed his brow.

Shinji raised his index finger and waved it to get his friend's attention. Then he picked up the pencil and scribbled on the back of the map. He was left-handed, and his handwriting sloppy. His chicken-scratch characters appeared along the edge of the paper.

[*I think they can hear us.*]

Yutaka's face went stiff. "Really? How can you tell?"

Shinji frantically put his hand over Yutaka's mouth. The boy understood and nodded, his eyes wide.

Shinji lowered his hand and said, "I just can. I know a lot about insects. That one wasn't poisonous." Then, just in case, he wrote some more.

[*We are looking at the map. Don't say anything to make them suspicious.*]

Providing a fake cover, he said, "All right, so, since my hack didn't work, we're out of options."

[*They heard me explain to you what I was up to and they cut off the Mac. I underestimated them. They expect some of us will try to resist. And monitoring our conversations is the easiest precaution. It's so obvious.*]

Yutaka took a pencil out of his pocket and wrote directly below Shinji's scrawl. His handwriting was much neater.

[*They've got monitoring devices all over this big island?*]

He seemed to have cribbed Shinji's kanji for "monitoring," and he'd written "devices" all wrong. Well, so what? This wasn't Japanese class.

"So," Shinji said, "I think we need to look for some of the others. The two of us can't do anything alone, and . . ."

He lightly tapped his collar. Yutaka's eyes bulged, then he nodded. Shinji wrote again.

[*I just looked at your collar. It doesn't seem to have a built-in camera. Only a microphone. And I haven't seen any signs of cameras about. All we have to worry about are satellites, but they won't be able to see us under these trees.*]

Yutaka's eyes widened again, and he looked up. The swaying tree-tops blocked any glimpse of the blue sky.

Then Yutaka's face stiffened as if in sudden realization. He clenched his pencil and brought it to the paper.

[*The laptop stopped working because you told me. If I hadn't been here, you would have succeeded.*]

With the hand holding his pencil, Shinji stuck out his pointer finger and poked his friend's shoulder, presenting him a reassuring grin. Then he wrote:

[*That's true, but don't sweat it. I should have been more careful. The moment the government was on to me, they could have blown our collars. In their benevolent mercy, they're letting us live.*]

Yutaka returned his hand to his neck and made a shocked expression. For a while, he gaped at Shinji, but then he pressed his lips together and nodded.

Shinji returned the nod, then said, "Seems like everyone is in hiding, but . . ."

[*All right. I'm going to write my plan here. I'm going to fake a conversation, so play along.*]

Yutaka nodded, then blurted, "Ah, but, there are so few we can trust."

Shinji thought, *Nice job*, and grinned. Yutaka returned the smile.

"Yeah," Shinji said. "But I think Nanahara would be one. I wish we could find him."

[*I have to warn you first. If my hack had worked, we might have been able to save everyone. But now, we can only think of saving ourselves. Are you fine with that?*]

Yutaka seemed to think for a moment. Then he wrote:

[*We can't look for Shuya?*]

[*We can't. I know it sucks, but we can't*]

Shinji wanted to write the kanji for "afford" but couldn't remember it. Shinji's grades in Japanese weren't that great either. He spelled it out instead.

[*a-f-f-o-r-d to worry about the others. Are you fine with that?*]

Yutaka bit his lip. But finally he nodded.

Shinji returned the nod.

[*But if my plan goes well, the game will be suspended for a while. That might give everyone else a chance to escape.*]

Yutaka bobbed his head twice. "Do you think everyone else is hiding in the mountains like us? I wonder if any of them have broken into the houses."

"Could be." Shinji was considering what to write next, when Yutaka jotted something instead.

[*What's your plan?*]

Shinji nodded, then gripped his pencil.

[*Actually, I've been waiting for something to happen since my failure this morning.*]

Instead of writing, Yutaka responded with a tilt of the head.

[*An announcement that the game has been suspended. I'm still waiting now.*]

With a look of surprise, Yutaka tilted his head again. Shinji gave him a smirk.

[*Before I told you all that stuff, when I first broke into those computers in the school, the very first thing I did was search for the backup copy of all their files. That, and their virus-scanning software. I found both right away. Before I downloaded anything, I infected both with a virus. An insurance policy.*]

Yutaka's lips formed the word, "Virus?"

Shinji thought, *C'mon, Yutaka, forget you can write too?*

[*My thinking was that if they realized something was wrong, they would either scan their files or restore them from a backup, and my virus would spread into their system. It would be chaos, and the game wouldn't be able to go on.*]

Yutaka nodded several times in admiration. The next bit Shinji wrote knowing it was only a waste of time, but he wanted to anyway.

[*I designed the virus myself, and it's badass. It's like if athlete's foot could spread through the air, only 100x worse.*]

Yutaka grinned as he fought to keep from laughing.

[*Once it gets going, it'll wipe all their data, then play "The Star-*

Spangled Banner" on infinite loop. With how much those bastards despise the American Empire, it'll drive them nuts.]

Holding in his laughter, Yutaka now had one hand on his stomach and the other over his mouth. Even Shinji had to struggle to keep from bursting out.

[*Anyway, when they discovered my hack, I thought they'd have to repair their files. Then this game would have to be suspended. But that hasn't happened yet. That means they only performed a cursory check. I guess it makes sense. I never did get to messing around in their main files.*]

Shinji said, "Wanna start with a thorough sweep?"

"But wouldn't that be dangerous?"

"Yeah, but we have a gun, so . . ."

[*That brings me to my plan. I'm going to make them have to recover their files. Then they'll trigger my virus.*]

Shinji pulled over the PowerBook 150 and showed Yutaka the document he'd been scrolling through—a text file with forty-two lines. His download had been interrupted, but of all the files that had made it through intact, this was the one he thought to be most important. The document was in plaintext, and at the beginning of each line ran a sequence, starting with "M01" through "M21," then "F01" through "F21." Each was proceeded by a ten-digit number resembling a phone number. These too were consecutive. Each line ended with another, seemingly random, sixteen-digit number. A single comma delineated the three fields. The file had a cryptic name: guadalcanal-shiroiwa3b.

Yutaka wrote, [*What? What's this?*]

Shinji nodded. [*I think these are the numbers that control our collars.*]

Yutaka nodded deeply as if to say, *Oohhh, I see.*

M01 would stand for student number one of the boys (Yoshio Akamatsu), and F01 would stand for student number one of the girls (Mizuho Inada, that somewhat kooky girl).

[*This is only my theory, but I think the collars work like cell phones. Each has its own number and its own pass code. I think the*

operators use the same numbers to detonate the collars. Therefore]
Shinji paused, looked at Yutaka, then continued, [*if my virus destroys
their data, and this file in particular, then we won't have to worry
about our collars blowing up. The virus keeps spreading deeper, so
even if they have a backup file somewhere, it won't help them. If they
have the numbers written down by hand somewhere, that might be
trouble, but even then, their whole system won't be functioning, so
we'll have bought ourselves some time.*]

Shinji said, "What if we flung pebbles at anywhere that seems suspicious? Anyone hiding would come running out."

"Hold on . . . What if it was a girl, and she let out a big scream?
Wouldn't that be dangerous for us—and for her? Well . . . if she wasn't
one of the bad ones, I mean."

"Hmm."

Yutaka wrote, [*How will you make them trigger it?*]

Shinji nodded. [*On your way out of the school, did you see that
room with all the soldiers?*]

Yutaka nodded, and Shinji continued, [*Did you peek in and see
the computers in there? Do you remember that?*]

Yutaka's eyes widened, and he shook his head. [*I couldn't
a-f-f-o-r-d to.*]

Shinji chuckled. [*I took a good look while keeping an eye on
those bastards. They had a whole long row of desktop computers and
one large server. One of the soldiers looked different from the others
though. He had a*]

*Wait, what was the kanji for "insignia"? How am I supposed to be
able to write that?*

[*symbol on his uniform that made him out to be a computer technical officer. That means what Sakamochi said is true: the computers
that run this game are inside that school. That's why we're going to
attack the school and at least*]

Shit, another I don't know.

[*make them think we damaged the data. If we can assemble the
proper ingredients, we can actually destroy the physical computers.*]

Shinji interrupted his writing to pretentiously spread his arms like a magician after his trick. Then he returned to the paper.

[*We're going to bomb the school. Then we escape by sea.*]

Now Yutaka's eyes really popped. He mouthed, "Bomb?"

Shinji grinned. "We might want to find some real weapons first. You're not going to be able to fight anyone with that fork of yours."

"Yeah . . . right."

[*What I really need is gasoline. I think there was a gas station at the harbor, but we can't get there anymore. I'm sure there must be several cars on the island. I don't know if they've still got gas, but finding out's our first step. At worst, we can use diesel too. We also need fertilizer.*]

Yutaka raised his eyebrows as if to ask, *Fertilizer?*

Shinji nodded, then tried to write the name of the fertilizer he needed, but yet again he didn't know the right kanji. Maybe he had gotten too used to typing in his word processor. *Oh, well. At least I know the name of the compound. That's good enough.*

[*It's for the ammonium nitrate. Who knows if we can find it. But with that and gasoline, we can make a bomb.*]

From his pocket, Shinji took out the knife and its attached cylinder and displayed it for Yutaka.

[*Inside this is a blasting cap. A detonator. Why I have it is a long story, so I'll skip it. What matters is that I have it.*]

Yutaka seemed to think for a moment. Then he wrote, [*Your uncle?*]

With an embarrassed smirk, Shinji nodded. With how Shinji went on and on about his uncle, Yutaka seemed to have formed his own image of the man.

Yutaka wrote, [*But how are we going to smash a bomb into the school? We can't get near it. Are we going to make a giant slingshot with some trees or something?*]

Shinji chortled. But no, that wouldn't be accurate enough. If they could keep firing, a slingshot would be fine, but with only one detonator, they only had one chance.

[*A rope and pulley.*]

Yutaka opened his mouth as it to say, *Ohhh.*

[*Basically, a ropeway. We can't go near the school, but the mountain on our side and the flat lowland on the other side are still open.*]

Shinji turned over the map to show Yutaka. Then he flipped it back over.

[*We'll run it from the mountains to the plain. No, that's wrong. We'll secure the lower end first and then pull the rope up to the mountain. I think we'll need a full 300m of rope. Then we pull the rope tight and send the bomb sliding down on a pulley. When the bomb's over the school, we cut the rope. Or just let it go slack. Our own special slam dunk.*]

Yutaka bobbed his head up and down in renewed admiration.

Shinji said, "It'll be easiest to find weapons if we start looking while it's still daylight."

"Yeah . . . you're right. It'll be easier than finding our classmates."

[*That'll be best for our work too. I feel like I saw a pulley in a well somewhere. We can collect the gasoline from cars. The trick will be finding rope and fertilizer, especially rope that long.*]

For a moment, the two boys fell silent, but quickly Yutaka wrote with enthusiasm.

[*But it's the only way, right? Let's go for it.*]

Shinji nodded. [*If everything goes well, the bomb might take out Sakamochi and his men. But like I wrote just before, all we have to do is make them think we damaged their data. That way*]—he pointed at his collar—[*they won't be able to kill us with these.*]

Yutaka wrote. [*Then we'll escape to the sea?*]

Shinji nodded.

[*But I can't swim good.*] He meekly looked at Shinji. [*Either way, at swimming speed we*]

Shinji stopped Yutaka's hand and wrote, [*Tonight's the full moon. We'll use the tidal current. I worked out the timing. If we do it right, the tide will move us at 6-7 kph. If we swim as fast as we can, it won't take us twenty minutes to get to the nearest island.*]

As if his wide eyes weren't enough to fully express his admiration, Yutaka shook his head. [*But what about the guard ships?*]

Shinji nodded. [*For sure, we'll risk being seen. But those bastards rely on those computers so much, I think the ones on the ships probably aren't keeping a close watch at all. They're already spread too thin with only one ship in each direction. That's how we'll get through. Anyway, once the computers are down, they won't know where we are. The ones on the ships will have to look for us with their own eyes. Even if the government is using satellites, their cameras will be practically worthless at night. And we won't have to worry about our collars blowing. We'll have a chance to escape.*]

[*It still won't be easy.*]

[*I have an idea about that too.*]

Shinji reached inside his daypack and pulled out a small walkie-talkie, another item he'd picked up inside one of the houses.

[*I've been thinking about making some adjustments to this to increase its output. It shouldn't take much doing. Then, once we get somewhere far enough at sea, we'll send out an SOS. We'll say we were on a fishing boat that capsized or whatever.*]

Yutaka's expression brightened. [*That might do the trick. We'll get some ship to come save us.*]

Shinji shook his head. [*No. Even those idiots in the government would catch on to something like that. But we'll give them a false location and swim in the opposite direction.*]

Yutaka shook his head again. He even bothered to write, [*Shinji, you're awesome.*]

Now Shinji shook his head and grinned. "All right then," he said, checking his watch. It was already four in the afternoon. "We'll move in five minutes."

"Okay."

Shinji dropped his pencil. He never usually wrote that much, and his wrist had started to hurt. The underside of his map was covered with enough writing to fill a computer's network log file. (He much preferred typing over writing by hand. If only Yutaka knew how to type, they could have used the 150.)

But then he picked the pencil back up and added, [*I can't say it's a* great plan. *Our chances of getting out unharmed are slim. But it's all I could come up with.*]

He shrugged and looked at Yutaka.

Yutaka grinned and wrote, [*We'll do what we have to.*]

22 STUDENTS REMAIN.

Seated among the thick vegetation on the southern slope of the northern mountain, a boy peered into his hand mirror and ran a comb through his thick hair to neatly arrange his pompadour. Since the game had started, he might have been the only one in his class—even including the girls—to feel he could afford the luxury. But this came as no surprise. Despite his rugged features, he paid an excessive amount of care to his appearance. You see, he—the boy who, for a reason known to very few in Class B, was called Zuki by his friends, or rather, at this point he *had been* so called, anyway, this boy was . . .

. . . queer.

As for his location, relative to some of the other students, he was nearly two hundred meters due west from where until recently Shinji Mimura and Yutaka Seto had been hiding, and roughly six hundred meters northwest from Shuya Nanahara's trio in the clinic. This put him just up the mountain from the farmhouse where Shuya had witnessed Hirono Shimizu shoot Kaori Minami. If he looked up, he would see, bathed in the light of the sunset, the observation deck where Yumiko Kusaka's and Yukiko Kitano's corpses were still sprawled.

This boy smoothing down his hair had seen Yumiko's and Yukiko's bodies, along with that of Kaori Minami. And not just those. Kaori's corpse had been his seventh.

Ugh, gross. There's still a grass leaf stuck up there. This happens every time I lie down.

He brushed out the grass with his pinky, then looked in the mirror at the bushes twenty meters down the slope behind him.

Still sleep-ing, Ki-ri-ya-ma-kun?

The boy's thick lips twisted into a smile.

Aren't you being careless? Well, not even you would ever guess that the boy you failed to kill is right here watching you.

But it was this "queer" holding a mirror and a comb who hadn't shown up at Kazuo Kiriyama's meeting place, thus escaping his slaughter, and was the only surviving member of the Kiriyama Family— Sho Tsukioka (Boys #14). And indeed, inside those bushes below was Kazuo Kiriyama, the boy who had already finished off six students since the game's beginning. He hadn't moved in more than two hours.

Sho returned his gaze to his own reflection. As he scrutinized his complexion, he recalled how his fellow Family member Mitsuru Numai always got on his case for calling Kiriyama "Kiriyama-kun." Mitsuru had said, "Hey Zuki, you've gotta call the boss Boss," or some-thing like that. But the fearless Mitsuru never quite seemed to know how to handle this "queerboy," who casually tossed him a lascivious look and said, "Don't be so sensitive. It's not very manly." Mitsuru made a sour expression and muttered something or other, but dropped the issue after that.

Call him Boss, huh? Sho thought, inspecting his own left eye and then his right. *But you got killed by that Boss of yours, didn't you? Because you're a total moron.*

Sho Tsukioka had been more cautious than Mitsuru Numai. Just before his death, Mitsuru had wondered if Sho had sensed Kiriyama's inner darkness, but he hadn't really. Sho had always held the basic belief that in this world, betrayal could come at any time. In that manner, compared to Mitsuru, a ruffian who tried to fight his way out of every problem, Sho, who'd been in and out of his father's gay bar since he was little, therein catching glimpses of the adult world, was the savvier of the two.

When Sho left the school, he didn't head directly for the meeting point on the island's southern tip. Instead, he took a course slightly inland, ducking from tree to tree. His way took more effort, but it only cost him ten extra minutes at the most.

He saw it from the woods overlooking the shore. Atop the outcropping, which rose from the ocean to split the beach in two, lay three bodies—two in boys' uniforms and one in a sailor fuku. Inside a hollow in the rock, shaded from the moonlight, Kazuo Kiriyama stood motionless.

Mitsuru arrived almost immediately. Then, on those blood-soaked rocks (the smell of it reached all the way to where Sho hid), after exchanging a few words with Kiriyama, he fell prey to that machine gun.

Oh my, Sho thought. *This is trouble.*

By the time he began following Kiriyama, walking away from the scene, Sho had already settled on his subsequent plan.

In this game, Kiriyama was undoubtedly the favorite for the finals. Sho couldn't hear what Kiriyama and Mitsuru had said, but whatever it was, as long as Kiriyama was playing the game, he would almost certainly outlast his opponents. On top of that, he carried that submachine gun (was it his, or had it belonged to one of the three he'd killed?) and Mitsuru's pistol, along with who knew what else. Sho figured that anyone who tried to take Kiriyama head-on would never win.

But Sho Tsukioka possessed one set of abilities in which he was confident: slipping into somewhere he wasn't supposed to be, catching people off guard to steal something, or even tailing someone (when he found a boy he liked, he was a serial stalker)—basically, all things sneaky. *Hey, who are you calling sneaky? How rude.* Besides, the weapon he'd pulled from his daypack was a two-shot .22 caliber High Standard Derringer. Though its magnum cartridges could probably inflict a fatal wound at close range, the pistol was not suited for a gunfight.

Then the idea came to him. Granted, Kazuo Kiriyama was barreling straight for the victory. But if along the way he were to face his match—probably that Shogo Kawada or maybe Shinji Mimura (*now he's my type*)—and if this foe were armed, Kiriyama would surely emerge with at least some injury. And all that fighting would pile on the fatigue.

In that case, if Sho managed to follow Kiriyama to the end, then at that final moment, he could simply shoot Kiriyama from behind with the Derringer—right when he drops his guard at his last kill. Surely Kiriyama would never imagine someone would try to follow *him*— especially the boy who stood him up at the meeting point.

This way, in this game of killing their classmates one after the other, he could survive without having to sully his hands. This aspect was by no means rooted in logic; he had merely thought, *I don't want to kill an innocent kid. Where's the elegance in that? Leave all the killing to Kiriyama-kun. I'm just following him. If he happens to kill someone while I'm there, it's not like I could stop him. That would be dangerous. When I kill him at the end, it'll be in self-defense. Why, if I don't, he'll kill me.* That about summed it up.

Tailing Kiriyama provided another benefit. If Sho stuck to Kiriyama's path, he wouldn't have to worry much about being suddenly attacked. And even if he did, all he had to do was escape the initial assault, and Kiriyama would respond to the commotion. If Sho could hide himself quickly enough, Kiriyama would deal with the attacker for him. This was, however, a course of events he hoped to avoid, because if he was unable to follow Kiriyama afterward, his plan would fail.

After deliberation, Sho decided he'd maintain a fixed distance of twenty meters between himself and Kiriyama. This meant that when Kiriyama advanced, he'd advance, and when Kiriyama stopped, he'd stop. Sho also had to take the issue of forbidden zones into consideration.

Kiriyama was certain to base his plans with those zones in mind and would stay well clear of any forbidden zone, so if Sho held to that basic distance, he wouldn't have to worry about crossing into one of those sectors. Whenever Kiriyama stopped, Sho could check his map to make sure they weren't inside one of the forbidden zones, and that would be enough.

And everything had proceeded as Sho had planned.

Kiriyama had left the island's southern edge and stopped at a few of the houses in the village (he must have found what he'd needed), then for some reason headed for the northern mountain, where he stopped to rest. In the morning, gunfire sounded in the distance, but perhaps too distant, because Kiriyama didn't move. But soon after, when Yumiko Kusaka and Yukiko Kitano began calling out with that microphone on the mountain just above, he acted quickly, and as soon as he determined that no one was going to respond to the girls' call (Sho had heard another gunshot then—apparently intended to get the two to stop. Sho thought, *Wow, incredible, a humanitarian out here.* The gesture moved him, though not enough to take action.) Kiriyama shot and killed the two. After that, he descended the mountain's northern slope.

That afternoon, Kiriyama heard another instance of gunfire, but this too he overlooked. Then, just a little bit ago, before three o'clock, shots came from their side of the mountain. But when Kiriyama followed the sound, he (and consequently Sho) found only Kaori Minami's body, dead on a farm shed floor. Kiriyama went down to check the body, probably to go through her belongings, but someone else appeared to have taken off with them first. After that, he moved a short distance away . . .

And now he's in those bushes below.

Kiriyama's strategy seemed simple, at least so far. Once he knew where someone was, he ran there and fired away. Sho had been somewhat repulsed by the way the boy had mercilessly slain Yumiko Kusaka and Yukiko Kitano. (*Listen, bub, your name is Kazuo Kiriyama, so dreadfully plain, yet your actions are out of control. Meanwhile, my name is Sho Tsukioka, worthy of a celebrity, and yet I'm this ordinary.*) But such quibbles weren't going to accomplish anything now. Sho figured he should just be happy that Kiriyama seemed to remain completely unaware of his presence.

Kiriyama appeared to be resting quietly. He might have been sleeping, as Sho had supposed.

Sho, on the other hand, would be entirely unable to sleep, but in that department too he felt confident. As well he should, since girls possessed better stamina than boys—at least he'd read so in a book.

The hard part was being a heavy smoker. The smell of his cigarette smoke, depending on the direction of the wind, might give him away to Kiriyama. The click of his lighter might prove even more fatal. He was practically beside the boy, after all.

From his pocket, Sho pulled out an imported Virginia Slim Menthol. (He liked the name. In this country, the cigarettes were hard to acquire, but they could be found, and then he only had to steal them. His apartment bedroom was piled with cartons of them.) He slipped the thin cigarette between his lips. The scent of tobacco and that particular mint eased his withdrawal. He so wanted to fill his lungs with that smoke, but he somehow managed to fight down the urge.

I can't die. There's too much waiting for me to enjoy at my age.

To distract himself, Sho held up his mirror and caught sight of himself holding the cigarette in his mouth. He turned his head to the side and appraised his own face with a sidelong look.

Oh, he thought, *how handsome I am—and how clever. Winning this game would only be natural. Only the beautiful survive. That's God's—*

Out the corner of his eye, he caught rustling in the bushes below.

Sho plucked the cigarette from his lips and put it back into his pocket along with the hand mirror and drew his Derringer. He picked up his daypack with his left hand.

Kazuo Kiriyama's slicked-back hair appeared at the edge of the thicket. He slowly moved his gaze from his left to his right, then looked to the north—directly on Sho's left—and up the slope.

Watching from the shade of an azalea shrub covered with pink blooms, Sho raised his eyebrows.

What's he doing?

Sho hadn't heard any gunfire. He hadn't heard anything at all. Had Kiriyama seen something?

Sho looked in the same direction and saw no unusual movement.

Kiriyama emerged from the thicket. His daypack hung from his left shoulder, and his submachine gun was slung from his right. He held the weapon's grip. Weaving his way through the trees, he climbed up the mountainside. Within moments he was on the same level as Sho, and then he ascended farther. Sho stood up and took pursuit.

Sho's catlike movements belied his husky build, at one hundred seventy-seven centimeters tall. Catching quick glances of Kiriyama's black uniform from behind every tree, he maintained his twenty-meter distance. In this point, Sho's confidence was well placed.

Kiriyama advanced with precision and haste. From time to time, he stopped behind a tree to survey ahead. Where the vegetation grew thick, he got on his knees and looked beneath it before he went on.

Your back's wide open, Kiriyama-kun.

After about a hundred meters of this, with that observation deck visible on the left, Kiriyama stopped.

A narrow, unpaved road interrupted the line of trees ahead. Not even two meters across, it was barely wide enough for a single car to pass—and even that depended on the car.

Oh, Sho realized, *this is the path that goes up to the summit. We crossed it before we found Kaori Minami's body.*

Then Kiriyama looked to the right, where a small clearing made way for a single bench and a beige prefabricated restroom for hikers on their way to the summit.

Kiriyama surveyed the area, even turning his eyes Sho's way, but Sho had already hidden himself in the underbrush. Then Kiriyama turned back to the road and dashed for the restroom. He opened the door, which faced Sho's direction, and went inside. He looked back out, making sure no one was near, then noiselessly closed the door, though he didn't shut it all the way, instead leaving it open a crack, maybe to be able to make a fast escape should anything happen.

Well. Sho put his hand to his mouth. *My, my.*

Still crouched in the bushes, Sho had to fight to keep himself from laughing.

The entire time Sho had been following him, Kiriyama hadn't stopped to do his business anywhere. He might have used the bathroom in the house he'd been in overnight, but either way, he couldn't be expected to hold it in for an entire day. Sho had assumed Kiriyama had taken care of it while stopped in those bushes. (That's what Sho had done. He had to work not to raise any noise.) But apparently, Kiriyama hadn't. Whatever else he was, he was a rich boy. Maybe he couldn't accept going without a toilet. He must have remembered passing by the toilet and returned.

So, even Kiriyama-kun has to pee. Ha ha. Kind of adorable, really.

Right away he heard the splash hitting the toilet. Again Sho had to swallow a chortle.

Then a thought came to him, and he turned over his wrist to look at his watch. He was pretty sure they were somewhere near D-8, which Sakamochi had said would become a forbidden zone at five o'clock.

On the face of his women's watch, with its elegant italicized numbers, the hands indicated four fifty-seven. (He'd synchronized the watch with Sakamochi's announcement, so he knew it was correct.) Sho hurriedly took out his map and traced his eye to the northern mountain. But the map only included the dotted line of the mountain road, with no symbol for the rest area and public toilet either inside the square area of D-8 or out.

For a moment, panic gripped him, and he reflexively raised his hand to that metal collar and felt compelled to go back down that path.

But he glanced back to that toilet where the splattering sound continued. He shrugged and let out his breath.

No matter how strong the call of nature, Kazuo Kiriyama—*the* Kazuo Kiriyama—would surely be aware of where he was. When he had stuck his head out from the bushes and carefully stared up in this direction, he must have made a visual determination that the toilet was not within sector D-8. And Sho was hiding only thirty meters west of the toilet Kiriyama was using. The rest area would be closer to the forbidden zone than where Sho was hiding, so if Kiriyama was over there, Sho knew he must be safe as well. If he let some groundless fear spur him away from Kiriyama, his plans would be ruined.

Sho took the Virginia Slim back out from his pocket and put it in his lips, then looked up at the near-dusk sky. At this time of year, the sun wouldn't set for another two hours or so, but to the west, orange had begun to mix into the darkened blue sky, and the few small clouds glowed bright orange around their edges. *It's beautiful. Just like me.*

The splattering sound continued. Sho made another smirk. *You must have been holding that in a while now, Kiriyama-kun.*

The sound still continued.

Oh, how I want to smoke you, cigarette. I want to take a shower, do my nails, mix myself one of my screwdrivers, sip the drink, enjoy the smoke, and—

It still continued.

Geez, get it over with already. Kiriyama-kun, quit peeing and get back to work.

But it still continued.

Finally, Sho frowned with his full, downturned eyebrows. He took the cigarette from his mouth and quickly stood up. Following the edge of the thicket, he moved a little closer to the restroom and squinted.

That splattering sound went on. And the door was still open a crack.

With impeccable timing, a gust of wind blew the door open with a creak.

Sho's eyes went wide.

Inside the restroom, a water bottle—one of the ones supplied to the students—hung from the ceiling by a string. The bottle swayed in the breeze. A thin stream of water was leaking out from a small hole, probably opened there by a knife or something. As the bottle moved back and forth, the water came splattering out.

Terrified, Sho looked all around.

Then he saw it—far off, the back of that black uniform passing through the trees and into the distance, the head with that unusual slicked-back hairstyle he'd recognize even from behind.

*What? What? Kiriyama-kun? What? What's going on? W-what?
But I—*

As Kiriyama disappeared into the woods, a dull *bang* of a noise filled Sho's ears. The sound resembled a gunshot muffled by a silencer, or maybe a pillow. He would never know if the sound came from the explosive inside the collar so carefully designed by the government for the Program, or if it had been the reverberations of the blast through his own body.

A full one hundred meters down the slope, Kazuo Kiriyama didn't look back. Instead, he glanced down at his watch.

The second hand had just made its seventh click past five.

21 STUDENTS REMAIN.

Noriko stirred, then opened her eyes. It was past seven in the evening. Her unfocused gaze drifted across the ceiling of the now dim room. Then she looked at Shuya by her side.

He half rose from the stool he'd pulled over and removed the damp cloth from her forehead. He placed his hand where the cloth had been. Just as when he'd checked not long before, her fever was nearly gone. Inside himself, Shuya let out a sigh of relief. *Thank you. Oh, thank you.*

"Shuya," Noriko said, still sounding a bit dazed, "what time is it?"

"Past seven. You got some good sleep."

"Oh."

Noriko slowly sat up in bed. Shuya took his hand off her forehead and helped her sit up.

She said, "I . . ."

Shuya nodded. "Your fever broke. Kawada says it probably wasn't sepsis. Just a really bad cold. You were exhausted."

That seemed to put her at ease. She slowly nodded, then turned to Shuya. "Sorry—to be so much trouble."

"What are you talking about?" Shuya shook his head. "It's not your fault." Then he asked, "Can you eat? We have rice."

Her eyes widened. "Rice?"

"Yeah. Just wait here a moment. Kawada cooked some up."

Shuya left the room.

He stood in the kitchen doorway. Kawada was sitting on a stool, leaning back against the wall. The last traces of sunlight came in through the window, and motes of dust floated in the blue, almost indigo light, which didn't quite reach the edge of the room where Kawada sat, leaving him submerged in near darkness.

Noticing Shuya, he asked, "Is Noriko awake?"

Shuya nodded.

"How's her fever?"

"I think it's gone. Her temperature hasn't gone back up."

Kawada gave him a slight nod, then stood, still holding the shotgun, which hadn't left his grasp for one moment. He lifted the lid of the pot on the gas burner. The two boys had already filled their stomachs with rice and miso soup—though all they had to add to the soup was some leaves from an unidentified plant growing in the backyard.

Shuya asked, "Has the rice gone cold?"

"Hold on for five or ten minutes. I'll bring it in when it's ready."

Shuya thanked him and returned to the examination room.

He sat back down beside the bed and gave Noriko a small nod. "It'll be a moment, but Kawada will bring you some rice—actual rice."

Noriko nodded, then said, "Is there a...bathroom here?"

"Yeah, uh, over this way."

Shuya helped Noriko off the bed, and holding her arm, he guided her across the front waiting room to the bathroom. She was still unsteady, but this was a great improvement from the pain she'd been in before.

When she was ready, he escorted her back. She sat on the edge of the bed, and he wrapped a blanket around her shoulders, as Ms. Anno used to do for him at the House of Mercy and Love when he was a little boy.

"After you've eaten," Shuya said, pulling the edges of the blanket snug, "you should sleep a little more. We'll have to leave here by eleven."

Noriko stared at him. Her eyes still seemed unfocused. "You mean . . ."

Shuya nodded. "Yeah. At eleven, this will become a forbidden zone."

Sakamochi had said as much in his six p.m. announcement. The others were G-1 at seven and I-3 at nine; part of the southwestern shore and the southern slope of the southern mountain. Since they couldn't know exactly where the sector boundaries lay, this meant that nearly the entire southwestern shore was now off-limits.

Noriko's eyes dropped to her knees, and she ran her hand between her forehead and her bangs. "I was sleeping like some idiot."

Shuya placed his hand on her shoulder. "What are you talking about? Of course you should sleep. You need rest."

But suddenly she looked up to him and asked, "Besides Kaori, did anyone die?"

Shuya pressed his lips together and nodded. "Chigusa and . . . and Tsukioka and Niida died."

According to Sakamochi's announcement, those four had died in the hours between noon and six, and the students had already dwindled to twenty-one. Only eighteen hours had passed since the game began, and the Shiroiwa Junior High Ninth Grade Class B had been halved.

Sakamochi had also proudly declared, "Tsukioka got caught in a forbidden zone. Be careful, everyone!"

Sakamochi hadn't said where Sho Tsukioka had died, and Shuya didn't remember hearing any loud explosion during the afternoon. But he couldn't think of a reason for Sakamochi to lie. So Zuki, the member of Kiriyama's Family who was kind of effeminate despite his burly form and rugged features, had been carelessly caught inside one of the forbidden zones and had his head blown off. Save for its boss, the Kiriyama Family was defunct.

Shuya thought about commenting on this, but seeing Noriko's sorrowful expression, he kept it to himself. He couldn't imagine that any talk about the boy whose head had been ripped off his body would have a positive influence on the rest of Noriko's recovery.

"I see . . ." Noriko said quietly. Then she added, "Thanks for this." Underneath the blanket she started to remove Shuya's jacket.

"You can keep wearing that."

"No, I'm fine now."

Shuya took his jacket and straightened the blanket over her shoulders.

After a little while, Kawada came in. He held a round tray, topped with a bowl, up at shoulder height like a waiter. Steam wafted up from the dish.

Lowering the tray, Kawada said, "Order's up."

Shuya grinned. "What is this, some soba noodle joint?"

"Sadly, this ain't soba noodles. But I hope it's all right."

Kawada placed the dish, tray and all, beside Noriko on the bed.

Noriko peered down into the bowl and asked, "You made rice porridge?"

"Yes, ma'am," Kawada said, in English. His accent sounded flawless to Shuya.

"Thanks." Noriko picked up the spoon he'd provided. Then she lifted the bowl to her lips and took a sip.

"It's delicious," she said. "You put egg in it."

Shuya looked at Kawada, who said, "It's our specialty, ma'am."

Shuya asked, "Where'd you find eggs?"

All of the fresh food in the refrigerator had gone bad, probably because the government had cleared out everyone well in advance. Shuya assumed the same would be true of every house on the island.

Kawada gave Shuya a sidelong grin. "I found a house where they'd been raising a hen—though she hadn't been fed in a while and looked pretty weak."

Shuya made an exaggerated shake of his head. "When we ate our rice, I seem to recall there being no eggs."

Kawada raised his eyebrows. "There was only the one. Hey, I'm nicer to girls. I was just born that way."

Shuya laughed out his nose.

Kawada went back to the kitchen and returned with some tea. As Noriko ate, the three of them drank the tea. It gave off a slightly sweet and nostalgic aroma.

"Damn it," Shuya groaned. "This feels too damn peaceful, the three of us sitting here drinking tea like this."

Kawada grinned. "I can put on coffee after this. But I think Noriko might want to stick with the black tea."

Noriko nodded, smiling around the spoon that was still in her mouth.

Then Shuya said, "Hey, Kawada."

Nothing had changed the fact that they were still inside this killing game, but Noriko's apparent recovery had made him talkative. "Someday, let's drink tea like this again, the three of us together. We can sit on some veranda and watch the cherry blossoms."

Maybe that could never be, but Kawada simply shrugged. "You're not talking like a rocker, Nanahara. You sound more like a geezer."

"I get that sometimes."

Kawada chuckled. Shuya joined in, and he thought Noriko did as well.

When she finished her meal, she thanked Kawada, and he took her bowl. With his other hand, he gestured for Shuya to pass over her empty teacup, and he did.

"Kawada," Noriko said, "I'm feeling so much better. Thank you, really. I'm sorry I caused you so much trouble."

Kawada grinned and in English said, "You're welcome, ma'am." Then, in Japanese, added, "But it looks like the antibiotic wasn't necessary."

"That's not true. I know this might sound weird, but they made me feel safe enough to fall asleep."

Kawada smiled again. "Well, we can't completely rule out the possibility you still have sepsis. Anyway, you should get some more rest. Don't push your luck."

To Shuya, he added, "Mind if I take a nap?"

Shuya nodded. "Are you tired?"

"No, but I want to get some sleep in while I can. After we leave here, I'll stay awake through the night. Okay?"

"Okay."

Kawada gave him a quick nod and was carrying the tray out of the room when Noriko said, "Kawada, you should sleep here." She gestured to the adjacent bed.

But from the doorway, he looked over his shoulder and gave her a smile that seemed to say no. "I'll let you two have some privacy. I'll sleep on the bench out here." He tilted his head and added, "But if you're going to be intimate, please be considerate of your neighbors."

Even in the low light, Shuya could see Noriko's cheeks turn red.

Then Kawada left. Through the half-open door, Shuya could hear him walk to the kitchen, then after a moment, walk back to the waiting room. Then silence.

Noriko grinned. "He's so funny." After her meal, some of the color had returned to her face.

"Yeah." Shuya smiled too. "I never really talked to him before, but he kind of reminds me of Mimura."

Kawada didn't resemble Shinji Mimura in the slightest, not in his physique or in his looks. But the way he talked, curt, yet not without humor, was a lot like The Third Man. And though both were the opposite of model students, they were incredibly smart and reliable.

Noriko nodded. "Yeah, he does. Totally."

Then she said, "I wonder where Mimura is now?"

Shuya let out a breath. He'd been trying to think of a way to contact his friend, but with Noriko sick, he hadn't been able to try anything.

"Yeah, if he were here . . ."

He felt that with both Kawada and Shinji Mimura, no one could match them. Add Hiroki Sugimura, and they'd be invincible, with nothing to fear.

Noriko said, "I remember the class match." She lifted her head and looked at a point on the ceiling. "Not this year's, but last. It was the finals. Mimura was practically on his own against Class D—four of their students were his teammates from the basketball team. Then after your softball game, you rushed over and joined in, and you two came from behind to take the win."

"Yeah." Shuya nodded, thinking, *Looks like she's feeling talkative too.* That was welcome news. "I guess we did."

"I cheered until I lost my voice. When you won, Yukie and us, we went wild."

"Yeah."

Shuya remembered it too—because the typically gentle Noriko was screaming louder than anyone. Yoshitoki Kuninobu, who wasn't very athletic—though he was no Yoshio Akamatsu—was standing apart from Noriko and the others. When Shuya glanced his way, Yoshitoki threw him the devil's horns. Shuya felt a little guilty toward the cheering girls, because Yoshitoki's tiny gesture moved him the most.

Yoshitoki . . .

Lost in the memory, he looked at Noriko and noticed she had dropped her head and begun to cry.

He put his hand on Noriko's blanket-shrouded shoulder and asked, "What's wrong?"

"I . . ." She sobbed once, faintly. "I told myself I wouldn't cry, but then I thought . . . I thought how wonderful our class was, and then this."

Shuya nodded. Maybe it was the last traces of her fever, or the medicine she'd been given, but she was having some rough emotional swings. He kept his hand on her shoulder until she stopped crying.

Then she said, "Sorry," and wiped her eyes. After her tears were dry, she said, "Shuya, I wasn't going to tell you this, because I didn't want it to upset you."

"Tell me what?"

She looked into his eyes. "Did you know how many of the girls had a crush on you?"

At this sudden change of topic, Shuya made an uneasy grin. "What are you talking about?"

But Noriko continued, her expression serious, "Megumi, and I think Yukiko too."

Shuya tilted his head in puzzled disbelief. *Megumi Eto and Yukiko Kitano. Two girls already out of the game.*

"Them?" Somehow, it felt wrong to call them *them*. "What about them?"

Noriko looked up at him and quietly said, "They both liked you."

Shuya felt his face stiffen. After some time, he forced himself to say, "Really?"

"Yeah." Noriko looked away, then nodded. "Girls can just sense that kind of thing. So . . . just remember that when you think of them."

She tilted her head and added, "Though it seems arrogant for me to say that."

Shuya pictured the faces of Megumi Eto and Yukiko Kitano. He committed them to just a small part of his memory—about half a teaspoon's worth each.

"Wow." The word tumbled out on his breath. Then he said, "You could have waited to tell me that until after we've escaped."

"Sorry. Did it come as a shock?"

"Yeah, a little bit."

"It's just . . ." Noriko tilted her head again. "If I were to die without telling you, you'd have never known."

Shuya's head jolted up, and he squeezed her left wrist tight. "Please. No more thinking like that. We're. Together. Until. The. End. Got it? We survive, together."

Startled by his sudden vehemence, Noriko said, "Sorry."

Then Shuya said, "So by the way . . ."

"What?"

"I know someone who likes you."

This time, Noriko's eyes widened a little. "Really? Someone who likes *me*?" she said innocently, but her expression immediately fell. The fading sunlight, filtered through the window curtains, cast a rectangular, barely perceptible catchlight in her eyes.

She asked, "Is he someone in our class?"

Thinking of his childhood friend's affable, goggling eyes, Shuya slowly shook his head no. *Damn it. How much simpler would it have been to stress over some love triangle with my best friend of ten years? But that won't be an issue now. No sir, not ever.*

"Nope," he said.

Noriko seemed somewhat relieved as she dropped her eyes down to her skirt near her knees. All she said was, "Oh."

Then she looked up again and said, "Who is it? I'm not in any of the clubs, and I don't really know any of the kids in the other classes."

Shuya shook his head. "I won't tell. Not until we escape."

She looked a little skeptical but didn't pursue the matter.

After they'd fallen silent for a while, Shuya looked up at the ceiling. Unbecoming for a medical clinic, where sanitation was supposed to be top priority, the lampshade over the hanging circular fluorescent light was covered with dust—not that the light worked. And even if it did, Shuya wouldn't turn it on anyway.

"Huh." he said. "Megumi . . . *san*." He added the polite *san* after her name. Boys can be so fickle. "And Kitano-san. If it's true, I don't know what they saw in me."

The room had gone almost dark, but Shuya thought he could see her smile a little.

She said, "Can I tell you what I think?"

"I'm all ears."

Noriko tilted her head. "What's good about you is everything."

Shuya laughed and shook his head. "What's that supposed to mean?"

Dead earnest, she said, "That's what it means to love someone. Isn't that how you feel about that girl?"

Shuya visualized Kazumi Shintani's face. He thought about what Noriko had said. At first, he wasn't sure if he should tell the truth, but he decided to stick with honesty.

"Yeah. You're right. I guess that's how it feels."

Sounding amused, she said, "If it doesn't, it's not the real thing," and laughed. She smiled, but only with her mouth.

"What's so funny?"

"Even in this situation, talking about it makes me jealous."

He looked at her, though now in the darkness, he could hardly make out her face. He again wavered over what to say to her, and again went with the truth.

"That guy who likes you—I can understand why."

Noriko looked up to him again.

"You're so wonderful," he said.

He thought he saw her well-shaped eyebrows twitch, and her lips formed a smile with a hint of sadness.

"Really?" she said. "Even if it's a lie, it's nice to hear."

"It's no lie."

Noriko was quiet for a moment, then said, "Can I ask you a favor?"

Shuya raised his eyebrows as if to ask her, *What?* But he didn't know if Noriko could see. Still seated across from him, she leaned forward and gently placed her hands on his arms and rested her head on his shoulder. Her shoulder-length hair brushed against his cheek and ear.

They remained like that for a long while, until the dwindling daylight outside the window transformed into moonlight.

21 STUDENTS REMAIN.

Before dusk completely faded into darkness, Hirono Shimizu (Girls #10) headed west from the thicket where she'd been hiding. She couldn't handle it anymore—her entire body felt hot, as if she were in a scorching desert.

Water.

I need water.

Kaori Minami had shot her in her upper left arm. Hirono had ripped open her blood-soaked sleeve and found that the bullet had passed clean through her arm. The exit wound was the worst of it, shredding a large patch of skin. But the bullet had narrowly missed any of her major blood vessels, and once she had bandaged the wound with her torn-off sleeve, the bleeding soon stopped.

But the wound became hotter and hotter, and the fever spread through her body. The initial chills came and went, quickly replaced by the burning heat. She had finished off the last of her bottled water by the time Sakamochi gave his six o'clock announcement. After she'd killed Kaori, Hirono had run for two hundred meters, fleeing Shuya, and hid inside a thick patch of bushes. There, she used quite a lot of her water attempting to clean the wound. (She deeply regretted doing that.)

Nearly two hours had passed since then. For a time, she'd been sweating profusely beneath her sailor fuku, but by now, she'd run out of sweat. She was severely dehydrated. To put it simply, unlike Noriko Nakagawa, Hirono had indeed developed sepsis, and since she hadn't disinfected the wound, the symptoms were rapidly progressing— though of course, Hirono had no way of knowing this.

All she knew was: *I need water.*

As she moved across the green-covered mountain with as much caution as she could muster, thoughts of hatred for Kaori Minami whirled in her head, their revolutions hastened by the fever throughout her body and the dryness of her throat.

Hirono Shimizu wasn't about to trust anyone else in this game. She had always been tight with Mitsuko Souma, and her seat number was only one ahead of Mitsuko's, so when she left the school, with only Hiroki Sugimura between them, she could have let him pass and managed to meet up with Mitsuko, but she didn't. Hirono knew exactly how fearsome Mitsuko was.

Here's an example: their group of delinquents had a dispute with a similar group from another school. A little later, the leader-figure of that other gang (who even at her age was a yakuza's lover) was hit by a car and ended up badly injured. Hirono had heard the girl had nearly died. Mitsuko never said anything about it, but Hirono understood that she had gotten one of the guys she knew to do it. Mitsuko had any number of men who were willing to do absolutely anything for her.

Hirono imagined that if she met up with Mitsuko, the girl would use her for everything she was worth, just to ultimately shoot her in the back in cold blood. Mitsuko might have been able to get the more laid-back Yoshimi Yahagi to trust her (Hirono remembered that Yoshimi was dead now—her intuition told her that Mitsuko had been the one to kill her), but Hirono would have none of that.

Neither could she imagine ever trusting any of the rest of her class either. The ones who tried to act like they were good were the ones who had no trouble kicking you to the curb. Hirono may have only been around for fifteen years, but she knew that much all too well.

But even so, she was reluctant to go around killing her classmates. She'd done prostitution and she'd tried drugs, and she'd fought and fought with her fed-up parents, but murder was taboo. Sure, under the rules of the game, killing was permitted; there was no crime in it.

But.

Maybe I've done a lot of bad things, but almost all of it never caused anyone any trouble. Sure, I sold my body, but unlike the girls who tried to act all pure while using those phone "dating" services (she knew Mayumi Tendo was one of those girls), *I went through Mitsuko Souma's connections to get into a ring of professionals—now that took real resolve. And if a person wants to try drugs, isn't that her personal freedom? Is a department store jeopardized so badly when some makeup gets stolen from the cosmetics department? Really, when they're backed by huge capital? And sure, I bullied some kids, but only the ones who were asking for it. I fought girls from other schools, but we all knew what we were getting into—none of us were new to the game. Anyway, I . . .*

I'm not the kind of girl who's okay with killing people. That much I know.

But . . . but . . .

Self-defense is different. If someone is trying to kill me, that leaves me with no other choice. And if I manage to survive this game that way and make it back home . . . then doesn't that call for some champagne? Or, if that time limit comes and I have to die—on this point, her thoughts weren't clear—*well, there's nothing to be done about that.*

And so Hirono hid herself in that farmhouse where she later had that shootout with Kaori Minami.

Once she was sure no one else was inside, she began to feel at ease. Occasionally, she looked out the window, and when she caught a glimpse of a figure in the storage shed, her heart raced with fear.

After several minutes of debate, she decided to leave the house. (After all, she was quite good at sneaking out of her own.) She just couldn't bear having someone so near. Since the house had no back door, and the only windows faced the shed, she quietly climbed through the endmost window.

But at that moment, that very moment, Kaori stuck her head out from the shed to take a look. And without warning she shot at Hirono, who hadn't done anything. Kaori's bullet caught her in the arm, and she tumbled out over the windowsill. Somehow, Hirono got to her feet, and for the first time, she held out the revolver she'd been given and fired. She was pinned there, against the wall at the corner of the house, when Shuya Nanahara appeared.

That bitch. Always playing innocent, shrieking over these boy bands, and she tried to kill me on sight. Well I took care of her. (It was self-defense. Not a jury on earth would convict me. No doubt.) But if the rest of the class is like her, I can't show any mercy, I think.

Then Hirono thought about Shuya Nanahara. At least he hadn't pointed a gun at her. (That's how she had gotten her opening to shoot Kaori.) And he'd said he was with Noriko Nakagawa.

Shuya Nanahara and Noriko Nakagawa. Have they been dating? They hadn't seemed to be. Are they trying to escape together?

Hirono reflexively shook her head.

Ridiculous. Out here, nothing would be more dangerous than being with someone else. Get in a group and you'll have no right to complain when someone shoots you in the back. And escape? Utterly impossible.

I didn't see Noriko Nakagawa, but if he was telling the truth, it wouldn't be long before he killed her, or before she killed him. Whichever. But if one of them ended up surviving . . . then maybe we'll end up having to kill each other. But who gives a damn about that right now? Right now, I need . . .

Water.

The next thing she knew, she had traveled a good distance. The faint sunlight in the western sky had disappeared. Now, as it had in the early morning of the game's beginning, the full moon, eerily bright, hung amid the jet-black sky and cast its pale blue light over the island.

Still gripping her .38 revolver, a Smith & Wesson Model 10, Hirono sprinted from one thicket to the next. She ducked and held her breath. She popped her head out from the shadow of the bushes. Beyond a narrow crop field stood a lone house. The northern mountain was to Hirono's back, and low foothills encroached on the other side of the home. She looked to her left and saw several more fields, with two similar houses far beyond, behind which the ground sloped upward into the southern mountain. According to her map, a relatively large east-west road divided the island at the foot of that southern mountain. And from where that mountain stood, Hirono seemed to have made it all the way to near the western shore. As she had confirmed before heading out, she wasn't near any of the forbidden zones.

Enduring her thirst, Hirono observed the house ahead. The area was silent and still.

Still crouched, she slipped through the field. The house stood on slightly elevated land. Hirono stopped at the edge of the field, looked to her rear, then observed the house again. It was an ordinary, old, single-story farmhouse. Unlike the house where she'd previously hidden, this one had a tile roof. An unpaved road led away to her left, and a single mini pickup truck was parked in front of the house, along with a moped and a bicycle.

The house where she first hid hadn't had running water. This one likely wouldn't either. Hirono looked to her left and right . . .

And there, to the right, at the back of the yard, the farthest side from the incoming driveway, she saw it—a well. It even had a rope and pulley. Several short, slender, and leafy fruit trees—tangerines or something—grew around the well, but none had any low branches for anyone to be hiding behind.

Since her left arm was out of commission, she tucked her revolver down the front of her skirt, and in the moonlight, she rummaged through the dirt, finding a rock just big enough to fit in her hand.

She tossed it high.

The rock traced an arc through the air and struck the roof with a *thud*. It clattered down the tiles and fell to the ground and made a dull *thunk*.

Hirono held her revolver and waited, keeping an eye on her watch. She waited longer.

Five minutes passed. No head appeared peeking out from the house's door or windows. Hirono clambered up to the yard and ran for the well. Her head spun from her thirst and her fever.

The well was a concrete cylinder extending eighty centimeters above the ground. Still holding the gun, she set her right hand against its lip.

A full six, maybe seven meters below, the moonlight pooled in a tiny circle. Her own silhouette reflected within.

Water. Yes, no dry well after all.

Hirono tucked the revolver back down the front of her skirt and used her right hand to unsling her daypack from her left shoulder. She let the bag fall to the ground. She took hold of the frayed rope that ran up through an ancient-looking pulley suspended from a wooden crossbeam before dropping back into the well.

She pulled the rope, and a small bucket popped up on the water's surface. Hirono desperately hauled up the rope. With her left arm too immobilized, she had to pull up a short length of the rope, then hold it in place against the concrete lip with her knee. But somehow, she managed to lift the bucket closer.

Finally, the bucket reached the top of the well. One last time, she held the rope with her knee and took the bucket by the handle and placed it on the rim of the well.

Water.

The bucket was brimming with water. She didn't care if it might make her sick. Her body needed the water and needed it now.

But then she saw something that made her utter a tiny yelp.

A frog, as big as her fingernail, was swimming in the bucket. Its black, beady eyes and slimy back glistened in the moonlight. In the sun, its skin would be some disgusting fluorescent green or a dirty mud-brown. She hated no animal more, and the very sight of this tiny, loathsome creature evoked the touch of its slimy skin. A shiver ran down her spine.

But Hirono suppressed her disgust. She didn't have the energy to pull the bucket up again. Her thirst had become nearly more than she could bear. Somehow, she needed to shoo away this frog.

Suddenly the frog crawled up the side of the bucket and leaped toward her. She let out a small shriek and twisted her body. Even in this life-and-death scenario, she couldn't stand what she couldn't stand. She successfully dodged the frog, but her hand let go of the bucket, which made an abrupt fall back into the well. The splash reverberated up the concrete shaft. And that was that.

Hirono groaned and looked to where the frog had jumped. *I'll kill you, I'll kill you, I'll fucking kill you!*

But then something else caught her eye.

A dark figure in a school coat stopped in his tracks four or five meters in front of her.

Hirono's back had been to the house, where behind the figure the back door stood open. A memory of a childhood game came to her unbidden—the one where the person who was "it" would turn and everyone else had to freeze.

But this was no time to reminisce. What caught her attention was the thin ribbonlike object held between the hands of the short, scrawny, frog-faced Toshinori Oda (Boys #4). In an instant, Hirono recognized that object was a belt.

See, look at this. Here's little Toshinori Oda, the sheltered son of a company president living in the nice part of town. Always such an average boy. He's good at the violin (he'd won some prefecture-wide competition) and is always oh-so-gracious and well behaved.

And he's trying to kill me!

Like a freeze-framed video image suddenly unpaused, Toshinori sprang forward, raising his belt in one hand to attack. Its large buckle flashed in the moonlight. Something like that could tear through flesh. He was only four meters away now and closing.

But that was far enough.

Hirono brought her arm to her front and grabbed the revolver. She felt the now-familiar texture of its grip inside her hand.

Toshinori was upon her. She fired. She fired three times in a row. All three struck his chest, making three clean holes in his school coat.

Toshinori spun halfway around and fell on his face. A cloud of dust flew into the air, and he was motionless, with not even a twitch.

Hirono stuffed the revolver back down the front of her skirt. The hot barrel burned against her stomach, but such pain was beyond her concern. Right now, water was all that mattered.

She picked up her daypack and went inside the house. She had been foolish to expose her back to the house, but she no longer had to worry about anyone being inside. And Toshinori must have had water.

Hirono debated over whether to take out her government-supplied flashlight, but she easily spotted Toshinori's daypack right inside the open doorway. Hirono knelt down and worked the zipper open with her right hand.

The water bottles were there. One was still sealed and the other still half full. *Oh, thank you.*

Still kneeling, Hirono took the cap off the half-full bottle, pressed her lips flush around the rim, and raised the bottle. *Is this an indirect kiss with a boy who tried to kill me—even better, one who's already dead?* Anyway, such matters were as remote now as somewhere south of the equator or the snow-covered flag at the South Pole—or even beyond the moon. *Houston, this is Armstrong. That's one small step for a man . . .*

Hirono gulped down the water. It was delicious—exquisitely delicious. She'd never had water that tasted so good. The tepid liquid felt like ice water as it gushed down her throat and into her stomach. Delicious.

She emptied the bottle in one drink and let out a satisfied sound.

Suddenly, something wrapped tight around her throat, just above that collar all her classmates wore. She coughed uncontrollably, and the water still in her mouth sprayed out from her lips.

With her good arm, she clutched for the object digging into her throat. As she tried to pull herself free, she twisted her head around. Just to her right, she saw a furious, grimacing face. *Toshinori Oda— but you were dead just now!*

Something was choking her hard. It took a few seconds for her to realize it was the boy's belt.

How how how—how is he still alive?

The darkness of the inside of the house began to turn red. Her hand clawed at the belt, and her nails were snapping off. Blood ran down her fingers.

My gun.

Remembering the weapon, she reached for the revolver tucked into the front of her skirt.

But her arm was kicked away by a foot in an expensive leather shoe. With a cracking sound, her right arm took after her left and went completely numb. For that brief moment, the belt loosened—but it tightened again. No longer able to grab at the belt, Hirono merely flailed her disturbingly contorted right arm.

But even that only lasted ten seconds. Her arm dropped, dangling there, and her body went limp. Though not in the same rank as Takako Chigusa or Mitsuko Souma, Hirono had been decently attractive, with an alluring maturity that sometimes got her mistaken for a young woman in high school or even college. But now her face bulged with the trapped blood, and her tongue, swollen to twice its normal size, slopped out from the middle of her gaping mouth.

Despite this, Toshinori Oda doggedly continued to choke her (though not without an occasional glance over his shoulder).

After more than five minutes had passed, Toshinori released the belt from Hirono's neck. No longer breathing, her body slumped forward and struck the lip of the raised floor with a *thud*—and a *crack*. Some bone inside her face must have fractured. Her hair, worn spiked in a kind of punk style, was now strewn in all directions, its ends fading into the darkness. Only the nape of her neck, peeking out from the collar of the sailor suit, and her left arm, where she had torn off her sleeve, emerged from the shadows, pale and clear.

For a time, Toshinori Oda stood there, panting. His stomach was still in pain, but it wasn't that bad. When he'd first opened his daypack and found that weird, rigid, gray vest, he hadn't known what it was. But it did exactly what the included manual had said it would.

Amazing what a bulletproof vest could do.

20 STUDENTS REMAIN.

Though the vicinity of the small hill at the foot of the northern mountain had fallen into complete darkness, the nearly full moon offered a commanding view of the sea. The islands of the Seto Inland Sea rose out of the black water, but no lights of any ships were anywhere near—probably because the government had restricted their access. Neither could the guard ships be seen. They must be anchored with their lights off.

He'd seen this before, only from a lower elevation, when he'd left the school. Not that he was feeling any nostalgia over it.

"All right," Shinji said. "Over here."

Shinji stuffed his pistol into his belt, climbed onto the rock, then helped Yutaka up. Yutaka was out of breath, largely from the mountain hike, but the constant fear of a foe springing out from the darkness hadn't helped. But he managed to take Shinji's hand and clamber atop the rock.

The two boys got on their stomachs and looked down the other edge of the crag.

Down below stretched a carpet of inky black trees, beyond which a faint light could be seen. It was the school where Sakamochi was. Very little light escaped the steel plates placed over the windows. The building was more than a hundred meters away. With the school's sector, G-7, long since designated a forbidden zone, the two boys would be killed instantly once they crossed the border, but they were more than far enough away. While some daylight had yet remained, Shinji used his map, compass, and a cross-bearing navigation technique to accurately locate the sector's boundaries. The school stood eighty meters from its nearest neighboring cell, F-7, where Shinji and Yutaka were. Neither F-7 nor H-7 on the opposite side had been included in the list of forbidden zones in the six o'clock announcement. Perfect.

Shinji remembered Sakamochi saying Sho Tsukioka had been caught in one of the forbidden zones. Though Shinji found him a repulsive fairy ("How 'bout a date, Shinji?"), and this was no time to be concerned about any of the others, he nonetheless felt a little sorry for the boy having his head blown off by a bomb. *Where had that happened?*

And the news of Takako Chigusa's death had left a knot of remorse in his chest. Sure, she had been the prettiest girl in class (at least according to Shinji's tastes), but more than that, she had been friends with Hiroki Sugimura since the two were little children. Contrary to the mistaken belief of many in Class B, Hiroki and Takako weren't dating (Shinji heard it straight from the boy himself), but even still, her death must have hit Hiroki hard.

Sugimura, where are you?

But Shinji decided to focus on the present. He took a good look at the school below and its surrounding geography. They would have to pull a rope across that school and all the way into the next sector. Seeing it in person, he realized how long a distance it would be.

As he observed the gentle light leaking from the steel-plated windows, Shinji thought, *Shit. Sakamochi and the rest, they're in there. It's dinnertime, and for all I know, they're lounging in there eating stir-fried udon noodles, those bastards.* (Shinji specifically thought of the fried udon because that's what he so badly wanted to eat; the dish had become one of his favorites after his uncle, who lived alone, invited him over for dinner a few times at his small rented house and made the noodles.)

Shinji and Yutaka had already gathered what they needed.

Though it wasn't specifically indicated on the map (which had marked the building with the blue dot used for private residences), the two boys had found a farmers' co-op just to the south of the school, near the main east-west road. Both its walls and roof were made of corrugated metal, and a sign on the door read NORTHERN TAKAMATSU AGRICULTURAL COOPERATIVE OKI ISLAND BRANCH OFFICE. (Shinji had long since known they were on Oki Island, off Takamatsu City, but Yutaka gave an astonished, "Huh.") The building didn't have any offices or co-op ATMs like Shinji would have expected, but instead was a simple warehouselike space, inside of which rested an assortment of heavy machinery, including tractors, combines, and threshers. One corner had been partitioned off into a small office space with desks and such sundries. Regardless, Shinji had easily found the ammonium nitrate. It was even fresh and dry. And the well-stocked gasoline storage tanks inside the warehouse meant that the two boys didn't have to go looking from car to car.

They'd found the pulley not too far east of the co-op, in a well next door to the house where Shinji had found the Macintosh PowerBook at the start of the game.

Their biggest challenge, besides finding the ammonium nitrate, was the rope. In order to span the entire sector of G-7, which lay before their eyes, the boys would at the very least need more than three hundred meters of rope. But in order to remain unnoticed by Sakamochi and his soldiers, it would be best to leave a great deal of slack, so they really wanted an even longer piece. Such a rope did not prove easy to find. Shinji came across a line of rope in the farmers' co-op, but it wasn't even two hundred meters long, and besides, the line seemed intended for use in greenhouses or something, and was less than three millimeters thick. Shinji didn't think it would be strong enough.

Luckily, by following the coast a little ways south of the harbor, which along with the village had been designated a forbidden zone, Shinji and Yutaka had found a fisherman's private storehouse. The sea-weathered fishing rope was over three hundred meters long, with the weight and bulk to match, but Shinji and Yutaka split the rope into manageable lengths that the two boys hauled back to the co-op.

Then, leaving everything hidden in that warehouse, they came to this rock.

Shinji squinted into the darkness. The foothills of the northern mountain fenced in this side of the school—the north—and off to the right—the west. To the left—the east—the woods extended past the north edge of the village and down to the shore. And the area beyond the school opened into rice fields, with a few scattered copses and houses in between. Beyond the fields, Shinji could barely make out the co-op warehouse. To the left of the building, the scattered rooftops gradually began to haphazardly crowd together, reaching across the border of the forbidden zone where they became the village proper.

Yutaka tapped Shinji on the shoulder, and Shinji turned his head to the right to look at him. Yutaka took his student notepad out of his pocket and began to write on the vertical ruled lines.

Before they'd moved out, Shinji had written his friend a warning not to say anything out loud that might give them away. If Sakamochi's men found out the two boys were still up to no good, they would not be so lenient this time and would certainly send that remote signal to blow up their collars.

Shinji had wondered why Sakamochi and his men hadn't done that in the first place. It was probably because the intent of the game was to, as much as possible, make the students fight each other. It might have had something to do with the rumor he'd heard that the higher-ups placed bets on the game. If that was true, then Shinji didn't know about Yutaka, but as the ace guard of the Shiroiwa Junior High basketball team, "The Third Man" would no doubt be one of the favorites.

For this very reason, Sakamochi couldn't kill him lightly. That was Shinji's guess, anyway. It followed that Yoshitoki Kuninobu and Fumiyo Fujiyoshi, who had been killed before anyone left the room, were irrelevant to the betting—that is, no one had bet on them.

Still, as long as Sakamochi (*that fucking Kinpati Sakamocho*) had complete authority over the game, he could detonate their collars at any moment. All the boys could do was hope that they could drop the bomb on the school before that happened. Naturally this was not an arrangement Shinji appreciated. His uncle taught him to be the judge of his own actions, and he hated having his fate in someone else's clutches.

But looking down at the light from the school, Shinji only shook his head. Complaining about it wasn't going to solve anything.

He remembered his uncle once telling him, "Don't worry about the things you can't change. Just do what you can, Shinji—even if you have almost no chance of succeeding."

Apparently finished with his writing, Yutaka tapped his shoulder again, and Shinji looked back to the notepad. He had trouble reading it in the dark, so he held the paper up to catch the moonlight.

Yutaka had written, [*How are we going to pull the rope?*]

Then, [*We can't throw that much rope far enough from here. And we didn't even bring it with us. What are we doing?*]

Shinji hadn't told him the next step of the plan. He'd left the explanation at gathering the materials to build a ropeway. Shinji gave him a small nod, took out his own pencil, and wrote in Yutaka's notepad.

[*I brought some string. We'll run it over the school, then attach the rope to the other end. Then we return here and pull on the string to bring the rope back across—just before we carry out the attack.*]

He handed the notepad back to Yutaka, who read it closely, then looked at Shinji and gave a nod of apparent satisfaction. Then he wrote.

[*You're going to tie the string to a rock or something and throw it across, right?*]

Shinji shook his head. Yutaka's eyes widened in confusion, and he thought for a while before writing again.

[*You're going to make a bow and arrow? Then tie the string to it and let it fly?*]

Shinji shook his head again, then took the notepad and began running his pencil.

[*That one might work. Not even I could throw a softball 300m anyway. But we can't afford to miss our target. What if I hit the school with the rock or arrow or whatever it was? Or what if I missed and*] *got the string tangled up in something, and when I'm trying to pull it back, it snaps? We don't have a backup. We're going to use a more reliable way.*]

Instead of picking up his pencil, Yutaka gave Shinji a questioning look. Shinji slid the notepad back to himself and continued.

[*We're going to tie one end of the string to a tree over here. Then we take the other end and go down the mountain. We don't need to draw it taut until we're on the far side.*]

Yutaka read this, but this time his eyebrows immediately lowered and he looked skeptical as he scrawled.

[*Not possible. Won't it catch on a tree or something for sure? Somewhere in the middle.*]

Shinji grinned.

Yutaka had good reason to think it impossible. The distance they'd traveled to get here had been covered with trees both big and small. If they ran the string avoiding the school's sector, G-7, then pulled it tight after, the string would catch those many trees and accomplish nothing but to draw a giant curve across the mountainside, like a bizarre piece of outdoor modern art.

This installation is quite large, but becomes imperceptible from five meters away, and it is therefore impossible to see the entire sculpture. This portrays the delicate balance in the relationship between man and nature, and . . .

And the dense woods continued into area G-7 itself, all the way up to the school grounds. Running the string across would be impossible, as long as Shinji couldn't cut down each and every tree, or unless he could turn into a hundred-foot-tall giant. (Now that he thought about it, he remembered an old special-effects monster movie his uncle had showed him on videotape—one where a superhero trampled a city as he fought to save the world from a kaiju. They don't make many of those movies anymore.) With such things so obviously beyond the realm of possibility, it was no wonder that Yutaka had asked how Shinji would throw the rope across (though that too, of course, was impossible).

In a flourish, Shinji spread his arms wide (since he was on his stomach, the gesture wasn't particularly effective). Then he wrote.

[*How about we launch some advertising balloons.*]

Yutaka read the note and knitted his brows again, and Shinji waved him to come down from the rock. After they had climbed down and sat at the base of the rock, Shinji reached inside his daypack. He pulled out its contents and lined them up on the ground.

There were half a dozen bug-spray-sized canisters, several hundred-meter rolls of kite string (he'd found the above inside the farm co-op), electrical tape, and a box of black garbage bags.

Shinji picked up one of the canisters and displayed it to Yutaka. It was blue, with bold red letters that read VOICE CHANGER. (Just below was the slogan, "You'll be the life of the party!" Wow, really.) Below all that was a drawing of a cartoon duck Shinji recognized as a knock-off of a Walt Disney character. An opening, like the mouthpiece of a flute, jutted out from the canister's top.

[*To tell you the truth,*] Shinji wrote, [*I only thought of this plan when I remembered seeing these in the house where I found the PowerBook. You know what this is, right?*]

Before Shinji took the pulley, they had gone to the house next door and retrieved the canisters. At first, Shinji wondered why the person living there had so many of the things. The files left on the PowerBook's hard drive offered a clue. Judging from their names, which included "5th Grade Science" and "3rd Term Report Card Incomplete," the computer's owner must have been an elementary school teacher—probably from *that* school.

Yutaka covered his nose and opened his mouth. Shinji nodded.

[*Right. It makes you sound like that duck. Anyway, it's filled with helium. And these were pulled from the market as defective. They've got a shitload of gas in them.*]

Yutaka still seemed unconvinced. Thinking a live demonstration would be the fastest way to explain, he tore open the pack of garbage bags and took one out. He opened the bag, put the canister's nozzle (actually a mouthpiece) inside, and sealed it with electrical tape. Then he depressed the canister's actuator and the garbage bag began to quickly expand.

As he held the button down, Shinji thought, *This would be funnier with a condom. Though I guess it would never get quite big enough. What? Do I have any on me? Well sure, this is a school trip, after all. Anything can happen, right? You want to know if I'm still carrying them even after I got rid of my extra clothes and everything else? Well, yeah, I am. You never know, they still might come in handy.*

When the bag was just about full, Shinji grabbed it right above the canister, twisted it, and taped it closed. He took out a roll of string and wound it over the tape, then removed the canister. Just in case, he folded over the end of the bag and taped it again.

Then he let go.

The garbage bag floated upward. It rose until the string was taut, and even seemed to nearly lift up the spool, but stopped at eye height.

Out loud, Shinji said, "See?"

Yutaka was bobbing his head. He had probably gotten the idea while Shinji was still working.

Shinji unwound the string from a second spool and tied the string to the one hanging down from the balloon. Just to be sure, he secured it with tape. He then took each string in both of his hands and moved the balloon as if it were walking on two legs. Then he pointed to a nearby tree. He moved the strings again. Here were his giant's legs—though these were too frail to crush a city and, at the moment, stood no taller than he.

Yutaka gave two deep nods. He seemed to have completely understood it now. Then he mouthed words without voicing them. Shinji thought he said, "You rock, Shinji," but it could also have been, "You suck, Shinji." Whatever, it didn't matter.

Shinji grabbed the notepad and wrote, [*We'll make one or two more balloons and attach them too. But I don't know how far up they can take the thread. And wind will also be trouble. But let's give it a shot.*]

Yutaka read the note and nodded.

Shinji looked up. Even in the moonlight, the black bags would never be noticed by Sakamochi's men. Right now, the wind was calm, though Shinji didn't know how it would be higher up.

Then he said, "Let's hurry."

Shinji signaled for Yutaka to hold onto the first balloon, and then he pulled out another garbage bag.

20 STUDENTS REMAIN.

48

Just past ten o'clock, Shuya heard Kawada get up.

Shuya had kept watch over Noriko as she slept on the clinic bed. Now he fumbled through the near pitch darkness and found his way to the adjacent waiting room.

Kawada looked at him, said, "I'll make some coffee," and strode down the hall. Apparently, he had much better night vision.

Shuya returned to Noriko's bed, where he found she had removed her blanket and was sitting herself up.

"You should rest a little longer," he said.

"Yeah . . ." She nodded. Then, hesitantly, she added, "Could you ask Kawada, if he's boiling water, to make some extra for me? Just a cup will do."

Within the faint moonlight filtering through the curtains, Noriko sat on the edge of the bed with her hands beside her legs. Her head was pointed a little down and to the side.

"Sure," Shuya said. "But why?"

Noriko seemed to hold back, but then said, "Well, I was sweating so much that I want to wipe myself clean. Maybe it's too indulgent."

"Oh, no." Shuya quickly nodded. "Okay, I'll go tell him."

He left the room.

Kawada was boiling water in the darkness of the kitchen. The flaming charcoals beneath the pot and the tip of Kawada's cigarette glowed red. They resembled some rare species of firefly—a swarm, and a lone stray.

When Shuya said his name, Kawada turned, and the burning tip of his cigarette moved, its afterimage a single fat line in Shuya's vision that quickly faded.

"Noriko was wondering if you could boil some extra water. She says just a cup will be enough—"

Kawada interrupted him with a laugh. The cigarette parted from his mouth, and in the dim moonlight from the window, Shuya could see him smile.

"Sure," Kawada said. "A cup or a washbasin, it doesn't matter to me."

He used a bowl to scoop out water from a bucket on the floor and added it to the pot. He repeated this process five more times. The low flames of the charcoal kept the water inside the pot hot, and Shuya felt the wisp of steam on his skin.

After he'd finished, Kawada said, "She's a girl."

Not as obtuse as Shuya was, Kawada had apparently perceived why Noriko wanted hot water.

When Shuya didn't say anything, Kawada continued, atypically forthcoming, "She wants to be pretty because you're here."

Kawada exhaled smoke.

After a pause, Shuya said, "Can I help you with anything?"

"No." Kawada seemed to shake his head.

Squinting, Shuya saw three cups on the kitchen table, along with a filter-lined drip coffee brewer. Kawada had also readied a tea bag, probably for Noriko.

"Hey," Kawada said.

Shuya lifted his eyebrows. "It's not like you to talk so much. What gives?"

Kawada said, "I understand how you feel about Yoshitoki, but don't neglect Noriko's feelings."

Shuya again remained silent for a moment, then spoke. Though he himself didn't really know why, a hint of irritation mixed into his tone. "Yeah, I know."

"Do you have a girlfriend?"

Shuya shrugged. "No."

"So what's the problem then?" Kawada continued to look out the window as he smoked. "It's not so bad to be loved."

Shuya shrugged again, then asked, "Don't you have anyone special?"

The cigarette's tip glowed bright red. Kawada didn't say anything. The smoke drifted through the darkness.

"What, is it a secret?"

"No—" Kawada started to say, but then he suddenly grabbed the cigarette from his mouth and tossed it into the bucket. He whispered, "Get down, Nanahara," and ducked.

Shuya hurriedly obeyed. *Are we being attacked?* His muscles tensed.

"Bring Noriko here," Kawada said. "And don't make a sound."

But Shuya was already on his way to the examination room.

Noriko was still staring at nothing, sitting on the edge of the bed. Shuya motioned her to get on the ground. Noriko immediately understood. Holding her breath, she got down from the bed. He gave her his hand, and half supporting her, he led her to the kitchen. On the way, he looked over his shoulder to the entrance but saw nothing outside the frosted glass door.

Kawada had already gathered their three daypacks, each restocked with fresh water and other supplies. Shotgun in hand, he was crouched beside the back door.

Shuya whispered, "What is it?"

Kawada held up his left hand to silence him. Shuya didn't say another word.

"Someone's outside. If he comes in, we'll go out the other way."

All Shuya could see was the charcoal brightly burning beneath the pot. But with the sink blocking it, Shuya didn't think the fire would be visible from the outside.

Finally, Shuya heard a rattling sound. It came from the entrance. Kawada had jammed the door shut with a broom, and it wouldn't open. But whoever was outside would have seen the broken glass and realized someone had gone inside—and could still be around.

Another rattle came, but let up quickly. The intruder seemed to have given up.

"Fuck," Kawada muttered. "It's going to be a pain in the ass if they try to burn us out."

They held their breaths and waited but heard nothing. But Kawada gestured them to the front of the building. His ears must have picked up some slight sound.

The three of them practically crawled their way down the hall.

As they made their way, Kawada, who was taking up the rear, reached forward to Shuya, who was in the lead, and stopped him. Shuya looked over his shoulder and found Kawada's face in the darkness.

"They're moving around front again." Kawada waved back toward the kitchen. "We'll go out the back."

They went along the floor back to the kitchen.

Just before they reached the room. Kawada stopped again.

"Damn," Kawada growled. "But why?"

Apparently, the person outside was returning to the back door.

The silence went on. Kawada held his shotgun at the ready, and Shuya, keeping Noriko between them, gripped Kaori Minami's SIG-Sauer. (He'd returned the Smith & Wesson to Kawada. They'd decided Shuya was better off with the one that held more bullets.)

But the silence was shattered when a voice called out from outside the kitchen window.

"It's Sugimura." Then, "I don't want to fight. Please answer me, you three. Who are you?"

Shuya recognized the voice. It really was Hiroki Sugimura (Boys #11), who was, along with Shinji Mimura, one of the few boys Shuya could trust.

Shuya let out his breath. "What the hell? How . . ."

Shuya had thought meeting up with Hiroki was too impossible to even wish for. He exchanged a glance with Noriko, who also seemed relieved.

He immediately went to stand, but Kawada restrained him.

"What?"

"Shh. Don't raise your voice."

Shuya studied Kawada's serious expression, then responded with an exaggerated shrug and a smile. "Don't worry. I can vouch for him. We can trust him."

But Kawada shook his head and said, "How did he know there are three of us?"

That question hadn't occurred to Shuya. As he watched Kawada, he thought it over.

He had no idea, but now that he knew Hiroki was near, he didn't care. He just wanted to see Hiroki's face.

Shuya offered, "Maybe he saw us coming inside from far away. But he didn't see who we were."

"Then why would he have waited until now to come?"

Shuya thought a little longer. "It must have just taken him a while to get up the nerve to find out who we were. In any case, he's Sugimura. We can trust him. Don't worry."

Kawada looked like he was about to say something else, but Shuya ignored him and turned toward the window and shouted, "Sugimura, it's me, Nanahara. I'm with Shogo Kawada and Noriko Nakagawa."

"Nanahara." Hiroki's voice came back relieved. "Let me in. How can I get in?"

Before Shuya could respond, Kawada said, "This is Kawada. Go to the front door. Put both hands behind your head and don't move. Understood?"

His tone critical, Shuya started to say, "Kawada—" but Hiroki immediately responded, "Understood," and the boy's silhouette crossed the kitchen window.

Kawada was the first to stand and move toward the front. Shuya helped Noriko follow.

Kawada ducked inside the front door and glanced through the

broken part of the glass. Then he held his shotgun ready as he swiftly released the broom and slid open the door.

Hiroki Sugimura stood there with his hands behind his head. He was slightly taller than Kawada and more slender. His hair was wavy, like Shuya's, and his bangs went halfway to his eyes. Resting at his feet were his daypack, and, for some reason, a one-and-a-half-meter-long pole.

It was really him. Shuya shook his head in disbelief. Hiroki saw this and grinned.

"I'm going to frisk you. Stay still."

Shuya started to protest, saying, "Kawada, come on . . ."

But Kawada paid no attention. He advanced with his shotgun still at the ready and circled behind Hiroki. He first checked the boy's hands, then used his free hand to pat down his uniform jacket.

Kawada's hands stopped at one of the pockets.

"What's this?"

Keeping his hands behind his head, Hiroki said, "You can take it out. Just give it back, please."

Kawada pulled out the object, the shape and size of a thick notepad, but made of plastic or maybe steel. Shuya noticed the moonlight catch the smoothed surface on one side.

Kawada fiddled with it for a while, then said, "Aha." Still holding the object, Kawada moved his body, and the moonlight reflected off the flat panel again. He nodded and returned the object to Hiroki's pocket. Then he thoroughly searched Hiroki's slacks all the way down to his pant cuffs. When he had finished, he looked through the day-pack. Finally, he said, "Okay. Sorry about that. You can lower your hands."

Hiroki released his fingers, then picked up his daypack and stick, which he seemed to be carrying as a weapon.

"Sugimura," Shuya said, grinning. "Come inside. We've got coffee, if you'll have some."

Hiroki nodded vaguely and went with them inside. Kawada looked out the door, then closed it.

Hiroki had stopped in the entryway. Kawada leaned against a shoe rack, filled with house slippers, beside Hiroki and stared at the boy. He'd lowered the Remington, but Shuya noticed his finger was still on the trigger and felt a little annoyed. But he decided not to let it bother him for now.

Hiroki looked at Shuya and Noriko, then threw a glance at Kawada. Shuya realized Hiroki was worried about him—not to mention Noriko—being with Kawada.

Kawada said what they were thinking. "Nanahara, I think Sugimura wants to ask you if you're safe around me."

Hiroki made a weak smile and turned to Kawada and said, "That's not it. You're just an odd combination, that's all." Still smiling, he added, "If you were the kind of guy who would turn on him, Nanahara wouldn't be with you. I know he can be a dope sometimes, but he's not that dumb."

Kawada grinned. His finger remained on the trigger, but at least the two boys had made it through their introductions.

Shuya grinned and said, "That's not a very nice thing to say, Sugimura."

Then Noriko spoke. "Come in. Please. It's not our house, so I can't really apologize for the mess."

Hiroki gave her a broad grin, but he didn't move from the entryway.

Shuya, his left arm supporting Noriko, gestured into the house with his right. "Come on in. We have to leave here soon, but we still have a little time. We'll throw you a welcome party."

But Hiroki still didn't move. Shuya realized he had something important he'd forgotten to tell his friend. Instead, he'd talked about a party of all things. Maybe that's what had stunned the boy.

"Sugimura, we can escape. Kawada's helping us."

Hiroki's eyes widened a little. "Really?"

Shuya nodded.

But Hiroki only looked down. Then, a few moments later, he raised his head. "No," he said, shaking his head. "I have something I need to do."

Shuya knit his brows. "What? Well, why don't you come in and we can—"

Instead of answering, Hiroki said, "Have you three been together the whole time?"

Shuya took a moment to think, then shook his head. "No. Noriko and I were together. Then . . ."

He remembered the morning's events. He hadn't thought of it in a while, but now the image of Tatsumichi Oki's split-open head formed in the back of his mind, and a chill ran down his spine.

"Well, a lot of things happened, and we joined up with Kawada."

"I see." Hiroki nodded, then said, "So you haven't seen Kotohiki?"

"Kotohiki?" Shuya repeated. *Kayoko Kotohiki? Girls number eight? The one who despite being into tea ceremonies is more playful than demure?*

"No," Shuya said, shaking his head. "I haven't seen her." He turned to Kawada, who also shook his head.

"I haven't seen her either."

Kayoko Kotohiki was certainly somewhere on the island. And since Sakamochi hadn't read her name in any of the announcements, she should still be alive—as long as she hadn't died after six p.m.

This reminded Shuya that his plan meant turning a blind eye to his classmates' deaths, and his mood soured.

Noriko asked, "What about Kayoko?"

Hiroki shook his head. "Ah, it's no big deal. Thanks. Sorry, but I have to go."

Hiroki gave Kawada a parting glance, then turned.

Shuya called out to stop him. "Wait, Sugimura! Where are you going? Didn't I tell you we can save you?"

Hiroki looked over his shoulder at Shuya. There was sadness in his eyes but also the glimmer of his familiar dark humor. Perhaps it was a twinkle common to all of Shuya's friends, including, of course, Yoshitoki Kuninobu (*but he's dead now, damn it*), and Shinji Mimura.

Hiroki said, "I have to see Kotohiki about something. So I'm going."

Something. What could be so important to go around risking your life for?

Putting his curiosity aside, Shuya said, "Hold on. If you're going, you need a real weapon. It's dangerous out there. Besides, how are you going to look for her?"

Hiroki curled in his lower lip. But then he pulled out a device that looked like a PDA and showed it to Shuya. "This is the 'weapon' that was in my daypack. Professor Kawada over there seems to know what it is. This guy can somehow tell where anyone with one of these is located." With the hand holding the device, he pointed at his own neck, where he wore the same shiny silver collar that was around Shuya, Noriko, and Kawada's necks. "I have to get really close first. They appear on the screen—though it doesn't give me any names."

Shuya finally had his answers as to how Hiroki had known there were three of them inside and how he had constantly cut off their movements. Just like those computers in the school, the gadget could pinpoint the collars' locations, even if, as Hiroki had said, it didn't reveal who the wearers were.

Hiroki put the device back into his pocket. "Okay, see you," he said, and was about to leave when he stopped. "Oh yeah, watch out for Mitsuko Souma." He gave a stern look to Shuya and then Kawada. "She's playing for keeps. I don't know about any of the others, but at least I'm sure about her."

Kawada asked, "Did you run into her?"

"No." Hiroki shook his head. "No, I didn't, but Takako—Takako Chigusa told me, before she died. Souma killed her."

When Sakamochi reported Takako Chigusa's death in his six o'clock announcement, Shuya had worried how Hiroki would take it. But in the joy of seeing his friend's face, Shuya had completely forgotten about her death and only now remembered it.

Hiroki and Takako Chigusa had been incredibly close—enough so that for a time, Shuya had mistakenly believed the two were dating. But when Shuya casually asked him about it, he laughed and said, "I'm not nearly good enough for her. We've been friends since we were little—you know, playing hide-and-seek, that kind of thing. And when we had fights, I'd be the one who ended up crying."

True, Takako Chigusa possessed an exceptional athlete's instinct for a girl and was strong willed too, but next to Hiroki, a black belt standing over a hundred eighty centimeters tall (the one time Shuya had gone to his house to play, he'd convinced a reluctant Hiroki to show him how he could split a thick wooden board with nothing but the palm of his hand), something about the mental image of her making him cry seemed hilarious.

But now the strong-willed Takako Chigusa was dead. And from the way Hiroki talked, he had watched her die.

Softly, Noriko asked, "Were you with her?"

Hiroki shook his head. "Only at the end. When—when I was sent out, I hid in front of the school and waited for her. But I was distracted when Akamatsu came back, and I lost sight of her. And when I went off searching for her, I missed my chance to meet up with you and Mimura."

Shuya nodded several times. So Hiroki had been in front of the school when Yoshio Akamatsu came back—probably hiding in the woods. He had taken a risk doing so. But that only showed how important Takako was to him.

Hiroki continued, "I found her. Only I was too late."

Hiroki's eyes dropped. His head swung left and right. He didn't have to say the rest; Shuya understood that when he found her, she was already dying, having been taken out by Mitsuko Souma.

Shuya considered telling him that Yoshio Akamatsu had killed Mayumi Tendo and had nearly killed Shuya himself, but it didn't matter much now. Yoshio Akamatsu was dead.

Noriko said, "I don't know if it helps, but you have my condolences."

Hiroki gave her a slight smile and nodded. "Thanks."

"Anyway," Shuya said. "Come in. Let's talk it over. You'll still have—"

Time, he was about to say, but the word caught in his throat. If Hiroki wanted to meet Kayoko Kotohiki while they both yet lived, time was what he didn't have. Shuya understood why Hiroki had searched for Takako, but why he was looking for Kayoko Kotohiki was a mystery. In any case, while they were talking here, she could be fighting someone, only moments from death.

Hiroki gave another small smile. Maybe he'd read Shuya's thoughts.

Shuya licked his lips. He shot Kawada a glance, then said, "If you insist on going—" He looked at Hiroki. "—we'll come help you find her."

But Hiroki shook his head dismissively. He pointed to Noriko with his chin. "Nakagawa's injured. It would be too dangerous. I could never ask that of you."

Shuya couldn't accept this. "But we can save you. If we separate now, how can we meet again?"

Suddenly, Kawada said, "Sugimura." He still held the shotgun, but his finger had left the trigger.

Hiroki turned his head, and Kawada took a small object from his pocket. He put it to his mouth, held the metal end between his teeth, then twisted the rest of it with his fingers.

Chi-ch-ch-chirp-chirp. It was a bird's cry—a brilliant, loud, and playful twitter, like a thrush or a chickadee.

Kawada lowered his hand, and Shuya got a look at the object—*A birdcall? Why would Kawada have something like that?*

Kawada said, "Whether you find Kotohiki or not, if you want to meet up with us again, build a fire and put fresh wood on it to make smoke. Build two fires. Of course you'll want to get away fast, because you'll only attract attention. And make sure to build them in a way you won't start a wildfire. Once we see the smoke, I'll sound this call for . . . fifteen seconds, every fifteen minutes exactly. Follow the call to find us."

He held out the birdcall for Hiroki to see. "This little noisemaker is your ticket out of here. Hop on our train whenever you like."

Hiroki nodded. "Okay. I'll do that, thanks."

"One more thing," Kawada said. He took his map from his pocket, unfolded it, and handed it to Hiroki along with a pencil. "I'm sorry to take some of your time, but could you write down where Chigusa died? And do the same for anyone else you might have run into."

Hiroki raised his eyebrows a little, set the map down in the moonlight on top of the shoe rack, and took the pencil in hand.

Kawada added, "Give me your map. I'll mark the locations of the bodies we've found."

Hiroki stopped writing and handed over his map. The two stood side by side and began marking the maps.

Noriko said, "I'll bring some coffee," and left Shuya's arm. Holding onto the wall for support, she limped down the hall.

As Kawada wrote, he asked, "Did Chigusa say if Souma had a machine gun?"

"No," Hiroki replied without looking up. "She didn't say anything about that. She'd been shot several times in the back, though—not just once."

"Okay."

Standing beside the two as they worked, Shuya explained what had happened with Yoshio Akamatsu, and Tatsumichi Oki and Kyoichi Motobuchi. Hiroki nodded along as he wrote.

When Kawada finished, he showed the map to Hiroki and explained, "Minami was killed here. Nanahara saw Shimizu running away. It might have been self-defense, but either way, watch out for Shimizu."

Hiroki nodded. Then, unlikely as it was, he said, "I saw Kaori too," and pointed on the map. "Just before noon. She shot at me without warning. But I think she was in a panic."

Kawada nodded and exchanged maps with Hiroki.

Noriko appeared from the hallway carrying a cup. With her legs still unsteady, Shuya met her halfway and relayed the coffee to Hiroki, who took in the aroma, made a quiet whistle, then took the cup. He thanked Noriko and took a sip.

In almost no time at all, he set the cup down at the edge of the waiting room's raised floor. It was still mostly full.

"Okay, see ya," he said.

"Wait," Shuya said. He pulled the SIG-Sauer from his belt. He offered it to Hiroki, grip-first. With his other hand, he took the spare magazine from his pocket.

"Here, take this, if you still insist on going, okay? We've got a shotgun and another pistol."

The Smith & Wesson, which had originally belonged to Kyoichi before Shuya had taken it, was down the front of Kawada's belt. Shuya handing over the SIG-Sauer would certainly lessen their team's fighting capability, but Kawada didn't comment.

But Hiroki shook his head. "You need that, Nanahara. Protect Nakagawa. That's something I can't take from you. I couldn't make myself use it." Then, with a slight tilt of his head, he looked at Shuya and Noriko, smiled faintly, and added, "I always wondered why you two weren't going out."

With that, he gave them each a nod in turn and noiselessly slid open the front door.

"Sugimura," Noriko said. Her voice was quiet. "Be careful."

"I will. Thanks. And good luck to you guys too."

Shuya was starting to get choked up, but he managed to say, "Sugimura. We'll meet again. That's a promise."

Hiroki nodded, then left. Shuya helped Noriko down to the entryway, where they watched Hiroki depart. He went straight off to the right, up toward the mountain, and out of sight.

Kawada ushered them back inside without a word and closed the door.

Shuya sighed and looked over his shoulder into the clinic. He saw the faint wisp of steam rising from the cup abandoned at the edge of the floor.

20 STUDENTS REMAIN.

The moon hung high in the center of the sky with not a single cloud. The white light of the nearly full moon cast a thin film across the sky that obscured the stars.

In front, Kawada stopped, and Shuya and Noriko, leaning on him, both stopped too.

Shuya asked, "Noriko, are you okay?"

She nodded. "I'm fine." But from the way she felt on his arm, Shuya could tell that her body remained unsteady.

Shuya looked at his watch. It was past eleven o'clock now, but they had already left the now-forbidden zone, G-9. Next up was to find another place where they could settle in.

For now, they'd been retracing their previous path through the sparse groupings of trees, back up to the base of the northern mountain. A little farther, and they'd come out onto the farm where Kaori Minami had died. Off to their left, a narrow fan-shaped patch of flat farmland dotted with houses began at the eastern village and tapered off to the west. The main road passed through what would be the fan's hinge and cut through the island toward the western shore.

Kawada turned to them and asked, "Well, what now?" He'd rolled up a blanket for Noriko and tied it to the daypacks hanging from his shoulder.

Shuya said, "You don't suppose we could hole up in another house?"

"A house . . ." Kawada looked away and narrowed his eyes. "In general, that's not a good idea. As more of the island gets closed off, there'll be fewer houses to choose from. Anytime anyone needs something, like food, or whatever, they'll go looking inside the houses."

"Hey," Noriko said. "If you're worried about me, I'm fine now. I'll be all right outdoors."

Kawada smirked, then silently looked over the flat land. Maybe he was mentally lining it up with the notes Hiroki left on his map.

Hiroki had written not only who he'd found dead, but also detailed descriptions of how they'd died. Kazushi Niida's corpse was right near Takako Chigusa's. Not only had his eyes been gouged out (*Wow!*), his throat had been stabbed with something. And Megumi Eto had died inside the village, now a forbidden zone. Her throat had been slit. (Now that Noriko had told him Megumi had a crush on him, hearing how she died gave Shuya a pang.) Then, between the eastern village and the southern mountain were Yoji Kuramoto and Yoshimi Yahagi. Yoji had been stabbed in the head, and Yoshimi had been shot. And on the southern coast, Izumi Kanai, Hiroshi Kuronaga, Ryuhei Sasagawa, and Mitsuru Numai had all died. Mitsuru Numai had been shot four or five times, and the other three's throats had all been slashed. Sho Tsukioka aside, who had been caught in a forbidden zone, Kiriyama's lackeys had all died together.

"Kawada," Shuya said. Kawada looked back at him. "Do you think Souma killed Kitano and Kusaka?"

As he asked the question, Shuya was again struck by how unreal this all felt. He didn't doubt what Hiroki Sugimura had told him, but it contradicted his inexplicable belief—almost a conviction—that girls would *never* commit a wrong.

"No." Kawada shook his head. "I don't think so. When Kusaka and Kitano died, the sound of that machine gun was followed by two single shots. That was the killer finishing them off. But after Chigusa was shot, she lived long enough to see Sugimura. Her killer was not as thorough. Though it's certainly possible whoever did it recognized she was a goner and left her to die. But considering the times and locations, I think Souma and the machine-gunner must be two different people."

Shuya recalled the sound of that machine-gun fire he'd heard before nine in the morning. Whoever that had been was still roaming the island. And then, a little later, there were those other, distant gunshots. Had that been Mitsuko Souma?

"Whoever it was . . ." Kawada said. His lips twisted into a smile, and he shook his head. ". . . we'll meet him or her sooner or later, I'm sure. Then we'll know."

Shuya thought of something else that had been bothering him. "That gadget of Sugimura's made me think. Sakamochi must know that we three are together—and where we are."

Looking out at the flat land, Kawada said, "That's right."

Shuya shifted his shoulders to redistribute Noriko's weight. "That's not gonna interfere with our escape?"

His back still turned, Kawada chuckled, then said, "No, it won't. Not in the least. Just leave it to me." He again looked down at the open land below and said, "Let's go back to where we were."

He continued, "A common strategy taken by the ones who decide to play this game is to show up anywhere they hear action. If it weren't for that twenty-four-hour time limit, they wouldn't have to go to such lengths. But because of that deadline, they have to kill when they can. Plus, if someone is going around killing everyone, that means they're on their own, so they won't have much opportunity to sleep. Another reason to keep the match short. If they hear something happening near them, they go there, and if the fight has already kicked off, they can sit back and watch, and then finish off any survivors. That's why we're better off where we can avoid confrontations. If we get mixed up with someone who's lost it out here, one of the star players is bound to show up. Back where we were hiding before, it'd have been unlikely for anyone to run into us. After all, the guys who were hiding there before, Oki and Motobuchi—

they're gone now. Plus, there are hardly any houses in the area at all."

"But Shimizu ran off in that direction," Shuya said.

"No, she wouldn't have gone as far as we're going. She didn't have a reason to."

Kawada pointed toward the flat land. "But we'll avoid the mountainside, where she might still be. We'll take another route."

Shuya raised his eyebrows. "Is it safe for us to move through the open?"

Kawada grinned and shook his head. "No matter how bright the moon is, it's nothing like daylight. Actually, it'll be safer than going through the wooded mountains."

Shuya nodded. Kawada took the lead and began descending the gentle slope. Shuya gripped the SIG-Sauer tightly and, supporting Noriko, followed.

The trees opened into a grassland. The first field they crossed grew with some kind of squash. The next was a wheat field. With an island this small, the crops might have been for commercial sale. The Republic of Greater East Asia incessantly issued edicts to increase the domestic food supply. Small fields like these could be for contributing to the effort. As they walked along the edge of the farm, the ground beneath Shuya's sneakers felt a little dry, maybe because the island had been uninhabited for the past few days. But Shuya was struck by the lush, pleasant scent of wheat drifting in the air of this near-summer evening.

It was a nice smell—especially after growing accustomed to the stench of blood.

Ahead of them and to the left, a tractor had been left sitting. Just beyond it was a house.

It was an ordinary two-story, if fairly new. It looked like one of those cheap, mass-produced numbers made by BanaHome or Wirbel House, all ticky-tacky and glue. Despite its location in the middle of the farm, the home was enclosed by the requisite concrete block wall.

Shuya returned his gaze to Kawada's back.

Something tugged at his mind.

He looked over his shoulder. Noriko was leaning on his left arm as she walked. His eyes caught something high in the sky above her head. It sparkled in the moonlight. And it was flying in a parabolic arc straight toward them.

20 STUDENTS REMAIN.

What had made Shuya the team MVP in his Little League days was nothing other than his superior ability to detect objects in motion. Even in this dim light, he could tell that the object hurtling toward them was some kind of can. And here in the serene Seto Inland Sea, this was no act of a tornado, and empty cans didn't just fall from the sky. Whatever this object was, it wasn't an empty can.

It couldn't be a—

Shuya ducked his left shoulder out from under Noriko's right arm. He hadn't enough time to call out to Kawada, but the boy spun around anyway. He must have sensed something wrong. Noriko stumbled at the sudden loss of Shuya's support.

Shuya sprinted a few steps and jumped high. And Shuya could definitely jump high. He leaped like he had in the bottom of the eleventh inning in the prefectural semifinals, when as shortstop he caught what should have been a winning run.

He caught the ball—no, the can—in midair with his left hand. He transferred it to his right, and just as he started to come down, he twisted his body and threw it as far as he could.

Before he landed, a white burst of light filled the night.

He felt the air swell, and a violent roar crashed against his eardrums. The blast knocked him back before he could land, and he tumbled, rolling on the dirt. If Shuya had waited to react until that thing—that grenade—hit the ground, he and Noriko and Kawada would have been shredded. Sakamochi's men had reduced the amount of explosives within to safeguard against it being used to assault the school, but the grenade still packed more than enough punch to kill.

Quickly, he raised his head. He realized he couldn't hear. His ears were messed up. In the silence, he saw Noriko on the ground to his left. He started to look back for Kawada, when his head turned up and he saw it—another of those cans flying toward them.

Another one! I have to—

But it was far too late.

A distinct though muffled bang reached his deadened ears, and an instant later, a second explosion erupted in the air. Its sound too was muted, and it was far enough away that Shuya didn't get blown back again. Directly beside him, Kawada was kneeling, holding his shotgun. He had shot the grenade like a clay pigeon, destroying it in midair, or at least knocking it back before it exploded.

Shuya ran to Noriko and sat her up. She was grimacing. She seemed to moan, but he didn't hear anything.

"Nanahara!" Kawada shouted. "Get back!"

Kawada waved him down with his left hand and fired his shotgun once with his right. Then Shuya heard another gun go *brattattattat-tattattat,* and right in front of him the stalks of wheat were shredded and scattered into the air. Kawada fired again, twice this time. Still not understanding what was happening, Shuya dragged Noriko behind the ridge separating the fields. He dropped to the ground. Kawada, shotgun in hand, slid down beside him. Then Kawada fired again. With another *brattattattattattattattat,* dirt erupted from the ridge. Several granules flew into Shuya's eyes.

Shuya drew his SIG-Sauer and popped his head above the cover of the ridge. He fired blindly in the direction Kawada was facing.

Then Shuya saw it. Not thirty meters away, that distinctive slicked-back hair ducked back behind an opening in the concrete block wall of the house.

Kazuo Kiriyama (Boys #6).

And though Shuya's ears were messed up, he remembered hearing that *brattattattattattattat* before—it was the distant rattle from when Yumiko Kusaka and Yukiko Kitano were gunned down on the mountaintop. Sure, more than one of the students might have been given a machine gun, but Kiriyama was here now, and he'd just tried to kill them without any warning—and with grenades, no less!

Shuya was positive that Kiriyama had killed Yumiko and Yukiko. He thought of the way they had died, and rage coursed through him.

"What the fuck!" Shuya yelled. "What the fuck does he think he's doing?"

"Stop shouting and shoot." Kawada handed Shuya the Smith & Wesson and reloaded his shotgun.

With a gun in each hand, Shuya started shooting at the concrete wall. (*Akimbo style! How wild!*) The Smith & Wesson ran out of bullets first, followed by the SIG-Sauer. *I have to reload!*

Kiriyama took the opening to stand up. He spat fire with the *brattattattattattat*. Shuya ducked his head, and Kiriyama stepped out from behind the wall.

Now Kawada's shotgun barked. Kiriyama vanished. The shotgun blast blew off a chunk of the wall.

Shuya ejected the SIG's magazine and inserted a fresh one from his pocket. Then he swung the cylinder open and pushed down the extractor rod in its center, ejecting the spent, swollen shells. One landed on the thumb of his hand holding the grip and nearly burned him. It didn't matter. He quickly loaded the .38 caliber bullets Kawada had rolled his way. Then he aimed at Kiriyama's house.

Kawada fired again. Another chunk of the wall went flying. Shuya shot a few more rounds from the SIG-Sauer.

"Noriko!" Shuya shouted. "Are you okay?"

Beside him, she answered, "I'm okay."

Hearing her reply, Shuya realized that his hearing had come back.

Out of the corner of his eye, he saw her lying facedown, reloading .380 ACP rounds into the SIG's empty cartridge he'd tossed. Of all the things he'd witnessed since the game began, this one sent him reeling. *How could a girl like Noriko take part in a gun battle like this?*

Suddenly an arm appeared from behind the concrete wall. At its end was that submachine gun. Again it barked, *brattattat,* and Shuya and Kawada ducked back down.

The moment they did, Kiriyama stood. Firing his submachine gun, he darted forward. In no time he'd reached the shelter of the tractor. He'd closed in on them.

Kawada fired once more. The tractor's side was to them, and the pellets shattered part of the tractor's instrument panel.

Shuya shot twice, then said, "Kawada."

"What?" Kawada said, reloading his shotgun.

"How fast is your hundred meter dash?"

Kawada fired again (disintegrating one of the tractor's taillights) and replied, "Slow. It takes me thirteen seconds. But I've got a strong back. Why?"

Kiriyama thrust out his arm from behind the tractor. He spit fire, *brattattattat,* and glanced out. But Shuya and Kawada both shot at him, and he ducked his head back down.

Shuya spoke quickly. "Running to the mountain is our only play, right? I'm in the low elevens. You take Noriko and go first. I'll keep Kiriyama pinned."

Kawada looked at him. That was all he did. He understood.

Then he said, "At the place we were, Nanahara. Where we talked about rock."

Kawada handed Shuya his Remington and crawled backward on his stomach, circling around to Noriko on Shuya's left.

Shuya took a deep breath and fired the shotgun three times into the tractor. On cue, Kawada and Noriko stood and ran in the direction they'd come. For a brief moment, Shuya and Noriko's eyes met.

Kiriyama sprang to his feet, revealing his upper body. Shuya fired his shotgun in quick succession. Kiriyama had started to aim at Kawada and Noriko, but now he had to duck. The Remington ran out of ammo, and Shuya took up the Smith & Wesson and continued to shoot. He quickly burned through its five rounds. He switched to the SIG-Sauer and kept shooting. Before long, the slide locked open, and he replaced the empty magazine with the one Noriko had refilled, and he kept on shooting. He had to keep shooting.

He saw Kawada and Noriko disappear into the mountainside.

Again the SIG's slide locked open. He didn't have another magazine ready. He had to stop to load bullets into one of the empties.

But in that moment, Kiriyama stuck his arm out around the front of the tractor. The Ingram barked, *brattattattattattattat.* Just like he'd done before. And now he was running at Shuya.

Shuya had to get out of this gunfight. Keeping only the SIG-Sauer (he still had seven loose .380 ACP rounds in his pocket), he turned around and ran. If he could make it into the mountain where there was plenty of cover, Kiriyama wouldn't be able to chase him so easily. But Shuya made a split-second decision to head east. Noriko and Kawada would be moving west to their previous hiding place. Shuya wanted to lead Kiriyama away from them, if only for a moment.

It all came down to their sprinting speed. Shuya had little time to get as far away from Kiriyama as he could. The submachine gun's spray of bullets meant a sure hit at close range. All that mattered was how far Shuya could get away first.

Shuya ran. He was the best runner in the class. (At least so he thought. He was a hair faster than Shinji Mimura, and Kiriyama too, unless the killer hadn't been trying during the fitness tests.) His legs were all he could count on.

Just five meters away from the tree line, he heard the *brattattattat* from behind. Pain exploded in his left side, like someone had landed a full-force punch.

Shuya grunted and nearly lost balance, but he didn't quit running. He ran into the tall woods and up the slope. Another *brattattattattattattat* came, and his left arm jerked up even though he hadn't told it to. He realized he'd taken a bullet just above his elbow.

But still Shuya ran. He raced eastward—*hey, hey, bro, that's a forbidden zone, ya know*. He turned north. Another *brattattattattat* came from behind. A thin tree just to his right cracked and burst into a spray of matchstick-sized chips.

Again came the *brattattattattattat*. Shuya wasn't hit. Or maybe he was. Shuya couldn't tell anymore. All he knew was that Kiriyama was chasing him. *Good. At least I was able to buy Noriko and Kawada some time.*

He ran through trees and bushes, uphill and down. He spared no concern for the possibility of an attack from some third party hiding in the shadows. He didn't even know how far he'd run now. Neither did he know where he was headed. Sometimes, he thought he heard that *brattattattat* again, and sometimes he thought he imagined it. Maybe his ears were ringing as an aftereffect of those explosions. Either way, he couldn't stop to relax yet. *Farther. I have to go farther.*

Suddenly, Shuya's feet slipped. Without realizing it, he'd run up a rise, and its slope suddenly dropped off. Just as when he'd grappled with Tatsumichi Oki, he tumbled down the steep drop.

He landed at the bottom with a *thud*. He realized the SIG-Sauer was no longer in his hand. And then he tried to stand . . .

. . . and realized he couldn't get up. *Am I blacking out from blood loss?* he wondered in a daze. *Or did I hit my head?*

Impossible. I'm not hurt so bad that I wouldn't be able to stand . . . up I need to get back to Noriko and . . . Kawada I need to protect Noriko I promised Noriko I—

Half arisen, Shuya slumped forward.

And he was out.

20 STUDENTS REMAIN.

In the near total darkness, Shinji was sitting in the faint moonlight beside the window. As he had many times before, he threw the object in his hand to the floor. The sound of its impact was muted by a thick, folded-over blanket on the ground. But it landed with a *pop*, like something inside it had burst, followed by a faint ringing noise.

Shinji quickly picked it up and took a small plastic shard from beside the blanket and inserted it into one end of the object. The ringing stopped.

Yutaka, who was watching over his work beside him, said, "C'mon, hurry up."

Shinji held up a hand to quiet his friend and repeated his test again.

Pop, riiinng. Shinji picked up the object and made it stop.

Maybe that's enough tests. But if this malfunctions, all our preparations will have been for nothing. Surely I can try it out one more time.

"Hey, if we don't hurry. . . ."

Irritation threatened to flash across Shinji's face, but he managed to suppress it. With some reluctance, he said, "Fine," and broke off his testing. He disconnected the leads that connected the battery to the small electric motor he'd been using for the dry run. Then he started unwrapping the electric tape that held them together.

Shinji and Yutaka were back inside the Northern Takamatsu Agricultural Cooperative Oki Island Branch Office.

Along with the school and the harbor's fishery cooperative, this warehouse was one of the largest buildings on the island, if not the largest. With the power out, darkness swallowed the interior, a space large enough that it could hold an entire basketball court. Here and there heavy equipment, including a tractor and a combine, littered the space. A mini pickup truck, possibly under repairs, had been lifted on a jack with its tires removed. Sacks of various kinds of fertilizers were stacked in one corner. (The hazardous ammonium nitrate was kept farther behind them, stored in a large cabinet behind a lock, which Shinji broke.) The corrugated metal walls stood a full five meters tall.

On the north side of the building, an open second-story space seemed to be suspended from the wall, where more heaps of fertilizer and chemicals and such were lying around. Along the east wall, opposite from where Shinji and Yutaka were, a metal staircase descended from the second-floor storage. Beside the stairs was the large, sliding-door entrance.

Beneath the stairs, in the southeast corner, partition walls set off an office area. The office door had been left open, and Shinji could barely distinguish the outlines of a desk and a fax machine.

Passing the kite string across sector G-7 had been hard work. Shinji had tied one end of the string around the top of a tall tree behind that first rock. He walked the other end through the trees, but the wind higher up seemed to be fairly strong, and the garbage-bag balloons had not been easily guided. More than ten times, Shinji had had to stop and climb a tree to untangle the string. Worse yet, without knowing where in the shadows their potential enemies lurked, he had to constantly keep an eye out for Yutaka. The work had left Shinji completely exhausted.

But after three full hours, he'd managed to set the string in place. As he stopped to catch his breath, he heard a terrific gunfight extremely close by. He even heard a couple explosions, but he couldn't afford to get involved. He hurried back to the farmer's co-op. Somewhere along the way, the gunfire stopped.

Then he finally got to work on the electric conductor for the detonator, but that too proved unexpectedly difficult. For one, he didn't have the proper tools, and moreover the device required a delicate balance—the impact of the bomb hitting the school needed to set off the electric spark, but it couldn't be so touchy that some bump along his ropeway—for example, the pulley passing over a knot in the rope— would trigger the detonator.

But again, he somehow managed it, and as he was testing his result, using a motor he'd removed from an electric shaver in place of the detonator, Sakamochi gave his midnight announcement. Only Hirono Shimizu (Girls #10), whom Shinji saw soon after the game began, had died. Shinji wondered if her death had anything to do with that ferocious gunfight he'd heard, but then Sakamochi said something far more urgent, at least to Shinji and Yutaka. Sector F-7, where the rock overlooked the school, would become a forbidden zone at one in the morning.

Yutaka had good reason to be impatient. Once that area became closed to them, all their preparations would amount to nothing. They'd be finished. Shinji didn't want to make an elaborate play that left his opponent one move away from checkmate only to blunder into a trap himself.

Working quickly, Shinji removed the two halves of the electric detonator from the case attached to his knife. He joined the cylinders, their metal skin a dull sheen in the darkness, and stripped the plastic sheath from one of the leads extending from the detonator's end. Then he taped in place the small plastic spring that would be serving as the switch for the electric conductor and wound the detonator's stripped lead around one of the conductor's wires. He wrapped the connection with enough tape for him to be sure the wires would absolutely not separate. Next, he attached to the battery case a piece of circuit board, capacitors and all, which he'd appropriated from a camera's flash mechanism. He needed the capacitors' large, high-voltage storage to reliably trigger the detonator. He made sure the connections between the circuit board and the battery were secure as well. To safeguard against an accidental explosion, he'd wait to attach the detonator's other lead until they were back on the mountain. For now, he stripped the insulating sheath and taped the wire's exposed end to the side of the battery case.

"All right," Shinji said. He stood and put the completed detonator into his pocket. "It's time. Get ready."

Yutaka nodded. Just in case, Shinji tossed his needle-nose pliers, some backup wire, and other tools into his daypack and lifted several of the divided-up piles of rope over his shoulder. Down at his feet was the jerry can he'd filled with a mixture of gasoline and ammonium nitrate. To supply more oxygen, he'd folded some bubble wrap into pleats and stuffed it inside. The spout had been snapped closed, but next to it, a rubber plug, for holding the detonator, dangled from a piece of plastic packing string tied to the handle.

Shinji looked at his watch. Nine past midnight—plenty of time.

All right, Shinji thought, trembling with excitement. The two boys had been through a lot, but now they had everything in place. They would rejoin the sections of rope, then secure one end to a tree in area H-7 they'd spotted from the mountain. Then, they would tie the other end of the rope to the end of the kite string that they'd held in place with a stone. They would unravel the rope and leave it there as they circled around the school, going up into the mountain at area F-7. There, Shinji would take the end of the kite string from the top of the tree and haul it in as fast as he could. The rope would be drawn in, and he could suspend the activated jerry can explosive from the pulley like a gondola lift, and then pass the rope through. He'd pull the rope taut over the school and tie it to one of the trees or something. And then *party time! Have fun! Oh yeah, we're gonna make it!*

Once they'd damaged the school's computer, or even its power systems or part of its wiring, and Sakamochi's men saw the system malfunction—or no, that much explosives would take out the computers themselves—actually, it'd be far worse than that. Once they saw the bomb obliterate half the school, Shinji and Yutaka would grab their inner tubes, which they'd already hidden behind the rock in area F-7, and run. They would use their boosted walkie-talkie to send out a distress signal and confuse the government, then, per Shinji's calculations, would reach the adjacent island in less than a half hour.

From there, they would go by boat. (Shinji had some experience with motorboats. He felt like he owed everything to all the wisdom his uncle had imparted.) Then, they would flee to Okayama or somewhere and land on some shore where they wouldn't be noticed. After that, their future would be their own. They could hop on a freight train running through the countryside. Or they could furnish themselves with a passing car. After all, they had a gun. *Carjacking. Awesome.*

Shinji looked down at the Beretta 92F stuffed down the front of his slacks. His plan was to lead the government astray with that walkie-talkie, but just in case they were spotted at sea, he'd filled several glass pop bottles with his special ammonium nitrate and gasoline mixture and, making sure their lids were good and tight, put them into his daypack. But without detonators, they didn't amount to anything more than extra-flammable Molotov cocktails.

In the event that they were about to be spotted, their best move would be to take the initiative and board the other ship and fight, even if they had to swim to get there. If everything went well, they could get their hands on their enemies' weapons, and if they could control the ship, the vessel could provide their means of escape. But for any of that to be possible, he'd have to be a good shot.

It bothered him a little—he had carried that Beretta all over the island, but he hadn't fired it once. Not even his uncle had had a gun, so he'd never been taught how to use one.

But Shinji shook his head and told himself, *You're The Third Man. Shinji Mimura. You'll be fine. Just like that first time you picked up that heavy basketball and shot a free throw. That ball didn't even touch the hoop as it went through.*

"Shinji," Yutaka said.

Shinji looked up at him. "Are you ready?"

His voice pitiful, Yutaka said, "No." Then he took out his notepad and started to write.

Shinji read it in the moonlight.

[*I can't find the pulley.*]

He looked at Yutaka. His expression must have been fearsome, because Yutaka shrank back a little.

Yutaka was supposed to carry the pulley and half of the rope. He'd been in charge of the pulley from the moment they recovered it from the well. He was supposed to have set it down somewhere in the warehouse.

Shinji dropped his rope and his daypack. He got on his knees and began to search. Yutaka did the same.

They groped about in the dark, even looking behind the tractor and underneath the office desk, but they couldn't find the pulley. Shinji stood and looked at his watch again. The minute hand had rounded the ten-minute mark and was well on its way to quarter after.

Shinji took the supplied flashlight from his daypack. He held his hands around the lamp end and turned on the light.

Shinji did his best not to let any excess light spill out, but its faint warm glow spread through the vast space of the self-styled farmers' co-op. He saw Yutaka's dismayed expression, and over his friend's shoulder, he easily spotted the pulley. It was on the other side of the desk, out in the open near the wall, in a shadow just out of reach of the moonlight coming in from the window—not even one meter away from Yutaka's daypack.

Shinji winked at Yutaka and quickly turned off the flashlight. Yutaka snatched up the pulley.

"Sorry, Shinji."

Shinji flashed a dry smile. "C'mon, Yutaka. Get it together."

Shinji again shouldered his daypack and his rope. He picked up the jerry can. Shinji had pride in his strength, but the combined weight of the last two was quite heavy. The rope was only going part of the way, but he'd have to haul the twenty kilogram gas can up onto the mountainside—and quickly too.

Yutaka picked up his half of the rope (no small amount; he looked like a turtle and its shell—not that Shinji was any different), and the two boys walked toward the sliding door on the east wall. They'd left the door ten centimeters open, letting in a thin curtain of pale blue moonlight.

"Sorry, Shinji," Yutaka said again.

"It's all right. Don't worry about it. Let's just make sure we do this right from here on out."

Shinji switched the jerry can to his left hand, put his right on the heavy steel door, and slid it open. The curtain of pale light widened.

Outside was a broad, unpaved parking lot. A narrow road—not the larger east-west road, which was beyond it, just a little farther to the south—ran alongside the building on the right, and a lone minivan was parked near the lot's entrance.

Opposite the sliding door, the parking lot opened directly onto farmland, where scattered houses made tiny dots among the fields. Farther away, the village's cluster of homes remained visible even at night.

Shinji looked left. A small shed stood at the rear of the property. Beyond it, fairly high up, Shinji could see the school, enveloped by the foothills. On this side of the school was a small grove beside a two-story house. One tree stood far taller than the rest; this was where they would tie the end of the rope. They had secured the end of the kite string beside an irrigation canal to the left of the grove. The string ran past the side of the school directly to the overlooking rock up in the mountainside, over three hundred meters away.

Damn, I'm good. Now will that kite string let me pull that rope up without it breaking?

Shinji sighed, then thought for a moment, and spoke. He didn't think it would matter if Sakamochi's men heard what he wanted to say.

"Yutaka."

Standing to his left, Yutaka looked up at him. "What?"

"We might die. Are you prepared for that?"

Yutaka was quiet for a moment, but not for long. "Yeah. I'm ready."

"Okay then."

Shinji renewed his grip on the jerry can's handle and gave Yutaka a grin.

But the grin froze when he saw something out of the corner of his eye. Someone's head popped out of a field, where the crops were growing shorter, off the eastern edge of the parking lot.

"Yutaka!"

Shinji grabbed Yutaka by the arm and started to run back inside the corrugated metal walls of the co-op. Yutaka stumbled, partially due to the heavy rope he carried, but he kept up. By the time Shinji had squatted behind the cover of the sliding door, his pistol was already drawn and aimed at the figure in the field.

The silhouette yelled, "D—don't shoot! Mimura! Please don't shoot. It's me, Iijima."

Only then did Shinji recognize the figure to be Keita Iijima (Boys #2). Keita got along relatively well with Shinji and Yutaka, as far as their classmates went (mostly because they had been in the same class since seventh grade), but what gripped Shinji was not the relief at their group gaining a third member. Instead, he felt only distress. At this moment, he realized he hadn't much considered the possibility of one of their classmates joining them. *Damn it, just as everything is on the line, he shows up now!*

Behind him Yutaka spoke, and the excitement in his voice seemed a little out of place. "It's Iijima, Shinji. Iijima!"

Keita slowly rose and emerged onto the parking lot. He held his daypack by the strap with his left hand and gripped something that looked like a kitchen knife in his right. Cautiously, he explained, "I saw the light."

Shinji gritted his teeth. Keita must have meant the flashlight he'd only momentarily turned on to look for the pulley. Shinji scolded himself for jumping to use the flashlight so quickly. It wasn't like him to be so thoughtless.

Keita continued, "And I came here and saw it was you guys. What have you been doing? What were you carrying? Was that rope? Let—let me join you."

Knowing that their conversation was being monitored, Yutaka knit his brow and looked over at Shinji. His eyes widened when he saw that Shinji hadn't lowered his gun.

"Shinji," Yutaka said. "Shinji, what's wrong with you?"

With his open right hand, Shinji signaled for Yutaka not to move forward, then said, "Yutaka. Don't move."

"Hey," Keita said. His voice trembled. "Why are you pointing that at me? Mimura?"

Shinji took a deep breath, then told Keita, "Don't move." He sensed Yutaka go stiff.

Keita Iijima took one step forward, his forlorn expression evident even in the dim moonlight.

"Why?" Keita said. "Tell me why. Have you forgotten who I am, Shinji? Let me join you."

Shinji cocked the Beretta's hammer with an audible click. Keita Iijima froze in place, still a good seven or eight meters away.

Slowly, Shinji said, "Don't come near us. We're not joining with you."

Beside him, Yutaka cried, "Why, Shinji? We can trust Iijima, can't we?"

Shinji shook his head. Then he thought, *Oh, that's right. You don't know, do you, Yutaka.*

It wasn't anything important. Indeed, it was trivial.

Last March, near the end of the last trimester of eighth grade, Shinji and Keita had gone to see a movie in Takamatsu (the town of Shiroiwa didn't have a theater). Yutaka was supposed to come with them, but he was home, sick with a cold.

After the movie, he and Keita had looked around the book and record stores in the main street's shopping arcade. (Shinji bought some imported computer books at a used bookstore—a lucky find. Due to the government's strict monitoring over Western publications, even the technical ones were hard to get.) They were starting to head back to the train station when Keita said he'd forgotten to buy a comic that he wanted, and he went back into the bookstore alone.

That was when three tough-looking high schoolers approached Shinji in an alley off the main road.

"Hey," one of the high school boys said. "You got any money?" He stood a full ten centimeters over Shinji's one hundred seventy-two. (For someone on the basketball team, Shinji was short.)

Shinji shrugged and said, "I've got two thousand, five hundred seventy-two yen."

The one who had asked the question gave the other two a look that seemed to say, *What a loser.* Then he leaned into Shinji's ear. Shinji was annoyed. Maybe it was from getting wasted on paint thinner or whatever else was popular these days, but the kid's recessed gumline left gaps between his teeth, and his breath reeked. *Brush your teeth, man.*

One of his buddies said, "Give us all you've got. Come on, what are you waiting for? Do it."

Shinji gave them an exaggerated look of surprise and said, "Oh, so you guys are homeless, are you? You should be happy to get twenty yen, then. Get on your knees and beg me for it, and I might even give it to you."

Gap-tooth made a face that said, *Look what we have here.* He looked at his friends, who were grinning, then said, "You're in junior high, yeah? Looks like you haven't learned how to respect your betters."

He grabbed Shinji by the shoulders and put his knee in Shinji's stomach. Shinji tensed his stomach muscles and withstood the blow. In truth, there wasn't much to withstand. The knee kick was more of a threat than anything. Shinji could tell these three punks never went up against anyone their own age.

Shinji said, "What was that, a love tap?"

Gap-tooth's narrow, vacuous face twisted and he snarled, "I've had enough of this crap."

He punched Shinji in the face. This one didn't hurt that much either, though Shinji thought he felt a gash tear open inside his mouth.

Shinji stuck his finger inside his mouth and felt for the wound. It stung a little. When he withdrew his finger, it had blood on it. *Not bad.*

"That's right, hurry it up," Gap-tooth said. "Give us your wallet."

Still looking down, Shinji broke into a grin. He looked up, and when their eyes met, fear flashed across Gap-tooth's face.

Enjoying this, Shinji said, "Remember, *you* started it."

With his imported hardcover book in hand, Shinji delivered a short-range hook to Gap-tooth's filthy mouth. His hand felt the punk's teeth break, and Gap-tooth rocked back.

He'd mopped up the rest in ten short seconds. How to fight was a subject covered in his uncle's lessons. They hadn't given him any trouble at all.

But what *had* troubled him was something else.

Ignoring the doubled-over high schoolers and the distant ring of onlooking passersby, Shinji returned to the bookstore and found Keita in the comics section, holding the store's shopping bag with the comic he'd been looking for already inside. He was wandering the section aimlessly, but when Shinji called out to him, he said, "Sorry, sorry, when I came back, I thought of something else I wanted too." Then his eyes widened. "What happened to your mouth?"

Shinji shrugged and said, "Let's go home."

But he knew that Keita hadn't needed to ask about his mouth. While Shinji was surrounded by the three goons, his friend's face had peeked out around the corner of the alley, then immediately withdrew. At the time, he'd wondered if Keita had gone to call the police. (Well, he wouldn't count on them anyway—the cops were more enthusiastic about suppressing the public at large than criminals.)

Gee, so you wanted another book, huh?

Shinji didn't much enjoy the train ride back to Shiroiwa.

Keita must have figured that Shinji could surely handle three measly high school kids. *And, well, he was right.* He probably hadn't wanted to get drawn into the fight and end up injured. *Oh, I see.* And if he called the cops, the high schoolers might have taken note of his face. *Uh-huh.* He didn't appear about to apologize to Shinji either. *Well, white lies make the world go 'round.*

There was nothing Shinji could do about it. Like his uncle always said, if somebody was cowardly or fainthearted, it wasn't their fault. Shinji couldn't go around holding everyone responsible for everything they did.

But the front cover of that technical book Shinji bought had torn. Even worse, those gapped teeth had left impressions along the edge and his saliva had stained the paper. That really got Shinji. Every time he took the book out, he had to remember that ugly mug. Even though he recognized he was being uptight, he despised it when his books were torn or dirty. Whenever he read a book, he always removed the dust jacket first to keep it in good shape.

His uncle had also said, "If we dislike the outcome, we need to punish the person responsible, Shinji. You can't keep your anger bottled up."

So Shinji decided to punish Keita Iijima by showing Keita the same level of friendship his pal had given him. *What's wrong, Iijima? It's not that bad a sentence. It's not like I'm refusing to see you—that wouldn't be very mature of me. We're both better off this way.*

That's how trivial the story was. He hadn't even told it to Yutaka.

But ignore the trivialities in this game, and you end up dead, right? This isn't out of anger, Uncle. This is that real world you always talked about. I can't have anything to do with him.

"Yeah," Keita said, playing off what Yutaka had said. "You can trust me." He spread his arms wide. The moonlight reflected off the *santoku* knife in his right hand. "I thought we were friends."

But Shinji didn't lower his gun.

Seeing Shinji's resolve, Keita looked like he was about to cry. He tossed the kitchen knife to the ground. Then he said, "See, I don't want to fight. You have to see that now, don't you?"

Shinji shook his head. "No. Scram."

Now anger bubbled to the surface of Keita's expression. "Why? Why don't you trust me?"

"Shinji—" Yutaka said.

"Shut up, Yutaka."

Then Keita's face went stiff. He fell quiet, then, his voice trembling, he said, "Is it . . . is it because of what I did that time? Huh, Mimura? Is that it? Because I ran away? Is that why you won't trust me?"

Shinji kept the gun aimed at him, not saying a word.

"Mimura . . ." Keita had switched his tone back to one of pleading. He nearly sobbed as he spoke. "Please, Mimura. Forgive me, Mimura."

Shinji pressed his lips together. For a brief moment, he wondered if Keita was being sincere or just putting on an act. But he shook off his doubts. *I'm not alone now. I can't endanger Yutaka.* He'd seen this doctrine attributed to the Department of Defense of some foreign nation: "Prepare against our enemy's capabilities rather than their intentions." Meanwhile, the one a.m. time limit was steadily drawing near.

Yutaka said, "Shinji, what's—" but Shinji held out his right hand to stop him.

Keita stepped forward. "Please. I'm scared to be alone. Let me join you."

"Don't come any closer!"

Keita shook his teary face left and right and took another step. Slowly, he was closing in on Shinji and Yutaka.

Shinji pointed his gun down and squeezed the trigger for the first time. The Beretta erupted with a dry *bang*, and the ejected casing traced a pale blue arc in the moonlight. A cloud of dust rose at Keita's feet. He stared at the dust cloud as if he were observing some novel science experiment.

But then he started walking again.

"Stop! Just stop right there!"

"Let me join you. Please."

Keita kept walking, like a clockwork toy built to do nothing but shamble straight ahead. He took another step. Right. Left. Right.

Shinji gritted his teeth. If Keita was going to draw another weapon, he'd use his right hand.

Can I make that shot? This time, it won't be a warning. Can I aim true? Am I absolutely sure?

Of course I can.

It was now or never. Shinji squeezed the trigger one more time.

And as he did, he felt his trigger finger slip.

In the instant before the *bang*, Shinji realized what had happened. *Sweat. I'm nervous and sweating.*

It all happened so suddenly. Keita's torso rocked back, as if he'd been punched in the upper right chest. He spread his arms like a shot-putter just before his launch, then the next moment, his knees buckled, and he fell on his back. Even in the dark, Shinji could distinctly see the small fountain of blood spurting from a hole in the right side of his chest. That too only lasted for a moment.

"Shinji!" Yutaka cried. "What'd you do?"

Yutaka ran to Keita, whose gaping mouth formed an O. He dropped to his knees, put his hands on Keita's body, then, after a brief hesitation, he moved his hand to Keita's neck. Yutaka's face sank. "He's dead."

Unable to move, Shinji was still holding out his gun. He felt like his mind had gone blank, but it hadn't. He heard a voice inside his head say, *How lame.* Not that it mattered, but the voice echoed the way it did when he talked to himself in the shower.

How lame. Aren't you supposed to be Shinji Mimura, The Third Man who never misses a shot? You know, Shinji Mimura, Shiroiwa Junior High's ace guard?

Shinji rose, then walked forward. His body felt heavy, as if he'd suddenly turned into a cyborg. *One day, Shinji Mimura awoke to find he had become the Terminator. Great.*

Slowly, he walked toward Keita Iijima's body.

Yutaka glared up at him. "Why, Shinji? Why did you kill him?"

Shinji stood motionless and answered, "I was worried he had another weapon besides the knife. I aimed for his arm. I didn't mean to kill him."

Hearing this, Yutaka started to check Keita's body. Then he made a show of looking through the boy's daypack. Then he said, "There's nothing! How could you, Shinji? Why didn't you trust him?"

Shinji suddenly felt weak. *But I had to do it. Didn't I, Uncle? Didn't I?*

He didn't say anything. He just looked down at Yutaka, who was looking back up at him. *But . . . yes, that's right—we have to hurry. This is no time to dwell on a single mistake.*

But before Shinji could speak, something changed in Yutaka's expression.

Yutaka's chin trembled in fear. "No . . . Shinji, you couldn't . . ."

Not understanding, Shinji said, "What?"

Yutaka scrambled backward, distancing himself from Shinji.

More quavering words came tumbling out. "Shinji, you couldn't . . . on purpose . . . it was really . . ."

Shinji pressed his lips together. He gripped the Beretta tightly in his left hand. "You think I—I shot and killed him on purpose because I was in a hurry? That's—"

But Yutaka shook his trembling head. As he retreated by one step, then another, he said, "No . . . no . . . You . . . you . . ."

Shinji lowered his eyebrows and stared at Yutaka. *What, Yutaka? What are you saying?*

"You . . . you . . . this whole escape is . . . is . . ."

Yutaka was incoherent, but the CPU inside Shinji's skull ran as fast as anyone's, and it had worked out what Yutaka was thinking.

He can't think that . . .

But that's the only answer that fits.

Yutaka was accusing Shinji of really playing the game—and of having no intention of escape. And so Shinji shot and killed Keita.

Shinji must have looked flabbergasted. His mouth might have even dropped.

But then he shouted, "Don't be stupid! Then why the hell would I be with you?"

Yutaka shook his head. "Because . . . because . . ."

Yutaka didn't finish, but Shinji knew what he was going to say anyway. *Probably something about my needing someone to keep lookout while I sleep, or anyway, that I'm using him just so that I can stay alive. But wait, didn't I use that computer to take on Sakamochi, and when that got disrupted, haven't I gone to all that trouble to put this plan in motion? Does he think that since I'm smart, this was all some secret plot—that I faked everything with the laptop and the phone just to gain his trust, and that the gasoline and fertilizer are just for my own protection? And that, added to my one pistol, these custom explosives will give me a powerful advantage on my way to being the last man standing? And that my plan is to stop and say, "Actually, let's not," just as we're about to bomb the school? Just like when I was hacking their network, only to say, "It's no good," and gave up? No, really, wait a second here—then what the hell's the point of that kite string I ran all the way around the school? Do you want to tell me I saw all the phones disconnected on this island and thought to myself, hey, why don't I start up a tin-can-and-string telephone company and make big money? Or had that too been a fiendishly clever ruse? Maybe I have some other use for it that your mind can't begin to fathom. Is that it, Yutaka?*

But when you said you would get revenge for Izumi Kanai, and I said I'd help you, didn't you cry? Was that another one of my tricks?

You're over-thinking it, Yutaka. Once you begin to doubt, you can suspect everything. But you're over-thinking it. That's stupid. Really, it's hilarious. Even funnier than your jokes. Are you so exhausted now that you're starting to lose it?

Such were Shinji's thoughts on a rational level. And if he were able to explain them step-by-step, even Yutaka would have realized how foolish all his suspicions were. And maybe none of this was what Yutaka was trying to say to him. Maybe with his exhaustion, and the shock of seeing his close friend Keita die right in front of his eyes, a single thought lurking in the back of Yutaka's mind had suddenly raised its head above the surface. But for that to have happened, the thought had to have existed there in the first place—a single hint of mistrust. And all the while, Shinji had never doubted Yutaka in the slightest.

The feeling of weakness that had washed over his body instantly redoubled, hitting him like a flat-twelve engine, turbocharged. *This class of fatigue will leave all the others in the dust. A real bargain if I do say so myself, sir.*

Shinji uncocked the hammer of his Beretta and tossed it toward Yutaka, who hesitated but picked it up.

Exhausted, Shinji put his hands on his knees and said, "If you don't believe me, then go ahead and shoot me, Yutaka. I don't care. Shoot me."

Yutaka looked at him, eyes wide.

With his head down, Shinji continued, "I only shot Iijima because I felt I had to protect you. Damn it."

For a second, Yutaka looked stunned. Then, tearfully, he blurted, "Oh, oh," and ran to Shinji. "I'm sorry! I'm sorry, Shinji. I was just . . . so shocked when Iijima died, that . . ."

Yutaka put his hand on Shinji's shoulder and started bawling. Shinji stared at the ground with both hands still on his knees. He realized that tears were filling his eyes too.

Somewhere from his subconscious, a part of Shinji was saying, *Hey. This is no time for that. Don't you see that while you're bickering, you're leaving yourselves wide open? Have you forgotten that you're surrounded by enemies? Look at your watch, man. You're out of time.* The voice sounded like his uncle's.

But, blocked by Shinji's frazzled nerves, exhaustion, and the shock of Yutaka doubting him, the voice didn't reach into his consciousness.

Instead, Shinji only cried. *Yutaka. I was trying to protect you. How could you suspect me like that? I trusted you . . . Oh, but maybe this is exactly how Keita felt—when someone he trusted didn't trust him back. I did a terrible thing.*

Amid this jumble of emotions—grief, exhaustion, regret—Shinji heard a *brattattattattattattat* sound, like from some old typewriter.

An instant later, he felt as if pierced by scorching-hot pokers.

Though these wounds were fatal, their pain brought him back to his senses. Yutaka, who had his hand on Shinji's shoulder, slumped to the ground. Beyond him, at the far end of the parking lot, Shinji saw a figure in a school uniform. The figure was holding a gun—something larger than a pistol, it looked more like a tin box. Shinji realized what had pierced his body—*bullets, of course, fuck*—and that they had penetrated through Yutaka before hitting him.

His body felt warm and stiff (*Well duh, I did just catch a bellyful of bullets*), but he reflexively fell to his left and picked up the Beretta Yutaka had taken and dropped. He flipped over, stood, and aimed for the figure—Kazuo Kiriyama (Boys #6). He fired several shots at the killer's stomach.

But Kiriyama had already shifted to the side and out of their path. With another *brattattattattattattat*, his hands radiated an out-of-season firework show.

The impacts in Shinji's right side, left shoulder, and left chest dwarfed those before, and the Beretta slipped from his hand.

But Shinji had already started running for the co-op building. For a moment, he staggered, but he ducked, kicked out his legs, and dove headfirst through the doorway. The stream of bullets chased after him, but he had managed to elude them. Or so he thought, when the tip of his basketball sneakers blew apart. This time true pain pierced through him.

He had no time to rest. He grabbed the jerry can from behind the sliding door, and crawling nearly by his left arm and leg alone, dragging the jerry can along in his right hand, he retreated into the darkness where the tractor and combine waited.

Blood filled his mouth. He figured his body had taken more than ten bullets. Despite the unrivaled pain shooting up from his right foot, he glanced down to where the tip of his sneakers should have been and thought, *I won't be playing basketball anymore. It's impossible now. Even if I did, I'd never be a star player again. The legend is over. The end. Full stop.*

But Shinji was more concerned over Yutaka. *Yutaka, are you still alive?*

Kiriyama, Shinji thought, as the blood bubbled from the side of his mouth. He gritted his teeth. *Well look at you. So you've decided to play the game. Then come and get me. Yutaka can't move now, but I can. You can finish him off later. Come get me. Please come get me.*

As if in response to his silent plea, a shadow passed into the slash of pale moonlight coming in through the sliding door. Shinji saw it through the tractor's undercarriage.

The next moment, that *brattattattattat* sound came with strobe-like flashes of light, and the bullets scattered throughout the building. A part of some piece of farm equipment blew apart, and a window across from Shinji shattered.

Then it stopped. The submachine gun had run out of bullets. Kiriyama wouldn't take long to replace the magazine.

Shinji picked up a nearby screwdriver and threw it off to his left, where it clanged against something and fell to the concrete floor.

He assumed Kiriyama would shoot that way next, but instead, Kiriyama fanned bullets around the screwdriver. Shinji shrunk himself and hoped he wouldn't be hit. Then it stopped. Shinji raised his head.

Kiriyama was inside the building now.

That's right. Shinji twisted his bloody lips into a smile. *I'm over here. Come here.*

Shinji lifted the jerry can with his right hand and placed it atop his stomach. Then, careful not to make any noise, he slid backward with his left arm and leg. His back struck some hard, boxlike object, and he slid around it and continued to retreat. He knew Kiriyama could hear him. Kiriyama already knew he was hiding in the shadows. Besides, with the trail of blood, Shinji had no hope of sending the killer astray.

Kiriyama was ducking down, peering beneath the farm equipment and the raised-up mini pickup truck and everything else. Each time he did, he got a little closer to Shinji.

Shinji looked around himself. On the opposite wall, he could make out the outline of the second-floor space and the metal staircase leading up to it from the entrance. If his body had been up to the task, he could have tackled Kiriyama from there as he'd entered. But it was too late for such things now.

Over near the eastern wall was a hand truck with a platform and four tiny wheels. Beyond it, the corner of the building had been par-titioned off into an office space, beside which was a side door leading outside. The main sliding door was large enough, when fully opened, for a vehicle to pass through, but this one was only for people. It was closed.

That door. I locked it, like I did all the windows and everything. How long would it take me to unlock it?

He didn't have time to think. He dragged himself toward the hand truck. When he reached it, he quietly lifted the jerry can on top of the cart. He removed the cap from the spout. Then he took the hollow rubber plug that had been dangling from a piece of packing string and stuffed it into the spout.

He took the detonator from his pocket. With his injuries, he had trouble moving his fingers, but he managed to peel off the electric tape from the side of the battery case. The lead coming from the detonator dangled freely, and Shinji connected it to the end of the cord coming from the capacitor board. He removed the plastic insulation pull tab from the battery case, and the capacitors quickly charged, emitting a faint, high-pitched hum. His fingers more sure now, Shinji pulled off the tape from the electric conductor's switch and stuffed the detonator deep into the rubber plug in the spout. Everything else—the conductor, battery case, and circuit board—he left on top of the jerry can. He didn't have any time to secure them in place. Kiriyama's feet had appeared to the right of the threshing machine.

Shinji knew this was a long shot. But he and Yutaka were both injured, and they would not be crawling their way up the mountain now.

I've got a special present for you, Kiriyama.

Shinji kicked the cart from behind with his left leg as hard as he could. Without waiting to see if the hurtling cart avoided the piles of junk between him and Kiriyama, he flung himself at the doorknob of the side entrance.

He unlocked it in two tenths of a second. He pushed with his legs—even the one that had lost its toes—and body-slammed the door open, diving through it and outside the building.

Behind him the corrugated metal wall suddenly swelled. Then a roar shook the night, far more terrible than the blasts from Kiriyama's grenades that had temporarily deafened Shuya. Shinji thought, *Well, there go my eardrums.*

Shinji had hit the ground, but the blast propelled him a fair distance across the dirt, scraping skin from his forehead. Fragments and detritus blew past him, but Shinji nonetheless looked over his shoulder and saw, where one of the walls had been, the pickup truck floating upside down in the air. The force of the explosion must have built up beneath the raised jack and sent the car flying amid the swarm of shards of glass, corrugated metal, and even concrete (Shinji thought he felt several of the fragments spear him—not the ones that had blown straight out, but the ones that had flown up into the air). Slowly rotating in the sky, the vehicle traced a parabolic curve before slamming onto its side in the middle of the parking lot. Then it fell over another ninety degrees, once again completely upended, and stopped. Half its rear bed had been torn off, and what remained had twisted like a wrung-out dishrag. Somehow, its tireless wheels spun around and around.

Shrapnel showered down. Within the billowing smoke, nothing remained of the Northern Takamatsu Agricultural Cooperative Oki Island Branch Office aside from its skeletal frame. Only a fraction of the northern wall stood, with the second floor, but beyond the smoke, the second floor had been left bare. Most of the roof and the southern side had been blown away, and the farming machinery and various equipment had been scattered, toppled over, and charred blacker than the night. A few flames burned brightly wherever something had caught on fire. The side door from which Shinji had made his exit still clung by its lower hinge to the wall's remains. It had bent over in Shinji's direction, as if making a bow to the boy. The partitioned-off office was gone without a trace. Nothing of it remained—well, except for the desk. Propelled by the blast, the combine had rammed into it, pinning it against a part of the wall that had survived the blast.

One piece of shrapnel had been sent soaring high into the sky. Finally it fell into the smoke, landing with a metallic *clang,* like a punchline delivered with bad timing—though Shinji could hardly hear it.

When he came back to his senses, Shinji sat up from under the pile of fragments of paneling and everything else. He stared at the building's remains and said, "Huh."

His homemade jerry-can bomb had turned out well. With that much force, it would certainly have wiped out the school.

But that was all over now. At least he had defeated the enemy before him. But more than that . . .

"Yutaka," Shinji said. Slowly, he rose. He put his right knee on the debris. When he opened his mouth, blood spilled over his teeth, and incredible pain shot through his chest and his stomach. He was amazed that he was still alive. But he pushed with both hands, brought his right heel beneath his leg, then extended his left leg, and he managed to stand. He looked to where Yutaka had fallen in the parking lot.

And then . . .

And then he saw the flipped-over truck's door groan open (the door must not have survived completely intact). (That Shinji could hear the sound meant his hearing had started to return.)

Kazuo Kiriyama hopped out onto his feet. He held that tin-box submachine gun as if nothing had happened.

Hey . . .

Shinji felt like he should be laughing. Those blood-soaked lips of his might even have been smiling.

You've gotta be kidding.

By then Kiriyama was already firing. Shinji took the 9x19mm Parabellum shower straight on and reeled backward onto the debris-covered ground. Something pressed into his back—the front of the parked minivan, not that it mattered anymore. The car had been thrown back by the blast, its rear plowing into a now-canted wooden telephone pole. Shrapnel had struck its windshield, spiderwebbing the glass.

Framed by the bright light of the flames inside the building, Kiriyama stood calm and still. Shinji saw behind him Yutaka lying on his face, half buried in the debris. Directly beside him, Keita Iijima was on his back, his head listed to the side, pointing right at Shinji.

Shinji thought, *Kiriyama. Damn, so I ended up losing to you.*

He thought, *Yutaka, I let my guard down for a moment. I'm sorry.*

He thought, *Uncle, how lame, huh?*

He thought, *Ikumi, fall in love and be happy. Big bro won't be finding true love now. Big bro wo—*

Kazuo Kiriyama's Ingram spouted fire once more, and Shinji's thoughts ended there. A bullet had torn through the language center of his brain. All around his head, the cracked windshield shattered. Most of it fell inside the car, but a mist of tiny fragments fell onto Shinji's already dust-covered body.

Then Shinji slumped forward onto his face, and a piece of debris bounced away. The rest of his brain died not even thirty seconds later. Smeared with the blood pouring out of his left ear, the memento of his revered uncle—the earring that had once belonged to a woman the man had loved—reflected the flames of the building, glistening bright and red.

And like that, Shinji Mimura, the boy known as The Third Man, left the game.

17 STUDENTS REMAIN.

PART THREE
THE ENDGAME

STUDENTS REMAIN.

Inside the bushes with her blanket over her shoulders, Noriko sat with her head down and her knees clasped to her chest. Deep within the heavy darkness, insects hummed like a fluorescent bulb moments before burning out.

Shortly after she and Kawada had returned here, Sakamochi gave his midnight announcement. He read only one name—Hirono Shimizu (Girls #10), who had fled after Shuya saw her kill Kaori Minami, though Noriko hadn't witnessed it herself. The forbidden zones were F-7 from one o'clock, G-3 from three, and E-4 from five—no mention of C-3, where she and Kawada were hiding. And he hadn't said Shuya's name, but . . .

Only ten or twenty minutes after the announcement, the sound of distant gunfire returned. When the machine gun fire followed, Noriko's heart froze.

No matter how hard she tried, Noriko would never forget that sound. Without a doubt, she knew it belonged to Kazuo Kiriyama's machine gun—assuming that no one else had been given the exact same weapon. She feared that Kiriyama had been still chasing after Shuya and had finally caught him.

But before she could say anything to Kawada, she was interrupted by the sound of an incredible explosion far surpassing that of those hand grenades Kiriyama had thrown at them. After that, the machine gun fired twice more, the bursts now comparatively a whisper. Then the silence returned.

Even Kawada seemed somewhat surprised by the sound. He was using a knife to carve some kind of arrow. But he stopped and said, "I'm going to go take a look. Don't move from this spot." He left the thicket and came back right away and reported, "Some building's on fire to the east."

Noriko started to say, "Could it—"

But Kawada shook his head and said, "It's pretty far south from where we ran into Kiriyama. Nanahara escaped into the mountains, so this wasn't him. We'll keep waiting for him here."

The news relieved her at the time, but that was nearly an hour ago. Shuya still hadn't returned.

Noriko held her wrist up to the coin-sized spot of moonlight coming in through the leaves. Her watch read twelve past one. For some time now, she had been repeating this action as if it were a magic ritual.

Then she buried her head back into her skirt.

A horrible image flashed through her thoughts. It was Shuya's face, his mouth open and his gaze distant, an expression not unlike when he'd sung "Imagine" (he'd said it was a rock standard) during one of the breaks in the music room while the teacher was away. But in this vision, he had a large black dot on his forehead like a Hindu's bindi. Without warning, a red liquid rose up inside the dot—which was actually an extremely dark, deep hole. From his brain at the bottom of the hole, blood oozed forth and spread over his face like cracks in a pane of glass.

Noriko shook her head and dispelled the vision. She looked over to Kawada, sitting beside her with his back to a tree, smoking his cigarettes. At his side, he'd set down his handmade bow, and several arrows stuck out of the dirt.

"Kawada," she said.

Almost a silhouette in the darkness, Kawada took the cigarette from his mouth and rested his hand atop his standing knee.

"What?"

"Shuya should have been here by now."

Kawada returned the cigarette to his lips. Its tip became red, and the faint light illuminated Kawada's expressionless face. She felt a flash of irritation at his lack of concern. His face sank back into the shadows, and smoke lazily drifted from his lips.

"Yeah."

His calm voice annoyed her too. But remembering how he had saved her and Shuya several times, she suppressed the emotion.

Then she said, "Something . . . must have happened."

"Probably."

"What do you mean, probably?"

Kawada's silhouette raised its hands. The smoldering end of the cigarette shifted.

"Hey, calm down. That machine gun earlier was definitely Kiriyama. Assuming there aren't two of that same gun going around out here, anyway. And with that explosion, Kiriyama wasn't fighting Nanahara, but someone else. Whatever happened, Nanahara escaped Kiriyama. That's for sure."

"Then why hasn't Shuya—"

"Because he's hiding somewhere, probably. Maybe he got lost."

Noriko shook her head. "He might be hurt, or worse."

A chill ran down her spine. That image of Shuya's face, with his gaping mouth and the widening red spiderweb replayed in the back of her mind. Despite escaping from Kiriyama, he could have been fatally wounded. He could be dying right now. And if not, he could have been attacked by another student as he fled over the mountain—or he could have passed out somewhere . . . and if somewhere fell inside one of the forbidden zones, he could die while he was unconscious. After all, area F-7, just to the north of the school, and at the base of the mountain where Shuya had likely run and hid, was designated to become a forbidden zone at one o'clock. And it was past one now.

Noriko shook her head again. *That's not possible. Shuya would never die. He's like a saint with a guitar. He's kind to everyone, and sympathetic, never losing that reassuring smile, and he's decent and innocent and he wears his heart on his sleeve, but he has an unyielding spirit. He's my guardian angel. How could someone like that die? He wouldn't. No way. But . . .*

Softly, Kawada said, "Yeah, maybe. But maybe not."

Noriko turned her wrist and nervously checked her watch again. Then, moving her aching leg, she inched closer to Kawada and took his left hand from his knee and gripped it with both hands.

"Please. Can't we go . . . can't we go look for Shuya? Will you come with me? I can't do it by myself. Please."

Kawada slowly lifted his hand and guided hers back to her knee and gave them a pat. "No can do. Even if you insist on going alone, I won't let you. If I do that, then Shuya asking me to look after you was for nothing. He'll have put himself in danger, letting us escape first, for nothing."

Noriko bit her lower lip and stared at him.

"Don't make that face at me," Kawada said. "It hurts, having a girl look at me like that."

He scratched his head with the hand holding his cigarette, then said, "You really care about Nanahara, right?"

Noriko nodded. She nodded with confidence.

Kawada nodded back at her and said, "So try to understand what he'd want."

She bit her lip again, then lowered her eyes and nodded. "All right. All we can do is wait, right?"

"Right." Kawada nodded.

After a brief silence, he said, "Do you believe in the sixth sense, Noriko?"

Noriko's eyes widened a little at the unexpected topic. *Is he trying to distract me by talking about something else?*

"Yeah," she replied. "A little. But I don't really know." Then she asked, "Do you believe in it, Kawada?"

He stubbed out his cigarette on the ground.

"No, not at all," he said. "Actually, I don't bother thinking about it. Ghosts, and the afterlife, and cosmic energy, and the sixth sense and fortune telling and supernatural powers, that's the talk of fools who escape reality because they aren't equipped to handle it. Sorry, you said you believed a little, didn't you? No offense. It's just my opinion. But . . ."

Noriko looked at his eyes. "But?"

"But sometimes, without any apparent reason, I'm certain about things that are still unclear. And I can't explain why, but I've never been wrong."

Without a word, Noriko watched his face.

Then he said, "Nanahara is alive. He'll come back. Somehow, I know this."

Relief softened her expression. Everything Kawada had just said might have been made up. But even if it was, she was happy he'd said it to her.

"Thanks," she said. "You're kind, Kawada."

Kawada shrugged. "I'm just saying how I feel."

Then he said, "Nanahara's lucky."

Noriko glanced at him. "Hm?"

"To be so loved."

She smiled a little. Only a little. "You've got it wrong."

"What?"

"It's one-sided. Shuya likes someone else. And she's wonderful. I'm nothing next to her."

"Really?"

Noriko lowered her head and nodded. "She's really cool. How can I put it? She's strong, and that's what makes her so . . . beautiful. I'm jealous, but I understand why he's attracted to her."

Kawada tilted his head. "I wonder." He struck the lighter a few times and lit his cigarette. "I think Nanahara likes you now."

She shook her head. "No way."

"When he comes back," Kawada said with a grin, "you should call him a jerk for making you worry. Really let him have it."

She smiled a little again.

Then Kawada blew out smoke and said, "You should lie down. You still haven't completely recovered. And if you get tired, you should sleep. I'll be awake the whole night. When Nanahara comes back, I'll tell him to wake you up with a kiss."

"Okay." Noriko smiled and nodded. "Thanks."

She sat there for another ten minutes, and then she wrapped herself in the blanket and lay down.

But she couldn't sleep.

17 STUDENTS REMAIN.

53

Hiroki Sugimura was utterly exhausted. He'd been walking without rest since the game began, so it was only natural that he would begin to tire. But with each of Sakamochi's announcements, he'd heard the numbers of the dead, and his exhaustion rocketed up to the next level. They were down to twenty now—no, as far as Hiroki knew, it was already seventeen. *The* Shinji Mimura had died. He had been together with Yutaka Seto and Keita Iijima.

After Hiroki left Shuya's group in the clinic, he headed toward the previously unexplored northwest shore. Hearing a pitched gunfight just past eleven, he followed the noise and ended up a little to the east of the center of the island. But the noise had stopped before he got there, and he didn't find anything. Then the midnight announcement added to the list of forbidden zones, and Hiroki decided to visit each in turn. Then, just as he had nearly reached the zone on the north side of the school, F-1, he heard a single gunshot—immediately followed by that machine-gun sound.

From his vantage point on the mountainside, Hiroki could see over to the flat land below. Lights—likely gunshots—flashed in a field just west of the village. As he descended the mountain, he heard an earsplitting roar. For an instant, between the trees, the night sky lit up. Again came that machine-gun *brattattattat*.

When he left the foot of the mountain, he saw a burning building near where he'd seen the flashes. He considered that his machine-gun-wielding foe might still be in the area, but just as it had been with Megumi Eto, he had to find out what had happened. Cautiously, he wove his way between the fields, until, where the fires yet burned, he found Shinji Mimura's corpse. A large building, maybe a warehouse of some sort, was in ruins—it must have been an explosion after all. Beside it, debris large and small littered the parking lot, where, in front of a lone minivan, Shinji was lying facedown. His body had been riddled with bullets. Nearby, Yutaka Seto and Keita Iijima had been buried by the rubble.

The machine-gunner, who must have been the one to kill Shinji, was gone. But Hiroki, knowing one of the other students playing the game could be attracted to the area, quickly left.

He crossed the east-west road and ran into the base of the southern mountain. There, the thought again hit him: *Shinji Mimura is dead.* Hiroki knew Shinji fairly well, and his death was hard to believe. Though it seemed crass now, Hiroki had thought of him as immortal—someone who would refuse to die even when he was killed. Hiroki learned martial arts at the town's dojo, but ultimately that amounted to nothing more than technique. He had nothing on Shinji's innate physical prowess and had always assumed that if the two ever sparred, even under the martial arts rules with which he was familiar, and even with his full ten-centimeter height and reach advantage, he wouldn't stand a chance against Shinji. On top of that, Shinji was much smarter. Even if Shinji had been unable to escape from the game (though that likely had been his plan), he never would have been killed by any of the others. But this unknown machine-gunner had done just that.

Hiroki didn't have time to mourn Shinji's death. He had to find Kayoko Kotohiki. If he didn't find her soon, and she got caught by the machine-gunner, she'd be killed in a split second.

Since zone G-3, which would be a forbidden zone after three o'clock, was located on the northern side of the south mountain's summit, Hiroki decided to hike there.

He'd been on this mountain several times now. Takako Chigusa's body would still be on the side of the mountain in zone H-4, not far from his destination. He hadn't even been able to give her a proper burial. Instead, he'd merely closed her eyes and folded her arms over her chest. She would still be outside any of the forbidden zones.

As he cautiously advanced through the darkness, Hiroki absently thought, *I'm an awful person. I wasn't even able to stay with my closest friend. And now I'm going to walk right past you again on my way to G-3.*

I'm sorry, Takako. But I still have something I have to do. I have to find Kayoko Kotohiki. Please forgive me.

Then another thought occurred to him. It was about Yutaka Seto.

Yutaka's seat number directly followed his, and he would have been the second to leave the school after him. But Hiroki had been scoping out the situation and frantically searching for a place to hide with a clear enough view of the entrance. Before he knew it, Yutaka had already vanished. That was when Hiroki decided Takako would be his priority. He let Haruka Tanizawa (Girls #12) and Yuichiro Takiguchi (Boys #13) pass by. (Then, after all his precautions, Yoshio Akamatsu's surprise appearance panicked him enough for him to lose sight of Takako.) Yutaka had managed to join up with his friends, Shinji and Keita Iijima. But now he was dead along with them.

I have to hurry, he reminded himself. Of all the others, he didn't want her to die.

Hiroki stopped beside a tree that hadn't many branches, and he looked at his handheld locator. The device's liquid-crystal display had no backlight, and he had some trouble reading it with only the moonlight. But he squinted and found the faint shadow created by the crystal molecules.

As per usual, the display remained unchanged, with the solitary star marking Hiroki's own presence. Hiroki let out a faint sigh.

Should I just shout for Kayoko? He'd asked himself that question many times now, and again he mulled it over. By the time he'd found Takako Chigusa, he was too late. What if calling out for her could prevent that from happening again?

No. That wouldn't work.

He couldn't do it. First of all, he couldn't be sure that Kayoko would respond. She might even run away. Besides, while he didn't care if someone attacked him, Kayoko could end up being targeted if she were to come at the same time.

He was left with no choice but to rely on that crude government-issued locator. But at least he had that; without it, his task would have been harder. He hated the government for throwing his class into this bullshit game—he hated them plenty—but on this one point he was grateful. There was a saying about finding a small consolation within a larger sadness. Did that make this a small gratitude within a larger outrage?

Hiroki crossed a knoll overgrown with tall grass, and he came upon a gentle upward slope with sparsely scattered trees. He knew he would soon enter zone H-4, where Takako now rested. Hiroki held up his locator and shifted it to catch the moonlight on its display.

In the center of the screen, he saw a blurred double image of his own star indicator. *Damn, I'm getting too tired. My eyes are starting to go.*

He was still looking down when he realized he was wrong. He spun, and the pole in his right hand flashed. Using the form he'd mastered in his martial arts training, his graceful movement traced a clean arc in the air.

The pole struck the arm of the figure standing behind him, who grunted and dropped something—a gun. In that brief moment when he'd been distracted by the locator, this person, gun at the ready, came up directly behind him.

The figure ran for the weapon. Hiroki thrust his stick into the assailant's path. The figure stopped and staggered back.

Then he saw her—first, the typical sailor fuku. Then, her face, beautiful in the bright moonlight, angelic and lovely, and unmistak-able—the face of the girl who had left the school directly after him, while he hid in a corner of the schoolyard, not yet able to find a proper hiding place—the face of Mitsuko Souma (Girls #11).

Mitsuko raised both hands to her face and stepped back. "Don't kill me!" she cried. "Please don't kill me!"

She stumbled and fell onto her behind. Her pleated skirt revealed her white legs nearly all the way to the top of her thighs. As she edged farther back, those legs moved seductively in the pale moonlight.

"Please! I was only trying to talk to you. I wouldn't even think of killing anyone. Please help me. Help me!"

Hiroki silently stared down at her.

Apparently taking his silence as a sign that he meant her no harm, she slowly lowered her hands below her chin and looked up at him with the eyes of a frightened little animal, glistening with tears.

"You believe me, don't you?" she said. The moonlight fell on her pitiful, teary-eyed face. A hint of a smile appeared at the edges of her eyes. It was not the triumphant smile of having deceived her opponent, but rather one of heartfelt relief.

"I . . . I . . ." she said. As if only now noticing her bare legs, she tugged down the hem of her skirt with her left hand. "I thought I could trust you, Sugimura. And I was so scared, being all alone . . . This is all so terrible . . . I'm scared . . ."

Without a word, Hiroki picked up the gun Mitsuko had dropped. He saw that the hammer had been pulled back, and so he uncocked it and walked over to Mitsuko. Holding it grip first, he offered it to her.

"Th-thank you," she said, timidly reaching for the weapon.

Her hand froze.

Hiroki had flipped the gun around in his hand and took the grip. Its barrel pointed directly between her eyes.

"W-what? What are you doing, Sugimura?"

Her face contorted in astonishment and fear—or at least, con-torted. It was incredible, really. No matter how many rumors spread about her, very few (particularly among the guys) would believe their eyes, seeing that lovely face twisted and pleading. Even if they didn't, they'd still probably be convinced to do whatever she asked. Another time and Hiroki may very well have been one of them. But right now, Hiroki possessed an exceptional piece of information.

"That's enough of that, Souma," he said. Holding the gun on her, he stood up straight. "I saw Takako—before she died."

She gazed up at him, trembling those large, perfectly shaped eyes. If she was regretting not finishing off Takako, not a hint of it appeared in her expression. Only fear was there—and an entreaty for understanding and protection.

"N—no," she said. "That was an accident. That's right, I . . . wasn't alone the whole time. But when I met Takako, she . . . It was her . . . She tried to kill me. That gun was hers, so . . . so I—"

Hiroki recocked the hammer on the Colt M1911. Her eyes narrowed.

"I know Takako. She's not the kind of girl who would kill in cold blood, and she's not the kind of girl to lose it and go around shooting at people. Not even in this game."

Mitsuko tucked her chin and tilted her head. She looked up at him, and then her lips suddenly formed a smile. It was a chilling smile, and yet, in that moment, she became even more beautiful than before.

She quietly laughed. "I thought she'd died instantly."

Hiroki didn't respond. He held the M1911 steady, pointed right at her.

Then, still on the ground, Mitsuko took the hem of her skirt between the thumb and pointer finger of her left hand. Slowly, she pulled it up, baring those seductive white legs once again.

She looked up at him and said, "Well? If you help me, I'll let you do whatever you want. I'm not bad, you know."

Hiroki didn't move. He just kept the pistol trained on her and stared directly into her eyes.

Casually, Mitsuko said, "So that's a no? Yeah, you're right. If you gave me an opening, I'd kill you. Anyway, you couldn't sleep with the girl who killed your girlfriend—"

"Takako wasn't my girlfriend."

Again Mitsuko peered into his eyes.

Hiroki continued, "But she was my best friend."

"Oh, I see." Mitsuko lifted her eyebrows. Then she asked, "So why haven't you shot me? You're too chivalrous to shoot a girl, is that it?"

Brimming with confidence, Mitsuko's face remained beautiful. She was something altogether different from Takako, whose well-honed beauty could have belonged to a war goddess of Greco-Roman myth. If there was such a thing as a fourteen or fifteen-year-old sorceress, Mitsuko would be her. Spirited and childlike, and charming too, but cold. Beneath the moonlight, an icy light filled her eyes. Hiroki felt he might become dizzy.

"How . . ." Hiroki's voice cracked, and his throat felt tight. "How can you kill so easily?"

"What are you, stupid?" She spoke as if she were completely indifferent to the gun pointed at her forehead. "Those are the rules of the game."

Hiroki narrowed his eyes and shook his head. "Not everyone's playing."

Mitsuko tilted her head again. After a moment, and still smiling up at him, she said, "Sugimura." Her tone was friendly and unadorned, the way a girl would say the name of her crush when sitting next to him before homeroom and had decided on something she could say.

"You must be a good person, Sugimura."

Not following, Hiroki raised his eyebrows. His mouth might have dropped open a little.

Lightly, almost singing, Mitsuko continued, "Good people are good people—in certain circumstances, anyway. But even good people can turn bad. Though maybe some of them stay good all the way until the end of their lives. Maybe you're one of those people."

Mitsuko looked away from him and shook her head. "But that doesn't matter. I just decided to take instead of being taken. I'm not saying it's good or evil, or right or wrong. All I'm saying is that's how I want to be."

Hiroki's lips twitched. "But why?"

Again Mitsuko smiled. "I don't know. But if you insist, well, there is one thing."

She looked directly into his eyes. Then she said, "I was raped when I was nine years old. Three different people taking three turns each. Or did one of them go four times? They were all males, just like you—though they were older men. Back then, my chest was flat, and my legs were like sticks. I was a frail, skinny little girl, but I guess that's what they wanted. When I started crying and screaming, it only excited them more. That's why now, whenever I'm with dirty old men like that, I pretend to cry for them."

Through this all, she never stopped smiling. Hiroki stared at her in horror, overwhelmed by her devastating story.

Hiroki might have been on the verge of saying something.

But before he could, a silver light flashed from Mitsuko's hand. By the time he realized she had reached her right hand behind her back, the double-edged diving knife was planted deep in his right shoulder. (The knife, of course, had been the weapon provided to Megumi Eto.) He let out a groan, and though he didn't drop the gun, he staggered back in pain.

Seizing this opportunity, she stood and ran past him and into the trees behind him.

Frantically, he turned and caught a glimpse of her back . . . and she disappeared into the darkness.

Though he knew if he didn't stop Mitsuko Souma now, Kayoko Kotohiki might become another of her victims, he couldn't make himself give chase. Instead he pressed his left hand against his shoulder, where the blood had begun to soak through his school uniform around the knife, and stared into the shadows where Mitsuko had vanished.

Hiroki realized that she obviously could have made up that story to catch him by surprise. But he couldn't believe that. Mitsuko had been telling the truth. And likely that had only been one small part of it. He had wondered how a ninth-grade girl, the same age as he was, could be so cold-blooded. But that wasn't really it, was it? At her age, she'd already acquired the psyche of an adult—a disturbed adult. Or was it that of a disturbed child?

Blood ran down the inside of his sleeve and onto the Colt M1911 in his hand, trickled from the muzzle, and silently soaked into the leaf mold below.

17 STUDENTS REMAIN.

Just after half-past three in the morning, Toshinori Oda (Boys #4) left the house where he'd been hiding. As soon as he'd first gone inside, he tried to determine where he was, which as far as he could tell was somewhere inside zone E-4. And Sakamochi had announced E-4 would become a forbidden zone at five o'clock.

Before he opened the back door, he glanced over to Hirono Shimizu's body, which he'd dragged into the corner of the entryway. But it was only a glance. He didn't particularly feel any pity for her. After all, this was a serious match. They were all playing by the same rules. She hadn't thought twice before shooting him the moment she saw him. Of course, he had been sneaking up from behind to choke her in the first place, but that was beside the point.

He had wavered for some time over where he should settle in next, but he decided to go east toward the village. According to the map, each zone spanned a square roughly two hundred meters to a side. Also on the map were scattered dots indicating houses in the fields of the narrow band of flat land extending out from the eastern village. Once he got far enough away from this zone, all he had to do was hide inside the first house that looked good to him. Hiding in the bushes was far too vulgar for him to bear—after all, he did live in one of the two nicest mansions in Shiroiwa. (Kazuo Kiriyama's might have been in first place, not that Toshinori would ever admit it.) He did risk going into a house where someone else was already lurking, but he wasn't too worried about it. No, he was wearing that bulletproof vest (proven to be effective), and he had taken Hirono Shimizu's revolver, plus he was wearing a full-face motorcycle helmet he'd found inside the house.

A thin cloud had begun to form in the sky, its tip slowly moving across the low full moon. Fully decked out, Toshinori double-checked the helmet's chin strap, then crossed the yard and made his way down to the edge of the small adjacent field.

From there, he could look out over the flat land that extended to the eastern shore. The area wasn't completely flat, however; the ups and downs of the hills were made visible by the pale, moonlit hues of the crop fields that claimed them. A hundred meters to his left, a house stood alongside the foot of the northern mountain. A further hundred meters to its right stood another house, and two more just beyond the left of that house. For some reason, the line of buildings broke off there for three or four hundred meters before houses began to dot the fields again. The mixed woodland, along with a foothill protruding from the northern mountain, prevented him from seeing any farther, but the farms and houses likely continued all the way to the eastern village. Shortly after Sakamochi's midnight announcement, Toshinori heard a tremendous explosion and saw rising flames just to the right of the base of the foothill. But the flames must have gone out, because the area had sunk back into darkness.

Ahead and to the right of Toshinori, on the south side of the flat land, two more houses stood adjacent. If he could trust the blue dots indicating private residences on his map, the buildings were right on the border between zones E-4 and F-4. Behind him, the northern and southern mountains met. Or, more accurately, the foot of the northern mountain extended in rolling hills all the way to the western shoreline. He couldn't see any houses in that direction, though according to the map, one or two were there up on the mountain.

If he hadn't misread the map, once he went three or four houses to the east, he should be clear of the forbidden zone—though if upon closer inspection the houses turned out to be filthy and vulgar, he would have to consider going farther. Firstly, he hated filthy homes, and secondly, vulgar places attracted vulgar people. Such was the will of the market.

For now, Toshinori decided he'd head that way.

Following the dirt ridges between the fields, he ducked low and advanced with caution. Soon the sensation of vulgar dirt clinging to his feet began to gall him. The dull pain in his stomach where Hirono Shimizu (*that slut*) had shot him fueled this irritation.

Why did he have to be thrown into this vulgar game to crawl around in the earth with this vulgar rabble? (That was a phrase often used by his father, who ran the largest food company in the eastern part of the prefecture. Toshinori himself loved using it to express his scorn for the "common man," though as the son of a good family, he had to act the part, and never ever said it out loud.)

Whether or not he was qualified to think that of his classmates, he still possessed a gift unique within the entire junior high. This included his talented classmates—who ranged from the star players of all the school teams and most gifted members of every club, to both the male and female leaders of the delinquents, and even a gay one (though he was dead now, and an incredibly vulgar example).

Toshinori had started taking private violin lessons at the age of four, and now was one of the leading junior high student violinists in the prefecture. He wasn't at the level of a prodigy, but neither could he be lumped in with the unexceptional. Arrangements had been nearly settled for him to enter a highly distinguished private high school in Tokyo that had its own music department. With his talent, he would at the very least go on to become the conductor of the state-run prefectural symphony orchestra.

Therefore—at least, so he believed—he could not die on this island. He would attain the status of a professional musician; he'd marry some gorgeous yet refined woman and keep company with rich, cultured people. (His older brother Tadanori was going to inherit the company. Being the wealthy head of a company had its appeal, but Toshinori thought, *I don't need it. Food companies deal with such vulgar things. I'll leave that to my vulgar brother.*)

Toshinori was different from his classmates, the common rabble. He was a person of worth, blessed with talent. To put it in biological terms, shouldn't the superior members of the species survive?

When the game began, he had been inexplicably handed a bullet-proof vest for a weapon, and he'd had no choice but to hide. But now he had a gun.

He would show no mercy.

What about the noble soul of the music lover, you ask? Please. Only a rank amateur would talk like that. Sure, I'm only fifteen, and I haven't seen much of the world, but I at least know what the music world is like. Unlike the prodigies, the merely gifted rely on money and connections. It's all about crushing your competitors and surviving without being trampled on yourself.

Whether or not any of this was objectively true, it was what Toshinori Oda believed.

He had no close friends among the rabble of Ninth Grade Class B. Far from it—he despised his vulgar classmates. And one particular cause of this was Shuya Nanahara.

Toshinori was not in the Shiroiwa Junior High Music Club, which was home to an especially vulgar rabble—a bunch of losers who played nothing but vulgar popular music. (Apparently, the music room was strewn with sheet music for illegal foreign songs.) And Shuya Nanahara was the worst of them.

Toshinori vastly outclassed the boy in terms of musical ability, given his well-trained sense of pitch and his understanding of the many different musical modes. Yet when Shuya Nanahara strummed a nursery-school-level beginner's chord on his guitar, those females in class erupted in squeals as vulgar as themselves. (And with the looks on their faces, as they listened to him play in the break before music class, they might as well have had extra-bold sans-serif writing on their foreheads that went **Oh, Nanahara, do me, right now, right here.**)

But when Toshinori skillfully accomplished an operatic passage, all he received was half-hearted clapping.

For one thing, the female rabble could never appreciate the rarefied pleasures of classical music. And for another, Shuya Nanahara was good-looking. (Though Toshinori had never admitted it to himself, on a deep psychological level, he hated his own ugly face.)

Fine. That's what women are like. They're just a different species. Women are nothing more than tools for producing babies (and of course for men to get pleasure when they need it). And the decently attractive ones are ornaments to be placed beside a successful male. All I need is money and connections. And talent like mine merits money and connections. Therefore . . .

I'm the one who deserves to win this game.

During the night, Toshinori had heard occasional gunfire and a tremendous explosion, but now the island, enveloped in darkness, had returned to utter silence. Before long, he had bypassed the first house and was approaching the second. Though he couldn't see much more than its silhouette, he could tell the building was very old. Planted trees of different sizes encircled the house, and on Toshinori's western approach, one particularly large broadleaf stood with outspread branches, seven or eight meters tall, its trunk probably four or five meters around.

No one could possibly be up in the tree.

Could they?

Toshinori gripped his gun, and keeping an eye on both the house and that tree, he slowly proceeded. And he wasn't so foolish as to forget to stop every now and then and look in all directions. *You never know where the vulgar ones might come from. Take cockroaches, for example.*

After taking a good five minutes to pass the house, he looked over his shoulder for one more glance at the tree-encircled house. Through the rectangular window of his visor, he saw no suspicious movements.

Good.

He looked ahead. The third house, his destination, wasn't far now.

Toshinori glanced over his shoulder one more time.

He thought he saw a round black shape stir near the ground among the trees of the house.

That's someone's head. But by the time he'd realized it, he had already pointed his gun at the shape. *Who in the hell would be loitering around here when it's about to become a forbidden zone?*

He didn't care who it was.

He squeezed the trigger. The Smith & Wesson Model 10's wooden grip kicked back in his hands—it felt good—and an orange flame came out of the muzzle alongside a not-too-loud *bang*. His spine tingled. Although he despised the vulgar rabble, Toshinori did have one hobby, quite dissimilar from the violin, which would not be considered elegant. He collected replica guns. His father owned several hunting rifles but had never let him touch them. This was the first time he'd ever squeezed a real trigger. *Hot damn! The real thing! I'm shooting a real gun!*

Toshinori fired one more time, but whoever the person was had ducked down and hadn't moved. And this opponent didn't shoot back. *Well of course not. If they had a gun, they'd have shot me when my back was turned. That's what let me safely fire at you, anyway.*

Toshinori slowly approached the figure.

A voice cried, "Wait!"

From the voice, he could tell it was Hiroki Sugimura (Boys #11), that lanky boy who did that vulgar karate or whatever. (Toshinori also hated tall guys. He was only a hundred sixty-two centimeters tall, the second shortest in class after Yutaka Seto. Toshinori couldn't stand guys who were: [1] good-looking, [2] tall, and/or [3] vulgar on the whole.) Hiroki was dating that Takako Chigusa, who put that foul dye in her hair and wore all that repulsive, jangling jewelry. *Oh, right, she's dead. Well, she had a halfway decent face.*

Hiroki continued, "I don't want to fight. Who are you? Takiguchi?"

Hiroki meant Yuichiro Takiguchi (Boys #13), the next shortest boy after Toshinori. The only other guys around his size who were still alive were Takiguchi and Yutaka Seto—Hiroshi Kuronaga was long dead.

Toshinori thought about what Hiroki had said. *You don't want to fight? Nonsense. If you don't want to fight in this game, you might as well decide to kill yourself. Is this a trick? Even if it is, you don't have a gun.*

Toshinori changed tactics. He lowered his revolver.

With his other hand, he lowered his helmet's chin guard a little and said, "It's Oda." *Oh, I should be stuttering.* "S-sorry. D-did I hurt you?"

Hiroki slowly rose. Like Toshinori, he had his daypack over his left shoulder. He held some kind of pole in his right. His right arm was bare, with the right sleeves of his jacket and his shirt both missing. Maybe they'd gotten torn, or maybe he tore them off himself. A white cloth was wrapped around his shoulder like a bandage. His bare arm holding the stick looked like it had been transplanted from a primitive, naked tribesman—a vulgar naked tribesman.

Hiroki tilted his head a little. "I'm fine," he said. Then, looking at Toshinori's head, he asked, "A helmet, huh?"

"Y-yeah." Toshinori continued his advance, walking through the farm soil. *All right, only three steps more.* "I-I was scared—"

Before he finished saying "scared," Toshinori raised his right hand. At this close range—only five meters away—he couldn't possibly miss.

Hiroki's eyes widened. *Too slow, too slow, you vulgar karate bastard. Die your vulgar death, get in your vulgar coffin, and go get buried in your vulgar grave. I'll bring vulgar flowers just for you.*

But Hiroki wasn't in the path of the flames spitting from the tip of the Smith & Wesson Model 10. A split second before, he'd unexpectedly shifted to the left—from Toshinori's point of view, he was falling over to the right. Toshinori had no way of knowing that this was a martial arts move, but he did know that Hiroki had moved incredibly fast.

Still leaning sideways, Hiroki pulled out a gun with his other hand. (Here was something else Toshinori didn't know: Hiroki was originally left-handed—though unlike Shinji Mimura, he'd had it corrected.) *If you had a gun, why didn't you use it in the first place, you idiot?* But he hardly had time for the thought to cross his mind before he saw the tiny flame.

The gun vanished from Toshinori's hand. Then excruciating pain exploded in his ring finger. With a shriek, he fell to his knees. He pressed his left hand to the source of the pain—and discovered that his ring finger was gone. Blood spurted out. Even with his bulletproof vest, and even with his helmet, his fingers had been unprotected.

Ah . . . he . . . my finger! On the hand that exquisitely guides my bow. It can't be. Nobody's fingers get blown off in the movies!

Hiroki approached, pointing the gun at him. Toshinori held his right hand and looked down at it through the visor with wild and terrified eyes. Suddenly, he was sweating, and beneath the helmet, his face was clammy.

"So you're really into this, huh?" Hiroki said. "I don't want to kill you, but I don't have a choice."

Toshinori didn't understand what the boy meant, and despite his terrible pain, he still felt confident. Hiroki's gun was pointed at his chest. That was to be expected. Toshinori had taken the helmet not because of its actual ability to protect against projectiles, but because it would lead his opponents to aim for his chest instead—where, under his uniform, he wore his bulletproof vest. As long as his vest stopped the bullet, he could wait for an opportunity to take back his gun—his trigger finger was still there—and he'd win.

His gun had fallen at his feet.

Toshinori glared up at Hiroki Sugimura, who waited a few seconds . . . but then pressed his lips together and calmly squeezed the trigger. Right up until that moment, Toshinori had been thinking back to his fight with Hirono Shimizu and considering how to make his death convincing.

But it ended much more simply than he'd expected. Hiroki's gun only made a small metallic click.

Hiroki looked confused and hurriedly recocked the pistol and squeezed the trigger. Another click.

Hidden behind the visor, Toshinori's mouth twisted into a smile. *You karate bastard. It's a dud. That's a semi-auto—you'll have to rack the slide and reload the chamber if you want to shoot.*

Toshinori dove for the revolver at his feet. For a moment, Hiroki seemed about to swing the stick in his right hand—but perhaps judging the distance to be too far, he turned on his heels and ran toward the mountain beyond the house.

Toshinori picked up the gun. His hand throbbed with pain, but he managed to take hold of the weapon. He fired. With his weakened grip, he missed the center of mass, but he could see Hiroki get hit in the back of his right thigh—near his ass. *Did I only graze him?* Hiroki lurched forward—but didn't fall. He kept on running.

Toshinori took off after him and fired again. This time he missed. Each time the previously pleasurable sensation of the revolver's recoil stabbed through his maimed hand, Toshinori became more and more enraged. He fired yet again. And missed yet again. Even with a bullet in the leg, Hiroki was still the faster runner.

Hiroki vanished into the tree line at the foot of the mountain.

Fuck!

For a few seconds, Toshinori debated whether he should chase after Hiroki—but decided not to. His opponent was wounded, but so was he. Blood pouring out from what used to be his ring finger slicked the revolver's grip. And now that Hiroki had entered the woods, he might be able to reload and return fire. For that matter, Toshinori was perilously exposed out in the open. Hurriedly, he ducked.

I have to get to that house—where I was first going. And I can't let Hiroki see me go inside.

Toshinori clutched his right hand, which still gripped the revolver. Enduring the pain, he staggered toward the house. As he crossed over a ridge between two fields, he began to feel dizzy from the intensifying, excruciating pain.

First is my hand. I have to treat this wound. Then I need to come up with a different battle plan. Ah, but damn it, even if I go through physical therapy and am able to play the violin again, everyone's going to notice my missing finger—especially when I get a close-up during televised performances. And I'll be lumped in with the handicapped. Find grace through overcoming adversity, and all that bullshit.

He was approaching the house. He looked over his shoulder again. He peered into the darkness and saw no sign of Hiroki Sugimura. *I'm clear. He's not following.*

He turned his head back to the house.

A boy was standing on the ridge at the end of the field, only six or seven meters away and directly in front of the house. He hadn't been there before; he seemed to have sprung up out of nowhere. He had slicked-back hair, a little too long at his neck, and cold, gleaming eyes.

By the time he realized it was Kazuo Kiriyama (Boys #6) (another of the sort Toshinori couldn't stand—category [1]: the good-looking), flames burst from the loathsome boy's hands with a *brattattattat*. Several bullets slammed into Toshinori's torso, knocking him backward and off balance. Because of the pain in his right hand, he didn't have a good grip on the Smith & Wesson, which now tumbled out of his grasp. He heard it clatter against something to his right. His back skidded across the dirt, and his helmeted head landed on the ground.

The gunfire's echo subsided, and silence returned to dominate the night.

But Toshinori Oda was not dead. He held his breath and lay there without even the slightest twitch of movement, resisting the impulse to chuckle. Between this wicked glee, the intense pain coming from his right hand, the irritation of having let Hiroki Sugimura escape, and the anger at being suddenly attacked by a Category 1 vulgarian, the part of his brain presiding over his emotions—the limbic system— was in a total mess. But just as when he'd been attacked by Hirono Shimizu, his body remained completely unharmed (save for his ring finger). Wearing that helmet had indeed been the right decision. Kiriyama had aimed for his chest, where the bulletproof vest protected him. And just as Hirono Shimizu had done, Kiriyama would assume him to be dead.

He slitted his eyes, and at the edge of his widescreen view, he saw the Smith & Wesson reflecting the dim moonlight. He could feel the firm, uneven shape of the kitchen knife (he'd taken this from the house where he'd killed Hirono Shimizu) tucked in the back of his pants. In less than a second, he could pull it free from its makeshift cloth sheath.

As the cold sweat—the one thing he was unable to control—trickled down his face, Toshinori thought, *Now come take my gun. I'll tear out your vulgar windpipe with my knife. Or are you going to turn around and leave? Will you go after Hiroki Sugimura next? In that case, I'll pick up my gun and blow a hole in the back of your vulgar head. Come on. Take your pick. Just hurry up and do it.*

But Kiriyama didn't move toward the Smith & Wesson. He walked toward Toshinori.

He kept coming straight to him, staring at him with those cold eyes.

But why? Toshinori asked himself. *I'm dead, aren't I? Look, have you ever seen anyone so dead?*

Kiriyama didn't stop. He kept on approaching. One step more. Two steps—

But I'm dead! Why are you coming to me?

The sound of his footsteps on the soft earth grew louder. Kiriyama's figure filled Toshinori's field of view.

No!

Overcome by panic and fear, Toshinori lost control, and his eyes flung open.

Aimed directly at Toshinori's helmeted head, Kiriyama's Ingram flashed once more. Some of the point-blank bullets ricocheted off the reinforced plastic surface, sending out colorful sparks. Others perforated Toshinori's skull and bounced around inside the helmet. His head shook about, and the helmet along with it. His body danced a bizarre boogie—a vulgar dance he doubtlessly would have despised.

By the time it was over, Toshinori's head had been pulverized within the helmet.

His body was still—only this time, he wasn't pretending to be dead. Blood dripped from the neckline of the helmet, which was now more of a bowl of soup or perhaps a sauce.

Having overestimated the value of his bulletproof vest, and underestimated Kazuo Kiriyama's levelheaded nature, Toshinori Oda, the foolish boy who detested the vulgar rabble, died an ignoble death. Had he paid better attention to Yumiko Kusaka's and Yukiko Kitano's deaths the previous morning, he would have recognized the possibility of his opponent delivering a coup de grâce.

But Toshinori had never been a particularly good student. What's more, he died completely unaware—not that it mattered anymore—that his killer, Kazuo Kiriyama, had some time ago, from the terrace of his mansion—the largest in Shiroiwa and larger than Yoshitoki's—played the violin with far more grace than Yoshitoki ever had.

And then tossed the violin into the trash.

16 STUDENTS REMAIN.

Of all the sounds Mitsuko Souma (Girls #11) could have heard—
voices talking, for example, or the sound of someone moving, or even
faint breathing that couldn't quite be fully suppressed—what she
heard was liquid splattering onto the grass. Very close, in the nearby
grove, someone was peeing (unless a dog was on the island). Dawn was
approaching, and when she glanced overhead, she saw an inky black
sky that had begun to take on a tinge of blue.

After she'd managed to escape from her encounter with Hiroki
Sugimura, Mitsuko's first thought was that she needed a gun. Her first
run-in with Megumi Eto had been an accident, but when she heard
Yoshimi Yahagi and Yoji Kuramoto fighting, she followed the sound,
killed them both, and got her hands on a gun. (If only she'd started
with a gun. Then she could have returned to the school and taken
everyone out as they left one by one.) With a firearm, she was able to
safely move about the island with little caution. And killing Takako
Chigusa after that girl's fight with Kazushi Niida had been simple. (She
did, however, regret just leaving Chigusa to die rather than finishing
her off immediately. She'd have to be more careful from now on.)

But now Mitsuko was unarmed. She'd even lost Megumi Eto's
knife. All she had now was that rice sickle provided to her at the start.

Mitsuko needed to get a gun, whatever it took—because she wasn't the only one playing the game. That machine-gunner who killed Yumiko Kusaka and Yukiko Kitano was still out there. She'd again heard its gunfire only thirty minutes ago.

At least that meant she didn't have to push herself whittling down her classmates. She could leave that to this other player and take the easy kills when they presented themselves. In fact, when she heard the machine gun going off after midnight, followed by that explosion, she decided to stay away. She decided to watch from afar, and on her way to a vantage point, she saw Hiroki Sugimura and followed him instead. And that should have been one of those easy kills . . .

Regardless, she would likely have to face that machine-gunner in the end. If she were unarmed when that time came, she would be at a severe disadvantage. A handgun versus a fully-automatic machine gun would be bad enough—a sickle wouldn't stand a chance.

Mitsuko felt confident she could have again followed Hiroki unde-tected, but she sensed that stealing back her pistol would have been difficult. He hadn't trained in that kempo or whatever for nothing. Her right arm still stung where he'd hit her with that pole. And if he saw her again, he probably wouldn't hesitate to shoot.

So Mitsuko followed the east-west road to the west, and from there moved north into the mountainside in search of someone else. Around three hours had passed.

And now at last she'd heard something.

Following the sound, she made her way into the thicket—but cau-tiously. She couldn't let herself be heard.

The grove opened into a small clearing not even eight square meters in size. More of the thicket lay ahead and on her right and her left—but there, at the edge of the clearing, a boy in a school uniform stood with his back to her. He looked nervously to either side as that pitter-patter sound continued.

He must have been worried about getting attacked. From his pro-file, she saw he was Tadakatsu Hatagami (Boys #18). He was on the baseball team and was an entirely unremarkable, average boy. He was on the tall side, with an athletic build, and his face was, well, average. His hobbies were— *Gosh, I wonder if he even has any. He never mentioned any. No point in asking him now.*

But what caught her eye was the object he held tightly in his right hand as he did his business.

It was a gun—fairly large. A revolver. That fallen angel smile returned to her lips.

Tadakatsu was still going. He must have been holding it in for quite a while. He repeatedly looked left and right as he waited for his bladder to empty.

Careful not to make a sound, Mitsuko slowly drew her sickle with her right hand, and then she waited. When he went to pull up his zipper, Tadakatsu would probably need to use both hands. And if he made himself struggle with zipping it up one-handed, she'd have her opening.

Either way, that'll be the end for you—just like I saw in that one detective show, where the guy got killed while pissing.

The sound became sporadic, then stopped. Then came another drop, then the flow stopped for good. Tadakatsu looked around one last time, then quickly moved his hands around front.

By then, Mitsuko was already sneaking up behind him. The back of his head, with its short-cropped hair, was right before her eyes. She began to raise the sickle.

Someone behind her said, "Whoa," and Tadakatsu gave a start and turned around. Mitsuko jumped a little herself. She lowered the sickle (of course) and turned in the voice's direction.

Yuichiro Takiguchi (Boys #13) was standing there. He was a size smaller than Tadakatsu and had a cute, boyish face. Holding a metal baseball bat lowered in his right hand, he gaped at Mitsuko.

Seeing Mitsuko, Tadakatsu also said, "Whoa," and then, "Shit," and he raised his gun, aiming at her. Since he didn't show surprise at seeing Yuichiro, the two boys must have been together. Mitsuko cursed herself. *Tadakatsu had only stepped away from Yuichiro to go take a piss. How stupid was I not to check first? Come on, you're both boys—you can piss in front of each other!*

But this was no time to argue. Not with the barrel of Tadakatsu's revolver (incidentally, a .357 Magnum Smith & Wesson Model 19) pointed straight at her chest.

Yuichiro cried, "Tadakatsu, stop it!" His voice was shrill, either from general confusion or from dismay over seeing someone about to get killed before his very eyes. Tadakatsu seemed like he would shoot, but his trigger finger froze a fraction of a millimeter before the hammer would fall.

With his revolver still aimed at Mitsuko, he glanced at Yuichiro.

"Why should I? She was going to kill me. L-look! See that sickle? She's holding a fucking sickle!"

Mitsuko squeezed her feeble voice from the back of her throat. "Y-you're wrong." She made her voice high-pitched, trembling at the end, and didn't forget to cower. Here was another chance for the star actress, Mitsuko Souma, to shine. *Keep your eyes open—you don't want to miss this.*

"I-I . . ." She considered letting go of the sickle but decided it would appear more natural if she appeared to have forgotten she was holding it. "I was only trying to talk to you. B-but then, I saw you were, ah, peeing." She lowered her head a little and made herself blush. "So I—"

"Don't lie to me!" Tadakatsu didn't lower his gun. "You were trying to kill me."

The revolver was shaking in his hand. He probably only hesitated because he dreaded actually shooting another human being. The moment he saw her, he might have shot her purely by reflex, but Yuichiro had stopped him, and he'd had time to think—and time for hesitation to surface. And that meant . . .

You've lost, Tadakatsu.

"Stop, Tadakatsu," Yuichiro pleaded. "Didn't you say we needed to join with the oth—"

"You've got to be joking." Tadakatsu shook his head. "Us, with a girl like her? Do you know what she's like? She could be the one who killed Kusaka and Kitano."

Mitsuko summoned tears. "N-no . . . I would never . . ."

Desperately, Yuichiro said, "But Souma doesn't have a machine gun. She doesn't have any gun at all."

"How could you possibly know that for sure? She could have run out of bullets and ditched it!"

Yuichiro was quiet for a while, then said, "Tadakatsu. You shouldn't raise your voice."

His voice was calm and gentle now, not at all like before. Caught off guard, Tadakatsu looked at him with his mouth hanging open a crack.

Well now, Mitsuko thought. Yuichiro sounded rather brave for being Ninth Grade Class B's resident anime geek.

Yuichiro shook his head. "And you shouldn't be so suspicious when you don't have any proof," he admonished. "Think about it. Maybe she tried to talk to you because she trusts you."

"Okay, then." Tadakatsu raised his eyebrows. He still kept his revolver aimed at her, but his trigger finger had relaxed. "So what do you suggest we do?"

"If you absolutely can't trust her, we can take turns watching her. I mean, even if we told her she could leave, that wouldn't settle your anxiety, right? She could just wait for another opening."

Mitsuko was growing more and more impressed. *Where'd that come from? Not bad, kid. You're being logical and persuasive—well, ignoring whether or not you're making the right call. (You really should shoot me now.)*

Tadakatsu flicked his tongue across his lips.

Yuichiro pressed on. "Come on. We need more people on our side. And we have to find some way to escape. Once we spend some time with her, we'll know whether or not we can trust her."

Finally Tadakatsu nodded, though he still eyed her suspiciously. Sounding weary, he said, "Fine."

Mitsuko acted relieved. She rubbed her teary eyes with her left hand. Yuichiro let out a sigh of relief too.

Tadakatsu said, "Drop the sickle." Mitsuko acted flustered, then quickly threw the weapon down. Nervously, she looked at Tadakatsu and then at Yuichiro.

Next Tadakatsu said, "Search her, Yuichiro."

Mitsuko returned her gaze to Tadakatsu and widened her eyes as if she didn't understand.

Then she looked at Yuichiro, who was standing stiffly, somewhat surprised. Tadakatsu repeated himself. He aimed the gun straight at her, then said, "Hurry up. Don't be bashful. Our lives are at stake. You understand that, don't you?"

"Yeah," Yuichiro said. "Okay."

Yuichiro set down his bat and timidly came forward. He stopped at her side.

"Hurry it up," Tadakatsu insisted.

"Y-yeah." Gone was his bravery. He was back to his normal self, a spineless *otaku* child. "But—"

"Now!"

With that, Yuichiro said, "U-um, Souma, I'm sorry. I don't want to do this, but . . ."

He lightly ran his hands down her body. Even in the dim early morning light, she could tell his face had turned bright red. *Aw, how cute,* she thought. But she remembered to affect her own embarrassment.

Once he had finished his cursory pat-down and had taken back his hands, Tadakatsu said, "Look under her skirt too."

Yuichiro gave him a critical look and said, "Tadakatsu—"

But Tadakatsu shook his head. "I'm not getting off on this. I just don't want to die."

So Yuichiro, blushing even more, said to her, "Um . . . I was wondering if you could maybe lift up your skirt a little?"

Oh my, don't give yourself a heart attack now, little boy.

But softly she said, "O-okay," and acting ever-so-shy, she lifted her skirt until just a hint of her underwear showed. Now this was just like one of those porno videos that would have on the cover, *Fetish Gold: Starring Real Junior High School Girls.*

I've actually been in them.

When Yuichiro was sure she wasn't hiding anything, he said, "Th-that's enough."

Tadakatsu nodded. "Good. Yuichiro, tie her hands together with your belt."

Yuichiro sent him another critical look, but Tadakatsu remained firm and kept the gun aimed at her.

"That's my condition, Yuichiro. If you can't accept it, I'll shoot her right now."

Yuichiro looked at both, then wetted his lips.

Mitsuko said to him, "Yuichiro . . . it's all right. Go ahead."

Yuichiro looked into her face, then gave her a small nod and removed his belt and took her hands. "Sorry, Souma," he said.

Tadakatsu's gun hadn't left her. He said, "You don't have to be so polite with her," but Yuichiro pretended not to have heard. He gently wrapped the belt around her wrists without another word.

As she obediently held out her arms, Mitsuko thought, *Despite everything, I'm lucky he saw me before I raised the sickle. (And that I had wiped the blood off it earlier. Now that's luck.)*

Okay. What's my next move?

16 STUDENTS REMAIN.

56

"And that's why I think we really need to find the others," Yuichiro said, and then glanced at Mitsuko. Now that dawn had broken, she could see the dirt on his face.

They were sitting next to each other in the bushes. Mitsuko's hands were still tied with that belt, and her sickle had been stuffed down the back of Yuichiro's slacks. Tadakatsu Hatagami was deep asleep nearby. Even asleep, he still clutched his gun—he'd even tied it to his hands with a handkerchief.

With Mitsuko in the mix now, Tadakatsu had suggested that he and Yuichiro take turns sleeping. "It'd be good for us to round up some allies," he'd said. "But let's get some sleep first. We've stayed awake this whole time now. We won't be able to think straight."

When Yuichiro agreed, Tadakatsu added, "Either me or you will sleep first, Yuichiro. Souma will be third."

Yuichiro said, "I can sleep second," and with that the order was decided.

Holding onto his gun (which he really should have given to Yuichiro, who was keeping watch, but Tadakatsu didn't mention it, nor did Yuichiro object), Tadakatsu lay down and fell asleep in a matter of seconds.

Mitsuko guessed that Tadakatsu hadn't slept from when the game began until he joined with Yuichiro, and he definitely hadn't slept after that either. He was probably afraid Yuichiro might strangle him in his sleep.

But now with a third person, even if she was a girl he trusted far less, Tadakatsu could sleep, and Yuichiro and Mitsuko would watch each other. As long as he kept his gun and remained cautious, he would be fine sleeping. (Mitsuko hadn't slept at all either, but she was just fine. She was raised to be tougher than your typical junior high weakling.)

Apparently Yuichiro hadn't moved around much during the day but had thought he could get away with it at night. (*It's a matter of personal taste,* Mitsuko thought. *Sure, at night it's harder for your enemies to detect you, but you can't see them either. Well, I suppose if you think you're in trouble and you need to escape, night is better for that.*)

When the sun set, he had begun to cautiously move about—and just two hours before Mitsuko found them, the two boys ran into each other. They had talked about escape but weren't able to come up with any decent plan. Then Tadakatsu stepped away to pee, and because he was taking so long, Yuichiro came to check on him. That's when he found Mitsuko. At least that's what she had been able to put together.

"I was scared at first," Yuichiro said. "I didn't believe I could trust anyone. But then I thought about it and realized that most all of us probably just want to escape."

After he said this, he glanced at her again. Ninth Grade Class B's resident otaku avoided direct eye contact when he spoke. Right away, he dropped his eyes again.

And yet from the way he was talking to her, he didn't seem to be wary of her—for whatever reason.

Making as if she'd relaxed a little herself, Mitsuko asked, "Tadakatsu had that gun, didn't he?"

Yuichiro nodded and said, "Yeah."

"Weren't you scared of him?" *Okay, now act a little more relieved, get a little more talkative.* "And aren't you now? He doesn't ever let go of that thing."

Yuichiro smiled a little. "Well, you see, he didn't shoot me right away, at least—though he did point it at me. But we've been class-mates before, in elementary school. So I know him pretty well."

"But . . ." Mitsuko tried to look like her face had turned pale. "You saw Yumiko—Yumiko Kusaka and Yukiko Kitano die, didn't you? Some of them are playing. You can't be sure that Tadakatsu isn't one of them." She lowered her head. "And that's why he suspects me."

Yuichiro pressed his lips together and made several short nods. "That's true. But if we just sit still, we'll end up dying anyway. I'd rather try something. I won't try Kusaka and Kitano's plan, but I was thinking it would be good to gradually build our numbers somehow."

He looked into her eyes for the briefest moment, then dropped his head again. This seemed to be more than just his typical shyness—it was almost like he wasn't used to looking at a girl's face this close up. (*That's probably because he isn't. And they don't get more beautiful than me.*)

Yuichiro said, "And you shouldn't blame Tadakatsu for holding on to that gun. He's probably so scared that he can't help it."

Mitsuko tilted her head and gave him a little smile. "You're a good person."

"Really?" Yuichiro said, looking at her from the corner of his eye.

Still smiling for him, she continued, "You're brave like that, and even in this situation, you still think about how other people feel."

This made him bashfully drop his eyes again. He nervously ran his hand through his unkempt hair and said, "That's not true."

Then, still averting his eyes, he added, "That's why . . . that's why you should cut Tadakatsu some slack for doubting you. I think he's scared. He has some trust issues."

Trust issues? Tickled by his phrasing, she smiled a little.

With a hint of a sigh, she said, "I suppose. With all the things I've done, people are bound to distrust me. You're suspicious of me too, aren't you?"

After a moment, he turned his head to look at her. This time, he kept his eyes on her a little while longer. Then he said, "No."

He faced the ground again. "When you get down to it, even Tadakatsu is suspect. And I'm suspect too. I mean . . ." He plucked a dew-slicked leaf of grass at his feet and started to tear it into thinner strands. "I mean, yeah, I haven't heard many good things about you. But . . . that doesn't matter out here. You wouldn't think it, but it's the ones who always act decent who'll do anything to save their own skin when it comes down to it."

He tossed the shredded-up grass near his feet. He looked over at her again and said, "I don't think you're such a bad girl."

Mitsuko tilted her head. "Why's that?"

When she met his gaze, he panicked and looked away. Then he said, "Well . . . it's, you see, your eyes."

"My eyes?"

He kept his head down and began pulling apart another blade of grass. "You always have this vaguely scary look in your eyes."

Mitsuko displayed a little smile. She tried to shrug, but with her hands tied, the gesture didn't quite come off. "Maybe so."

"But . . ." One leaf had become four, which became eight. "Sometimes your eyes are really sad, and sometimes really kind."

She stared into his profile, letting him talk.

"That's why . . ." He tossed the leaf. His voice sounded embarrassed and nervous, as if he were confessing his feelings to a girl he loved, and though he stumbled a few times along the way, he managed to say, "I always thought you weren't as bad as they all say. I'm sure that even if you've done bad things, it was only because you had some reason that you had to. It doesn't make you a bad person."

Then he added, "At the very least, I didn't want to be one of those guys who couldn't understand that."

Mitsuko sighed inside herself. *You're too naïve, Yuichiro*, she thought. But then she smiled and said, "Thank you."

The sweetness in her voice surprised her. She had of course meant to sound sweet, but if there was a part of her who thought she might have overacted it, it might be—*just maybe*—because mixed in with those words was the tiniest bit of *real emotion*.

But that was all it was.

After a little while, Yuichiro asked, "What were you doing, Souma—before you met us?"

Mitsuko said, "Well . . ." She dragged the word out. She shifted and felt the morning dew soaking into the cloth of her skirt. "I've been running away from everything—like when there were gunshots nearby. So when I saw Tadakatsu, I was scared . . . but I was also scared to be alone any longer. I wasn't sure if I should call out to him. Since it was Tadakatsu, I thought he'd understand. But I just wasn't sure if it was the right thing to do . . ."

Yuichiro nodded again. He glanced into her eyes, then looked down and said, "It looks like you did the right thing."

She smiled and said, "Yeah. It looks like it."

Their eyes met, and they exchanged smiles.

Then Yuichiro said, "Oh, sorry, I should have asked you earlier—are you thirsty? You lost your things, right? You must not have had anything to drink for a while now."

She'd left her daypack behind after her fight with Hiroki Sugimura. He was right—she was thirsty.

She nodded. "Can I—can I have a little?"

Without looking at her, he returned her nod, then reached for his nearby daypack and picked it up. He took out two water bottles, and after comparing them, he kept the unopened one and returned the other to the bag. He opened the sealed bottle.

Mitsuko held out her bound arms. Yuichiro started to hand her the bottle, but then abruptly stopped. He glanced at the slumbering Tadakatsu, and then back at the plastic bottle in his hand.

He then set the bottle down beside his leg.

Hey now, aren't you going to let me have a drink? Change your mind because if you spoil the prisoner, big Sergeant Hatagami will get mad?

But without a word, Yuichiro took her hands, lifted them a little, and grasped the belt. He started to remove it.

"Yuichiro," Mitsuko said, as if she were surprised (actually, she was, a little). "Are you sure about this? Tadakatsu will be mad."

His eyes intent on her wrists, Yuichiro said, "It's all right. I have your weapon after all. Besides, how can you enjoy your water when you have to drink it with your hands tied up?"

Yuichiro looked up at her face. When she said, "Thank you," his cheeks flushed again, and he dropped his eyes.

The belt came free. Mitsuko rubbed one wrist and then the other. Since the belt had been tied fairly loose, her wrists hadn't suffered any harm worth mentioning.

Yuichiro offered her the water bottle. She accepted it, took two demure drinks, and held it out to him.

He had been looping the belt back through his slacks, but he stopped and asked, "That's all? You can have more if you like. If we run out, we can always get more from a house with a well."

Mitsuko shook her head. "No, that was plenty."

"Okay."

Yuichiro took the bottle, put it back into the daypack, then returned his hands to his waist and fastened his belt buckle.

As he did, Mitsuko said to him, "Yuichiro."

Yuichiro looked up.

She reached to him with her newly liberated hands and gently took his right hand. Yuichiro seemed to tense up—likely not because he worried she was going to try some scheme, but because a *girl* was holding his hand.

"W-what?"

Mitsuko smiled warmly. She opened her shapely lips and cooed, "I'm so glad I met someone like you. I've been shaking scared this whole time—but I'm safe now."

Self-conscious and embarrassed, he opened his mouth timidly and closed it several times before he finally said, "You're safe."

Yuichiro seemed to want to take back his hand, but Mitsuko held firm. Again he had trouble making himself speak, and when he did, his voice was tense, but he said, "I'll protect you, Souma."

He went on, "And we have Tadakatsu too. He's a little jumpy right now, but once he settles down, he'll see you're not our enemy. Then the three of us together will look for the rest of the class. And we'll come up with a way to escape."

Mitsuko gave him a warm smile. "Thank you. I feel better now."

She squeezed his hand tightly between hers. His face turned even redder, and his eyes looked everywhere that wasn't her.

Then he spoke, this time not looking at her at all. "U-uh, you're . . . really p-pretty."

She raised her eyebrows. "Do you really think so?"

He nodded repeatedly—though it seemed less like nodding than shaking from extreme nervousness. She smiled again at this. And then she realized her smile held no malice.

Well, almost none.

16 STUDENTS REMAIN.

Sakamochi's six a.m. announcement woke up Tadakatsu. He'd had less than two hours of sleep but insisted it was enough, and untied the handkerchief from his wrist, took a proper hold of the gun, and sat down next to Mitsuko and Yuichiro. Yuichiro offered to let Mitsuko sleep, but she declined, and he ended up lying down. (Incidentally, the broadcast informed them of four new deaths: Keita Iijima, Toshinori Oda, Yutaka Seto, and Shinji Mimura. None of the forbidden zones pertained to Mitsuko's group.)

Seeing the belt unfastened from her wrists, Tadakatsu had complained, but Yuichiro persuaded him to let it go—though if Tadakatsu hadn't allowed her to remain untied, she had plans to get herself freed again—*by Tadakatsu.*

All right, what now?

She couldn't afford to take time choosing a course of action. If Hiroki Sugimura showed up, she'd be done for. *(What is he doing wandering around like that anyway? Is he trying to find someone to join with, like Yuichiro and Tadakatsu are doing?)* And that machinegunner also came to mind.

With a grin, Yuichiro had said, "I might not be able to sleep," but he was deep asleep within five minutes. Given that he was an otaku, he probably didn't have much physical stamina. He must have been tired. While Tadakatsu had snored a little, Yuichiro slept with the quiet breaths of a baby.

Tadakatsu sat with his back against a tree a good three meters to Mitsuko's left. He had short-cropped hair and light acne over his cheekbones. And his eyes watched her warily. The barrel of the revolver in his right hand wasn't pointed at her, but he kept his finger on the trigger. He seemed to be telling her, *I could shoot you at any moment.*

Mitsuko waited another half hour, and then, after making sure Yuichiro, who was lying down with his back to her, was still asleep, she looked at Tadakatsu and softly said, "You don't have to look at me like that. I won't do anything."

Tadakatsu snarled, "You never know."

Yuichiro stirred. She watched his back like Tadakatsu was staring at her. Quickly, Yuichiro's breathing steadied.

Without looking at Tadakatsu, she sighed, pretending to have gotten uncomfortable in the way she was sitting, and she moved her legs. She rested her right leg on the ground and brought in her left, standing it up a little.

Her pleated skirt glided down her thigh, revealing most of her pale legs, but she kept looking around as if she hadn't noticed.

Tadakatsu stiffened. *Ha. Can you see the edge of my panties? They're a nice sexy pink, and silk too.*

Mitsuko remained in that position for a while. Then slowly, she turned her head to Tadakatsu.

He was looking up. He seemed a little panicked. Without a doubt, his eyes had been glued to her legs.

But Mitsuko continued to act as if she hadn't noticed. "Hey, uh, Tadakatsu," she said.

"What?"

He seemed to be doing his best to preserve an intimidating attitude, but there had been a slight tremor in his voice.

"I'm . . . really scared," she said.

She expected him to say something nasty to her again, but instead, he just stared at her.

"Aren't you scared too, Tadakatsu?"

Tadakatsu's eyebrows twitched, but then after a short pause he said, "I am. That's why I'm watching you."

Mitsuko made her eyes look sad and glanced away from him. "You still don't trust me, do you?"

"Don't hold it against me," he said, but his voice had lost half its edge. "I know I'm repeating myself, but I don't want to die, that's all."

She quickly looked back at him. With a little more force now, she said, "It's the same for me. I don't want to die. But if you don't trust me, we'll never be able to work together and find a way to save ourselves."

"Yeah, well . . ." He nodded, almost in defeat. "I know . . ."

Mitsuko smiled warmly at him. She looked him in the eyes and turned up the corners of her red, shapely lips. This wasn't like the smile she'd given Yuichiro during their more idyllic conversation. This was Mitsuko Souma's bona fide fallen-angel smile. Falling under her spell, Tadakatsu stared at her, his eyes glazed.

"Hey, Tadakatsu." Mitsuko resumed the face of a frightened little girl. When it was called for, she could switch her expression from virgin to whore, day to night. *There's a movie title in that somewhere.*

"W-what?"

"I know I said it before, but I'm just so scared."

"Y-yeah."

"So . . ." She looked him straight on.

"So?"

Any trace of hostility or suspicion had vanished from his voice and his expression.

Mitsuko tilted her head and asked, "Can we talk a little?"

"Talk?" He scrunched his eyebrows in bewilderment. "Aren't we talking right now—"

"Silly," she said, talking over him. "Don't make me say it out loud, silly."

Without taking her eyes off him, she gestured to Yuichiro with her chin and said, "Not here. Okay? Somewhere a little away. I want to talk to you without Yuichiro around."

Tadakatsu cracked his mouth open and stared vacantly over at Yuichiro. Then he looked back at her.

She said, "Okay?" and stood, looked around, and found a suitable-seeming patch of bushes behind Tadakatsu. She walked up to him, gave him a tiny tilt of her head, then proceeded ahead. It all came down to whether or not he took the bait—but after a moment, she sensed that he had.

About twenty meters away from where Yuichiro was fast asleep, Mitsuko stopped inside a similar small glade.

She turned around to see Tadakatsu emerge from the thicket with those glazed-over eyes. But whether he was conscious of it or not, he still held the gun.

Without hesitation, Mitsuko lowered the zipper on the side of her skirt. The pleated garment dropped to the ground and her pale legs took in the faint morning light. Tadakatsu made an audible gulp.

Next she took off her scarf, and then her sailor top. Unlike the other girls, she didn't do anything so unsexy as to wear a T-shirt layered underneath, so with that, she was down to her underwear. *Oh, wait, I forgot to take off my shoes.* She tossed her sneakers aside and leveled her fallen-angel smile at the boy.

He spilled her name from his tense, slightly gaping mouth. "S-Souma . . ."

Mitsuko decided to make sure she had him. "I'm scared, Tadakatsu. So . . ."

Tadakatsu took one, then two awkward steps toward her.

Pretending to only just now notice, she dropped her eyes to his right hand and said, "Just leave that thing somewhere over there."

He raised his hand and squinted at it as if he'd never seen it before. Then he hurriedly set it down a little off to the side.

He stepped toward her once more.

She smiled at him warmly and reached her arms toward him,

and quickly his neck was inside them. His body trembled, but when she offered him her lips, he took them and didn't let go. She followed along, breathing heavily.

After a while, their lips parted.

Mitsuko looked up into his eyes and said, "It's your first time, isn't it?"

"So what if it is?" His voice trembled at the end.

Then they fell to the grass, with Mitsuko on the bottom.

Tadakatsu's hand went immediately for her breasts.

Don't you know you should kiss me a little more before that, you idiot?

But she didn't say this—instead, she moaned. His rough hands pulled aside her bra and clutched at her exposed, ample breasts. Then he slid his face down there.

"Ahhh. Oh, yes . . ." she gasped, pretending to be turned on. (She played it up a little, like in a porno.) But meanwhile, her right hand was reaching to the right side of her panties, a little to the rear.

Her fingertips reached something hard and thin.

Most of the bad girls these days had likely abandoned such a cheap, unhip weapon. But it had been Mitsuko's weapon of choice for a long time now. In this kind of situation, a girl needed something she could hide inside her underwear.

Tadakatsu was still fumbling around with her breasts. The top of his head was beneath her eyes. His left hand reached between her legs. She moaned for him—and his eyes were focused entirely on her breasts.

Slowly, she moved her right hand to the side of his neck.

Sorry, Tadakatsu. But hey, at least you get to go out happy. Sorry for not letting you go all the way.

Her ring finger brushed against the side of his neck, the weapon between her pointer and middle fingers.

A bird chirped—and it came from her right side.

Startled by the noise, Tadakatsu looked up and over in its direction.

It had only been a bird's call, but Tadakatsu's eyes opened wide.

Right before his eyes, he'd seen the razor blade in her hand.

Shit!

Of all the timing, Mitsuko thought, but she swung the razor blade regardless.

Tadakatsu grunted and pulled away from her. The edge of the blade scraped his neck, but made only a light scratch—nothing remotely fatal. *My, what fast reflexes. No wonder you're on the baseball team.*

Tadakatsu stood, eyes wide open, and stared down at the rising girl. He looked like he wanted to say something but couldn't find the words.

Mitsuko didn't concern herself with his reaction. Instead, she sprang to her feet. Her eyes darted to the revolver lying on the ground to her right.

But Tadakatsu's body flew past her in a headfirst dive. He scooped up the gun and spun around into a crouch. *You might have taken Shuya Nanahara's position* (Shuya's fame as the Little League's "ace shortstop" had reached even her elementary school), *but our school's baseball team is still in good hands, isn't it? Well, you're just lucky this happened before you took your pants off. That move would've looked ridiculous in the nude.*

As soon as she recognized that he would beat her to the revolver, Mitsuko did an about-face and ran for the bushes. She heard a gunshot behind her but made it into the thicket unscathed.

She could hear him chasing her. He was catching up. That was no surprise.

She was out of the thicket. Yuichiro was ahead. He must have heard the gunshot and stood, and having noticed her and Tadakatsu's absence, was looking in all directions. When he saw her, his eyes went wide. *(Well of course they did. I'm half naked and giving him quite a show, aren't I? Mitsuko Souma live, one night only! Well, morning now.)*

"Yuichiro!" she cried, running to him. She didn't forget the tears.

"S-Souma, why are—"

By the time Tadakatsu Hatagami emerged from the bushes,

Mitsuko had gone behind Yuichiro's back. Yuichiro was only four or five centimeters taller than her, so she couldn't completely hide herself behind him, but it would have to do.

"Yuichiro!" Tadakatsu howled. He stopped and held out his gun. "Move."

"W-wait," Yuichiro said in a panic. Having just awoken, he seemed not to have grasped what was going on. Mitsuko put her hands on his shoulders and pressed herself, half naked, against his back.

"What's going on?" Yuichiro asked.

"Souma tried to kill me—just like I told you she would!"

Hiding behind Yuichiro, Mitsuko said in a feeble voice, "N-no. Tadakatsu, he tried to—to force me . . . He threatened me with that pistol. Please, Yuichiro, save me from him!"

Tadakatsu's face twisted in astonishment. "She's lying. It's not true, Yuichiro! Hey, yeah, look—look at this." Tadakatsu pointed at his neck with his free hand. A faint trace of blood ran from the tiny scratch. "She cut me with a razor blade!"

Yuichiro turned his head and looked at Mitsuko out of the corner of his eye. She shook her head (in a cute way, natch, and scared—she was back to the virgin), and said, "I . . . was desperate. I scratched him with my nail. Then Tadakatsu got mad—he tried to shoot me."

She had already tossed the razor blade into the undergrowth. Even with a strip search (and she was nearly stripped already), Tadakatsu wouldn't come up with any proof.

Now Tadakatsu's face was flushed crimson with anger. "Move, Yuichiro!" he yelled. "I'm shooting her."

"Wait," Yuichiro said, trying to make himself sound calm. "I, uh . . . can't tell which of you is lying."

"What?" Tadakatsu snarled.

But Yuichiro stood firm. He held out his hand to Tadakatsu and said, "Give me that gun. Then we'll get to the bottom of this, okay?"

Tadakatsu's expression contorted. He appeared despondent and on the verge of tears. He cried out, "We don't have time for that! She'll kill you too if we don't take care of her now."

Mitsuko cried, "That's awful. I would never do that. Help me, Yuichiro, help me." She squeezed his shoulders.

Yuichiro patiently extended his hand. "Give it to me, Tadakatsu. If you're not lying to me, hand it over."

Tadakatsu's face twisted again.

But after a moment, he let out a deep sigh that lifted and dropped his shoulders, and he lowered the gun. With his finger in the trigger guard, he flipped the gun over grip first, and offered it to Yuichiro in surrender.

Though Mitsuko didn't drop her forlorn expression, a glimmer appeared in her eyes. Once the gun was in Yuichiro's hands, she'd have won. Taking it from him would be easy; she only had to decide how.

Yuichiro nodded and stepped forward.

But then—

It was the same move Hiroki Sugimura had pulled on her with the Colt M1911. The gun flipped around in Tadakatsu's hand like some magic trick. At the same time, he dropped to his knee and leaned sideways. The barrel pointed over Yuichiro's left shoulder and straight at Mitsuko. When he'd stepped forward, he left her exposed.

Yuichiro's eyes followed the line extending from the gun barrel and looked over his shoulder to Mitsuko.

Her eyes widened.

I'm dead.

With no hesitation, Tadakatsu squeezed the trigger.

A gunshot. Then another.

She watched as Yuichiro collapsed, seemingly in slow motion.

She looked beyond him to Tadakatsu, his face crumbling in dismay.

And she was picking up the sickle Yuichiro had set down while he slept.

She threw it. The sickle spun through the air, and its banana-shaped blade dug into Tadakatsu's right shoulder. He grunted and dropped his gun.

Not wasting a moment, she picked up the metal bat next and

rushed Tadakatsu. She hurtled Yuichiro's prone body. Tadakatsu was tottering and clutching his right shoulder. She sprinted at him and put that momentum into a full-force swing directed at his head.

Look what we have here. It's your old friend, the baseball bat. I hope you like it.

CRACK. The end of the bat landed right in the center of his face. The cartilage in his nose shattered, several of his teeth broke off, and his jaw and cheekbones caved in. The impact of it all transmitted through the bat and into her hand.

Tadakatsu went down then and there. She brought the bat down on his forehead. His skull dented in. His eyes nearly flew out of their sockets, and his hands balled into fists at his sides. Mitsuko swung once more, aiming for the bridge of his nose again. *Mitsuko Souma's special training—a marathon fungo session. Stay sharp, this next one's heading for center field.*

The hit sent blood spraying from his nose.

Mitsuko lowered the bat. His entire face was drenched in blood. Thick rivulets of blood came dripping out from his ears and his buckled nose.

He was dead.

She tossed the bat aside and picked up the revolver lying to her left.

Then, she walked over to Yuichiro, who was face down on the ground.

Beneath him, a spreading pool of blood wove through the spaces between the leaves of grass.

He had shielded her in that split second.

Slowly, she knelt beside his body. She leaned in and saw he still breathed.

She thought for a moment, then moved over to where she would block Yuichiro's view of Tadakatsu's corpse. She grabbed Yuichiro by the shoulders and turned him over.

He groaned and opened his unfocused eyes. His school jacket had two holes, one on his left chest, and the other on his side, from which blood came pouring out, to be absorbed by the black fabric. Mitsuko held him up.

Yuichiro's eyes searched for a while, then saw her face. His breaths came short and intermittently, as if keeping time with his heartbeat.

"S-Souma . . ." he said. "What . . . what happened . . . to Tadakatsu?"

Mitsuko shook her head. "After he shot you, he freaked. He ran away."

Since Tadakatsu had been trying to kill her, this answer didn't hold water. And she was glossing over which of them had been lying. But Yuichiro probably wasn't thinking very well anymore. He gave her a barely perceptible nod.

"Oh . . ." His eyes didn't seem to be focusing on the same point. He probably wasn't able to see her very clearly. "Are . . . are you hurt?"

She shook her head. "No, I'm fine."

Yuichiro seemed to smile. "I . . . I'm sorry. I . . . won't be able to protect you . . . anymore. I c-can't . . . move—"

Blood bubbled from his mouth. His lungs must have been punctured.

Mitsuko said, "I know." She leaned over and gently held him. Her long, black hair fell onto his chest, and the blood pouring from his wounds wetted its tips. Before she placed her lips on his, his eyes moved slightly, but then they shut.

This kiss was not at all like the whore's kiss she had given Tadakatsu only moments before. This was a soft, warm, sincere kiss—even though it did taste of blood.

Their lips separated. Yuichiro opened his glazed eyes and said, "S-sorry . . . I think I'm—"

"I know."

BLAM! BLAM! BLAM! came the three muffled gunshots, and Yuichiro's eyes opened wide.

Staring up into her face, and probably without having any idea of what had just happened, Yuichiro Takiguchi died.

Mitsuko slowly withdrew the smoking barrel from his stomach, and she held him again. She looked into eyes that no longer saw her and said, "You were pretty cool back there. You even made me a little happy. I won't forget you."

Almost as if she were reluctant to leave him, she closed her eyes and softly kissed him once more. His lips were still warm.

The sunlight was finally beginning to shine on the western slope of the northern mountain. Beneath Mitsuko's head, which shaded him from the light, his pupils rapidly dilated.

14 STUDENTS REMAIN.

58

Shuya Nanahara (Boys #15) suddenly opened his eyes. He saw the blue sky bordered by verdant grass.

He sat up with a jerk. There, beyond the patch of grass that surrounded him, bathed in the gentle sunlight, stood the familiar building of Shiroiwa Junior High.

On the school grounds, several students in gym clothes were playing softball and cheering each other on.

Shuya was in the garden at the side of the school's courtyard. The large leaves of a date palm tree fanned out overhead. He often napped here during lunch break, or sometimes when he skipped class.

He stood up and looked at himself.

He was completely unscathed. Small bits of grass had gotten on his school uniform, and he brushed them off.

A dream.

Shuya shook his head to clear his mind. Then he knew for certain: *It was a dream. It was all a dream. All of it.*

As was always the case after having a nightmare, he was drenched in sweat. He wiped the back of his neck and his hand came back wet.

What a terrible dream to have—that we were all killing each other, and that we'd been chosen for that Program.

Then the realization came to him. *Those students over there . . . Is that gym class?*

He looked at his watch. It was well into the afternoon class period. *I overslept!*

Shuya hurried from the garden and trotted toward the school building. *Today is . . . today is. . . .* As he ran, he checked his watch again and saw it was Thursday.

First period after lunch was Japanese. That made him feel a little better. He enjoyed Japanese class, and since his grades were all right, the teacher, Kazuko Okazaki, liked him more than most of the others. Shuya wouldn't be in any real trouble—an apologetic bow should be enough.

Words drifted across his mind with a deep and unidentified nostalgia.

Japanese. Like the class. Grades. Ms. Okazaki.

Shuya did enjoy studying Japanese. Even though pro-Republic slogans and the platforms of its ridiculous so-called ideologies pervaded the stories and essays in his textbook, Shuya discovered words he liked between the cracks. Words to him were of equal importance with music. After all, rock needed lyrics.

Lyrics . . . That reminded Shuya of Noriko Nakagawa, the best student in Japanese class. Her poems were beautiful. While he struggled to come up with lyrics for his own songs, she could always find the perfect words, vivid and gentle and kind, and yet with intensity and power. To Shuya, it was as if everything that encompassed what a girl was to him had been transposed into the realm of language. If nothing else, this part of her had caught his heart—despite the fact that his friend Yoshitoki Kuninobu had a crush on her.

Then Shuya remembered his friend was still alive. Though he knew the thought was silly, for a moment there, as he jogged to the school, he felt like he could cry with relief. *Ridiculous. Yoshitoki dead? What kind of stupid dream was that?*

And why was I with Noriko in that dumb dream? I know there must have been a reason. Does that mean I have just a little bit of

*feeling for her beyond liking her poetry? Come on now, that'll mean a
big fight with Yoshitoki. That's trouble.*

Lost in these idle thoughts, Shuya grinned despite himself.

Shuya entered the school. With the afternoon classes in session,
the hallways were quiet and still. He bounded up the stairs two steps
at a time to the third floor.

At the top of the stairs, he took the right-hand hallway. The second
classroom belonged to Class B.

He paused in front of the door to prepare his excuse for Ms.
Okazaki. *I wasn't feeling well . . . No, I had a dizzy spell when I stood
up. That'll do it. I had to lie down and rest a moment. Will she believe
that story from me—a young man in perfect health? Yoshitoki will give
me a theatrical shrug, someone like Yutaka Seto will say, "I bet you
were sleeping," or some such, Shinji Mimura will snicker at me, Hiroki
Sugimura will fold his arms and look vaguely amused, and Noriko will
smile at me as I rub the back of my head out of embarrassment. All
right. That's fine with me. I can live with a little embarrassment.*

Shuya put his hand on the door. He stood stiffly and lowered his
head, trying to look sincere and apologetic, then slowly began to open
the door.

But before he could look up repentantly toward the teacher's
podium, the smell of blood assaulted him.

He lifted his head and threw the door open.

The first thing he saw was someone lying on the podium.

Ms. Okazaki—

It wasn't Ms. Okazaki. It was their class's head instructor, Masao
Hayashida. And . . .

His head was missing, replaced by a pool of blood. One half of his
eyeglasses rested in the puddle.

Shuya pulled his eyes away from Mr. Hayashida's corpse and
jerked his head toward the inside of the classroom.

The rows of desks and chairs were there as usual.

What was not usual were all of his classmates, who were slumped
over on their desks.

Blood covered the entire floor. The stench was overpowering.

For a moment, Shuya stood frozen, but then he quickly reached for Mayumi Tendo, at her desk nearest the door. Then he noticed the silverish bolt standing up like an antenna from her back. Its tip came out the front of her sailor top, and blood dripped down from her stomach to her skirt, and from the skirt's hem to the floor.

Shuya walked forward. He shook Kazushi Niida's body. Kazushi flopped to the side and his face turned up toward Shuya.

A chill shot through Shuya. Kazushi's eyes had become two dark-red cavities oozing a mixture of blood and a slimy egg-white-like substance. Some kind of metal spike with a thick handle on its end had been stabbed into his mouth.

Shuya screamed and ran to Yoshitoki Kuninobu's seat. Three large holes had torn through the back of his uniform, each blooming with a flower of blood. Shuya held him up, and his neck flopped onto Shuya's shoulder. His goggling eyes stared vacantly up at the ceiling.

Yoshitoki!

Shuya cried out and looked around the room in confusion.

Every single one of his classmates was either slumped in their chairs or had spilled onto the floor.

Megumi Eto's throat had been slashed open like a watermelon. A sickle was planted in Yoji Kuramoto's head. Sakura Ogawa's head had burst apart like an overripe fruit. Yoshimi Yahagi's head was half gone. A hatchet split Tatsumichi Oki's face into two lopsided halves like a cracked-open peanut shell. Kyoichi Motobuchi's stomach looked like a slop bucket at a sausage factory. Tadakatsu Hatagami's face was pulverized and covered in blood. Hirono Shimizu's face was swollen and black, a tongue the size of a sea cucumber lolling out the side of her gaping mouth. Shinji Mimura, The Third Man, had been riddled with bullets.

Everyone was dead.

Then something else caught his eyes—a knife plunged deeply into the chest of Shogo Kawada, that standoffish transfer student with the bad reputation. His half-lidded eyes stared down at the floor, seeing nothing.

Shuya gulped and looked at Noriko's seat. Her desk was directly behind Yoshitoki's, so he should have noticed her sooner. But Shuya felt as if all the desks and bodies of his classmates were spinning around him, and he only just now saw her.

Noriko was still in her chair, sitting with her head on her desk.

Shuya ran to her and sat her up.

Her head fell off. Leaving the rest of her body and her sailor suit behind, it thumped down on the floor and rolled through the pool of blood. When it stopped, it looked up at him with eyes forlorn and resentful. *Didn't you tell me you'd save me, Nanahara? Well, I'm dead now, even though I loved you. I really loved you.*

His eyes were glued to her face. He put his hands to his head and his mouth dropped. He felt like he was losing his mind.

A scream was building up deep inside him.

Suddenly, he saw something white.

As he regained awareness of his own body, he perceived that he was horizontal. His eyes focused, and finally he realized he was seeing a ceiling. It even had a fluorescent bulb at the rightmost edge of his vision.

A hand gently touched his chest.

He realized he was breathing heavily. His eyes followed the hand to an arm, and the arm to a shoulder, and he saw the sailor fuku, the braided hair, and the warm, serene smile of the class leader for the girls, Yukie Utsumi (Girls #2).

"You're awake," she said. "What a relief."

14 STUDENTS REMAIN.

Shuya tried to sit upright but was immediately met with sharp jolts of pain all over his body, and he fell back down. He realized he was lying on a soft bed with fresh sheets.

Yukie gently touched his chest again, then pulled a fluffy blanket up to his neck.

"Stop that now," she said. "Don't overexert yourself. You've been hurt pretty bad." Then she added, "You were moaning in your sleep. Were you having a nightmare?"

Still too disoriented to provide a proper response, Shuya turned his head to survey the room. It was a small space. The wall directly to the left of his bed was hung with cheap-looking wallpaper. On his right, behind Yukie, was another bed, but the room had no other furnishings to speak of. Down past the blanket and his feet was a door, but it was closed. Its wooden frame looked very old. A window seemed to be above his head, through which dull light came in and illuminated the room. With the way the light felt, it might have been cloudy outside. *But where am I?*

"Well this is weird," Shuya said. At least now he knew he could talk. "I don't remember checking into a hotel with you."

He was still in a half stupor, but Yukie gave a sigh of relief. Her full lips widened into a smile, and she laughed and said, "That sounds like something you'd say. That's a relief, actually." Then she looked into his face and added, "You were out for a long time. It's been—let's see . . ." She looked at the watch on her left wrist. "About thirteen hours."

Thirteen hours? Thirteen hours. Thirteen hours ago, I was . . .

His eyes opened wide. His memories and the here and now were two gears that suddenly clicked into place. Now Shuya truly had awoken.

There was something he needed to ask her before anything else.

"What about Noriko—Noriko Nakagawa? And Shogo Kawada?"

After he asked this, he gulped. *Are they still alive?*

Yukie regarded him with a curious look, then said, "Noriko and Kawada are both fine, I suppose. At least, we just heard the noon announcement, and their names weren't called."

Shuya let out his breath. Noriko and Kawada had escaped. Kiriyama followed Shuya and lost them. *And Kiriyama is . . .*

Shuya looked up at Yukie. "Kiriyama. It's Kiriyama!" Panic edged into his voice. "Where are we? Are you alone? You have to be careful!"

He'd lifted his right hand from under the blanket. She patted his hand and said, "Calm down." Then she asked, "Did Kiriyama do this to you?"

Shuya nodded. "It was him. He attacked us. He's completely playing the game."

"I see." Yukie nodded slightly, then said, "We're safe here. There are six of us here, not counting you. Everyone else is keeping watch now. You don't need to worry about them—they're all my friends."

Shuya raised his eyebrows. *Six of them?*

"Who's here?" he asked.

"Yuka Nakagawa, of course," Yukie said, meaning the perky girl with the same last name as Noriko. Then she added, "Satomi Noda and Chisato Matsui. Haruka Tanizawa. And Yuko Sakaki."

Shuya touched his tongue to his lips. Noticing his expression, Yukie asked, "What's wrong? Can't you trust them? Which one? All of them?"

"No." Shuya shook his head. "If they're your friends, I trust them."

But how were six girls—who were all friends, no less—able to find each other?

With a sincere smile, Yukie squeezed his hand and said, "I'm glad to hear it."

Shuya smiled a little too. But almost immediately, he realized his smile had gone. Another question remained. He had missed the midnight, six a.m., and noon announcements.

He opened his mouth.

"Who died? I . . . Well, there've been three announcements today, right? Midnight, six, and noon? Did anyone die?"

Yukie pursed her lips tightly and picked up two pieces of paper from the small side table next to her. It was a map and the class roster. He recognized the dirt stains and way they were folded. They were the ones he'd been keeping in his own pocket.

Yukie ran her eyes down the list. "Shimizu and Iijima. Oda, Seto, Takiguchi, Hatagami, and Mimura."

Shuya's mouth dropped—in part because the game had proceeded to whittle them down to little more than a dozen survivors, and he had played in Little League with Tadakatsu Hatagami.

But.

"Mimura . . ."

Shinji Mimura, The Third Man, was dead. He could hardly believe it. He'd thought that no matter what else happened, Shinji would never die.

Yukie nodded softly.

Shuya thought it strange that he wasn't that shaken. *I've gotten used to this. That must be it.* He pictured Shinji's grinning face—and his serious expression, back in the classroom, when he signaled Shuya to settle down.

So I won't be seeing any more plays by Shiroiwa Junior High's ace guard, The Third Man, Shuya thought with a twinge of sadness.

He asked, "When was Mimura's name read?"

"In the morning," Yukie answered. "Iijima and Seto were in the morning announcement too. They might have been together, since they were friends."

"Oh."

That meant that Shinji had still been alive at midnight. And like Yukie said, he might have been with Yutaka Seto and Keita Iijima.

"During the night," she added, "there was a huge explosion—and gunfire. That might have been what happened."

"An explosion?" Shuya recalled that Kazuo Kiriyama had thrown a hand grenade at them. "Do you think . . . Kiriyama had some hand grenades. Do you think that could have been it?"

Yukie lifted her eyebrows. "Oh, so that's what that was—after eleven o'clock, right? This one—the one after you were brought here— it came just after midnight. It was way bigger than the ones at eleven. The girls who were keeping watch said the sky lit up over the middle of the island."

Shuya pressed his lips together, then remembered that he still hadn't gotten an answer as to where he was now.

Before he could ask, Yukie held out his map and class roster and said, "These are yours. I updated your map too."

Oh, right, Shuya thought, *the forbidden zones.* He unfolded the map.

"At the place we were," Kawada had said. *"Where we talked about rock."*

Like so many other squares on the map, that sector—C-3, near the western shore—had been scribbled out with diagonal pencil lines. Small writing inside the grid read: *23rd, 11AM.* This morning, while Shuya was unconscious, their meeting place had become off-limits.

Shuya pressed his lips together. Noriko and Kawada weren't there now. *That is,* Shuya thought, his mind having recovered into working order, *unless they died after noon.* He knew they had to be alive, but he recalled how he'd dreamed Noriko's and Kawada's corpses next to those of Yoshitoki and Shinji. Though he knew it was irrational, Shuya shuddered.

Anyway, for now, I have to believe they're still alive. But how in the hell am I going to find them again?

Shuya set the map down on his chest. To waste time thinking it through now would be a fool's errand. He needed more information first. Together with these girls, he might be able to find a way to reach Noriko and Kawada.

He looked up at Yukie and asked, "Um . . . where are we, anyway? How did I end up sleeping here?"

She bobbed her head, then looked up at the window and said, "This is a lighthouse."

"A lighthouse?"

"That's right. We're on the northeastern side of the island. Maybe you saw it marked on the map? We've been here this whole time—since the very start."

Shuya looked at his map again. The lighthouse was, as Yukie had said, on the island's northeast, where part of the shoreline jutted out in sector C-10. None of the surrounding area had yet been designated forbidden.

"As for the rest, Nanahara, it was last night. There's a cliff in front of the lighthouse. You came falling down it. The girl on watch found you, and she dragged you inside. You were really badly hurt—covered with blood. I thought you'd die right there."

Shuya realized he wasn't wearing a shirt, and the top of his left shoulder—where he was in excrutiating pain—had been bandaged. From how his shoulder felt, a bullet must have shattered his shoulder blade and remained inside. On the right side of his neck, just below that ever-present collar, his skin seemed to burn. He could feel another bandage there, where another slug had probably only grazed him. A third bullet had torn through his left arm, just above the elbow. It must have shredded some of a bone or tendon on its way out, because his arm remained heavy and almost entirely immobile. One more shot had passed through to the left of his stomach, near enough to his side that it had *probably* missed any internal organs. Shuya awkwardly moved his untouched right arm and lifted the blanket far enough to see the many bandages that covered his body.

He lowered the blanket and said, "You patched me up."

"Yeah." Yukie nodded. "The lighthouse was stocked with your standard first-aid supplies. And about your wounds—I sort of stitched them. I'd never done that before, and it shows, and the only needle and thread I could find was from a sewing kit. I think the bullet that went into your shoulder is still in there, but I couldn't do anything about that. I was worried you were going to need a blood transfusion, you were bleeding so badly."

"Sorry to put you through all that."

"Oh, no," Yukie said with a warm smile. "I was psyched—I got to touch a *guy*. I even got to take off your clothes."

Shuya chuckled. Yukie Utsumi was quick-witted, perceptive, and considerate, but it was also just like her to say something so brash. She'd been that way ever since he'd first gotten to know her, back in elementary school, on a rainy day when his Little League team negotiated with the girls' volleyball team to share the gymnasium for indoor practice. He even remembered telling Yoshitoki once, "Utsumi in Class Two is pretty cool. I like a girl who gets things done."

But this was no time to bask in idle sentimentalities.

Then Yukie said, "Oh, here, have some water," and offered him a cup. Shuya whistled. He himself had only just realized he was thirsty. She must have had the cup ready and on the sideboard where he couldn't see.

He thought, *That's just like you, Class Leader. You'll make someone a fine wife someday. You'll be a fine woman someday. Or maybe you already are one. I suppose I've thought that about you for a long time now.*

He took the cup, lifted up his head, and drank the water. When he swallowed, his neck wound hurt and he grimaced. But he drank the entire cup.

"Sorry if I'm asking for too much," Shuya said, "but I think I need to be drinking a lot more water. And if you have any painkillers, could I have some? I'll take anything. Just something to help for right now."

Yukie nodded. "All right. I'll go get some."

Shuya wiped his lips, then said, "It's really cool that everyone was so understanding—letting me be carried in here, even though I might be one of the bad guys."

Yukie shook her head. "You were dying before our eyes. It's hard to argue against saving a life. Besides . . ." She looked into his eyes and flashed him a mischievous grin. "It was you. I'm pretty much the leader of this group, so I made them all agree."

Does that mean she's also thought there's something special about us, ever since that afternoon in the elementary school gym?

He decided not to say anything about this suspicion, but instead probed another. "Does that mean some of the girls were against it after all?"

"Only because of the situation we're in." Yukie dropped her eyes. "Don't take it the wrong way. Everyone's so rattled."

"Yeah." Shuya nodded. "I can understand."

"But I convinced her." She looked up and smiled again. "You'd better be thankful."

Shuya started to nod, but then he noticed that despite her smile, tears were welled up in her eyes. *What's that about?*

"I was worried sick. I thought you might die, Nanahara."

Taken somewhat by surprise, Shuya watched her expression.

She continued, "I didn't know what I'd do if you died." She was nearly crying now, and her voice quavered. "Do you understand what I'm saying? Do you see why I'd do anything to save you?"

As he gazed into her tear-filled eyes, he slowly nodded once. Then he thought, *How do I handle this? And how popular can one guy be without his even knowing it?*

Certainly this might just have been some kind of cabin fever. With death a looming possibility (a certainty, rather—Shuya had never heard of anyone surviving this Lord-and-Leader blessed Program save for the winner), and their numbers dwindling, maybe a little crush on a boy she'd talked to in the corner of the gymnasium one day could turn into a love for which she'd be willing to die.

But no, he didn't think that was the case. If she didn't truly care for him, she wouldn't have stood against her friends to save him—nor would she have trusted in him in the first place.

"I understand," Shuya said. "Thank you."

Yukie wiped her eyes with the heel of her hand. Then she said, "I have to ask you something. Just now, you asked about Noriko and Kawada, didn't you? And you said 'us.' Were you with them? Were you actually with them?"

Shuya nodded.

Yukie tightened her brows. "Noriko's fine, but you were really with *Kawada*?"

Shuya could guess what she was getting at. "Kawada's not a bad guy. He saved my life. Noriko and I are still alive only thanks to him. I'm sure he's still protecting her now—but I forgot, there's something more important I have to tell you."

With eagerness in his voice, he said, "We're going to be saved."

"We're going to be saved?"

Shuya nodded deeply. "Kawada's going to save us. He knows a way off this island."

Yukie's eyes widened. "Really? For real? How?"

That cut him short. Kawada had said he couldn't reveal the plan until the end.

Now that Shuya thought about it, he realized he had nothing to back his claim. He of course trusted Kawada, but he'd been with Kawada this whole time. Yukie hadn't. He doubted that she would take his word for it. Kawada had said as much himself—it was conceivable that he was simply using them.

But for now, Shuya decided to tell Yukie everything that had happened.

And he did. He told her about getting ambushed by Yoshio Akamatsu as soon as he left, how he and Noriko were together the whole time after that, about his fight with Tatsumichi Oki, about Kawada saving him when Kyoichi Motobuchi attacked, how the three of them had stuck together and talked about escaping, and that Kawada was the survivor of last year's Program, about Noriko developing a fever and taking her to the clinic, and even about Hiroki Sugimura, and how he said that Mitsuko Souma was a threat, and then, about Kazuo Kiriyama ambushing them while they were on the move.

But when he'd finished, the first thing Yukie said was, "So Oki . . . was an accident?"

"Yeah, like I just told you." Shuya lifted his eyebrows. "What about it?"

She shook her head, said, "It's nothing," then quickly changed the subject. "Sorry if this seems blunt, but it's hard to trust Kawada all of a sudden—or believe that he knows how to escape."

Shuya wondered why Yukie had asked about Tatsumichi, but thinking it relatively unimportant, he let it slide, and he conceded to Yukie's skepticism.

"I don't blame you for thinking that. But I believe Kawada can be trusted. I wish I had a better way to put it, but he's not a bad guy." He made an impatient gesture with his unrestrained right hand. "Once we've met up with him, you'll see."

Yukie touched her fingertips to her lips, then said, "Okay. I agree it's worth hearing him out. It's not like we have any better options."

Shuya looked at her. "What were you planning on doing?"

She shrugged. "I'd pretty much lost hope. All of us talked it over, but we weren't able to decide if we were better off taking our chances with an escape or waiting here a little longer."

Shuya remembered another question he'd meant to ask. "How did you all gather together—the six of you?"

"Oh, right." Yukie nodded. "I came back to the school, and I called out to them as they left."

This was a surprise. "When?"

"I guess it would have been right after you and Noriko fled. I saw Niida running away. Actually, I had hoped to get back in time to find you. And then I saw the two bodies outside the school—right by the entrance."

Shuya raised his eyebrows. "But Akamatsu was just unconscious, right?"

Yukie shook her head. "I didn't get a close look, but I think he was dead by then. He had an arrow sticking from his neck."

"That means that Niida . . ."

Yukie nodded. "Yes, it does."

Shuya asked, "Weren't you afraid? Didn't you worry about someone else doing what Akamatsu did?"

"Yeah, I considered it. But I knew I needed to form a group, and I couldn't think of any other way. You remember the woods directly in front of the school? I figured that if I hid there, I'd be hard to spot. And even if it did mean I'd be found, I didn't see any other choice."

Shuya deeply admired her for that. Admittedly, he had had to look after Noriko, who was injured, but he left all the others behind and ran. Hiroki Sugimura had waited for Takako Chigusa; but unlike Yukie, he was a boy, and he knew kempo.

"Wow. You're incredible, Class Leader."

Yukie smiled. "So you call Noriko by her name, but I'm Class Leader."

"Um, well . . . it's—"

"It's fine. You don't have to say anything." She gave him another smile, but it seemed a little lonesome. "Anyway, Yuka Nakagawa came out of the school, and I called out to her."

"Were you able to convince her right away? I mean, I don't doubt that you could. People like you, Class—uh, Class Leader."

"Yeah." Yukie nodded. "And I hadn't returned alone either. After I first left the school, I was totally shaken up. But then I knew that I had to go back to the school, and on the way, I ran into Haruka completely by chance. She's my best friend, you know."

Shuya nodded. Yukie and Haruka Tanizawa were on the volleyball team together.

"I talked with her, and I told her I was going back. She was against it at first, but since I was armed—I had found a pistol in my bag—she said okay. I think Yuka trusted us because we were together."

"But . . ." After brief consideration, Shuya decided to broach one of the game's tenets. ". . . in this game, you can't trust two people just because they're together."

Yukie nodded. "True. We ran into that."

"What do you mean?"

"Well, first off, we decided to leave out the boys—no offense, but I talked it over with Haruka, and we decided that boys mean too much trouble. So anyway, skipping the boys, next was Satomi, right, and then Fumiyo—" Yukie stopped. Fumiyo Fujiyoshi (Girls #18) had died inside the classroom. "After her came Chisato. That made five strong. When Kaori Minami came out, we called for her, but . . ."

Shuya picked up the rest. "She ran?"

"Yeah. She ran."

Shuya realized he hadn't told her that he'd watched Kaori Minami die. He thought about saying it now but decided against it. Now that her killer, Hirono Shimizu, was also dead, it didn't matter. Neither did he want to revisit the memory. And besides, though it might seem crass, he couldn't afford to waste time talking about the dead.

Shuya asked, "And then Yahagi ran just like Minami?"

Both Kaori Minami and Yoshimi Yahagi, the last girl to leave, were dead now, and speaking their names side by side gave him the chills. *The names of the dead. Both of them dead. Two-for-one special.* It had been a while since that smiling man in the black suit appeared in his mind's eye. *"Hey there, Nanahara. Still alive, are you? Stubborn boy."*

"Well." Yukie looked away from Shuya and drew in her lips and pressed them together. Her eyes narrowed. "That was different."

"How so?"

She let out her breath. "I told the others we should call out to her. But a few of them were against it. Yahagi's one of Souma's girls, right? So the other girls felt we couldn't trust her."

Shuya didn't say anything.

Still turned to the side, Yukie said, "But she's dead now, isn't she? We left her to die."

"No, you didn't."

Yukie looked at him.

"Some things can't be helped. It's not anyone's fault." He knew what he was saying didn't really make any sense, but it was all he could think to offer her.

Yukie smiled bitterly and sighed. "You're kind, Nanahara. You're always so kind."

Their conversation threatened to lapse into awkward silence, but Shuya found something to say. "You should have let Mimura join you."

Shinji Mimura (dead now) was toward the end of the seating list. They would have been able to call out to him.

Shuya added, "You could have trusted him."

Yukie sighed again. "I thought so too, but Mimura was never popular with the girls. I mean, you have to admit, he came off as a bit of . . . a playboy. And he was so smart that it became kind of scary, I guess. So you remember how he helped Noriko when she was hurt? Well, one of the girls suggested he might have done it as a calculated move."

That was almost exactly what Kawada had said when he mentioned he'd seen Shinji that first night.

"Before we could come to a decision, he was already gone." Yukie shrugged. "Anyway, we'd decided at the start not to take any of the boys. We didn't even call out to Yamamoto."

Despite his handsome looks, Sakura Ogawa's boyfriend, Kazuhiko Yamamoto, was unassuming and as warmhearted as could be. He must have been popular with the girls. But Yukie's group hadn't reached out to him. Given this policy, no wonder there'd been a dispute over bringing Shuya inside.

Shuya realized Yukie's account had ended with a group of five. She hadn't mentioned Yuko Sakaki (Girls #9).

"What about Yuko? How did you find her?"

Yukie nodded and looked at him. "That was also pure luck. We came inside here yesterday morning—it's pretty good for a fortress, right? Anyway, it was last night, around eight I think. Yuko just happened to pass right by. She was terrified."

Yukie paused. Something seemed to have stopped her. Shuya was about to ask her what was wrong, but before he could, she spoke.

"Anyway," she said, "All of us know her really well, so there wasn't a problem."

That ended her story. Shuya considered pressing her about Yuko but decided against it. If Yuko had been on her own until last night, she might have witnessed something horrific. Maybe she had been attacked and managed to escape, or maybe she had seen two of the students trying to kill each other. She could have even come across some gruesome corpse left in the aftermath of a battle.

Shuya bobbed his head. "That all makes sense."

"There's still something I don't understand," Yukie said. Shuya looked up at her, and she continued. "It's not a big deal, but you said that Sugimura was trying to find Kayoko. And that's why he didn't stick with you."

While Shuya had been filling Yukie in on what had happened, he found himself thinking about Hiroki. Hiroki was still alive, as was Kayoko Kotohiki. Had he found her yet?

Yukie said, "And he told you he had to see her about something. I wonder what it is."

Shuya shook his head. "We didn't ask him. He was in a hurry. It was just as curious to us."

Something tugged at the back of his mind. *Has Hiroki found Kotohiki yet? If he has . . .*

Kawada's voice came back to him. *"This little noisemaker is your ticket out of here. Hop on our train whenever you like."*

Shuya's eyes widened, and he said to himself, "The birdcall."

"What?"

He looked up at Yukie. "I have a way to meet up with Noriko and Kawada."

"You do?"

Shuya nodded deeply. He tried to get moving. The explanation could wait. "I have to send them a message. I have to go."

"Hold on there. You need to rest."

"I can't do that. While I'm lazing around here, something could—"

"I said hold on. Listen to the girl who's in love with you."

Her cheeks flushed a little, but she managed to say this and follow it with a playful smile. "We put you in here assuming you wouldn't be able to move even when you did wake up. You'll scare some of the girls if they see you've got that much strength."

Shuya's eyes widened. But what she said did make sense. That was probably why the other girls accepted Yukie being alone with him.

She continued, "So just stay put a little while. I'll go and tell everyone what you told me. And I'll convince them that they can trust you—and Kawada as well. As for you contacting him and Noriko, I can't let you go alone. It's too dangerous. I'll have to discuss that with the girls too. So wait here."

Then she added, "Can you eat?"

"Yeah."

He *was* hungry. He was worried about Noriko and Kawada, but getting some food into his stomach sounded like a good idea. It would help his gunshot wounds to heal.

"If you can spare anything," he said, "I'd be grateful. I do feel pretty weak, as you'd expect."

Yukie smiled. "We were just preparing lunch now. I'll bring some for you. I think it's some kind of stew. Does that sound all right?"

"Stew?"

"Yeah. This place is loaded with food. Well, whatever was in the pantry at least—you know, cans and pouches. But there's water and fuel tablets too, so we can cook."

"Wow," Shuya said. "That sounds great. Thanks."

She gently withdrew her hand from the side of his bed. She stood and was walking toward the door when she said, "Sorry, but I'm going to lock the door."

"Huh?"

"I'm really sorry. One of the girls won't feel safe if I don't. Sorry. Just wait here."

She gave him a warm smile, then opened the door and left the room. Her two braids swayed like twin tails of some strange and unknown animal. He caught a glimpse of her pistol, tucked down the back of her skirt.

After the door shut, he heard another click. It didn't sound like a lock but some kind of latch. Had they put it on the door just for him?

Shuya leaned on his right elbow and forced himself upright. He looked up and over his shoulder at the window, which had been barricaded with pieces of squared lumber. Sunlight entered through the gaps. The intent had certainly been to keep intruders out—but right now, to Shuya, they were like prison bars.

Beneath the blanket, the fingertips of Shuya's nearly immobile left arm reflexively formed a chord progression. The chords were from "Jailhouse Rock," a hit song by the rock star worshipped by the man who had given Shuya his guitar.

With a sigh, Shuya lay back down on the bed. That movement alone was enough to send sharp pain through the wound on his side.

14 STUDENTS REMAIN.

The Oki Island lighthouse was old but sturdy, with a single-story brick residence extending south from the seventeen-meter-high tower. The living quarters were arranged from north to south, starting with a combined living, dining, and kitchen space adjacent to the tower, followed by a storage room, bathroom, and toilet. Farther south and near the entrance were a large and a small bedroom and another storage room. A hallway connecting all the rooms ran along the west side of the building. Shuya was in the smaller bedroom closest to the entrance.

A table, its small size ill suited to the large space of the living room/dining room/kitchen—which was as big as a school classroom—had been pulled over to one corner. Yuko Sakaki (Girls #9) was sitting on one of the stools around the table. She was slumped over the white tabletop and appeared have dozed off. The past night had not done much to alleviate the exhaustion of having roamed the island for so much longer than the other five girls. But this was no surprise, considering that something had kept her from getting much sleep.

Yukie Utsumi's group kept to this single room and had even slept there. They had to keep a lookout atop the lighthouse tower, but Yukie had decided that it would be best for everyone else to stick together.

Directly behind Yuko, Haruka Tanizawa (Girls #12) and Chisato

Matsui (Girls #19) stood at the cooktop, busily preparing a meal out of preserved foods, with fuel tablets substituting for the shut-off gas. Haruka, who as a hitter on the volleyball team made a great duo with Yukie as the setter, stood one hundred seventy-two centimeters tall. With her height and her short hair, and Chisato's petite frame and long hair, the two girls almost looked like a boy and girl couple.

On the menu was packaged soup mix with canned vegetables. The muted light of the cloudy day came in through a frosted glass window above the cooktop. To keep intruders out, the girls had hastily boarded up the window with lumber from the storage room. As soon as they had arrived at the lighthouse, the girls had sealed off every possible entrance from the inside. (They had designated the front door as their solitary entrance and exit, which was how they had brought Yuko and Shuya inside. They had since rebuilt the makeshift desk-and-locker barricade in the entryway.)

In the opposite corner of the open room was a writing desk with a fax machine and personal computer. To the left of the desk, Satomi Noda (Girls #17) sat on a sofa that had been pushed against the wall; its matching coffee table had been mobilized for duty at the front door. Satomi was a gifted student on par with Yukie, and although she usually seemed calm and collected, fatigue had started to set in, and she had lifted up her round-rimmed glasses and drowsily rubbed her eyes.

The door to the main hallway was to the left of the couch. The opposite door, to Yuko's right, led to the base of the lighthouse tower. The open doorway revealed a glimpse of the first few steel steps of the spiraling staircase to the lantern room. Yuka Nakagawa (Girls #16) would be up top keeping watch. Yuko hadn't taken her turn up there yet, but Yukie had assured her there wasn't much to it. The sea was to the lighthouse's back, and in front, a single narrow path led up from the harbor, and the rest was all mountain. Right now, Yukie was in the front bedroom where they were keeping Shuya Nanahara.

Shuya Nanahara.

A flicker of her previous terror returned, and she again saw the scene that she would never forget—the cracked open head, the bloody hatchet withdrawn, and the boy holding that hatchet.

The memory chilled her. And that boy, Shuya Nanahara, was inside the lighthouse, under this very roof. *That's—*

No, that's fine. It's fine.

Yuko stared down at the white tabletop, trying to keep herself from shaking. *That's right,* she thought, *he's nearly dead. With those injuries, and that much blood loss, he won't be waking up.*

She felt someone tap on her shoulder. She lifted her head.

Haruka Tanizawa sat in the stool next to her, looked into her face, and asked, "Were you able to get a little sleep?"

She must have been taking a break from cooking. Chisato Matsui was scrutinizing the label of one of the pouches of soup mix—maybe she was looking at the recipe. (Chisato had quietly wept in the corner of the room this morning. She was crying because Shinji Mimura's death had been listed in the morning announcement. At least that's what Haruka had whispered. Yuko hadn't known that Chisato had a crush on him. Her eyes were still red.)

Yuko forced a smile and replied, "Yeah, a little." *I'm fine here. We all know each other. As long as the six of us girls are together, we're fine. I can rest safe here, even if it only lasts until the time runs out. It's just that . . .*

"Hey," Haruka said. "About what you told me yesterday."

"Oh." Yuko smiled. "It's all right now."

Yes. It's all right now. She didn't want to think about it anymore. Just the memory of that scene sent chills down her spine. A shiver came from deep down inside her.

But no, she told herself, *Shuya Nanahara won't be waking up again. So there's no problem now. None at all.*

Haruka made an ambivalent smile. "Okay. If you're sure."

When Shuya was discovered unconscious in front of the lighthouse last night, Yuko had vehemently opposed taking him in. She had explained (shrieked, rather) to the other girls what she'd witnessed— Shuya Nanahara pulling the hatchet from Tatsumichi Oki's split-open head. She warned them that if they let him live, he would try to kill them all.

Yuko and Yukie Utsumi had come perilously close to a big fight, but Haruka and the rest of the girls interceded, saying that whatever the case was, they couldn't leave someone to die. And so they brought Shuya in. As the others carried the bloody boy, Yuko watched from a distance, her face ashen. It was like welcoming into their house some unfamiliar monster from a childhood nightmare. Exactly like that.

But as the hours passed, Yuko had managed to calm herself down. *Shuya Nanahara is nearly dead. With those injuries, he won't wake up.* Even with him near death, she was still upset, but she had somehow been able to control her emotions—though she had insisted upon locking his door.

Haruka continued by asking a question she'd been repeatedly asked the day before. "You said you saw Nanahara kill Oki. But couldn't it have been in self-defense?"

That was true. She'd been hiding in the bushes only a few meters away when she heard the dull thud. When she looked out, she only saw Shuya Nanahara pulling the hatchet out of Tatsumichi Oki's head. She immediately left.

What Haruka meant was (and Yuko had said it herself) that Yuko had only seen the aftermath. Shuya may have acted out of self-defense.

But no matter how many times Haruka or Yukie told her this, her mind couldn't fathom the idea—or rather, she refused to accept it.

What do you mean, "May have"? I saw it with my own eyes—that cracked-open skull; Shuya holding the hatchet; the blood running down the hatchet; the dripping blood.

The memory took hold deep within her mind. She was no longer capable of rational thought, at least regarding Shuya Nanahara. Her fear was like a flood, or a tornado—a force of nature that swept away all lesser thoughts, leaving only a single and almost palpable theorem: *Shuya Nanahara is dangerous.*

But this was not entirely without reason. Yuko didn't like violence.

In fact, she couldn't stand it. One time, she heard her friends talking about some slasher film in their old classroom and got so sick she had to be taken to the nurse's office. (She thought it was Yuka Nakagawa who said, "Sure I was laughing, but come on, it was pretty tame. You gotta have more gore than that. Spill some organs, ha ha.")

Memories of her father likely played a role. Her father—and not even a stepfather but her biological father—was a drunk who physically abused her mom, her older brother, and Yuko herself. She was too young at the time to understand why, and to this day, she'd never asked her mother. She didn't want to remember. Maybe he didn't have a reason to hurt them in the first place. She didn't know. When some gambling trouble got him stabbed to death by a yakuza—this would have been when Yuko was in first grade—she was more relieved than sad. And after he was gone, her mother, her brother, and she lived in peace. She could even start to have friends over. Without him, their home felt safe.

But even now, she sometimes dreamed about when he was around. She dreamed of her mother, her head bloodied by a golf club (even though they were poor, that was the one extravagant item in their house), and of her brother, nearly blinded by a thrown ashtray, and of herself, too terrified even to scream as the lit cigarette pressed into her flesh. (Her mom had intervened and was struck again.)

Maybe this was why, or maybe it wasn't, but right now, all she could think was, *Shuya Nanahara is dangerous.*

"Right?" Haruka prompted. The word reached Yuko's ears, but not her awareness. A chill came upon her as she saw a vision. All six of the girls, including herself, were dead. All of their heads were split open. And Shuya Nanahara, with hatchet in hand, smiled.

No. No. It's all right now. Shuya Nanahara will never leave his bed again.

"Yeah." Yuko lifted her head and nodded. She had no idea what Haruka was talking about, but since Shuya Nanahara would never awaken, she didn't need to upset the harmony of their group. She searched for something to say that would satisfy Haruka. Then she said, "Right. You're right. I don't know what was the matter with me. I was just so tired."

Haruka seemed relieved. "Nanahara's a good guy. I don't think there are a lot of boys out there as good as him."

Yuko stared at her as if she were looking at a mummy on exhibit at a museum.

Until the day before, Yuko had thought much the same thing. Though he had his quirks, Shuya Nanahara was on the whole a very likable guy. She'd even thought he was a little cool.

But now her mind had shed any memory of ever feeling that way about him. Or rather, the memory had been blotted out by the sight of that split-open head.

What? What was that, Haruka? He's a good boy? What are you talking about?

Again Haruka regarded Yuko with a puzzled expression. Then she said, "So if he wakes up, don't cause any trouble, okay?"

Yuko shuddered. *Him, wake up? Impossible. But if he does . . .*

But she utilized the remaining functional portion of her thoughts to nod and say, "Don't worry. I won't."

Haruka returned the nod. "Okay. That's a relief." Still seated, she turned to Chisato and said, "That smells good."

White steam and the smell of stew wafted from the pot atop the range.

Chisato looked over her shoulder and replied in her gentle and delicate voice. "Yeah. I don't think it'll be half bad—maybe better than last night's soup."

Though she'd cried for a long time over Shinji Mimura, Chisato seemed to be doing all right for the moment. Even Yuko in her current state could sense that much.

Then the door to the hallway opened, and Yukie Utsumi strode in with her back held straight and her steps brisk. After Yuko had arrived, she saw Yukie act as an admirable leader, but the girl had seemed in a way dispirited. After they had taken in Shuya Nanahara, her expression had become increasingly clouded. (In reality, her expression had been one mixed with happiness over reuniting with Shuya, and with worry over seeing him near death—but Yuko hadn't thought of that possibility.) She hadn't seen Yukie this lively in a long while. But more than that, Yukie's face was bright.

Yuko felt as if a hairy caterpillar were creeping up her spine. This couldn't be good.

Yukie stopped on her heels, put her hands on her hips, and sent her gaze across the girls. Then she jokingly cupped her hands around her mouth like a megaphone, and she announced, "Nanahara has awoken."

Haruka and Chisato cried out in surprise, and Satomi sat upright on the sofa.

And Yuko turned pale.

14 STUDENTS REMAIN.

"Really?" Haruka asked. "Can he talk?"

Yukie nodded. "Yeah. And he says he's hungry." Her eyes went to Yuko. "It's all right. I locked him in his room. I didn't want to worry you."

She wasn't being snide. From the tone of her voice, she had done what she thought was necessary as the leader.

But skipping past Yukie's demeanor, Yuko immediately began to think about what she would do—though over the past night, she had already thought about it, over and over. She was certain he would never wake up, but what if he did? How would she respond? And then the smell drifted to her nose.

Perfect timing. It's almost lunch. And who would think anything of a gravely wounded boy suddenly taking a turn for the worse?

Yuko contrived a smile (and impeccably so) and shook her head. "I'm not worried at all." Then she said, "Sorry about last night. I was a little crazy. I don't suspect Nanahara anymore."

Looking relieved, Yukie let out a breath. "If I'd known that, I wouldn't have had to lock the door." She gave Yuko a smile. "He told me it was an accident—what happened with Oki."

Hearing Tatsumichi Oki's name again caused the scene to replay in the back of her mind. Another chill ran down her spine, but she managed to keep her smile in place as she nodded. *An accident. Well, that was a pretty serious accident for Tatsumichi Oki, wasn't it?*

To Haruka, Yukie said, "Hey, would you go get Yuka? There's something I want to discuss while we eat."

"Is it okay for us to go without anyone keeping watch?"

"Sure." Yukie nodded. "We've got the building sealed off, anyway. And it'll only be for a little bit."

Haruka nodded and disappeared into the tower room. Her footsteps clanged up the steel staircase.

Satomi and Chisato asked Yukie, "How is he?" and, "Can he eat the same food as us?" Simultaneously, Yuko quietly stood and approached the sink.

White, deep ceramic dishes were stacked beside the steaming stewpot. Chisato and Haruka had found them in the cupboard.

Yuko slipped her right hand into her skirt pocket and gripped the object inside. A telescoping tactical baton had been the weapon provided in her daypack, but this little number had been in there alongside it, labeled EXTRA BONUS. She hadn't expected to find a use for it inside the game. And when she was welcomed into this group, she hadn't seen any point in mentioning it. Then when Shuya Nanahara showed up, she'd had this idea and had kept the item a secret.

Once upon a time, her father's tempestuous violence had vanished from their home suddenly and by chance. Her family had found peace again.

Now Yuko found herself in the presence of another specter of violence. This time, it fell upon Yuko to put it to an end. Only then would she find peace again. She would no longer need to fear.

She had no reason to hesitate. Strangely, she was calm.

Inside her pocket, Yuko furtively removed the cork from the tiny little bottle with one hand.

14 STUDENTS REMAIN.

"Hey," Yuko said to Yukie.

Yukie, who was still talking Satomi and Chisato, turned to her.

"Shouldn't we bring Nanahara his food first?"

Yukie beamed. "Yes. Let's."

Yuko added, perfectly casually, "The stew looks ready. How about I serve us up?"

She was holding onto the plate. *The* plate.

"Sure," Yukie said. Then, seeming to remember something, she added, "Oh, right. The first aid kit's in that desk, right? I think I saw some some painkillers in there. Would you get it for me? We need to bring him some with his meal."

"Okay." Yuko set the dish down. It clinked against the lip of the sink. "Hold on, I'll find it."

Yukie had meant the writing desk, with the computer and phone, in the far corner of the room. Yuko swung around the table and headed for the desk.

The clanging of footsteps on metal stairs echoed in the room. Yuka Nakagawa and Haruka appeared. Slung from Yuka's shoulder was a gun that looked like an oversized pistol with a stretched-out back end and a short barrel. (It was an Uzi 9mm submachine gun. The weapon had been Satomi Noda's, but since it seemed the most potent of their weapons, they decided it would remain with whoever was keeping watch.)

Yuka set the Uzi on the table and asked in her usual bright voice, "I heard Nanahara's awake?"

She was a little on the chubby side, and her time on the outdoor tennis courts had given her a deep tan. Even in these circumstances, she hadn't lost her good cheer.

Yukie nodded happily. "He is."

"Well, good for you, Class Leader," Yuka teased.

Yukie blushed. "What are you talking about?"

"Come on now. Look at how happy you are."

Yukie made a face at her and shook her head. But then Yuka looked at Chisato and fell silent. Having just lost the boy she liked, Shinji Mimura, Chisato was standing there with her head down a little.

Paying little attention to this exchange, Yuko rummaged through the desk drawer and pulled out the large wooden first aid kit. She placed it on top of the desk and opened it. The box had been jam-packed with a variety of pharmaceuticals, gauze, and poultices and the like. All that was missing were the bandages, which had been almost entirely used on Shuya Nanahara.

The painkillers . . . where were those painkillers? Not that it matters, of course. It didn't matter. Because . . .

"Wow, that smells great," Yuka was saying. Her attempt to brighten the mood was obvious even to Yuko, barely paying attention.

Painkillers . . . Ah, here. This one. Used to temporarily relieve headaches, menstrual cramps, toothaches. I do have a bit of a stomachache, now that I think about it. I'll take some of these later—after it's all over. Yes, after it's all over.

"So what do you want to talk about?" This was Satomi's slightly husky voice. She must have been asking Yukie.

"Oh, right," Haruka said. "I want to hear this."

"Oh, yes, about that," Yukie said. "Where should I begin?"

But when Yuka said, "Which one's mine? I want a little taste," Yuko's head snapped up.

She looked over her shoulder. She saw Yuka standing at the sink, holding a dish of stew up to her mouth. If all she wanted was a taste, she could have used the ladle. But instead, she had to put *that* dish against her lips. The dish sprinkled with that semitransparent powder.

The blood drained from Yuko's face. She started to speak out—but before she could, it happened.

Yuka dropped the dish. The plate crashed to the floor, shattering noisily, and the stew splattered. All eyes were on her.

Yuka gripped at her throat and coughed up the stew she'd just swallowed. She coughed harder, and more came spraying out onto the white table. Only now it was bright red. The radial splattering of round, red droplets resembled the flag of the Republic of Greater East Asia. Then, not even a second later, she crumpled to the stew-covered floor.

"Yuka!" they all shouted—all save for Yuka herself, who could no longer speak—and the girls rushed to her.

Curled on her side, she coughed up blood again. Her tanned face turned pale as they watched. Red foam spilled from the edge of her mouth.

Yukie shook her. "Yuka! Yuka! What's wrong?"

But all that came from Yuka's lips now were the bubbles of dark red. Her eyes were open nearly as wide as could be, as if they could pop out at any minute, and their whites were turning crimson. Whether from a sudden rush of blood or her capillaries bursting, several dark red spots appeared on her face, transforming it into a grotesque monster mask.

But something else became evident. They could tell just by looking at her.

Yuka had stopped breathing.

Nobody said a word. Yukie touched her trembling hand to Yuka's throat. Then she said, "She's dead."

Behind Haruka and the kneeling Yukie, Yuko stood still, pale-faced. Her entire body shook.

Oh, how could this happen? A mistake, it's a mistake! She only had a tiny sip . . . I didn't know it would be so strong . . . I killed her . . . killed her . . . by mistake . . . I didn't mean for this . . . Yukie said, her voice quavering, "This . . . couldn't have been because the food had gone bad, could it."

Chisato responded, "I tasted it a few minutes ago. It was perfectly fine. But this . . . this . . . this is . . ."

Haruka finished for her. "Poison?"

That set everything in motion. All of the girls (to be precise, all of the girls except for Yuko, though the other four didn't notice) looked at one another.

There was a clatter. Satomi Noda had grabbed the Uzi and pointed it at the others. Reflexively, the other four—including Yuko—moved away from Yuka's corpse.

Satomi's eyes were wide and hard behind her round glasses. She shouted, "Who was it? Who did this? Who put in the poison? Which of you tried to kill us?"

"Stop it!" Yukie yelled. Yuko saw her immediately begin to reach for the pistol tucked in the back of her skirt. (She had a Browning Hi Power 9mm. The weapon had been hers from the start, and since she was essentially their leader, she'd kept it). But Yukie resisted the impulse and brought her hand back to her side. "Put down the gun," she said. "This has to be some kind of mistake."

"This is no mistake." Satomi shook her head. She had always kept her cool but was in a blind fury now. "You heard the last announcement—we're down to fourteen of us. That's not that many. The timing's right for some game-playing traitor to show her true colors."

She glanced at Haruka and said, "You were the one cooking."

Haruka hastily shook her head. "Not just me. Chisato—"

"That's horrible," Chisato said. "I would never do something like that." She hesitated, but then said, "Anyway, Satomi and Yuko had the opportunity too."

"She's right," Haruka said, turning back to Satomi. "You seem *too* upset. You're acting funny."

"Haruka!" Yukie cut her short, but she was too late. Satomi's face turned red with anger.

"What did you say?"

"You heard me," Haruka said. "You haven't slept at all. I know you haven't. I woke up in the middle of the night and you were awake. What, couldn't you trust us? That proves it!"

Again Yukie pleaded, nearly shouting now, "Haruka, stop! Satomi, put down the gun!"

Satomi pointed the Uzi at Yukie. "Oh, please. Stop acting like you're in charge. Or are you just doing that to trick us after you blew your plan to poison all of us? Is that it?"

Yukie's jaw dropped. "Satomi . . ."

Yuko raised her hand to her mouth and took three dazed steps back. With this all happening so suddenly, her body had gone numb. *I have to say something. I have to explain the truth. If I let this go on . . . something awful . . . something dreadfully awful is going to happen.*

Then Chisato moved. She ran for the sideboard table against the wall to the right of the sink. There they had left the only other firearm the girls had been provided—a Czechoslovakian CZ 75 pistol, originally Yuka's.

The *thmpthmpthmp* of automatic gunfire rang through the room. Three holes opened in Chisato's back. She slammed into the sideboard and slid down, hugging its edge, and then fell facedown on the floor. No one needed to check her—she was dead.

Yukie's eyes went wide and she shrieked, "Satomi! What are you doing?"

"What's the problem?" Satomi said, glaring at her and still holding the smoking Uzi at the ready. "She went for the gun—because she was guilty."

"You went for *your* gun too!" Haruka yelled. "Yukie, shoot her! Shoot Satomi."

Satomi whirled the submachine gun on Haruka. Satomi's expression had darkened. She seemed ready to pull the trigger at any moment.

Yuko saw Yukie's face in profile. She seemed to anguish over something, but then in the next instant, her hand was on the Browning in the back of her skirt. After her hesitation, she must have decided to aim for Satomi's arm or somewhere less fatal.

Satomi whipped the Uzi to the side and pointed it at Yukie.

With a *thmpthmpthmp*, Yukie was knocked backward. Blood sprayed from the chest of her sailor fuku, and she landed on her back.

For a second, Haruka stood there, frozen. Then she was running after the Browning Yukie had dropped. Satomi's Uzi followed her motion and then barked, *thmpthmpthmp*. The side of her blouse burst open and sent fabric and blood flying. Her body slid along the floor.

Then Satomi pointed her gun across the table at Yuko and said, "What about you? You're different, right?"

Yuko could only tremble. She shook as she looked into Satomi's face.

She heard a bang and saw a hole open in the left side of Satomi's forehead. Satomi's mouth opened, and she looked to her left. Blood streamed from her forehead. The river of it stopped briefly at the edge of her eye, behind those round-rimmed glasses, then resumed its journey down.

Like an automaton, Yuko stiffly swiveled her head to see where Satomi was looking. There, on the floor, Haruka was sitting upright, apparently in terrible pain—but she had a firm grip on the Browning.

Satomi's Uzi barked, *thmpthmpthmpthmpthmpthmpthmp*. She might have fired on purpose, or it might have been a death spasm. Either way, the trail of bullet holes ran up the floor and across Haruka's body, knocking her back and twisting her around. A mist of blood scattered in the air, and above her collar, only half of her neck was still attached to her head.

Then, slowly, Satomi toppled forward. With a thud, she slumped atop Yuka Nakagawa's crumpled-up corpse. And then she was still, with not even a twitch.

Yuko, now alone in the room, only stood there shaking. As if her body had turned to stone, she remained frozen and trembled. Like a little child who'd wandered into a museum of oddities, she stared around at her five classmates dead on the floor.

9 STUDENTS REMAIN.

When Shuya heard the sound of something shattering, he figured it was something innocent, such as one of those clumsy girls making lunch dropping a plate. But then when he heard the voices arguing, he sprang upright in his bed.

Sharp pain struck his left side and shoulder. He grunted but managed to use his right arm to pull himself from the bed. Still wearing only his school slacks, he put his bare feet on the floor. The argument carried on. He thought he could hear Yukie shouting amid the voices.

Shuya walked to the door. He put his hand on the knob, turned it, and pushed the door open—but after a centimeter, it stopped with a jolt. Through the narrow opening, he saw a wooden beam running aslant across the other side. As Yukie had warned him, they had barred him inside with a makeshift crossbar.

He took a better grip on the doorknob and gave it a good rattle, but the door refused to budge. He pushed his fingers through the crack, but whatever the girls had done to fix that beam in place, it didn't move.

Just as he gave up and sighed, a *thmpthmpthmp* sound came through that crack—gunfire, like he'd heard so many times now. There were more screams.

The blood drained from Shuya's face. *An attack? But then why is . . . well, whatever it is, something's wrong!*

In spite of his injuries, he was able to lift up his right leg and hold himself steady, while he kicked the door with the ball of his bare foot, following a technique Hiroki Sugimura had once taught him. But the stalwart door rebuffed his attack, and Shuya lost his balance and fell on his rear. Pain shot up from the wound in his side. On top of it all, he realized he needed to pee; but that would have to wait.

Another *thmpthmpthmp*. And again, *thmpthmpthmp*.

He quickly looked over his shoulder to the bed, then stood and lifted the metal pipe bed frame with his good arm. The bed crashed over on its side, and the blankets and sheets fell.

He dragged the bed to the door, went around behind it, then rammed it into the door as hard as he could. The wood creaked in protest, and the door tilted. *One more time.*

Another gunshot. *BANG!* This time, it was only one.

The bed frame smashed into the door. Wood snapped, and the door, nearly bent in half, spilled open into the hallway. Shuya yanked the bed back and let it fall over on the floor.

With another *thmpthmpthmpthmpthmpthmp*, the gunfire came loud and clear through the open doorway.

Shuya stepped out of the room. With the electricity out and the windows shaded and boarded over, the hall was dark. The front door was on his left, and at his right were three more doors along the long hallway. The farthest had been left ajar, and the light leaked into the hall. Its reflection formed a cold puddle of light on the floor.

The beam that had been blocking the door had split in two. The larger piece was about a meter long. He picked it up and dragged his aching body down the hall. There wasn't a sound now. *What the hell is going on? Did someone attack?*

Shuya cautiously approached the third door. He put his eye up to the opening. Through the crack he saw a room with a kitchen and Yukie Utsumi and Haruka Tanizawa sprawled out beside the center table, and behind them Yuka Nakagawa (*What the fuck happened to her face!*), and Chisato Matsui against the right-hand wall, and another girl facedown in the table's shadow. That one must have been Satomi Noda, because unless Shuya's eyes were mistaken, the slender girl with silky shoulder-length hair, standing motionless with her back to him, was Yuko Sakaki.

Several guns were scattered among the fallen bodies. The stench of the splattered blood assaulted him.

Shuya froze in shock. The feeling of complete and utter paralysis was identical to what he had felt seeing Mayumi Tendo's corpse in front of the school.

What the hell! What happened here? Yukie—the same Yukie who had told him, "Listen to the girl who's in love with you," was sprawled on the floor. And four more were with her. *Are they . . . dead? Are they all dead?*

Yuko, her back still to him, wasn't holding a gun. All she did was stand there, like a girl from Venus suddenly dropped on Pluto.

In a daze, Shuya took the doorknob, slowly opened the door, and set foot inside.

Yuko spun to face him. For an instant, she stared at him with bloodshot eyes, and then she was diving for the pistol on the floor between Yukie and Haruka.

In that same moment, Shuya snapped out of his trance. Putting force into his uninjured right arm, he hurled the piece of wood at her the way he used to throw a perfect fastball in Little League. (He doubted now that such a sport existed on this earth. No, that must have been somewhere in a land far, far away, near the Andromeda Galaxy, where they used three of their five arms to play—except in the final inning, when they were permitted use of their tails.)

Shuya grimaced as pain shot through his body, but the wood hit the floor right in front of her and bounced up, and she stopped running and shielded her face with both arms, only she slipped on the bloody floor and landed on her backside.

Shuya ran for the same gun. He couldn't make sense of what was happening, but he was certain that Yuko picking up that gun would only complicate matters even further.

Yuko screeched and backed away. She sat upright, then turned over and scrambled for the opposite doorway. She made it past the table and disappeared through the open door. He could hear her footsteps clacking on something metallic. *Stairs?*

For a moment Shuya watched the doorway after her, but before he followed, he ran to Yukie Utsumi and knelt beside her.

He saw the holes in the front of her school uniform. Blood had begun to spread beneath her, and her eyes were closed peacefully, as if in slumber. Her mouth was barely open.

But she wasn't breathing.

"No," he said. He reached his hand to her tranquil face, and for the first time since the game began, he felt tears welling up in his eyes. Was it merely because they had been talking just minutes before, or was it something else?

"I didn't know what I'd do if you died . . . Do you understand what I'm saying?"

"So you call Noriko by her name, but I'm Class Leader."

Her face then had been teary-eyed yet filled with relief, and later, tinged with sadness. Now her face was eerily peaceful.

Shuya looked around. He didn't need to check on the others. Yuka Nakagawa's face was discolored, and bloody foam overflowed from her mouth. A pool of blood had formed beneath Satomi Noda's face-down head. Holes riddled Chisato Matsui's back, and Haruka Tanizawa's head had nearly been torn off.

How could this happen?

Shuya looked back at Yukie. With his numb left arm even managing to pitch in, he sat her up. Maybe it was a pointless gesture, but Shuya had to do it.

As he held her, he could hear blood from the exit wounds in her back dripping to the floor. Her neck lolled back, and her braided hair touched his arms.

"Do you understand what I'm saying?"

Teardrops spilled from his eyes and made tiny splashes on her sailor fuku.

Sobbing, Shuya pressed his lips together and gently laid her back down on the floor. He picked up the Browning Yuko had tried to grab. He walked to the open door at the end of the room where she had disappeared. His body felt far heavier than his many injuries could justify. Holding the gun in his right hand, he rubbed his eyes with his bare forearm.

Through the doorway was a cylindrical space with exposed concrete walls. *A lighthouse. This is the lighthouse.* A steel staircase wound around a thick steel column in the middle of the room. Without windows, the tower was dim. A faint light fell from above.

Shuya yelled, "Yuko!" and began up the stairs. "What happened, Yuko?"

He saw no sign of her above. But then he heard her scream echo through the cylindrical space. Shuya knit his eyebrows and hurried his pace. The wound in his side pulsated with pain. He thought he might be bleeding because he felt the bandage grow damp.

9 STUDENTS REMAIN.

64

Yuko Sakaki raced up the stairs and was out of breath when she emerged at the top of the tower. The lantern room had just enough space to walk around the Cyclopean eye of the Fresnel lens in the center. The storm panes offered a view of the cloudy sky. To her left, a low door led to the outside catwalk. Yuko desperately opened the door and went outside.

This high up, the wind was stronger than she'd expected and smelled strongly of the sea.

The water unfolded before her. The sea reflected the overcast sky in a muted indigo upon which white waves wove an intricate fabric. Yuko moved to her right around the lantern deck. Across a small clearing at the front of the lighthouse, the northern mountain loomed. A little to the left, an unpaved access road wove around the base of the mountain. A lone white minivan had been left beside a meager gate at the mouth of the road.

Yuko held the steel railing. Beneath, she could see the roof of the attached single-story building—and of the room where she had been only moments ago. She followed the handrail around the lantern deck but did not find what she had expected—a ladder. She hadn't taken a turn on watch yet and wasn't familiar with the outside of the lantern room. There was no way down. She'd trapped herself in a dead end up in the sky. Panic nearly overcame her, but she gritted her teeth and fought it down. With no ladder, she'd have to jump.

Breathing heavily, she returned to where the building lay below, and she looked down again.

It was a long way down—not as bad as to the ground, but still a very long way. It was, in fact, too far to jump, but before she could reach a rational decision, that image flashed through her mind again. Only this time, the other girls were gone, and it was just her there with her head split open. Blood sprayed up and covered Shuya Nanahara's face. She *had* to escape—no matter what it took. She couldn't *not* escape. And she was out of time.

Yuko crouched down and slipped herself through one of the wide gaps between the posts in the carelessly constructed railing. Then she was on the other side. Holding onto the railing, she carefully stood on the ten-centimeter-wide lip of the balcony.

The view beneath her feet was dizzying. *This is really high. I can't jump from here. It's high . . . It's so high.*

Suddenly her body jolted. Her foot had slipped. Below the hem of her pleated skirt, the side of her bare shin struck the edge of the concrete walkway (she felt her skin scraping off), and her body was in air. She shrieked and flailed her hands and wrapped her arms around the bottom of a narrow metal railing post. The rest of her dangled below the balcony's edge.

Her arms were wrapped around the pole, and she was panting for air. *I almost . . . died.*

Yuko swallowed and willed her arms to hold. *Okay, first, I need to pull myself up and get back on the other side of the railing. Then I need to figure out a way I can stand up to Shuya Nanahara. That's my only—*

A strong gust of wind shook her. She let out a futile scream. Her hands slid from the steel pole and barely hung on to the edge of the concrete. The pole was beyond her reach now.

Her palms began to sweat. Overcome by terror and dismay, she

began to panic. *How how how how can I be sweating now? My hands—*
they're slipping—

Her right pinky lost hold and fell.

"No!" she yelled. Her ring finger went next. Then her whole right
hand dropped. (She felt the nail of her pointer finger catch, but it broke,
and that was that.) Her body swung in the air, pivoting on her left
hand. And now that hand was—

She screamed as she fell. A dreamlike sensation came over her.

But then her arm jolted and pulled at her shoulder, and her drop
halted less than half a meter after it began.

Dangling from her outstretched left arm, she looked up dumbly—
and saw Shuya Nanahara, who was sticking halfway through the
railing and had caught her by the wrist.

For an instant Yuko stared at him blankly. Then she screamed,
"No!"

Of course if he let go, she would die, but it was *Shuya Nanahara.*

"No! No!"

With her eyes open wide and her hair shaking wildly, she kept on
screaming, and she thought, *Why? Why are you trying to save me? Is
it to use me to stay alive? Or . . . oh, that's it. You want to kill me with
your bare hands!*

"No! Let me go!" Whatever remaining traces of rational thought
she possessed were in tatters now. "No! I'd rather die like this than be
killed by you! Let me go. Let me go!"

Whatever he thought about this—or maybe he didn't think anything—his expression didn't change. "Keep still," he barked.

Again she looked up at him, and then she noticed it. Blood oozed
from the bandage around his neck, just below that silver collar, and
trickled down his shoulder.

The blood dribbled all the way down his arm and onto her hand.

Shuya grunted and redoubled his grip. His face was clammy with
sweat. And he wasn't just hurt in his neck, but all over his body. Not
only was he holding her weight with one arm, he was trying to pull her
up. He must have been in extraordinary pain.

Yuko's jaw dropped. *Why? Why are you trying to save me, when it must hurt that bad? It's because—*

The answer came to her all at once. The black fog enveloping her mind cleared as if blown by a sudden gust of wind (much like the sea breeze buffeting at her now). Scattered was the image of Shuya holding that bloody hatchet as he gazed down at Tatsumichi Oki's corpse. Once again, she saw the cheerful boy she used to know back in Class B until only two days ago. He was laughing as he traded jokes with Yoshitoki Kuninobu and Shinji Mimura. He was looking serious as he repeated a tricky guitar riff in the music room. He was grinning as he struck a victory pose from second base, after she'd happened to glance outside the gymnasium during volleyball in gym class and saw him make a perfect hit straight down the third base line. And he was gazing at her with concern, when in class, she'd turned pale from an attack of terrible cramps, and he gently asked her, "What's wrong, Sakaki? You don't look so good," and interrupted their English teacher Mr. Yamamoto's reading to get the attention of the nurse's aide, Fumiyo Fujiyoshi.

Oh. Yuko finally grasped what was really happening. *It's Nanahara. Nanahara is trying to save me. Why did I think I had to kill him? Why did I think that? He's Nanahara. I always thought he was kind of cool and kind of nice.*

Then another thought began to coalesce—what she had done, and what she had brought about. Again her face paled.

I lost my mind . . . and because of me, everyone's . . .

She started to cry. Noticing this, Shuya looked puzzled.

"Nanahara!" she yelled. "It was me. I . . . I . . . tried to kill you."

Tears filling her eyes, she looked desperately up to him. He seemed surprised.

She continued, "I—thought you killed Oki. I saw it. I was scared. I was so scared. So I tried to poison your food, but Yuka ate it. And then everyone . . ."

Now Shuya understood everything. She had been in some nearby bushes and witnessed him fighting Tatsumichi and pulling the hatchet from his face. But that was all—she hadn't seen Kyoichi Motobuchi and Kawada show up. Sure, she could have interpreted it as self-defense or an accident. But she had been so completely terrified that she had no choice but to fear him. She'd tried to poison him, but Yuka Nakagawa ate *his* food by mistake, and all the girls fell into a paranoid panic. Only the poisoner herself survived.

"That doesn't matter now!" Shuya yelled. "It's all right, so just don't move. I'll pull you up!"

Shuya was lying nearly flat on the concrete balcony, with his body passed between the bars of the handrail. With his left arm disabled, he couldn't grab on to the posts. But he twisted his body and managed to tuck his right knee beneath himself to get leverage for his back muscles. Still holding firmly to her wrist, he began to pull. In his side, and his shoulder, and his neck, and every part of him that hurt, the pain surged.

But then with tears streaking down her face, Yuko shook her head. "No. No. It's my fault they're all . . . they're all . . ."

She wrenched her hand about, trying to pull free. His firm grip on her loosened, and he quickly he squeezed tighter—but the blood trailing down from his neck made his hand slip.

Her hand left his. The weight on his arm suddenly vanished.

Yuko's face, looking up at him, fell away.

Then with a thud, she was on her back on the roof of the building below. Rather than fall from his hand, she seemed to have appeared down there like a jump cut in a film.

Her body, in the sailor blouse and pleated skirt, splayed out on the roof, and her head was turned in an unnatural way. Her head appeared oddly distant from her body. A red splash extended from the top right of her head like an elongated, abstract-art maple leaf.

"Ah . . ."

For a while Shuya remained there, his arm still hanging from the balcony as he stared at the sight below.

8 STUDENTS REMAIN.

Hiroki Sugimura (Boys #11) held his breath.

He'd heard the intense gunfire about ten minutes ago. Having been wandering in the northern mountain, he hurried to the east, toward the source of the sounds. When he came upon the lighthouse, silence had fallen.

Hiroki had noticed the lighthouse on his map, but thinking Kayoko Kotohiki would never hide by herself in such a conspicuous location, he hadn't bothered to investigate. He hadn't been sure if this place was the source of the gunfire, but when he looked down from the surrounding clifftop, he saw a girl sprawled on the roof of the brick building connected to the lighthouse. Even at this distance, he could see the red stain beneath her head. She was dead. Much like with Megumi Eto, her short hair and petite body might have belonged to Kayoko Kotohiki.

He slid down the cliffside. From below, he couldn't see the body on the roof, so he went around to the front entrance. Inside the open door, desks and chairs were jumbled in a pile, like someone had built a barricade, and then for some reason tore it down. Cautiously, Hiroki proceeded down the hallway of boarded-up windows (next to the entrance was a room with a bed and a broken door), and the display of his locator changed. Six stars. Alert, Hiroki shifted his broomhandle-staff to his right hand, withdrew his gun from his waistband with his left, and slowly advanced.

When he reached the room with the kitchen and the standing pools of blood, he froze.

The bodies of five girls were strewn about the room. The girls' class leader, Yukie Utsumi, was face up next to the center table. Haruka Tanizawa, with her head nearly torn off (*yikes!*) was to her right. Yuka Nakagawa, her face a sickly black, was near the back. Chisato Matsui had fallen forward by the sideboard table to his right, and her pallid face was turned toward him. A fifth girl lay facedown in the blood in the shadow of the table.

The four whose faces he could see were clearly dead. But he couldn't be sure about the other.

He carefully scanned the room once more. He looked toward the open door on the far side and listened. No one seemed to be in hiding.

He returned the pistol in his left hand to the back waistband of his slacks, walked between the bodies of Yukie Utsumi and Haruka Tanizawa, passed by Yuka Nakagawa, and circled around the table. The soles of his shoes made splashing noises as he walked through the blood spread all over the floor. He crouched beside the face-down girl, set down the broom handle in his right hand, and put both hands on the girl. When he began to turn her over, sharp pain shot out from where Mitsuko Souma had stabbed him in his right shoulder. Toshinori Oda's bullet had only grazed his thigh and hadn't bled or hurt much at all. But Hiroki ignored the pain and turned over the body.

Satomi Noda. A red hole had opened in the left side of her forehead, and the left lens of her glasses, askew but still on her face, had shattered, possibly when she'd hit the floor. Dead.

Hiroki laid her back down and looked to the open doorway at the rear of the room. That led to the lighthouse tower and up to the lantern room.

The sixth blip on his detector would be the girl on the roof. She too was certainly dead, but he had to find out who she was—chiefly because she resembled Kayoko Kotohiki.

Hiroki drew his gun and stepped through the door to find a steel staircase. He rushed up the stairs—taking care for his footsteps not to make any noise. Someone might still be up there. In his right hand, he held the detector along with the broom handle and kept an eye on the display.

But the device showed no change as he came up into the lantern room. Hiroki put the detector back into his pocket and the pistol into his back waistband, and he went out to the lantern deck.

He put his hands on the steel railing, gulped, and thrust his head over the railing and looked down.

He saw the body of a girl in a sailor fuku. Her neck was twisted in an unnatural way, and blood had splattered beneath her—but she wasn't Kayoko Kotohiki. She was Yuko Sakaki.

And yet, he thought, as he felt the sea breeze on his face and gazed across the water, *the six girls here died all at once.* He hadn't seen any guns in the room below, but from their wounds, and the many holes in the walls and floor, he was certain that the gunfire had come from here. He tried to imagine what had happened—somehow, the girls had gathered together and shut themselves inside, but then someone attacked them. That was plausible. The other five downstairs were killed first, and Yuko fled to the tower, but she fell to her death before the attacker got to her. And that assailant had left before Hiroki arrived.

But then there was the barricade at the front door. *If they'd boarded up every window and blocked every way in,* Hiroki wondered, *why did the girls tear down the front barricade when the attacker showed up? The attacker could have done it on the way out. . . . But no, that wouldn't explain how he—or she—got inside. Could it be that there were* seven *girls, and one of them suddenly betrayed the rest or had her plans revealed? No, that couldn't be. And Yuka Nakagawa—she wasn't shot. She looked like she'd been strangled or something.*

And I can't figure out the blood splattered all over the table. How did that much blood get up there? But that's not all—what about the door by the front entrance? How did it get broken?

No matter how much he thought about it, he wasn't going to find any answers. He shook his head, gave the roof one last look, and returned to the lantern room.

Hiroki tramped down the winding metal staircase in the dim tower and gazed at the walls without paying attention to them. He felt a little dizzy, as if his spiral descent were a part of him. Maybe it was his fatigue, or maybe it was his realization.

We're down another six now. At noon, Sakamochi said there were fourteen of us left. Now there are eight, at most.

Is Kayoko Kotohiki still alive? She wouldn't have died sometime since noon, somewhere I haven't found yet, right?

No, he thought. *She has to be alive.*

Though he had nothing on which to base this belief, for some reason he felt nearly certain. Only eight of them remained—or less. But he was still alive. And Kayoko Kotohiki was surely still alive. Only finding her was taking too much time. A full day and a half had passed since the game began, and he still hadn't found her. But he *would* find her. Of this too he was nearly certain.

Hiroki thought of Shuya Nanahara's little group. None of the three's names had been in the announcements. And Shogo Kawada had told him, "Hop on our train whenever you like."

Is there really a way out? And can I really reach that station with Kotohiki?

Of that he wasn't sure. But whatever it took, he wanted to get her aboard that train.

Shall I offer you my hand, Mademoiselle?

Ha, that sounds like a line Shinji would use.

He could see how Shinji Mimura could be friends with Yutaka Seto. Shinji liked to joke—though his sense of humor was a little different from Yutaka's. Shinji was more sarcastic, at times biting. But he knew the importance of being able to laugh things off. Back in second year, while some government official from the regional school board was droning on during the closing ceremony for their winter term, he and Hiroki were talking, and he said, "My uncle used to say that laughter is a crucial element for harmony, and it might be our only means of release. Do you understand that, Sugimura? I still don't quite get it."

Hiroki felt like he vaguely understood but couldn't get a good grasp on it. Maybe he was just too young. Whatever the case, Shinji Mimura and Yutaka Seto were dead now. Hiroki would never be able to give Shinji his answer.

Lost in his thoughts, Hiroki found himself standing in the kitchen with the five corpses. Once again Hiroki looked over the blood-soaked room.

Because of the overpowering stench of blood, he hadn't until now noticed the enticing smell coming from the pot on the cooking range. With the gas surely shut off, the girls must have been cooking with some kind of solid fuel or something. He walked over and took a look. The flame beneath the grill had gone out, but steam still rose from the stew inside.

He'd had nothing to eat aside from the government-issue bread (and he'd run out of water and had to retrieve more from a well outside a house), and he was hungry, but he shook his head and tore himself away from the pot. He couldn't bring himself to eat—not in this room. Besides, he needed to hurry and find Kayoko Kotohiki. He needed to leave now.

He staggered to the hallway. The sleep deprivation had left his legs unsteady.

Someone was standing at the front door at the end of the long corridor. In the darkness of the hallway, the figure stood silhouetted by the bright outside light.

Before his eyes had time to go wide, Hiroki dove sideways, back into the kitchen. At the same time, violent flames burst from the figure's hands, and a stream of bullets flew past Hiroki's feet.

His expression twisted with alarm, Hiroki rose to one knee, slammed the door shut, and turned the lock.

He'd heard that gunfire before. He'd heard it right before and after that incredible explosion. He'd heard it behind him after he ran from Toshinori Oda—whoever this was had killed Toshinori. He'd also heard it when Yumiko Kusaka and Yukiko Kitano were killed. And he'd heard it many other times. Which meant that this was *that* classmate. Like Hiroki, he must have heard the gunfire and come to investigate—or he'd come to take out the person who had killed Yukie and her girls. Or maybe *he* was the attacker, now returning.

Still kneeling, Hiroki put his left hand around to his back and gripped the pistol. He'd found spare ammo in the daypack Mitsuko Souma had left behind and filled the magazine, but he hadn't found a spare magazine—maybe Mitsuko had kept it in her pocket. The weapon was a single-action semi-automatic Colt M1911. The magazine housed seven rounds, and he had one more in the chamber. He would not likely have time to reload. The moment he tried, he'd be mowed down by that machine gun—or whatever other firearms his attacker carried.

He pressed himself against the wall beside the door and looked across the kitchen where the girls' corpses lay. All the windows had been boarded up from the inside. Tearing down the barriers to get outside would take time. He looked at the door to the lighthouse tower. But no, that wasn't an option either. The upper platform was too high for a jump—if he did, the best he could expect was a long sunbath next to Yuko Sakaki. Hiroki wondered what this unknown attacker was doing now. *Is he sneaking up to the door? Or is he going to wait for me to come out? No, he must be in a hurry too. If he doesn't end this quickly, someone else coming to investigate the gunfire might catch him from behind, so he'll—*

Hiroki was right. Bullets tore through the wooden door around the handle. (Several of the rounds struck Chisato Matsui's corpse, directly in front of the door, and shredded flesh from her shoulder and side.)

The door crashed open.

The next instant, a dark figure dove into the room.

The figure sprang to his feet, and Hiroki saw that it was Kazuo Kiriyama (Boys #6). Paying no heed to anything else in the room— not even the corpses—he aimed his machine gun at his blind spot to the side of the door. By the time it was pointed there, he was already firing.

Five or six bullets dug holes in the wall—and then the shooting stopped. No one was there.

Not missing this opportunity, Hiroki raised his broom handle and attacked Kiriyama from above. In a snap decision, he had climbed atop the tall, wall-mounted shelves beside the door. He had put away his pistol, having decided not to rely on the unfamiliar weapon. What mattered now was not to let his opponent—Kiriyama, he now knew—shoot.

Kiriyama sensed his movement and looked up. He began to raise his gun, but before he could, Hiroki smashed his wrist with the broom handle. The 9mm Ingram MAC-10 clattered to the floor, slid, and came to a stop on the other side of the table, near Satomi Noda.

Kiriyama started to pull another gun from the front of his slacks (a large semi-automatic pistol—not Toshinori Oda's revolver). But Hiroki landed in a fighting stance and immediately flicked his pole, slapping this second gun from Kiriyama's hand.

Keep striking! Don't stop until he's down!

Hiroki swung again, but Kiriyama leaned back and went straight into a backflip. With a finesse fit for a kung-fu movie, he bounded over Yukie Utsumi's body, did a flip, and landed on his feet in front of the center table, with a revolver in hand. Hiroki recognized it as Toshinori's gun.

But Hiroki's move must have taken even Kiriyama by surprise. In an instant, Hiroki had rushed forward, closing within eighty centimeters of the killer.

Hiroki shouted, "Hyah!" and swung his pole, slapping a gun from Kiriyama's hand for the third time. The revolver sailed through the air, and before it landed, Hiroki wheeled the other end of the pole at

Kiriyama's face. Kiriyama's back was to the table—he wouldn't be able to dodge backward again.

But the broom handle stopped mere centimeters before it struck the killer's face. And then a third of the pole's length skimmed past Kiriyama's head as it went flying. Only then did Hiroki hear the wood snap. Kiriyama had brought up his left palm and chopped the broom handle in two.

The killer immediately followed with a right spear-hand strike to Hiroki's eyes.

Kiriyama's hand moved so quickly that it was a miracle Hiroki managed to duck in time.

But he did duck it, and as he did, now that he had dropped the broom handle, he grabbed Kiriyama's wrist with both hands. He twisted it back while at the same time driving his right knee into Kiriyama's stomach. The killer grunted but remained expressionless.

Keeping Kiriyama's wrist bent backward with his left hand, Hiroki drew his pistol with his right, cocking the hammer. He pressed the muzzle into Kiriyama's stomach and squeezed the trigger.

And he kept shooting until every last bullet was gone. Kiriyama's body shook with each shot.

When the pistol's slide locked, the eighth spent cartridge clattered to the floor, where it rolled and clinked against one of the others.

Still holding Kiriyama's wrist, Hiroki felt the strength slowly drain from his opponent's body. Kiriyama's head, with that slicked-back hair, went limp. Were Hiroki to release his wrist, his body would likely slump onto the corner of the table and slide to the floor.

But instead Hiroki stood fixed to the spot, facing his foe, breathing heavily, as if the two were locked in some strange dance.

I won.

He had won against *the* Kazuo Kiriyama—the same Kazuo Kiriyama who boasted an athletic ability superior to Shinji Mimura and maybe even Shuya Nanahara, and who, from what Hiroki had heard, had never lost a fight.

I beat the *Kazuo—*

Suddenly, sharp pain pierced through his right side. He grunted . . . and his eyes went wide.

Kazuo Kiriyama was looking up at Hiroki. And the knife in his left hand was digging into Hiroki's stomach.

Slowly, Hiroki's eyes moved from the knife back to Kiriyama's face. Kiriyama stared at him with those handsome, yet cold eyes.

How . . . is he . . . alive?

Hiroki had no way of knowing it was because Kiriyama was wearing Toshinori Oda's bulletproof vest. And right now, there wasn't any point in trying to figure it out.

Kiriyama twisted the blade, and Hiroki moaned. Hiroki started to lose his grip on Kiriyama's wrist.

Oh no, this is bad. Really bad.

But Hiroki summoned the strength to renew his grip. He swung up his other arm, which still held the emptied pistol.

His elbow connected with Kiriyama's chin.

Kiriyama flew back and skidded across the blood-covered white table. The blood splatter, which had resembled the flag of the Republic of Greater East Asia, now looked more like the stripes of the American flag. The knife came free, gouging out about thirty grams of flesh. Blood gushed out from the wound. Hiroki let out a gasp that emptied his lungs.

But the next moment, he was turning on his heels and running for the hallway door.

Just as he was passing through the doorway, he heard a gunshot, and the doorframe cracked. Kiriyama hadn't had time to pick up one of the many guns from the floor. He must have been carrying a fourth (probably strapped to one of his ankles).

Ignoring the gunfire, Hiroki ran.

He hurtled over the scattered chairs and desks at the entrance. The moment before he emerged outside, he heard that all-too-familiar machine-gun fire, but he was in a crouching run, and Kiriyama's shots missed.

The cloudy sky threatened to rain at any moment, yet seemed so terribly bright.

Hiroki sprinted for the thicket beyond the gate where the minivan was parked. Behind him, his red blood speckled the white earth.

He heard the machine gun again, but he had already burst into the thicket.

He didn't have time to rest now.

8 STUDENTS REMAIN.

It had begun to drizzle. In pale daylight muted by thick clouds and raindrops, the rain-washed island foliage took on a dark sheen.

Shuya slowly wove his way through the bushes. To his right, he had an open view of the sea, a dull gray beyond the white curtain of rain.

He was wearing his own shirt, uniform, and sneakers, which he'd found in the room where Yukie and her girls had been. Raindrops fell from tree branches and soaked his school coat. He carried the Uzi submachine gun slung from his shoulder, his right hand on its grip, and had tucked the CZ 75 pistol in the front of his slacks. The Browning—along with all the ammo he'd collected—was in the day-pack on his back.

Shuya had quickly distanced himself from the lighthouse. Some fifteen minutes later, when he had begun collecting branches to light the two signal fires near the northern cliffside, gunfire came from the direction of the lighthouse. He was not surprised. Even though the massacre had occurred inside, two of his classmates had likely heard the repeated gunfire, gone there, and ended up fighting.

After some indecision, Shuya decided to return to the lighthouse. The shots had sounded like Kazuo Kiriyama's machine gun—a sound he knew only too well. He doubted that Noriko and Kawada would have rushed toward the scene of the massacre, but few players remained. If one side of this battle was Kiriyama, then the other could very likely be Hiroki Sugimura—though it could of course also be Mitsuko Souma.

But the gunfire quickly ceased. Shuya reconsidered and decided not to return to the lighthouse. He didn't think he'd find anyone there now—except for possibly one more corpse added to those of Yukie and her girls.

The rain had started to fall just as Shuya had finished preparing the two signal fires atop the cliffs. He had found a lighter in the light-house, but with the rain, he hadn't been able to get the fires going.

When the rain worsened, Shuya gave up and moved on. Noriko and Kawada probably hadn't moved far. Sector C-3 was a forbidden zone now, but the adjacent D-3 and C-4 remained safe. They should still be somewhere in that area. He could make the fires once he was closer.

With that plan in mind, he began walking. But when the northern shoreline turned toward the west he heard the faint sound of a chirping bird far in the distance. This was near two-thirty in the afternoon. Shuya stopped to listen—and hurriedly looked at his watch. The second hand ticked seven times, and the faint chirping stopped. Kawada had said he would sound the birdcall for fifteen seconds. Once Shuya accounted for how long it took him to check his watch, that seemed to be about how long the chirping had lasted. And Shuya had the impression that most birds didn't chirp in the rain. At the very least, the occasional tweets he'd heard the afternoon before were otherwise entirely absent now.

Shuya continued along the northwest shore—and again he heard that chirping. This time, the sound was distinct. This call came exactly fifteen minutes after the last—and stopped after exactly fifteen seconds. *Kawada*. Without waiting for a signal fire, Kawada had been sending Shuya the call.

Three minutes had now passed since the third call. Shuya was getting close. According to his map, he was just entering Sector B-5 from B-6.

Shuya rested his feet for a moment. He put the Uzi's barrel under his left wrist and used the gun to lift his arm so he could see his watch. This way was easier than straining his muscles to lift the arm on its own. The watch's hands, distorted through the raindrops on the glass, indicated five after three.

The birdcall sounded like it came more from the mountain than near the shore. Shuya sent the sea one more glance, then proceeded up the gentle slope. He looked up and noticed that the shape of the northern mountain appeared different, and he realized how far he'd circled around the mountain and was now deep into the western shoreline.

Just a little more now. He hadn't walked a kilometer and a half, but he was feeling the effects of losing so much blood. His body was weak, and the severe pain from all his wounds was nearly enough to make him throw up. (He really needed to not be moving.) *But I'm almost there—almost there.*

He entered the thicket. Having to push his way through the bushes intensified his exhaustion. The danger of someone attacking from the undergrowth of course remained. But he couldn't afford to worry about that any longer. If that did happen, all he had to do was squeeze the trigger of his Uzi.

The thickly layered leaves became sparse, and the thicket suddenly opened into a clearing. Shuya froze. No gun-wielding foe awaited in this small open space—but he did find something unexpected.

At first, he thought they were two gray boulders. But they were moving. And when he really looked, he saw the legs, in sneakers and black slacks.

Corpses. Two boys had died here.

A small flash of red rose from one of the stiff gray clumps and cried, "Kaw!" It was a medium-sized bird—about as large as a heron— with its head stained red. They were feeding on the bodies.

Reflexively, Shuya raised the Uzi toward them and pressed his finger on the trigger . . . but he stopped himself. He walked toward them.

The birds flapped their wings and flew away from the bodies.

Shuya stood beside them in the rain. He felt a sudden urge to vomit and instinctively raised his right hand (which still held the Uzi) to his mouth.

It was a chilling sight. The birds had picked away at their exposed faces. Here and there, red flesh poked out through the skin. They were covered with blood.

Shuya managed to hold back his nausea while he looked at the bodies. They seemed to be Tadakatsu Hatagami and Yuichiro Takiguchi. Then he noticed that through no fault of the birds, Tadakatsu's face, which was by far the worse of the two, had been brutally mangled. Even his nose, which had so far escaped the birds' beaks, was crushed.

Shuya looked around and saw a bat lying nearby in the grass. Despite the rain, the bat's tip was still tinged red. Between the bat and Tadakatsu's face, the boy had apparently been beaten to death—the baseball player killed by the implement his sport depended on.

Yuichiro's face was in comparatively good shape—though it seemed to have been stripped of its lips and eyeballs.

Shuya heard flapping, and one of the birds returned to land on Tadakatsu's face. Then a few more came to join it. Since Shuya had been standing still, they must have thought it was safe.

You think you're safe, you bastards?

Shuya tightened his finger on the Uzi's trigger, but he stopped himself. Getting back to Kawada and Noriko was the most important thing now.

More of the birds returned.

Were the other bodies all over the island being eaten by birds like this? Or was it just because these two were near the sea?

Shuya tore his gaze away from the two bodies, walked unsteadily around them, and entered the thicket ahead. The birds cawed behind him.

As he walked farther, he felt another sudden urge to puke. He had become accustomed to people dying, but seeing them eaten by birds—by those filthy birds . . .

I'll never again be able to stand on a beach and feel at peace watching the birds fly. When I write my own songs, I'll never again sing about seabirds. I don't even think I'll want to eat poultry for while. Birds . . . suck.

But then he heard that chirping again. He looked up. Fat raindrops hit his face.

Well, birds suck . . . but maybe I can give the little ones a pass.

After exactly fifteen seconds, the chirping stopped. It seemed very close now.

Shuya looked around himself. The undergrowth continued up the gentle slope. *They must be . . . they must be around here. Kawada and Noriko must be right nearby. But where?*

Before he could think of an answer, the nausea he'd suppressed at the back of his throat resurged. *The two corpses and their sagging faces. And the birds making an afternoon snack of their soft flesh. Yummy.*

He knew he shouldn't puke. It would only weaken him further.

But.

Shuya fell to his knees and vomited. Since he hadn't eaten anything, all that came up were gastric juices. The sharp, acidic stench struck him.

Shuya threw up more. Something pink was mixed into the yellow liquid, like spilled paint. He wondered if his stomach was messed up too.

"Nanahara," a voice said.

Shuya looked up. Reflexively, he pointed the Uzi toward the voice. But then he slowly lowered the muzzle back toward the ground.

Amid the bushes was that face that would have been at home behind a carnival food stand. *Kawada.* In his left hand, he held a bow which he seemed to have carved from wood, and he was lowering an arrow in his right. Shuya realized, *Oh, that's right. I must have caught on his tripwire.*

"Bad hangover?" Kawada joked, but his voice was infused with a deep warmth.

With a rustling of leaves, Noriko appeared behind his shoulder. She gazed at Shuya, and beneath her rain-drenched hair, her eyes and mouth trembled.

Halfway knocking Kawada aside, she dragged her leg and ran to Shuya.

Shuya wiped his mouth and shakily rose. He let the Uzi drop on its sling and met her with a one-armed embrace. He didn't care that the impact of her body sent pain shooting through his side. He didn't care that their reunion came atop a fresh pile of puke. She clung to him, a warmth in the cold of the rain.

Buried in his chest, she looked up at him. "Shuya, Shuya, I'm so glad . . . I'm so glad." She was crying. Teardrops fell from the corners of her eyes and mixed with the raindrops that struck her face.

Shuya gave her a grin. Then he realized he too was nearly crying. Too many had died in this damn game. But he was happy the two of them were alive. He was as happy as could be.

Kawada walked over to them and thrust out his right hand. For a moment, Shuya was puzzled by the gesture . . . but then he understood. He held out his right hand past Noriko and shook Kawada's hand. It was large and thick.

His voice gentle, Kawada said, "Welcome back."

8 STUDENTS REMAIN.

A little down the slope toward the western shore, an outcropping of rock formed a low, seaward-facing wall amid the trees. Two large sticks stuck out from the rock face. (If Kawada had put them there, it must have taken him a lot of work with his knife.) Leafy branches stacked across the two sticks formed a shelter from the rain, and raindrops dripped from their tips.

After taking some potent painkillers Kawada had taken from the clinic, Shuya told them what had happened in the lighthouse. Kawada boiled water in a tin can using some charcoal. The sound of it bubbling melded with the falling rain.

When Shuya had finished his story, Kawada said, "I see," then let out a deep breath and put another Wild Seven into his mouth. He'd rested the Uzi between his legs. They'd decided to have him hold the submachine gun, while Shuya had the CZ 75, and Noriko carried the Browning. Kawada lit his cigarette.

With a feeble shake of his head, Shuya said, "It was awful."

Kawada blew a small puff of smoke and took the cigarette from his lips. "Yukie forming a big group ended up backfiring."

Shuya nodded bitterly. "It's hard . . . to trust someone."

"Yes, it is." Kawada dropped his eyes and nodded. "It's very hard."

He appeared to think about something as he continued to smoke in silence. Then he said, "In any case, I'm glad you made it out alive."

Shuya recalled Yukie's face. *I'm alive. Thanks to those girls, I'm alive. But now they're out of the game.*

Shuya looked at Noriko, who was sitting to his left. The news of the deaths of her friends, Yukie Utsumi and Haruka Tanizawa, had hit her hard, but now she was tending the water. When she saw it was boiling, she took out some bouillon cubes (also found by Kawada) and plopped two into the can. The scent of broth soon came drifting up.

Noriko asked, "Can you eat, Shuya?"

He looked at her and raised his eyebrows. He knew he needed to eat, but he had just thrown up—and besides, the image of those stiff gray lumps that were Tadakatsu Hatagami and Yuichiro Takiguchi still flickered in his mind. He couldn't summon an appetite. (Shuya hadn't mentioned the lumps, which were likely still wriggling a mere hundred meters away. He said that he had thrown up because of the pain he was in.)

Cigarette in mouth, Kawada said, "Eat, Nanahara. Noriko and I already had lunch."

Shuya looked at him. His stubble had thickened. Finally, Shuya nodded. Using a handkerchief, Kawada lifted the can by its lip and poured the soup into a plastic cup that he offered to Shuya.

Shuya took the cup and slowly lifted it to his mouth. The taste of broth filled his mouth, and the warm liquid slid down his throat and into his stomach. It didn't feel as bad as he'd expected.

Noriko held out a bread roll. Shuya accepted it and took a bite. And once he started, he was surprised to find out he was able to eat it. Just like that, the roll was gone. Regardless of his mental state, his body had been starving.

"Do you want more?" Noriko asked.

Shuya nodded and raised his empty cup. "A little more soup."

This time Noriko filled it.

He took the cup and said, "Noriko."

She looked up at him. "What?"

"Are you feeling better?"

"Yeah." She smiled. "I've been taking more of that cold medicine. I'm fine now."

Shuya looked at Kawada. He was facing to the side, smoking. Without looking back at Shuya, he nodded. He'd taken another of the antibiotic syringe kits when they left the clinic, but she must not have needed it.

Shuya turned to face Noriko again and returned her smile. "That's great."

Then she asked the same question she'd been repeating ever since he rejoined them. "Shuya, are you really all right?"

He nodded. "I'm all right."

He really wasn't, but what else could he say? Sticking out from the cuff of his uniform, his left hand was a different color than his right. He didn't know if it was because of the wound in his shoulder or the one in his upper arm. It might have been nothing more than the tight bandage around his elbow. His left arm felt like it was becoming more and more stiff.

Shuya took another sip of the soup and set the cup down by his feet. Then he called Kawada.

Kawada was inspecting the Uzi's condition. He raised an eyebrow and looked at Shuya. "What is it?"

"It's about Kiriyama."

As he contemplated the events of the past day, the question occupying his thoughts just before he was forced to split up with Kawada and Noriko suddenly came back to him. He was also thinking of that gunfire he'd heard after leaving the lighthouse. It was the same question he'd shouted when Kiriyama attacked them: *What the fuck does he think he's doing?* In other words, what kind of human being was Kazuo Kiriyama?

As far as Shuya could tell, Kiriyama wasn't the only student playing the game. There was Tatsumichi Oki, who Shuya had fought, and Yoshio Akamatsu. And if Hiroki Sugimura were to be believed, Mitsuko Souma would fall into the same camp. But Kiriyama was so lacking in mercy or hesitation, so cruel, and so calm. Shuya had always felt a strange otherness in Kiriyama, but inside this game, that feeling expanded to full size and came at him head-on. Shuya recalled those cold eyes he saw behind the flames erupting from the machine gun's muzzle, and shuddered.

Kawada hadn't said anything, so Shuya continued, "What's . . . what's up with him? I can't understand it."

Kawada looked down. He fidgeted with the safety switch, which was combined with the fire selector for the automatic and single shot modes.

Then Shuya remembered him saying that they didn't need to understand it. He expected to hear that same answer again.

But Kawada had a different response now. He looked up and said, "I've seen people like him before."

"In the last game?"

"No." Kawada shook his head. "Somewhere else. Somewhere completely different. When you're the son of a doctor in the slums, you see a lot of things."

He took out another cigarette and lit it. He exhaled smoke and then said, "I think he's a very hollow man."

Noriko asked, "Hollow?"

"Yeah." Kawada nodded. "There's no place in his heart for morality or love. No—for any kind of values at all to take root. That's the kind of person he is. And I doubt there's any reason for the way he is."

No reason, Shuya thought. *Does that mean he was born that way?*

Kawada took another drag and blew out smoke. "Sugimura mentioned Mitsuko Souma, right?"

Shuya and Noriko both nodded.

"We can't be sure she's really playing the game because we haven't seen her ourselves. From what little I've seen of them in school, they're similar. But Souma has purposefully rejected morality and love and all that. I'm sure there's some reason behind it. I don't know what it is. But Kiriyama doesn't have a reason. That's a big difference. He doesn't have a reason."

His eyes still on Kawada, Shuya murmured, "Scary."

"Yeah, it's scary," Kawada agreed. "Just think about it. It's probably not his fault. I mean, sure, you can say that nothing is anyone's fault—but at the very least, I don't think he has the capacity to grasp the unknown future. What would be scarier than to be born that way?"

Then he continued, "What I mean is, even an ordinary guy like me sometimes can think that everything is pointless. Why do I wake up and eat? It all ends up shit in the end. Why do I go to school and study? Even in the unlikely chance that I become successful in the future, I'm still going to die. You can dress nice and make people envious, or get rich, but none of it means anything. It doesn't mean a damn thing. Anyway, maybe such meaninglessness is appropriate for this shitty nation.

"But—and here's the 'but'—you and me, we have other emotions like happiness, right? We can find enjoyment. It's nothing that amounts to much—but isn't that what fills the emptiness inside us? At least for me, that's the only answer I know. So . . . I think Kiriyama lacks those emotions. And without them, he has no criteria around which to form any values. So all he does is choose. He chooses what to do. He doesn't have a fixed rudder. He just chooses at random. Take this game now, for instance. I think there was a good chance he could have chosen not to take part in the game. But he decided that's what he was going to do. That's my theory, anyway."

Then he added, "Yeah, it's scary—both that that kind of person could possibly exist, and that we have to go up against that kind of a person now."

Silence fell over the three. Kawada took one more drag on his shortened cigarette, then rubbed it out on the ground. Shuya picked up his cup of soup and took another sip.

Then Shuya looked up at the cloudy sky over the edge of Kawada's tree-branch canopy and said, "I wonder if Sugimura's all right."

He had already told the other two about the gunfire he'd heard after leaving the lighthouse, but he was still worried about it.

Noriko said, "I'm sure he is."

Shuya looked at Kawada and said, "I wonder if we'll be able to see his smoke."

Kawada nodded. "Don't worry. From here, we can see smoke from anywhere on the island. I'll check periodically."

This reminded Shuya about Kawada's birdcall. It had led him to them, but why did Kawada possess such a strange object in the first place? He intended to ask Kawada, but before he could, Noriko spoke.

"I wonder if Sugimura has been able to find Kayoko."

Kawada replied, "If he did, we'd be seeing smoke."

Noriko nodded, then softly said, "Why does he need to see her?"

They'd talked about this before they left the clinic. Now, as he had then, Shuya said, "Beats me." Then he added, "They didn't seem all that close."

But then Noriko said, "Oh," as if suddenly realizing something.

Shuya looked up at her. "What is it?"

"I don't know for sure." She shook her head. "But maybe . . ."

She let her sentence trail off. Shuya's eyebrows drew together. "Maybe what?"

Kawada interjected, "That's . . ." Shuya looked over to him. Kawada was staring down at a freshly opened pack of cigarettes. "That's too sentimental for this bullshit game."

"But," Noriko said, "it's Sugimura, so . . ."

Completely lost, Shuya looked back and forth between the two.

8 STUDENTS REMAIN.

Kayoko Kotohiki (Girls #8) sat in the bushes hugging her knees. She was halfway up the southern slope of the north mountain, in Sector E-7.

Evening was approaching, but the light coming into the brush remained largely unchanged. It just stayed dark. Heavy clouds descended after noon, and two hours ago it finally began to rain.

Kayoko wrapped a handkerchief over her head to shield herself from the rain. Thanks to the branches above, the rain didn't hit her directly, but the shoulders of her sailor fuku were drenched. She was cold. But more than that—she was scared.

She had first hidden directly east of the northern summit, in Sector C-8. She was practically close enough to have witnessed with her own eyes Yumiko Kusaka and Yukiko Kitano getting killed. She had held her breath and kept still. She knew their killer was near, but her intuition told her that moving would have been even more dangerous. She kept absolutely quiet, and the afternoon passed, and then the night, without anyone attacking her.

She had moved twice due to the forbidden zone announcements. The second time had been just after this noon, because Sector D-7, to the south of the summit, was going to become a forbidden zone at one o'clock. She was starting to get boxed in.

She hadn't run into anyone else yet. Sometimes distant, and at other times perilously close, she had heard gunfire and even explosions, but she remained still and quiet. And the broadcast every six hours announced her classmates' diminishing numbers.

At noon, fourteen remained. And after that, she heard more gunfire. Was it twelve left now? Or maybe ten?

Her pistol (a Smith & Wesson Model 59—though Kayoko couldn't have cared less what it was called) was heavy in her right hand, so she set it down at her feet and stretched out her fingers with her other hand. Having kept a tight grasp on the gun this whole time, her finger muscles felt like they might fall off. She turned over her hand and saw her palm, flushed red and with the distinct imprint of the textured pattern of the weapon's grip.

She was completely exhausted from the near total lack of sleep along with her thirst and hunger. Because she had been too afraid to enter any of the houses where her classmates might be hiding, the only food and drink she had was the supplied bread and water. Foremost was her grossly inadequate water intake. She had tried to stretch her allocated water as far as she could, and since the game began, she had only drunk a little more than a single liter. The one good thing about the rain was that she had been able to collect the rainwater by placing her empty bottle where the rain came off one of the branches. But even this didn't amount to a third of the bottle. Occasionally she took the wet handkerchief from atop her head and used it to moisten her dry lips, but that did nothing to alleviate her dehydration.

Kayoko let out a long, feeble sigh, brushed her shoulder-length hair over her ear, and gripped the M59. Her mind wandered.

Again she pictured his face—a face she'd visualized many, many times since the game began. She wasn't as close to him as she was to her parents or her sister, of whom she'd also been thinking, but the image of his face carried a great importance to her.

She had first seen him soon after she had begun studying the tea ceremony. It was in the fall of her seventh grade year, at a holiday event held for tourists at the request of a prefectural park. The performing of the actual ceremony was left to the adults, so Kayoko and the other students her age had all been assigned various small jobs like setting up the outdoor seating or preparing the sweets to be served with the tea. But *he* was one of the masters of the ceremony.

He had shown up rather late in the afternoon. He was handsome yet still boyish, and he looked like he could be in college. She had assumed he was one of the helpers, but he told her forty-two-year-old instructor, who was in one of the tea master's seats, "Hey, sorry I'm late," and the two switched places, and he began preparing the tea.

He was wonderful. He had mastered the tea cloth and moved the whisk with skill and grace, and he sat with impeccable posture. Despite his youth, he looked perfectly natural in traditional Japanese clothes.

She neglected her own tasks to gaze at him when someone tapped her on her shoulder. She turned and saw the girl, her senior in the Shiroiwa Junior High Tea Ceremony Club, who had dragged her into the tea ceremony classes.

"He's pretty hot, huh?" the girl said. "He's the headmaster's grandson. Well, actually, the headmaster's *mistress's* grandson. I'm a fan of his too. I'm still taking lessons pretty much because I want to meet him."

She told Kayoko that he was nineteen, and that by the time he graduated high school, he was already something of an assistant instructor, with many students of his own. At the time, Kayoko had simply thought, *He's from a different world,* and *So there are people like that out there.*

But whenever she heard he was going to make an appearance in one of her classes, she spent more time in front of the mirror. Given her age, makeup was out of the question, but she made sure her kimono was just right, and she combed her hair and carefully put in her favorite dark-purple hair clip in the perfect placement. *My flowing eyebrows; my long, tapered, if not large eyes; my well-shaped, if a little*

*short nose; my wide, firm lips . . . Okay, I might not be stunning, but
I do look pretty mature.*

He had scores of admirers, from girls her own age to middle-aged
women. The reasons she became ever more smitten with him didn't
have to be anything complex. After all, he was handsome and intelligent, cheerful and always considerate—the kind of ideal man that was
hard to believe existed. And what's more, Kayoko heard he didn't even
have a girlfriend.

But two particular encounters with him were memories she treasured (though to anyone else, they likely would have seemed trivial).

The first was at one of her tea ceremony school's regular demon-
strations, in the spring soon after she entered eighth grade. The
demonstration was being held at the headmaster's home in the town
of Shido, near Shiroiwa. But almost immediately after the ceremony
began, a problem arose. An official from the central government—a
representative on the regional cultural committee—who had been
invited as a special guest, suddenly began complaining about the way
the ceremony was being conducted. That kind of thing happened all
the time. Civil servants had their slogans, like "Serve the nation with
honesty and integrity," and so on, but many used their authority
for personal profit—for example, offering to arrange increased support from the national traditional arts fund to a tea ceremony school
in exchange for a kickback. The headmaster had politely declined.
Maybe this official was lashing out at the demonstrator for the headmaster's affront.

But the headmaster himself was in the hospital at the time. His
two heirs, one of whom he had left in charge in his absence, both fell
into a panic, and their lack of any competent response endangered
the future of the school. And who saved the day? Kayoko's crush. He
was only nineteen at the time. He escorted the problem official into
another room, and then after a little while, the young man returned
alone and said, "The gentleman has gone home. There's no need to
worry, everyone—he seems to have left in a more agreeable mood."

The young man said no more, and the seated higher-ups in the school didn't ask. The rest of the ceremony proceeded smoothly. But Kayoko was concerned. He might have assumed full responsibility, saying something like, "I'm in charge of today's ceremony," And if he did, he might have provoked that official into retaliating against him—a fabricated report could see him arrested for antigovernmental spiritual pollution (which would get him sent to one of those re-education camps).

After the tea demonstration concluded with no further interruptions, he led the cleanup. He was carrying some seat cushions when she caught him alone in the hall. Behind him, she worked up the nerve to say, "Hey." Still holding the cushions, he stopped and turned to her. His cool, clear eyes landed on her, and her heart raced. But she managed to speak. "Um . . . is everything all right?"

He seemed to understand what she meant and gave her a smile and said, "Thanks for your concern. But it'll be fine."

Her concern, meanwhile, had quickly been replaced with elation at having her first real conversation with him. Still, she continued, "But . . . but . . . that official looked so mean. What if—"

He stopped her and said something sophisticated, almost lecturing her. "That man doesn't act like that because he wants to. Sure, that kind of thing happens all over the world . . . but the way this country is structured—it twists people. We as people must seek harmony, and maybe that's what the art of tea is about."

Then, almost to himself, he added, "But in this country, it can be very hard."

He looked at her and continued, "Tea and its trappings have no power. But it's not such a bad thing either. You should enjoy it while you can."

He smiled kindly, turned, and walked away.

Enthralled, Kayoko stood there for a while. His unperturbed manner had put her at ease, and though she didn't completely understand what he was saying, she thought *Wow, he's so mature.* She was completely smitten by him.

In any case, she might have made some sort of impression on him, because ever since that encounter, he always gave her a warm smile whenever their eyes met.

The second—and to Kayoko, deciding—encounter came in the winter of eighth grade. At another tea ceremony—this time in a temple—Kayoko stepped outside and was gazing off at the camellias in the traditional garden. (Actually, she was thinking of him again.)

Suddenly from behind, she heard the airy voice she longed to hear.

"Beautiful, aren't they?"

For a moment, she thought she had imagined it. And when she turned, she could hardly believe he was standing there . . . and smiling at her. This was the first time he'd addressed her outside of tea ceremony lessons and organizational meetings.

And so they talked a little while.

"How are you liking it—the Way of Tea?" he said. "Do you think it's interesting?"

"Yes. Very. But I'm not that good at it."

"Really? I've been impressed with your excellent posture when you're preparing the tea. And I don't just mean that you keep your back straight—I guess I'd call it a kind of dignified air about you."

"What? Oh, no, not me . . ."

With his hands tucked into his sleeves and the gentle smile on his face, he looked up at the camellias and said, "No, I really do think so. You're just like these flowers—they're stiff, but in a way that's beautiful."

Sure, it might just have been an empty compliment for a fellow enthusiast. After all, she was still a child. Yet she thought, *All right!* (She didn't snap her fingers with glee until she was in the bathroom alone.)

Kayoko increasingly devoted herself to her practice. *I got this,* she thought. *I may still be a girl, but when I'm eighteen, he'll be twenty-four. That's a close enough match.*

Those were memories now.

Kayoko buried her face into her pleated skirt. Warm droplets wet the fabric at her knees—but this wasn't rainwater. She realized she was crying. Her hand holding the gun trembled. *Why is all this happening to me?*

She wanted so badly to see him. Yes, she was only a kid. But in her own adolescent way, she felt like she truly loved him. She had never seriously loved anyone until him. Just a single moment with him was all she wanted—being able to tell him how she felt would be enough. He had described her as beautiful, even if he was only referring to her manner at the tea ceremony, and she wanted to tell him, "I'm still a child, and I might not know what it is to be in love with someone, but I'm pretty sure I'm in love with you. I love you."

Even if it came out like that, she wanted to tell him.

Leaves rustled. She looked up. Wiping her tears with her left hand, she stood up. Her legs, moving of their own accord, took one step away from the sound.

A boy in a school uniform—Hiroki Sugimura (Boys #11)—emerged from the bushes, first his face and then his upper body. The right sleeves of his jacket and shirt had been torn off, leaving his arm bare. Red blood seeped through a white bandage at his shoulder. The rain had turned the red into a broad patch of pink. In his hand, she saw a gun.

Hiroki's face was smeared with dirt, and his mouth cracked open, but her eyes were drawn immediately to his. They seemed to glare at her.

Fear surged within her. *How did he get so close without me noticing? How did—*

"Kayoko," he said.

She screamed and turned on her sneaker heels. She ran into the bushes. She didn't care about the branches scratching at her face and tangling her hair. She didn't care about the rain soaking her. She just ran. She had to run, or she'd be killed. She knew it.

She emerged from the thicket and onto a winding, two-meter-wide mountain trail. She immediately decided to run downhill. Uphill, and he was sure to catch her. But downhill, maybe—

The leaves rustled behind her. "Kayoko!" Hiroki shouted.

He's catching up!

Kayoko spurred on her exhausted body and ran for her life. *I can't believe this. If I knew this was going to happen, I would have taken up cross-country instead of tea.*

"Kayoko! Please wait. Kayoko!"

If she had been calmer—that is, if she had been munching on popcorn while watching actors play out this scene in a movie, she would have recognized that he was pleading with her. But instead she took it to mean: *"Kayoko! Stop right there! I'm gonna kill you!"*

She wasn't about to stop. Ahead, the path forked. She chose the left.

On her left, the woods opened onto a terraced tangerine grove. The irregular rows of low trees spread out in the dreary light of the misty rain. Beyond them she saw another thicket. *If I can make it into there, I might . . .*

No, it's impossible.

Fifty meters separated her from the thicket. It was hopelessly far. He'd catch up to her while she was still stumbling her way through the uneven rows of tangerine trees—and he'd shoot her in the back.

Kayoko gritted her teeth. She didn't want to do this. But it was her only choice. He was trying to kill her.

She stopped on her right foot and spun around to her left.

By the time she had turned around, she was holding her gun in both hands. She'd turned off the manual safety, it was called, as soon as she read the instructions, and she'd left it that way. The instructions had said she didn't need to cock the hammer, only pull the trigger. The rest came down to whether or not she could actually handle the thing.

Seven or eight meters up the sloping path, Hiroki froze with his eyes wide.

Too late. What, did you think I wouldn't shoot?

Kayoko held her arms locked straight out. She squeezed the trigger. With a bang, a small flame rose from the muzzle, and her arms jerked up from the recoil.

The well-built Hiroki spun and fell on his back.

Holding on to her gun, she ran toward him. *I have to finish him off. I have to! I can't let him get up again.*

She stopped about two meters away from him. A small hole had opened in the left side of his chest. (She had aimed at his stomach.) Around the hole, the fabric of his jacket was starting to turn dark red. His arm had been flung out onto the ground, but he was still holding the gun. He could raise it at any moment. *His head. I have to aim for his head.*

He turned his head and looked at her. She aimed her pistol down at him and squeezed the—

Her finger froze. Hiroki had tossed aside his gun. If he had that much strength left, he could have fired at her. What was going on?

His gun rolled over once, then fell on its side.

Huh?

As the rain fell on her wet, shoulder-length hair, and she held the gun steady in both hands, she stood there, motionless.

"Listen to me," Hiroki said. He was lying on the uneven path where rain puddles had begun to form. He seemed to be in pain, but he held his eyes fixed on her. "Burn fresh wood. Two . . . fires. There's a lighter in my pocket. When . . . you do that, you'll hear a birdcall."

Kayoko heard what he was saying but couldn't begin to understand. She didn't even understand what was happening.

Hiroki continued, "Go toward the bird's call. You'll find Nanahara . . . and Noriko Nakagawa, and Kawada. And they'll save you. Got it?"

"W-what?"

He almost seemed to be smiling. Patiently, he repeated, "Make two fires. Then follow the bird's call."

He stiffly reached his hand into his pocket, took out a cheap one-hundred-yen lighter, and tossed it toward her. Then he winced and closed his eyes.

"Okay," he said. "Now hurry."

"*What?*"

He flung his eyes open and shouted, "Run! Get away from here! Someone might have heard the gun. Run!"

Then, as if the pieces of a far-too-complicated jigsaw puzzle had fallen into place and revealed a picture, Kayoko finally understood what was happening. This time, she got it right.

"Oh . . . oh . . ." she said.

The pistol dropped from her hand. She fell on her knees beside him. She scraped her knees, but she didn't care about that now.

"Hiroki! Hiroki! I . . . what have I done?"

Kayoko didn't realize it, but she was crying. Sure, Hiroki Sugimura was a little intimidating. He seemed like he'd be violent, since he studied kempo or some kind of martial art. He rarely talked, and when he did he was curt. When he was talking with other boys—like Shinji Mimura and Shuya Nanahara—sometimes he smiled, but otherwise, he was generally surly. Kayoko had heard he was going out with Takako Chigusa, and the two did seem to be very close, but Kayoko thought, *I really don't get her tastes. Maybe when you're as pretty as she is, you're attracted to dangerous boys.*

In any event, that was her impression of him. And in this game, where her classmates were dying one by one, he absolutely terrified her. But then . . . this happened.

He closed his eyes again and said, "It's all right." He was smiling. He looked *happy*. "I was going to die soon anyway."

Finally Kayoko noticed another wound in his right side, thoroughly soaked in a liquid that wasn't rain.

"So . . . go now," he said. "Please."

She began to sob. She gently touched his neck. "Let's . . . let's go together. Okay? Stand up."

Hiroki opened his eyes and looked at her. He seemed to be smiling with his eyes too.

"I'm fine now," he said. "I just wanted to see you. That's enough for me."

"What?"

Kayoko opened her teary eyes wide. *What? What was that? What did he say?*

Her voice trembling, she said, "What . . . what do you mean?"

He exhaled deeply, as if to help endure the pain—or maybe it was just a long sigh.

"If I tell you, will you go?"

"What? Tell me what you mean."

He told it to her plain and simple. "I love you, Kayoko. I've always loved you."

She still couldn't process it. *What is he talking about?*

Looking up at the rain, he continued, "That's all I wanted to tell you. Now hurry—run."

Kayoko's next words tumbled from her lips almost without her knowing it. "But . . . you . . . and Takako . . ."

He gazed into her eyes one more time. "I love *you*."

At last she understood. The truth crashed into her mind with a tremendous impact, like getting struck by a wrecking ball.

You love me? You wanted to tell me? You weren't searching for me, were you? If you were, then what have I done?

Several times she tried to speak, but her voice came as only air rasping through her throat. But then finally words came.

"Hiroki! Hiroki!"

"Hurry," he said, and then he coughed out a mist of blood that sprayed Kayoko's face. He opened his eyes again.

"Hiroki . . . I . . . I . . . I . . ."

The lack of drinking water had left her thoroughly dehydrated, but her tears kept coming and coming.

"It's all right," he said gently. He closed his eyes. "Kayoko . . ." He said her given name, which he'd never dared use before, as if it were a precious treasure. "If I die because of you, I don't mind at all. So, I'm begging you, run away from here now. Or else—"

As the tears streamed from her eyes, Kayoko waited for him to continue. *Or else what?*

When Hiroki didn't say anything, she reached out for him. She took hold of his shoulders and shook.

"Hiroki! Hiroki!"

When people died in television shows, they would always stop mid-word, like "Or el—" But Hiroki had managed to say, his voice pained but distinct, "Or else." He must have had more to say. *Or else what?*

"Hiroki! Come on, Hiroki!"

She shook him once more and finally realized he was dead.

And the instant she did, the dam inside her restraining her torrent of emotions suddenly ruptured. She felt a cry force its way out her throat.

Then the cry became a wail. Kneeling on the ground beside him, she fell over him and wept.

He loved me. He ignored everything but his feelings, and searched for me, putting himself at risk of becoming someone else's target. What hardships had he faced? Anytime he ran into someone else, they could have attacked him. That's why he had that wound in his side . . . and the one in his shoulder . . . Because he was looking for me.

But that wasn't all. For a moment, Kayoko's gasping sobs ceased.

I attacked him—at the very end, just as he'd finally realized his goal.

She shut her eyes tightly and wept more.

He loved me. Just as I wanted to tell my love how I feel about him, so did Hiroki. And he went looking for me. A boy in my class cared for me that much. But I . . . but I . . .

Suddenly, a memory came back to her. During the student cleaning period after the last class of the day, Kayoko was wiping down the blackboard with a damp cloth. When she couldn't reach the top, Hiroki—who had been slacking off, resting his chin on his hands atop the end of a broom handle—said, "You're short, Kayoko." Then he snatched the cloth from her hand and wiped the blackboard for her.

Only now had she remembered it.

Why hadn't I recognized his nice side? Why hadn't I noticed his feelings, when he loved me so much?

If I'd only tried to think about it, I would have asked myself why, if he wanted to kill me, he hadn't shot me right away. But I didn't understand that. I couldn't understand that for you. I'm so stupid.

Another memory came to her.

Talking to her friends in class, she was squealing over her crush, when Hiroki, who was looking out a nearby window, muttered, "You're making a fool of yourself." That made her mad at the time, but he had been right. She was a fool. And yet he'd told this foolish girl, *I've always loved you.*

She couldn't stop crying. His cheek still felt warm against hers as she wept and wept. He'd told her to run, but she couldn't bring herself to even try. *I'm going to keep on crying—crying over the sincere dedication of the boy who loved me (I wouldn't trade that for anything), and crying over my own stupidity (I really am such a child—how could I have ever thought I'd be a match for someone six years older). I'm just going to keep on crying right here—even if it's suicidal in this game.*

A voice whispered in her mind. *"So you're planning on a murder-suicide?"*

"Yes, yes I am," she said aloud to herself. "I'm going to die with him—with his love for me, and with my stupidity."

Then someone else said, "All right then, go ahead."

A shiver ran through her. She looked over her shoulder, and Mitsuko Souma (Girls #11), with her long, beautiful, black, wet hair, looked down at her—holding a gun.

With a dry-sounding *bang bang,* two holes opened in Kayoko's right temple, and her body slumped over that of Hiroki Sugimura.

Blood slowly flowed from the holes in her temple. As if in defiance against the washing rain, it kept coming and coming and trickled down her face.

Mitsuko lowered the .357 Magnum Smith & Wesson Model 19 she'd taken from Tadakatsu Hatagami. Then she said, "You really were a fool, Kayoko. Why couldn't you understand him?"

Her eyes landed on Hiroki's face. "Long time no see, Sugimura. You got to die alongside your love. Are you happy now?"

She shook her head in disgust. She started walking toward the Smith & Wesson Model 59 Kayoko had dropped, and the Colt M1911 Hiroki had tossed aside (that had been in Mitsuko's possession earlier).

Mitsuko glanced down at the two bodies and put a finger to her lips. "Now what was that about building a fire?"

She shook her head again. Kayoko's skirt was covering part of the M59. Mitsuko kicked the cloth aside and was reaching down for the gun, its metal surface gleaming blue in the rain, when she heard the typewriter-like *brattattattattattat*.

6 STUDENTS REMAIN.

At the same time, several impacts jolted Mitsuko's back. The front of her sailor blouse was shredded, and her blood sprayed out. She staggered, and a burning sensation quickly spread through her body, like smoldering embers had been pressed into her.

She didn't feel so much surprised or confused by the pain as she felt indignant. *How could I not have heard him sneaking up on me through all this mud?*

Though she had already taken more than one person's share of bullets, Mitsuko managed to turn around.

A boy in a school uniform was standing there. He had long, slicked-back hair, grown out in the back, a handsome, well-defined face, and those clear, frigid eyes. Kazuo Kiriyama (Boys #6).

Mitsuko tightened her grip on the M1911 in her right hand. The muscles in her back were all but useless now, but she mobilized whatever strength she had left and tried to raise the gun.

But then, amid this life-or-death battle, her thoughts suddenly plunged into another time and place. It all might have lasted but an instant.

She had told Hiroki Sugimura, who was now lying at her feet, "I just decided to take instead of being taken."

When did I start living that way? Was it like I told him—when I was nine and those three men raped me? When I was in that shabby apartment in the run-down district at the edge of town, where they had that video camera, and they raped me? Or was it when my own drunk mother (she never had a father) *brought me to that room, then took a fat envelope from those men and left before they began? Was that when it started? Or was it not until the one elementary school teacher who I trusted came to me, after the terrible trauma had left me feeling dead inside, and when I finally told him what had happened the look in his eye changed and he raped me too? Was it there, in the dark, confined archival room? Or was it when my best friend saw it (or at least part of it), and instead of comforting me, she spread rumors about it (and the teacher went away)? Or was it three months later, when my mother tried to take me to do* that *again, and I resisted her and accidentally killed her? After I got rid of all the evidence and knew to make it look like a burglary, and I was sitting alone on a park swing? Or was it after that, when I was taken in by my distant relatives, and their daughter did nothing but bully me, and when she slipped and fell from the roof of an old, tall building, and her mother accused me of killing her because I was there with her? Or how about when her father intervened and defended me, but then a little while later, he too started molesting me? Or was it after that, when—*

Little by little—no, a lot by a lot—they all took from her. No one gave her anything. Mitsuko became a hollow shell.

But none of that matters.

I am right. I will not lose.

Strength filled her arm, and she raised her pistol. The tendons of her wrist rose up and looked like violin strings. And then she squeezed the—

With a *brattattattat*, flames erupted from Kiriyama's Ingram MAC-10. From Mitsuko's chest to the middle of her face, four holes opened in a vertical line. Blood spurted from the split in her upper lip, and she bent back.

But even after that, Mitsuko smiled. She stood up straight and squeezed the trigger, again and again.

Each one of the four bullets she had left went into his chest.

Though his body made tiny jerks, he remained unperturbed. Mitsuko didn't know why. Then his Ingram spat fire one last time.

Her once-beautiful face exploded, and she looked like she'd been hit with a strawberry pie. This time, her body was flung backward, and she landed in the mud. By now she was dead. She might have been dead for a while now—physically, a few seconds before; spiritually, a long, long time ago.

Kazuo Kiriyama walked up to her and calmly pried the gun from her fingers. He also picked up the M1911 lying by Hiroki Sugimura's hand, and then the Model 59 Kayoko had discarded. As the rain beat down on the three corpses, he didn't give them a single glance.

5 STUDENTS REMAIN.

70

Mizuho Inada (Girls #1) peeked out from the shade of the bushes. The ceaseless rain had plastered her neatly trimmed bangs to her forehead.

Beyond the bushes was a small planting field. Through the gauze of rain, she could see the back of a uniformed boy in the middle of the field. Like hers, his slicked-back hair was also wet. It was Kazuo Kiriyama (Boys #6).

Kiriyama had formed two piles of various branches. He was sitting in front of one of the piles, shaping it.

Mizuho steadied her breathing. She was cold and tired, but she didn't mind it much. After all, the time had come for her to carry out her greatest mission . . .

. . . as an anime space warrior.

The voice of the God of Light, Ahura Mazda, came to her.

ARE YOU READY, WARRIOR PREXIA DIKIANNE MIZUHO?

The voice seemed to emanate from the spindle-shaped mystical crystal Mizuho wore around her neck. (Actually, the mail-order item was glass, but Mizuho *believed* it was a crystal.)

Of course, Mizuho replied. *I saw the demon walk away from where he killed Yumiko Kusaka and Yukiko Kitano. I lost track of him for a while, but I just now found him again. And I saw him kill that other demon, Mitsuko Souma, who killed Kayoko Kotohiki. He is an enemy who must be defeated. And now I've followed him here.*

SATISFACTORY. AND YOU UNDERSTAND YOUR MISSION?

Of course. I received your message from the fortune teller—that I was destined to battle evil for the sake of the planet. At the time, I didn't understand what you meant. But now I know.

SATISFACTORY. ARE YOU NOT AFRAID?

No. I follow your guidance and have nothing to fear.

SATISFACTORY. YOU ARE THE LAST SURVIVOR OF THE HOLY TRIBE DIKIANNE. YOU ARE THE CHOSEN ONE. THE LIGHT OF VICTORY WILL SHINE UPON YOU. . . . HM? WHAT IS IT?

Oh, no, it's nothing. It's just . . . O Great Ahura Mazda, my fellow warrior Lorela Lausasse Kaori died. (Kaori Minami, who sometimes hung out with her in class, always had to stifle a yawn whenever Mizuho told her she was "the warrior Lorela." But anyway.)

She—

SHE FOUGHT TO THE END, MIZUHO.

Oh. Oh. I thought she would have. But . . . but she lost, didn't she—to the evil.

AH. WELL. YES, SHE DID. UMM . . . BUT YOU SEE, THE THING ABOUT THAT IS, UH, SHE WAS ONLY OF COMMON BIRTH. YOU'RE DIFFERENT. ANYWAY, DON'T FUSS OVER THE DETAILS. THE IMPORTANT THING IS FOR YOU TO FIGHT. DO IT FOR HER SAKE AS WELL. AND WIN, MIZUHO. UNDERSTOOD?

. . . Yes.

OKAY THEN. IT'S TIME FOR THE LIGHT. BELIEVE IN THE COSMIC LIGHT—THE LIGHT THAT ENVELOPS YOU.

Light filled her with the warm cosmic power that engulfed all things.

Finding her inner peace, Mizuho nodded. *Yes. Yes. Yes.*

She unsheathed her double-edged knife (she had found it in her daypack and considered it an appropriate weapon for a warrior) and held it in both hands in front of her face. A white light filled the bluish blade. She looked through that light at Kiriyama.

His back was turned. He was defenseless.

NOW. NOW IS THE TIME TO SMITE YOUR ENEMY!

Yes!

Mizuho weaved through the bushes so as not to make any noise, then she sprinted at Kiriyama. The light sprang out from the fifteen-centimeter-long blade, and the knife transformed into a meter-long sword of legend. The sword of light would pierce straight through the evil monster with a single thrust.

As Kiriyama straightened the branches with his left hand, he drew his Beretta 92F with his right. Without turning to look, he extended his arm behind his back and squeezed the trigger twice.

The first shot hit Mizuho in the chest, stopping her, and the second caught her in the face.

As she fell backward, blood spurted, tracing gentle curves of red in the air. The rain immediately began washing away the blood. The warrior Prexia Dikianne Mizuho's soul transmigrated to the Land of Light.

His back still turned to her, Kazuo Kiriyama put away his gun and continued arranging the branches.

4 STUDENTS REMAIN.

71

The rain continued. Shuya was slumped against the wet rock wall as he watched the raindrops dripping from the edge of the thatched canopy. About twenty minutes ago, he'd heard a lot of gunfire. Then five minutes ago, two single shots rang out. Neither of these had sounded nearby, but they hadn't seemed very far either. They had probably come from somewhere else on the same northern mountain where Shuya's group of three were keeping watch.

A large raindrop slid from a leaf of their shelter's would-be roof. The bead of water landed on the ground right next to Shuya's extended right leg and sent up a muddy splash on his Keds sneaker.

Noriko had said, "Maybe Hiroki's in love with Kayoko. If I were him . . . I'd do the same thing." She glanced at Shuya. "I'd look for the person I cared about."

Is that true about Hiroki? Is he in love with Kayoko Kotohiki? He was always with Takako Chigusa, the hottest girl in class, so why would he fall for a girl as utterly plain as Kayoko?

Well, I guess falling for someone can work like that. After all, Billy Joel sang of loving a girl just the way she was.

Shuya wondered who was involved in those two shootouts—though the latter had seemed more like one student shooting another.

Including the gunfire that came soon after leaving the lighthouse, he'd heard shooting on three separate occasions since midnight (not counting what happened with Yukie Utsumi's group). The reasonable assumption would be that at least three others had died. That would mean only five were left.

Which three had died? Or had no one died at all, and everyone had managed to escape the various confrontations? Then there'd still be eight students remaining.

Shuya, Noriko, and Kawada were sitting next to each other along the rock wall. From the far side of Noriko, Kawada asked him, "Are you tired?"

Shuya looked over at the two.

"Maybe you should sleep a little," Kawada offered.

"No." Shuya gave him a smile. "I slept all the way till the afternoon. I bet you're the one who hasn't slept."

Kawada shrugged. "I'm fine. But Noriko—she didn't sleep at all, waiting for you."

Shuya looked at Noriko, but she waved her palms at him, and with a smile, she said, "That's not true. I'm pretty sure I was dozing off. But Kawada—he stayed awake all night for me."

She looked at Kawada, who grinned and shrugged. He put his hand to his chest in a dramatic salute and said, "I shall always guard you, Your Highness."

Noriko grinned at this, then put her hand over his and said, "Really, thank you, Kawada."

Shuya's eyebrows raised a little as he watched the two of them. He found it strange how close Noriko and Kawada seemed. When they first met Kawada after the start of the game, she had only talked to him through Shuya. But now everything was completely different—the two of them made a good team on their own. Shuya figured that was only natural, though, since the two had spent over half a day together while he was gone.

Kawada suddenly pointed at Shuya and said, "Hey, look, Nanahara is getting jealous 'cause we're acting friendly."

Noriko's eyes widened as she looked at Shuya. Immediately, she grinned and said, "No way!"

Shuya blushed. "Am not. What are you talking about?"

Kawada shrugged. He raised his eyebrows and, with mock surprise, said to her, "Oh, he's saying he trusts you. Because he loves you."

Shuya opened his mouth, but was caught speechless. Kawada started to laugh. He cracked up. Then Shuya, who was still trying to think of a response, began to laugh with him. Noriko smiled too.

It was a brief but blissful moment. This was the kind of conversation and laughter longtime friends might share after school in their favorite café—even if he couldn't shake the feeling that it was a reunion after the funeral of a mutual friend.

With the laughter still in his expression, Kawada looked down at his watch, then went out to check for Hiroki Sugimura's signal.

Noriko gave Shuya the hint of a smile and said, "Kawada's always joking."

Shuya smiled back. "Yeah, but . . ."

He looked up.

Maybe I was *jealous.*

He faced Noriko again. He was about to tell her—to pass it off as a joke—"Maybe I *was* jealous." And then she'd laugh and say, "No way!" again.

But Kawada was back outside the shelter. His stubbled face was wet from the rain.

"I saw smoke," he said and quickly turned around again.

Shuya scrambled to his feet. He lent Noriko his uninjured arm and helped her stand. The two of them joined Kawada where he stood.

The rain had eased up, enough so that Shuya could see the smoke drifting in the sky. He followed Kawada's eyes, and there, on the opposite side of the northern mountain, he saw two columns of white smoke.

Without thinking, Shuya let out a quiet version of a rock-and-roll shout. "Right on!"

His and Noriko's eyes met. Grinning as much as he was, she said, "Hiroki's all right."

Facing the smoke, Kawada took the birdcall from his pocket and chirped it. The cheerful sing-song call took to the air and spread into the rain that enveloped the island. He kept an eye on his watch and stopped sounding the call after precisely fifteen seconds.

Then he looked at Shuya and Noriko and said, "Let's wait here a while longer. I don't think he'll be able to hear this until he's really close. This'll take time."

They got back under the roof of their shelter.

Noriko said, "He must have found Kayoko."

Shuya was about to nod, but he saw Kawada purse his lips and stopped. Noriko lost her smile.

Shuya said, "Kawada . . ."

Kawada looked up and shook his head. "It's nothing. I just think there are other possibilities."

"Huh? But . . ." Shuya turned over his right palm and gestured with it. "Hiroki's not the kind of guy who gives up."

Kawada nodded. "Maybe so." He paused, then looked away from them. "But Kayoko might have been dead when he found her."

Shuya frowned. Kawada was right, of course. Kayoko had at least lived until noon, but there had been all that gunfire—and then those two single shots not long ago. After combing the island for her for two days straight, he could have found her dead.

"Or," Kawada continued, "everything could have gone differently."

Noriko asked, "What do you mean?"

Kawada answered as he took the pack of cigarettes from his pocket. "Kayoko might not have trusted him."

Shuya and Noriko both fell silent.

Lighting a cigarette, Kawada continued, "Anyway, all we can do is pray he reaches us here. I just don't know if he'll be with Kayoko or not."

Kawada didn't need to tell Shuya to pray; he already was—for Hiroki to come back with Kayoko Kotohiki.

Then we'd be five. Five of us can escape.

Only five.

Then Shuya remembered that Mizuho Inada was still alive—or at least she had been alive at noon.

"Kawada," he said.

Kawada looked at Shuya without turning his head.

"Inada is still alive," Shuya said. "Do you think we can contact her somehow?"

Kawada shrugged. "I know I'm repeating myself, but you shouldn't be too trusting of others in this game. Honestly, I don't even trust Kayoko—my apologies to Hiroki."

Shuya bit his lip. "Yeah, but—"

"If circumstances allow, we can think up a way to reach Inada." He blew out smoke. "But don't forget, there's no guarantee *we'll* live long enough to try it."

Kawada had said that he had a way out—but only at the very end, when everyone else was dead. That meant they would have to battle Kiriyama one more time—or possibly Mitsuko Souma. Shuya wasn't sure about her, but he knew there'd be no avoiding Kiriyama—that boy wouldn't die so easily. And Shuya's three might not all survive.

Kawada took another drag from his dwindling cigarette and said, "I'm going to ask you again, Nanahara."

He exhaled a puff of smoke and watched Shuya's eyes as he continued. "Even if we manage to meet up with Hiroki, we'll have to fight Kiriyama again, or maybe Souma. Are you prepared to be merciless?"

That's how it was going to be. Any attempt to make contact with Mizuho Inada would have to come after they'd killed Kiriyama and Mitsuko. No matter what the circumstances were, Shuya didn't like how used he'd become to the thought of killing his classmates.

But he nodded and said, "I am."

4 STUDENTS REMAIN.

72

Kawada sounded the birdcall. This was the third time. The rain was letting up; drops fell less frequently from the edge of the canopy. It was already past five o'clock.

Shuya had heard Kawada's birdcall four times before he'd been able to rejoin him and Noriko—but that was only because he already had a general idea of where they'd be. Without the same clue, Hiroki Sugimura might take longer to find them.

When Kawada came back into the shelter, he put another Wild Seven between his lips and lit it.

He blew out a single puff of smoke. Out of the blue he asked, "Where do you want to go?"

Shuya looked past Noriko at Kawada. Kawada turned his head to him.

"I didn't think to mention this before," Kawada said, "but I know a guy. When we first get off this island, we'll hide out at his place."

"A guy?" Shuya asked.

Kawada nodded. "He's a friend of my dad's."

He continued, "He'll get us out of the country. I'm sure you won't object. If we stay in the country, we'll be caught sooner or later. We'll be hunted down and killed like rats."

With some surprise, Noriko said, "We can really do that—escape the country?"

Shuya asked, "Who is this guy, this friend of your father's?"

Kawada put his hand to the cigarette and looked thoughtfully at his two companions, but not for long. He took the Wild Seven from his mouth and said, "I think it's best if I don't tell you that."

He added, "If we get split up while we're on the run, and the government catches you two, it would be bad if you talked. Now hold on, I'm not saying I don't trust you. But once they start torturing you, it's only a matter of time before you spill. So I'll have to lead you to him myself."

Shuya thought about it a moment, then nodded. It seemed like the right call to him.

"But . . . let's see," Kawada said. He returned the cigarette to his lips and pulled a sheet of paper from his pocket.

It was one of those sheets on which they'd all had to write, *We will kill each other.* Kawada tore it in half and began writing something in pencil on both the pieces. He neatly folded them into two small pieces and gave one each to Shuya and Noriko.

Shuya asked, "What's this for?" and started to open his up, but Kawada stopped him.

"You don't need to look at that yet. It's just a way we can reach each other if we get split up. There's a time and a place. Every day, go to that place at that time. I'll do what I can to make it there."

Noriko asked, "Can't we read it now?"

"Nope," Kawada said. "It's only for if we get split up. Don't look at it until then. You see, your notes are different. It's best if neither of you knows what I wrote for the other—just in case one of you gets caught."

Shuya and Noriko looked at each other, then back to Kawada.

"I'm not leaving Noriko's side," Shuya said. "No matter what."

"I know that," Kawada said with a pained smile. "But it happened when Kiriyama attacked us. We can't be sure it won't happen again, right?"

Shuya pressed his lips together and looked at Kawada—but in the end, he nodded, then sent Noriko a glance and put the note in his pocket. Noriko did the same.

Kawada was right. Anything could happen. Just escaping the island in the first place was going to be incredibly difficult.

But then, Shuya thought, *shouldn't Noriko and I come up with our own meeting place—without telling Kawada? Then again, if he gets captured, Noriko and I will have nowhere to turn.*

His thoughts were interrupted when Kawada said, "So . . . where do you want to go?"

Shuya had forgotten the question. He folded his arms and took his time thinking about where he'd want to go once they'd fled the country.

Then he said, "I suppose America, after all. The birthplace of rock. I've always wanted to go there at least once."

I just never thought I'd be escaping to there.

"Uh-huh." Kawada nodded. "And you, Noriko?"

"I don't really have anywhere in mind, but . . ."

She glanced at Shuya, who nodded and offered, "Let's go together. Right?"

Her eyes went wide. She made the most modest of smiles and nodded. "Yes, of course—if it's all right with you."

Kawada grinned. He took another drag on his cigarette and asked, "What are you going to do in America?"

Shuya thought a little more, then answered with a wry smile. "I'll try my hand at busking with a guitar to start, and save up a little money."

Kawada chuckled. "You should become a rocker. You've got the talent. I hear immigrants and refugees aren't at too much of a disadvantage in America."

Shuya sighed and made a pained expression. "I'm nothing special. I don't have what it takes to be a pro."

Kawada shook his head and offered him a reassuring smile. "Don't be so sure about that." Then to Noriko, he asked, "What about you? Is there anything you want to do?"

She pursed her lips tightly, then said, "I've been thinking about becoming a teacher."

She'd never mentioned this before, so Shuya was taken by surprise. "Really?" he asked.

She nodded to him, and he asked, "You wanted to be a teacher in *this* lousy country?"

She looked a little hurt. "There are good teachers here too." Her eyes dropped. "I thought Mr. Hayashida was a good teacher."

It had been a little while since Shuya had last thought of their teacher's dead body and his caved-in head. *He died for us. The "Dragonfly" died for us.*

"Yeah, he was," Shuya agreed.

"Well," Kawada said, "it might be tougher for a refugee to become a teacher. But you might be able to do research in some university. Ironically enough, the rest of the world is very interested in our country. So in a way, you'd be able to do some sort of teaching."

Gazing ahead with his face in profile to the two, he tossed his cigarette butt into a puddle at his feet. He lit up a fresh one and replaced it, then continued, "Go for it, both of you. Be what you want to be. Follow your hearts and give it your all."

Shuya liked the sound of that. *Follow my heart. Give it my all.* He was reminded of his friend Shinji Mimura—he was dead now—who would sometimes say things like this, things that hit upon a truth of the way the world should be.

He liked the sound of it. But then another thought took over. *Something's missing in the way Kawada's talking.*

He quickly realized what it was.

Panic edged into his voice as he asked, "What about you? What are you going to do?"

Kawada shrugged. "I told you already. I owe this country payback. Actually, no. It owes me, and I'm going to collect—whatever it takes. I can't go with you."

With sorrow, Noriko said, "No . . ."

But Shuya's thoughts went in a different direction. He clenched his teeth.

"If you're taking action," he said, "let me help."

Kawada peered into his face for a moment, but then he dropped his gaze and shook his head with a dismissive snort. "Don't be stupid."

"Why not?" Shuya pressed harder. "I'd like to get back at this shithole of a country too."

"He's right," Noriko added, a little to Shuya's surprise. She looked at Kawada and continued, "We'll do it together. All of us."

Kawada looked from one of them to the other, then lifted his shoulders and lowered them with a deep sigh.

He lifted his head and said, "Listen. I think I told you this before. This country may be a shithole, but it's a well-made one. Taking it down won't be easy. Hell, right now, it's likely impossible. But I . . ."

He craned his neck to look out from the canopy. The rain was letting up, and the sky was white. He looked back to Shuya and Noriko.

"I'll get in at least one good slash. I'll have my revenge. Even if it's only for my own satisfaction, that's not so bad."

He paused, then repeated, "That's not so bad."

Shuya started to say, "But—"

But Kawada held up his hand and said, "I haven't finished talking."

Shuya went quiet, and he continued.

"I'm telling you that you will die if you come with me. And you just now told Noriko you'd go together." He looked at Noriko and then back at Shuya. "That means you still have her. Protect her, Nanahara. And if it ever looks like she's in danger, fight—whether you're up against a burglar, the Republic of Greater-fucking-East Asia, or a spaceman."

Then he looked at Noriko. Tenderly he said, "The same goes for you. You still have Nanahara. Protect him, Noriko. Pointless deaths are for fools."

He faced Shuya again, his voice firm now. "Do you understand? I don't have anything anymore. What I'm going to do I will do for me. You two are different."

Kawada glanced at his watch, then tossed his cigarette into the puddle, stood, and walked out from the shelter. The *chirp chirp* of the birdcall rang out.

As Shuya listened to the call, he remembered a rock song from the continent, "Yi Wu Suo You," which meant, "I Have Nothing." Can you love someone who has nothing, the lyrics asked.

But what did Kawada mean when he said he had nothing?

Exactly fifteen seconds later, the birdcall stopped, and Kawada came back into the shelter and sat down.

Noriko asked him, softly, "Don't you have someone you care about?"

Shuya had been about to ask the same thing.

Kawada's eyes widened a little. He gave them a smile, but something seemed sad about it.

"I wasn't going to tell you, but . . ." he said with a sigh. "Maybe that's what I want to do."

He reached into his back pants pocket, produced his wallet, and took out a worn photograph.

Noriko took the picture and held it so that she and Shuya could both see.

It was a photo of Kawada from the chest up. He wore a school uniform and had long hair like Shuya's, and he was smiling. It was a bashful, happy smile hard to imagine on the Kawada they knew. And a girl in a sailor fuku stood at his left. Her jet-black hair was gathered over her right shoulder. She seemed strong willed and had a very charming smile. They seemed to be on a major street—behind them were a row of streetside trees (gingkoes, maybe), a billboard for a brand of whiskey, and a yellow car.

"She's pretty," Noriko said with admiration.

Kawada scratched the tip of his nose. "Really? I don't think she's what you'd call conventionally beautiful. But I always thought she was."

Noriko shook her head. "Well, I think she *is* beautiful. She seems so mature. Is she your age?"

Kawada smiled, and it was a little like that bashful smile from the picture. "Yeah. And thanks."

Shuya looked at the two happy, side-by-side faces and thought, *What was that all about before? You* do *have something.*

But Shuya was failing to remember a critical piece of information.

"So is she in Kobe?" he asked.

Kawada grimaced and shook his head.

Then he said, "Did you forget, Nanahara? I've been in this fucking game once before. And I won."

Now Shuya made the connection. Noriko must have too, because her face went stiff.

Kawada continued, "She was in my class. I wasn't able to save her. Keiko."

They fell silent. Shuya finally felt he understood Kawada's anger and how deep it ran.

"You should see now," Kawada said, "that I don't have anything left. And they're going to pay for what they took from me—for killing Keiko."

Kawada put another cigarette in his mouth and lit it. Smoke drifted by.

After a moment, Shuya said, "So her name was Keiko."

"Yeah." Kawada nodded several times. "It means 'joyful child.'"

Shuya noted, in the back of his mind, that her name would be written with one of the same kanji as Yoshitoki's.

"Were you . . ." Noriko asked gently, "with her? Until the end?"

Kawada smoked in silence for a while, then said, "That's a painful question."

But he went on. "Her family name was Onuki. That time, girls' number seventeen was the first to leave. Well, the details aren't important. What matters was that her number was ahead of mine. She left three ahead of me."

Shuya and Noriko listened without a word.

"I thought she might be hiding somewhere near where we started, waiting for me. Just maybe, you know? But she wasn't around. Well, that couldn't be helped. Just like this time, hanging around the starting place wasn't safe."

He took in smoke and let it out.

"But somehow, I managed to find her. We were on an island like this one, but somehow I found her."

He took in smoke and let it out.

Then he said, "She ran away."

Startled, Shuya looked at Kawada. Behind the stubble was the expressionless face of someone fighting to conceal his feelings.

"I tried to chase after her, but then somebody attacked me. I took him out, somehow—but I lost sight of her."

Again he took in smoke, and again he let it out.

"She didn't trust me."

He kept up his poker face, but the corners of his eyes were almost imperceptibly quivering.

He continued. "And still I looked for her. When I found her again she was dead."

Now Shuya understood Kawada's troubled expression when he told Kawada, "It's hard . . . to trust someone," and Kawada said, "Yes, it is. It's very hard." He also saw why Kawada had said that Hiroki Sugimura might only have found Kayoko Kotohiki's body—or that she might not trust him.

"You asked me, Nanahara," Kawada said, "why I trusted you. You know, when we first met?"

"Yeah." Shuya bobbed his head. "I did."

"I believe I said you two looked like a nice couple."

Kawada looked up at the thatched canopy. By the time he lowered his eyes, his expression had relaxed. "That was the truth. That's what I saw. So I decided, unconditionally, to help you two as best I could."

Shuya nodded. "I see."

After a time, Noriko said, "I'm sure that . . ."

Shuya looked at her, and she continued. "I'm sure that Keiko was terrified . . . and she wasn't thinking straight."

"No." Kawada shook his head. "I loved her, but I know there

must have been something about the way I treated her when we were together. That must have been why."

With a little force, Shuya said, "You've gotta be wrong."

Kawada kept his hands clasped in front of his pulled-up knees as he looked at Shuya. A wisp of smoke, delicate as silk thread, rose from the cigarette in his hand.

"It was a misunderstanding," Shuya said. "Just a small misunderstanding, I'm sure of it. It's this fucking game. These awful circumstances. That's gotta be it."

Kawada grimaced again. "I don't know," he said. "I'll never know."

He tossed the cigarette into the puddle with the others and took the birdcall from his pocket.

"See this?" he said. "Keiko was a city girl, but she liked mountain hiking. The week we had that fucking game, that Sunday, she was going to take me bird watching."

Holding the red birdcall between the thumb and forefinger of his right hand, he put it up to his eye like a jeweler appraising a gemstone.

"She gave this to me."

He smiled and looked at Shuya and Noriko. "This is all I have left. It's my lucky charm, though I can't say it brings back good memories."

Noriko waited for him to put away the birdcall, then handed him back the photograph. He returned the picture to his ID wallet, and the wallet to his rear pocket.

When he'd finished, Noriko said, "Hey, Kawada." He looked back up at her.

"I don't know how Keiko felt at that moment. But . . ." She wet her lips. "I think she loved you in her own way. She had to have—I mean, she looked so happy in that picture. Don't you think so?"

"Yeah?"

"Yeah." Noriko nodded. "And if I were her, I'd want you to live. I wouldn't want you to die for me."

Kawada grinned and shook his head. "That's just a matter of personal taste."

Noriko insisted, "Just keep it in mind as a possibility. Okay? Please?"

For a while, Kawada remained silent. He opened his lips as if to speak . . . but then shrugged and smiled—only it seemed sad.

He looked at his watch again and stepped from the shelter to sound the call.

4 STUDENTS REMAIN.

73

By the sixth time Kawada had sounded the birdcall, the rain had completely stopped. Though it was five minutes to six, compared to the previous hours, the island seemed terribly bright. The three kids dismantled the tree-branch canopy.

After sitting back down against the rock wall, the open sky above, Noriko said, "It's nice out now," and Shuya and Kawada nodded.

The gentle breeze rustled the trees and bushes.

Kawada put another cigarette in his mouth and lit it.

Shuya watched Kawada in profile, deciding whether or not he should say what he was thinking. He decided to speak.

"Kawada."

Kawada looked up. The cigarette dangled from the side of his mouth.

Shuya said, "We didn't ask about you—about what you want to be in the future."

Kawada chuckled, and smoke came from his lips. "I thought I'd become a doctor," he said. "Like my father. I figured that even in this shitty country, a doctor can still help people."

This answer gave Shuya enough confidence to say, "Then why don't you? You've got the knack for it."

Kawada tapped the ashes from his cigarette and shook his head as if to say, *That discussion is over.*

"Kawada," Noriko said.

He turned his head to her.

"I know I'm repeating myself, but I'm going to say it one more time. If I were Keiko, I'd say this." She looked up at the sky, now beginning to take on orange, and continued, "Please live. Talk, think, act. Listen to music now and then, and—" Her words caught, then she continued, "and look at paintings and be moved by them. Laugh often, and at times, cry. And if you find a good girl, pursue her and find love with her."

It's like poetry, Shuya thought. *Pure poetry.*

These are her words. And words, when combined with music, have a great, godlike power.

Kawada quietly listened.

Noriko continued, "Because that's the person who I really loved."

She looked at him. She seemed a little embarrassed as she added, "That's what I'd think, if I were her."

The ashes on the end of his cigarette had grown long.

Shuya said, "Hey, Kawada. There are ways to take down this country without dying, right? Even if it's in a roundabout way."

Then he added, "After all, we just got to be friends, yeah? It'll be lonely without you. Come with us—to America."

Kawada remained silent for a long time. Then, realizing his cigarette had burned down to the filter, he tossed it aside.

He looked up at them, about to speak.

That's it, Kawada, Shuya thought. *Come with us. We'll stick together—because we're a team.*

But then that all-too-familiar voice came ringing out.

"Hey there."

Sakamochi.

Shuya lifted his limp left arm with his right and looked at his watch. Beneath the muddy glass, the hands read five seconds past six p.m.

"Can you hear me, all of you? Well, I say all of you, but there aren't many left now, are there? All right, I'll announce who died. Here's the boys."

Shuya was already thinking. *We were down to only four boys left: me, Kawada, and Hiroki, and Kiriyama. And only four girls, too—Noriko, Kayoko Kotohiki, Mitsuko Souma, and Mizuho Inada. Kiriyama won't have died so easily. Hiroki signaled us. So there should be no boy fatalities.*

"Only one died. Number eleven, Hiroki Sugimura."

Shuya's eyes went wide.

4 STUDENTS REMAIN.

PART FOUR
FINISH

STUDENTS REMAIN.

74

"And now for the girls. Big numbers there. Number one, Mizuho Inada; number two, Yukie Utsumi; number eight, Kayoko Kotohiki; number nine, Yuko Sakaki; number eleven, Mitsuko Souma; number twelve, Haruka Tanizawa; number sixteen, Yuka Nakagawa; number seventeen, Satomi Noda; and number nineteen, Chisato Matsui."

Shuya and Noriko's eyes met. Hers were trembling. They had been prepared to hear the names of Yukie's group . . . *but Hiroki and Kayoko? And Mitsuko Souma and Mizuho Inada? That means only us and Kiriyama are left?*

"That can't be," Shuya uttered. *We didn't hear any gunfire after the smoke signal went up. Was Hiroki killed by a knife or something? Or did I hear Sakamochi wrong just now? Are my ears playing tricks on me?*

He hadn't heard Sakamochi wrong. The announcement continued.

"All right. We're down to four now. Are you listening, Kiriyama, Kawada, Nanahara, and Nakagawa? You've done so well. I'm really proud of you all. Now then, I'll announce the new forbidden zones."

But before Shuya could dutifully mark his map, Kawada said, "Gather your things."

"Huh?" Shuya asked, but Kawada waved him to hurry.

Sakamochi continued, "From seven p.m. . . ."

"Get your head in this," Kawada said. "It's Kiriyama. He could have somehow figured out how Sugimura was going to contact us. We might have been leading Kiriyama to us this whole time."

Shuya scrambled to his feet and put his and Noriko's daypacks over his shoulder.

Sakamochi was saying, "All right then, keep it up. Just a little more to go—"

At that very moment, Shuya saw Kawada's eyes dart over to their alarm system—the thread inserted into a notch on the side of a tree trunk.

The thread fell from the wet bark.

"Down!" Kawada yelled as the *brattattattattatatat* barked.

Shuya and Noriko ducked as sparks blossomed on the rock face behind them and fragments of rock sprinkled their heads.

Kneeling, Kawada fired his Uzi into the brush.

Shuya didn't know if Kawada hit him, but Kiriyama (because who else could it be?) didn't return the fire.

Kawada said, "This way. Hurry!" and the three ran south along the rock wall, away from where the shots had come.

When they reached the end of the wall, from where Kawada had been sounding the birdcall, that *brattattattat* came again from behind. Unharmed, the three flew into the bushes ahead.

They came upon a waist-deep cleft in the rocky ground a little less than a meter wide. Dirt and leaves covered the fissure's base as it stretched on toward the south. Shuya hadn't known about the formation, but Kawada had likely taken it into consideration when selecting their hiding place. Kawada prompted them to jump down into the naturally formed trench, and they did. Kawada took the rear, firing the Uzi behind. They heard that other *brattattat* again, and just beside Shuya's head, the trunk of a thin tree that had taken root on the edge of the cleft shattered.

"Run!" Kawada yelled, and they ran along the base of the cleft. Shuya's foot caught on a dead branch, but he managed to catch his balance and follow Noriko. Behind them, the two guns exchanged rapid gunfire.

Suddenly, Noriko stopped as if something had hit her, and she moaned and crouched over. Shuya, who had been about to look back at Kawada, rushed to her. Had she tripped over something?

She hadn't. A horizontal cut ran below her left eye, and blood poured down her cheek. Her right hand must have been cut too, because blood was dripping from her closed fist. The Browning semi-automatic she'd been carrying was at her feet.

Shuya put his hand on her shoulder and looked up.

And then he saw it.

A thin, twisted wire had been stretched across above the cleft. Leaving aside the question of where Kiriyama had found it (he had probably untwisted a wire rope that had been used to secure some object), the killer had anticipated they'd escape through the trench. Had Shuya run into the wire, it would have sliced through his neck. Noriko escaped such a fate, but if she'd been unlucky, she might have lost her eye.

A red anger blossomed in Shuya's mind. He didn't know what Kiriyama was. Kawada had said he only chose what to do at random. Whatever he was—normal or abnormal, prodigy or madman—hurting Noriko was too much.

I'm going to fucking kill him!

But first he needed to help Noriko to her feet. He stuffed the CZ 75 into his slacks, picked up the Browning, and with the gun in his hand, he put his arm around her shoulder. Though dazed, she was already trying to stand.

Kawada, still firing behind, caught up with them and gave them a glance. His eyes darted about, and he must have spotted the wire, because he clenched his teeth. Then Shuya, who had turned his head to look at Kawada, saw behind his comrade's back Kazuo Kiriyama jumping down into the trench.

Kawada said, "Heads down!" as he fired. Kiriyama, machine gun in hand, quickly ducked back into a fold on the side of the cleft. Kawada's shots tore into the rock, and dust flew up.

Again Kawada said, "Run!"

Shuya stood Noriko up, and they ducked under the wire and started running. Unable to know if more wire traps awaited them, they let up on their pace.

Shuya was frustrated. If he only had use of both his arms, he could have still supported Noriko while filling Kiriyama with lead.

Kawada kept on firing as he stuck close behind them. Kiriyama was shooting back at them as he slowly but steadily advanced.

A good five or six meters later, the cleft came to an end. Shuya scrambled up to the ground first, then took Noriko's uninjured hand and pulled her out of the ditch. Her face was tight with determination, but the left side of it was covered with blood.

"Don't stop!" Kawada shouted over the gunfire. Shuya pulled Noriko by the hand and charged into the bushes ahead.

They came out in the yard of a house, an old single-story building that seemed to cling to the side of the mountain. A white mini pickup truck was parked near the front door, just off the driveway. For some reason, an ancient washing machine and refrigerator were on their sides in the cargo bed—maybe the owner had been about to throw them away.

"Behind the truck!" Kawada yelled. Shuya and Noriko ran hand in hand across the muddy ground and made it behind the vehicle.

Shuya had sat Noriko down and had drawn the Browning by the time Kawada dove into cover behind the truck. Shuya caught a flash of black moving through the bushes and started firing. The recoil jarred his left shoulder, where the bullet was still lodged, and sent waves of searing pain through him. But right now he couldn't let that stop him.

Kawada loaded a new magazine into the Uzi, offered it to Shuya, and said, "Shoot this. Keep him pinned down."

Shuya set the Browning down at his feet, took the submachine gun, and fired in the direction he had seen Kiriyama.

Kiriyama didn't shoot back. While Shuya edged his eyes over the top of the pickup's bed, Noriko moved closer to him. She was holding the Browning tightly in her bleeding hand.

Watching for any movement in the bushes, Shuya asked, "Are you all right, Noriko?"

"Yeah. I'm fine."

He glanced around her to Kawada. He'd opened the truck's door and was leaning over into the driver's seat, rustling around inside the cab.

Suddenly the engine revved up, and Shuya felt the truck vibrate. The roar quickly settled into a low rumble. Raindrops loosened by the gentle vibration began to trickle down the side of the truck.

Kawada pulled his head out to shout, "Get in! We're getting out of here. Hurry, Noriko!"

Noriko took his hand and climbed into the cab. Kawada scrambled up after her and into the driver's seat.

"Nanahara!" he shouted. "Get in the passenger's side!"

Kawada backed the truck, aiming its tail in the direction Kiriyama had been, then turned the wheel and brought the passenger side facing Shuya. Noriko opened the door.

Just as he reached up his hand to climb inside, that *brattattattat* rang out—but this time, accompanied by a hammering. Holes punctured through the inside roof of the confined cab, and the bullets that made them blew out the windshield directly in front of Kawada. Shuya threw himself against the side of the truck, aimed the Uzi high into the mountainside, and squeezed the trigger. The black figure ducked back into the trees. Kiriyama had gone up the mountain.

Shuya jumped into the passenger's seat, and Kawada hit the gas. The truck swerved onto the unpaved driveway. Another *brattattattat* tore the hose off the washing machine on the back of the truck. The hose twisted snakelike in the air, then landed behind them—and was left in the distance.

The gunfire ceased.

Shuya asked, "Are you all right, Noriko?"

Noriko was sitting between them, her face painted bright red, but she gave him a nod and said, "Yes."

But she was still tense, and she clutched the Browning with both hands. Shuya rested the Uzi between his legs, took the bandana from his pocket, and wiped her face. Blood continued to gush from the pink flesh of her open wound. Without substantial surgery, it would likely leave a scar. *To do this to a girl . . .*

"Damn it," Shuya said, looking over at Kawada. "He knew where we were a while before. That's how he anticipated our escape route."

But Kawada shook his head. Working the gearshift as he navigated the winding road, he said, "No, he must not have known until just when he attacked. Otherwise, he would have come before Sakamochi's announcement. If we'd still had our guard down and came out to meet him thinking he was Sugimura, he could have wiped us out without a hitch. But he didn't know where we were, so he passed the time between the birdcalls setting up that trap wire. That probably wasn't the only place he did it."

Oh, Shuya thought, *that might be. For him, it was just passing time. And now Noriko has that terrible gash on her face.*

"Noriko," he said, "let me see your hand."

Only now did she let go of the gun. The grip too was bright red. She held out her right hand, so small and delicate. The cut, a diagonal slash across the base of her ring and little fingers, was deep. The pattern of the Browning's textured grip had imprinted into her skin, and her blood filled the meshlike grooves. The wire had probably cut her face first. Then, when she started to fall, she had reflexively raised her hand and sliced it on the wire. It might have been a lot worse had she not been holding the gun at the time.

Shuya had intended to bandage her with his bandana, but he stopped when he realized he couldn't without his left hand.

Noriko said, "It's all right. I can do it." She took the bandana, shook it open with her left hand, then wrapped it around her right and tied the ends. Then she gripped the Browning again.

The view beyond the spiderwebbed windshield suddenly opened, revealing farmland sandwiched between the wooded foothills and leading down to the flat land, all beneath an evening sky. Their truck had come down from the mountain.

Shuya realized where they were and said, "Kawada—we're heading into a forbidden zone."

"Don't worry. I'm aware of it," Kawada said, looking ahead. "Did you hear the new zones? From seven, B-9. From nine, E-10. And from eleven, F-4. Add them to the map, will you?"

Amazingly, Shuya had remembered the locations. He took the now tattered map from his pocket, spread it open on his lap, and, as he bounced inside the cabin, he scribbled off the forbidden zones.

They passed a house on the way down, then came onto another road, equally narrow, but paved. Beyond the fields, Shuya could see the southern mountain now. To their right were the low foothills of the northern mountain. To their left, about two hundred meters away (inside the forbidden zone), stood a single house, and two more were ahead and a little to the left. Beyond those, scattered homes led all the way to the village on the eastern shore. Not too far on this side of the village, though hidden by a hill, would be the field where they first encountered Kiriyama. The school was one more hill over from there, also not visible from this location.

Kawada slowed the truck a little and proceeded down the road. They had come down quite far now. The wide east-west road lay ahead.

Kawada cut across the fields, and then they were up onto the pavement. He cranked the wheel and cranked it back, and brought the truck to a stop in the center of the road, leaving the engine idling. Then he smacked the cracked windshield with his fist and the whole thing popped out and fell in front of the truck, shattering noisily on the pavement.

He put his hands back on the wheel, then said, "Check the map."

Shuya took his map out again.

"As I remember it," Kawada said, "we can take this road all the way east. Am I right?"

Shuya and Noriko looked at the map together.

"Yeah," Shuya said, "but F-4, just ahead, is off-limits starting at eleven."

"That won't matter," Kawada said, staring ahead. His gaze was as straight as the white lines on each edge of the black, rain-slicked asphalt. "So aside from that, we can take this road all the way to the village?"

"Yeah. We're fine until just before the road curves."

Kawada nodded.

Shuya put his head out the window and looked back. "Do you think Kiriyama will—"

Kawada only now looked at him. "He'll come. He has to come. Keep a good eye—"

Before he could finish speaking, a car appeared around the bend of the mountain road. Shuya recognized the old, faded yellow-green minivan from one of the houses they'd passed on the way down.

Kawada turned the rearview mirror to look and said, "See?"

The minivan was approaching fast, and the moment Shuya could see Kiriyama's face behind the wheel, violent sparks blossomed in front of that face. Shuya pulled his head back inside the window. The bullets hit the truck somewhere and clanged against the metal. Kawada put the truck into gear and the vehicle jolted into motion, speeding east down that wide road.

Shuya looked out the window again just as the minivan came onto their road. He held out the Uzi and squeezed the trigger. The van swerved right, taken over by Kiriyama's fast reflexes.

"Aim well, Nanahara," Kawada said.

But Kiriyama's van gained speed and closed in on them.

"Kawada!" Shuya said. "Can't you go any faster?"

"Calm down."

Kawada began slowly turning the wheel left and right—probably to prevent their tires from being shot out. Kiriyama fired again, and Shuya ducked back into the cab. The killer had knocked out his own front windshield in order to more easily shoot at them. Shuya leaned out again, aimed at Kiriyama, and squeezed the trigger. Kiriyama swerved again and dodged the gunfire. He hadn't even ducked.

The stream of ejecting empty shell casings ceased. The firing mechanism clicked, the magazine out of bullets.

Kawada reached in front of Noriko to hand him a preloaded magazine. But before Shuya could take it, Kiriyama's minivan was nearly upon them. Shuya drew the CZ 75 from the front of his slacks and fired. Undeterred, Kiriyama kept gaining.

"Damn," Kawada said with a faint grin. "If you think you can beat me driving, you're dead wrong."

Kawada flicked the wheel and yanked the handbrake. Shuya's body pressed against the door. Just like straight out of a movie, the pickup truck was doing a full turn inside the width of the road.

As they spun, Kiriyama's minivan came hurtling past. Sparks burst from the passenger window, accompanied by that familiar *brat-tattattat*. The rearview mirror shattered in front of Noriko's face.

"Duck!" Kawada shouted.

But Shuya was busy firing the CZ 75 at Kiriyama. That none of Kiriyama's submachine-gun volley had hit Shuya was a miracle, but Shuya didn't hit him either. As the truck's front bumper skimmed past the front-left side of the minivan, Shuya was close enough to see Kiriyama's eyes, as cold as ever.

The truck's tires screeched on the wet pavement, and Kawada pulled out of the turn—and now the hunter and the hunted had reversed. Kawada had evaded the minivan and pulled off a full three-sixty turn. Now the van was ahead. Kawada didn't miss a beat as he slammed the truck into gear and took on speed. The engine roared with a power it likely didn't even know it possessed, and the pickup quickly caught up with the back of the minivan. Kiriyama looked back at them.

"Fire, Nanahara!" Kawada said. "Give it everything you've got!"

But Shuya didn't need to be told. He had reloaded the Uzi and was firing on full auto. He knew the hot empty casings were being ejected toward Noriko, but he couldn't worry about that now. The van's rear window shattered. There was a pop, and the rear hatch lifted. Then the rear right tire burst. Shuya's magazine was empty, but the van listed, starting to drift toward the shoulder.

Kawada floored it. He brought the pickup alongside the minivan and flicked the wheel, slamming the truck's right side against the van's left.

The impact rattled them, but it did far worse to Kiriyama's van. He lost control of the vehicle and went careening off the right shoulder. The next instant, the van's nose was planted in the dirt of the low-lying roadside field. Cabbage leaves scattered into the air.

Then everything was still.

Kawada slammed on the brakes and brought the pickup to a stop even with the van, where they could look down on its roof.

"Give me the gun, Nanahara," Kawada said.

Shuya gave him the Uzi. Kawada replaced the magazine, held his arm out window, aimed at the minivan with Kiriyama still inside, and squeezed the trigger. His arm shook up and down. Even from the passenger seat, Shuya could see the minivan was being riddled with holes.

Again Kawada replaced the magazine, and he continued to fire. He reloaded once more and emptied it again. Meanwhile, Noriko had loaded loose ammo into one of the empty magazines with her injured hand. Kawada took the magazine and fired it as well. Noriko kept on reloading. Shuya rose in his seat and looked from her to Kawada's hands and to the minivan below.

Noriko and Kawada repeated the process and repeated it again, and even one more time after that. The Uzi fired nine millimeter rounds, the same as Shuya's CZ 75 and Noriko's Browning, and by the end, Kawada had shot every loose round they had.

The Uzi's firing mechanism gave one last click. They were all out of spare ammo. Kawada curled his arm, holding the Uzi upright. Blue smoke drifted from the end of its short barrel, and the gunpowder smell filled the cab.

How many rounds did Kawada fire? Shuya wondered. *That Uzi came with five spare magazines and plenty of extra rounds—add the CZ 75 and the Browning to that, and you get, what? Two hundred and fifty? Three hundred?*

What Shuya could see of the minivan—the roof and passenger

side—looked like a honeycomb, or a net—or maybe a bizarre insect cage in the shape of a car.

The sky had turned a deep orange. Shuya didn't have time to look, but he supposed the western sky would be in a beautiful sunset.

"Did you get him?" Shuya asked.

Kawada opened his mouth, when—

The minivan moved. It was backing up. The vehicle crossed the edge of the field and climbed back up onto the road. It was behind them again.

Shuya was dumbstruck. Not only was the van's engine still working, but Kazuo Kiriyama was still alive—and driving it. Kawada had put all their ammunition on the line to make sure they'd won, but Kiriyama still lived.

On the other side of the bullet-ridden hood, Kiriyama popped up like a jack-in-the-box in the driver's seat. And he was holding the machine gun. With a *brattattattat*, the small window behind Noriko's head shattered, and two holes appeared on the metal panel to its side. Shuya was surprised the truck's flimsy, domestically produced body had remained unscathed for this long. But maybe it was because of the washer and fridge on the rear bed. And maybe Kawada had put them there in the first place, having foreseen this eventuality.

With a curse, Kawada put the truck into gear and started driving. "Shoot, Nanahara! Shoot back!"

Shuya aimed the CZ-75 at the minivan, now right on their tail, and began firing. Kiriyama returned fire. One shot landed right next to Shuya's head and sent up sparks from the truck's steel frame.

Shuya's pistol was already empty. He replaced the magazine and fired more—but as he did, he realized, *This is the last of my bullets. Once this runs dry, all we have left is what's in the Browning and its one spare magazine.*

While he hesitated, Kiriyama fired. Shuya heard that *brattattattat*, and with a *twang*, sparks flew from the refrigerator in the back. The small freezer door flew open and fell out.

Shuya yelled, "Kawada, I'm out!"

Kawada remained calm at the wheel. "He'll be running out too. He doesn't have time to reload his magazines."

Just as Kawada said, Kiriyama's next shots came one at a time. Next to Noriko's shoulder, the seat exploded.

"Noriko!" Shuya cried. "Get down!"

He stuck his arm out the window and fired at Kiriyama, who now held a pistol in one of his hands. Shuya ran out of bullets and took the Browning from Noriko. He fired again.

Ahead and to their left, a black husk of what seemed to have been a warehouse appeared between the houses and fields. It must have been the source of the explosion late last night that Kawada had mentioned. Not two hundred meters separated them from the curve in the road leading toward the village on the eastern shore.

"Hey," he said, "Kawada, that's the—"

"I know," Kawada replied. He yanked left on the wheel. Beneath Shuya, the left side of the pickup seemed to lift up. But when all four wheels were back on the ground, they had turned onto an unpaved road, another path winding through fields on its way up the northern mountain. Kiriyama skillfully steered the minivan after them.

Shuya took aim and fired. Kiriyama ducked, and then was upright again, returning fire. This time, a hole opened in the steel panel next to Kawada's head.

"Nanahara!" Kawada yelled. "Just keep firing until you're out. Don't let him shoot!"

Kawada was leaning over the wheel now. Shuya noticed blood oozing out of a tear in the left shoulder of his school jacket. Kiriyama had hit him.

Shuya nearly objected, but instead he leaned out the window and fired.

Is Kawada trying to escape into the foothills? Then I have to keep Kiriyama from shooting until we get there . . . or get lucky and kill him first.

He fired again.

The Browning locked open. It was empty.

The mountain drew near, and with it, a sight that seemed strangely familiar—a farmhouse with a concrete block wall. And a field. And a tractor.

This is where we first came up against Kiriyama, Shuya realized. *Only we're looking at it from the opposite side.*

"Kawada, I'm out of ammo," he said. "Are we going to escape into the mountain?"

Kawada was looking straight ahead. Shuya thought he saw a smirk.

"Oh, we *have* ammo," Kawada said.

Shuya frowned, not knowing what he meant.

The truck turned off the driveway leading to the farmhouse and took a footpath between the fields. They passed the tractor. The path ahead was too narrow for a vehicle.

But Kawada kept driving onward. Kiriyama kept a fixed distance behind them—only twenty meters. He fired at them again.

The pickup careened into the field and came to a stop with Shuya's passenger side facing Kiriyama's van. Kawada kicked open his door, yelled, "Get out—this way!" and jumped out of the cab.

Shuya prompted Noriko to move. They were crawling across the front seat when Shuya glanced over his shoulder.

Kiriyama's minivan was coming straight at them.

A loud gunshot came from somewhere near.

Kiriyama's left front tire exploded. He was only ten meters away.

The minivan slowly tipped, then rode up on the lip of the elevated field on the left like a surfboard catching a wave. Its front lifted into the air and the next instant was on its roof in the field.

But before the van came to a complete stop, a black blur leaped from the driver's side. It flipped in midair and landed in a crouch. Shuya saw it was Kiriyama, and he then heard two gunshots as sparks blossomed from the gun in the killer's hands. At the same time, that first loud gunshot blasted again.

Still inside the truck, Shuya had to crane his neck to see outside the passenger window. Kazuo Kiriyama was bent over and flying backward.

His back hit the field with a thud. He didn't move a muscle.

In the back of Shuya's mind, the memory of Kyoichi Motobuchi's death came to him—the boy's stomach transformed into a sausage factory slop bucket. At this distance, Shuya couldn't see what had happened to Kiriyama's stomach, but having been directly hit by what must have been a shotgun blast, he couldn't still be alive.

Shuya finally emerged from the truck, and there was Kawada, rising from behind the pickup's bed, holding the shotgun Shuya had abandoned when he ran from Kiriyama.

Oh, we have *ammo,* he'd said. Kawada had picked up the shotgun, swiftly loaded it with some of the cartridges he had kept with him (he'd likely only had time to load the two shells), and fired. And he took Kiriyama down.

"Right at the beginning," Kawada said slowly, "he missed his chance to surprise us. That was when he lost. He had to take on all three of us."

He let out a deep breath, then set the shotgun down beside the fridge in back of the pickup. He took the pack of Wild Sevens from his pocket, then got one out and lit it.

"You're bleeding," Noriko said, pointing at his shoulder.

"Yeah." He glanced at the wound and grinned. "It's nothing big."

He exhaled smoke.

Bang.

Kawada tipped forward. The Wild Seven fell from his mouth, and the languid smoke trail drifted in the air. His stubbled face contorted. His eyes seemed to be staring off somewhere near Shuya's feet.

Down in the field behind him, Kazuo Kiriyama was sitting up, holding a gun in his right hand. *He's alive! But he was blown back by a shotgun blast into his stomach!*

Kawada slowly sank to the ground. Kiriyama turned the gun on Shuya. Shuya realized that he too was now in front of the truck. And he was unarmed. He didn't even have any bullets. Too late to reload the shotgun on the pickup's bed. No, far too late now.

A good ten meters away, the little muzzle of Kiriyama's gun seemed a giant tunnel—a black hole sucking everything in.

Bang.

Shuya closed his eyes. He felt something pierce his chest, and he thought, *I'm dead.*

He opened his eyes.

He wasn't dead.

Kiriyama stood in the orange angled light of the setting sun. A red dot had been carved into his cheek. The gun fell from his hand. Again his body tilted backward. He fell.

Slowly Shuya looked over his left shoulder. There was Noriko, holding the Smith & Wesson Chief's Special revolver in both hands.

While Kawada had been loading the shotgun, she must have picked up the revolver he'd also left behind and loaded it with the remaining .38 Special rounds.

Her hands were shaking.

Kawada grunted. He got back on his feet before Shuya could offer him a hand.

"Are you all right?" Shuya asked.

Without a reply, Kawada picked up the shotgun, loaded it with another shell from his pocket, and walked toward Kiriyama. He stopped exactly two meters away, aimed at the killer's head, and pulled the trigger. Kiriyama's head shook only once.

Kawada turned and walked back to Shuya and Noriko.

"Are you all right?" Shuya repeated.

"It's nothing big."

He approached Noriko. She was still holding the gun straight ahead. Gently, he put his hands around hers and guided her to lower the revolver.

Just above a whisper, he said, "He's dead. I killed him, not you."

Then he turned to look at Kiriyama. "He was wearing a bullet-proof vest."

Now it all made sense.

"Kawada," Noriko said, her voice trembling. "Are you all right?"

He grinned at her and nodded. "I'm all right. Thanks, Noriko."

He again took out the pack of cigarettes. It must have been empty, because he looked around, then picked up the one that had dropped from his mouth. It was still lit. He put it to his lips.

Shuya turned to look out across the island in the light of the sunset. It was over—or at least this happy little game was. Scattered across the island, starting with Kiriyama directly in front of him, were the bodies of thirty-nine of his classmates.

Once more a feeling like dizziness came over him. A hollow feeling numbed his thoughts. What had this all been for?

One after another, faces appeared in his mind. *Yoshitoki Kuninobu screaming, "I'll fucking kill you!" Shinji Mimura's faint smile when he left the room. Tatsumichi's bloodshot eyes as he raised the hatchet. Hiroki Sugimura saying, "I have to see Kotohiki," and then slipping into the darkness outside the clinic. Hirono Shimizu shooting Kaori Minami and then running from his sight. Yukie Utsumi crying as she confessed to him, "I didn't know what I'd do if you died." Yuko Sakaki, prying his fingers loose as she said, "No, no. It's my fault they're all dead." And Kazuo Kiriyama's cold eyes as he hunted them down until this very moment.*

They were all gone. They'd lost their lives, and they'd probably lost much more.

But this wasn't the end.

"Kawada," Shuya said. Kawada looked over at him, shortened cigarette in hand. "Let's do something about those wounds."

Kawada smiled. "I'm fine. I just got grazed. Look after Noriko's wounds."

Then he said, "I'm going to get Kiriyama's weapons."

He took another drag from the stub of his cigarette and turned around and walked toward the minivan.

3 STUDENTS REMAIN.

75

Kawada led the way up the mountain. He'd stuffed his pick of Kiriyama's weapons into the daypack over his shoulder. He hadn't offered them to Shuya and Noriko. There was no need for that now.

Shuya walked on Noriko's left, supporting her as they followed Kawada. For now, they had washed the cut on her cheek with water and covered it with four band-aids in a line. Kawada had said they were better off not making a poor attempt at suturing it themselves. They'd also washed the wound on her hand and wrapped the bandana back around it. Kawada had also quickly attended to his own injuries.

The mountainside was already growing dark, but they no longer needed to make their way through the brush, and they ascended the mountain with comparative ease. Beneath their feet, layers of leaves in varying stages of decomposition were wet from the afternoon-long shower.

They had covered a long distance since Kawada had announced without explanation, "We're going up the mountain."

"Kawada," Shuya said, and Kawada turned over his shoulder. "How far are we going?"

Kawada grinned. "Just a little farther. Just keep following me."

Shuya readjusted his arm around Noriko and quietly obeyed.

The summit, near the observation deck where Yukiko Kitano and Yumiko Kusaka were killed, and the area to its south had already become forbidden zones. Kawada stopped just outside the sector's edge fairly high up the mountain. Now that he thought about it, he realized that the farmhouse where he'd witnessed Hirono Shimizu shoot Kaori Minami was not far below.

"I think here should do it."

A steep drop below broke the tree line and offered a picturesque view to the south. Shuya looked across the island, now immersed in the blue twilight, where the fierce battle of the students of Shiroiwa Junior High Ninth Grade Class B had unfolded. But the school where their final foes dwelled—Sakamochi and his men—remained hidden among the rolling hills.

Shuya let out his breath, then asked, "What's up here anyway? How are we going to escape?"

Kawada smiled without looking at him. Then he said, "Relax. Take a look over there."

Shuya and Noriko looked to where he pointed.

In the darkness beyond the southern mountain, Shuya could see the outline of several smaller islands, and in the distance, a larger landmass with points of light scattered across it. Were he closer, he'd be able to tell which were neon and which were the lights along the coastal highway.

Now Shuya knew they were on Oki Island, off the shore of Takamatsu City. The island formed a small north-to-south chain with Megijima and Ogijima. Oki Island was the most northerly, and the farthest from shore of the three. Looking past the southern mountain, the closer island would be Ogijima, followed by Megijima, and then followed by the Shikoku mainland—and Kagawa Prefecture.

Kawada said, "I wasn't there very long, but it's your home. Shiroiwa will be over that way, I suppose. You won't be seeing it again, so take a good look."

Right, since we're escaping the country, I guess we'll never be coming back. But still . . .

Shuya looked at Kawada. "Don't tell me we came all the way up here just for the view."

Kawada chuckled. "Don't be in such a hurry." Then to Noriko, he said, "Let me see your gun. I need to check something."

She was still holding the Smith & Wesson. She held it out, and Kawada took it. He opened the cylinder and checked to see if it was loaded. Noriko would have reloaded it after taking that single shot at Kiriyama.

He didn't return it but kept it in his right hand. He took a single breath and let it out.

Then he said, "Do both of you remember what I told you all those times? That maybe I simply wanted partners but would try to kill you in the end?"

Shuya raised his eyebrows. *Yeah, we had that talk, but what about it?*

"You did," he said. "So what?"

"So," Kawada said. "You lose."

He pointed the Smith & Wesson at them.

3 STUDENTS REMAIN.

76

Shuya felt a strange expression spread across his face—like a simultaneous mix of amusement and bewilderment. Noriko was probably experiencing the same emotion.

"What's this?" Shuya said. "After all that, you're going to joke around?"

"This is no joke," Kawada said.

He pulled back the hammer.

Shuya's grin melted. His right arm was around Noriko, and he felt her stiffen.

Then Kawada said, "You can enjoy the view a little longer if you'd like. I told you, it's the last time you'll see it."

A faint smile was plastered across Kawada's stubbled face, a sinister expression he hadn't shown before.

Somewhere a crow cawed. It might have been flying above them in the darkening sky.

Finally, Shuya spoke. He was having trouble emotionally coping with the situation, and his voice sounded tearful. "What? What are you saying?"

"You're a slow one," Kawada answered with a slight shrug. "I'm going to kill you both. I win. That'll be two in a row for me."

Shuya's lips trembled. *It can't be. It just can't be.*

His words came tumbling out. "Don't be ridiculous. So you're telling me all this was some act? Didn't you—didn't you look after us? Didn't you save us all those times?"

Calmly, Kawada explained, "You two saved *me*. If I hadn't had you two around, Kiriyama would probably have killed me."

The more Shuya tried to keep the shaking out of his voice, the louder it became. "You . . . and I suppose that story about Keiko was all made up too, yeah?"

"Yep," Kawada admitted. "It's true I was in last year's Program in Hyogo Prefecture, and I did have a classmate named Keiko Onuki. But there was nothing between us at all. The girl in the photo *is* my girl, Kyoka Shimazaki. She's still in Kobe. She doesn't have a lot going on upstairs. Well, anyway, she insisted I carry her photo. Not a bad lay though."

Shuya swallowed. The light, early summer breeze felt chilly against his skin. Weakly, he added, "But the birdcall . . ."

"Was just something I picked up at that general store. I thought it might come in handy. And it did at that."

The light continued to fade.

Kawada continued, "Do you understand now? You two lost the moment you started to trust me."

Shuya still couldn't believe it. *It can't be. It . . . can't.*

Finally, a thought crossed Shuya's mind. *This, this is . . .*

But before he could say something, Noriko spoke.

"Kawada . . . is this some test to see if we really trust you? Is it because Keiko didn't?"

Kawada shrugged. "Incredible. You're really going to believe that crap until the very end."

He was done talking now. He casually shifted the gun in his hand and slowly squeezed the trigger.

Soon after the echoes of the two shots had faded, the island fell into darkness.

1 STUDENT REMAINS.
GAME OVER
END OF PLAYER MONITORING SYSTEM REPORT
PROGRAM HEADQUARTERS/SHIROIWA JUNIOR
HIGH NINTH GRADE CLASS B

Shogo Kawada (Boys #5) reclined in the soft chair. His body gently rocked as the ship carried him across the choppy waves.

The room was fairly spacious for being inside a small patrol ship. The ceiling was low, but the floor covered a good eight square meters. A low table sat in the center of the room, flanked by two armchairs. Kawada was sitting in the one farthest from the door.

The room was below deck and hadn't a single window. Kawada couldn't see outside, but it must have been nearly half past eight. The ashtray on the table reflected the yellowish light from the ceiling, but Kawada was out of cigarettes.

When the game ended, the forbidden zones were nullified, and Sakamochi's voice instructed him to walk back to the school. In the schoolyard, Yoshio Akamatsu and Mayumi Tendo's corpses remained untouched, as did those of Yoshitoki Kuninobu and Fumiyo Fujiyoshi inside the classroom.

At last he was freed from the metal collar, and after recording the video clip of the victor for the news, the soldiers escorted him to the harbor, where two ships were docked. One was for the winner, the other a transport ship to carry away the soldiers who had been crammed inside the school. The majority of the men—the ones who had been stuck waiting in the faculty room—boarded the transport ship. Only the three who had been in the classroom at the start of the game boarded the other ship along with Sakamochi and Kawada. A cleanup crew would come the next day to dispose of the other students' bodies. The speakers that had been placed across the island and the computers in the school would be taken away within a few days—though the software and data related to the game had likely been retrieved by now. Everything had followed the same procedure as after the Kobe Second Junior High Program Kawada had been in ten months before.

And now he was being made to wait in this room. The ship was south of Oki Island on its direct route to Takamatsu Harbor. The soldiers' transport ship would have peeled off to head for their base in the west.

The door handle turned with a click. The soldier standing guard (the unimpressive one called Nomura or something) peered in, then quickly withdrew to the side. Kinpatsu Sakamochi appeared. He was carrying a tray with two teacups.

"Hey," he said, "did I keep you waiting?" and entered the room. Behind him, Nomura closed the door from the outside.

Sakamochi conveyed himself in on his stubby legs and placed the tray on the center table. "Here," he said. "It's tea. Have all you want."

He took a flat, letter-sized envelope from under his left armpit and sat in the armchair opposite Kawada. He tossed the envelope onto the edge of the table in front of him and brushed his shoulder-length hair behind his ear.

Kawada gave the envelope a disinterested glance, then put his eyes on Sakamochi and said, "What the hell do you want? I'm tired and I just want to be left alone."

"Now now," Sakamochi frowned. He raised his teacup to his lips. "That's no way to speak to an adult. You know, I had a student once, named Kato, and he used to give me a lot of trouble. But he's a respectable man now."

"I'm not one of your dogs."

Sakamochi's eyes widened a little, as if he were taken aback, but then he smiled again. "Don't be like that, Kawada. I just wanted to have a little chat with you."

Kawada remained silent as he leaned back in the armchair with his legs crossed and his chin resting on his hand.

"Let's see, where should I begin?" Sakamochi put down his teacup and rubbed his hands together. "Ah, yes," he said, his eyes glimmering. "Did you know we have a betting pool over the Program?"

Kawada narrowed his eyes in disgust and said, "I wouldn't be surprised. You are a bunch of tasteless bastards, after all."

Sakamochi smiled. "And you see, I had my money on Kiriyama. Twenty thousand yen. On my salary, that's quite a lot. But because of you, I lost."

"My sympathies," Kawada said, his tone entirely unsympathetic.

Again Sakamochi smiled. Then he said, "I explained to all of you, didn't I, that those collars let me know where everyone is at all times?"

They both knew he had. Kawada didn't respond.

Sakamochi looked him in the eye and said, "You were with Nanahara and Nakagawa the whole time. What you did at the end— you betrayed them, didn't you?"

"You got a problem with that? There are no rules in this happy little game. Surely you're not going to criticize me for that. Don't make me laugh."

Another broad grin spread across Sakamochi's face. He brushed back his hair, took another sip of his tea, and rubbed his hands together.

Then, speaking as if he were sharing a secret, he said, "Hey, Kawada. I really shouldn't be telling you this, but those collars have built-in microphones. It's the truth. We can hear everything the students say during the game. I bet you didn't know that."

Until now, Kawada had responded with indifference, but now he showed a reaction. His eyebrows lowered and his lips tightened.

"How the hell would I?" he said. "So, you heard everything then— how I tricked them."

"Uh huh, that's right." Sakamochi nodded. "But that wasn't nice, what you said. 'I bet the government wouldn't think twice before writing off someone like Sakamochi as an acceptable loss.' Maybe it doesn't seem like it to you, but the Program Administrator is an important position. Not everyone can do this work."

Ignoring Sakamochi's complaint, Kawada asked, "Why are you telling me this?"

"Oh, I don't know. I just, well, I guess I was just impressed by your brilliant performance and wanted to let you know."

"Bullshit."

Kawada turned his head away, but he soon turned back when Sakamochi said, with emphasis, "It *was* a brilliant performance."

Sakamochi continued, "But there *is* something that's bugging me."

"What?"

"Why didn't you shoot those two immediately after you took out Kiriyama? You could have, couldn't you? That's the one thing I don't get."

Without hesitation, Kawada said, "It's like I told them. I figured the least I could do was let them have one last look at their homes before they died. Even I know the value of common courtesy. After all, I was able to win because of them."

Sakamochi continued to smile as he made an odd-sounding, "Hmmm."

He brought the teacup back to his lips. Keeping the cup in his hand, he settled back into the armchair and said, "By the way, Kawada, I requested the records from the Kobe Second Junior High Program. You know, the one you were in last year?"

He stared at Kawada for moment. Kawada returned his gaze without a word.

"And, you see, as far as I could tell from the records, you didn't have any special connection with Keiko Onuki."

Kawada cut in. "Onuki? Like I said, I made that—"

"You—" Sakamochi talked over him, and he shut his mouth. "You came across her twice, like you told Nanahara and Nakagawa. The first was only for a moment, and the second was right before you won—and she was already dead. I read the transcripts, and you didn't even mention her name—not once. Do you remember that?"

"What's to remember? It's like I said—there was nothing between me and Onuki. Weren't you listening?"

"But here's the thing, Kawada. The second time, you remained there for two hours."

"That was a coincidence. It was a good place to hide, that's all. Anyway, that's why her name stuck with me. She died gruesomely."

With that ever-present grin still plastered on his face, Sakamochi bobbed his head attentively. "The other thing is," he said, "during the eighteen hours of your first game—and that's quite fast, actually. I think the battlefield might have been a little too small for that one. Anyway, you didn't talk to anyone in your game. Well, you said things like 'Stop' and 'I'm not your enemy,' and so—"

"Also just a means to an end. Wasn't it obvious?"

Sakamochi ignored the interruption with a smile. "And so I can't figure out what your approach to that game was. You did an awful lot of moving around, and—"

"It was my first time. I didn't know the smart moves."

Sakamochi nodded again. The corners of his lips contained an amused smile, as if he found something terribly funny. He took a sip of tea, then returned the teacup to the table.

He looked up again and said, "By the way, how about that photo? Do you mind if I have a look?"

"What photo?"

"Come now, you showed it to Nanahara and Nakagawa, right? The one you told them was of Onuki. Oh, but you said it was really of . . . Now what was her name? Shimazaki?"

Kawada sneered at him. "Why should I have to show you that?"

"Come on, let me see it. You're making me feel left out. Please. Come on, please. Look, you're making me beg." He put his hands on the edge of the table and bowed to Kawada.

Resigned, Kawada reached behind his back and searched his back pocket, then raised his eyebrows and brought his hand out. It was empty.

"It's not there," he said. "I must have dropped it when we were fighting Kiriyama."

"You dropped it?"

"Yeah. It's the truth. ID wallet and all. Well, it wasn't that important, anyway."

Suddenly, Sakamochi burst out laughing. As he laughed, he said, "Right." He clutched at his sides, slapped his knees, and laughed and laughed.

Kawada looked on in confusion.

But then he narrowed his eyes and looked up to the ceiling of the windowless room.

Though dampened by the military ship's thick walls, he could hear the quiet but distinct roar of an engine—and it wasn't from the ship.

The sound grew increasingly louder and then softer again. And then it was almost entirely gone.

Kawada's lips twitched into a frown.

"Is that noise troubling you, Kawada?"

Sakamochi had stopped laughing, but the twisted smile remained in place.

"It's a helicopter," he said. He reached for his cup, slurped the rest of his tea, and placed the cup back on the table. "It's flying to the island—the one where you all fought."

Kawada's eyebrows tightened again, but with a hint of an emotion he hadn't yet displayed. Disregarding this, Sakamochi leaned back in the chair, crossed his arms, and shifted topics.

"Hey, Kawada. Let's talk some more about those collars. They have a name, you know. Guadalcanal 22. Well, not that it matters. Anyway, you told Nanahara that they couldn't be hacked."

When he saw that Kawada wasn't going to respond, he continued, "In fact, your speculation was right on the mark. They're built with three redundant systems, and even supposing a one-percent failure rate for each system, only one in a million will fail. In reality, the failure rate is even smaller. In any case, what you said was correct. Nobody could possibly escape from them. Any attempt to remove them would trigger the explosive, you see, killing the wearer. Rarely does anyone try it though."

Kawada still didn't speak.

"But, and there *is* a 'but,'" Sakamochi said, sitting forward. "You see, I'm a curious kind of guy, so I thought I'd get in touch with the Nonaggressive Forces R&D center this time around. And when I did . . ." He looked Kawada in the eye. "Guess what I found out. If someone knew their way around electric circuitry, he could use parts from a common radio to easily unlock the device. Of course, he'd have to know what was inside the collars."

Kawada remained silent, but as Sakamochi continued to stare, he spoke up, as if a thought had occurred to him, and in a voice unnaturally flat. "But nobody does know that, so that shouldn't be a problem."

"Right." Sakamochi nodded with a small grin. "Well, anyway, if someone did unlock his collar that way, what would happen next is incredibly simple. The collar transmits the same signal as if the student had died. Supposing that—just supposing, mind you—one of the students removed his collar without triggering the explosive, then that student could wait for the game to end and the soldiers to pull out, and then escape at his own leisure. What you told Nanahara was right—in the event that the game ends after noon, the procedure is for the cleanup crew to come the next day. That leaves plenty of time, wouldn't you say? And this time of year, the water's not too bad for swimming."

Sakamochi gave Kawada a meaningful stare.

Right away, Kawada said, "Huh," and Sakamochi leaned back into the armchair.

"None of that means anything," Kawada said. "The collar's electronics are classified, right? No junior high student would know what was inside them."

But Sakamochi said, "Wrong."

Kawada looked at him.

"That's the real issue here," Sakamochi said. "All that information I looked up—your records from the last game, the stuff about the

Guadalcanal device—now, normally, I wouldn't have looked into any of that. I would have just thought, 'Oh, that Kawada is a clever boy,' and that probably would have been the end of it. But this time, you see, I was contacted by the Secretariat and the Nonaggressive Forces before the game. Just before, actually—the message came on the twentieth."

Kawada's eyes were locked on him.

Sakamochi continued, "They told me someone hacked into Central Processing sometime in March."

He left a pause, then said, "I think the hacker believed he got away undetected. He was good too—when he ran into the administrator inside our system, he even remembered to delete the access log before he fled. But . . ."

Sakamochi left another pause. Kawada didn't say anything.

"But the government's systems aren't so easy to beat. They keep a second, hidden log—a backup of all operations in the system. Usually, nobody bothers to check it, and the administrator didn't think anything was wrong at the time, so the discovery came quite late. But they found out. Oh, they certainly found out."

Kawada's lips tightened. He watched Sakamochi's face. Almost indiscernibly, his Adam's apple moved.

"Let me just say," Kawada said, "I really did hear about how they dispose of the bodies from one of the workers. I met him having a few drinks and we got to talking. And I knew that hardly any of the games end due to the time limit because the guy in your role told me in my last game. You can ask him."

Sakamochi covered his mouth with his fist and stared at Kawada. "Why are you telling me this? I wasn't asking you."

Kawada's Adam's apple moved again—and this time, it was obvious.

Sakamochi chuckled and got back to talking. "So anyway, the data that hacker stole included information about the Program—including technical information on the Guadalcanal collars. Now why do you think he would want to know about a boring little thing like that? That would be pointless, right? If he let it get out to the public, the government would simply make a new design, and that would be that. Anyway, there's been no sign of the plans being leaked as of yet. But what we can say is this: for whatever reason, the intruder must have really wanted that information. Am I wrong?"

Kawada didn't respond. Sakamochi sighed and picked up the envelope he'd tossed onto the table. He turned it upside down, shook it, and pulled out what was inside. He placed the contents side by side on the table in front of Kawada.

There were two photographs, both black-and-white and roughly the size of notebook paper. One was too dark for Kawada to make out anything in the picture, but the other clearly showed a truck surrounded by three black dots. From the overhead angle of the shot, the dots must have been the tops of three people's heads.

"You know what that is, right?" Sakamochi asked. "That's the three of you from just a little bit ago. It's right after you killed Kiriyama. It was taken by a satellite—not that we usually bother to do that sort of thing. Now what I want you to look at is the *other* photo. Well? What do you see? Almost nothing, right? This one is part of the mountain. It's a picture of you shooting the other two. It's too dark, and the trees block almost everything. Do you understand? There's nothing to see."

Silence fell. The boat swayed a little, but Kawada and Sakamochi stared at each other without moving a muscle.

Then Sakamochi sighed and brushed his hair back behind his ear. He grinned and said in a chummy tone, "Hey, Kawada. I've been keeping track of this whole game. And when you shot Nanahara and Nakagawa, well, when you shot, at least, Nanahara took fifty-four seconds to die, and Nakagawa took a full minute and thirty seconds. I'd expect them to die immediately, since you only need one shot to finish each of them off. So then, what's that delay?"

Kawada remained silent. Whether he was aware of it or not, his face had stiffened. But still, he managed to say, "It can happen. I *thought* they'd died immediately, but—"

Sakamochi interrupted him. Perhaps it was overdue. "Just stop, Kawada." His voice was firm. "Okay? Let's get this over with."

He looked into Kawada's eyes and gave him an admonitory nod.

Then he said, "Nanahara and Nakagawa are still on that island. They're alive. They're hiding on the mountain. You're the one who broke into the government network. You knew how to remove the collars. And you knew we could hear you, so you staged that radio drama of you shooting the other two. Then you took off their collars. Am I wrong? I shouldn't have said it *was* a brilliant performance—because it *is* one. You're still putting it on."

Kawada watched Sakamochi with narrowed eyes. His teeth were clenched, and it showed.

Still smiling, Sakamochi continued, "You gave them each a note with a place they could contact you, right? So you were going to meet them later, were you? Well, it's all over now. That helicopter went to spray the island with poison gas. It's a newly developed composite poison and mustard gas called Republic of Greater East Asia Triumphant Victory #2—or GREAT Victory #2. I've also kept the guard ships in place. Nanahara and Nakagawa are finished."

Kawada's fingers were digging into the synthetic leather of the armrests. Sakamochi sighed again and sank deep into his chair.

"There's no precedent for this," he said. "Strictly speaking, you're not really the winner. But I owe a favor or two to one of the officials on the education committee who has bet an awful lot of money on you. I've decided to handle this as an internal matter. If that official spreads around a good word about me, I can go far. So, officially, you're the winner, and you killed those two. That must feel satisfying, eh, Kawada?"

Kawada had gone completely stiff, as if he might start shaking at any moment. But as Sakamochi raised his eyebrows, Kawada forcefully turned his head away, dropped his gaze to the floor, and said, "I . . . don't know what you're talking about."

Nervously, he clenched and unclenched his fists. His eyes flicked back to Sakamochi. With his voice sounding a little anxious, he said, "Why don't you call off that helicopter? You're just wasting tax money."

Sakamochi chuckled. "We'll see about that after it's done."

Then he added, "Oh, and one more thing." He drew a small pistol from his breast pocket. He pointed it at Kawada.

"I've decided to handle you as an internal matter as well. You have dangerous ideas. I don't think that allowing someone like you to live would be in our country's best interests. If you find a rotten tangerine in the crate, you throw it away—and the sooner the better. Before we could get you to the hospital, you died of injuries received during the game. How's that sound? Oh, and don't you worry—if you have any allies, we'll find them. We don't need to bother with an interrogation."

Kawada slowly looked from the barrel of the gun up to Sakamochi's face. "You . . ."

He bared his teeth. Sakamochi grinned.

"You bastard!" Kawada howled, his voice filled with rage and despair, and maybe even a little fear in the face of the incomprehensible. What he really wanted was to get his hands on Sakamochi, but with the gun aimed at him, all he could do was clutch at his knees.

"You . . . Don't you have any kids? Don't you see how fucked up this game is?"

"Sure I have children," Sakamochi said, utterly calm. "You know, I like to have a good time, so we're about to have our third."

Kawada didn't acknowledge the wisecrack. Instead, he shouted, "Then how can you accept this? *Your* children might end up in this fucking game too! Or—or is that it? Do you rank high enough that your kids are exempt?"

Sakamochi shook his head as if he were shocked by the accusation. "That's preposterous. What are you saying, Kawada? Didn't you read the Program guidelines? Did you see any exceptions? Sure, sometimes I do things that are less than entirely honest. I've used my connections to get my daughter into a prestigious elementary school. I'm only human. But there are certain rules to which a human must adhere. Oh, that's right, you didn't get far enough to steal that document, did you? Some of the top secret files contain information on the Program. Well, since you didn't get to read them, I'll fill you in.

This country needs the Program. And no, not as some military experiment—that's a fabrication, of course. Come on, why do you think we broadcast video of the winners on the local news? Sure, seeing that, a person might feel sorry for the child, and maybe they're thinking about how the poor kid probably didn't even want to play the game. But the child was left with no choice but to fight the others. It serves to remind everyone that in the end they can't trust anyone. And soon, nobody's even thinking about banding together and staging a revolution. The Republic of Greater East Asia, and its ideals, will live on forever. And for the sake of such a lofty goal, everyone needs to die equally. I've taught my own children as much. My oldest—she's in second grade now—she's always saying how she'd give her life for the Republic."

Kawada's cheeks were trembling. "You're mad," he said. "You're insane! How can you live like that?" He sounded on the verge of tears. "The government should serve its people. We don't live for the sake of the system. If you think this country is right . . . then you're insane!"

Sakamochi waited for Kawada to finish. Then he said, "Listen, Kawada. You're still a child. It sounds like you've talked about this before, but I want you to really think about it. This is a magnificent country. No other country anywhere in the world is as prosperous. Sure, overseas travel is a little restricted, but the quality of our exports is second to none. When our government boasts about our per-capita GDP, that's no mere propaganda. It's the truth. We've the highest in the world. But the thing is, and listen to this now, that prosperity can only be achieved through a strong government and a people united around it. A certain level of control is a constant necessity. Otherwise, we'd decay into some third-rate country, like the American Empire. You've heard what things are like over there, haven't you? The country is a total mess, rife with drugs and violence and homosexuality. It's surviving only on its past legacy, but it'll collapse soon enough."

Kawada remained silent for a time. He appeared to be clenching his teeth. Then, quietly, he spoke.

"Just let me say one thing."

Sakamochi raised his eyebrows. "What is it? Go ahead, say it."

"Your kind might call it prosperity . . ." His voice sounded weary but possessed a core of conviction. "But it'll always be a fraud. Even if you kill me here, that truth won't change. You'll always be a fraud. Remember that."

Sakamochi shrugged. "Are you finished speaking?"

He pointed the gun straight between Kawada's eyes. Kawada pressed his lips together and stared not at the barrel of the gun but at Sakamochi behind it. Maybe that was his way of saying he was ready.

"Bye, Kawada."

Sakamochi gave him a small nod of farewell. His finger tightened on the trigger.

A typewriter-like *brattattattat* shook the air.

Sakamochi's finger froze. For a split second, his eyes went to the door—along with his attention.

By the time he looked back, Kawada was right in front of him. Table or no table, the student had appeared a mere ten centimeters away. It was as if he'd teleported there, like a wizard, or at least someone with supernatural powers.

The *brattattat, brattattattat* continued outside.

With one hand, Kawada forced down Sakamochi's gun. With the two of them close enough to kiss, Sakamochi, strangely still, watched Kawada's face. His long hair didn't fall out of place. He didn't try to shake free from Kawada's grasp. Without a word, he simply watched Kawada.

Again the *brattattattat* came.

The door opened. The soldier, Nomura, started to say, "It's an attack—" but when he saw Kawada and Sakamochi, he began to raise his rifle.

Still clutching Sakamochi's hand, Kawada twisted the man around as if they were dancing the tango. As he did, he pushed Sakamochi's finger down on the trigger and fired. Nomura took three bullets just above his heart, groaned, stumbled back and collapsed. The next *brattattattat* sounded far louder with the door open.

Kawada looked into Sakamochi's eyes. With their bodies pressing together, Kawada brought his clenched hand under Sakamochi's chin and twisted his fist.

Staring at Kawada with his eyes wide open, Sakamochi coughed out blood. The red liquid spilled out from his lips, ran down his chin, and dripped to the floor.

"I told you it was a waste of tax money."

Shogo Kawada twisted his hand again. Sakamochi's eyes left Kawada as they slowly rolled upward.

Kawada stepped back, and Sakamochi slumped into the armchair. His chin tilted back to reveal a brown stick poking out from his windpipe like some bizarre necklace. A closer inspection would find the small, silver letters, "HB," etched near its end. The pencil was, of course, one of the very same ones with which Kawada and Shuya and everyone else had written, *We will kill each other*. But Kinpatsu Sakamochi likely died not even knowing it was a pencil at all.

Kawada held his eyes on him for only a brief moment before tucking Sakamochi's pistol into the front of his slacks. He ran over to Nomura, who was face up on the floor, and he scooped up the soldier's rifle. He swiped the spare magazines from Nomura's belt and exited the room. Down the corridor to the right were two doors. He opened one, and then the other, but each led to a room lined with bunk beds on either wall—and both rooms were vacant.

Another *brattattattat* came from somewhere nearby, and a soldier tumbled down the ladder at the end of the hall. He was the one called Kondo, now dead, and weaponless save for the sidearm in his hand— he must have assumed he'd be safe inside the ship now that the game had ended.

Kawada stepped around the body and into the ladderway. He looked up.

Shuya Nanahara (Boys #15), Ingram MAC-10 in hand, and Noriko Nakagawa (Girls #15) stood side by side, looking down at him. Both were sopping wet from head to toe.

78

Shuya had heard gunfire that wasn't his own and was worried he and Noriko were too late. Seeing Kawada safe at the bottom of the ladder, Shuya cried out in relief, "Kawada!"

Kawada came running up the stairs, carrying a rifle he must have taken from one of the soldiers.

"Are you all right?" Shuya asked.

"Yeah." Kawada nodded. "Mr. Sakamochi is dead. But did you take care of the others?"

"Everyone above deck. But we didn't see Nomura—"

"Then that's all of them. I took out Nomura."

Having said that, Kawada slipped past them and ran down the corridor toward the bridge. Shuya and Noriko followed.

Along the way, they came across one dead soldier in the corridor, and two more inside and outside the briefing room below the bridge. One was Tahara, and the others were navy men assigned to the vessel. Only Tahara was armed, and only with his sidearm. Shuya had dispatched them with the Ingram's automatic fire. Another two were out on the deck. They had been the first to die.

Kawada put his hand on the railing of the ladder leading up to the bridge. He glanced down at Tahara's corpse and said, "You were merciless, Nanahara."

"Yeah." Shuya nodded. "I was."

They followed the ladder up to the bridge, where two more sailors lay dead. The windows separating the three students from the darkness bore several holes from bullets that had either gone astray or had passed through the soldiers' bodies.

The ship was passing by an island—probably Megijima—lit with the lights of people in their homes. Shuya wondered if the sound of their gunfire had carried to the island or, for that matter, far across the surrounding sea. But even if it had, he wasn't concerned—sudden bursts of gunfire weren't an unusual occurrence in this country.

Kawada peered ahead. Shuya and Noriko followed his gaze and saw what seemed to be a gravel barge approaching them on the right. Kawada took the wheel and made a small adjustment on the lever sticking out from its side.

As he steered, he said, "I hope the two of you didn't catch a cold."

"I'm good," Shuya said.

"And you, Noriko?"

She bobbed her head. "I'm fine."

The gravel barge was near now. Kawada watched ahead and said, "I'm sorry. It looks like I had the easy part this time."

"That's not true," Shuya said, looking back and forth between Kawada's hands at the wheel and the passing ship. "I wasn't in any condition to take on Sakamochi and his gun unarmed. No, we had the right man in the right job."

The barge's silhouette loomed larger and larger. But soon the ships glided past each other without event. The gravel barge's lights receded into the distance.

Kawada sighed in relief and let go of the wheel. Then he began working a complex array of buttons next to a gauge Shuya didn't understand how to read. Kawada kept his eyes on the panel until one of the indicator lights went out. Then he picked up the radio transceiver's handset. A voice came from the speaker.

"This is the Bisan Seto Vessel Traffic Service Center."

Kawada responded, "This is the Nonaggressive Forces Naval Vessel Registration DM245-3568. Requesting our current position."

"We cannot confirm your position at this time, DM245-2568. Are you having mechanical issues?"

"We seem to have a malfunction in our DPS navigation system. We're going to remain in position for an hour while we attempt a repair. Can you notify the other ships in our area?"

"Understood. What is your current position?"

Kawada read off the numbers from the gauge he'd been working at before. Then he ended transmission.

This must have been a ploy to buy them time to move elsewhere. He put his hand to the wheel and spun it into a hard left. The ship rocked into the turn.

As he carefully manned the wheel, Kawada said, "That bastard Sakamochi was on to us. I'm glad I told you to come to the ship."

Shuya nodded and droplets of water fell from his bangs.

After Kawada had fired those two shots into the air on that mountainside, he raised his finger to his mouth, signaling the wide-eyed and blinking pair to stay quiet. He then took the map from his pocket and wrote on the back with his pencil. It was dark out, and the writing was hard to read, but they managed it. Kawada removed their collars, using only a cable and a part that looked like it came from a radio—where he obtained those, Shuya didn't know—along with his knife and a small flat-head screwdriver. Then Kawada pulled a crude ladder of bamboo and rope from his daypack. Shuya had no idea when he'd managed to prepare that.

Kawada wrote again on the back of the map.

[*Sneak onto whatever ship they put me on. It's night, so no one will see you. Swim into the harbor from the sea. You'll find an anchor on a chain coming down from the ship. Attach this ladder to the chain and hold on. Once they raise the anchor and start the boat moving, climb up to the deck and hide behind the lifeboats at the back of the ship. When you sense the time is right, attack.*]

When the ship took on speed and started kicking up waves, holding on to the flimsy ladder as it dragged them through the water hadn't been easy. Surmounting the last few dozen centimeters between the top rung and the edge of the deck had also posed trouble. With his left arm out of commission, Shuya found himself unable to do what otherwise would have been an easy task. But even with her wounded hand, Noriko climbed ahead of him and practically lifted him above deck. Her strength took him by surprise.

And so they had made it.

Shuya said, "I just wish you had told us your plan earlier than that."

Kawada spun the wheel to the right and offered an innocent shrug. "It would have made your reactions less natural. I'm sorry."

He released the wheel. Ahead lay only the black, open sea. For the time being, no ships were coming to pass them by. Kawada began checking the various gauges and displays on the console.

"It's amazing, though," Noriko said, "how you managed to hack into the government's computers."

"Yeah," Shuya agreed. "That was some lie about you being no good with computers."

A grin flashed to Kawada's face in profile. "Sakamochi figured it out anyway—or at least he came close enough."

Seeming satisfied with the readings, Kawada stepped away from the instrument panel. He walked to one of the fallen sailors. As Shuya and Noriko looked on, he began to dig through the soldier's pockets.

"Damn," he said. "These days, even the soldiers have started to quit smoking."

Shuya realized he was looking for cigarettes.

But then, in the front pocket of the other soldier's shirt, Kawada found a crumpled-up pack of Busters. Ignoring the blood splattered on the outside of the packaging, he drew one of the cigarettes, put it to his lips, and lit it. He leaned against the side of the helm, narrowed his eyes, and let out a pleasurable puff of smoke.

Watching him, Noriko said, "If there were many more of us, we wouldn't have been able to escape like this."

Kawada nodded. "Yeah. And it had to be after dark too. But there's no point in dwelling on it. We're alive. Isn't that enough?"

Shuya nodded. "That's right."

Then Kawada said, "Why don't you two go take a shower? It's in front of the ladder. It's small, but there should be hot water. You can steal the soldiers' clothes to wear."

Shuya nodded and set the Ingram down on a small table beside the wall. He put his arm around Noriko and said, "Let's do that, Noriko. You can go first. We don't want your cold to come back."

Noriko nodded, and the two of them started for the ladder.

"Nanahara," Kawada said, stopping him. "Actually, hold off on that for a second." He rubbed out his cigarette on the underside of the helm. "Let me show you how to steer this thing first."

Shuya raised his eyebrows. He'd expected Kawada to take care of steering the ship. But now that he thought about it, he realized Kawada might want a shower too, and Shuya and Noriko would have to steer.

Shuya nodded, and he and Noriko returned to Kawada beside the helm.

Kawada let out a breath and tapped the wheel with his palm. "Right now, the ship is on manual control. It's simpler than trying to fumble with the autopilot settings." He gestured to the lever coming out of the side of the wheel. "Now this is like an accelerator and brake all in one. Push it forward to make the ship go faster, and pull back to slow down. Easy, right? And over here . . . Take a look at this."

Kawada pointed at a round gauge above the wheel. Inside it, a needle pointed forward and to the left. The edge of the circle was lined with numbers and the four familiar letters that marked off each cardinal direction.

"This guy here is a gyrocompass," Kawada explained. "It'll tell you which way you're going. Here, take a look at this sea chart."

He showed them the route leading through the islands from their current position east of Megijima toward the Honshu mainland. Then he told them they should find some inconspicuous beach somewhere in Okayama Prefecture to make land. He followed that with a brief rundown of the radar and depth finder systems.

Kawada put his hand to his chin. "That about does it for the crash course. That's enough to steer this thing. Remember to always steer to the right of an oncoming ship. Another thing, ships take time to stop. Be sure to lower your speed enough before approaching the shore. Got that?"

Shuya raised his eyebrows again. He wasn't sure why Kawada was bothering to tell him how to dock, but he nodded anyway.

Kawada added, "Do you both still have the notes I gave you? I really did write your contact's information on them."

"Yeah," Shuya said, "We have them. But you're coming with us, aren't you? Of course you are."

Kawada didn't answer immediately. Instead, he took the pack of cigarettes from his pocket, put one in his lips, and lit it. It lit up right away, but then Shuya noticed something wrong. Kawada's hand, holding the lighter, was trembling.

Noriko's eyes widened. She must have noticed it too.

"Kawada, you—" Shuya said.

"You guys asked me . . ." Kawada said, speaking over him. The cigarette was still in his mouth. His trembling hand tossed the lighter down beside the helm. ". . . if I would come with you to the States."

His hand still shaking, he took the cigarette from his mouth and exhaled smoke. "I thought it over. But . . ."

Kawada put the cigarette back in his mouth, interrupting himself. He took it out again and blew smoke. "It looks like I won't have to give you an answer."

Suddenly, his body slid down. His head slumped forward as he fell to his knees.

"Kawada!" Shuya yelled, running to him.

He wrapped his right arm around Kawada's and held him up. Noriko also ran over and held Kawada from the other side.

The strength drained from Kawada's body, and he was heavy in their arms. Shuya realized the back of Kawada's school uniform was soaking wet. A tiny, tiny hole had torn open in the cloth below his neck. Kiriyama's work—that one shot. Kawada had said it was only a graze.

Why? Why hadn't he tended to it right away? Did he already know it was fatal? Or did he ignore it in order to get us to the ship on time?

In their arms, Kawada slowly dropped and sat on the floor.

"I'm tired," he said. "Please let me sleep."

"No, no, no, no!" Shuya shouted. "You can do that at the nearest hospital! They'll be able to take care of—"

"Don't be ridiculous." Kawada laughed, and like the two soldiers at the edge of the room, he slumped onto his back.

Shuya got on his knees and shook Kawada's shoulder. "Please! Get up, please."

"Kawada," Noriko cried.

"Noriko!" Shuya barked. Her eyes snapped to him. "Don't cry. Kawada's not going to die."

"Nanahara." Kawada reproved him in a mild voice. "You shouldn't yell at her over nothing. You have to be kind to your girl." Then he added, "And, sorry, but . . . well, I'm g-going to die."

Kawada's face was turning more pale by the moment, the scar above his left eye a dark red caterpillar in sharp contrast.

"Kawada . . ." Shuya said.

"I still hadn't d-decided," Kawada said. His head was trembling, but he continued to speak. "If I . . . I was going to join you. But I w-want to—to th-thank you. B-b-both."

Shuya shook his head, *no, no*. But unable to speak, he just stared at Kawada.

Kawada lifted his trembling right hand. "G-g-goodbye."

Shuya took his hand.

"You too, N-Noriko."

Holding back the tears in her eyes, she took his hand.

Now Shuya knew Kawada was dying. He had already known, but now he accepted it. He hadn't any other choice. He tried to think of something he should say. He found it.

"Kawada."

Kawada's eyes drifted from Noriko to him.

"I'm going to tear down this country for you! I'll fucking tear it down!"

Kawada smiled. His hand slipped from Noriko's grasp and fell limply to his chest. Noriko took it again, holding it there, squeezing tight.

Kawada closed his eyes. He seemed to faintly smile again. Then he said, "I t-told you, Nana—Nanahara. Y-you don't—don't—don't have to d-d-do that. J-just—just—just live—live on. T-t-together. Keep on—on t-t-trusting and—and—and hon-honoring one—one—one an-another. P-p-p-please."

Kawada took in a deep breath. His eyes remained closed.

"That's what I want."

That was the end. He stopped breathing. The lights of the wheelhouse ceiling cast their unnatural yellow glow over his pale, white face. He seemed at peace.

"Kawada!" Shuya yelled. He still had more to say. "You'll see Keiko! You'll be happy with her! You'll . . ."

Too late. Kawada heard nothing now. Besides, his expression looked so peaceful.

"Damn it," Shuya said, the tremble in his lips working into his voice. "Damn it."

Noriko was crying as she held on to Kawada's hand.

Like her, Shuya laid his hand atop Kawada's thick hand. A thought struck him, and he searched through the pockets of Kawada's school uniform. He found what he was looking for—the birdcall. He pressed it into Kawada's hand and closed his friend's fingers over it. Then he wrapped his own hands around Kawada's fist.

And finally, he cried.

Within the crowd of people, each hurrying through with their own purpose, Shuya Nanahara (Boys #15, Ninth Grade Class B, Shiroiwa Junior High, Shiroiwa Town, Kagawa Prefecture) stepped off one of the escalators that flanked the wide staircase into Osaka's Umeda Station and heard the broadcaster say, "We now bring you this report on the murder of a Program Instructor in Kagawa Prefecture." He nudged Noriko Nakagawa (Girls #15), who was beside him, and came to a stop.

On the giant screen, which was next to the escalator and just as tall, appeared a news anchor in his fifties with neatly parted hair.

Shuya and Noriko stood side by side in front of the screen. It was Monday, a little past six in the evening, and students and suited salarymen were among the many congregating there waiting for someone to meet them. Shuya and Noriko were not in their school uniforms. Shuya wore jeans and a denim jacket over a patterned shirt. Noriko, also in jeans, had on a dark green polo shirt under a gray lightweight hoodie. (Their sneakers, however, were the same ones they'd worn in the game—washed clean, of course.) Shuya had flipped up his jacket collar to hide the bandage around his neck. Similarly, Noriko had pulled down her black leather baseball cap to conceal the large bandage across her cheek. Her right leg still had a limp, but it wasn't so conspicuous anymore. Still unable to move his left arm, Shuya used his right hand to adjust the strap of the messenger bag over his left shoulder.

Kawada's note to Shuya gave the name of a doctor, and the one to Noriko contained the address in Kobe. It was a small, backstreet clinic, probably not all that different from where Kawada had grown up. The doctor, who still seemed to be in his twenties, welcomed them warmly and treated their wounds.

"Kawada's father was something of a mentor to my dad when they were in medical school together," the doctor said. "And he did a lot for me too."

The doctor seemed to be well connected. He let them stay with him overnight, and the next day—yesterday, that is—he made the arrangements for them to escape the country.

He'd said, "We'll be using the money Kawada left with me in case of an emergency." From a small fishing village in Wakayama, they would take a fishing boat out to the Pacific Ocean. From there, they'd get on a ship heading to the Democratic Republic of the Korean Peninsula.

"Getting to America from the DRKP won't be a problem," the doctor had said, looking concerned. "But the trick will be transferring to that second ship."

Either way, Shuya and Noriko hadn't any other option.

Today, before they left the doctor's house, Noriko talked to her family over the phone—to be precise, she first called a friend of hers from another class and had the friend relay a message to her family, instructing them to call her at the doctor's house from a pay phone in case her family's phone had been tapped. Shuya gave her some space so that she could talk in private, but he heard her crying voice coming from the hall. Shuya didn't try to contact the House of Mercy and Love. Inside himself, he gave Ms. Anno his thanks and bid her farewell. He did the same with Kazumi Shintani.

The news anchor continued, "Inspection of the site where the Program was held, Kagawa Prefecture's Oki Island, was delayed until this afternoon due to the presence of poison gas sprayed by a Nonaggressive Forces helicopter. Now, two days since the incident occurred, the inspection revealed that two of the students are missing."

The image on the giant screen changed. It was the island. A telephoto-lens shot from the sea, of policemen and soldiers searching the island where Shuya and his classmates had fought for their lives. The broadcast cut to another long-distance shot of the harbor, where the corpses of his classmates were piled. The view only lasted a brief moment, but Shuya recognized two of the bodies. At the edge of the mountain of black uniforms and sailor suits, two faces were turned toward the camera—Yukie Utsumi and Yoshitoki Kuninobu. Because they had both died indoors, their faces remained pristine, untouched by the effects of GREAT Victory #2. Shuya clenched his right fist.

"The missing students are Shuya Nanahara and Noriko Nakagawa, both ninth grade students of Shiroiwa Junior High School in Kagawa Prefecture."

The giant screen changed again, now displaying the same portrait photographs they each had on their student IDs. Shuya looked around, but none of the other people watching the report seemed to have noticed him or Noriko.

Next up was footage of an unpopulated shore where the mountains extended all the way to the sea. The camera zoomed in on a small military patrol ship that had run aground in the shallows just off the beach where more policemen and soldiers were looking on. This seemed to be an older clip from when the ship had first been discovered.

"In the early morning hours of the twenty-fourth, the ship of Instructor Kinpatsu Sakamochi, Program Administrator for Kagawa Prefecture, was found stranded off the coast near the town of Ushimado in Okayama Prefecture. The bodies of Instructor Sakamochi, along with nine Nonaggressive Forces soldiers, including Private First Class Tokihiko Tahara, as well as the Program's winner, Shogo Kawada, were found on board."

The image changed to a portrait picture of Sakamochi and his long hair.

"Police and military officials launched a joint investigation into the cause of their deaths. Authorities now believe that the two missing students may possess information critical to the investigation and are searching for—"

The newscaster went on, but the image on the screen captured Shuya's attention.

It was a short video clip with a caption below that read TWO-TIME WINNER SHOGO KAWADA FOUND DEAD. Under normal circumstances, it would only have been shown on the local news in Kagawa, and with a more generic caption like MALE STUDENT WINNER. Shuya and Noriko had watched the news in the Kobe doctor's house several times but had only seen photos of Kawada. This was their first time seeing this footage.

Confined by the soldiers at his sides, Kawada stared into the camera.

Then, at the end of the ten-second clip, he grinned and gave a thumbs-up.

A distressed murmur spread through the crowd of people watching the report. They probably assumed he was gloating over his victory.

They were wrong. As Shuya stared vacantly at the face of the reporter now back on the screen, he thought, *Was that a message for us? When he stood in front of that government camera, did he already know he was going to die? Or was it simply another display of his ironic humor?*

Just like Kawada once said—I'll never know.

Shuya's and Noriko's pictures returned to the screen.

"Any sightings of these two should be—"

"Let's go, Noriko," Shuya whispered. "We should hurry."

He took her hand, and they turned their backs on the screen and started to walk away.

As they held hands, Noriko said, "Kawada . . . said something to me. Before you came back—when you were with Yukie's group."

Shuya tilted his head and looked at her.

She looked up at him. Her eyes, dark in the shade of her cap, brimmed with tears. "He said he was glad to have made such good friends."

Shuya looked ahead and nodded. He just nodded.

They let a group of six or seven students cut across them. When they started walking again, Shuya said, "Noriko, I'll stay with you forever. I promised Kawada I would."

He sensed her nod.

"For now, we escape," he said. "But one day, I want to tear this country down. I won't break my promise to Kawada. I want to tear down this country—for Kawada, and for you, and for me, and for Yoshitoki, and for everyone. When that time comes, will you help me?"

Noriko squeezed his hand and said, "Of course."

They slipped through the crowd. Soon, they reached the ticket vending machine. Noriko looked up at the fare chart, then took her change from her pocket, counted out the correct amount for two tickets, and got in the back of the line at the machine.

Standing alone, Shuya waited for her turn to come. It soon did. Noriko pressed her coins into the slot.

Shuya casually turned his head to the left.

His eyes narrowed. Outside the doors of the station's concourse, and past the busy street where taxis and cars came and went, the feet of Osaka's high-rise buildings stood. In front of this backdrop, a tall man in a black uniform was walking straight at them. Deftly weaving through the flow of the crowd, the man kept his eyes fixed in their direction.

His uniform could only be that of a policeman, the golden peach insignia shining in the center of the front of his cap.

Shuya searched for an escape route as he slowly reached for the Beretta 92F tucked in the back of his jeans, concealed under his jacket. Another street ran alongside the concourse's opposite entrance. If they could get outside, they could find a car, and . . .

Noriko returned with the tickets. Shuya whispered, "We can't take the train."

Noriko understood. She turned her head, and her eyes widened when she saw the man.

"Let's go out that way," Shuya said.

The policeman started running.

"Run, Noriko! Run as fast as you can!"

They took off running, and Shuya thought, *Hey, I think I've heard something like that before.*

He glanced over his shoulder. The cop was holding a gun. Shuya drew the Beretta, and the officer fired two shots in a sweeping motion. By luck, neither hit Shuya or Noriko—or anyone else in the crowd. Several people screamed, and some in the crowd dropped to the floor, while others, not knowing where the shots had come from, scattered and ran in every direction. The cop lowered his weapon and started running toward them again, but he collided with an overweight woman carrying shopping bags and tumbled to the ground. The woman fell with him, and various vegetables and packages spilled from her bags and slid across the floor.

Having seen enough, Shuya again looked ahead.

And as he ran alongside Noriko, a thought came over him. The screams, the pounding of their feet, the shouts of the policeman ordering them to stop, all of that faded away, then vanished, and this thought filled the entirety of his mind.

It might have been inappropriately tranquil. Even worse, he'd plagiarized it. *Oh man.*

But he thought it anyway.

Together, Noriko, we'll live with the sadness
I'll love you with all the madness in my soul.
Someday girl I don't know when
we're gonna get to that place
Where we really want to go
and we'll walk in the sun.
But till then tramps like us
baby we were born to run.

The screams and angry yells returned at once, accompanied by Noriko's heavy breathing and his heart's thumping.

This isn't over. Not even close.
All right, I'll play your game now.
And I won't stop until I win.

ONCE AGAIN, TWO STUDENTS REMAIN.
BUT OF COURSE, NOW THEY'RE WITH YOU.

AFTERWORD TO THE 2009 EDITION

Greetings. I'm the author, Takami. It's already been ten years since I wrote this book. Well, to be more precise, the novel originated as a contest entry and underwent several revisions before debuting in Japan ten years ago. As I have come to always admit in articles like this, and feel compelled to include here as well, I haven't written a single new novel in the ten years since. I know, it's unusual. I suppose by now a majority of those in the Japanese publishing industry feel like I'll never write another novel. (Apparently, the Japanese Wikipedia has even said as much.) (Wonderful.)

When VIZ asked me to write something to put in this new edition, I was a little hesitant. In the first place, I don't give a damn about authors. When deciding what to read next, I will seek out works by the author of a novel I've previously enjoyed, but the personal background of an author is essentially irrelevant, and any story—or for that matter, a work in any creative form—that needs foreknowledge of its creator to be enjoyed is fundamentally poor.

Also, and this is more my own problem, I haven't written anything else in these ten years, and so the only things I can discuss directly pertain to this book. To be frank, I've become a little bored with it. Revealing myself, feeling the way I do, could disrupt the fantasy built up around the novel. (Some may think that's not a big deal, but to hell with them.) But, well, I started writing, and how should I put it? I decided this would be the last time I would ever write about this novel. I'll write everything I can write about it, and then I will say goodbye to this novel that has accompanied me—or, perhaps, haunted me—for these ten years. Just like an exorcism. Will I also say goodbye to the royalties? No. No way has yet been invented to say goodbye to royalties.

Well, where should I begin the exorcism? To save my mind from unnecessary strain, VIZ has prepared several questions for me. Let's start with the first one.

What sort of economic system does the Republic have? It sounds like a mix of fascism and communism. Was that purposeful?

Wow, there's a tough question right from the start. Hmm . . . to answer this, I first need to explain how I came to write this novel. I quit my job at a newspaper after five years to become, of course, a novelist. (Not possessing enough talent—or stamina—to do both at once.) I tried writing some short stories as a kind of warm-up, but I didn't have the slightest idea of what I would write after that. Before I had worked at a newspaper, when I was a student, I mostly wrote detective stories, or horror, as best I could, or some variation...Like something that felt like horror, but with a detective as the main character, or maybe more like the investigation of an incident straight out of a horror story. But all those ideas had structural problems and could hardly be called stories. (Couldn't the same be said for the book you now hold in your hands?) A short story I wrote in college made it to the second selection (or so) during a minor competition, but the competition had somewhere around six rounds. Sure, it took sound determination to abandon my career with so little experience, but determined or not, I still didn't have any ideas.

And, well, I remained without any until one night, possibly after a particularly late night, I was lying in my futon, half asleep, half awake, and I got the mental image of a teacher from a school drama I saw on TV long ago. He said, "All right class, listen up." (He speaks like this throughout the book too.) "Now today, I'm going to have you all kill each other!" The image of him grinning as he spoke was so vivid, I laughed, but was also terrified. (As Rumiko Takahashi, the creator of *Ranma 1/2* and *Inuyasha* says, the difference between humor and terror is paper-thin.) And with just that, I knew I had something to write about.

When I shared this idea with a number of my friends, they all said it sounded like a manga (a nice way of saying it was unrealistic), but they were interested by it. At that point, however, I was working under a serious misconception. You see, I was something of a pro wrestling fan, and even though I had seen any number of "battle royal"–style matches (or possibly because I had seen so many), I didn't understand the true meaning of the rule, "Anyone can face off against anyone else." Soon I would come to realize this while talking with a friend. I don't have any record of the conversation, but it basically went like this:

"Let's say there's a shack in the forest, and the toughest guy is holed up inside."

"What do you mean, toughest?"

"He's like a killing machine. He's already killed a lot of people."

"Hmmm . . . Well, we'd better do something about him."

"Yeah, and even worse, he's got a machine gun!"

"Oh, that's cool, that's cool."

"So we have to work together to take him out."

"And we have to come up with a plan, right?"

Oh, how terrible. But it's kind of fun, isn't it? Please note how sportsmanlike our speech was, like a huddle in a football game. (Now that I think about it, *Force 10 from Navarone* was the same kind of sportsmanlike.) And it was at that point in the conversation that it hit me. Suddenly. Yes, suddenly.

"Wait a minute. When we talk about working together to go after that toughest whoever, shouldn't I be worried that you might suddenly start making moves against me?"

"Why? It's important to deal with that guy right now, isn't it? We can worry about each other later."

"Sure, you might say that, but what if you're just trying to trick me?"

"Wait, look, here, I set down my weapon. See, you don't need to worry."

"What does that prove?"

You may already have guessed what I felt as my friend innocently insisted that he'd never turn on me. I was struck by a premonition that what I was about to write would be so completely different from my assumptions that it would become bleak. (Just to be clear, you initially intended this to be lighthearted?) (Yes, *sir!*) Someone you thought was your friend could suddenly turn against you—as I wrote in the story's introduction, that sort of thing happens in a pro wrestling battle royal. But there is a huge difference between being double-crossed by your friend and being defeated by pinfall for the crowd's enjoyment, and being double-crossed by your friend and being killed. The level of distrust for your fellow man wouldn't even be comparable. I had arrived at the realization that it wasn't sportsmanlike at all. And I think it was at that point that it became possible for me to write this story.

Let me take a moment to protect the honor of my friend. I know he was telling the truth. He isn't the kind of guy who would betray me. If the two of us were put on the rack, I would absolutely betray him first. I'm sure of it, sir!

This backstory has gotten long, but I hope you understand that whether or not it was going to be sportsmanlike, I had just wanted to put Sakamochi's "It's a fight to the death!" into a concrete form. In the end, I chose unsportsmanlike, and so I tried to imagine a world that would encourage such actions—and quickly I thought it would have to be some sort of totalitarian regime. Doubtlessly, I had Stephen King's

The Long Walk in mind. In other words, the nation that would serve as the setting for the novel was added later. That's not to mention details like the economic system, which were almost not considered at all, and, well, since it would still make up a novel without it, you're holding the result. (Those who think the story still doesn't make up a novel may be correct, but to hell with them too.)

Still, I thought that figurative country couldn't be written any differently. I don't know if I can explain it well enough for you to understand, but this fictional country, "The Republic of Greater East Asia," is in part Japan. I wanted to write about the trapped feeling of living in Japan I've felt clearly since childhood—at the very least, from middle school on—and that's what I attempted to do. Here in Japan, being different from other people makes you a potential scapegoat when anything goes wrong. It's still true to a certain extent to this day! Even if a rule is clearly ridiculous, nobody will speak out against it, because people think, "If I say something, others will think I'm different," and the rule continues unchanged. Eventually, that oddity becomes a tradition that everyone seems to think of affectionately. (Regarding this, Motoharu Sano sang, "again and again and at some point you'll love me.") (Probably.) Shogo Kawada puts it best when he says in Chapter 31, "Even if everyone were against it, no one could say it out loud. That's why nothing changes. There are a lot of screwed-up things in this country, but they all boil down to the same thing— fascism." Or, "Blind submission. Dependence on others and group mentality. Conservatism and passive acceptance . . . They can't think for themselves. Anything that's too complicated sends their heads reeling. Makes me want to puke."

When I was born, near the end of the '60s, there existed even in Japan the sort of culture where a college student would throw Molotov cocktails at police. But in the '80s, when I was a teenager, that environment had vanished. Maybe everyone became disillusioned when they discovered that even throwing Molotov cocktails at police didn't change anything. This may be related to my feeling of trapped hopelessness. (And it's why I had such a reaction upon finding messages like "Beat the System" and "Keep Questioning" written on the jackets of Motoharu Sano's records in the late '80s.) Furthermore, the phrase "successful fascism" appears in this novel. It's based on something Beat Takeshi said—he once described Japan as "successful socialism." In this context, "successful" likely means, "Most everyone can eat." It may be successful, and it may be purposeful, but even when you can eat, don't you care if you're a slave or a prisoner?

Oh, and while I'm at it, here's a little-known story. The ruler of the country gives an address at the beginning of the novel. I derived it from propaganda that North Korea would broadcast at Japan at that time (and to this day as well, I suppose). Aside from North Korean spies, the Japanese police agencies, the media, and a few hobbyists, I was probably the only person in Japan intently listening to those broadcasts. Furthermore, Dylan's "Blowin' in the Wind" appears, translated into Japanese, at the end of the manga edition of *Battle Royale*. (It was not my idea, but rather that of the manga's author Masayuki Taguchi and our editors. For some reason, it didn't make it into the English edition.) Kiyoshiro Imawano, who translated into Japanese and covered "Blowin' in the Wind" in Japanese, wrote his own song, "Wanna be in North Korea" (Akogare no kitachousen), in which he sings, "They'll take you [to North Korea] for freeeeeeee." Those who are interested should definitely study East Asian geopolitics.

Now, on to the next card.

What English-language authors do you like to read?

Oh, this looks like it might turn into another long answer. But it's an important topic to me.

For a time, I had something of a "seat of honor" on my bookshelf. Well, I say bookshelf, but it was really just a cheaply cobbled together bit of furniture, and one of the shelves had a glass door to keep out the dust. Mixed in among the Japanese novelists I'll mention later were the works of Stephen King and Robert Parker (as well as books by Thoreau, Whitman, and Kerouac due to Motoharu Sano's influence— as well as Lovecraft (!) and Chandler as classics. Finally, I added Orwell to the list, but by that point my personal library grew too large to keep updating the "seat of honor").

I became interested in reading fairly late and didn't start King and Parker until college, but those two masters influenced me greatly. Not only was Parker's dialogue interesting, he showed me that it can be fine to set the story aside for a debate (usually some kind of social commentary) between characters. As for King, and I apologize for so commonplace an observation, I was astonished by the skill of his story-telling—no, rather, I became so engrossed that I kept on reading, unaware of my own astonishment.

This would be a good time to confess that Shogo Kawada's final line in this book, "That's what I want," is nothing more than an overt copy of the last line of *Rita Hayworth and Shawshank Redemption* (or to be more precise, Hisashi Asakura's translation of that line into Japanese). When Shuya Nanahara recalls reading an old American paperback in Chapter 0, he is referring to *The Body*, and the name of the city the children are from, Shiroiwa, is a direct translation of "Castle Rock." If I had never read *Needful Things*, the introduction by the pro wrestling fan (who is basically just myself) might have been filled with bland explanations of pro wrestling jargon.

Readers of Parker's Spenser series may have noticed that Shogo Kawada's lines in Chapter 45 resemble what Hawk says to Spenser and Susan in the Las Vegas hotel in *Chance*. I made an effort to keep it from being exactly the same, but the situation was quite similar. Shogo's manner of speaking was modeled after Hawk. Or, to be more precise, after Hawk's way of speech as translated by Mitsu Kikuchi, as crazy as that is. At any rate, if you considered the mix of dialogue and narrative as a percentage, and thought it felt like Parker, you wouldn't be wrong. Mitsu Kikuchi also translated *The Silence of the Lambs*; although possibly because someone didn't think he would fit the work, a Hiroshi Takami (no relation), a well-known translator in Japan, did *Hannibal*.

Well. Let's keep at it. The next question:

When you were writing *Battle Royale*, did you have a movie in mind with all the characters and points of view?

I feel like I wrote with camera angles in mind. While this book is written in third-person perspective, each scene is almost like first-person, and we basically view each scene through the eyes of one character. Of course, the "camera" sometimes pulls back, allowing us to see everything, such as the scene with Shuya and Noriko at the end of Chapter 45. We're talking about movies, but people who grew up with television as well (and manga) can't escape that influence. I was aware of how tall each character was, and their build, but I don't think I went as far as forming detailed images of their faces.

On the subject of perspective, only Shogo Kawada's part in Chapter 77 is noticeably awkward. That part is neither from Shogo's point of view, nor is it from that of his opponent, Sakamochi. They each have a secret plot they want to spring on the other, and if it was a true first-person perspective, I would have to reveal one of those plots to the reader. It was very difficult for me to write that scene. Does anyone know a clever way of solving that problem?

If I had to say what movies I was conscious of while writing, and you may have noticed this, one would clearly be *Terminator 2*. In Chapter 0, two mysterious males—Shogo Kawada and Kazuo Kiriyama—appear. One is the main character's ally, the other his enemy. That's why Shogo Kawada has a shotgun. Also, when the girls are arguing with each other in Chapter 62, I recalled John Carpenter's version of *The Thing*. It's just like "I know I'm human. And if you were all these things, then you'd just attack me right now, so some of you are still human. This thing doesn't want to show itself, it wants to hide inside an imitation."

Next card. Ah.

Who is your favorite pro wrestler of all time and why?

I wonder if the typical reader will understand this, although I believe Mitsuharu Misawa's group, Pro Wrestling NOAH, sometimes appears over there in America. I may be digressing here, but of the wrestlers whose names I listed in the opening of this book, at least three have already passed away. In America, Road Warrior Hawk and Davey Boy Smith. Both of them seemed wrapped in armor made of muscle, but I think their sudden, premature deaths (both in their forties) were related to that very muscle. When Ben Johnson's world record for the hundred-meter dash was rescinded, I foolishly told my friends, "If only he had doped up more, he could have run it in five seconds!" The world of pro wrestling has similar stories. As a pro wrestling fan, I will say up front they didn't need to go that far for us, but they did, and in so doing, they were an inspiration to us in our youth. For that I thank them from the bottom of my heart. In Japan, Shinya Hashimoto left us, also at a young age. I hope all three are in a better place.

Back to the question. It's very hard to narrow it down to just one person, but I'll start out with one Japanese wrestler, Jumbo Tsuruta, and an American, Stan Hansen. I think the appeal of pro wrestling can be summed up, as Giant Baba once said, as "big, strong men charging at each other." Tsuruta had a substantially large build for a Japanese man. As an amateur wrestler, he competed in the Olympics, and his execution of Lou Thesz's back drop was beautiful. (He came down with hepatitis and died due to complications in transplant surgery.) He was typically calm, and his face was free of maliciousness even inside the ring.

I'm sure some of you know who Stan Hansen is, but when he entered the ring in All Japan Pro Wrestling, what a shock it was! All sorts of foreign wrestlers have done it since then, but watching him devastate one Japanese wrestler after another—even my idol, Asura Hara—with his lariat was really the biggest shock. (Had I seen the Road Warriors before Hansen, my reaction might have been different.) On top of that, he had a rugged, Western appearance that remained somehow charming, no matter how tough his performances in the ring.

While it's hard to narrow down the wrestlers, choosing an entrance theme is easy. No matter what anyone says, the best one was the song used by Dynamite Kid and Davey Boy Smith, Tom Scott's "Car Wars."

When I was making a movie in high school, I really wanted to use this song for a fight scene between the protagonist, his partner, and some evildoers, but I didn't know who recorded the song. Eventually, I had to make do with something else...while in tears. (I guess I should have just called All Japan Pro Wrestling.) (Well, at that time, I was still starting out, and I didn't have any connection with the world of superstar wrestlers.) For the opening theme, I used the theme from Clint Eastwood's *The Gauntlet*, "Bleak Bad Big City Dawn." (Of course, without permission. But at least it was a nonprofit "educational work.") I didn't own a record of it and instead used an aircheck of an FM radio broadcast.

Hmmm, what's the next question? Ahh.

Did you do a lot of weapons research for the book, or were you a gun enthusiast in your early life?

A lot of people seem to wonder about that. To reveal my secrets, the only resources I had on hand were a few issues of gun magazines I purchased from a secondhand bookstore. I didn't have any money at the time. I really don't know that much about firearms, and just about the only thing I planned out ahead of time was to make most of the weapons nine millimeter to make ammo supply convenient. (That's why Kiriyama's Ingram isn't a 45mm like normal, but a 9mm model instead.) Due to my lack of research material, after the book was published I received many corrections from gun enthusiasts, such as, "That kind of gun doesn't exist. That's the part number from a model gun."

Anyway, I only used weapons that appeared in my magazines or that I already knew about beforehand. But how much could I have known? Consider that in Japan the average citizen cannot, aside from some hunting rifles, possess any firearms.

I'm a fan of an anime series called *Lupin III*. Anyone who watched that show regularly (and really, any Japanese person who isn't aware of *Lupin III* must live in a hole in the ground) probably knows that

Lupin's gun is a Walther P38, and anyone who calls himself a fan had better know that his partner Jigen carries a Smith and Wesson M19. (In Japan, Lupin and Jigen have such a strong cultural resonance that I decided not to include those weapons in this book.) The creators of that anime didn't cut corners when it came to these details, and their fans took notice. But that's not where all of my firearms knowledge comes from. To explain further, I need to tell you a little more about my history as a reader.

The "Seat of Honor" I mentioned earlier was actually domi-nated by Japanese authors, such as Haruka Takachiho (space opera), Toshihiko Yahagi (Japan's finest writer of Chandler-esque hard-boiled fiction, who also wrote the story for one of Katsuhiro Otomo's manga), Saeko Himuro (girls' novels!), Hideyuki Kikuchi (sci-fi action, horror, fantasy, and to this day a master of the impartial viewpoint), Baku Yumemakura (fantasy, action, etc.), and . . . Haruhiko Ōyabu (let's just say he's a type of picaresque/romance novelist). (There's also Haruki Murakami, but his books were in hardcover, and there wasn't room in the bookcase for them. The "Seat of Honor" was only big enough for paperbacks.)

Before I entered middle school, I had read only a few sci-fi and mystery novels off and on. (I had hardly any interest in "literature." The truth is, I still don't have much.) I don't know what caused it, and it could have been as simple as the word "detective" being in the title of the first book I grabbed, but for a part of middle school I started reading a large number of books written by Haruhiko Ōyabu, though I'm sure I've only read a fraction of his large body of work. I'm wandering off topic here, but he was also from the same prefecture as me, Kagawa, in Shikoku (just think of it as the fourth largest island in Japan). That may have been another reason for me to read so many of his books. Lion Avenue, a street in Takamatsu City, Kagawa, appears in one of his works as "L Avenue." (Takamatsu City also served as the setting for Haruki Murakami's *Kafka on the Shore*, but, unfortunately, no spe-cific street names are mentioned.)

His literary style could be summed up by a single word: violence.

(Albeit a violence of a slightly different tenor as discussed by Kinji Fukasaku.) He paid an extraordinary amount of attention to guns and cars, and when a weapon or a vehicle enters the story, his descriptions go on and on. Incidentally, he got arrested for illegal possession of firearms . . . Anyway, I later stumbled across the author I still revere most, Hideyuki Kikuchi, and while he didn't go as far as Ōyabu, he too gave detailed descriptions of firearms (not so much with cars, however). If I were to follow the proper tradition of the novels I had read, I couldn't get by with describing firearms as just a "revolver" or "automatic." The reason Sakamochi's gun at the end of the story doesn't have a name is because I felt like it should be a domestic, official military firearm, and I didn't want to disrupt the story with a long description of his weapon's name.

By the way, Ōyabu was still alive when I worked at the newspaper and was once hired as a judge for the newspaper's literature award. I didn't work in the entertainment section, and I didn't have a chance to meet or even speak on the phone with him, but this man, who sent out violent story after violent story (*Monsters Must Die, The Long Hot Vendetta, The Cursed Lugar P08*) out into the world, was here judging harmless novels about family relationships in the countryside and such. Don't you find it heartwarming?

That's not enough of an explanation for you? Here's another. Since weapons were going to be appearing left and right, if I kept saying "revolver" and "automatic," it would get boring. Also, if I didn't even know how many bullets a gun could fire, I couldn't feel comfortable writing about it. Still not good enough? All right, to be perfectly honest, I myself don't see firearms as mere tools. I have a sort of nostalgia for them, or possibly even a childlike affection for them, let's say. I've already talked about my connection to Westerns and detective novels, but can you think of a Western where there weren't any guns? Or a samurai without a sword? Or even Bruce Lee without nunchaku? Even now, I bet that if you went to an outdoor booth at a Japanese festival, you could buy a flimsy cap gun or a plastic katana. (That reminds me, Ōyabu wrote a particularly intense story, *Red Shuriken*, about a samurai that used both a katana and a gun.) Or nunchucks . . . well, I doubt they sell those, but regardless, boys like those kinds of things! (Well, that's politically incorrect.) (I think literary prize judges hate me because I talk about such vital matters so flippantly.)

While I'm at it, here's a little-known story about the manga version of *Battle Royale*. When the manga was first serialized in the magazine *Young Champion*, a "hanging ad" campaign was launched, a relatively rare treatment for a manga. Hanging ads are small posters hung from the ceilings of trains. The manga's creator, Masayuki Taguchi, came up with an image of Shuya Nanahara and the rest holding guns, but the train company's advertisement oversight committee rejected it, and we eventually settled on a lineup of the characters' faces in various states of anger, joy, grief, and so on. It's the design used on the jacket of the recent Japanese hardcover edition. (That's a blatant advertisement for you.)

This made Mr. Taguchi angry, since no one seems to mind if the aforementioned Lupin or James Bond carry guns. For some reason, those guns aren't seen as tools used to kill people, but rather as icons representing those characters. But if a child in a school uniform has a gun, that means trouble. I suppose. Setting aside the validity of that reasoning, it's not incorrect to think that the pistols carried by Lupin or Bond have become iconic. Those two don't jump out of the TV or movie screen and start killing people in real life. And if a kid like me starts to grow fond of those icons . . . well, in the end, the weapons manufacturers might make some money. Didn't Spenser and Rachel Wallace talk about this too?

And yet my somewhat metaphysical (?) support is restricted to handheld weapons only. I am not at all interested in tanks or missiles. In *Commando*, Governor Schwarzenegger's walking-arms-market amount of ordinance barely makes the cut. (I can hardly say that with a straight face.) Whatever sort of meaning it has for me comes from him being on foot. I have to think that if he climbed into a tank, he would have definitely lost something. (Stagecoaches aside, would Wyatt Earp ride a tank? Would Doc Holliday push the button to launch a nuclear missile?) And just to make sure all the bases are covered, I don't carry firearms in my own hands. After all, it's against the law. My apologies if I disappoint. I don't have nunchucks either. Please purchase them from a specialty store.

Well, let's look at the next card. Whoa, another tough one. . . .

You worked for a newspaper before becoming a novelist; do you see the media as complicit in the crimes of governments in the real world the way they are in the world of *Battle Royale*?

Um, please don't hope for a particularly journalistic opinion from me. I was definitely not a first-rate journalist. My opinion just as a regular person? Well, it's relatively pessimistic. But Japan isn't a total-itarian country or one ruled by a single party. It's a country of free speech, right? And part of that freedom covers information closely related to current governmental policies. Don't you think there are often things that just seem dumb, even malicious? To give a relatively nonviolent example, yes, with the current worldwide recession spurred on by America's sub-prime loan crisis, Americans have stopped buying as many things (oh, thank you to everyone who purchased this book), and many companies here in Japan, starting with Sony and Toyota, have suffered serious losses. People can now explain that several loans bundled into unidentifiable securities spurred on distrust and then a collapse, or that it started because of dangerous loans that relied on real estate prices continuing to rise in perpetuity, and it's not that hard to understand.

But did even a single media institution in the entire world make a campaign to warn us of it ahead of time? It seems that some experts were trying to point out the problem, but when they did, there were other economists who found personal success by not pointing it out. The media has yet to seriously take on these economists. In the end, the only defense I can propose is not believing everything the media tell us and promoting critical thought and "media literacy" in early edu-cation. The members of the media, or the government, or Congress, or the judiciary, aren't all that smart, sadly enough. Oh, and neither are authors.

While I'm on the subject, please allow me to give a more major example. Whether we're talking about the emergence of the Nazi party or the national system of our "glorious" (I'm not patriotic enough to say that without quotes) Japan some sixty years ago, there was freedom of speech before those politicians took power. As a child, my mother lived through Japan's final war (not counting oddities like the War on Terror), and when anyone goes on TV or the like and says, "The citizens supported that war because they were drunk from our last victory," she gets indignant and responds, "They're wrong. We were against the war, but we just couldn't say it."

The problem isn't with any individual leader—and of course some politicians, members of the military, and even regular citizens had their own reasons to want a war—but I want you to understand how awful it feels to be caught up in an atmosphere of massive social change. Well, you all know about McCarthyism, so I'm preaching to the choir. And when the national system is transformed like that, the media can be very fragile.

Okay, on to the next.

You also have a degree in literature, but *Battle Royale* is a bloody, pulp-fiction thrill ride. Have you ever heard from your old teachers and classmates?

While it's true that I was in the literature department in college, my major was in aesthetics of the fine arts, or to be more precise, I only studied aesthetics in philosophy (Kant, Hegel, etc.) and design. I learned not by creating, but by looking. Even worse, I didn't have many colleagues. I wasn't a very good student, and I haven't spoken to my professors since, but my friends enjoyed my work. As for why I majored in aesthetics, I thought it would be cool to write "Majored in Aesthetics" on my bio. That's all! (My professors never knew what to say when I told them that.) The dream came true when I published my novel, but looking back, I should have been a good student and studied Chandler in the English literature department. I'm not sure if it was just youthful indiscretion, but that's the kind of fool I am.

All right, next. I feel like I'm starting to hear Dylan's voice.

If you type the words "battle royale" into Google.com, your book and movie dominate the listings, beating out the classic pro wrestling battle royal-type match and even the famous battle royal scene from Ralph Ellison's classic novel *The Invisible Man*. How does it feel to have your creation be so famous?

I don't personally search for the name of this book or my own name in Google. I used to do so, happily, when the book first came out in Japan, but I've since stopped. Of course, I like it when people enjoy my work, but there will always be some who say negative things, and when I see something like that, I can't shake it off. I'm easily hurt. Partly for that reason, I don't have much of a sense that my work is famous.

By the way, I have a story about looking up phrases. At first, I had decided to make the English name of this book *Battle Royal*. But, when I was talking to a friend (not the one who set his weapon down) and explained the idea to him and asked what he thought of the "pro wrestling term, written in English, Battle Royal" as the title. He said, "You mean Battle Royale?" with what was probably a French accent. My friend, who didn't know a single thing about pro wrestling, was probably making an association with café royale, but based on that conversation, I decided to make the Japanese title in the French style, and I kept the "e" on the end for the English title. That reminds me, a friend, upon reading a rough draft of the novel, critiqued, "Isn't that title too gaudy for this kind of content?" But I intended the title to be silly. I hope all of you in English-speaking countries will pronounce it through your noses.

Incidentally, Google, I use your search engine day after day (I even used it while writing this afterword), but I don't know what I think about you scanning every book in the world. It's not just a matter of copyright. I think that authors have the right to control access to their work, at least while they are still alive. But you probably don't understand.

All right, well, next, is this the last one? Yes.

What will it take for Hollywood to remake the movie with American actors? Would you like to see such a remake?
Having something I wrote turned into another form of media makes my heart dance. But I have to take the opportunity to admit that I'm not as enthralled with Hollywood as I used to be in the '80s. (Although I use an Apple computer, ride a Dahon bicycle, and am fairly Americanized.) The following is business talk, but I am not currently in discussions to make an American version of the movie. And if it does come about, I have already decided who I want to work with. Therefore, people in the industry, please stop asking me. No, really.

Well, it's time to wrap up. I did have one more request from VIZ. I've been asked to write a new episode for this novel. Of course, I have several ideas that never made it into the book ten years ago. In particular, I had a scene above the lighthouse where the girls are holed up. Yukie Utsumi and Haruka Tanizawa have a conversation when they are changing guard shifts. Yukie Utsumi's father was a soldier in the Special Defense Army... and something like that. The two of them probably talked about boys and politics. But I can't write it anymore. This novel is incomplete in many ways, but if I start trying to add to it now, it may lose something special by removing those very deficiencies. So instead, let me show you a part that got cut out in revisions that I particularly like:

> Noriko wasn't in the literary club, and Shuya first became aware
> of her talent when they shared the same class in second year. Ms.
> Okazaki, their Japanese teacher, instructed the students to write

poems on any theme they wished, and then the teacher read the best ones aloud.

At that time, Shuya had already written several of his own songs. He also had a number of lyric fragments he couldn't quite make into songs yet and managed to put a few of them together for the assignment. He was confident. And when his was read first, he raised up his hands with a cheer and waved at the rest of the class, but when Ms. Okazaki announced her favorite poem, it was Noriko's.

If I could have my way, I would fashion a tale
I would fashion a tale about everything surrounding me
The cherry blossoms, the crybaby dog next door, the wind
    chime I bought before, the sea from that one day, the man
    I spoke with at the fish market,
If I could, I would fashion a tale about it all
Yes, that's what I think
And if everyone would protect that tale
The world would be always at peace.

It was that sort of poem.

Okay, well, that about does it. I still think that the author doesn't matter a damn when it comes to the story, but still, I'm glad I got to talk to you all. I feel blessed to have my story undergo the process of translation and be read by people of another tongue. Completely blessed. Thanks again to VIZ and to Mr. Oniki. And to you readers, however much you enjoyed this book, I give my utmost appreciation. Thank you.

I just have one more piece of business. Whatever is written in Wikipedia, or whatever people in the industry might think, or even whatever gets scanned in by Google (well, that might be unrelated), I will return. I wonder if I will produce something worth translating. I don't know, but I have to aim for that level of quality or there's no point. The truth is, I didn't include much rhyming or wordplay in the original manuscript of *Battle Royale*. Even while writing it I was working under the fantasy that it would be translated someday. Yes, I had been waiting! Therefore, I will leave you with the line said by Lupin III at the end of each episode for the past thirty years.

"See ya!"

March 2009
Koushun Takami

ABOUT THE AUTHOR

Koushun Takami was born in 1969 in Amagasaki near Osaka and grew up in Kagawa Prefecture of Shikoku (the fourth largest island in Japan), where he currently resides. After graduating from Osaka University with a degree in literature, he worked for a newspaper company, Shikoku Shinbun, for five years, reporting on politics, police reports, and economics. Also, he attended Nihon University's liberal arts correspondence-course program and acquired an English teaching certificate for junior high school and high school.

Battle Royale, completed after Takami left the newspaper company, was his debut work and his only novel published so far. With its publication in Japan in 1999, it received widespread support and became a best seller. *Battle Royale* was serialized as a comic, made into a feature film in 2000, and has been translated into more than ten languages. Since its initial release, *Battle Royale* continues to be a cult favorite in Japan and internationally.

In 2012, *Battle Royale: Angels' Border,* a spin-off manga scripted by Koushun Takami, was released.

THE
BATTLE ROYALE
BR
SLAM BOOK

EDITED BY HAIKASORU

Koushun Takami's *Battle Royale* is an international best seller, the basis of the cult film, and the inspiration for a popular manga. And fifteen years after its initial release, *Battle Royale* remains a controversial pop culture phenomenon.

Join *New York Times* best-selling author John Skipp, *Batman* screenwriter Sam Hamm, Philip K. Dick Award–nominated novelist Toh EnJoe, and an array of writers, scholars, and fans in discussing girl power, firepower, professional wrestling, bad movies, the survival chances of Hollywood's leading teen icons in a battle royale, and so much more!

$14.99 USA // $16.99 CAN // £9.99 UK   ISBN: 978-1-4215-6599-6

BATTLE ROYALE ANGELS' BORDER

STORY BY KOUSHUN TAKAMI // ART BY MIOKO OHNISHI & YOUHEI OGUMA

A BATTLE ROYALE MANGA

FINALLY, DISCOVER THE POIGNANT, TRAGIC STORY OF THE GIRLS IN THE LIGHTHOUSE.

HARUKA TANIZAWA IS AN AVERAGE JUNIOR HIGH STUDENT. SHE PLAYS ON THE VOLLEYBALL TEAM AND JUST FELL IN LOVE FOR THE FIRST TIME. BUT HER LOVE IS ALSO HER BEST FRIEND AND CLASSMATE, YUKIE, AND HARUKA DREADS THE TRUTH COMING OUT AND RUINING THEIR RELATIONSHIP.

AND THEN HER ENTIRE CLASS IS DRUGGED, DRAGGED TO A DESERTED ISLAND, AND FORCED TO PARTICIPATE IN THE BLOODY SPECTACLE OF THE PROGRAM.

WHILE MOST OF THE STUDENTS SCATTER AS SOON AS THEY'RE RELEASED FROM THE STAGING GROUNDS, YUKIE COMES BACK FOR HARUKA, AND TOGETHER THEY GATHER SOME OF THE OTHER GIRLS IN THE DUBIOUS SAFETY OF THE ISLAND'S LIGHTHOUSE.

THEY KNOW SURVIVAL IS UNLIKELY.
BUT WHAT ABOUT HOPE…?

$12.99 USA // $14.99 CAN // £8.99 UK | 5.75" x 8.25" | ISBN: 978-1-4215-7168-3